A CAULDRON OF BITTERNESS

A PRACTICAL GUIDE TO SORCERY
BOOK FIVE

AZALEA ELLIS

To Jared.

I dreamed the smell of fresh flowers
At the end of time.
And you told me to climb on
Ever upward.

JOIN THE INNER CIRCLE**

Become part of the Inner Circle.
Instantly receive a free excerpt from Siobhan's illustrated grimoire.

https://www.azaleaellis.com/newsletter

I will send you new release updates, exclusive content like pre-release or deleted scenes, as well as news about giveaways or contests I'm doing (signed paperbacks, posters, etc.) and other cool stuff I think you might enjoy. Sometimes I tell weird stories about my life.

Plus, you get discounts on all products sold through my online shop, many of which you can't get on other retailers.

Support me on Patreon

https://www.patreon.com/azaleaellis

Read along chapter by chapter as I write the next book in the series, with early access chapters not available elsewhere, plus exclusive short stories/bonus chapters, and other goodies like various illustrated excerpts from Siobhan's grimoire.

NOTE TO READERS

The world-building for this story is extensive and can be quite complicated. If you find yourself forgetting terminology or wanting a little more detail about a term, the end of this book holds a Glossary of Magical Terms.

Thank you for reading!

Azalea

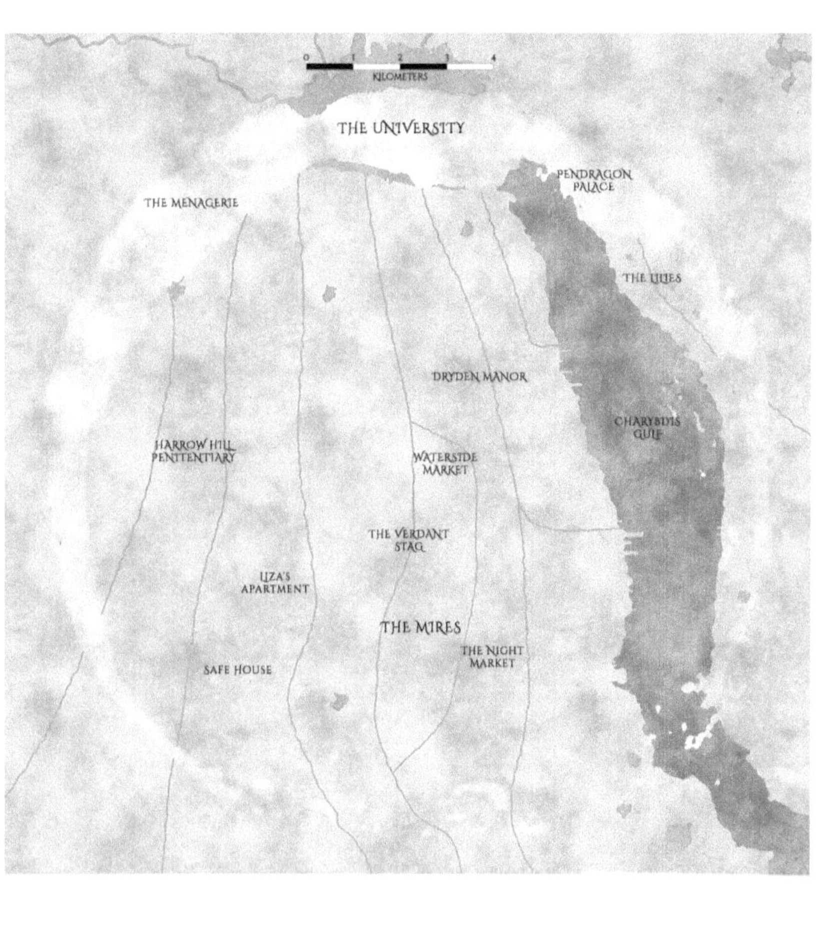

KILOMETERS
0 1 2 3 4
THE UNIVERSITY
PENDRAGON PALACE
THE MENAGERIE
THE LILIES
DRYDEN MANOR
CHARYBDIS GULF
HARROW HILL PENITENTIARY
WATERSIDE MARKET
THE VERDANT STAG
LIZA'S APARTMENT
THE MIRES
THE NIGHT MARKET
SAFE HOUSE

A PRACTICAL GUIDE TO SORCERY
RECAP

If you have not read the first three books in the Practical Guide to Sorcery series, spoilers lie ahead.

Previously, in *A Conjuring of Ravens*:

Siobhan Naught unwittingly becomes a wanted criminal when her father steals a mysterious book during their visit to the Thaumaturgic University. Her hopes of becoming a student dashed, she runs from the coppers with the book. Later, in danger from being caught by their ambush, she meets Oliver Dryden, who tries to help her escape.

When the coppers corner them, she accidentally activates a transformation amulet that had been hidden in the stolen book, turning herself into a young man who looks nothing like her original form. With this new body, she deceives the coppers and escapes arrest. To have a chance at entering the University under a new identity, she takes a huge loan—one thousand gold— from Oliver and Katerin at the Verdant Stag, the criminal organization they run.

Oliver helps her create a new identity for herself as Sebastien Siverling, but she makes a bad first impression on Damien Westbay and his group of Crown Family friends upon their first meeting.

When Siobhan learns the coppers caught her father Ennis, she and Oliver enlist the help of local illegal thaumaturge Liza, who helps Siobhan contact Ennis with a spelled raven messenger. To Siobhan's disappointment, Ennis has tried to sell her—and the stolen book—to the Gervin Family in marriage, in exchange for benefits for himself.

Much disillusioned, Siobhan studies for the University entrance exam and works for the Verdant Stag, who actually seem to serve and help the people within their community. When young Theo, Katerin's nephew, injures himself, Siobhan unthinkingly uses some harmless blood magic learned from her grandfather to heal the boy, earning both Katerin and Oliver's ire for the reckless use of illegal magic that could get her executed, and them implicated by association.

As Sebastien Siverling, she takes the University entrance exam, but her results are poorer than she hoped, and the panel of professors who administer the verbal portion of the exam plan to deny her entrance. In a fit of rage, she refuses to be dismissed, casting a hastily prepared spell to prove that she has the only thing that matters to a potential sorcerer—a strong Will.

Professor Thaddeus Lacer, a famous free-caster and Siobhan's childhood hero, takes an interest in her and overrides the panel of other professors, forcibly admitting Sebastien Siverling under special circumstances.

Sebastien falls into her University classes with glee, learning with feverish enthusiasm. She keeps to herself except for a budding new friendship with Anastasia Gervin, a Crown Family heiress, and Damien Westbay, who remembers their first meeting and finds Sebastien abrasive, nurturing the pseudo-rivalry between them. One of their student liaisons, Newton Moore, also extends an olive branch of friendship, believing her to—secretly—be a poor student just like him.

When she is not studying, Sebastien brews alchemical concoctions for the Verdant Stag to pay back the debt she owes them.

Oliver makes moves to expand the power of the Verdant Stags, but things backfire when the Morrows, a rival gang, attack one of his warehouses with the help of a mysterious sorceress. Oliver sets off Sebastien's alarms, waking her in the middle of the night to give emergency aid to his people.

Returning to her female form, Siobhan uses the minor spell exercises she's been practicing for Professor Lacer to sling balls of shattered glass at the Morrows. When the fighting is over, she tries to help the Verdant Stag warehouse workers, some of whom have been severely injured. Unable to do much, she patches up what she can before the coppers arrive.

Trying to give the others a better chance to escape, Siobhan uses a harmless esoteric spell that controls her shadow, molding it into a frightening creature of tattered darkness with a huge raven's beak. The coppers are successfully frightened, but one of them shoots a grasping spell at Siobhan, tripping her and cutting her hand.

She and Oliver escape to a safe house owned by one of Oliver's subjects, but the coppers found some of her blood left behind at the scene and use it to cast scrying magic on her. Siobhan's warding medallion, given by her grandfather, holds off the scrying attempt—at the cost of Siobhan's Conduit—and they go to Liza for a more permanent solution.

Liza creates a divination-diverting ward, anchored in five disks that she inserts underneath Siobhan's skin. The ward uses her blood for power, and can activate at low efficiency on its own or be further empowered by Siobhan's conscious efforts.

Thaddeus is called to the scene of the crime to consult on the investigation at Titus Westbay's request. Given the available evidence and witness accounts, they come to some erroneous conclusions. Siobhan Naught—codename Raven Queen—is a free-caster with some unknown, nefarious purpose that involves curses and blood magic.

She fascinates Thaddeus.

Siobhan, now without a Conduit, contacts Ennis in jail again, hoping to retrieve her mother's Conduit from him, but learns that he gave it to the Gervin Family as a bond for his word in the marriage agreement he gave on her behalf. Enraged and desperate, she spends most of her remaining funds to buy a dinky, overpriced replacement Conduit, then breaks down in tears.

But she isn't the same person who came to Gilbratha with Ennis those months ago. She's no longer under his—or anyone else's—control. She takes ownership of her life and her choices, pulls herself back together, and returns to the University.

In *A Binding of Blood*:

Sebastien does her best to keep her Will-strain concealed, but she remains concerned about future attacks from the Morrows. To better prepare, she experiments with ink-and-paper spell arrays with some success.

One day, while practicing slicing spells, Damien distracts her, causing her to accidentally injure him. She uses her flesh-mirroring spell to heal him, concealing the mechanics and the fact that it is technically blood magic. The effort re-strains her already fragile Will.

Feeling guilty and impressed, Damien resolves to befriend her.

Sebastien then begins to develop a sleep-proxy spell that will allow her to avoid her nightmares, as another sleeps on her behalf.

Professor Lacer sets up an in-class tournament for the sphere-spinning spell and becomes dissatisfied with her sandbagging against Damien, believing she does so to ingratiate herself with a powerful peer. Sebastien insists neither of them tell Professor Lacer the truth.

When the rogue magic sirens go off, the frightened students shelter in the library, and Sebastien discusses named Aberrants with Damien, asserting that they are more dangerous and less well-contained by the Red Guard than it might seem.

As classes continue, delving deeper into the details of both transmutation and transmogrification, Sebastien researches divination in the hopes of stealing or destroying the blood sample the coppers have been using to scry for her. When she manages to take advantage of a scrying attempt to trace her blood back to Eagle Tower on University grounds and only a short distance away, Damien stubbornly follows her.

Damien believes Sebastien is going on an "adventure," and is surprised and intrigued to learn he is spying on an attempt to find the Raven Queen, his imagination leading him to some dramatic conclusions.

Their student liaison, Tanya Canelo, interrupts the scrying attempt with an explosion just as Sebastien is becoming concerned. After talking about the situation with Oliver, Sebastien inducts Damien into a fake secret organization and together they hire their other student liaison, Newton, to help them keep tabs on Tanya.

While contemplating the foiled attempt on the Raven Queen, Thaddeus has an epiphany: When Sebastien refused to cast to her full ability, she had Will-strain. He interrogates Damien, who hints that Sebastien needs a better Conduit. Thaddeus wakes Sebastien in the middle of the night to lend her a Conduit and threaten her against similar recklessness.

After putting a tracker in Tanya's boot, Siobhan goes to a meeting with Lord Lynwood, leader of the Nightmare Pack gang, whom Oliver allied with. Lynwood and his prognos sister Gera give Siobhan a tribute of a black star sapphire, and request she help Millennium, Gera's cambion child who cannot sleep. As this happens to be Siobhan's area of expertise, she develops a spell to help the boy, leaving the Nightmare Pack leaders both fearful and in awe of her.

Later, following Tanya's suspicious activity, Siobhan discovers a secret organization of thaumaturges and joins. Her divination-diverting ward activates for the entrance interview, leaving the administrators convinced that she is the Raven Queen and frightened by her abilities.

Together with the Nightmare Pack, Oliver is planning an attack on the Morrows, who have become more aggressive toward people in the Verdant Stag's territory. He hires Siobhan as a healer's assistant for this.

In the meantime, Sebastien competes in the Practical Casting tournament and performs well, but sees the first classmate dead from Will-strain.

She knows they will not be the last.

The day of the battle arrives, and as Siobhan helps to heal the injured enforcers and civilians, Oliver attacks the Morrows' main warehouse and kills Lord Morrow, only to discover a storage room filled with beast cores and magical supplies all meant for the University.

Ana rushes home to comfort her little sister Natalia, who is being badly bullied by her adult cousin and uncles, as they hope to discredit Ana and her sister in their father's eyes, so that neither can become the Fourth Crown Family's heir.

Newton reveals that some of his family members were injured in the fighting and their house was lost. Desperate for coin to continue studying at the University, he accompanies Tanya to one of the secret meetings.

Siobhan is trailing them, keeping tabs on them with the tracker in Tanya's boot. Paranoid, Tanya realizes they are being followed and decides to attack.

Despite Newton's fear, the three of them are in a stand-off, but Tanya calls for backup from what few Morrows were not killed or captured in the earlier battle. When the Morrows come, they decide to capture all three of them, despite Tanya's protests, hoping to receive a ransom for them.

But when one of the Morrows sees Siobhan's face and recognizes her as the Raven Queen, fear causes them all to attack. In the confusion, Siobhan casts her shadow-familiar spell to draw attention and spell-fire away from herself.

Newton loses control of the spell he was casting and experiences a break event, turning into a string-based Aberrant. When the strings touch a human being, they unravel them alive.

Together with Tanya and the surviving Morrows, Siobhan works out how to pass somewhat safely through the strings and helps move them to safety.

But her bag is still with the Aberrant, and she decides to go back for it, as it could be used to find her, and she does not want to give up her place at the University to flee the law again. She manages to retrieve her bag and return to Sebastien's form, but the Red Guard has arrived and, when they notice strange divination readings, knock her unconscious.

Professor Lacer arrives to monitor her questioning and they are quickly joined by Gera, who misleads the investigation. As Professor Lacer takes Sebastien, cleared of suspicion, back to the University, she tells him her suspicions of Tanya and some of the other University faculty.

Not knowing Sebastien's fear of sleep, he then knocks her unconscious.

In *A Sacrifice of Light*:

Red Guard agents have captured and entombed two Aberrants for transport. One was once Newton.

Thaddeus Lacer investigates the coppers' investigation into the Raven Queen, and her father Ennis reveals that Siobhan's mother died after casting through her own flesh, and later their home village was destroyed by an Aberrant incident from which only Siobhan escaped. Ennis tracked her down and found her traumatized and in jail some months later, and took her on the road with him.

Siobhan takes some time to recover from the trauma of Newton's death, and back at school is subjected to Grandmaster Kiernan's probing questions about the Aberrant incident, which she refuses to answer. People everywhere, including the newspapers, are gossiping that Newton must have been doing morally bankrupt magics to corrupt his Will and become an Aberrant, which enrages Sebastien and her friends.

Meanwhile, Oliver runs into an incident of the coppers using excessive force on a civilian. Percy Irving, a teenager with unusually, ridiculously bad luck, accidentally takes a photograph of the incident. Upon learning that Percy also took a photograph of the Raven Queen but has been keeping it secret, Oliver decides to hire Percy to work for his new newspaper, *The People's Voice.*

Ana requests that Sebastien help her in a risky plan to frame and overthrow her uncles, who encourage abuse toward her and her little sister Natalia. Sebastien replies rudely, making Ana angry, but Ana comes back with an offer Sebastien cannot refuse. If she helps depose Ana's uncles, Ana will ensure the textile sub-commission that Oliver needs.

Sebastien negotiates with Oliver for payment and a stake in the textile company he will set up, and then she, Ana, and Damien begin Operation Defenestration.

They break into Malcolm Gervin's office and take photographs of his documents. (Sebastien secretly steals back her mother's heirloom ring that her father gave them as collateral for her hand in marriage.)

Then, they have Sebastien dress up in a costume of the Raven Queen to meet with the uncles and frame them for collusion with a criminal.

Siobhan discovers that the ring she retrieved actually has a thaumaturge-created diamond instead of a celerium gem, and concludes that Ennis must have switched them out and sold the celerium at some point. Enraged, she disowns and curses him.

As Sebastien learns new concepts in her classes and works on output detachment with Professor Lacer, Oliver pulls her into working as a healer's assistant to "seal the tongues" of the Morrows who they will be turning over to the coppers for sentencing and imprisonment.

However, Grandmaster Kiernan and the Architects of Khronos, who desperately want the stolen book that started everything, betray Oliver. They attack the prisoner convoys with several powerful thaumaturges, including an old man that casts an almost unfathomably powerful spell to trap everyone inside Knave Knoll and infect them with spores that affect their minds.

Siobhan and the enforcers work together to escape, and as she is trying to escape, the old man captures her satchel. She sets off the disintegration mine inside and kills him along with his companions.

Soon after, the friend trio confronts Malcolm Gervin to place the final nail in his coffin as he attempts to kill them to escape, and Ana plants a fake journal in his handwriting detailing his crimes and plans to kill her father, the head of their Crown Family.

While she's still unrecovered from these events, the coppers try one more scrying attempt on Siobhan, which is so powerful it forces her to leave the city. She's unable to cast her dreamless sleep spell that night, and has a nightmare of a twisted mirror locked away in her childhood house.

Finally gathering her courage, Sebastien visits Newton's family, only to find that they have had their memories and opinions modified—poorly—by the Red Guard. They, too, now believe that Newton was experimenting with unethical magic and deserved to turn into an Aberrant.

Sebastien goes to Professor lacer, and is horrified to learn that this is standard practice for the Red Guard.

To follow up that blow, Oliver lets slip the idea to create a scapegoat for the Raven Queen to divert attention and suspicion, leading her to suspect that he did the same to her. She considers all the evidence for and against this new theory, and vows to uncover the truth.

Thaddeus Lacer contacts Oliver to pass along a request to meet the Raven Queen. He secretly stole her mother's heirloom ring and replaced it with a fake, and plans to give the original to her as tribute when they meet.

In *A Foreboding of Woe*:

Thaddeus meets with Grandmaster Kiernan and agrees to help decrypt Myrddin's journals.

During their Defense exam, Sebastien uses Damien's fallen Conduit through a tear in her pants, which Professor Fekten misinterprets as flesh-casting until Professor Lacer intervenes. Later, Sebastien's impressive tree sculpture during her Practical Casting exhibition earns her seventy contribution points and confirms her apprenticeship with Lacer.

Before leaving the University, she learns that students who succumb to Will-strain are sent to the Retreat at Willowdale.

When Damien confronts Sebastien about Oliver Dryden, revealing Titus's investigation into their relationship, she assigns him to research Aberrant incidents as a distraction. Oliver also reveals Titus's outlandish suspicions. Deciding to be proactive, Sebastien writes to Titus, the Retreat at Willowdale, and the High Crown.

Siobhan assists Liza with testing the sleep-proxy spell and proposes hiring her to retrieve the blood sample from Eagle Tower by impersonating the Raven Queen. She brings Tanya and Gera into the plan.

Professor Lacer shares his theory that Myrddin's journals require identity verification and pure Will rather than spells to access. When he dismisses the possibility of splitting one's Will to cast multiple spells simultaneously, Sebastien remains silent, knowing *she* can split her Will. She discovers Myrddin's journal requires recognizing multiple glyphs simultaneously, confirming that he too could split his Will.

Sebastien masters the Refinement of the Nine Heavens spell, which cleanses and strengthens her body and mind with light.

Siobhan gives Tanya a spelled raven to deliver a message to the Edictum Council. When leaving, she experiences an inexplicable compulsion to attend Ennis's sentencing. Miles rescues her from a copper, revealing that he and several allies are fleeing from Pendragon operatives targeting him. As they attempt to escape, a magical trap explodes, and they're captured.

Trapped in sensory deprivation, Siobhan confronts the being sealed in her mind by her grandfather. She resists its manipulation, escapes, and uses her shadow-familiar to bribe and frighten Pendragon Corps guards into helping her rescue the other civilians. They raid the armory, providing Siobhan with gold and high-quality celerium. During their escape, Parker is captured by the pursuing captain.

From the white cliffs, Thaddeus watches the Raven Queen escape by boat. He secretly kills two pursuing operatives and sabotages their boat, earning what he believes is an acknowledging look from her before she disappears.

Siobhan leads her group to safety through the Mires. Unknown to her, the rescued captives gather to discuss their escape, portraying her as more powerful and eldritch than she realizes. They speculate about her abilities and agree to support her future revenge against the High Crown.

At Pendragon Palace, Thaddeus nearly attacks the High Crown upon learning his apprentice was targeted. A guard's memory display shows a frightening, warped version of the Raven Queen's shadow abilities, while a traumatized operative rants about her shadow companion's hunger and coldness. The advisors debate whether she has Aberrant influence. Upon returning home, Thaddeus finds a letter from the Raven Queen requesting an exchange of information.

Disguised as Liza's niece, Siobhan visits the Retreat at Willowdale and learns that Myrddin left *five* journals, not four. The fifth was stolen by another expedition member before returning to Gilbratha. Siobhan suspects Oliver orchestrated the theft and resolves to question Grandmaster Kiernan.

In a private mentorship session, Professor Lacer reveals to Sebastien and Damien how transmogrification relies on society's collective understanding rather than individual interpretations, which is why she has struggled so much with it.

After days of exchanging coded letters with Oliver and Professor Lacer, Siobhan confronts Grandmaster Kiernan as the Raven Queen. He confesses to betraying the Verdant Stag and reveals that Myrddin's journal contains instructions for purifying beast cores into celerium—critical knowledge as Lenore's mines will be depleted within five to ten years.

Sebastien then confronts Oliver about stealing Myrddin's journal and using her as a decoy. Their argument escalates until she declares she'll only interact with him through formal tribute like other Raven Queen supplicants. Oliver collapses at his desk after she leaves, mourning their lost friendship.

To fulfill her promises, she successfully heals Anders' dying dog using multiple stray dogs as components.

Damien presents Sebastien with his research into suspicious rogue magic incidents, sharing his theory that the Red Guard uses blood magic and possibly Aberrant components. Sebastien confirms his suspicions by revealing what happened to Newton's family.

Using her split Will technique, Sebastien successfully accesses Myrddin's journal.

Siobhan warns Oliver about the Architects' planned kidnappings in Osham, despite their strained relationship.

Walking home from Liza's in the rain, Siobhan is caught in a spell. A masked Red Guard agent confronts her in a magically created space, wielding a grotesque pink flesh-glove that negates spells.

Despite her creativity and desperation, Siobhan cannot defeat the agent. When cornered, she detaches her shadow-familiar's output. Her shadow rises up with glowing amber eyes, confronts the Red Guard agents claiming to be the Raven Queen, and allows Siobhan to escape. Upon returning and reattaching to her, it reveals it used power from the beast core she swallowed when the Pendragon Corps captured her to temporarily escape its seal. She can feel its emotions and tell when it's lying. It wants to be remembered.

Siobhan visits Professor Lacer as the Raven Queen. He presents her mother's ring as tribute and offers tentative protection from Red Guard scrutiny in exchange for continued cooperation.

At Theo's birthday celebration, Oliver apologizes for his deceit and manipulation. He mentions the growing worship of the Raven Queen among commoners. He suggests managing the movement since it cannot be stopped.

A Cauldron of Bitterness begins directly after these events.

1

SPECIAL AGENT LACER

THADDEUS
Month 8, Day 15, Sunday 6:00 a.m.

THADDEUS HAD NOT SLEPT.

The Raven Queen—Siobhan, as she had told him to call her—had left his cottage hours before, disappearing into the trees during the darkest hour of the night when most of the city slumbered. Theoretically, there had been time for him to catch a bit of rest, but Thaddeus had not even attempted to lay down. He knew sleep would not come. Even now, he was still buzzing with the energy of her visit.

He was walking through Waterside Market so early because Siobhan had made triply sure to impress upon him the need for urgency.

Thaddeus scratched at one eyebrow in embarrassment as he remembered their first meeting. He had done his best to react to her unexpected arrival with aplomb, but with his more instinctual responses of cutting cynicism and some measure of disdain off the table, he had been off balance.

It had taken him a regrettable amount of time to recover from the surprise of her presence. He would have wagered his Conduit that she had noticed and found him amusing. Her unfathomably dark eyes had been knowing, the set of her lips hinting at a shared secret, as if she could taste the surface of his emotions. He did not believe she could truly do such things, but she certainly *was* insightful.

Siobhan Naught had been little like the rumors, and yet, more intriguing than he had hoped. Unlike her reputation might have suggested, she had staged no spectacle in an attempt to cow him with awe or fear. She had been polite, completely sane, and looked nothing like a creature out of nightmares. In fact, she had treated him more familiarly than many of his fellow professors, and without either the hero worship or animosity of many of the agents in the Red Guard. If one could overlook a few strange behaviors, her company was quite pleasant—even if she *was* a degenerate heathen who ruined her coffee with both milk and sugar.

His perception of her had not changed when he cast several spells meant to cleanse and protect the mind from outside influence. Such things were never foolproof, of course, but he was inclined to believe that she had been honest.

As he turned down one of the market's side streets, he pulled a short incense stick from one of his pockets, which he then used to free-cast a minor compulsion that would prevent people from recognizing him as Thaddeus Lacer. Despite the precautions the Red Guard took to keep the entrances of their field bases secret, a celebrity being seen entering the cover building was an unnecessary risk. It was unfortunate that Gilbratha's primary field base was in the direct center of the city and on the edge of Waterside Market.

His destination was a rather ordinary, if slightly run-down, building that failed to properly advertise what goods or services it provided. One of its wards created a subtle compulsion to find the building uninteresting and somewhat off-putting. Once that took effect, anyone who got too close to the front door would abruptly be reminded that they had forgotten something urgent that required their attention elsewhere.

Thaddeus shrugged off the attempts to turn him from his purpose. The front door shrieked with poorly oiled hinges and set off an irritating bell jingling above, creating enough racket that there was no possible way anyone inside would miss his entrance.

The area beyond was arrayed with cheap, kitschy fake artifacts and spell components chosen more for their decorative ambiance than their properties. A woman glamoured to look both older and rounder than she actually was looked up from a desk in the corner, separated from the rest of the shop by a curtain of cheap beads. "Come to get your dreams read?" she asked, after an awkward pause where she tried to pretend she didn't recognize him. She gave him a gap-toothed smile. "Only six gold." The price was outrageous.

The Red Guard agents working here were trained not to break character. Manning the face companies that secured the non-emergency access points to a field base was considered a leisure assignment. Agents were assigned to the job on rotation, or after a traumatic event that required a break from more directly serving the organization.

Some of the agents had taken the responsibility to deceive, discourage, and drive away civilians as a personal challenge, turning it into a game of one-upmanship among several of the field bases.

Despite his lack of interest in the endeavor, Thaddeus had picked up a detailed understanding of their work simply from idle chatter during the meetings he was required to attend.

This agent pretended to be a dream diviner. To those few determined clients who made it past all the discouragement and forcibly purchased her services, she would give horrible dream interpretations, such as, "Oh, the signs are clear. I'm so sorry. You are haunted by a tenacious and deadly fate." Of course, such a thing could only be escaped by moving away from Gilbratha entirely. Their misfortune would certainly be made far worse if they ever returned for another dream divination, as the "evil force" haunting them had marked their visit and would attempt to keep them from receiving further advice.

Thaddeus had heard her bragging about how many superstitious people she had actually convinced to pack up their entire lives and move away from the city.

He gave her a sharp nod but otherwise ignored her, walking toward the doorway at the back of her shop. He suppressed the sudden and somewhat urgent need to urinate, which was connected to an impulse to look at the sign announcing that there were no bathrooms in the building and displaying a map to the nearest location one could relieve themselves.

If one made it past the dream diviner, the next area housed another agent who acted as a supposed alchemical researcher with an obviously fake license. The man beyond was in the middle of eating a sandwich, and when Thaddeus opened the door, tried to inhale and stand at the same time. He ended up choking, red-faced and leaning over his desk.

Anyone who made it to this agent would be non-violently accosted as the agent tried to get them to accept a position as a research subject to test the effects of his potions.

This room was filled with shelves of ancient, pickled animal components and dozens of the scariest-looking concoctions known to the Red Guard. The kinds of things commoners imagined when they thought of a blood sorcerer's lair.

The poorly paid job required the prospective research subject to read and sign an entire binder of waivers for possible side effects, starting from every hair on the body growing backward into the dermis and ending with all nine natural orifices melting closed into a seamless patch of skin.

And it was non-paid.

The agent had been reported to the coppers for illegal experimentation and suspicion of using blood magic eight times already by people who had escaped his clutches.

Thaddeus forcibly cleared the man's windpipe with a small spell and waved at him to sit back down again. "I am here for a beauty treatment," he said somewhat sardonically, opening the door to the stairs at the back of the room. He ignored the sudden intrusive knowledge that he had forgotten any and all forms of possible payment at home, as well as an unpleasant smell that was hard to place, but which made him sure that continuing to breathe it in would give him a horrible headache and perhaps kill some of his brain cells.

Down the stairs into the basement, a prospective customer would find a day spa that specialized in the therapeutic uses of aquatic creatures. Specifically, the carnivorous sort. The agent there was happy to recommend their cleansing foot baths to any amazingly stubborn customer who managed to reach them.

The man was slightly less harmless-looking than his two coworkers, ready to magically accost anyone who seemed a little too interested in certain parts of the room with mind-altering spells.

The foot baths used fish to eat the dead skin off of whatever was immersed in the water, leaving behind skin "as smooth as a baby's bottom." He would demonstrate their miraculous function by dropping some crusty, dehydrated animal appendage or other into one of the foot baths and letting the customer watch as the fish completely devoured it, leaving not even bone behind.

He had a stellar record; no civilian had ever managed to watch this display while in the presence of the man's unnaturally shiny smile and twitchy eyes and still decide that they wanted to stay in the building.

Thaddeus gave him a nod of respect. "Hello, Mike. No time to chat today."

The agent deflated—he did not receive many visitors—but waved Thaddeus on.

With his badge out, Thaddeus walked through the invisible barrier around one of the glass fish tanks that held some particularly vicious-looking spiny eels and stepped down into the water. It was all an illusion, of course. There was no water and no eels. In reality, a hidden ramp had reacted to his badge, melting out of the stone floor and leading down into the darkness.

The ramp was wide enough for a few people to walk side-by-side and spiraled outward into a descending hallway. The spiral, somewhat strangely, grew continuously wider and more shallow as he descended. It took a few minutes before he finally came to a heavily warded metal door. This was not the only access point to Field Base One, but it was the only one sanctioned for non-emergency purposes.

The door took a complex password, a tiny sliver off the end of his finger-nail, and thirty seconds of contact with his Red Guard badge to open up. Finally, it revealed a large cylindrical cavern of Gilbratha's white stone. It was a smaller, concentric Circle nested within the much larger one that people called the white cliffs. That did not necessarily mean anything, but some considered it strong evidence that the whole city was once a massive spell array.

After the Red Guard had discovered this space and taken it over, the organization had partitioned off large sections for various functions. Despite the many subdivisions, much of the space was still open and airy, with light crystals set into the high ceiling creating the illusion of natural light. It helped to keep the agents who spent too much time here from going insane.

Thaddeus moved past the lobby and recreation area, with its potted plants, dueling board games, and snacks preserved within Shipp evidence boxes. Someone had even brought in an aquarium, and a giant-sized rocking horse took up enough space for a dining table, for some unknowable reason.

He brushed off any vain attempts to distract him with conversation and walked past the desks where a couple squads of agents were filling in research reports, doing paperwork, or chatting with each other, ignoring the sudden silence that spread as they noticed him. The quarantine zone and the debriefing rooms were adjacent to each other in this base, and he made his way to the latter.

As Siobhan's story had led Thaddeus to expect, there were two teams in one of the debriefing rooms, sitting in their individual cubicles in front of the shield spell that bisected the room. It was a surprise that they were still there, several hours after their altercation with her. It was even more of a surprise, and not a pleasant one, to see Captain Goldfisch on the other side of the shield.

The short, dark-haired man sat next to the much taller and fairer Captain Aisling, the half-jentil in charge of this base. A horn of speech rested on the table in front of the mismatched pair, most likely connected to Captain Rashell, the captain of Field Base Two. With the other two captains in physical attendance, she could not be there in person due to the risk of an attempt to decapitate the Red Guard's local leadership. It was a paranoid safety measure, but it had paid off more than once.

Both captains and all four of the agents being debriefed wore the bulky helmets meant to suppress memetic effects. All of this signaled, unfortunately, that they were on high alert and discussing a potentially dangerous threat.

Thaddeus opened the glass door and stepped into the room.

"Special Agent Lacer," Captain Aisling said with mild surprise, his voice deep but somehow still mellow.

Captain Goldfisch's features twisted together into a dark scowl. "What are you doing here?"

"I am here to pass on a message from the Raven Queen," Thaddeus said.

The air in the room seemed to tighten as multiple strong Wills reacted to his announcement.

"What do you mean?" Captain Goldfisch asked.

"Exactly what I said," Thaddeus responded. "The Raven Queen was displeased by how her interaction with a few of our agents went last night, and contacted me to pass on a message to those in charge."

"Were you accosted?" Captain Aisling asked calmly.

"To the contrary," Thaddeus said. "I have been in contact with her for some months now. When she found herself in sudden opposition to the Red Guard, she simply reached out for a small favor."

A woman's voice, somewhat metallic, came from the large brass horn artifact on the table as Captain Rashell spoke. "You've been in contact with the Raven Queen?"

Captain Goldfisch's deep-set eyes narrowed dangerously. "You've been secretly colluding with an enemy of the Crowns?" he whispered.

Thaddeus lifted an eyebrow sardonically. "It was not a secret. I already reported, and even later confirmed again, that Siobhan Naught is not the kind of threat the Red Guard was created to deal with. I have taken no vows restricting who I can associate with beyond that." He allowed the tone of his voice to grow darker, the inflection of his words more cutting as he stared at Captain Goldfisch, as if the weight of his gaze could squeeze the man down until he lost a few more inches. "Or are you, perhaps, suggesting that the Red Guard is subordinate to the Crowns? That Lord Pendragon's enemy is naturally our enemy as well?"

Captain Goldfisch flushed but, to his credit, did not glance shamefully at Captain Aisling, who was currently the highest-ranked agent in Gilbratha. "Do not put words in my mouth, Special Agent Lacer. We were merely examining a legitimate potential threat. And judging by the events that transpired last night, it seems obvious that we were correct to do so. It's my own folly that I didn't realize the danger the Raven Queen presented earlier. It seems the rumors hold more water than hot air."

"What rumors would those be?" Thaddeus asked.

"Blood magic rituals with civilian victims, a girl who is really some sort of ancient monster, and hints of a budding cult. And tonight, strong evidence that she's either controlled by or working with an Aberrant. What if she's the source of the civilian disappearances we've been investigating?"

"Is there anything to connect her to the disappearances?" Captain Rashell asked over the horn.

"There is not," Captain Aisling replied succinctly.

Captain Goldfisch did not look away from Thaddeus. "We've pulled the reports from the Pendragon Corps about what she did to their men. The evidence is all there, even if you want to deny it. She's a threat and needs to be neutralized. If we cannot control her, we must destroy her."

Thaddeus swallowed down a surge of hot, angry acidity. "Of the claims you have made, I believe I can firmly refute at least three and a half of them."

There was a moment of silence, and Captain Goldfish's scowl wavered in confusion.

"What claim do you believe to be half-correct?" Captain Rashell asked, as he had hoped she might. Of Gilbratha's three captains, she was the most level-headed and unbiased.

Thaddeus did not answer directly. "I am quite sure we do not have clear evidence that she has performed any blood magic rituals with civilian victims. Blood magic, yes, but almost all turned toward the purpose of healing, to my knowledge. And the laws against any and all forms of blood magic are not our own. We do not enforce the will of the Crowns, or the will of whoever happens to be the current ruler."

Thaddeus paused just long enough to let that barb sink in. "What you call hints of a budding cult I call desperate and misguided ignoramuses, creating their own hope through superstition. Miss Naught has not cultivated their numbers or encouraged any form of worship, but is aware of the potential problems and willing to take measures to mitigate them. And, again, we do not interfere in political or religious movements unless they become an existential threat. By no means can you make that claim at this point."

Behind the shield barrier, the four field agents were watching their conversation, tracking the movement of Thaddeus's mouth and the body language of the captains with weary interest.

Captain Goldfisch opened his mouth, surely to make some offensive statement, but Captain Aisling waved indulgently for Thaddeus to continue. The huge, golden-haired man always seemed slightly amused in Thaddeus's presence, and even more so when Thaddeus's tongue was sharp with irritation or fatigue. Thaddeus had at first believed it to be patronizing and despised it— for who was Aisling to patronize him—but eventually realized that the man looked at the entire world with earnest interest.

Thaddeus moved on to his next points. "That she would be involved in the civilian disappearances is not only baseless speculation but contrary to the character she has displayed until now. She acts against those who offend her, and otherwise is at worst capricious and at best benevolent. As for the creature of shadow that you believe to be an Aberrant, I examined that ingenious spell only a few hours ago. It is fascinating, and holds certain implications for those who know what to look for, but it is still only a product of power and Will, with some aspects of an artifact that allow it to mimic certain actions in defense of its owner. But of the one accusation you brought forth that might have a partial basis in reality…"

He paused as he considered how best to word his revelation. "Siobhan Naught's existence has always been shrouded in…discrepancies. She should be a young woman without significant magical training, and yet she is a powerful free-caster with mysterious abilities. We have found no evidence that her background is fraudulent, and she put herself at risk with what seems to be a genuine emotional connection to her father, but the theft of the book seems impossibly coincidental. There are some hints that suggest Raaz Kalvidasan had more of a motive than altruism for adopting Miss Naught's mother, and there are rumors that the bloodline of the Naughts has some resistance to casting through their own flesh. I have considered that there might be some kind of connection to the research of the Third Empire."

Captain Goldfisch drew in a sharp breath.

Through the horn, Captain Rashell chuckled. "It seems I have been missing out on all the fun. Well, don't leave us hanging, Special Agent Lacer."

"Additionally, Siobhan Naught's childhood village was destroyed in a Blight-type Aberrant incident. This is an open Red Guard record, and I do not believe she was tainted by the incident, but it does make one wonder what exactly might have led to such a powerful break event, and of whom. And finally—"

"Oh, there's more?" Aisling murmured, rubbing his palms together.

"She has displayed an interest in the concept of how one might magically encapsulate and store a consciousness."

Captain Aisling frowned. "That is a fascinating line of inquiry, but how is it relevant?"

"Consider the origin of the books that were retrieved from the Black Wastes. Even if you are not a historian and have no particular interest in Myrddin, I think we all know the most common legends. Who has not heard of Carnagore, the steed of white metal, an artifact so complex that it was indistinguishable from life?"

"You think the books hold the secret to such a thing?" Captain Goldfisch asked, his stubborn reticence beginning to melt away.

Thaddeus smiled thinly. "I have, perhaps, left out the most relevant pieces of information. One, she assures me that she can open and read Myrddin's journals, a feat that some of the best minds of the University, and even I myself, have failed to accomplish after months of effort. Two, she agrees that her adoptive grandfather's research may have some relation to how Carnagore was created. Three, I have personally watched Siobhan Naught cast two different spells, from two separate spell arrays, at the same time. She claims to be capable of splitting her Will."

To their credit, none of the Red Guard captains spoke immediately or spewed thoughtless exclamations.

Captain Aisling crossed his arms and tapped one finger against his bicep. "Do you believe her?"

"She claims that the Raven Queen does not lie, but I cannot be sure. She is resistant—perhaps immune—to divination. The other explanation would be that she houses two consciousnesses within the same mind, each with a distinct Will. I do not know which is most likely. I was once a skeptic, but I have come to believe that Myrddin's research must be more important than I would have ever originally guessed. Perhaps there is more truth to his legend than rumor."

Thaddeus allowed the silence to linger for a few seconds, then added, "I see the potential for great benefits to whoever works with her. I would hope that we do not alienate and make an enemy of one who could otherwise be a potent ally. And, quite fortuitously, she has asked me to act as a liaison."

Captain Goldfisch snorted. "Of course, the great Thaddeus Lacer, always greedy for merit and influence," he muttered, just quietly enough that Thaddeus could pretend he did not hear.

Thaddeus raised one side of his lip in a sneer, but did not call the man out. There were more important things at stake here than a petty game of one-upmanship.

Captain Rashell spoke hesitantly. "Special Agent Lacer, do you think it is possible that Myrddin trapped the consciousness of a powerful sorcerer who calls herself the Raven Queen within the book? If that were so, and the sorcerer maintained a working Will and was then somehow able to escape into the mind of a willing host…"

According to Grandmaster Kiernan, Siobhan had intimated as much, but Thaddeus still had his doubts. Just because the woman supposedly could not lie did not mean she could not deceive. "I think we still know too little to form any coherent hypothesis. However, even if that is not the case, there is something behind her ability to split her Will, an ability that presents the kind of galvanizing opportunity that might only come once in a generation, if we are able to convince her to share her secrets."

"It seems to me the attempt to reach out to her was quite botched," Captain Rashell said. "Despite the rumors, your agents underestimated her resourcefulness, Captain Aisling, and frustration at the difficulty of contacting her may have led them to be more aggressive than necessary. Agent Lacer, are you sure she is still amenable to a friendly relationship? Would she join as an agent, or perhaps a consultant?"

Captain Aisling's fingers tapped silently against his own arms. "We could ensure her good intentions through our vows. She would be an asset, if she can be controlled."

Thaddeus was surprised by the visceral rejection that rolled through him, and he shrugged his shoulders slightly as his body forced a physical reaction to the emotion. He had spent a very long time within the bindings of the Red Guard, and many of those years had been spent loosening the hold of his vows, increment by increment. He would not see her go through the same, if he had the choice. "She very much values her freedom, and our agents did not make a good impression on her. But they also did not make enough of an enemy of her that she has decided to take vengeance. I doubt she would be willing to submit herself to our vows and restrictions, but we might be able to get a loose consultancy agreement out of her. Or, at the least, the promise of a couple of favors." Thaddeus chuckled. "Though she might call them boons."

Captain Goldfisch was already shaking his head. "That's not acceptable. We cannot allow someone so dangerous to go free."

Captain Aisling frowned at him. "Is it not even more dangerous to forcibly bind a dragon, as they say?"

"Yes," Thaddeus agreed quickly. "There is a reason why even we, knowing the critical importance of our purpose, have allowed Aberrants like the Dawn Troupe some leeway. I give my sincere testimony and advice at this moment, and I can only hope that you listen." He met the gaze of Captain Aisling, who would be the one to make this decision in the end. "Do not make an enemy of her. Those who have already done so will surely come to regret it."

Goldfisch turned to look at Captain Aisling with frustration, but even he, that self-righteous prick, knew that continuing to display his grudge against Thaddeus when the matter was this important would be to his detriment.

Captain Rashell remained silent as well.

Finally, Aisling spoke. "I would know more before we set our course. Please, tell me of your interactions with the Raven Queen, Special Agent Lacer."

Thaddeus had expected this demand and prepared for it. He recounted, more or less, his correspondence with her and their conversation when she visited his cottage the night before. However, he left several things out. He did not tell them about her interest in shamanry or the hints he had given her about it, what he had done with the Naughts' heirloom ring, or a number of other small details he found distasteful to share.

They were most interested in the magic he had witnessed, as well as her claim of access to the contents of the journal in her possession.

At his urging the night before, she had cast what she called her "shadow-familiar" spell for him to observe and examine. His memory of the moment remained vivid. "It is not truly a familiar," she had warned him as he set up a few diagnostic spell arrays that would be too difficult to free-cast. "This spell merely allows me to take control of my own shadow. When I was young, it was one of the first esoteric spells I learned, and I would form it into the shapes of various creatures and pretend to have conversations or go on adventures with them. That is why my grandfather took to calling it my shadow-familiar, and the name stuck. I find it useful for distractions, concealment, and occasionally to cause fear, but it is not corporeal and cannot actually cause any damage."

Siobhan borrowed some of his spellcasting supplies to draw out a rudimentary sound-muffling spell, not dissimilar to the one he often free-cast. Her handwriting was careful and slow, as if she did not spend much time with a pen, but elegant and beautiful. At first, he had been curious about why she would do so when she was known by all to be a free-caster, but then she cast that spell, using it to contain the sound of her voice, while simultaneously casting the shadow-familiar spell with her mother's ring and her hands cupped in a Circle around her mouth.

Her shadow darkened ominously, but Thaddeus was too shocked by the display of dual-casting to pay full attention to it. He examined the spell array again for the signs that she had cast that spell as an artifact, but found none. The strictures and containment required by an artifact could not be free-cast. Artifacts required physical spell arrays.

She smiled up at him, and he realized he was gaping. He shut his mouth immediately. "I will examine your shadow-familiar first, but you must demonstrate your ability to dual-cast more fully afterward," he said, his words coming out harsh, more a command than a request.

Siobhan lifted one warning eyebrow but did not argue or admonish him further. Instead, she turned her head to her shadow, and it peeled off of his floorboards like a black sticker. Then it filled out, becoming three-dimensional.

She grimaced, and it quickly moved beyond mimicking her form, stretching up into the nightmarish, spindly, beaked form Thaddeus recognized from reports and the memories of the Pendragon Corps.

Entranced, Thaddeus cast a few diagnostic spells, then stepped forward and swiped his fingers through it. "As I thought, it is incorporeal. Enemy spell-fire would pass right through. But several people have reported being touched by it."

"Well, that is most likely a misconception based not on the sensation of pressure but of cold." And just like that, the creature began to suck the heat from the air. Almost immediately, the air around its perimeter began to grow foggy as water vapor froze from contact with the area of her shadow.

After confirming that it was safe to do so, Thaddeus swiped his fingers through its form again. It was true. The cold created an illusion of sensation, likely aided by the very distinct delineation between the area within the shadow, which sucked heat from his flesh with almost painful speed, and the surrounding area. With careful control of the shadow to create the illusion that it was interacting with his flesh, Siobhan was able to easily mimic the sensation of it running an ice-cold claw down his forearm.

"How far can it extend away from your body? Can you increase the absorption of heat fast enough to cause frostbite, or perhaps kill someone by flash-freezing them? Can it absorb other things beyond light and heat? What about spell-fire? Was the spell modeled off of Myrddin's void-shield?" Thaddeus stopped himself before more questions could shoot out, then turned to stare at her impatiently when she did not answer.

Her lips, which were larger than the current fashion, stretched into a slow smile. In his opinion, they complemented the rest of her features perfectly and made a wonderful canvas to paint with the color of blood and fear. "I will not give away all my secrets, Thaddeus. I can extend it some distance from my body. I have never attempted to give anyone frostbite or flash-freeze them to death. And as for Myrddin's void-shield…" She laughed. "I am nowhere near as powerful or skilled as he was. To be able to absorb spell-fire is a distant dream, at best."

But when Thaddeus watched as she drew out two simple spell arrays—of his choosing—and simultaneously cast both the light-based illusion of a blooming flower along with a spell that desiccated a piece of fresh squid that had been kept in his cold box, he could only think that from an outsider's perspective, she was not as far from the feats of Myrddin as she seemed to believe.

It was some small consolation that the effort seemed to strain her.

When she dropped the spells, Thaddeus sat back in his chair, pressed his fingertips together, and stared at her. "Is there any chance that you are, biologically, part brillig? Either through birth or some other method?"

Siobhan had stared at him blankly, then blinked a few times. "That seems exceedingly unlikely, but I suppose it could be possible, somewhere far, far back in my ancestry, from a time before the brillig were culled. Though I was under the impression that they could not interbreed with humans."

Thaddeus frowned. "Are you entirely sure that Ennis Naught is your biological father? Forgive me for stating it so insensitively, but you do not look like him."

"Ennis No-Name," she reminded him. "I have cast him out." She raised a hand, idly playing with one of the red-orange feathers sprouting from between the dark strands of her hair. "I have previously used some of my hair to partially anchor a locating spell for him. I suppose my mental model of him could simply be good enough that the hair was unnecessary, but I find it unlikely that the spell would have worked were he not my biological father."

"In that case, are you entirely sure that you are splitting your Will? I asked you about this once before, but you would not answer me. Grandmaster Kiernan mentioned your conversation to me. He suggested that perhaps there was some consciousness held within the book. A consciousness separate from Siobhan Naught. One with a Will of its own, perhaps?"

She paled. "That is a terrifying thought."

He noted that she still did not actually deny the claim.

Siobhan swallowed. "But I can assure you, I am myself, and my Will is my own. Every speck of it. I am not two entities casting two different spells. It is merely a splitting of attention. I understand why the concept might be hard to grasp, because the act of enforcing your Will seems to require such force that it seems only logical that the entirety of one's consciousness must be bent to creating that force. However, I have found that I can enforce my Will just as irrevocably without actually turning one hundred percent of my concentration to the task. I am hesitant to suggest that others experiment with getting past this mental block. I believe we can both imagine the consequences if it were to go wrong." She shuddered.

"It would almost certainly go wrong ninety-nine times out of a hundred," Thaddeus agreed.

"Do not attempt it," she warned him, clasping her hands together and leaning forward.

"I do not wish to meet death, nor am I curious about what Aberrant form I might take," he assured her. "Your abilities fascinate me, but I find a singular, complete Will to be enough to serve my purposes. Still, I wonder if we might find some knowledge of the topic within Myrddin's journals."

She released her clasped hands and showed him her empty palms. "I could not say, but I am eager to find out."

"You are sure you can open them, then?"

"If they are all protected with the same method as the one within my possession, yes."

It was Thaddeus's turn to lean forward urgently. "Tell me of what lies within the pages of your journal. We believe them to be grimoires. Is that accurate?"

She nodded easily. "Yes, though mine is not structured like any sort of instructional text. Myrddin did actually use it as a journal for random musings, and he seems prone to tangents and stopping halfway through a thought as he had some new idea or epiphany. He was more knowledgeable than I am, and some of his inventions and discoveries are difficult to understand. But if you wish to know more than that, we would have to come to an agreement about what you could offer me in return. Acting as my liaison with the Red Guard will not suffice."

They had spoken for some time afterward, and discussed how best each should handle the current situation, but as soon as Siobhan had left, a half-dozen topics that were left uncovered and questions unanswered had tumbled through Thaddeus's mind.

He had looked around at his empty cabin, in which her presence lingered indelibly, and wondered if perhaps it was more than sentimental perception, or if she really did have some control of the shadows, and had left some of her attention behind.

When he finished telling his nominal superiors everything he was willing to pass along, and they had discussed it from every angle and questioned him thrice more, he said, "The Raven Queen is willing to meet and has agreed to a basic assessment so that we can be at ease toward her nature and her intentions. But the meeting will be on her own terms."

_2_

MUTUALLY ASSURED
DESTRUCTION

Siobhan
  Month 8, Day 15, Sunday 3:15 p.m.

'It is amazing _how even adults—thaumaturges!—can be so easily impressed by the simplest of magic, when cast by the Raven Queen with a bit of added flair and mystery,_' Siobhan thought.

She had needed a momentary break from the edge of helpless pressure building into insanity inside her, and so had descended among the children to perform some party tricks for Theo's birthday. And, well, she _had_ turned on her divination-diverting ward to do it, because the attention of the party-goers —mostly surreptitious peeks and whispers, but a few blatant and almost avaricious stares—had made her uncomfortable. Siobhan had also taken careful control of her shadow to make sure there was no chance the thing inside her could use it to break free again. She hadn't wanted to risk any harm to the children, to the point that she maybe went a little overboard, not allowing it to touch them or their own shadows even when the physics of light should have demanded it do so.

And yet, the adults, who one might have reasonably thought would be more logical, composed, and knowledgeable about magic than the children, were the ones who seemed to be most affected by her presence and demonstration of simple spells.

The children started off afraid and mildly awed but quickly took their cue about how to feel and behave around her from Theo and Miles. One little brat of a girl even kept doing her absolute best to step into Siobhan's shadow, and even ignored Siobhan when she admonished her. The girl's mother looked like she was about three seconds away from wetting herself until Siobhan drew her entire shadow underneath her feet and took away the little girl's temptation.

"Wow, you're an idiot," Theo told the girl, hands on his hips.

For once, Miles agreed with him immediately. "You know that shadow can turn into a monster and crawl inside you, right?"

Gera cleared her throat loudly, and Miles sighed like a middle-aged man. "I'm not allowed to talk about it with *outsiders*."

"Yeah, *outsider*," Theo echoed, and was quickly followed by several of the other children.

This sent the little girl crying off to her mom, who clamped a hand over her mouth, bodily lifted her under one arm, and backed away while bowing repeatedly and stammering apologies to Siobhan.

If not for the adults, maybe playing with the children would have helped to relax Siobhan. Instead, she found herself growing even more uncomfortable, and ended up escaping while the children fought over who could play a simple puzzle game with the handful of ravens she had summoned.

Theo was glowing like he'd swallowed the sun, puffed up with enough pride that he might have been violently deflated with the prick of a needle, so Siobhan decided that she'd done enough. She turned up the power of her divination-diverting ward, ignored Gera's wince and shudder, and escaped back up to an empty private box on the floor above.

The woman gave a blind, single-eyed glare to several people who moved as if they wanted to intercept or follow Siobhan, disabusing them of that notion with surprising effectiveness.

Siobhan was grateful, and actually managed to get about a half-hour of peaceful solitude. She remembered the anti-anxiety potion she'd been prescribed by the University healers and took a small sip of it, and when she felt how nice it was to relax a bit, used Newton's esoteric humming spell to unwind the tension in her body. She rearranged the box's chairs, leaning one back against the wall and turning the other so that she could rest her feet on it.

She tilted her head back and closed her eyes. '*I have too many problems and not enough answers,*' she mused. '*Seems to be the story of my life. Is that ironic or just depressing?*'

She peeked one eye open to watch Oliver and Lynwood talking in another private box on the other side of the arena. When Oliver glanced at her, she made a subtle, lazy motion of invitation: an encouragement to come talk to her when he was free. '*I'm not growing more powerful nearly fast enough to keep up with my problems, but Oliver once told me that people are power, too.*' She had seen the truth of that during Operation Palimpsest, even if everything had gone horribly wrong before the end. *'If I can call on enough of my contacts, and their contacts, and pour enough gold on the situation, maybe I can squeak by somehow.'*

One of Siobhan's biggest obstacles was that she knew she was in danger but didn't fully understand that danger or how it might manifest. That was true of a lot of her problems, but most notably, and most importantly, it was true of both the Red Guard and the thing trapped in her mind. *'I just need infor-mation and time. If I can get those two things, I'll find a way to handle everything else.'*

She began to catalogue possible resources, things that could help her directly and ones that might give her a hint about where to look next. A few minutes passed in quiet contemplation before Oliver's soft steps joined her in the box once more.

He looked down at her, his dark blue eyes shadowed and a lock of hair falling forward across his forehead. He remained silent for a few long seconds, his gaze trailing across her face gently before returning to meet her own. "Have you already considered my offer, then?" he asked, his voice as soft as his nameless blend of an accent and something inscrutable in his expression.

"I need to know what's going on with my 'believers,' yes. I'll want to meet with them. You were right that I can't let the mythos of the Raven Queen continue to spread unchecked. But that's not what I wanted to talk about right now." Siobhan stood, took some supplies from her pockets, and pushed aside the draped curtains to draw a large sound-muffling spell array on the wall. The floor was carpeted in a sound-dampening material that would inevitably break the Circle if she tried to use it as a surface.

When the spell was up, she took out a bottle of moonlight sizzle, shook it until it glowed, and surrounded them in a bubble of her shadow, just to make doubly sure their conversation would be private.

Oliver's mouth flattened into a grim line as he waited for her to speak.

"I'm able to read Myrddin's journal. The one I have, anyway." When Oliver stared at her blankly, she added, "And if you want, I can probably get past the defenses on yours, too."

Oliver opened and closed his mouth in shock, which Siobhan found some-what vindictively satisfying, then narrowed his eyes. "Did you already offer that deal to the Architects of Khronos?"

"I did," she admitted, her satisfaction leaking away.

"That explains the weird preparations Kiernan has been making. He must realize the possibility of a leak, if he's being so secretive," Oliver mused, raking his fingers through his hair.

"The possibility of a leak, like from one of the spies you planted?" Siobhan asked.

"I wouldn't call them spies. More like…informants of opportunity." Her unamused look didn't faze him. "That, or a double-crosser now loyal to the

Crowns. Who knows if one of the many, many people the coppers brought in for interrogation agreed to be an informant? Hells, they might even be worrying about spies from some other country. I should have known something had changed when he started giving strange orders and buying rare warding components."

"Have you managed to talk to him, yet?"

"Apparently he's out of the city at the moment, doing Myrddin knows what. If I cannot get ahold of him within the next couple of days, I'll reach out to one of the others I believe are influential members of the Architects." His eyes were shadowed with worry. "Every day, it seems I come up with some increasingly worse scenario in my imagination. Hopefully whatever they're doing is, if not innocuous, then at least not likely to draw the wrath of Osham's leadership."

Oliver shook his head, putting aside the line of conversation. "But how did you manage to succeed in accessing the book where Kiernan's entire team of people, including Thaddeus Lacer, did not? Does it have anything to do with your transformation amulet?" Oliver stepped closer, staring greedily down at the spot where it hung beneath her clothes. "Is it a key?"

Siobhan reached up to press the amulet against her skin protectively. "It's part of the answer, but it's not actually necessary. The University already found out how to spoof the part of the authentication that recognizes the identity of the reader. But the second part requires an ability that, apparently, is specific to me."

Oliver tilted his head to the side like a curious bird. "How is that possible?"

"It's a surprise to me, too. I suspect that others would be able to develop the ability, with careful research and training from the start of their journey as a thaumaturge, but as of right now, I'm the best option. That might not last, as I'm sure they'll be searching for anyone else who can split their Will, but I plan to take advantage of the situation while I can." She explained the deal she had made with Thaddeus and Kiernan, and through the latter to the Architects of Khronos.

Oliver let out a low whistle. "Wow. Okay, I can see how that would be valuable, especially to someone like you. It's too bad the Red Guard didn't buy the diversion the Architects tried to create in Silva Erde. Maybe if the rumors about you had developed differently…"

Siobhan shrugged helplessly. "I'm hoping to get Professor Lacer to act as my liaison to them, but—" She hesitated, and then admitted, "I'm worried. He said they would probably insist on a meeting so that they could do an assessment. A test, of sorts. And even if they decide I'm not the kind of existential threat they need to erase…the Red Guard wouldn't have survived so long if their agents didn't seize power and opportunities wherever they arose. I won't let them enslave me." Silently, she added, *'I won't let them kill me.'*

Oliver winced, then rubbed the back of his neck, looking down at his shoes in the soft blue light. He thought for a moment, then said, "Your best bet is to bribe them."

Siobhan let out a short, sharp laugh. "That's what Thaddeus said! Professor Lacer, I mean," she corrected.

Oliver squinted at her. "Do you have any ideas?"

"Oh, several. I'm insisting that I will choose the time and location of the meeting, and I plan to use every single resource at my disposal to stack the odds in my favor. But I'll be balancing on a thin string above a very deep chasm. And…you are one of those resources."

"Oh?" Oliver raised one eyebrow, his lips quirking up in a subtle smirk.

"What do you plan to do with your volume of Myrddin's journals?" she asked without preamble. "What are you going to do with the knowledge to create celerium from beast cores, if that is indeed what it contains?"

His smile spread wide and then kept going, curling up at the edges in gleeful slyness. "I will become the known lands' major supplier of celerium. Silva Erde will still have their working mine, and the Thirteen Crowns are organizing a half-dozen expeditions into the wilderness and unknown lands beyond to search for more celerium deposits, but even if they manage to find an untapped mine, just one won't be enough to keep up with demand in Lenore alone, not to mention the other countries."

Palms facing up, he spread his hands to the side. "As a thaumaturge, you should have some idea of how desperate individuals, factions, and entire countries might become for more celerium once they really begin to feel the pinch. Even those who have been stockpiling in preparation for this day will eventually begin to run out. Can you imagine the leverage that will give me?"

His fingers curled slowly into grasping fists. "It's enough power to make my plans a reality…" He dropped his hands and shrugged. "As long as I handle it carefully, don't get assassinated, and can manage to keep the conversion method confidential. Even twenty years of exclusivity would probably be enough. Maybe thirty years, considering how long some thaumaturges live."

"What are your plans, exactly? I mean, I know you want to take over Lenore and improve the lives of civilians. But how, exactly, does stealing the book and converting celerium come into it? Are you hoping to make the Crowns into a puppet leadership and blackmail or bribe them into enforcing the laws you want?" Siobhan watched Oliver's expression as she asked, and knew that her suggestion was incorrect.

The tiniest hint of what might have been sadness passed over his face. He hesitated, probably considering the wisdom of sharing his secret plan—which could be ruined if the wrong person found out—with her. Finally, he said only, "I don't plan to share it with the Crowns."

Siobhan had suspected as much, but the skin of her back grew cold, not because of his statement, but because of what it actually meant. The Thirteen Crowns would not, *could* not, simply allow anyone else to have that kind of power. They ruled by the philosophy that there was a limited amount to go around. If Oliver gained more, then they would lose some of their own. And eventually, they would starve and die.

Oliver's voice was low and intense, and his gaze had turned to look beyond her into the darkness of her shadow. "I don't want a puppet rulership, though I wouldn't object to having people of questionable morals in lower positions as long as they are willing to take extensive vows regarding the allowed ethics, and submit to external oversight. I want to tear out the current system by its rotten, putrid roots. Anything that resists has to be destroyed."

He refocused on her and gave her a lopsided, humorless smile. "Of course, I am not against handing out a bit of power to the right people. Ones that will act toward my interests—whether they realize they are doing so or not."

Siobhan frowned. "The Crowns and those that work for them could turn on each other, if given the right incentive," she said slowly, trying to see if that was what he meant, or if his plans ran layers deeper than she could comprehend.

"The principle extends anywhere there are people who care more about their own interests than the greater good," he replied.

She raised an eyebrow. "So, everywhere."

His lopsided smile filled with some actual amusement. "Well, yes. My exclusive access to large amounts of celerium will allow me to make alliances, destroy certain people, take control of Gilbratha and then, ideally, the whole of Lenore. In the future I envision, every single person in the country will have access to basic education, including magical training. Upon completing that training, and perhaps taking certain vows, every applicable citizen should have a way to obtain a Conduit suited for Apprentice-level magic. Can you imagine a country where every single person is able to produce as much value as you do, Siobhan?" he asked fervently. "We can eliminate illness and poverty. We could eradicate governmental corruption. We could extend the standard lifespan by decades and, well, it might sound trite, but we could give people happier lives."

He took a deep breath, his hands clenching until they trembled. "In a world like that, we would teach people to look back and be appropriately horrified by what will eventually be considered atrocities of indifference. We could achieve feats that you and I are both too ignorant to even dream of." He hesitated, then added, "With enough minds turned toward the problem, we might even be able to find a way to stop Aberrants from forming."

The cold feeling on Siobhan's back increased as she considered his dream. It was wondrous, to be sure. But it would make an enemy out of those who did not share his vision. That kind of world would require their current one to be torn asunder and rebuilt from the foundation. And she could not even imagine the kind of power and resources it would take to achieve. Even an endless source of celerium might not be enough.

Siobhan didn't consider herself a strategist or particularly knowledgeable about how politics—or even people—worked. But even she knew it wouldn't be just the Thirteen Crowns who had a problem with it. If Oliver really did take over Lenore, then what of Osham, Silva Erde, the northern islands, the people of the Tataroc Desert, or the countries of the East? Countries needed people, even commoners. What country could survive its people emigrating en masse to join a promised wonderland of opportunity? He would have to defeat and unify at least those closest to Lenore.

'It is possible,' a thought whispered insidiously, even as her dread grew. 'The Blood Emperor did it, after all.' She swallowed. "There will be bloodshed. No matter how clever you are, no matter how many deals you make or schemes you put in place, I don't think there's any way to avoid that."

"People are already dying. And not just that. Tell me, how much pain and despair must ten people feel to balance out to the equivalent of one person's life? How much from a hundred people? If a million people die young, of preventable causes, what is the worth of their unrealized years?" Oliver shook his head. "Most people don't see how bad it is because they're inured to reality. It's how things have always been, for as long as they've known. No. Better to let blood be shed quickly and decisively, and ideally in greater proportion by those who deserve it most."

Cold sweat trickled down Siobhan's back as she had a realization about something even more important than Oliver's plans.

The Raven Queen would be a major point of interest for…possibly every single major player in the city. Maybe even powers outside of Lenore, if they had reason to believe she knew how to create celerium. And several of those players were about to become increasingly desperate, which might encourage them to take risks or extreme actions they would have otherwise hesitated to commit to.

Siobhan was not a skilled politician or manipulator. It was unlikely that she would be able to maintain the delicate balancing act between powerful forces that would keep her safe.

She swallowed, noting how dry her throat had grown. "And if the blood of your allies is also shed to enact your plans?"

"Sacrifice is inevitable. As a thaumaturge, you should know, you cannot gain something for nothing. I won't give up even a drop of innocent blood without making my enemies pay for it a thousand-fold." Oliver's conviction shone bright in his eyes. He looked at her, but she thought that he was actually seeing a vision of his dreams for the future.

Siobhan suppressed a shudder. His ideas were nice, but she found his answer horrific. *'That is the difference between us. I, too, have grand dreams of power, but I would not willingly sacrifice even a drop of the things that truly matter to me to reach them. Is he an altruist, or am I simply greedy?'*

She set that thought to the side to focus on a more immediate problem. "So, Myrddin's journal? Would you like me to unlock it for you or not? I assume you haven't already found a way to do so on your own."

"I am certainly interested in your services. But what would you wish in return?"

"I understand that you wouldn't give the knowledge within to any political power. But would you be opposed to sharing it with the Red Guard?"

Oliver's eyes narrowed. "You need a bargaining chip. That kind of knowledge certainly *seems* like the kind of thing they would be interested in. Though who knows for sure with the Red Guard?" he added. But he shook his head. "My original plan was to wait until someone decrypted any of the other four journals and then come to an agreement with the thaumaturge in question. I had thought it might be Thaddeus Lacer. I would be willing to allow you to unlock the book in exchange for sharing the information with you alone. But if you want to pass that on to the Red Guard, you will have to offer me something additional, and significant."

Siobhan smirked. "Oliver, the person who unlocks it being able to read literally every page is a requirement of accessing the contents. It is not like some chest, where the key can be passed around and the contents remain available while it is unlocked. Myrddin's journals require constant effort to maintain their clarity, with an additional test at literally every turn of a page. You cannot offer that as repayment. And in this situation, I think you need my services quite a bit more than I need the additional danger of having that knowledge in my head. I have no need of extra celerium, after all. What I need is something that can make me safer. And forgive me my lack of faith, but I don't believe you have much to offer in that regard."

Oliver turned his back on her as if to pace, but found himself restricted by the borders of her shadow. After a few moments of fidgeting, he turned back around. "What if I could offer you something else that the Red Guard would definitely be interested in?"

He paused for a dramatic silence and she waved at him impatiently.

"The Red Guard places a very high value on chasing down their rare defectors," he said. "What if I could get you information about one of those defectors? That would be a way to show your goodwill while also making it very hard for them to refuse you."

"Can you do that?"

"I believe I can. Give me three days and I'll know for sure."

Siobhan's eyes narrowed. "Unless your information is so amazing that the Red Guard are willing to literally turn around and offer me their ongoing protection, I'm not sure it really balances the scales between us."

Oliver scoffed. "Access to the knowledge within should be enough."

"Knowledge that people have been trying to capture or kill me for since I got to this city. If you start producing celerium, those same people are going to make the obvious connection. And they are going to be desperate."

After a long moment, Oliver said, "I would be willing to negotiate with the Red Guard if they would agree to maintain an apolitical stance to my satisfaction. I have no grudge against them using celerium to keep us all safe from Aberrants, and I am sure they could offer me many things of value in return. Perhaps an assignment as my exclusive and sole representative in our dealings would be enough to keep you safe long term? They would have a personal, vested interest in maintaining their access to celerium, and thus in your safety. Then all you have to do is convince them you're not so big of a threat that they need to deal with you anyway."

"That *might* work," she said dubiously.

Oliver laughed. "You're such a pessimist."

Siobhan scowled. "It's not pessimism if the world really is out to destroy you." Their discussion continued for a few more minutes, after which she let her shadow-familiar and the sound-muffling spell drop.

Oliver returned to mingling with the other partygoers, and Siobhan fell into contemplation. Despite the agreement she had just made, her anxiety was far from settled. In fact, their conversation had left her even less sure of her safety than before. She might be able to call on the Red Guard for protection, if she trusted them, because as an organization they were magically stronger than either the University or the Crowns. And they were international, so they could stash her almost anywhere. But she didn't trust them. Even Thaddeus didn't fully trust them, if she considered the advice he'd given her.

And, of course, Siobhan had what she was ninety-five percent sure was an Aberrant, or a piece of one, locked inside her head.

'Is this the calm before the storm, the last moment where I could make a different decision before everything goes horribly, horribly wrong?' she wondered. After what had happened to Newton, she had looked back on her decisions and decided that she was a fool.

'What are the possible outcomes, and what is the likelihood of each of them?' She pulled out a piece of paper from her satchel and began to do the math, estimating the weight of both positive and negative outcomes. Staying alive, but not getting to stay at the University or otherwise continue making progress on any of her goals had a weight of zero. Getting to stay at the University, read all of Myrddin's journals, and peruse the restricted archives at her leisure had a

weight of positive eight. All that, plus having the thing in her head magically dealt with by someone more powerful and competent than her had a weight of positive ten. The Red Guard catching her and taking away her life, her autonomy, and her name, while discovering the thing in her head, had a weight of negative nine, because it was foolish to imagine there literally couldn't be anything worse. There was always something worse that could happen.

She came up with a dozen or so other possible outcomes and then multiplied each by its likelihood—as best she could guess it—to come up with what she called the utility value.

She was horrified by the results of the math. Even if, technically, she couldn't accurately predict the likelihood of any future, common sense, in black and white ink, showed her that things were looking grim. Taken together, the negative utility values far outweighed the positive.

Siobhan burned the paper. *'Should I just run? If I went to Silva Erde and set up a new identity there, what's the chance I could survive long enough to successfully fix my other problem? I have the gold, and I've learned so much useful magic already, I could make it by. But the problem with that is the thing in my head. I cannot cast the sleep-proxy by myself. I need Liza, or someone equally powerful and ethically questionable.'*

Rubbing at her burning eyes, Siobhan tilted her head back. She was not tired, even after all the exertion of the day before. It was still wonderful, but the gratification of her success there could not stand up to the weight of everything else. *'I can go a few more days without sleep until the raven bound to me needs to be released or risk death. But maybe Liza and I could cast the spell with two ravens at once, allowing them to stagger being the sleeper and recovery. That might allow me to eliminate the need for sleep indefinitely. Or, even better, why not create a whole network of interconnected ravens? Enough that they barely feel the extra weight of my fatigue.'*

Professor Lacer's voice resounded in her head, her subconscious calling up an appropriate response to her idea. *'Hare-brained twit. Would that idea get you added to the pages of* 100 Clever Ways Thaumaturges Have Committed Suicide?' her imaginary version of him asked acidly.

Siobhan pinched her chin between forefinger and thumb as she considered it. *'It's based on the principles of binding magic, not sympathy. There's an agreement and exchange between myself and the ravens, but none of them are conceptually "me." Which means that they shouldn't be able to be used to find or affect me. Right? The most someone who wanted to hurt me could do is break the binding. It's the same reason you can't use a person who's cursed as a component to track down the person or object cursing them.'*

Her frown deepened. *'Is that right? It seems like that idea is too easy a solution to be workable. Nothing ever works out so easily for me.'* She tried to find the flaw, but any problems she came up with seemed to have rather simple solutions. This left her even more suspicious. If there was a danger there, it was something she didn't have the knowledge or experience to anticipate. Which meant it would be a surprise. And that was the worst kind of danger.

But a network like that would be self-sustaining. She would no longer need to rely on Liza once it was set up. It wouldn't solve her real problem, but it might give her time. Time to grow stronger and more knowledgeable. Both of those things would be significantly harder away from Gilbratha, especially considering the new resources Thaddeus and Grandmaster Kiernan had offered her.

However, being free to grow and learn *at all* was more important.

3

―――――――

ECHOES AND ANXIETY

Siobhan
Month 8, Day 15, Sunday 7:00 p.m.

THOUGH IT WAS A HASSLE, since she planned to talk to Professor Lacer that evening, Siobhan changed into her other form to travel back to the University. She didn't have confirmation that the Red Guard were willing to wait until the meeting time she would set, or even that they would be amenable to a conversation at all. And though it might not hold true if they changed methods, they had indicated that they were unable to find her as Sebastien.

She looked out of the window of her hired carriage, though her mind was occupied elsewhere. *'If I left Gilbratha, where would I go? What would I do?'* There was only one Thaumaturgic University of Lenore, but Osham and Silva Erde had their own institutions of learning. It was possible they really were inferior to the University, but after learning more and more about how politics played a role in such things, she thought it was equally possible that the Thirteen Crowns simply couldn't admit there were viable alternatives.

After hearing some of Oliver's stories and reading newspaper articles about Osham, she wanted to avoid spending significant amounts of time there. Besides, access to their schools was much more regulated and restricted, and would probably require her to take certain vows of service that would come into play after she graduated. She did not want to end up being conscripted.

Silva Erde didn't put as much focus on modern sorcery in favor of what many considered "softer" crafts, but surely there was still plenty to learn there. Some of her most useful spells were esoteric, after all. They might even be more inclined to teach "creative" solutions to certain unusual problems. However, she'd heard it was a lot harder to get certain spell components they considered unethically sourced, and they even fined people for foraging components from the wild without the proper licenses. Like Osham, Silva Erde was not particularly fond of Lenore, though for very different reasons.

'I could buy a space-expanded traveler's pack, take my gold and my celerium and everything else, and pick one of the false identities I had the Nightmare Pack get papers for. I have the gold to buy my way into a year or two at most institutions, or an apprenticeship with someone powerful. I might even be able to guide my own studies, buying rare or expensive books and trading information with other thaumaturges I meet on the way.' There was a certain appeal to the idea, especially because coin in hand would make all the difference from when she had traveled with Ennis.

While the thought of leaving behind the danger of Gilbratha and the Raven Queen's identity enticed her, there were other things she would be reluctant to part with: Oliver, Liza, Theo and Miles, Damien, Ana, and even Professor Lacer; her little attic apartment that she had so many plans for; and the University library. Without quite realizing it, she had begun to build a life here. If she left, she would also be abandoning the kind of opportunities that many would kill for: access to the restricted archives and relationships with powerful people, whose contacts might help her find a way to deal with the thing inside her head.

The thought of walking away from all of that was almost painful.

'But it would be better than several of the worse possible outcomes,' she reminded herself. Another, more cynical side of her thought, 'Except leaving doesn't guarantee my safety. It just cuts me off from possible solutions.'

She would be giving up her apprenticeship. Thaddeus Lacer was a Grandmaster, a free-caster, and the type of person who didn't mind if she happened to dabble in a bit of harmless blood magic. That would not be replaceable.

Liza was a discreet source of powerful artifacts and a skilled collaborator who could bring Siobhan's ideas to fruition.

And Siobhan would lose the small circle of friends—yes, friends—that she had accidentally built up. If she left now, she would probably never see any of them again.

And if she stayed, maybe one or several of the resources she'd painstakingly gotten her greedy claws in could help her fix things.

When she arrived at the University, she found that all of the library's private rooms and many of the empty classrooms of the Citadel, the University's cylindrical main building, were occupied by other students. So Sebastien retreated to her cubicle, pulled the curtain, and set up a sound-muffling spell that she pre-charged as a nominal artifact with the most basic of functions and then set to slowly run dry.

She spent the long hours until sunset trying to finish her homework. Unfortunately, she found that all her practice splitting her Will made it quite easy to continue worrying over her many problems while simultaneously writing essays and drawing diagrams. Even math was not enough to require her full concentration.

She forced herself to wait until after the poorly enforced curfew, when the dorm lights were shut off and most of her classmates were asleep, before taking up her satchel and slipping away to the bathroom. There, she turned on her divination-diverting ward, then crept out of the University and into the darkness of the trees to the east, away from the cobblestone paths. Using her shadow to further block any potential sight, she changed back into her Siobhan form and fumblingly dressed herself. A cloak with a hood concealed her features. She made sure to exit the cover of her shadow-familiar spell several meters away from where she had entered it, even though no one was around and the precaution was probably unnecessary.

When she had reached the edge of the trees, she looked out toward Professor Lacer's cottage, gauging the distance. *'Two hundred meters? I can see light through his window. I think I can make that.'*

Squinting slightly to make out details, Siobhan re-cast her shadow-familiar spell with exceeding care, then sent it forward slowly through the darkness. She was ready to stop and drop the spell at the first sign that something was wrong, but the distance was barely a strain. She let her shadow rise up to the window, and when Professor Lacer's silhouette passed by, she sent her shadow through the glass.

His silhouette froze.

Siobhan formed her shadow into the shape of a cute, unassuming raven. She hoped the shape took form like she imagined. She'd never tested her precise control at such a distance, when all she could see was a little blob of darkness at the end of her tether. When she was pretty sure that Professor Lacer had seen it and knew who she was, she formed words in a looping script instead. *May I visit? Turn on your porch light to invite me.* Then she let her shadow retreat through the glass and dropped the spell.

The cottage's porch light came on thirty seconds later.

Belatedly, she realized that if Professor Lacer had been entertaining company, her shadow might have gotten him into trouble. Siobhan took one last glance around to be sure no one would see her, then strode quickly to the cottage's front door.

Professor Lacer opened it before she could knock. "I did not expect to see you tonight," he said as she swept past him. "Are you so impatient to meet again?"

Siobhan thought she detected a hint of amusement in his voice, though she wasn't sure if he was trying to make a joke. "I am impatient to know the outcome of your endeavor today. I am *trying* to curb my reckless tendencies, and I realize that if the leadership of the Red Guard is unfavorably inclined toward me, it would be very dangerous to make your organization an enemy in truth. It is a fight I am not certain to win. I am considering leaving the country, and if it is necessary, it would be best to do so as soon as possible."

"You cannot leave!" The words burst from Thaddeus in a harsher tone than she had expected.

She turned away from restlessly examining the room to look at him.

He cleared his throat. "I meant…leaving now would be a foolish and *unnecessary* decision."

She narrowed her eyes but resisted the urge to let her emotions froth from her lips in their raw, blistering state. "The agent that I tussled with threatened to take from me my name, my autonomy, and my life." She swallowed and again tried to regulate her voice to keep the rage from it. "I will not allow that. If they come after me again…" She wanted to make outlandish threats that she definitely couldn't back up but instead allowed the silence to stretch and linger. "I have an unfortunate amount of experience with the way things can spiral out of control after a few regrettable decisions. So tell me, Thaddeus, do I truly have no need to worry?"

"To be cautious, yes. To worry?" He hesitated. "I do not believe so. While certain individuals among my colleagues do hold some amount of animosity toward you, as a whole, the local leadership has been convinced of your value. The rest will be up to you."

"They agreed to the meeting?" she asked.

"They did, and seemingly in good faith, though that does not mean they will not take precautions."

Siobhan frowned, running her tongue over the back of her teeth as she gazed into the darkest shadows of the room.

"It would be foolish to abandon the knowledge and power you stand to gain here. Think of the work we could do together. And, might I remind you, you have already given your word that you would aid in my research of Myrddin's journals. Doing so from afar seems implausible."

Siobhan relaxed slightly. "I would also prefer not to leave. Please, tell me what you have learned."

"Would you like coffee? I have purchased milk and sugar."

She gave him a small, surprised smile. "Yes, please."

Something of the tension in his shoulders seemed to ease, and when he returned, he told her what he could of his meeting with the Red Guard captains and their plans for her.

With every small piece of information, Siobhan's anxiety uncoiled. Perhaps she had been overreacting. The Red Guard was a terrifying opponent, but as long as she could convince them that she was neither an existential threat to the world nor so valuable that they should try to enslave her, everything should be fine. Probably.

"Will they expect me to take vows?" she asked, sipping her obviously very expensive coffee and savoring the slightly nutty aftertaste.

"They will certainly push hard for that concession. If you wish to adjust the terms, you may need to give up other bargaining points. The Red Guard quite loves their vows," he added with a wry, bitter twist of his mouth.

Siobhan really hoped that Oliver would come through with some intel on a rogue agent, because the excessive interest in the method to create Carnagore, or otherwise quantify and encapsulate a consciousness, that Professor Lacer had hinted at wasn't something she could actually provide. Not unless she happened to find that information within her entry of Myrddin's journals. And she certainly couldn't let them inspect her warding medallion or the disks under the flesh of her back. *'Perhaps there will be other knowledge in my entry that I can use to bribe them. If I can manage to read and understand enough of it before our meeting.'*

"Helping me like this does not violate your own vows?" she asked.

"There is wiggle room within any binding, if you are tenacious enough," he said lightly, though his eyes were shadowed. "While it is true that I have taken vows to work toward their best interest, I do not consider this a violation. Both sides have more to benefit from alliance than strife."

"Do you have any advice for me, then?"

Professor Lacer was silent for a long moment, and then a thin, toothless smile stretched his lips. "Be yourself."

She blinked at him, then let out a low chuckle at the trite counsel.

"Do not let them control you," he added firmly. "They will try."

Siobhan didn't stay much longer; she had gained what she could, and any more would just be useless repetition. After confirming when they would make an attempt on the University's three entries from Myrddin's journals and reminding Thaddeus to hurry with her access to the restricted archives, she returned to her previous form within the darkness of the trees, then sneaked back into the dorms.

For about half an hour, Sebastien stared out at the night sky, where patches of stars hid behind sparse clouds that felt almost close enough to climb to.

Sebastien was not tired, but she was still afraid.

She rummaged in her satchel and the chest at the bottom of her bed, compiling a handful of components. She considered exactly what she hoped to do, and then began to bear down with her Will, though she channeled no energy and cast no spell.

Then, under the light of the stars and a vial of moonlight sizzle, Sebastien cut a finger-width strip from a piece of soft mermaid leather she had saved from in-class spell practice. The giant magical cephalopods excelled at disguising themselves, and with enough time, the cord would begin to visually blend into its environment, even without any added enchantments.

She used the rest of the leather to protect her hands as she massaged the strip with ghost pepper oil, allowing its burning heat to sink in. Beeswax made from honey gathered from magical flowers that were aligned with mundane light carefully sealed the leather surface. Then, she used her silver athame to cut a few notches in the leather on one side and to narrow a section of the other side, allowing her to weave the two together.

Finally, she fit the leather band inside the Circle of her two joined hands and raised it to her mouth. "Life's breath, shadow mine. In darkness we were born. In darkness do we feast. Devour, and arise," she whispered slowly. She repeated this three times. When she had an iron grip on her own shadow, she lowered her hands and separated them from around the leather Circle.

The spell held without appreciable strain, and a wild grin split her face. This was what hundreds upon hundreds of hours of practice brought you.

Control.

And from now on, she would practice constantly. Sebastien slipped the leather over her foot and tightened the cord until it fit snugly as a slightly chilly anklet. She would maintain her shadow-familiar spell at all times, using just a small part of her Will. Several uses had already confirmed that it was seemingly safe to cast the spell, and this felt like a much more acceptable alternative than trying to avoid danger by never casting it again. If she was in constant, total control of her shadow, nothing else could be. With the barest trickle of power through the spell, her ankle wouldn't grow too cold, and her shadow would remain visibly normal.

The need for sleep would be her only weakness. And as time went on, her mastery over her shadow would only grow. If she ever needed to fight for it again, she would win.

She spent the remainder of the night meditating over her shadow's vague perception and, when that grew tiring, twisting it into increasingly complex shapes.

In the morning, she ate every morsel provided at breakfast, then supplemented more from her personal stores of dried meat, fruit, and crackers. Not sleeping meant that she needed more food than ever, since she dearly wanted to avoid another attempt at intervention from Professor Lacer.

She was somewhat distracted during classes, both by her shadow-familiar spell and her plans, but she did her best not to let it show.

Damien was likewise distracted, and tired enough that he dozed off during class, drawing most of their friends' concerned attention to himself. Professor

Lacer ended up sending him to the infirmary for a dose of sleep potion rather than allowing him to practice during class time, despite the young man's fervent protests.

After school, Sebastien went down into Gilbratha and put together another civilian disguise, which she used to visit Liza.

Perhaps because of the sleep-proxy spell's effects, the woman was in one of the least grumpy moods Siobhan had ever seen her in. Her dark skin was glowing with health and her mane of curls was shiny and barely frizzing at all. She didn't even scowl when she saw who had knocked on her door. Siobhan grimaced and then proceeded to ruin Liza's cheer.

After she was done explaining the situation with the Red Guard, and how she hoped Liza would help her prepare for the meeting, Liza stared at her, blank-faced and eyes slightly unfocused. "How do you get yourself into such trouble? Have you been cursed?" she muttered.

"Will you help?" Siobhan asked.

Liza scowled, grinding her teeth for a dozen seconds before she spoke. "I can place wards at the location and lease you a bevy of protective artifacts, but I will not be present for your meeting or in any way act personally."

"That's enough," Siobhan hurried to assure her.

They spent the next hour discussing everything while Liza brought out some breadsticks slathered in garlic butter. They narrowed down the best location that the other side would reasonably agree to—a magical hedge maze in the Lilies that the Red Guard could secure from civilians and which would give Siobhan a reasonable chance of escape if something went wrong. Siobhan would be renting a ridiculous amount of warded jewelry, as well as purchasing an enchanted set of armored clothing with embedded shielding from one of Liza's acquaintances. Liza had never been in the Red Guard but had worked with them a few times during the latter part of her stint in the army. She had several ideas for wards that might help counteract what the woman drolly labeled the Red Guard's "nefarious schemes" or help Siobhan to escape if necessary.

Before Liza could bring up the issue of payment, Siobhan said, "I have access to notes on several methods Myrddin used to create self-charging artifacts. I can make a copy for you."

Liza froze and then agreed without haggling. "But you must pay me before your meeting. In case you never come back from it."

Siobhan was almost as disturbed by the lack of haggling as she was by that ominous statement. *'Is it possible that I just agreed to grossly overpay her?'* She had expected the fee to be well over one thousand gold, and unlike some of Myrddin's other feats, self-charging artifacts were not completely lost. She crossed her arms and added, "In addition, I also want you to help me develop and then apply a new version of the sleep-proxy spell. One that doesn't rely on a single raven or have any single point of failure."

When Siobhan explained her plan, Liza tried to argue that Myrddin's notes weren't worth that much, but when Siobhan offered to pay her in gold or celerium instead, the woman's protests died a sudden and mysterious death.

"Do you have any other advice for me about how to handle the meeting?" Siobhan asked, as she had done with Professor Lacer.

"The Red Guard is full of sanctimonious, hypocritical, covetous pricks," Liza said, waving a breadstick around violently. "Don't let them think they can control you."

Siobhan's eyebrows rose at the identical advice.

"They have a history of conciliation and pacification when they have no better option," Liza explained. "So you need to make them believe they have no other, better, option. But you won't be able to lie to them. They love their truth compulsions and unbreakable vows. If things look to be going wrong, better to escape, even if you have to fight your way out, than to get trapped in an unacceptable vow. If you can find anyone willing to risk themselves for you, take backup."

Siobhan nibbled on her lower lip, nodding slowly. "One last thing. Can I get the contact info for your shaman? I have some questions I would like to ask about his craft." Getting access to the library's restricted archives would be invaluable, but for someone as ignorant as her, they were also likely to be difficult to navigate and beyond her understanding. Even better would be a knowledgeable shaman. Though she would wait to meet him until after her assessment from the Red Guard. If Liza was right, Siobhan wouldn't be able to lie to them, after all, and they took offense to certain uses of shamanry.

4

RED GUARD MEETING

Siobhan

Month 8, Day 21, Saturday 6:35 a.m.

One unexpected benefit of no longer needing to sleep was that Siobhan could set appointments at times that would be inconvenient for others. Such as before the sun rose on a weekend morning.

It had been a week of intense preparation since she last spoke with Professor Lacer. She had divided her time between collaborating with her handful of allies, shopping for supplies, practicing her spellwork, and rehearsing any and all possible variations of the upcoming conversation while observing herself in the mirror. Hopefully, the last of those would allow her to seem composed no matter what they threw at her.

Earlier that morning, one of Oliver's people had ferried her across the Charybdis Gulf in a four-person speedboat. Oliver himself was gone from Gilbratha entirely. By this time, he would be well on his way to Osham. Apparently, someone powerful within the Architects—not Kiernan, according to his assertions of innocence—had gotten it into their head that it would be a good idea to kidnap a group of military recruits that included the child of a powerful noble. Oliver hadn't given her much detail, but even someone as politically ignorant as her could understand why that was a bad idea. He and a group of combat-experienced enforcers were on their way to try to catch up to and stop the Architects, by force if necessary.

Oliver's stable of erythreans might be able to make it possible. Apparently, with the right enchantments on the saddle and gear, a well-trained erythrean could travel well over one hundred kilometers a day. For land-based mounts, that was second only to Carnagore.

Siobhan put that niggling worry from her mind. She needed to focus on what she could control. The speedboat driver would be waiting to take them all back from the Lilies in an hour if all went well. The two men escorted her toward the place she had chosen for her meeting with the Red Guard—an enormous magical hedge maze.

As they approached one of the entrances, which was barred by a Red Guard cordon and a repelling compulsion, Siobhan's eyes widened.

Gera was waiting for her, which they had agreed on and Siobhan had expected. The woman had agreed to accompany Siobhan to the meeting as her remaining payment for saving Millennium's life. She would keep the agents from successfully lying as well as secretly give Siobhan some insight into the opponent.

But Siobhan had not expected that Gera would allow Miles to get anywhere close to anything involving the Red Guard. And yet, the boy stood beside his mother, grinning brightly as Siobhan and her two bodyguards approached.

Siobhan raised her eyebrows at Gera, who shook her head with weary defeat and gave a minuscule shrug.

"Nice outfit," Miles said when she stopped in front of him. He reached forward to run the luxurious blue-black fabric between his fingers, then peered at one of the subtle spell arrays embroidered into the fabric.

"Thank you," Siobhan replied automatically. Except for Liza's work examining and warding the maze itself, this dress had been Siobhan's single most expensive purchase. It was luxurious enough to fit the image she wanted to portray, was designed for a woman to fight in, and contained several additional minor enchantments. All that, in addition to being self-repairing. If not for Liza's connections, she wouldn't have had a chance to buy it, no matter how much gold she could throw around. It was a horrible waste of money, but if it increased her chances of successful negotiation, or of escaping alive in the case of failure, any amount of gold would be worth it.

It also didn't show moisture as Siobhan wiped her sweaty hands on it. "What are you doing here?" she asked bluntly.

"I came to listen beforehand and let you know if I heard anything important. The Red Guard agents are already here, waiting for you inside," Miles said.

Gera clenched and unclenched her fists. "I tried to stop him, but he was...insistent."

Miles scrunched his face at her. "I *know*. I'm not going in with you. But I can still help a little."

"The whispers?" Siobhan asked, unconsciously lowering her voice. "What have you learned?"

"They have three people inside. One of them you know, and the whispers know him, too. People like to talk about him."

'*Thaddeus Lacer*,' Siobhan guessed.

"He likes you, so you don't need to worry about him, but the other two sound like greed and trickery and…something. I can't hear clearly enough. And they hid another eight people all around the outside of the maze. But, since you hid some too, I think that's fine?"

"Can you point out the hidden agents? Discreetly?"

Miles did so, though the whispers were too capricious to give him exact details.

Siobhan placed them on her mental map of the area. It wasn't ideal, but it could have been worse. "It's fine. We expected that. Is there anything else?"

"They have a plan. It kind of sounds like…making you slip, or pulling the ground out from under you so you fall over. And then when you're down they'll trap you in a net." He closed one eye and tilted his head. "And the strings will…wrap you up and make you dance like a little puppet?" He shook his head, wincing and pressing his hands against his ears as if he'd heard a loud, jarring noise that was inaudible to the rest of them. "Sorry. I'm still not very good at this. But they talked about it beforehand, and they are who they are. The wind hears everything." He shuddered, then rubbed at his arms and the back of his neck.

"If it hurts, stop listening," Siobhan said.

Miles gave her a sad, wry smile. "I can't. Not really. But you're known to the wind, too. So what you should do, it's like, smile with blood-painted teeth. And, um, if you trip, just lean into it and keep spinning all the way around? Make yourself look big and win in a staring contest."

"Did the whispers say that?"

"Oh, well they don't really talk. I mean, I can hear speaking, but it's just memories that got trapped by the wind. I…I don't know how to explain it. Uh, maybe it's like when you watch a stage play and the music goes along and changes with what's happening? The wind changes with meaning, too." Miles jerked his head to the side again, pressing harder against his ears. "Ugh!" he squeaked with pain. "It's *too much* meaning. The wind wants me to hear *everything*, but my head is too small."

Gera let out a low, suppressed moan of distress.

Siobhan sank down onto one knee, pressing her own hands over his to better protect Millennium's ears. "You can't stop the wind from blowing, but you can stop listening. What's your favorite meditation exercise?"

Miles hesitated, but eventually whispered, "My tintinnabulating sand. But I don't have it here."

"You can still imagine it. Close your eyes and meditate. Focus in until everything else is just background noise."

"Can you hum? Do the humming magic," Miles requested, his eyes clenched shut tight and wetness shining on his lashes.

As soon as she understood what he meant, Siobhan tugged him closer, spinning him around so that he was crouched in front of her, his back pressed against her front. She pressed the Circle of her hands against the boy's chest to cast Newton's vibrational calming spell.

Miles hummed along with her, his voice much higher pitched and wavering at first, but slowly settling into a steady tone.

"I knew I shouldn't have brought him," Gera murmured to herself, her voice distant and her blind eye staring sightlessly down at them. "But I was afraid he would sneak out alone. I can't stand not knowing where he is. Not after what happened last time. I *told* him I would pay the debt on his behalf, but he wouldn't..."

Siobhan couldn't speak past the humming, but she tried to convey some comfort in her expression before realizing that whatever magic Gera used to perceive the world couldn't see Siobhan past her divination-diverting ward.

But Miles had already calmed, and so with a few more breaths, she released the magic. "I'll teach you how to do this spell yourself one day," she whispered to him.

Gera's face tightened. "I'm sending my son home now."

A squad of Nightmare Pack enforcers stepped forward from the shadows across the street at Gera's commanding motion.

Siobhan nodded. "One of you, go with them," she said to her own escort. When Gerard opened his mouth to protest, she added, "You cannot come with me past the maze entrance anyway. Go, and come back to escort me when I am finished." Really, her guards' presence was more for show than anything. Even if one of them left, she would still have the aid of the other people Oliver had placed along her various pre-planned escape routes.

Gerard drew the short straw and limped off after Miles, scowling like a bulldog with indigestion.

"I'll be fine," Miles called back over his shoulder as he patted his breast pocket.

"You got him a battle wand?" Siobhan asked as she and Gera watched them leave.

"Two. One is hidden in a calf sheath. And every bead on his necklace is a single-use shield artifact. They're all charged with the strongest spells gold and favors can buy, and we've hired a tutor to teach him some footwork and technique. If someone tries to harm my son again, it is my dearest hope that they are reduced to a fine mist of blood and bone marrow."

Siobhan hoped that Miles was never forced to witness something like that, and even more so that he wouldn't be the cause of it, for his own sake. She looked to the east, where the white cliffs still blocked the hint of an oncoming sunrise, and took a deep breath of the briny air. It was too bad that there was no fog this morning; it would have fit the mood. "Shall we go?"

Gera steeled herself, checked her warding artifacts, and linked arms with Siobhan. Together, they stepped past the Red Guard's cordon.

Siobhan walked slowly, her head held high, quite conscious of all the warded jewelry that she was renting from Liza. It was all rather bold and somewhat gaudy, and she would have felt silly, like some noble showpiece, if not for the extremely pragmatic purpose it served.

As they neared the center of the ten-foot-tall maze, one of the tiny golden dragons curved around the shell of her ear let out a soft sound, alerting her that one of her four anti-compulsion artifacts or three anti-memetic effect artifacts was actively protecting her from outside influence.

The muscles in Siobhan's back tightened. '*Relax,*' she warned herself. '*You need to seem totally confident, not rigid and on-edge.*' Much of Siobhan's spell practice this last week had been spent on light-refinement. She hoped this might help to bolster her mind against any compulsions the Red Guard managed to slip past her wards. She wished she had some way to gauge how much practice she needed with the spell to create a noticeable effect, but knew that, like growing the Will from scratch, whatever effects the light-refinement spell had would likely take hundreds or thousands of hours to become truly impactful. Still, any edge could be used to cut, with the right application of force.

As they got closer, the dragon let out another sound. '*Two artifacts activated. It's not surprising, but I'm still somehow in awe of this kind of blatant manipulation attempt.*' As Siobhan stepped into the center of the maze, which held a game board big enough for life-sized game pieces, she ran through a series of mental questions to determine if she was affected. '*A ward against untruth and a compulsion to speak freely,*' she determined. '*If the casters are strong enough to get anything past Liza's wards, those compulsions might be enough to leave me a gibbering mess if I were unprotected. What they're doing is illegal, but they're the Red Guard. Who's going to stop them? I wonder if a piece of an Aberrant is fueling the effect, or if their artificer is simply that much stronger than the spells Liza can put into a piece of jewelry.*'

Professor Lacer stood beside two other Red Guard agents. He wore his usual long jacket over a simple white shirt, while they wore crisp, fully equipped red uniforms.

One of the agents had two fluffy tails, marking him as a kitsune. He wore a sly, amused smile and carried a luggage case of supplies.

The other was...big. Large enough that he might have had some jentil blood. They all turned to watch as she and Gera stepped from between the hedges onto the checkered marble game board.

To her credit, Gera did not falter, and Siobhan retained the faintest of smiles. It was just enough to make her seem as if she thought everything she looked at was under her control. She had practiced in a mirror beforehand.

Professor Lacer made introductions. The kitsune was Agent Marcurio, and the large man was Captain Aisling.

Gera reached into the purse at her side and drew out two small pieces of fabric. They unfolded an unreasonable number of times and fluffed up into square pillows, which she placed on the ground. Their surfaces were embroidered with yet another protective spell array. She and Siobhan sank down onto them as if they did such things every day.

Professor Lacer reached into his pocket for a beast core, moved to the side, and then sat in an invisible chair, halfway between Siobhan and the other two agents.

Agent Marcurio and Captain Aisling shared a look. "Should have brought chairs," Marcurio muttered before they both sat down on the marble board, legs crossed. To Siobhan's disappointment, neither seemed particularly discomfited by the arrangement.

"I am here as a mediator," Professor Lacer said. "My presence is meant to ensure the safety of either side in case the other tries to go against the agreement of neutral ground."

Gera didn't give the pre-agreed symbol that she'd sensed a lie, but Siobhan still raised an eyebrow. "You are also a Red Guard agent. Somehow, this arrangement does not seem truly equal."

Captain Aisling cleared his throat. "If it came to a fight, Special Agent Lacer's abilities are overwhelming enough to take on both myself and Agent Marcurio, and probably you two as well, all at the same time. And he has been known to reinterpret commands to his preference before. Seeing as he's a large part of the reason we're having this amicable meeting, I think his presence is appropriate."

That answer was less than satisfactory, but Siobhan gave a one-shouldered shrug.

"Shall we begin?" Captain Aisling asked.

Agent Marcurio opened the case of supplies and brought out an artifact with several different lenses. He put it on his head so that one of the lenses was over his right eye.

Siobhan immediately felt the effects of the divination magic sweeping over her. Her divination-diverting ward was already active because of Gera's presence, but the disks in her back grew colder and began to prickle painfully as they absorbed her blood to power themselves.

Gera shuddered, Agent Marcurio's eyes widened, and Professor Lacer looked on in fascination as the ward's spillover effect strengthened, too. Only Captain Aisling remained stoic, though Siobhan sensed something like a large, patient predator waiting for its prey to make a mistake behind his gaze.

She considered attempting to maintain the divination-diverting ward. Being able to get away with a lie during the questioning would be immensely useful. However, she doubted that she had the capacity to maintain its effect in the face of their efforts.

If they had been trying to find her location, of course she would have failed immediately. Here, they were trying to scan her for anomalous effects and later, ensure the results of their assessment were accurate. The divination would scan her physical form and calculate any of a long list of anomalous effects that might emanate from her.

Likely, once the questions started, they would want to ensure she didn't somehow manage to lie despite their compulsions. For that, their divination would catalog and translate the meaning of her micro-expressions, her heart-beat, and tiny shifts in her muscles. All of this should be slightly easier to fight against than a divination as simple as finding her location, but she was still a relatively weak thaumaturge.

Before Agent Marcurio could increase the power, Siobhan reached forward as if grabbing the hem of a long, invisible veil and lifted it. She and Liza had discussed the possibility of the agents using invasive divinations beforehand, and Liza had made some slight tweaks to the disks in Siobhan's back. It had required the use of a scalpel, some blood-clotting potion, and some carving tools, and overall been one of the more unpleasant experiences of Siobhan's life.

But the improvements allowed Siobhan to adjust the output of the disks to cover only themselves, just in case the agents tried to scan the composition of her body to make sure Siobhan wasn't secretly made out of raven feathers on the inside or something.

"Human, no anomalous effects," Agent Marcurio reported.

Professor Lacer leaned back and crossed his arms as a quick smirk flashed across his face, and Siobhan tried not to seem relieved.

"We'll ask you some questions now," Captain Aisling said.

Siobhan waved one hand with graceful nonchalance.

"What is your name?"

"Siobhan Naught," she answered immediately.

Marcurio and Aisling shared a look, and Marcurio gave a subtle nod. "Truth."

"Have you ever been called by another name?" Captain Aisling asked.

Siobhan nodded easily. "Many times. Here, they also call me the Raven Queen."

"Are those your only two names? Have you always gone by Siobhan Naught?"

Siobhan raised her eyebrows. *'What are they getting at? Surely they don't know about Sebastien.'* Aloud, she said, "Siobhan Naught is my name. But I often go about in disguise, and I use other names then." This was even true. She had half a dozen identity papers with different names for her female form.

"All truth," Agent Marcurio muttered again.

Captain Aisling crossed his arms and tapped one finger against his elbow. "Is it true that you do not lie?"

Siobhan's body tried to blurt out, "No," under the effects of the compulsion, but she was able to guide her words to a more useful truth. "I mislead and deceive people often. I have found that one need not lie to make someone believe an untruth. With the right guidance, some people will do all the work of beguiling themselves better than I ever could."

"But do you lie? Are you able to lie?"

"I can, and I do," she grudgingly admitted. "But I strive never to make promises that I do not keep."

"Why?"

She hesitated. "Because I feel like it."

With another confirmation from Agent Marcurio, Captain Aisling continued. "How old are you?"

Siobhan frowned. *'What kind of questions are these? Are they just trying to get a baseline of what truthfulness looks like, or does this have some kind of unfathomable purpose?'* "I believe I'm twenty."

They shared looks. "Is your mind also twenty? All parts of your mind?"

Gera tapped her left pinky finger against her thigh, the signal they had come up with to convey that the agents were particularly emotionally invested.

Siobhan had thought they might try to hide fear or anger, but if she was reading the situation right, they were…fascinated? But the question left a cold stone at the pit of her belly. "I can't say," she admitted, as she had no other choice. "Such a strange question, I am unsure how to answer. But I certainly think of myself as twenty, no matter what disguise I may be wearing at the time or what name I answer by."

"Have you ever met Myrddin?"

Siobhan blinked slowly, feeling like she was sliding down a steep, muddy incline into surreality. "Is that question relevant and necessary to determine if I am or am likely to become an existential threat to the world?"

"Yes," Agent Marcurio tried.

"Lie," Gera rebutted immediately, in a twist of irony that Siobhan found deeply satisfying.

Captain Aisling shifted and cleared his throat, but his expression remained undaunted. "You have been accused of multiple and varied crimes, some of which may be relevant. Have you ever performed blood magic on a sapient being?"

Siobhan suppressed a cringe, but remembered Millennium's advice and answered boldly. "I have. I can heal using blood magic, but I have also used modification spells on ravens that Sacrifice other ravens, and used ravens for the Lino-Wharton messenger spell and the like."

"Is that all? Have you ever cursed anyone? There are accounts of nightmare curses, strange blood magic rituals, and strange misfortunes that befall your enemies."

Colloquially, people called several kinds of battle magic "curses," generally due to the severity of an effect or the difficulty in shielding against it. But by technical definition, a curse was a long-lived spell, usually cast with a piece of the victim or an effigy of them. Many curses worked on the principles of binding magic, and would get harder to break after they had had time to settle in.

The battle magic Siobhan had used, such as the disintegrating spell she had attacked the Red Guard agent with, would technically be considered a hex—a short-term, actively cast spell with moderate to severe negative effects. The delineation between the two terms often grew hazy, but Siobhan felt she could answer truthfully.

"I have cursed someone. But only once, and with an insect-attracting spell that was ultimately harmless. Technically, I cursed the threshold of his house, so I would suggest that it does not even count. As for nightmares, perhaps some people have experienced them after meeting me, but not because I have gone tiptoeing through their dreaming minds. I accept no responsibility for their lack of mental fortitude. I have hexed a few people here and there, but almost universally to their faces and with their knowledge."

"Truth," Marcurio said.

Even Professor Lacer seemed to find that surprising.

Captain Aisling's eyes narrowed. He turned to Gera. "Madam, do you believe that to be the truth?"

Gera flinched. "My lady would know better than I. It is not the answer I would have expected, but I accept the words that pass her lips."

Captain Aisling turned back to Siobhan. "Do you, or any companions or associates of yours, have some sort of natural fear or other mind-affecting aura or other passive effect—anything that might have caused this recurring *misunderstanding* that you bestow nightmares and even madness on your enemies?"

"Not to my knowledge. My best guess is that people are quite gullible and fall prey to my theatrics."

"Truth," Marcurio said, though even he seemed to doubt the word.

"Have you colluded with other rogue magic users?"

"I have attended some underground thaumaturge meetings, and I have a working relationship with an artificer I often call on for various projects, but I feel like the word 'collusion' might be somewhat excessive."

"Do you consider yourself to be a possible existential threat to the world?"

"Yes," she said immediately. When they tensed, she smiled. "Every single thaumaturge is a possible existential threat to the world. Without us, there would be no Aberrants."

"Do you consider yourself to be significantly more likely to meet the requirements for a threat that the Red Guard would generally deal with than the average thaumaturge?"

Siobhan's thoughts jumped to the thing sealed in her mind, and "Yes," had slipped out of her before she could stop it. She smiled again, even larger. "The majority of thaumaturges spend most of their lives after schooling casting the same spells over and over, never really stretching their Wills. More importantly, they do not engage in magical conflict with other thaumaturges. I will continue to actively improve my Will and explore new magic for the rest of my life, and at the moment, it seems likely that I will also end up in more than my fair share of magical conflicts. The easiest way to shatter celerium is to oppose another's Will, after all."

She paused long enough to let that set in, but continued before they could respond. "But here's the answer to the question I think you really want to ask: I will do everything in my power to keep myself from becoming an existential threat to the world, and I would do the same for other thaumaturges, where possible. I am not *mad*."

Captain Aisling let out an almost inaudible snort. "Are you in contact with or aware of anyone who meets the previous criteria?"

"I am not. I would have already acted if that were the case."

"What is your purpose for the organization that calls itself the Undreaming Order?" Captain Aisling asked, the "Ah-ha!" of trying to catch her off guard obvious in his tone.

Siobhan pressed her lips together. The Undreaming Order was apparently the edgy, villainous-sounding name that Deidre and the others had recently come up with. "I have no purpose for them. I was not involved in their creation. I will do my best to keep them from doing anything crazy, dangerous, or too fanatical."

Agent Marcurio's tails swished back and forth violently. "How could it be that you are uninvolved with them?"

"I *have* presumably met them. And saved some of their lives. But I certainly did not encourage them to create an organization or start calling themselves by such a...*fanciful* title. Truly, if I did not know it to be happening, the idea of such a thing would be almost unfathomable."

She tapped a finger thoughtfully against her wine-red lower lip. "I suspect the common person's willingness to become infatuated with the idea of me might be an imprecation against their quality of life under the rule of the Thirteen Crowns. Either that, or the average person has a much more active and childish imagination than I realized, and is bizarrely willing to indulge it.

Or…" Siobhan grimaced. "Or these 'followers' of mine simply happen to be the strangest outliers of society, and a bizarre confluence of events has allowed them to come together and start feeding each other's faults."

Frowning, Agent Marcurio adjusted his divination artifact, then tapped it a couple of times as if he suspected it wasn't working properly. At Captain Aisling's pointed look, he grunted and said, "Truth. Everything so far has been the truth."

Captain Aisling was now repeatedly tapping three fingers against his elbow. "Do you have any plans or the intention to do anything that would be considered a crime, or require our involvement?"

"This is getting ridiculous," Siobhan said. "I refuse to be judged based on things I have not done and may not do. I am certain to commit crimes of some sort, as it seems that the Thirteen Crowns are willing to take anything I do and belatedly label it a crime. But I can freely confirm *once more* that I have no desire to cause harm to the innocent or endanger this world. Beyond that, I will actively work to ensure my own safety, that of those I care about, and the livable state of the world within which I must continue to exist. Working rules of society, production pipelines, and basic safety for everyone are simple principles that also make my own life bearable."

Professor Lacer nodded as if all of this was common sense.

"What is your relation to Sebastien Siverling?"

Siobhan felt the blood drain from her cheeks but forcefully stopped herself from responding. "I refuse to answer," she said, baring her teeth in something like a smile.

Gera tapped her pinky finger again, and then blinked for an abnormally long moment. This was the trap, or one of them, and they believed they had caught her.

Captain Aisling smiled back at her triumphantly. "Do you admit that you bestowed a boon upon the boy?"

"I provided him the ability to resist divination," Siobhan replied slowly. It was even basically true, if one accepted the fact that she had purchased that ability for herself, and that she was Sebastien.

"How did you do that?"

She met the captain's gaze unblinkingly. "I did not do anything dangerous or unethical to provide the ability. Next question."

"Why did you do it?"

"I like him. Something like that could help keep him safe." Siobhan had been told several times that she loved herself too much, and was, in fact, a narcissist. Did this count as close enough to the truth?

"Partial truth," Agent Marcurio said, showing cute snaggle-toothed canines as he grinned.

"The device you used in your fight with Agent Gale recently, the one that contains fabric spell arrays that can be released or retracted at will… We tracked that back to a craftsman who had been working with Mr. Siverling to develop the devices. How did you come into possession of it?"

Siobhan's heart was pounding and her mouth had gone dry. She tried to come up with an excuse, but the artisan himself was the weak link, and she was not willing to commit murder to keep him silent. Under the pressure of the compulsions and the threat of being caught in a lie, she didn't have enough mental power to come up with a good lie that kept her two identities separate. Not without noticeably pausing long enough to come up with something plausible. But she remembered Millennium's advice. She forcefully loosened her muscles, tilted her head to the side, and smiled right back into Captain Aisling's smug face. "I got it from the craftsman, of course. However, I have to admit that the man would not remember giving a second prototype to me, if you were to ask him."

Professor Lacer uncrossed his legs and sat in a more upright position.

Gera plucked at the cuticle of her forefinger's nail.

Captain Aisling tried to act nonchalant, but Siobhan could smell him almost slavering, believing she was trapped and wounded and ready to take a bite of her flesh. "Are you aware that we do not allow thaumaturges to practice memory manipulation on others? It is very easy to cause mental collapses and break events when such delicate work frays or unravels. In fact, this is some of that very blood magic we asked about earlier."

Siobhan's mind flitted to the new battle wand in a holster on her thigh. She could reach it through the open seam in the left hip pocket of her dress. And Liza had given her the strongest three-hundred-sixty-degree battle shield she could make. As soon as something activated it, Siobhan would have ten minutes to get herself and Gera to safety. If they could use the hedge maze to escape direct line of sight, Siobhan thought they could make it.

Siobhan leaned forward, as if telling a secret. "I am aware that you restrict that particular privilege to your own agents, and that they do indeed occasionally lack the skill and delicate touch required. Why, just earlier this year, poor Newton Moore's family became positively *unhinged* after your peoples' tender care."

Captain Aisling's smile slipped, but he, too, leaned forward toward her. "And as for your other claims of harmlessness… We have extensive, repeated, and confirmed testimony from several Pendragon Corps operatives of the dangerous nature of the thing you call your 'shadow-familiar' and the long-term effects it causes. My own agents who confronted it recently reported that it caused a deep discomfort and existential dread within them. Special Agent Lacer has relayed your insistence that it is a simple, harmless trick spell, but I have my doubts. How did you break the mind of a Pendragon Corps operative who had been trained to withstand torture?"

Siobhan opened her mouth and closed it again. "I...did not? Are you saying one of the High Crown's men had nightmares? Well, I suppose my shadow-familiar can be made to seem quite frightening, but I've never 'broken anyone's mind.'" She hesitated, "Or, if I did, it was by accident due to a variety of possible extenuating circumstances. Maybe that operative had pre-existing mental conditions."

"Truth," Agent Marcurio said.

But Gera pressed her lips together to signify that the men did not actually believe Siobhan.

Siobhan resisted the urge to throw up her hands in exasperation. *'What is the point of their truth-telling divination, then!?'* She let out a sharp sigh. "I can prove it," she said aloud. "I would be willing to demonstrate my shadow-familiar spell if it would put this to rest. I assure you, it is perfectly harmless."

5

FUNDAMENTAL ATTRIBUTION ERROR

Captain Aisling and Agent Marcurio shared a look of surprise and distrust at Siobhan's offer of a demonstration.

"Totally safe," Siobhan repeated.

Agent Marcurio's tails lashed back and forth in agitation. His voice was tight, and his accent came through more thickly. "You want to show us the spell you used against the other agent who fought against you? The same one you used on the Pendragon Corps. The creature of shadows that everyone talks about."

Siobhan deflated slightly. "I had thought you would want to examine it." She'd gone so far as to ask Liza to run some diagnostic spells on her shadow while it was under her control, ignoring the woman's strange, angry stares. Siobhan had wanted to be sure that, after what had happened, there were no lingering effects or hints at the true nature of the shadow woman the other agent had met that night.

"We do want to examine it," Captain Aisling replied, but there was something obviously left unsaid in his tone. He stared at her, but Siobhan didn't know what that unsaid thing was, and so after an awkward while of gazing into each other's eyes, he waved graciously to her. "Please."

Siobhan had been in control of her shadow the entire time, a tiny part of her Will spent on maintaining the spell through her new mermaid-leather anklet while leaving the rest of her concentration for high-stakes human inter-action. Magic had rules, but with practice and skill, those rules could be bent. It was very convenient not to have to keep her hands in front of her mouth constantly, especially as she had been maintaining the shadow-familiar spell for several consecutive days.

Now, she looked down at her shadow, which stretched out insubstantially in several directions at once from the maze's various light crystal lamps. At a wave of the hand that now wore her mother's celerium ring, each copy of her shadow snapped together into one and shrank closer to her body. Then, a small black raven rose up from the puddle of darkness.

The raven took a cute hop forward, and both Red Guard agents took a simultaneous step backward.

"Stop!" Captain Aisling barked, one palm outstretched toward her and the other reaching for the battle wand at his waist.

Siobhan and the raven both froze.

Agent Marcurio pulled out and used three divination artifacts on the bird, one after the other. Finally, he announced, "It is a shadow. An extremely, abnormally lightless shadow, but that is all."

The edges of Professor Lacer's mouth twitched with amusement.

Captain Aisling pointed at the adorable raven as it cocked its head to the side and wiggled its tail feathers. "*This* is what drove several trained men half-mad and terrified my agents?"

"I can make it more frightening," Siobhan offered. Though she kept the size the same, she molded the shadow into the standard battle form she had been using since she came to Gilbratha, then used it to absorb the heat and create a foggy aura. The six-inch horror hunched menacingly and flexed its clawed digits.

Agent Marcurio took out his divination devices again, but after another round of testing, asked, "Are you trying to make a joke right now?"

Siobhan blinked. "Is this funny?"

"It seems like you are insulting our intelligence," Captain Aisling said.

Siobhan frowned. She considered making her shadow bigger but had a feeling they would still find some way to be dissatisfied. They were expecting her to display some menacing, spine-chilling magical abilities, so when she told the truth, they thought she was mocking them. They had decided who she was before the meeting and were judging all of her actions through that lens. '*So maybe the answer is not to try to seem as harmless as I actually am and instead play the Raven Queen.*'

She closed her eyes, took a deep breath, and opened them again. "The only way to *truly* recreate the psychological effects of a battle would be to fight. But if you want me to try to frighten you, I am willing to try." She smiled, slow and wide. "If you can promise you will not lose your wits and try to kill me."

"Will the effects remain harmless?" Captain Aisling asked.

"Yes. It might get somewhat cold, but not enough to kill you. I have no intention to harm you unless you attempt to harm me."

"May I leave for this?" Gera asked.

"Of course." Siobhan waved to the grassy area beyond the edge of the over-sized game board. "I will contain any active effects to this space."

Gera pressed her lips together for a moment. "Is it alright if I go some-what…farther?"

Siobhan was surprised by her apprehension, but quickly realized it was a good idea. "You may. The extra distance will provide you some additional protection if the agents forget themselves and start shooting battle spells around."

Professor Lacer was smiling openly now. "I will stay near the edge of the game board. I want to watch."

Agent Marcurio shuffled his feet and looked up at his superior to whisper, "Are we sure this is a good idea?"

Gera stood, picked up her cushion, and folded it back into a small square of cloth.

"It is just a demonstration. Not a spar," Siobhan reminded them, handing her own cushion to Gera. "But if you are willing to take me at my word about this spell, I need not go to the effort."

"No. I want to see this," Captain Aisling said. "Do your worst, Queen of Ravens."

Siobhan chuckled. "Well, I am definitely not going to do that. But it might get *slightly* frightening. Please remember that you are not actually in any danger."

Gera shook with a full-body shudder, spun on her heel, and hurried off without another word.

Agent Marcurio looked after her longingly. "Maybe I could watch from outside, too." The fur of his tails lay abnormally flat as the two appendages tried to hide behind one of his legs. "It's just, I've heard so many of the stories already, I feel like I know what to expect. And wouldn't it be beneficial to have an outside perspec-tive to do scans and take readings while the action is ongoing, so to speak?"

Captain Aisling placed one mitt-sized hand on Marcurio's shoulder and squeezed. "No need. We will examine it together, from the inside. Special Agent Lacer is enough for external observation."

The other three took some time to prepare while Siobhan planned out something that would match the sensational rumors that seemed to be spreading about the Raven Queen, even if only a little. *'I hope I can pull this off.'*

When the agents were ready, Siobhan let her shadow collapse back into a puddle around her feet. It rose up slightly from the ground and began to spread like a real liquid, and then to bubble like thick, viscous sludge in a cauldron. Except instead of steam, cold fog rose from its surface.

Every second, it grew thicker and spread further, until it enveloped the agents' feet. As it spread, Siobhan slowly and subtly bent her knees, lowering herself toward the ground within the visual shield of her midnight dress. If she was doing it right, she imagined it looked something like she was sinking down into the darkness.

The spell gave her no hint of struggle or lack of control. Over the last week of almost constantly casting it, she had become increasingly certain that the thing in her mind could not simply take over at any point. It needed certain requirements to be met.

When the faux liquid had spread far enough, and she had sunk low in a smooth, molasses-slow dip that might not have been so effortless without all of the practice with the light-refinement ritual, she cued the shadow liquid to explode upward in front of the agents, revealing a hint of giant teeth and tentacles below. At the same time, the edges of her shadow rose up in a giant dome, cutting off the meager light from the outside. She left a second inner wall of darkness around the agents, as they would surely bring out a light of some sort and she didn't want them to see her just yet.

Rather than follow through with anything else immediately, Siobhan dug around in her satchel. She pulled out a vial of moonlight sizzle that had already spent most of its magic, her modified light-crystal coaster, and her last philtre of darkness with the proprioception modification, which she had decided to call a philtre of shadow-perception. She hesitated before using the latter, but knew that due to the short shelf life, she would need to create a new batch soon, anyway. One with slightly diminished side effects, ideally.

She needed to be able to move around freely within the darkness, both to ensure the agents didn't retaliate against her and to more effectively demonstrate that she could be scary. They would have divination spells going, so it would be beneficial for her to be able to track them as well. *'It would be silly if something went wrong after the immense effort I put into preparing for this meeting just because I was reluctant to use a potion worth a handful of gold and a few hours of my time.'*

Siobhan unsealed the vial and took a small sip of the roiling darkness, allowing the majority of the philtre to billow steadily from its small glass container. She was lucky—there was barely a breeze this morning, and the philtre would hang around unless something artificially cleared the air.

She formed a shell of shadow around her body, a duplicate of herself to her left—though the act made her shudder, it could be useful to deceive the agents—and created her standard semi-avian shadow-familiar to her right.

Then, she activated the heat absorption ability on all three. The Red Guard might otherwise be able to tell which one was her by some sort of thermal divination. She didn't think she could perfectly fool them, but it was best to put in the effort.

Her skin immediately cried out in discomfort from the cold. Siobhan did her best to guide her shadow to pull from the air and not from her body, but otherwise ignored it. It would take a lot of concentration to control three forms at once, especially with everything else she planned to do.

"Is this it?" Captain Aisling called out from within their inner area.

Siobhan shook her depleted vial of moonlight sizzle to get the bubbles and light going, unsealed it, and began to walk in a circle around them, each step slow and deliberately soft so as not to give away her movement. Her two extra shadow forms followed beside her. She dribbled little splashes of the weakly glowing potion on the marble. A little bit of light, just enough to feed the imagination, could be more terrifying than complete darkness.

As the philtre of shadow-perception continued to fill the area, she gained a clear sense of what the agents were doing within the smaller barrier she had created around them. To free one hand, she tucked the philtre in one of her dress's many pockets.

"Oh, by the sun and moon above, what is that?" Agent Marcurio asked, his voice breaking. "Can you sense it?"

"Show yourself!" Captain Aisling snapped, looking around at the veil of darkness with the light of a headlamp beaming from his forehead.

Marcurio was frantically working with his divination artifact, and suddenly his head jerked up. "Behind us!"

Siobhan grimaced and threw away the remaining moonlight sizzle, allowing the vial to break across the ground where she hadn't yet made a full circuit.

Both agents flinched at the sound, but spun to face her rather than the distraction. Without any communication that Siobhan could perceive, they stepped forward to test the barrier of darkness. Finding it incorporeal, they stepped through it. The modified philtre of darkness filled the air, but there were a few areas where it was thin enough for their bright lights to partially pass through. Enough to make out her form. They flinched at the sight of her.

Siobhan probably would have also flinched at the sudden beam of light to the face, but her shadow was covering her eyes completely.

"The one in the middle is her," Agent Marcurio announced immediately. His tails stretched out and grew longer, then formed a Circle in front of his mouth. He whispered a few words, took a deep breath, and then blew some sort of esoteric gust spell that cleared most of the air between them, though the dark miasma continued to seep through her dress from the vial in her pocket.

Siobhan sighed, but supposed that at least immediate discovery meant she didn't need to continue freezing herself to hide. She let the shadows covering her body fall away, leaving only a small covering over each eyeball to protect against the light and freeing up quite a bit of her concentration for the other two.

"Her eyes," Agent Marcurio whispered.

Captain Aisling ignored him, his own narrowed eyes flicking around to take in every detail of the situation.

Siobhan created a few simple barriers of darkness in irregular shapes around the edges of the dome, then flashed them across the space between herself and the agents, almost too fast for the eye to track. They would see only indescribable movement.

Both of them jumped and looked around, but they didn't take their attention off her for long.

Even so, by the time they looked back, the Siobhan-facsimile shadow was gone and the looming, semi-avian shadow began to skitter toward them with jerky, zig-zagging movements.

Captain Aisling calmly said something that sounded like "netrah," pointed a battle wand at it, and released a beam of light so bright that Siobhan could see it even through the shadows protecting her eyeballs. It overcame the light-blocking philtre of darkness, pierced through her shadow-familiar's monstrous form, and continued on and out through the outer edge of the shadow dome and into the sky beyond.

The sudden influx of light energy forced Siobhan almost to the edge of her thaumic capacity and left her shadow-familiar flush with power—and if possible, even more utterly black and lightless than it had been before.

Agent Marcurio had immediately closed his eyes on Aisling's verbal signal but now shook his head. "No damage."

Siobhan tilted her head to the side. "Breaking promises so quickly?" she asked, her voice coming out with a strange echo past the philtre that wafted up from her stomach and spilled from her mouth. She suppressed the urge to cough. That would not be very intimidating.

Both men shifted warily, and Captain Aisling even grimaced as if he had seen something disgusting. "It was just a test, not an attack. If I'd shot you with that spell, you might have gotten a little warm and been temporarily blinded."

The Siobhan-duplicate shadow rose up from the shadows stretching out behind them, moving too quickly for them to react.

Marcurio's eyes had just begun to widen, his head turning to look back, when the Siobhan-duplicate brushed a frigid hand the color of the void against the back of Captain Aisling's neck, just below the curve of his ear.

To his credit, Captain Aisling did not scream, and even Agent Marcurio clamped his mouth shut to muffle an involuntary screech of surprise. Captain Aisling spun around, swinging his battle wand like a baton at her shadow.

Agent Marcurio spun in the other direction, his back to Aisling as he scanned for another surprise attack. It was a response that spoke of both a lot of training and an impressive amount of trust toward his partner.

The Siobhan-duplicate slid back from Captain Aisling's attempted blow as if gliding across ice or floating half an inch above the ground. Its mouth opened wider, and wider, and wider still, until the jaw appeared to unhinge and its head split almost in two.

From within its throat, a small form struggled upward. A raven clawed its way out of the Siobhan-facsimile, then perched on the edge of its dislocated jaw and shook itself as if after a bath. Then, its beady black eyes locked on Captain Aisling. It launched itself straight at him, flying faster than any corporeal raven could have.

He tried to move out of the way but was too slow, and a puff of fog burst outward from his chest as the bird seemed to fly into him.

Of course, in reality, this was all a complex illusion. Sweat beaded on Siobhan's forehead as she struggled to create both realistic form and movement in so many places at once.

She let the Siobhan-duplicate sink into the ground and created a few more flashing silhouettes against the scattered, faint glow that barely illuminated the outer areas of the game board. With the mental power she had freed up, she created thin, tattered spiderwebs of shadow scattered through the area, stretching around haphazardly as if from the long-abandoned nest of some giant beast.

Those, her harrowing avian shadow-familiar used to climb up and around, moving as fast and unnaturally as only a creature without mass or true form could.

While it moved above, she created some vague forms nearer to the floor, hinting at feathers and insects, quick movement and seething, treacherous footing. Just enough so that the agents didn't know where to focus their attention, as seeming danger could come from anywhere.

Siobhan reached into her pocket, grabbed the light-crystal coaster, and gritted her teeth. With extreme care and only a tiny amount of power sourced from the light-crystal itself, she used the array drawn on the back to create two small glowing orbs slightly inside one of the clouds of darkness beside the agents. Just as Agent Marcurio—who seemed to be the more observant of the two—caught sight of the glowing orbs, she made them appear to blink. Like the reflective eyes of a nocturnal predator, they blinked twice, and the second time did not appear again.

"Prekshak!" Marcurio announced tightly.

"New?" Captain Aisling asked, confirming Siobhan's suspicion that the unfamiliar words were some kind of short-code used among the Red Guard.

"Glowing eyes in the darkness."

Siobhan began walking again while the men were distracted, putting a shield of darkness between them to hide herself and activating her dowsing artifact. Her divination-diverting ward activated, and would hopefully make them less likely to focus on her past all the other distractions.

She wished she had some ability to create illusory sound, or even that she knew how to throw her voice, but alas, all she knew how to do was create a loud, screeching alarm, which didn't have the subtle effect she was going for.

She called up the memory of an old lullaby that she vaguely remembered in her mother's voice. Like many old rhymes and children's stories, the tune was soft and lilting, but the lyrics were fairly disturbing. She began to sing. Her voice still came out strange and warbling, which Siobhan thought somewhat enhanced the effect, while also masking the fact that she didn't really know how to sing.

"HUSH NOW, child, do not weep.
　　Close your eyes and sink to sleep.
　　In slumber's realm, you may roam,
　　But heed me, child, stay close to home."

"WHY DID I VOLUNTEER FOR THIS?" Agent Marcurio asked. "Why couldn't I just let that idiot Berg come instead?" He bit back a shriek and jumped to the side as an enormous beak of shadows rose up from the ground around him and pretended to try and snap shut around his legs.

"Keep it together, Agent!" Captain Aisling snapped. But when the Siobhan-facsimile stepped out of the cloud of darkness beside him, reaching out for a passionate kiss, he bent almost all the way backward in an impressive feat of flexibility to avoid it.

"FOR SHOULD you wander far and wide,
　　Your soul may find a place to hide.
　　In the realm of dreams, beware,
　　Dark creatures roam with wicked stare."

SIOBHAN PUNCTUATED the last word by dropping the semi-avian shadow from where it had been skittering above. It landed on all four spindly limbs behind the two men, its cloaked head bowed toward the ground. Siobhan sent a cold tendril of shadow to caress their backs and draw their attention.

Both spun to face it, breathing hard despite the lack of real exertion. Another blast of light did nothing except provide more power in an easy-to-absorb form. She was prepared for it this time and let the excess energy shoot harmlessly into the distance.

The shadow-familiar slowly raised its head. But where usually there was only an enormous beak and endless void under the cloak, now glowing red eyes stared out at them from the darkness, pulsating and flickering like two distant, malevolent stars.

Siobhan resumed her lullaby.

"FOR IF YOU stray too far, too deep,
In the land where nightmares sleep,
Your soul may wander, lost and torn,
And those you've left behind, forlorn."

THE SIOBHAN-FACSIMILE STUMBLED out of the darkness, giggling silently as it approached its beaked, wretched counterpart. Its silent mirth grew until it was holding both hands over its mouth and convulsing hard enough to lose its balance. It seemed to catch itself on the side of the battle-familiar, which cowered as if in fear, but was not so bold as to pull away.

Siobhan had traveled almost all the way around the men once more. The shadow-perception philtre had run out and was fading from the air.

Both men watched in horror as the semi-avian shadow began to convulse as well.

"Permission to use the shield spell, Captain?" Agent Marcurio asked, his voice high and tight.

"It won't work. Do you want to encourage her!? And before you ask, I already triggered the anti-corruption and compulsion artifacts. No effect."

Siobhan took a deep breath and sang the final verse as she sent thin tendrils of shadows to chill their skin in random caresses, always from the most unexpected angle. The shell of an ear, the ankle just under their pant leg, and the base of their spines through their clothes.

The men twitched with every simulated touch, but Agent Marcurio shook his head, grim-faced, and they kept their attention on her shadow-familiars.

"SECRETS IN THE DARKNESS KEEP,
For with the dawn, all shadows flee.

Sleep now, child, do not fear.
Morning comes soon, bright and clear."

BOTH OF HER SHADOWS FROZE, then turned slowly and seemed to look at something behind the men. Siobhan dabbed away the sweat on her forehead, allowed the semi-avian shadow's red eyes to sputter out, and put the light coaster back in her pocket. Siobhan put as much fear into her shadows' body language as possible, then yanked both of them out of sight so fast they almost seemed to disappear.

Captain Aisling and Agent Marcurio turned to face her.

She stood still, silent, and expressionless, simply staring at them in the spotlight of their headlamps for long enough that the wait grew uncomfortable.

Finally, she allowed the dome of shadow around them to fall and her shadow to return to its normal form, spreading out from her feet in the faint dawn light. Able to see clearly again now that the shadow over her eyes was gone, she smiled.

Captain Aisling glared at her, and Agent Marcurio was examining his and his captain's shadows with marked suspicion. "Thank you for that demonstration," the larger man said stiffly. "It was most…illuminating."

To the side of the game board half a dozen meters away, Professor Lacer snorted. He had dismissed his invisible chair and was holding his Conduit in one hand and a beast core in the other. His expression was one of distinct displeasure. He strode across the board toward them, stopping by Siobhan's side.

Agent Marcurio's tan skin had a wan, greenish pallor to it, and his tails alternated between lashing around with agitation and wilting down to hide behind his silhouette. Captain Aisling's fingers were trembling, and as soon as the man realized, he crossed his arms and clamped his hands around his biceps.

And so, belatedly, Siobhan noticed the obvious signs. She realized that Red Guard agents would be almost guaranteed to have experienced harrowing, traumatic situations time and time again through the course of their work. Many of those horrors would leave marks. She had seen beast hunters who had come back as the only one in their party left alive. Sometimes groups met opponents beyond their capabilities and their prey hunted them in return.

The agents probably had trouble responding to perceived threats without immediately resorting to excessive violence. She was lucky that they had managed to restrain themselves so well.

"Thank you for humoring me," she said. She hesitated, then reached into her satchel. "Would either of you like a dose of anti-anxiety potion?"

Professor Lacer's fingers tightened around his Conduit. "Surely my colleagues are not in need of such coddling."

Siobhan was dubious. Obviously, they were experiencing some symptoms of a war neurosis or lingering combat stress reaction.

Captain Aisling raised his palm to stop her, bowing his head as if to gather strength. "No, thank you."

6

A DEAL WITH DARKNESS

Siobhan
Month 8, Day 21, Saturday 7:15 a.m.

Professor Lacer turned on Siobhan and scowled. "I distinctly remember mentioning that I would be observing from the edge of the board. So why, I wonder, did you start casting your anti-divination spell halfway through your demonstration?"

Siobhan remained awkwardly silent. She hadn't even considered what activating the divination-diverting ward's full effects might do, even though she knew that it protected her shadow as well as her physical body. Trying to be inconspicuous, she reached into her bag and turned off the dowsing artifact.

"If I were a more paranoid man, or less insightful, I might have taken it as a sign of ill intent. Thankfully, I am skilled enough to bypass your spell's effects without having to break it, and I was able to put together a good model of what was happening within your dome of darkness by sending probes through the ground and specifically leaving out the places where your knowledge-devouring magic touched. I had to keep the backup forces from attacking you twice after you pulled that arrogant, foolhardy stunt."

Before she could respond, Professor Lacer turned on the Red Guard agents. "And you! Despite giving your word not to use offensive spells during the demonstration, not once, but twice, you attacked with a beam of Radiance!"

Agent Marcurio shuffled and shrank like a scolded puppy.

Captain Aisling's mouth firmed. "It was light alone, and would not have harmed her—"

Professor Lacer slashed his hand through the air as if it were a knife, effectively cutting off the other man's words. "Please do not defend your actions with irrelevant information. While your spell might not have killed Miss Naught herself, it could very well have catastrophically disrupted her shadow-familiar spell and caused backlash."

Gera had returned from the edge of the maze path she had retreated down, but hesitated at the obvious tension between them. Looking toward Siobhan, she steeled herself and moved to stand on the Siobhan's other side, opposite Professor Lacer.

"Considering the power and abilities she has displayed, that was very unlikely," Captain Aisling replied evenly.

Gera did not indicate a lie, so it must have been the truth.

"And I daresay our probing response was a very measured reaction to the Raven Queen's oppression." The huge man turned to Siobhan. "How is it that your 'completely harmless' shadow-controlling spell managed to bypass our wards against mental effects? Or, perhaps, did you slip in some secondary magic with an artifact or this…'dual-casting' you claim to be capable of?"

Siobhan coughed roughly, though she managed to keep from expelling any visible darkness from her lungs, then stared at him for several long seconds. Finally, she hesitantly asked, "And exactly what 'mental effect' are you talking about? Because I assure you, I did not cast anything like that. Are you, perhaps, suggesting that, because you were frightened by my display, I must have been casting a compulsion of some sort?"

Beside her, Gera took an exceedingly deep, slow breath and released it again, and Siobhan thought her face was beginning to hold some derision for the agents.

Professor Lacer gave Captain Aisling a scathing look that held none of the respect for a superior that Siobhan suspected he was supposed to display. It was surprising that he got away with it. "The philtre. They began to display the physical signs of excessive agitation when it reached them," he explained.

Siobhan reached into her pocket and pulled out the vial, from which the barest traces of wispy darkness escaped. "This? I admit it is getting a bit old, maybe on the edge of losing effectiveness, but it should not have had any direct fear-inducing effects. It simply gives me knowledge of what is within its touch. At most it…" Siobhan trailed off, staring at the bottle with wide eyes. "Well, maybe if you breathed it in, it would give you a sense of me in return."

Professor Lacer waved a finger at the vial, followed by a faint frown at the results of his free-cast divination spell. "I have not encountered a philtre of that nature before. How does it work?"

"I created it myself. But if you want the recipe, we will have to negotiate a suitable trade."

Professor Lacer's eyebrows rose. "I did not know you were a Master of alchemy."

Siobhan waved her hand, tucking away the empty vial again. "Oh, nothing of the sort. I dabble."

Aisling shot Marcurio a questioning look, and the kitsune nodded his head. "Truth," he whispered, almost soundlessly.

Gera crossed her arms and glared at him.

Marcurio looked at Siobhan and shuddered, oblivious to the other diviner's growing dislike. "So, that extremely unnerving, horrifying sensation of being watched, seen, *known* by some spine-chilling eldritch creature, was all a result of our subconscious feeling a connection to…you? It wasn't a memetic effect at all, just an instinctive response?"

Siobhan squinted at him. "It sounds very insulting if you word it like that."

"I am sure he only meant that your awe-inspiring nature can be overwhelming to witness first-hand," Gera said quietly. She threw Marcurio a wordless, forceful expression, her lips pinched tight together.

Marcurio's eyes widened. "I meant no offense, Queen of Ravens. Only— exactly what your attendant said."

Gera nodded. "And I'm sure you only continue to doubt the truth of my lady's words, for even the smallest statements of fact, because of protocol. Not because you are accusing her of being honorless."

Marcurio hesitated, looking at Siobhan doubtfully. "That too," he agreed reluctantly. "Everyone knows the Raven Queen is *deeply* honorable."

Aisling pinched the bridge of his nose as if to push back a headache. "Lady Raven Queen," he said, pulling her attention back to him. "We would like to examine the artifact from which your shadow-familiar spell stems. You said it was created by your grandfather?" Captain Aisling asked.

"I will not agree to that," Siobhan replied promptly. "The artifact my grandfather left for me is precious, and it contains proprietary secrets." In truth, she couldn't allow them to see it because they would realize her shadow-familiar had nothing to do with it, and thus that the creature that had risen wearing her form had not been simulated by it.

Captain Aisling raised his eyebrows and nodded meaningfully, as if he had taken some deeper meaning from her refusal. "I suspected as much. Would you be willing to demonstrate your ability to 'dual-cast' for us, then? With something other than your shadow. Not to suggest you would cheat, but you have indicated the artifact could take over the burden of guiding it. I hope you understand."

Siobhan was loathe to drop her shadow-familiar spell, but she didn't want to attempt splitting her Will in three directions, no matter how little of that

Will was going toward keeping her shadow under control. However, proving that she really could cast two spells at once would go a long way to disabuse them of any suspicions that might lead them to the thing sealed in her mind. "Fine, but let us be quick about it." She pulled out a soft wax crayon and drew out two spell arrays on the marble board, taking care to keep her handwriting different from the natural scrawl she used as Sebastien.

Despite knowing about it ahead of time, they seemed stunned and disbelieving when she cast a basic float spell at the same time as she used a variation of one of the many small spells she had learned in her classes this term to force a seed to sprout.

Only Thaddeus watched impassively, though the tiniest hint of a smirk slipped out as he observed the others' reactions.

Even Gera's blind eye grew wider as she observed Siobhan's demonstration, though she settled quickly. "I do not know why I continue to be surprised by the feats you display," she said, and then spent some time nodding rapidly to herself.

After running several divination scans to ensure Siobhan was truly casting both spells separately and not free-casting a single spell that somehow combined both very dissimilar effects, the agents grew strangely excited.

"Is the ability to dual-cast something you can bestow as a boon, just as you gave a weaker version of your protection against divination to Sebastien Siverling?" Captain Aisling asked.

"This is not the kind of ability I can simply hand out. At best, I could attempt to teach someone, but I fear the results of failure would be...regrettable."

"And this ability is required to read Myrddin's journals?"

"It is the only way I know of to access the protected contents. That is not to say there are no other methods."

"What about your anti-divination boon? You have already given it once."

"That I could, technically, provide to others. But it comes at quite a high cost." Quite literally, she would have to pay an exorbitant amount to have Liza do the same work for someone else. "Before you ask, I have no intention to do so, regardless of what you offer." It would be tantamount to giving away one of her most precious secrets.

"Are there other boons of a similar nature or value that you might bestow?"

"My boons are catered to the circumstances and the individual. There is quite a lot I can do, but even more, perhaps, that I cannot. I doubt much that I could offer would be of real use to your organization."

Agent Marcurio looked at the sudden response of his divination artifact and gulped. "Lie," he whispered.

Gera's face snapped toward him.

Siobhan frowned. She had spoken without thinking—and without meaning to lie—but obviously, some part of her knew that she had value to offer. It was only that she was so used to being destitute and knowing only a few magical tricks that it was hard to leave behind that mindset.

"I was not attempting to be deceitful. But I suppose, perhaps, leaving behind the need for sleep could be useful. And some of my other magical knowledge." Almost anyone would benefit from mastering light-refinement. "And my non-magical knowledge. And some of my personal resources and connections," she added, just to be safe. She did know some useful people and own several rather high-capacity celerium Conduits, after all.

A muscle in Captain Aisling's broad jaw clenched and unclenched several times in the ensuing silence. "I have been an agent of the Red Guard for several decades, but you are one of the most brazen thaumaturges I have ever met," he said, his voice hard with anger.

Shocked, Siobhan slid her gaze slowly over to Professor Lacer.

He raised his eyebrows at her, as if wondering why she was surprised.

Siobhan turned to Gera instead, but the woman was staring at Captain Aisling defiantly and didn't seem to notice Siobhan's consternation.

"Not only do you manage to lie during our interview, you are so obsessed with being recognized as exceptional that you unveil your deceit in the most defiant manner possible," the man continued. "Did you so badly want us to know that you can lie or tell the truth as you please? This, in addition to the admission that you may have cast memory-affecting spells on civilians. I also find it concerning that you performed nonconsensual, permanent magic on Sebastien Siverling, a civilian known to be connected to one of our agents. Are you compulsively compelled to taunt those around you despite the danger, or do you really hold no regard for the threat we embody?"

Siobhan's thoughts reeled as if she had been slapped, though she tried not to show it. Beside her, Gera had begun to breathe harder, but on Siobhan's other side, Professor Lacer still seemed relatively calm. He was holding his Conduit and a beast core, but looking at her, not Captain Aisling. As if he expected her to be the one more likely to burst into violence. Before she could come up with a response, Captain Aisling continued.

"I believe you have lied about quite a lot today, although for what purpose, it is not entirely clear to me. But it *is* obvious that you do not take us seriously. And that is a mistake," he added dangerously.

'*What is he even talking about? Where did this come from? I take them so incredibly seriously that I prepared for this meeting to the point of abandoning almost all other distractions and spending a large chunk of my newly gained fortune for even the slightest improvement in the chances that I walk out of here safely.*' For a moment, hot, acid panic began to rise up in her stomach. But then she remembered the advice she had been given, not just by Miles, but by Liza and even Professor Lacer. If she acted weak, they would treat her as someone they could walk over. And when they surprised her, she needed to roll with it.

So she smiled as genuinely, sincerely, and gently as she could. "If you really wanted to do something to me, you would be doing it, not talking about it. Which means you want something from me. Why not set aside the bluster and just ask?"

Agent Marcurio actually flinched, but Captain Aisling retained the general composure he had displayed from the start. He paused, but showed no hint of shame, confusion, or frustration. When he spoke again, most of the anger was gone from his voice, suggesting that it, too, had been mostly an act. "We believe you know something about the way that Myrddin created Carnagore. Which might have been just a prototype. And that you might even hold the answers within yourself."

Siobhan felt the blood drain away from her face. She could only hope they didn't notice.

Unfortunately, they were too perceptive. Agent Marcurio gave a single nod, which Captain Aisling picked up on. The huge man gave her a small smile.

Gera tapped her left pinky finger against her thigh. This, then, was what the agents hoped to gain from this meeting.

"We are interested in that knowledge. How would one transfer a consciousness into another vessel?" Captain Aisling asked, paraphrasing one of the questions she had asked Professor Lacer via letter.

Siobhan threw Professor Lacer a dirty look. He had warned her that he would have to speak about their correspondence but had told her he would keep the most important things secret. Did he not consider that frankly alarming question to be *important?*

"Special Agent Lacer believes you are likely to unearth the answer, given the chance. We want you to share it with us, whether the knowledge comes from one of Myrddin's journals, your own experience, or from personal research into the matter. When you have satisfactory information, you will bring it to us."

"I think your expectations are rather unreasonable," Siobhan replied, trying to keep the tension from her voice. "Would it not be better to ask such a question of those most knowledgeable and likely to be able to find an answer? I share your curiosity, but I do not know the answer and have only the barest inkling of where to look to find it."

Captain Aisling didn't even look at Marcurio or his truth-divining artifact. Apparently they really didn't trust that they could tell when she was lying or not. Or they just didn't care. "If you prefer, you can turn yourself in for more extensive testing and questioning. That might allow us to find the answer ourselves, and from there possibly even discover the secrets of dual-casting."

Siobhan clenched her jaw, once again considering the best move to surprise them and successfully escape. But a suspicion tickled her brain, and she forced herself to wait and think things through. *'If they knew I had an Aberrant sealed in my mind, is this the conversation we would be having? Why are they so calm? And why do they think this has anything to do with my ability to split my Will?'*

She took a mental step back and encouraged her emotions to calm with a deep breath. *'Oh. That's what the questions about my age and identity were about. Did they hear something from Professor Kiernan? Or perhaps second-hand, from Professor Lacer? Because I did, at one point, intimate that perhaps the Raven Queen had been what was hidden in the book. I thought it might let me, as Siobhan Naught, go free from any crimes that could be foisted off onto her. But I didn't expect this outcome. What, exactly, do they think Myrddin was doing?'*

She decided to probe Aisling's intentions. "Trying to capture me right now would be in violation of this neutral ground."

"Oh, you are free to go, since you do not seem to be the kind of threat we need to remove from existence. But that does not mean we cannot find you again later," he said.

She reached up to run her fingertips over the red and black feathers sprouting from her hair. "Perhaps. However, I am not particularly inclined to give boons to those who have been unfriendly to me," she said boldly. "Do not presume that you can intimidate and control me, squeezing for more and more until I am wrung dry."

She leaned forward subtly, allowing all emotion to slip from her face. "I do not play games I cannot win."

Captain Aisling matched her not-so-subtle threat in both word and tone. "That we allow you your freedom is a gesture of goodwill. We can track you down anywhere in the known lands, if necessary. Do not think that, if we truly turn all of our resources to it, we will be as ineffectual as the local law enforcement." He leaned back again, suddenly more pleasant. "But this task shouldn't be that much of an imposition, my lady. If the information happens to be in Myrddin's journals, you will get off basically free. If you need help with research, Special Agent Lacer has volunteered his services. And if you cannot find the answer yourself, you can simply let us take charge of the research."

By that, he meant that the Red Guard could take charge of her body and mind. Siobhan considered lying—agreeing and then immediately leaving the country. Even if she had to travel beyond the borders of the East, beyond the known lands, it might be safer. But she couldn't lie without them knowing, despite what they thought. Perhaps an acknowledgement that was not true agreement would let her slip by.

"We will complete the vow here, now," Captain Aisling added.

Siobhan's hope collapsed. "I would never agree to trade away my freedom.

And the fact that you need a vow makes me suspect that you are not truly so confident you can track me down and take me by force."

"This vow would allow you your freedom in exchange for some reasonable promises."

She let out a breathy, humorless laugh. "Reasonable promises? You mean chains that restrict my actions and cut off my future, and the assurance of knowledge you so desperately want. It seems a miserly bargain to gain only what is already mine in exchange for something so valuable."

"And yet, you value your freedom so much, it seems more felicitous than anything else I can offer you."

Siobhan's fingers flexed, aching for the Conduit she had left behind in case Professor Lacer recognized it. "Freedom cannot be given. It is mine by right." Anger was beginning to replace her fear.

Professor Lacer cleared his throat. "Might I remind you both, despite your inclination to force outcomes in which you completely sweep the board, compromise is possible. I know you both came willing to at least partially accommodate the other."

'*He's right,*' Siobhan realized, chagrined. '*I prepared several possible bribes. And…maybe I can get something out of this, too.*' At that thought, at least half of her reluctance drained away. '*Actually, could this be the perfect opportunity?*'

Captain Aisling pressed his lips together. "Indeed. What we have learned about you suggests you are almost always willing to trade. We have access to extensive resources and could provide you quite a lot, within reason. Is there anything you might be interested in, or some problem that you would like us to solve?"

Siobhan briefly considered asking them to get all of her crimes pardoned. They probably had the power. But then she remembered that they were supposed to be politically neutral. Besides, just being generally connected to the interests of the Red Guard gave her some protection against the Thirteen Crowns. There was something she wanted even more than that. "If I am to find the answer to this question, I will need leeway to research topics that would otherwise be too…delicate. Forbidden," she clarified.

Seeing the frown already growing on Captain Aisling's face, she continued before he could deny her. "I want to clarify that I have no plans to harm innocent sapients—except perhaps for a few ravens and other creatures that might otherwise be considered mere animals. You may not be willing to take my word as my bond, but I am not mad, nor am I a monster. Any potentially harmful research would be theoretical only. I have no intention to do anything that would require the Red Guard's efforts in disaster management or cleanup."

Captain Aisling's eyes narrowed. "That is…acceptable. We will have to hash out the details, of course. I can see a few ways to get around a vow with the terms you've stated. And I must mention that, with this allowance, you will agree to bring us *actionable* information, not random results that only vaguely involve the question. That being said, if actionable information would require dangerous experimentation, you may do so under our supervision."

"I can offer you something else in exchange for forgoing the vow," Siobhan said.

"We need the vow. Without it—"

"Without it, you can just track me down and do what you threatened to do before, right? And if you're unable to do that, you really have no way to force me to take the vow in the first place. But I think I have something of equal, if not greater value."

"What, exactly?"

"I know who stole the book purported to contain the solution to transforming beast cores into celerium. I have agreed to access the contents and extract the relevant knowledge. The owner is willing to let the Red Guard have that information in exchange for the right offer, and I have the authority to broker that deal."

Captain Aisling hesitated, but then shook his head. "We would be willing to bargain for the knowledge, but you overestimate our interest."

That...had not been the answer Siobhan expected.

"You have no need of celerium?" she asked, wishing her gaze could bore through his eyes and extract the truth directly from his brain.

"Oh, we do. But we are confident that as soon as anyone discovers the answer, we will be able to access the information ourselves as well. Keeping secrets that we are determined to discover is...difficult."

Agent Marcurio smiled. "As they say, two can keep a secret when one of them is dead."

Captain Aisling threw the man a disapproving glance. "To clarify, we will *not* kill people simply for possessing this information. We would be happy to pay a certain amount for it, as well. But not enough to simply let you go without a vow."

Siobhan wished she had something to sip while she stalled for time to think. She had prepared another piece of information that she was quite sure they would be interested in. It seemed a shame to give up something so valuable just to get away without a vow, but the only other way to do so would be to fight her way free. Then, even if she succeeded, she would have made an enemy of the Red Guard. In her situation, what she really needed was time and access to rare and possibly forbidden knowledge. And if this meeting went well, she would have both.

She raised one eyebrow. "What about information on a pipeline funneling Aberrant parts into Lenore?"

Both Captain Aisling and Agent Marcurio froze. Even Thaddeus's eyes snapped to her like a hawk that had seen movement in the grass.

She had asked Oliver to look into any Red Guard defectors. Instead, he had found her this little piece of juicy information. She didn't know if he had convinced the Architects of Khronos to give up one of their own sources, or if he had found someone else; she hadn't had much time to talk to him as he frantically prepared a team and enough erythreans to chase down the Architect's strike team before they could get to Osham. Hopefully, when he got back, they would begin delving into Myrddin's other stolen journal.

"Are you…certain?" Captain Aisling asked.

"Reasonably. And my information is *actionable*. I would even be willing to take a vow that I will tell you the truth of it, since it seems you have chosen not to believe a single word out of my mouth."

It turned out that this was, in fact, irresistible.

Half an hour later, Siobhan followed Gera's lead out of the moving hedge maze, both of them unmolested. The Red Guard were free to chase down whoever was selling pieces of Aberrants, and Siobhan was free to research the forbidden secrets of shamanry—which might hold some answers about how the thing in her head had been sealed—and any other topic she wished, unbeholden to anyone.

Siobhan had gotten what she wanted, but she couldn't help but feel that she had come out of the whole bargain on the losing end. It was a shame that she didn't have the power to treat with the Red Guard on equal terms.

7

CALIGINOUS MOTIVES

Thaddeus
Month 8, Day 21, Saturday 8:00 a.m.

As Thaddeus, Captain Aisling, and Agent Marcurio forced their way free from the ever-changing hedge maze that tried to trap them within, Captain Aisling spoke. "I do not believe I've ever said this before, but I think we came out of that negotiation on the losing end. The Raven Queen controlled the flow from start to finish, and I am only now beginning to realize how skillfully."

Thaddeus agreed. Captain Aisling had undoubtedly gone through the same training courses as other Red Guard captains, but Thaddeus gathered that interrogation and negotiation were not the man's primary talents. Aisling was too easily distracted and did not dig as deeply or as persistently as Thaddeus would have done if he were in the man's position.

Captain Aisling was also inexcusably trigger-happy. That his Radiant battle spell would have been harmless was a ridiculous excuse. If it had hit someone in the eyes, it almost certainly would have done damage, and even a short time under a sustained beam could have caused burns.

Using it outside of battle, against a nominally friendly counterpart, was not only honorless—which Thaddeus did not care so much about—but also foolish. He would have taken further umbrage at the attack if Siobhan herself had not been so nonchalant about it. Evidently, she had not felt threatened.

Instead of saying any of this aloud, Thaddeus merely grunted. When they got to the communications staging area, the pair of agents stationed there gave all three of them a sound-recording device. Unlike the phonograph artifacts currently available on the open market, the Red Guard's version was small enough to fit in a single hand and captured the sound inside of tiny black beads, which were extruded along an even smaller string. This string coiled up inside the device, providing enough space for several days of recording.

With these, each of them walked to a different corner of the room and gave their individual reports on the mission they had just completed. It was best to keep impressions to themselves until they had a chance to say everything; group testimony was famously untrustworthy.

When Thaddeus was finished, he moved to look over a diviner's shoulder into the mirror the operations-focused agents were using to keep tabs on the area. This one was linked to another mirror they had hung in the sky, and could show anything caught in its partner's reflection.

Several suspicious characters, who they suspected to be allies that the Raven Queen had prepared in case of an altercation, were beginning to withdraw, some of them trying to pass themselves off as random civilians.

The woman, her prognos companion, and a couple of superfluous bodyguards were already on a small boat heading south through the Charybdis Gulf.

"The spell's efficiency is unnaturally low because of whatever wards she has, but we haven't lost sight of her," the agent in charge of divination explained. "It's hard to disappear when someone has been watching nonstop the entire time. I'm not even blinking both of my eyes at the same time, just in case."

Captain Aisling sighed as he moved to stand beside Thaddeus, soon followed by Agent Marcurio. They stared at the image of fishermen hauling in their catches as the Raven Queen passed by unnoticed. "Repeat your basic report to me." The captain turned to Marcurio expectantly.

The kitsune hesitated at first, but he quickly fell into telling the story of what they had just experienced. Captain Aisling stopped to ask for clarification and detail several times, especially about the Raven Queen's demonstration of her shadow-familiar spell.

"Now you, Special Agent Lacer," Captain Aisling asked.

Though it was tedious, Thaddeus obliged. Again, Aisling seemed particularly interested about what Thaddeus had seen—or divined—of her shadow display.

Agent Marcurio's eyes were wide, and his tails swished violently. "Do you suspect she somehow managed to tamper with our memories *during* the assessment?"

Captain Aisling shook his head. "I did consider it, but I don't think that's the case. No, I was more suspicious that what she showed us wasn't actually shadow-manipulation at all, but some kind of waking nightmare spell. It would explain the control, the uncanny details, and even the insidious sensations quite cleanly if they were all sourced from our own imaginations. Alas, all three of us experienced the same thing, so that theory is unlikely, though perhaps still not entirely impossible."

"Alternatively, perhaps that level of control and detail is nothing special for a woman who can cast two spells at the same time," Thaddeus suggested.

His colleagues' expressions darkened.

"I would like to once again point out," Agent Marcurio said, "that if she was telling the truth about how that philtre worked..." He looked to Thaddeus questioningly.

"I did a basic analysis of the ingredients. Even for me, it can be almost impossible to discern what components went into a potion once it is fully completed, as a potion is more than the sum of its parts, but I detected some lingering particles of crushed onyx and what might have been algae...or mold. None of the highly conductive, more inert components like metal or celerium dust. No traces of anything that might be cause for concern, for what little that is worth."

"Okay," Marcurio said dubiously. "That's good, I suppose. At least it's some tiny measure of peace of mind that I probably didn't just breathe in some liquified fetus or something. But I would like to reiterate that I find the implications—that simply being aware of her consciousness made us feel the way we did—quite telling. Maybe it was just a trick. But maybe... Well, if we didn't think it likely that Myrddin worked some potentially very psychotic magic to create the 'Raven Queen,' I would say it is rather compelling evidence that she's one of the shapeshifting creatures of dreams and shadow my great-grandmother used to tell me stories about."

Captain Aisling let out a humorless huff. "Who's to say *what*, exactly, Myrddin trapped in that book?"

Agent Marcurio's mouth fell open slightly, revealing his canines. Then, he shivered. "I've seen too many things, so my imagination is more exaggerated than some ignorant commoner's. Now I almost hope she's just some random person Myrddin experimented on. But if she has been imprisoned for centuries, her deep desire for freedom in all aspects makes a lot of sense."

Captain Aisling turned to Thaddeus. "Tell me your impressions. Did you notice anything relevant?"

Thaddeus looked down at the distant reflection of a small boat nearing the edge of the mirror. Tiny Siobhan seemed to be watching the sun rise over Gilbratha's eastern wall, standing tall despite the motion of the boat cutting through the water. "She was showing off her control—the clarity, forcefulness, and soundness of her Will—rather than its capacity. She managed everything she showed us today with less than a thousand thaums, even though there is no way she became a free-caster without at least a few thousand at her command. It says something about who she is, that she believes this to be more impressive than brash displays of capacity. And I would hazard a guess that she could have put on an even more impressive display, if she were not hesitant to push *you* beyond the limits of your self-control," he added, a small hint of his scorn slipping into his tone.

Agent Marcurio pursed his lips, then tapped his forefinger against his chin. "Is it possible that Siobhan Naught's body can't keep up with higher thaumic requirements, and so the Raven Queen is restricted to those low-level spells? Like using a low-capacity Conduit."

"Who knows how it works?" Captain Aisling said. "But if the rumors are true, some of the magic she's shown would be rather difficult to accomplish on a thousand thaums or less. It could also be something to do with identity. Do you think we were talking to Siobhan Naught or the Raven Queen? What distinction is there between them, if any? I heard the Undreaming Order believes that if the Raven Queen manifests fully within an acolyte, it can be damaging to the acolyte's body. She may have been keeping the magic light to protect the girl."

By now, Siobhan and her companions had passed out of sight of the mirror. No doubt trying to find her again with any conventional form of divination would be strangely impossible.

Thaddeus turned the thought of her over in his mind a few times. Who had he been interacting with? He found that he *hoped* it was some combination of both personalities, melded to become one. It would be a shame if Siobhan Naught were trapped away within her own body, screaming soundlessly for help. Or if the girl had been crushed out of existence by the weight of the Raven Queen's consciousness. A combination of personalities might also explain why the Raven Queen sometimes acted with strange immaturity or made reckless decisions based on emotion.

At least she had not shown any signs of psychosis or a split personality. Except for, perhaps, the ability to split her Will.

As the other agents began to pack up, the three of them descended to the heavily warded and illusion-covered carriage that would deliver them near a field base entrance.

Agent Marcurio tucked his tails over his lap as they sat. "I do have to wonder, if she could lie as she pleased without us realizing, why did she let slip about wiping that artisan's memories?"

It was a good question, but not the right one.

"Why did she use such a device at all?" Captain Aisling asked. "Several times, and even today, she's shown off her free-casting ability. Surely she wouldn't need such a thing."

That was a better question, but still seemed to be lacking some critical insight.

"It might make it safer to dual-cast," Marcurio offered, perking up. "Did you notice, she drew out the spell arrays to show her ability to us? Maybe that wasn't just so we could confirm what and how she was casting, but for her own sake as well."

Captain Aisling nodded as if everything suddenly made sense, but Thaddeus had an instinct that he was still missing a piece of the puzzle.

Not only had Siobhan openly used a device designed by his apprentice, Sebastien, she had almost purposefully drawn their attention to that fact, even to the point of implicating herself. It was strange. Almost as strange as the original boon she had given the boy. All because she liked him? But no, that had only been a *half*-truth.

Thaddeus frowned, breathing out slowly as disparate pieces of information began to come together into something that formed meaning. What if she had not lied to them freely at all? She was clever with her words to the point of manipulating people's understanding as she wished, but she also liked to play games with hidden clues and subtext.

Perhaps she *had not* damaged the memory of the shop owner. Technically, her statement could have meant that she stole from the man, came in a disguised form and bought from him, or even took the schematics and made a copy for herself.

But if that was true, it meant that she had implicated herself in a serious crime—one strangely connected to his apprentice—on purpose. And that she had given the boon to Sebastien for a reason beyond just liking him. Thaddeus had thought *he* must have been the reason behind her initial actions toward the boy, for what other reason could she have to be interested in a random University student? He had thought that she knew his reputation or had learned some hint of his work and found herself intrigued. But what if that was not the case? What if there was some other connection between Siobhan and Sebastien?

As if the obvious had been waiting for him to open his mind to the possibility all along, Thaddeus saw a clear memory of Siobhan Naught's dark, unfathomable eyes, illuminated by the soft light of dawn. They were so like those of his apprentice, though he and she were dissimilar in almost every other way. In fact, unless Thaddeus was mistaken, that unusual eye color was almost…identical.

8

BOOK OF SECRETS

SIOBHAN
Month 8, Day 21, Saturday 8:35 a.m.

SIOBHAN FELT the moment when they escaped whatever method the Red Guard had been using to track her from the maze. As the strain on her divination-diverting ward fell to the normal low-level prickle and coldness of working against her dowsing artifact, her shoulders relaxed and her jaw unclenched. "We are clear," she announced, triggering a simultaneous sigh of relief from everyone else in the small boat.

Beside her, Gera looked up from where she had seemed to be staring pensively into the water despite her lack of actual sight. "Did that meeting… go as you planned? I am uncertain if my presence was actually useful. Your designs run so deep, I feared to disrupt them by acting in a way that might go against your hidden purpose."

"Your presence served its purpose," Siobhan said. "If you had needed to interfere more directly, it would have been a consequence of the situation going wrong."

Gera stared somewhere to the right of Siobhan's arm. "But is this…truly enough to pay my debt? This does not feel equal in weight to what you did for me."

"You also helped me manage the aftermath of the High Crown's anger and fulfill the boons I promised, as well as fencing some items and procuring several false identities for me, remember? In fact, it is I who owe you. The spell I promised you, the one to handle Millennium's sleep issues even once his power grows—and without hiring sorcerers to guard his sleep through the night—is ready." Siobhan listed the basics that Gera would need to prepare before they could cast the sleep-proxy spell. "When you are ready, I will visit with the spell instructions and guide them through the first casting."

Gera bowed deeply. "Words cannot express my gratitude."

"It is an equal exchange. There is no need to be grateful."

"An exchange that you gave me the opportunity for. There are many others who would have jumped at the chance to barter with you. And…if I might be so bold, I wonder if there is any other task you might set me to? I have a favor to ask of you, my lady."

Siobhan raised an eyebrow. "Oh? What is it?"

"Would you be willing to teach me the spell you used with Millennium? The one in which you place your hands over his chest and hum? I appreciate your offer to teach him directly someday. It's only that I am his mother, and I would like to be able to comfort him in the meantime." The muscles around Gera's eye and mouth tightened, creasing her skin with faint wrinkles. "I—I feel that I've been so useless in that aspect. Never able to fix things for him."

Siobhan's stomach clenched. Would Ennis have made a request like that for her? Had he ever noticed her, *thought* about her, enough to know when she was struggling silently? Several different responses sprang to the tip of her tongue, but Siobhan suppressed them all, and eventually only said, "I would be willing to teach you that spell. It is not difficult, though you must be careful with it. One might be enticed to use it during times of greatest distress —times when a mistake can be most fatal," Siobhan said meaningfully.

Despite the heat, the hair on Gera's arms rose visibly. "I take your meaning, my lady. And in exchange?"

Siobhan hummed thoughtfully, then waved Gera to join her at the back of the boat, where she spoke in a low voice. "There *is* something that I have found troublesome lately. But I do not want to potentially endanger your life or sanity by exposing you to it. I want to gather information about something that deals with the realms of dreams, consciousness, and memory. I wonder, perhaps there are more abstract forms of divination that might be able to give me information about the seal containing something without actually touching the thing trapped inside? Is there a way to…place blinders on yourself, metaphorically? Nothing to do with dream-walking. I think that might be…hazardous."

Gera had gone distinctly pale and was crumpling the fabric of her skirt with both fists.

"I would not require you to perform this divination," Siobhan hurried to assure her. "For such a small favor of my knowledge, I only wanted your expertise on the subject."

Gera relaxed only slightly, looked around, and then leaned closer to Siobhan to whisper. "Is this about the request the Red Guard made of you?"

Siobhan nodded, though considering it a "request" was generous.

If anything, Gera grew even more tense. Siobhan could almost hear the woman's muscles creaking against each other like old bone, she was so stiff. "Prying into things that should not be known is one of the most common ways for a diviner to die. One of the first things we learn is to allow null answers as outputs to all of our spells, and that if we receive one, we should *stop*. I would suggest some preemptive divinations about the danger of prying further into this 'seal,' if even that can be done without accidentally accessing whatever is within. I know you are incredibly powerful, my lady, and this research seems to lie within your domains of sovereignty, but I caution against trying to do this investigation yourself, if it is truly so dangerous. I…could put some feelers out for skilled diviners who are, for whatever reason, desperate enough to risk their lives in exchange for a boon from you."

Siobhan sighed and waved away the offer. "The situation is not so dire yet. I will consider other, less risky favors that you could do for me."

Gera straightened and smoothed down the section of her skirt that she had wrinkled, though she did not seem fully relieved.

Normally, Siobhan might have asked the woman for some restricted spell information, but as soon as she got access to the rest of the University's restricted archive, that need might disappear. Perhaps she could have the woman sell a stolen Conduit or two on her behalf. Even though she had paid Liza for her latest work in knowledge rather than coin, Siobhan had been spending like a profligate mistress of the High Crown lately. Her stash was down to less than a thousand gold. These extravagant expenses were worth it for even a small increase in her safety, but it was a sharp reminder that her current funds would not last forever.

By the time she became Sebastien once more and returned to her attic apartment, she was feeling a bit of mental fatigue, if not exactly the profound exhaustion that she had once been so familiar with. She stared around listlessly for a bit. Despite her work to fix it up, the place was still so empty, with the only items beyond mere necessity being the small shelf of books she had accumulated. Sebastien let out a deep sigh, feeling empty for some reason. She cast her dreamless sleep spell, used the vibrational calming spell to forcefully relax, and took a short nap to relieve the burden on the raven she was currently bound to.

When she woke, she was ready.

Rather than re-cast her shadow-familiar spell, Sebastien took out Myrddin's journal, ran through a few exercises to limber her mind, and then passed the book's test after only three attempts. Over the past week, she had transcribed the first thirty or so pages for Liza, which contained the three methods

Myrddin had recorded to create self-charging artifacts. The task had been both slow and arduous, as trying to maintain her concentration on both glyph meanings while also understanding the contents of the page well enough to write them down on a separate sheet of paper was at the edge of her capabilities. And then, after every few pages, she would need to rest, recuperate, and then attempt to access the contents once more.

But when Liza had received the pages, the woman's hands had trembled, and as they discussed the work to prepare for the meeting, her eyes had strayed toward them every time she thought Siobhan wasn't looking.

Now, as Siobhan ran her forefinger over the thick paper, she wondered what else she might be able to get someone like Liza to do with the enticement of Myrddin's knowledge. Gold could be earned anywhere. This particular knowledge was accessible through Siobhan alone, and with secrecy vows, would hopefully remain so for quite some time.

She only wished that she could gain from it, too. Even though she had transcribed Myrddin's notes by hand, all she could say was that she vaguely understood the concepts of what he had created. The actual mechanics of his spellwork shot so far over her head that she might as well have been a toddler. He used glyphs that her huge lexicon had no reference for, frequently interspersed with complex math. To this, he added notes in a truncated shorthand that made little sense even when she recognized all the individual letters. That, and, since he was not writing this for others' consumption, he often stopped halfway through a thought and made a logical leap either to the conclusion or to another thought entirely.

Truly, an eccentric genius.

After the self-charging artifacts, Myrddin's focus shifted, prefaced by a note:

It escapes me why everyone recommends brownies for household work. It's one of the first things people suggest when they learn I'm a bachelor, right after they hear that I have no plans to marry or hire some pretty young girl to take care of the house and warm my bed. It's ridiculous! Brownies are profoundly unreliable. This is the third time this month that mine has somehow become offended and decided to leave my shoes out in the rain, and that's not even counting the time it "accidentally" vomited on my pillow and "forgot" to clean it up. Someone should come up with a more reasonable

THE NOTE CUT off abruptly there in favor of several detailed sketches of a two-foot tall, fully articulated humanoid mechanism made of metal. It was meant to be powered by a beast core and follow what Siobhan guessed was a complex set of commands built into artifact wards that were—once again—so complex she couldn't understand them.

'Did Myrddin invent any potions? Surely I could understand that,' she lamented. *'Probably,'* she amended, noticing one sub-spell array that was only half built out. Knowing her luck, Myrddin would feel that the number of stirs and how finely to grind his potion's hellcat feathers were so obvious that he didn't actually need to write it down.

The designs for his brownie-replacement continued for a few pages, but then Myrddin wrote some questions about how to define *when* certain actions should be taken based on other criteria, and the next dozen pages were nothing but incomprehensible, incredibly detailed spell arrays that seemed to be sub-arrays of other sub-arrays, all calling on each other in a hierarchical web. Even that much she wouldn't have understood if Myrddin hadn't drawn a mind-map to keep track of their connections.

At that point, her mind grew too strained and she lost control, causing the book to snap back into incomprehensibility. Siobhan rubbed her temples as she let out a hissing breath. She closed Myrddin's book and put it back in the warded chest, then took a stance in the center of the room and began light-refinement. This, too, had become even easier with practice. She completed nine full cycles of refinement, and when she was finished, let out a final deep breath that almost seemed to glow.

Covered in sweat, she felt as if she half floated down the back stairway, every cell in her body filled with a gentle, buoyant energy. She bought a big meal at one of the local restaurants, ate until she was stuffed, then ordered a second meal that they packed away in a lunch box. Then, she returned to her attic apartment and opened Myrddin's journal again.

The reaction-array work cut off halfway through one page, and when Sebastien turned to the next, she found a map drawn out across both pages. This, she carefully copied down, because it could hold a clue as to when, exactly, Myrddin had written the journal.

Several more maps of various regions followed, with question marks around the edges where the known lands ended and the wilderness began. Those borders had changed in the thousand years since, and some of the countries didn't even exist anymore. Then, Myrddin had drawn what he knew of the planet, calculated the equator, and estimated the planet's diameter.

Sebastien stared at that drawing for a long time. She had never realized how small a part of the planet the known lands were. Then, her eyes were drawn to the notes Myrddin had scribbled beside his rendition of the world.

Sixty to seventy percent water? I wonder if other continents exist. The Starpeak
Mountains were probably formed from the unnaturally violent collision of two
continents, but they are too tall. Unnaturally so. I can only guess what could
have caused such a thing. Maybe the Cataclysm. My Will isn't strong enough to
do a planet-sized divination, even now. No new epiphanies about how to
possibly bounce a light-based divination off the moon. Does magic even extend
out that far?

Sebastien stared at the last line until a headache bloomed through her
skull and her concentration slipped once again. Instead of moving on to light-
refinement to boost her recovery speed, she stared up at the sky through the
ceiling window. *'Why would Myrddin even suspect that magic doesn't extend to the
moon?'* It was a possibility so far outside of her understanding of reality that
she would have never expected it.

'Does magic…need air to exist?' That seemed absurd. But Myrddin's understanding of the cosmos had been advanced far beyond his time. And she knew
his understanding of magic was the same. *'Maybe magic doesn't exist where there's
no life. If it's some kind of byproduct of thought, or requires the common consciousness as
a medium, then it might make sense that there would be none on the moon. Wow.'* A
slow, giddy smile stretched across her face.

This was a hint at a profound secret. A tiny brick in the foundation of her
goal of being the world's most powerful sorcerer. She bounced up, laughing to
herself as she began the first cycle of light-refinement in the beam through the
window. After nine more cycles, her muscles were beginning to complain that
she could only practice this particular magic so many times per day.

She had trouble getting past Myrddin's protections this time, making
seven or eight attempts as she ran into rare glyphs that she had not yet
memorized. But the next part of his journal filled her with even more delight.

He was developing a personal flight spell. And not just any flight spell—
one that could take the user into the stratosphere, providing both oxygen and
insulation. And she could *almost* understand the beginning iterations, until he
started adjusting it to create a semi-automated flight backpack that would
adjust its output based on the surrounding conditions and the health status of
its wearer.

Sebastien carefully copied down the actively cast version of the spell, even
though she probably didn't have the capacity to cast it even if she could
unravel how it worked.

This took her to the end of her concentration once more, and after a final
round of light-refinement from the setting sun, Sebastien forced herself to
take another short nap before returning to the book once more.

After the flight spell, Myrddin had worked on a long-distance magnification spell that could outperform most telescopes, which he then modified with a divination spell that would filter out visual impurities caused by particles of dust, water, and other atmospheric pollutants.

She was fascinated. *'Was he developing this to look closer at the moon, or perhaps other distant celestial bodies? Is he about to invent a way to bounce a divination off of the moon?'* But before she could learn the answer, her Will gave out once more. Her head was throbbing too badly to even be upset about it, however.

Sebastien soothed her overworked and aching body with several salves and potions, completed all of her homework, and then practiced with the three things Professor Lacer had tasked her to transmute. By this point, she felt that she was approaching expertise. Transmuting diamond was the easiest, because it had such a uniform internal structure, but she still struggled to create even the tiniest speck using air as the component.

Her scab-root *looked* more edible than the naturally grown samples, but it was equally disgusting, and no matter how she attempted to cook it, it left the lingering taste of soap and blood behind on her tongue and coated her teeth with a film she had to brush to remove.

The orb-weaver silk was somewhat easy to make but often looked like it had been woven by a fat-fingered blind woman. She tried to ensure she grew the threads evenly, wove the fabric consistently, and kept the color uniform. Silk was the most fun to play with, though, and she had given herself a side project to augment it.

Using the same methods, Sebastien could transmute filament-thin gold wire and weave it through the silk to create an even more conductive thread. She planned to practice until she could create tiny gold tubes, through which she could force a thinned-down mixture of magical beast blood and other conductive material. She theorized that it would end up being able to handle a lot more power than the current arrays that filled out her spell rod, while maintaining a small size and being relatively cheap to produce. *'Maybe one day, I could even create a battle outfit full of spell arrays for active casting rather than enchantment effects.'*

Sebastien filled her Sunday with more attempts to get through Myrddin's journal. He started off with a spell that worked together with the previous two, adding multiple images taken at slightly different angles together to create a coherent composite. He noted that it was useful to see details on the moon, even looking at it during the day.

After that, his focus jumped to a series of data points and a long essay on the migratory patterns of birds. Apparently, birds had tiny magnets in a spot on their beak, which allowed them to sense where they were in relation to the planet's own magnetic field.

This digressed into a study and dissection of a cockatrice, complete with detailed sketches. Myrddin noted:

> I think the feathers are actually a mutation of the scales. Or the scales are unexpressed feathers, like a latent genetic trait. Proto-feathers? Did a dragon breed with a chicken? How, even? Genital-transformation magic?
>
> I can't believe I just wrote that. I wish it weren't so plausible. It reminds me of that time Tharraxaron took an interest in me.

SEBASTIEN SNORTED. The next dozen pages were filled with several drawings of sky-kraken and other sea-creature-like beasts that Sebastien had never seen before.

That was all she managed to get through on Sunday, but she slept the night at her apartment and got in a final session early on Monday morning.

Myrddin's next area of interest was again aligned with her own childhood fascination, though rather than trying to ride one of the sky-kraken, he designed a wing-suit that would work with his previous backpack propulsion artifact. But he stopped development halfway through, with another note:

> Too uncomfortable for long periods of use. I'm old. I want to poop on a proper heated chamber pot.

AND WITH THAT, Sebastien had accomplished all she could for the moment and was forced to hide away the book and hurry across most of the city to the University. The day started off normally, though Damien looked haggard and sallow when he murmured that he would have a report for her soon.

For once, it was she who made sure that he was eating enough during the cafeteria mealtimes. Even Alec noticed and tried to cheer Damien up by assuring him that there was no way he was going to fail the end of term exams with how hard he had been studying.

"Are you in some sort of competition with Sebastien?" Brinn asked.

"That's exactly it," Sebastien lied. "Because Professor Lacer still isn't impressed enough to take Damien on as an apprentice, provisional or otherwise."

Damien nodded, his mouth pinched as if he had bitten into an unripe persimmon.

Then they arrived at the Practical Casting classroom. Professor Lacer was often a few minutes late, but this time, he hadn't arrived even after half an hour.

Tanya Canelo went to the administrative office and returned with a note that he was taking a personal day. As casting without supervision was considered too dangerous—especially this close to the end of term when students were most likely to be both exhausted and desperate—she made the executive decision to release the class early amidst rumors and gossip about where Professor Lacer could be.

"An Aberrant," Damien muttered bleakly. "He probably got called away to deal with the aftermath of some poor sod breaking like a piece of crystal. Dashed upon the ground and ruined. All the beauty and potential of a life, wasted."

Ana raised both eyebrows, sharing a glance with Sebastien over Damien's head. "Damien, do you remember that time you started memorizing sad poetry and then tried to run away from home?"

Damien blinked. "I was twelve. I didn't pack an umbrella, and I got rained on, and—"

Sebastien flinched, her back tightening as the warding disks under her skin activated. Both Ana and Damien looked at her, and she tried to settle her expression into a nonchalant grimace. Almost as soon as the divination had started, it faded again. "Muscle spasm," she explained.

She did her best to pay attention as Ana subtly tried to dig into Damien's dark mood and encourage him, but then another weak pulse of divination washed over her. As Ana was in the middle of convincing Damien to go out to the latest comedy play, Sebastien "suddenly remembered" that she had a book to return to the library and scurried away to the abandoned second floor classroom, where she set up her reverse-scrying spell and waited for another pulse.

She caught it as soon as it appeared and traced it back to the same building her dormitory was in. A little closer detail revealed it was another of the first-floor dormitories, and that was all she needed to take down her reverse-scrying spell and storm out of the Citadel.

If she had been wearing something like Professor Lacer's climate-controlled long coat, it would have flared out behind her as she threw herself through the dormitory doorway and scanned for whoever was scrying for her.

She found them almost immediately.

A group of girls sat in a circle around a divination spell array. Its components were a daisy, a very accurate, if slightly too handsome, drawing of Sebastien, and a fountain pen that looked suspiciously like the one Sebastien had recently lost.

One of the girls looked up at her and paled. Soon after, the rest noticed her, which set off a dramatic scene full of shrieking and flailing as they tried to hide the drawing, smudge out their spellwork, and physically block her line of sight with their bodies.

But Sebastien had already seen it all. She ran through her mental image of the memory to parse the shape of the glyphs and the written instruction around the outside.

'*I'm the focus, obviously, but the divination wasn't to find me. It was to reveal if I had any...desire? Oh. It was to reveal if I had any romantic interest in whoever was doing the casting. Were they taking turns?*'

Sebastien stalked forward and ripped the drawing of herself out from under the leg of the girl who had tried to hide it by sitting on it.

She held it over the flame of the scented pink candle they were using for power. As the drawing curled away into blackened soot, she stared them all down. "Let me answer the question you were all so desperate to know that you decided to invade my privacy and steal from me. *No, I do not.*"

One of the girls flinched as if she had been slapped, most couldn't meet her gaze, and big tears rolled down the cheeks of the girl closest to Sebastien's feet.

If Sebastien were her father, she probably would have spat on the ground to show her displeasure, but she had always found that disgusting, and besides that, she didn't trust what they might do with her saliva. "Do not do this again," she bit out.

Then she took her fountain pen back and left.

She found her Crown-family friends in her own dorm room, all gathered around Alec's bed.

Ana immediately narrowed her eyes and stood up when she saw Sebastien's stormy expression. "What's wrong?"

Sebastien explained, though she made up a random student that had tipped her off to the situation to cover up how she had actually learned what was happening and where. She had expected sympathy, but instead, both Damien and Alec turned as red as tomatoes before spluttering out laughter.

They guffawed so hard they fell off the bed, and Alec started drooling on the floor, open-mouthed and struggling to breathe. If she hadn't known better, she would have thought he was sobbing in horrible pain.

Ana coughed several times, until that, too, devolved into laughter, and then all was lost.

Rhett and Waverly hugged each other for support, while the tiny girl slapped Rhett's arm over and over as if trying to smack the amusement out of him.

Brinn was the only one who managed to keep it to a few chuckles, and he patted Sebastien's back sympathetically.

Alec crawled his way back onto his bed and wiped the tears from his cheeks. "I peed myself, just a little."

Sebastien grimaced at him with disgust. "Why would you admit that?"

Ana coughed again, then tucked her hair behind her ears and lifted her chin like she had never found anything funny at all. "Those girls are taking this too far. Writing stories and drawing pictures was one thing, but at this rate, someone will be trying to slip you a love potion."

'Wait, drawings and stories? What is she talking about?'

That sobered Damien, at least. He lifted his head from where it had been resting on his knees in a recovery position. "Anyone who was discovered doing such a thing would be arrested for blood magic! Love potions tamper with a person's free will."

Ana stared at him, blank-faced, Rhett chuckled, and Waverly rolled her eyes.

Damien sighed. "Okay, so stupid people will do stupid things. And most people are a little bit evil when it suits them and they think they can get away with it. I'm learning this. But surely they wouldn't be able to find a recipe?"

Ana rubbed her temples. "Maybe not. But that might not stop them from trying. And if they botch some illegal concoction and end up *poisoning* Sebastien instead, does that make it better?" Before anyone could respond, she huffed, pulled her hair around so that it hung artfully over one shoulder, and nodded at them like a general giving the order for battle. "I will handle this. I'll need to pull in Tanya Canelo and a few others."

She took a single step, then hesitated, turning to Sebastien. "If that's alright?"

Sebastien buried her head in her hands. "Yes. Stop them. Thank you."

Alec lounged back on his bed as he watched Ana leave, then turned to Sebastien. A mischievous grin grew across his face. "So we now know those girls have no chance with you. But you're still an eligible bachelor. If you were to pick the most desirable romantic partner, who would it be, Sebastien? Do you have a type? Someone you like?"

Sebastien rolled her eyes. "I'm not interested in romance. I'm going to become a free-caster, and an Archmage. That's much more enticing than any foolish dalliance."

Alec waved away her words as if they were buzzing gnats, then leaned forward conspiratorially. "But if you had to pick, who would it be?"

Rhett shook his head sadly. "I think a better question would be to ask Sebastien if he remembers anyone's *name*. That's a more realistic stepping stone for our emotionally stunted friend."

"Just hypothetically," Alec urged. "What makes a desirable partner?"

Seeing that Alec wouldn't stop until she gave him something, Sebastien thought for a moment. "Well, probably someone intelligent, and driven, who you could have interesting conversations with. And maybe a bit older, so they would have matured beyond the emotional level of a *child*," she added with a sneer.

Only then did she notice that several of their dorm mates were obviously listening in on the conversation from the walkway and nearby cubicles.

A young man called out, "He's talking about Professor Lacer!" from behind the cover of a cubicle wall, and several of the eavesdroppers let out gasps and muffled giggles. At least they had the good sense to scurry away before Sebastien could burn them alive with her gaze alone.

Alec clapped a hand to his mouth, wide-eyed. *"Professor Lacer?"* he asked in a stage whisper.

Sebastien took a deep breath and pinched the bridge of her nose. "Thaddeus Lacer is too old for any of us, and having a relationship with a professor is against the University's ethical rules."

The whole group stared at her, and Waverly hadn't even tuned out the conversation to start reading a book.

Alec's grin grew larger. "But if it wasn't against the rules?"

Sebastien pointed at him threateningly, as if her finger were a battle wand. "I am *not* romantically interested in Professor Lacer. And he would never consider such a thing, either. He's a professional, and I'm sure he has *standards*. I'm just saying, if you had to pick someone, someone *like* him would be better than those girls. Hells, even my nemesis Nunchkin would be better!"

Damien coughed awkwardly and, thank the stars above, changed the subject.

9

SIMPLE MATH AND COMPLEX SUSPICIONS

DESPITE THADDEUS'S attempts at efficiency, paperwork and in-depth after-action reports still took longer than they had any reasonable right to. It consumed almost two hours before he could depart Field Base One. By that time, he already had his next steps firmly in mind.

Using his fame and his identity as a frequent consultant for the coppers, it was fairly easy to get access to the records at the city's archive. According to what little information they had on him, Sebastien Siverling was an orphan of unremarkable parents. Other than his date of birth, his records were nonexistent until he came to Gilbratha.

Harrow Hill was similarly lacking, containing only information Thaddeus already knew. The boy was easily influenced by those he considered his friends and had repeatedly put his safety at terrible risk for them. And he had met the Raven Queen in passing on the same night that Newton Moore broke.

Thaddeus was about to replace Sebastien's records and leave when Titus Westbay slid around one of the record shelves. "I heard you were visiting, but you didn't come to see—" He broke off as his gaze trailed over the label on the file in Thaddeus's hands. Thoughts raced behind his eyes for two seconds, and then he said, "Is something wrong?"

Thaddeus remained silent for a moment, considering his words. "I have reason to be concerned for my apprentice. I am merely...ensuring there is nothing I have missed."

Titus shifted on his feet then smoothed his hair back. "I did a private investigation into Mr. Siverling, as well."

Thaddeus's eyes narrowed.

"I was worried he might have bad intentions toward Damien!" Titus hurried to explain, holding his hands out as if to stop Thaddeus, though Thaddeus had not moved at all.

"Why bring it up?" Thaddeus asked. "You must have discovered something relevant."

"Well...I don't know about that. Perhaps if you were more specific about the reason for your concern?"

Thaddeus closed the file and put it neatly back in its place. "What do you know?" he asked, his voice low and his words slow.

Titus swallowed. "Oliver Dryden, who is sponsoring Sebastien's way through University, is inappropriately *interested* in him. Damien was worried that Sebastien might be being taken advantage of. Fortunately, Dryden doesn't seem to have managed to act on his interests, and Sebastien is at least moderately wary of him. Sebastien has friends at the Silk Door, and grew up poor, but until now he's kept himself alive by practicing small, illegal magic as he traveled through rural towns rather than prostituting himself."

Titus ran out of air, took a deep breath, and continued to spew everything he knew. "Mr. Siverling is an orphan and was taken in as a small child by a man who taught him some magic. No known blood relation. That man later died in a fire that Mr. Siverling suspects was arson. I don't know a lot of other details about Mr. Siverling's past, except that he experienced some severely traumatic events which he doesn't like to discuss. If you're concerned that he's scheming for influence and power, you can put those worries aside. He strongly prefers to achieve success through his own merits alone and face obstacles head-on. He's got an abrasive mouth and he gets irritated easily, but he's excessively kind to those he considers weaker than himself. And..."

Titus looked left and right, cleared his throat, and added, "When he was little, he used to collect newspaper clippings of you and pretend you were his father!"

Thaddeus took a moment to process all of that. He reached up to press on his eyes, pushing back the pressure building behind them. For once, he found himself at a loss for anything to say. Aching, grating, sympathetic embarrassment rasped against his insides. He understood the kind of lack that could lead a child to do something like that all too well. Thaddeus resolved never to mention it to Sebastien. He would pretend he did not know. "Okay. Tell me more about Oliver Dryden. And the man who took Sebastien in. And the arson."

"Well...I really only know a little more about Lord Dryden. I think he's infatuated with your apprentice. I have reason to believe he's hired prostitutes to impersonate Mr. Siverling, and when I confronted him, he had a rather strong protective reaction for the boy. I don't believe he means your apprentice any *harm*, per se, but Mr. Siverling did come clean about some wariness toward the man. He isn't oblivious to Dryden's manipulative nature. Damien was hoping that his friend could come to stay with us over Harvest Break, so that he would not be forced to sleep at Dryden Manor."

Thaddeus pressed harder on his eyes. Why had Sebastien never mentioned any of this to him? It was just like the underpowered Conduit situation all over again. Was Thaddeus not trustworthy in Sebastien's eyes? Was he not reliable? Or was his apprentice too ashamed to tell the truth, perhaps? Thaddeus took a deep breath and opened his eyes. "Alright. Thank you for informing me. I must be off." He nodded to Titus and brushed past him, striding toward the exit.

"Ah? Sure. But wait, what's going on?" Titus asked, turning belatedly to follow Thaddeus.

"It is still unclear. I will inform you if I need further assistance."

"What? Wait, there has to be a reason for this. Did Dryden do something? Did Sebastien *say* something?"

Thaddeus ignored him, and as soon as they were among others who might overhear, Titus was forced to shut his loose lips. The man was delayed by his subordinates stopping him to talk, and Thaddeus exited and got into a carriage alone.

As the suspensionless, uncushioned carriage rattled beneath him on a path back toward the base he had just left, Thaddeus pondered.

He had examined the boon the Raven Queen had given Sebastien extensively. Based on his observations of her own anti-divination magic during the meeting that morning, he strongly suspected they were exactly the same. Which meant that, during the short period of time they had crossed paths, and without Sebastien noticing, Siobhan had cast complex magic on the young man. But how?

Thaddeus had considered it before, but he ran the questions through his mind again, searching for some new revelation now that his understanding was deeper.

It seemed that, from a distance, she had placed a long-lasting anti-divination ward on Sebastien while somehow avoiding any physical traces of its existence. The sheer implausibility of this, verging on impossibility, was part of the unfathomable reputation that led so many to find her frightening.

It was also possible that it was no ward at all—at least not by the definitions of modern sorcery. Changing a person's intrinsic nature to give them some of the unconscious magical qualities of a beast was not *totally* unheard of, but to do it so late in life, and without any other obvious side effects or physical mutations…doubtful. No, perhaps impossible, and likely even harder to accomplish than the first option. On top of that, Thaddeus was no magizoologist, but he could think of no beasts with that precise effect.

More plausibly, Siobhan had somehow shared her own abilities with Sebastien, likely through some kind of binding magic. Perhaps she was even actively casting the ward on the boy from a distance, whenever some kind of alarm alerted her to the need. But how would she have done so without Sebastien's knowledge? Either there was some deeper intrinsic connection between the two that allowed her to give such a powerful boon to Sebastien—without the young man realizing he had accepted anything or given anything up in return—or something else was going on.

Of the two options, Thaddeus leaned toward the idea that some deception had been perpetrated. And Sebastien was very likely complicit.

Back at the Red Guard base, Thaddeus took a few hours to pore over all of the information they had compiled about the Raven Queen's actions and abilities. Their intelligence was more thorough and accurate than what the coppers had put together, but held no particular revelations. He noted that she was rumored to never sleep, and had given boons of a similar nature, though the details were unclear.

Thaddeus's gaze grew distant as he remembered the spell Sebastien had been developing the previous semester. A blood magic binding spell that would allow someone or something else to sleep in his place. From what Thaddeus remembered, the spell had been strangely advanced for a first-term student. Truly, it would have been more realistic coming from a Journeyman. Furthermore, it used principles none of Sebastien's professors would have taught him, since Thaddeus knew that he himself had not.

The Red Guard's investigation had also confirmed that the Raven Queen very likely made use of several physical forms. How she accomplished this was uncertain.

Some suggested that her body was merely like a pair of clothes, a chosen acolyte that had agreed to host her for a time. But all of them looked fairly similar, which was suspicious. Based on the flesh-molding blood magic that she had used to heal—even giving one man a thumb-shaped forearm in a bit of perverse humor—Thaddeus guessed it was well within her displayed capabilities to moderately adjust her physical form.

Again, he considered that if he had no reason to believe otherwise, he might suspect that the real Siobhan Naught was long dead and her body devoured by the denizens of the Charybdis Gulf.

However, such a capability, along with her proven mastery at outclassing all traditional divination, meant that she could probably travel the city freely, one woman amongst the many. In fact, someone naive like Sebastien might have met her without even knowing who she was.

It was growing dark already, and, somewhat stymied for epiphanies, Thaddeus returned to the University. He could sense the signs of excessive sleep deprivation and stress sending his thoughts spiraling in unproductive loops, so he forced himself to sleep. In the morning, he found that Sebastien was gone from the dorms, though this in itself was not particularly alarming. Many students flouted the rules over the weekend, with or without approved absences from the dormitories.

Still, something about not being able to see Sebastien set Thaddeus on edge.

Thaddeus was forced to go to a faculty meeting where his colleagues argued about inanities, ate mediocre pastries, and tried to get Thaddeus to volunteer for extra work in various forms. After that, he was stuck in back-to-back consultations with his students, several of whom in the upper terms were signed up for the exhibitions. By the time he was finished, it was already late.

Scowling, he walked to the administrative center. Along the way, he frightened several student couples who were having romantic moments along the gently lit cobblestone path. He ignored the administrative desk attendant who tried to flirt with him every time he visited and pulled Sebastien's records.

Sebastien's file was not as thick as some of the worst troublemakers, but still thicker than average. His professors, in general, had taken special note of the young man, perhaps as a courtesy to Thaddeus.

Most of the notes were consistent. Sebastien had trouble socializing, but had made friends with Damien's group, as well as a few others, namely Tanya Canelo and the unfortunate Newton Moore. He had many "fans" among the other students, though he interacted with them as little as possible. And his Will's capacity was growing with abnormal speed, leading several to worry that he might be pushing himself to the breaking point. The healers had even left a note about him being underweight, and several prescriptions for anti-anxiety potions.

Thaddeus slowed down and read those notes again. Sebastien had started the first term barely over two hundred thaums. But his most recent test placed him at six hundred eighteen.

Thaddeus commandeered a piece of paper from the administrative desk and did the math. Generally, Will-growth followed a simple equation that most students would be able to compute by the time they gained their Mastery.

He stared down at the results, then scratched his beard.

Either Sebastien had been lying about his capacity at the start of term, couldn't bring his full Will to bear because of a sub-par Conduit, or had been working himself to the bone ever since. Or…he was one of the few humans with a calculable smidge of extra talent. Like Thaddeus.

Thaddeus realized his heart was pounding and took a deep breath to calm himself.

But even for Thaddeus to make that kind of advancement, he would have had to practice almost six and a half hours per day. Extensive studies had shown that the safe limit for active casting was only six hours, ideally to be completed over an eight-to-twelve-hour period. One could safely surpass that on occasion, but to do so consistently was dangerous. It was possible to extend the six-hour limit slightly with special treatment and a rigid program meant to maximize physical and mental health, but it still required a lifestyle without other mental stressors or distracting efforts.

And Thaddeus knew that Sebastien's life did not even come close to such conditions. No University student's did.

For a normal student, the growth Sebastien had displayed would have required eight hours per day, and they would likely already be dead.

Thaddeus considered that maybe Sebastien had already mastered the light-based healing spell Thaddeus had translated for him, somehow cutting the average initiation time for an adult to pick up their first success within the gestura's movement-based magic from about two years down to a few months. Still, the results should be relatively negligible, because the effects were diluted throughout the entire body, not only focused on the mind. And in addition to that, the very act of casting that spell would be considered time spent actively casting.

It was possible, Thaddeus supposed, that this allowed Sebastien to eke out an extra half hour of casting per day, but not enough to reach eight.

Perhaps, instead, his apprentice's first measurement had been well below his true capacity. By over one hundred thaums. Otherwise, Sebastien was a monster. Likely even more so than Thaddeus. And Thaddeus knew well that *he* was a special circumstance.

Thaddeus stared down at the wooden grain of the table for a while, tracing the natural pattern with his eyes. The former explanation was more likely. Thaddeus knew that. But he was unable to put aside the small possibility of the latter. He put the scattered papers of Sebastien's file back together and returned it to its place among the student records, then walked through the darkness to the transport tubes.

He made his third trip in two days to one of the local Red Guard bases, like a bee returning to the hive. He was careful to keep his mental agitation from showing through in his body language. Anxious fidgeting was a sign of weakness.

The other agents tried to gossip with him about the Raven Queen, now that news of their meeting had spread, but he waved them off. Something of his mood must have leaked through, because none of them persisted.

Within the records, Thaddeus began an in-depth search for information on Sebastien's parents. Several times, he had to use his relatively high-level access authority to get paperwork magically transferred from one of the non-Gilbrathan bases, and the administrative agents were becoming increasingly irritated with his demands for instant fulfillment. Such magic was not without effort or cost, and they were beginning to doubt his assurances that this was an emergency.

He searched for anything on Sebastien's parentage in the Red Guard's internal records, which included information about their agents, their experiments, and their many, many missions to eliminate dangers to the world. When he found nothing, he looked for clues that might suggest that Sebastien's parents had been recruited by one of the major countries. Osham would be the type to have done something like this.

Unfortunately, Thaddeus found almost no information about them, and what did exist were merely mundane census records pulled from a small village. By all accounts, they had been completely normal citizens who just happened to have died in a beast attack, along with several other casualties on that same day. The only strange thing was that there were no records of what had been done with their child after their death.

The unnamed man who had, according to Titus, taken Sebastien in had never formally adopted him. This was not unusual. Especially if he had hoped to use the young boy as a source of unpaid magical labor.

Thaddeus was aware that the surname Siverling was vaguely notable, but from what Thaddeus could find, Sebastien's ancestors had been illiterate commoners, and the spelling of their surname had changed several times over the generations before reaching the current iteration. They were not even interesting enough to have a connection to the original Siverlings, who had once produced several proficient thaumaturges.

Thaddeus's fruitless research lasted well into the morning hours, but unwilling to concede defeat, he sent out a disguised Red Guard messenger to inform the University that he was taking an unplanned personal day.

He scoured birth, death, and marriage records, as well as various confidential reports for any mention of programs dealing with children or experiments to enhance magical aptitude. He looked up articles about arson and strange fires. He even strained his bloodshot eyes combing for mention of anyone with unusually fair coloring, or magical side-effects that resulted in strange pigmentation.

Evening had approached by the time Thaddeus was finally forced to concede defeat.

To learn more, he would need to speak directly to a source.

As he made his way back to the University, his weary mind mulled over the purpose behind Siobhan sending him on this fruitless hunt. The only reason he could think of that she would have gone out of her way to bring attention to the connection between herself and Sebastien was because she wanted both Thaddeus and the Red Guard to keep a closer eye on him.

Maybe Thaddeus was searching in the wrong direction.

Based on everything Thaddeus knew about her, he doubted that she held any ill will toward the boy. The only reason he could think of for her to do this, then, was that *someone else* intended to harm him. Siobhan hoped that he would discover it and protect the boy.

But why would Sebastien be in danger? What did she know that Thaddeus did not?

His first inclination was to ask Sebastien, but he quickly changed his mind. He had an inkling that Sebastien might lie about it. And, in fact, might have been hiding something for quite a while. It would be best to gather as much information as he could and then spring the trap around his apprentice.

He could reach out to Siobhan herself, but it would take time for her to respond, and Thaddeus was not willing to wait.

First, he would speak with Damien. The foolish boy was one of the few that Sebastien confided his harebrained schemes to. And if he knew any secrets, Thaddeus would pry them free.

1 0

———

A SWARM OF SPARKS

Damien
   Month 8, Day 23, Monday 6:00 p.m.

When Ana returned from whatever social warfare she had been engaged with, her hair was frizzing out around her temples from sweat, but she was holding back a grin and flitting around with excess joy. She poured this energy into getting all of Damien's friends to agree to accompany them out for a play that evening, despite the fact that a few of them might have been better off spending that time studying.

Though Alec probably also needed a break to destress, and Waverly wouldn't study any extra even if given the chance, unless the topic happened to be magizoology or witchcraft.

The play was a dark comedy about a young man fighting to keep his idiotic family from falling into ruin and crime, with each incident accompanied by horrible social embarrassment.

Waverly fell asleep about twenty minutes in, her tiny, dark-haired head falling backward and her mouth hanging open.

Brinn pulled a light blanket from his satchel, tucked it around Waverly, then guided her insensate form over so that her head rested on his shoulder. All without waking her.

Undisturbed by the uproarious laughter all around her, she drooled on his arm until the fabric was soaked through, but Brinn smiled happily the whole time.

When the play let out, Alec and Rhett kept laughing as they reenacted the funniest parts. Alec mimed his pants splitting open at the seat seam, then laughed so hard that he choked on his own saliva.

Sebastien looked on with concern as Alec's face grew increasingly puce. With a put-upon sigh, Sebastien used an esoteric spell to forcefully clear Alec's airways. He stepped back with a grimace of disgust as Alec spat out a huge mouthful of snot, saliva, and—somehow—a few bits of food.

Alec stared down at the globulous mass with fascination as he regained his breath. "Thanks, man."

Sebastien rolled his eyes and moved to Damien's other side, as far away from Alec as he could get.

"What did you think of the play, Sebastien?" Brinn asked.

Sebastien moved over to him and idly used the same spell to pull Waverly's saliva from Brinn's sleeve, leaving behind a thin crust where the edges of the wet spot had been. "I didn't really understand the humor. Why do people think it's so funny when they see others meet misfortune? Every time, all I could think of was how those situations would be so stressful, painful...and mortifying." He cringed, then shuddered. "It was an overall unpleasant experience."

Brinn gave him a small smile. "I think that's called empathy."

Sebastien raised his eyebrows dubiously as he put away his spellcasting supplies. "I don't think most people would describe me as empathetic," he said, his tone making it obvious that he thought Brinn had no idea what he was talking about. "Ah!" Sebastien smacked one fist into the other open palm. "It must be because I'm not a sadist." He turned his head and peered speculatively at Rhett and Alec, looking them over from head to toe as if searching for physical signs of moral depravity.

Sebastien nodded to himself, satisfied that his suspicions were confirmed, though Damien noticed the small quirk at the edge of his lips and knew that he was joking.

Alec's mouth dropped open, and he raised one arm, pointing at Sebastien with outrage. "I'm not a sadist! You just have no sense of humor!"

"I am a sadist," Rhett announced, shoving his hands into his pockets. He added an exaggerated wink. "In the *bedroom*."

Waverly gagged, then shot Rhett the middle finger.

Alec reached into his pocket and threw a handful of candy at Rhett. "Booo!" he jeered.

Rhett dodged, then ran away down the sidewalk, cackling loudly, which enticed Alec to give chase.

Sebastien stared after them with dismay. "Why am I friends with you lot?" he muttered to himself.

Ana gave him her lopsided grin. "Because we make your life interesting."

Sebastien looked up at the sky and breathed almost silently, "My life is already *too* interesting."

Damien nudged Sebastien with his elbow, and Sebastien nudged him back. It was the most relaxed Damien had seen Sebastien in the last couple of weeks.

This was why someone like Professor Lacer would never be a good match for Sebastien.

Sebastien should be with someone lighthearted, kind, and outgoing. As part of a couple, Sebastien should be the mature, serious, driven one. Otherwise, his relationship would probably consist of nothing more than studying, discussing, and practicing magic, with nary a romantic moment. There was a good reason for the saying, "opposites attract," in Damien's opinion.

After that, their group went to a fancy restaurant that specialized in exotic food from the East. Rhett ate some kind of blood-chunk and intestine soup, grinning at the looks of fascinated disgust from the rest of them. Well, the rest of them except for Sebastien.

"Food is food. Much better to use it than waste it," he said.

Brinn looked green. "I just can't help but think of the animal it came from whenever I eat meat. Have you ever been hunting? Ever dressed and cleaned your own kill?"

"I have," Sebastien said calmly.

"I went with my uncle when I was eleven. Some kind of rite of passage. Asserting dominance and all that. I had nightmares for months afterward. The feel of the warm meat, the smell, the sensation of skin and muscle parting under my knife..." Brinn shuddered. "I agree that, if you're going to do that to a living being, you shouldn't waste a single gram. But I'd just rather *not*, entirely."

Waverly patted Brinn's hand and passed him an egg boiled in tea. "You still need your protein."

"What's the most disgusting thing you've ever eaten?" Alec asked.

"A rat," Sebastien said. He looked just as startled as everyone else, as if he hadn't meant to say that.

"A *rat?*" Alec echoed, leaning forward across the low table as if he wanted to grab Sebastien by the lapels and shake more information out of him.

Rhett looked down at his soup, suddenly disappointed.

Even Waverly was morbidly fascinated. "How? Why? *How?*"

Sebastien hesitated, but seeing that everyone had stopped eating to stare at him, he looked away, rubbed his arms as if he were cold, and reluctantly spoke. "There was a time during my childhood when I was on my own."

"Because you're an orphan? Was this after your parents died?" Waverly asked.

Brinn tried to pinch her side, but she slapped away his hand and returned her attention to Sebastien. "What? Everyone knows he's an orphan. It's not like it's news to Sebastien."

Brinn pressed his lips into a thin line, pushed past her attempts at defense, and gave her a hard pinch as punishment for her tactlessness.

Waverly remained unrepentant, though she pouted as she rubbed her side.

"…Yes. After they died," Sebastien agreed, still looking away. "I had to provide for myself for a short time. And hunger… If you've never been truly hungry, you can't imagine how it will drive you to do things you've never considered. It's like a compulsion. It erases your reservations and tests your principles. I managed to capture a rat. I won't go into the details. But then I cooked it and ate it."

"What parts?" Alec asked.

Sebastien looked back at him, ate a bite of his own food, and said, "The whole thing, of course. It tasted horrible because I didn't drain the blood ahead of time, and I didn't have any spices. I wasn't very skilled at butchery, so the meat had hair all over it. I ate the organs, the brain, the eyeballs…even the tongue. The only things I didn't eat were the skin, the bigger bones that weren't soft enough for me to chew my way through, and the intestines. I wanted to eat the intestines too, but I knew they might make me ill, and I didn't know how to clean them thoroughly enough that it would be safe."

Sebastien's gaze grew distant again as he added, "I also tried to eat a stray dog, which would probably have taken the number one spot among my most unpleasant meals, but I wasn't strong enough to capture it. And then I was found and taken in, and didn't have to catch my own food anymore."

Sebastien returned to eating, and Damien knew the conversation was over. Both Alec and Waverly opened their mouths to toss out more questions, but Damien, Brinn, and Ana, working together, managed to glare and pinch them into silence. Soon enough, the matter was buried under an attempt by Waverly to force Alec to swallow an entire foot-long piece of artisanal bread without chewing.

Damien imagined a young, tiny version of Sebastien, thin and dirty, crouching somewhere hidden as he gnawed on rat bones. His eyes burned, and he looked away so that Sebastien wouldn't see as he blinked back tears.

When they were finished with the meal, Sebastien paid for both himself and Damien, reaching into his coin purse and taking out a few gold as if it were nothing. "I lost a bet," Sebastien explained when Ana looked at them strangely. But Damien knew that it was because *Sebastien* knew that he had spent all of his savings and his allowance for the term on newspapers and couldn't afford extravagant meals.

After the meal, the restaurant workers invited their customers up to the roof, where a fire witch was doing a nighttime show. The witch's familiar, instead of manifesting as a coherent being of flame, had a body that was just a dense collection of sparks in different colors. It danced through the air in a beautiful, mesmerizing display, twinkling in and out of visibility like a swarm of fireflies.

Waverly was at the front of the crowd, gleeful as the fire witch directed their familiar to brush teasingly through the air around her.

Sebastien and Damien watched from farther back. "Do you think we could accomplish the same effect with a slightly modified version of the spark-shooting spell?" Sebastien asked.

"*You* probably could," Damien said. "I would need a bit of practice to handle the complexity. And I don't know how to distance my output yet, either, so I'd have to have a really big Circle."

Sebastien nudged him, then jerked his head to the back corner of the roof, where it was darker and more secluded. Damien followed, and they looked out over the city in silence for a moment.

"Are you alright?" Sebastien asked.

Damien blinked. He had just been about to ask Sebastien the same thing.

Before Damien could respond, Sebastien continued. "I've noticed that you're stressed. You're sleeping less than usual, you keep leaving food behind at meals, and a few of your hairs have split ends."

Damien's hands flew up to smooth back his hair. "I have split ends?" he asked, his voice strained. "Do you have a mirror?"

Sebastien ignored his request, gazing softly down at Damien. "Is it because of the mission?" he asked, his voice low enough to be almost drowned out by the crowd on the other side of the roof.

Damien lowered his hands reluctantly. "It is."

Sebastien let out a huff of frustration. "You know that you can set aside the mission until after the term ends? You should have done so as soon as the stress began to build. No one needs you to take on more than you can reasonably handle."

Damien snorted. Sebastien was such a hypocrite. If there was one person between the two of them who didn't know how to relax, who attacked every problem like it was life or death, it was definitely Sebastien.

"I'm serious," Sebastien said, grabbing Damien's shoulder as if to jostle him.

"It's not the exams or a lack of time that's stressing me out," Damien admitted reluctantly. "I don't want to say anything until I'm ready, but when I am you'll be the first to know. I just need a few more days."

Sebastien squinted, peering at him as if he could read the thoughts behind Damien's eyes.

Damien tried to hold his gaze but ended up looking away and taking a half-step back.

Sebastien let his arm fall to his side, then looked down at the flat rooftop for a few long seconds.

Damien didn't want to say it, because it would likely either alarm Sebastien or spark his curiosity, but what he was working on was much more important than any exam score. He wasn't sure if the higher-ups knew what he might find when they set him the mission, but he could see the outline of something world-shaking. That was why he needed to be cautious. To be sure.

And it wasn't as if one term's scores dipping a little would matter, especially so early in their schooling. Furthermore, Damien was insulated from certain consequences by the advantage of his Family name. He would never struggle to find a job.

Sebastien sighed. "Alright. But if you need help, I have resources that might surprise you. I can deal with a wide array of problems, both mild and severe."

Damien chuckled. "What if I need to break into the University records and adjust my exam scores?"

Sebastien frowned. "It's not just the scores we'd need to adjust, but the professors' memories. It would be easier to bribe them to get them to agree. Or blackmail them. It should be possible." He crossed his arms and brought a thoughtful hand to his chin.

Damien lifted both his hands, palms outward, to stop Sebastien before his friend could actually start planning a criminal operation against their professors. "It was just a joke!" he said, but a soft warmth was spreading outwards from the center of his chest.

Sebastien shrugged. "Sure. But if you needed something *like* that, I could probably make it happen. I'm just saying. You can ask me for help if you need it," he said, stressing the last sentence.

Damien swallowed. Not trusting himself to speak, he nodded silently.

He had exceedingly good taste in friends.

11

AT THE THRESHOLD

DAMIEN
Month 8, Day 23, Monday 9:20 p.m.

BACK AT THE University in time for curfew, they found Tanya Canelo waiting at the entrance to their dorm room, doing what looked like a practice exam. This would be the end of her fifth term, and she would receive her Journeyman certification if she passed. She looked up at Damien expressionlessly as they approached. "Professor Lacer is looking for you, Westbay. He wants you in his office."

Damien checked his pocket watch. "This late?"

Tanya shrugged, standing up and brushing past Damien to talk to Sebastien. "Miss Gervin reported the situation with some of the other students to me," she told Sebastien. "I'll do what I can to keep an eye on them. I may not be a student liaison anymore, but being Professor Lacer's student aide still has some weight."

Damien narrowed his eyes. Was it just his imagination, or did she seem a little too eager for Sebastien's approval? Did she like Sebastien, too? The two of them even had similar hairstyles, though Sebastien's was getting a bit long. Was Tanya enough older to be considered "mature?" Damien let out a snort and left.

When he arrived at Professor Lacer's office, the man was still there, though his low ponytail was a bit disheveled and his face was drawn with fatigue. He scowled down at a stack of student papers, holding a mug in one hand and his Conduit in the other as a free-floating pen filled with red ink made angry scribbles and slashing marks across the paper.

The pen dropped. Half a second later, Professor Lacer gestured to a chair, which scuttled across the floor and settled ominously in front of his desk. He gestured again, at Damien, and Damien almost expected that he, too, would be magically picked up and moved. In the end, however, he had to take the inauspiciously placed seat of his own volition.

Professor Lacer put down his mug, steepled his fingers together and pressed them against his lips, then stared at Damien silently.

Damien gulped. "Why am I here, sir, if I may ask?"

Professor Lacer reached into one of his desk drawers and took out a casting band—a clear hoop with several bubbles of components arrayed at one end, with the other end molded to fit in the grip of a fist. Free-casters used them to cast powerful spells that required components.

"Did you just cast a spell?" Damien asked.

"A divination spell. It will help me better assess your response."

Damien's throat grew tight and his voice came out strained. "A *lie-detecting* spell?"

"Not exactly. A spell to improve my understanding," he replied emotionlessly.

It was better than a compulsion spell, but the fact that Professor Lacer felt the need to cast any sort of spell just to have a conversation with Damien was deeply ominous. "Did I do something?" Damien asked, squeezing the chair's armrests tighter as the urge to wipe his sweaty palms over his pant legs became almost unbearable.

"That is not what this is about. You are in no trouble, Mr. Westbay. Please be at ease."

Damien wasn't sure how that was possible, but he nodded jerkily anyway. Showing Damien that he was casting a divination spell was a courtesy and a sign of respect. Either that or the man *wanted* to put Damien on edge for some reason—it could be a warning.

Professor Lacer leaned back in his own chair, moving the hand with the component band beneath the table, as if not being able to see it might allow Damien to forget it existed. "I hope you are not inebriated, Mr. Westbay. You need to be at your best for the exams next week."

Damien blinked. "No! We just went out to a play and then dinner. Something to get our mind off things. I've been kind of stressed lately—well, we all have."

Professor Lacer nodded easily, as if they were having a conversation about weather patterns in Silva Erde. "Has Sebastien been stressed as well?"

Damien shrugged and chuckled nervously. "He lives in a rather constant state of stress, doesn't he? So I'm not sure if it counts."

Professor Lacer raised one eyebrow. "You are his best friend, correct?"

Damien remained silent, unsure how to respond.

"As far as I have seen, you are the person he spends the most time with and speaks most freely with. Would you say that is accurate?"

"I...guess so."

"Why do you think Sebastien is stressed?"

"Maybe because he's worried about performing well enough on the exams? He seems to think that if he's not at least in the top five percent and outperforming people several terms above him, he's a failure. He's really concerned about living up to your expectations."

Professor Lacer frowned slightly. "Is that all?"

Was Sebastien being considered for some kind of special opportunity, and Professor Lacer wanted to judge whether he had the energy for it? Maybe he thought Sebastien would agree to more work no matter how overloaded he already was.

Or maybe Professor Lacer had heard some of the rumors and gossip floating around the school and thought that Damien should be the one to do something about it.

He couldn't possibly have already heard some mutated and scandalous version of Sebastien thinking Professor Lacer was the ideal romantic partner, could he?

Damien found himself smoothing back his hair as his thoughts raced, suddenly remembered that he apparently had split ends, then forced his hands together in his lap. "Probably not," Damien admitted, "but I don't know the details of the rest. He always seems to be juggling half a dozen projects or practicing some spell. Maybe he's having trouble with the extra exercises you assigned for this term."

Professor Lacer kept staring silently. Expectantly.

Damien cleared his throat. "Or maybe he's just tired? He always has trouble sleeping."

"Tell me more about that." Professor Lacer's expression didn't change, but perhaps that was why Damien could tell he was so interested in the answer. Normally, Professor Lacer would have scowled, scoffed, or made some scathing comment. Restrained neutrality was abnormal for him.

"He...has nightmares. I don't know the specifics, but he wakes up in the middle of the night a lot." Damien paused, then added, "What is this about?"

Professor Lacer ignored his question. "Nightmares? Have you noticed anything unusual? Is this something new for him, or has he always been an insomniac? Has he mentioned anything about the contents of his dreams?"

Damien was shaking his head, as he didn't know the answer to any of those questions.

"*Think*," Professor Lacer urged.

"Why are you asking me? If you want to know, why not just ask Sebastien?" A sick, squirming feeling was growing in Damien's stomach, as if he had swallowed a live nightcrawler.

Professor Lacer's expression remained inscrutable. "I do not wish to make him uncomfortable by prying into delicate matters."

The squirming feeling grew stronger, edging into nausea. "But you'll go behind his back and try to get me to gossip about him?" Damien snapped. He took a few sharp breaths, shocked at his own boldness, to say such a thing to Thaddeus Lacer. Sebastien must be rubbing off on him.

Professor Lacer gave Damien a condescending look. "This is not gossip. I am his master and mentor. I need to know if my apprentice might be in danger, either from his own actions or due to outside influences."

Damien's mouth watered, and he swallowed compulsively. "Why would Sebastien be in danger?"

"You tell me."

Damien's thoughts began to race, flitting around but landing on nothing. Why was it so hot in here? "Are you worried he might be placing too much pressure on himself to succeed? I don't think you have to worry about a break event or anything—"

"Stop," Professor Lacer said softly. Somehow, it was more disturbing than the normal dagger-sharp chop of his cursory commands. "You know something. How is Sebastien in danger, Damien?"

Damien remembered the divination spell. The man must be cataloguing all of Damien's involuntary responses and using them to gain insight into his emotions and thoughts. And the obvious reason that Sebastien might be in danger was the secret that only Damien knew. Sebastien was a member of their secret order. Damien took a deep breath and forced himself to calm.

He focused on Professor Lacer like the man was his father.

There was no use trying to avoid anger or punishment. He accepted that things might go wrong beyond his control. He allowed the certainty that he would survive, no matter what happened, to carry him through. A slow, cold dread crept through him, numbing his fingers and leaving sounds more distant, as if he heard them through a wad of cotton. But he was calm, and neither a panicked, flighty mind nor improper fidgeting would bring otherwise avoidable punishment down on him.

As far as Damien knew, Sebastien wasn't currently taking any hazardous missions for their secret order. So, technically, that shouldn't be a truthful reason that Sebastien was in danger. Probably. But Damien didn't know if he could get away with saying that when he felt it was a misdirection, at best.

Professor Lacer was still expressionless, and hadn't even leaned forward over the desk, but Damien still felt that the man was watching him like a cat looming over a stunned mouse.

The best option was to stay silent.

Damien swallowed, then leaned even further into the numbness. What was the worst that could happen to him? He remembered Sebastien's promise earlier that evening. Would Sebastien blackmail Professor Lacer on Damien's behalf, if the man tried to get him expelled? Would Sebastien confront Damien's father, just like he had stood up in front of Malcolm Gervin?

They were absurd thoughts, but Damien couldn't imagine that Sebastien would stand by silently, even if he had no chance to actually save Damien. Strangely, this helped Damien to calm even further. He stared Professor Lacer down.

The silence stretched on until Damien felt a trickle of sweat slide down his side.

Finally, Professor Lacer sighed. "Do you think Sebastien will be in trouble if you tell me?"

Damien's voice was rough with stress, but he spoke without hesitation. "I think if you want to know personal details about Sebastien, you should ask him yourself. Frankly, it's insulting that you would come to me. Do you think I'm an idiot, or just a faithless friend?" Being so rude sent a spike of anxiety shooting through his calm, but he accepted it and let it go.

Something about the way Professor Lacer stared at him after that made Damien wonder if, perhaps, a compulsion spell was coming next.

He realized that, despite his complaints, their secret order *still* didn't have robust communication methods. And after they had burned their bracelets to keep whoever had tried to kidnap Sebastien from tracking them down, Damien had no way to let Sebastien know he might be in danger.

Damien made a mental note to, if he got out of this unscathed, submit an official suggestion that members of their secret order take compulsory vows to help them resist interrogation. Or would that be even more suspicious? But if an enemy were willing to go as far as blood magic—taking away a sapient being's free will—then the person being questioned was probably screwed, and any method to keep the others safe would be better than nothing.

But that reminded Damien that compulsion spells *were* illegal. Was Professor Lacer questioning him on behalf of the Red Guard?

Damien's detached calm began to tear like a shield made of spiderweb. Was there any piece of information he could give that would lead the man away from the truly important secrets?

But then Professor Lacer sighed, and whatever undecided action had been waiting *in potentia* subsided. "You are a good friend," he said begrudgingly. "Let me explain my sudden interest. I recently met with the Raven Queen. She intimated that there was some threat to Sebastien—one I had missed. And after considering it, I realized that Sebastien may, for some unfathomable reason, be keeping relevant secrets. Things I should know as his guardian.

Whether that might be because he thinks he will be punished for his actions, or there is some other reason he will not...or *cannot*, be open with me..." He trailed off.

Was he really suggesting that Sebastien might be under a geas, or being blackmailed, or had taken some restrictive vows? Or was that only Damien's paranoia talking?

"Damien, I hope you know that I only want what is best for Sebastien. I take my responsibility to ensure his safety and general well-being very seriously. If you have any reason to believe that Sebastien might be in danger, please tell me."

Damien considered continuing in silence. What would happen then? Professor Lacer would probably confront Sebastien. But Sebastien had a boon from the Raven Queen, right? Damien still wasn't sure of the details, but Sebastien had once mentioned that it could ward off divination. Professor Lacer might not be able to tell if he was lying. Would the man force Sebastien to talk with a compulsion, then, thinking it was all for Sebastien's good? Illegal or not, someone like Thaddeus Lacer wouldn't be punished for doing so, especially not if the Raven Queen was in any way involved. Only his own morals bound him.

Maybe, if Damien could steer things in the right direction, it would be a net positive. But what could he reveal? He considered giving over the specific details of what they'd done to entrap Ana's uncles. Surely, if the Raven Queen knew about someone impersonating her, she wouldn't be pleased? But even the idea made Damien shudder. With all the newspapers he had been reading lately, he had been exposed to more examples of how unhinged thaumaturges could exact malevolent retribution than was good for his mental health.

And it was the kind of thing that really *might* get Sebastien in trouble if the Raven Queen ever found out. But suddenly, Damien realized a possible solution.

"You know," Professor Lacer said. "Or you have a good idea. Tell me." His command was so strong it almost seemed to hold a compulsion of its own.

Damien was worried that this was not, in fact, the optimal solution.

"You will not leave this room without sharing this information with me," Professor Lacer said, his voice hard. "*Speak.*"

"The High Crown!" Damien burst out.

Professor Lacer's eyes and nostrils both flared. "What happened?" he asked softly.

"During Sowing Break, when the Raven Queen made that huge ruckus and rescued a group of people from the Pendragon Corps... They had kidnapped civilians. Children."

Professor Lacer's knuckles grew white as he squeezed his large spherical Conduit within a fist.

Damien continued. "Sebastien said that he had been trampled by a crowd during the panic. But…that was a lie."

"How was he injured?"

"A Pendragon Operative tried to kidnap him. He fought back and was injured. And…someone else, I don't know who, saved Sebastien. That person used a memory-modifying spell on the Pendragon Operative so that they wouldn't realize they failed. I guess just to make them think they couldn't find him."

"Why did he not say anything to me?" Professor Lacer asked, still strangely calm.

"Because if anyone knew, then they might try to come after him again. And memory-modification spells are illegal."

"Who saved him?"

Damien shook his head, dread building in his stomach again as he realized that this was the failure point of revealing what he had. "I don't know. I'm not sure Sebastien knows, either. I don't think that person wanted anyone to know who they were. I… Please don't say anything about this. You can understand why we kept it secret, right? It's not just the danger from the High Crown. Sebastien can't say anything about the person who saved him, and if he knows I told you—"

Damien wouldn't actually keep what he had revealed a secret from Sebastien, of course, but this desperate attempt was the best way he could think of to keep Professor Lacer from digging in a direction that would lead him to the secret order.

"Yes, I understand," Professor Lacer said. He stood slowly, dropping the component band and squeezing his Conduit even tighter. He slammed his fist down on the table. In a flash, a wave of force rolled out from his body.

Damien's eyelids fluttered, and his heart clenched so hard he thought he might pass out under the force of Thaddeus Lacer's Will.

Everything in the room rattled and jumped in place as the man's anger came to life.

Sound disappeared.

The air froze, trapping Damien's breath in his lungs.

The light dimmed strangely in a way that reminded Damien of the moon passing in front of the sun, and Damien wasn't sure if it was because he was on the verge of passing out or if it was real. He saw multicolored stars that reminded him of the fire witch's show earlier that evening.

Damien's skin seemed to ripple strangely despite the stillness of the air, as if he had gone thrill-jumping off of the white cliffs. He began to hear a phantom sound. Something more sensation than noise, approaching from a great distance.

He caught a glimpse of Thaddeus Lacer's eyes and had the sudden, intense certainty that someone was going to die.

And then, just as suddenly as it had come, the pressure receded.

Damien was in his chair, unscathed.

Professor Lacer dropped his Conduit, letting the celerium sphere clatter onto his desk. He blew out a long breath, just on the edge of a whistle, before lifting his head to meet Damien's gaze again. "I apologize, Mr. Westbay. It has been a long time since I allowed my emotions to overtake me so shamefully."

Damien pressed his trembling fingers into his thighs, blinking rapidly as he took a few deep breaths to reassure himself that he was okay. His jaw ached where he had been clenching his teeth together, and his heart beat like a small drum, but there were no real sensations of pain. "Are you…going to do something?" he croaked.

"To the High Crown?" Professor Lacer closed his eyes and took another deep breath. "Sebastien's injuries… He had my apprentice beaten, and if not for—" He cut off again.

Damien's bladder tightened shamefully, and his eyes stung with the prickle of oncoming tears as he realized how close beneath the surface Thaddeus Lacer's rage still was. "Sebastien is safe," he forced out. "The Pendragon Corps never took him."

"But he is still in danger." Professor Lacer looked up at Damien, then adjusted his chair and sat back down. "Was Sebastien attacked only because of his positive interaction with the Raven Queen? Just because he could have been used as bait? Or is there something more?"

"It—it's possible the High Crown is paranoid and thinks Sebastien could be a threat? Ana, she looked into Sebastien's background, and we think maybe he's connected to the original Siverlings. And Princess Krell…could have had a baby that survived, possibly. With the promise Sebastien has been showing, maybe the High Crown believes Sebastien could be long-lost royalty. Technically, he would have some kind of claim to a…kingship?"

Professor Lacer shook his head. "No. I am aware of the original Siverlings, but Sebastien is not of royal blood. Or at least not…that…kind." His gaze went distant.

"Sir?" Damien asked, confused.

Professor Lacer ignored him, staring at nothing.

12

WONDERFULLY RIGHT (OR HORRIBLY WRONG)

DAMIEN REMAINED silent while Thaddeus escorted him back to the dorms and all the way to the end of the walkway between sleeping cubicles, but as soon as they arrived at the far end of the room, the young man stepped forward and ripped back Sebastien's curtain. As Sebastien bolted up in alarm, Damien blurted, "I told him about the kidnapping attempt and the stranger who saved you. I'm sorry, I just thought it would be better to have someone on your side to keep you safe."

Thaddeus turned his head slowly to look down at Damien. He was *quite* sure that he had instructed Damien to keep his mouth shut about their conversation until Thaddeus had a chance to talk with Sebastien.

Damien pressed his lips together until they turned white, but did not remove his gaze from Sebastien, who looked between the two of them, his confusion rapidly morphing into suspicion and anxiety.

Thaddeus sighed. "I would like to talk with you, Mr. Siverling. Accompany me to…my cabin." He would normally use his office for something like this, but the unconventional setting might remind his apprentice that Thaddeus had helped him with other problems, such as his sub-par Conduit, and suggest that Thaddeus was playing a non-official role and could be trusted.

Sebastien picked up his school satchel, then reached inside and pulled out a small disk. With a twist, it glowed to life, revealing a thirteen-pointed star design that he directed at the ground to provide light for their walk. Sebastien gave Damien a pointed, probing look. "Are you coming?"

"He is not," Thaddeus said.

Damien pressed his lips even tighter together, opened his eyes wide, and shook his head deliberately, as if he was the one in charge of the decision and could have tagged along against Thaddeus's will.

Sebastien turned his attention to Thaddeus and adjusted the satchel's strap on his shoulder. "I'm ready, Professor."

By the time they left, Sebastien had suppressed all signs of nervousness, and they walked to Thaddeus's cabin in silence, almost as if they were sharing a tranquil evening stroll. Thaddeus noted that, when it suited him, Sebastien could display remarkable self-control. This was a young man who could keep secrets. Traumatic childhoods often resulted in such a skill. Thaddeus once again mused on the fact that his apprentice was remarkably like a younger version of himself.

When they reached his cabin, Thaddeus waved Sebastien in.

The boy looked around the small interior and then, without asking, moved to sit at one of the two chairs at the small kitchen table. He kept his satchel on his lap, as if clutching onto a shield.

Thaddeus followed him into the kitchen and pulled the component band out. Though it might seem like catching lies in secret would be most practical, it was often more effective to let someone know that they would not only be caught in a lie but that even small clues could give them away. Something about the increased pressure made them more likely to make mistakes.

But as Thaddeus explained what he was free-casting, the edges of Sebastien's lips barely tightened. His apprentice's breathing remained deliberately even, his hands hidden beneath the edge of the table, and his gaze steady.

Thaddeus felt the resistance of the Raven Queen's boon and shattered straight through it, noting Sebastien's flinch. Depending on how the magic had been placed on Sebastien, Thaddeus knew it was possible *she* might be alerted to its activation and failure, but he did not care. "The Raven Queen can dual-cast," Thaddeus said casually. "Did you know this?"

To Sebastien's credit, rather than try to seem oblivious or come up with some tissue-thin lie, he remained quiet. Even now, the physical signs of his distress were extremely muted compared to what Damien had shown in the same position.

"I ask," Thaddeus continued, "because I recall how surprised you were that dual-casting—splitting one's Will in two different directions—was not something that everyone could do."

Sebastien's posture was painfully straight, his chin raised high, but the divination spell allowed Thaddeus to notice the otherwise unnoticeable twitch in Sebastien's nostrils.

"I recently had the opportunity to examine the Raven Queen's anti-divination magic. Curiously, it seems to be the exact same magic that powers the boon she bestowed upon you. Was the day Newton Moore died the first time you met her?"

At this, Sebastien seemed genuinely confused, his eyes flicking around as if searching in different parts of both his memory and imagination for answers but finding none. Again, he did not respond.

Thaddeus had expected a stronger reaction, but kept his own composure. "If necessary, I can force you to speak."

"I don't know how to answer your question," Sebastien said. Strangely, this seemed to be mostly the truth.

"Because you do not know how best to lie about it?"

Sebastien's eyelids drooped by a millimeter, turning his alert expression into one of calm laced with subtle defiance, despite the pulse beginning to pound in his neck. When challenged, his apprentice consistently responded with aggression, even when it would be eminently wiser to remain meek.

Thaddeus repressed his instinctive urge to speculate. Answers would come soon enough. "Do you know what binding magic is?" He could see that Sebastien did. "Then you must understand that it cannot be used without some form of consent, purposeful or accidental, from *both* parties. And yet you reported to the coppers and the Red Guard that this bizarre magic somehow attached itself to you without your knowledge."

Strangely, Sebastien seemed to start calming down again. Had Thaddeus mis-deduced something? Perhaps Sebastien really had no memory of the agreement. Or the boy simply believed that Thaddeus knowing the truth held no real danger for him.

He would try another test, then. "The Raven Queen recently got into an altercation with the Red Guard, during which she used the array-device *you* came up with. Which, I might add, has not been patented or approved for general sale yet."

Sebastien appeared entirely unperturbed—which itself was a clue. Even if Sebastien knew that the Raven Queen had a prototype of his design, surely the knowledge that she had used it, and against the Red Guard at that, should have been surprising. "But you knew that already," Thaddeus said flatly.

Sebastien's eyelids fluttered and a muscle in his throat pulsed as he stopped himself from swallowing nervously.

Perhaps a slight change in tactics was in order. Thaddeus leaned back, settling himself more comfortably into the kitchen chair, and gave Sebastien a slight smile.

Sebastien flinched.

"Are you familiar with the limits on Will-growth?" Thaddeus asked.

Sebastien blinked twice, then opened his mouth as if to ask an involuntary question, but closed it again before any sound could come out.

"It is well known that the Will grows faster in those who are already powerful. What the general public might not be aware of is that there is a formula one can use to calculate the maximum rate of growth based on a person's current Henrik-Wilson capacity. Your records indicate that you have considerably exceeded this growth limit, even if you were to spend the maximum safe amount of time casting since the first term. Explain this."

"I…didn't actually hit my maximum on that first test."

Thaddeus stared at his apprentice. "And?"

Sebastien swallowed. "And?"

"What else?"

"I've been using that light-refinement spell you translated for me."

Thaddeus leaned forward. "How long did it take you to be able to cast?"

Sebastien leaned back slightly. "A…week?"

Thaddeus's eyebrows twitched. "A week? To successfully cast a light-based gesturan spell?"

"Well, maybe not *successfully*. It wasn't until you helped me understand how transmogrification works that I was able to really grasp the spell."

"Have you ever cast any spells developed by the gestura before?"

"No."

Thaddeus stared at his apprentice. He had known the boy possessed some talent with light, but apparently Sebastien was a kinetic genius. This talent needed to be nurtured. It might even bode well for early success with free-casting. However, that was not the point of this conversation. Thaddeus cleared his throat. "That still fails to explain your growth." He had picked up the subtle reticence in Sebastien's answers. The boy was still hiding something.

Sebastien took a deep breath, closed his eyes, and then admitted, "I got help completing that sleep-proxy spell. It means…I can cast more, safely. Longer."

"And you have been sacrificing your sleep to do so," Thaddeus stated, feeling as if a stone had settled in his stomach. "Who helped you?"

Sebastien's eyes darted to the side before he deliberately brought them back to stare at a single spot on the table. "I can't talk about that."

"You took a vow?"

Sebastien nodded.

The stone in Thaddeus's stomach grew heavier. "Let me guess. A raven has taken on the burden of your sleep?" He did not need Sebastien to respond to know the answer. And being aware of Sebastien's aversion to sedatives, supposed nightmares, and the suspected abuse and trauma of his childhood added nuance to the boy's desire for such a spell. Thaddeus scowled. "Do you have any idea how dangerous that could be? To cast an untested blood magic spell on yourself... Are you an idiot?"

A flash of defiance tightened Sebastien's face. "It's definitely safe."

"Do you actually trust the Raven Queen not to mislead you?" Thaddeus scoffed.

Sebastien's lips curled back and he opened his mouth, probably ready to spit out something foolish, but had the unusual self-control to stop himself.

Sebastien's guard had fallen somewhat. It was time for Thaddeus to drop another explosive spell, metaphorically. "The Raven Queen came to visit me here, recently." He nodded to the couch a few meters away. "But when I checked the records, I saw that my cabin's wards had reported a passage...by *your* student token."

Finally, Sebastien seemed truly shocked. Though the signs were subtle, to Thaddeus they screamed like the death shriek of a dragon diving from the sky.

"In fact, your student token has left and returned to the University at strange times more than once."

Sebastien's arm muscles tightened as he clenched his fists, probably recriminating himself for his carelessness.

"That is not all I know. Not about you, nor about the Raven Queen. I know you have been keeping secrets and lying for some time now. Possibly even from the very beginning. Tell me the truth."

Sebastien looked up from the table to meet Thaddeus's gaze. "Why don't you ask me your real question, instead of telling me all the things you know?"

"Very well. I think I can state it quite succinctly. What is your connection and history with the Raven Queen?"

Sebastien's jaw muscles pulsed as he clenched his teeth together. He had no intention of answering.

"You can tell me," Thaddeus said. "I do not work for the coppers or the Thirteen Crowns, and the Red Guard has no quarrel with you or the Raven Queen. My concern here is you and your wellbeing." Thaddeus hesitated, then added, "Whatever you tell me, I will not punish you. And the Raven Queen can protect herself. She does not need you to do so."

To Thaddeus's frustration, his words seemed to have no effect.

"I can compel you to speak," Thaddeus offered calmly. "I know a spell that will push past weaker compulsions of silence. And if she has threatened you, I can protect you. So long as you tell me everything."

Sebastien had turned his gaze back to that spot on the table. A frustratingly long stretch of time passed before he finally said, "I am not going to talk about this."

"Why?" Thaddeus asked, his voice hard.

"I have taken some vows. But even more than that, I can't talk because I'm afraid of what will happen if I do." Sebastien clenched the top of the satchel in his lap, raised his chin calmly, and without even the barest hint of untruth, said, "If you force me to talk, I am going to bite off my tongue. I know an esoteric spell to muffle the pain, and I am quite certain I can manage it."

Thaddeus heard his heartbeat in his ears and felt it in his temples. He had seen someone bite off their tongue before in a misguided attempt to commit suicide. While it was not an efficient or effective method of ending one's own life, it would certainly delay any attempts to make Sebastien speak. "Do your vows of silence compel you to such extremes? Or are your secrets so great?"

Sebastien remained expressionless and determined.

Perhaps the answer was both. Thaddeus sat back, trying to figure out how to navigate this situation. It was so much worse than he had thought. He felt like the stone in his stomach had turned to lead, heavy enough to drag him through the kitchen chair and down to the floor. Thaddeus stopped casting his social insight divination, released the component band, and tucked his Conduit into one of his vest pockets. "What about now, when I am less likely to infer more than what you mean to share?

Sebastien's eyes grew slightly glassy. "I like this life. I don't want to lose it. I want to keep going to classes, spending time with my friends, and learning from you."

Thaddeus wanted to vomit. It had been a very long time since his body responded so viscerally to his emotions. He had thought such weakness mastered, or at least turned toward sudden and devastating violence rather than the shameful betrayal of his mortal flesh.

He bared his teeth with frustration. "I cannot help you if you will not speak to me. Do you think me so useless that I cannot deal with your secrets? Whatever problems you may have, I assure you they are trifling in comparison to my abilities."

Sebastien sighed softly, the gentle fall of his chest and the flutter of a strand of hair that had fallen into his face the only indication of his feelings.

Thaddeus rubbed his chin. "You do not trust me," he realized. He did not know why this was so surprising. Would Thaddeus have acted any differently, in the boy's position?

However, usually, his own responses were not a good metric to judge others by. Thaddeus was quite singular. He suppressed the urge to ask Sebastien what his nightmares were about. He knew the boy would either refuse to speak or would lie.

But even without Sebastien's cooperation, Thaddeus had his own theories. Why would the Raven Queen place such emphasis on the boy? He had considered that they might be related, and Sebastien the product of some dalliance of her father's. Only, *neither* of them looked anything like Ennis Naught, and nothing like each other, either, except for the eyes. Eyes which

Ennis did not share. If they were related, it would have had to be through someone else.

This led him to consider what value Sebastien might provide someone like the Raven Queen. What could be worth the things that she had given and done for him? When Thaddeus asked himself that question, several clues he had initially not even recognized as strange lit up like a beacon in his memories. Thaddeus stood. "Follow me."

Sebastien hurried to catch up as Thaddeus left his cabin. They walked in a straight line toward the library, ignoring the winding cobblestone paths to cut across the grounds.

The library was closed, but Thaddeus's faculty token gave him access to the building, and then to the restricted archives beneath.

Their footsteps echoed in the empty tunnels, but Sebastien's anxious, heavy breaths remained audible.

Thaddeus took Sebastien deep into the white cliffs, to the place he and Kiernan had prepared for the Raven Queen to help them with Myrddin's journals. It was a small room, which had made it easier to ward to the gills. It was both a physical and mental struggle to get past the doorway, and would be again to leave through it.

The room was a perfect bubble, sealed in seamless iron, with air-refreshing artifacts at the corners of the ceiling. Neither Kiernan nor Thaddeus were ward-masters, but one of the other members of the Architects had helped with the design, and they were competent enough to implement it.

The ward used a spell array layered with both a tetragram and nonagram, for stability against authority and the creation of a conceptually separated space. A smaller circle of ever-burning dark red flame surrounded a pedestal of pure salt, atop which lay the three books.

Sebastien's breath was coming even faster.

"Come in," Thaddeus said, making the necessary offer to allow the boy past the threshold.

Sebastien's gaze was glued to the books.

Thaddeus took Sebastien by the arm, guiding him forward. They stopped in front of the pedestal. Thaddeus slid his hand down to Sebastien's wrist, then pressed Sebastien's fingers to the bottom edge of the central book's leather cover.

Sebastien's breath hitched.

Silently, Thaddeus guided his Will to match the meaning of the changing glyphs on the front. Soon enough, they split into two.

Thaddeus's spine tingled at the confirmation of what he had considered, at first, a rather unrealistic theory. He was not sure if he was satisfied or disappointed to be correct about this, in particular.

He dropped Sebastien's wrist. "These are Myrddin's journals. You may remember that I mentioned they have an identity lock. We developed a way to spoof a positive response. However, I have not used that method tonight. Which means that the books recognize your identity and authority over them."

Sebastien stumbled back, passing the inner Circle of red flame. It illuminated his features from below, giving his dark eyes an eerie tint. He looked to Thaddeus, his bewilderment clear.

Thaddeus clasped his hands behind his back. "This evidence suggests an extraordinary conclusion. It is possible that you are a direct, if distant, descendant of Myrddin. I would also suggest that the Raven Queen knew of this, and it is why she approached you, and why she was willing to give you aid on multiple occasions."

Sebastien swallowed. "Ahh…"

"Has she been using you to help open the journal in her possession?"

Sebastien's eyes widened, then narrowed. After a few long seconds, he gave the tiniest of nods, so minimal that Thaddeus might have missed it if he were not paying avid attention.

Thaddeus kept silent the fact that he was not entirely sure Sebastien's bloodline was natural, as Thaddeus even now knew nothing about the boy's parentage. Sebastien could still have been a more *deliberate* product. Thaddeus's mind ran wild for a moment with outlandish speculation. How would someone have been able to match Myrddin's bloodline? Did they have a sample from the man? Or, perhaps, they had tried to create a Myrddin imitation in a completely different way. It was even possible that it was a combination of both—Myrddin's bloodline discovered and experimented on. Thaddeus forcibly reined himself in. He had no evidence, and the reality could be something entirely different and more mundane. "Do you know anything of Siobhan Naught's bloodline?"

Sebastien shrugged, his fingers bone-white around the strap of his satchel. "The same things as everyone else, I think."

"I had considered that she might be a descendant of one of the experiments carried out by the Third Empire. Or that the People were hiding an advantage thought long-lost. Did you know that you and Siobhan Naught have almost exactly the same eye color?"

Sebastien stared back at Thaddeus like a deer caught in the light of a high-powered search-lamp.

"On her, it looks natural, but on you, it is quite unusual. Almost as if it were an unnaturally dominant genetic trait."

"You think Siobhan Naught might…*also*…be distantly related to Myrddin?" Sebastien asked, his voice high-pitched with disbelief.

"Who knows? She has one of his extraordinary abilities. That is not enough evidence to say for sure. But it is some moderate evidence that she was chosen for a reason." Thaddeus scratched his beard as a wild hypothesis jumped to mind. What if the Raven Queen identity was lying dormant within Siobhan Naught all along, and merely *released* with proximity to the book? He set this idea aside, because it would require her to either be basically immortal but have no memory of her past, or for Myrddin to have figured out how to pass memories extensive enough to contain an entire personality down to descendants. It was too outlandish.

"Will you tell anyone?"

Thaddeus returned his thoughts to the present, raising his eyebrows derisively. "Of course not. Did you think my assertions of your safety were merely lip service? Or that I would be so enamored by the idea of a descendant of Myrddin that I would lose my mind?" He snorted. "I am interested in seeing if you can develop the ability to split your Will, however. But *do not* go trying such a thing until I have given the matter more thought. We have no way to assess if it would be safe. And..."

Thaddeus sighed. "You judged correctly that you should never tell another of this matter. Not everyone is as rational as I, and those who are may still be swayed by greed."

13

PROPERLY ACCESSORIZING

Sebastien's mind was spinning so fast and intently that she seemed to blink, look up, and find that they were already outside of the warded room in the depths of the white cliffs, walking back to the University library. 'How did this happen?' she wondered, catching herself as she started to trip on a rough segment of the floor.

Professor Lacer gave her an exasperated look. "Please do not forget how to walk because you are too busy thinking. Keep your attention on the present."

Sebastien cleared her throat and gave a small nod, refusing to meet his gaze. She still couldn't see how Professor Lacer had managed to figure so much out, yet still come to such a strange, erroneous conclusion. She, as Sebastien, had been in contact with the Raven Queen, who had been using her to get into Myrddin's journal? And as payment, the Raven Queen had given her a boon and protected her from the Pendragon Corps? And, perhaps most ridiculous of all, Sebastien was possibly descended from Myrddin? Professor Lacer had embedded enough clues in his questions that she had some idea of the "evidence" he had used, but it still felt like she was missing some critical connective tissue that could have led from A, to B, all the way to Z.

Furthermore, she couldn't believe she had been so careless as to leave such blatant clues linking her to her secret identity. Growing up with Ennis had taught her that when one was doing something secret—and usually bad—it was very often growing lazy and sloppy that got one caught.

Which sometimes meant packing up and leaving—running—again.

Sebastien could only be thankful that Professor Lacer hadn't managed to deduce the real truth. In a way, it made sense that Professor Lacer had thought the Raven Queen simply borrowed Sebastien's student token. Sebastien had spent so much time as a student, much of that in Professor Lacer's presence, and obviously lacked the Raven Queen's prowess. It would take a big leap for anyone to realize that Sebastien and Siobhan were the same person. But that didn't mean no one *could* make that leap if she kept screwing up and handing out clues like they were candy.

As they exited into the library, Sebastien's mind returned to the room below. Myrddin's other three journals looked strangely, *exactly* the same as her own, to the point that she might not be able to pick hers out of a lineup. That had to have been deliberate on Myrddin's part, and it also helped to explain why the University wouldn't have known that one of the five books was missing before they even got to Gilbratha, once it was removed from the expedition records.

'But if that were the case, how was everyone so certain that the book I held was the one that could answer their questions about celerium production? There must be some reason I don't know about—something that sets my journal apart from the rest. Maybe they marked or labeled them in some way.'

Outside of the dormitory building, Professor Lacer pointed imperiously to the door. "Go to sleep. Take your anti-anxiety potion if you need it." He paused for emphasis, then added, "Do not do anything foolish or *incriminating.*"

She guessed that he was trying to tell her not to panic and contact the Raven Queen or something similar. If the Red Guard had the same kind of suspicions as Professor Lacer, they could be watching her.

As she walked in, she crossed her arms and curled her hands into fists to suppress the trembling in her fingers. This couldn't calm the sour feeling in her stomach or the bone-grinding tension in her neck and shoulders. She took a deep breath and let it out slowly, but this made her eyes sting, and she gritted her teeth together to shove the emotions back down.

Damien was waiting up for her. As she passed by his cubicle, he darted out, looking from right to left for observers while he waved his hands in what looked like a frantic interpretive dance.

She grabbed him by the elbow and dragged him into her cubicle, since his was overrun with newspapers. She closed the curtain, violently shook a bottle of moonlight sizzle, and then drew out the sound-muffling spell array they had gotten from Professor Lacer.

As soon as she cast the spell, words spilled out of Damien's mouth with the force of a breath held until the edge of suffocation. "He was using some kind of divination spell on me, I couldn't lie, but I had to tell him something, and he was so frightening, I couldn't *think*, and it was totally obvious why he got his reputation, it's embarrassing to say but I almost peed my pants from the pressure, and he knew *something* so I ended up telling him about the Pendragon Corps trying to kidnap you and the person who saved you but I'm pretty sure he thought it was the Raven Queen who saved you." He sucked in a deep breath, then winced and held a hand to his forehead as if holding back a wave of dizziness.

"It's fine. Of the things you could have told him, that was probably the best."

Damien nodded hesitantly. "Taking out the thirteen-pointed star was a sneaky way to ask me if I let anything about that slip, right? Because I didn't. He shouldn't have any idea about it."

"Yes. Thank you." Damien had picked up on Sebastien's indirect question with surprising alacrity. "I don't think he knows anything. But we need to be even more careful."

"What did he say to you?" Damien asked.

Sebastien hesitated. "He asked me a lot of questions…"

Damien stared at her with wide-eyed expectation that slowly morphed into a speculative squint as she tried to figure out what she could say. "Does this have anything to do with the big secret you're hiding?"

Sebastien stared at him with silent misery.

"Alright, alright," Damien said, waving his hand between them as if to shoo away a fly. "You don't have to tell me. But is there anything specific that I *should* know? I just went through a traumatic experience. Surely I deserve *something*."

Sebastien scratched the nape of her neck, where some of her fine blonde hair had stuck to her skin with sweat. "You do," she admitted, before Damien could grow upset. "It's just… I don't know what I can say." Almost everything she had talked about with Professor Lacer was either something she needed to keep secret or a clue to something she needed to keep secret.

"He told me the Raven Queen said you were in danger."

Sebastien let out a slow breath between pursed lips. "Okay. Well, there was that. But he also was concerned that my Will is growing too quickly." She decided to give Damien something that seemed big but that wasn't related to her real secret. Perhaps it would help to lead him off the trail, because she very much doubted he would be able to stop speculating if he thought there was some huge mystery that he was being left out of, with the clues lying all around him. She crooked her finger to draw Damien closer, then leaned in and cupped her hands around his ear to cut off any possible sight of her next words. "He thinks I might be distantly descended from Myrddin." She pulled back.

Damien's eyes had grown as wide and round as two silver coins.

"You can't tell anyone," she added. "Not even a hint. Pretend you don't know. It might not even be real."

Damien inhaled sharply, then started coughing. When his violent fit had passed, he sat staring at the cubicle wall for a minute, then looked at her, and then back to the wall. "Wow." After a long pause he said, "Wow," again. Finally, he seemed to regain some of his wits. "Does anyone else know?"

Silently thankful that he had refrained from asking for further details about this "discovery," Sebastien shook her head. *'Though, technically, I guess the Raven Queen knows.'*

"Is…anything going to happen? I mean, are there any implications?"

"Not unless anyone finds out. But Professor Lacer thinks it could be very dangerous."

Damien nodded thoughtfully. "I don't think I'm going to be able to sleep tonight. This is…a lot."

Sebastien knew she too would not be sleeping, though, for once, she almost wished for the oblivion it could bring. A reset of sorts.

Damien puffed out his cheeks like a chipmunk stashing nuts, then slapped them hard enough to force all of the air out and leave his cheeks red. He cleared his throat and straightened, turning to her like a cat who had just done something embarrassing and was determined to pretend it had never happened. "I think we need to discuss the communication issue. I know that ever since we got rid of the bracelets, neither of us has really been doing any dangerous missions, but stuff like today can still happen. Did you pass along my previous feedback to the higher-ups? We need a better way to communicate with each other during emergencies. This isn't a small matter. You and I may just be low-level members, but leaving us stuck out in the metaphorical wilderness to fend for ourselves endangers not only us but the organization as a whole."

Sebastien was already nodding before Damien could finish. "I know. I'm a bit of a special circumstance because of…" She leaned forward and whispered, *"the boon.* It's caused difficulties. Most sympathetic magics just won't work on me unless I cast them myself. But I already have a plan to improve communications. I'll handle it tomorrow." Damien was right—she should have handled it long ago. She had been preoccupied with other things…and, to be honest, she had gotten sloppy, despite thinking that she was being more careful than ever.

When Damien went somewhat reluctantly back to his cubicle, Sebastien used Newton's humming spell to calm herself down, then took a few hours to plan out everything she needed to do when the rest of the world was awake.

The next morning, Damien was like a huge squirrel, exhausted to the point of jitters but still breaking out in random smiles, juxtaposed by bouts of looking around suspiciously, as if he expected to find people who wanted to kidnap Myrddin's descendant hiding among the student populace.

At breakfast time, Sebastien snatched away Damien's coffee, made him drink an entire glass of water and a quarter dose of her anti-anxiety potion, and ensured he finished the same amount of food she did. Damien fell asleep for the last twenty minutes before classes started and drooled on the table.

While Damien slept, Alec drew whiskers on one of his cheeks with a dull-tipped fountain pen. If not for Ana shooing Alec away, the whiskers would have been accompanied by even more embarrassing scribbles.

After classes, Sebastien took her shopping list into the city and bought one third of the items from her huge list of components, potions, and various supplies. She stopped by her apartment and spent a few hours creating sympathetically linked bracelets. Unlike her initial creations, her improved design was made of several linked metal segments. These were significantly larger than her old bracelets but would only require one for each person within the network.

Each bracelet carried dozens of small pieces that could be removed. Doing so would trigger a response in one or all of the other bracelets and convey various meanings. She had labeled each piece with enamel paint in various colors, which could even glow in the dark if necessary. If any of the pieces were activated, they would only need to be replaced, and the single-use sympathetic spell attached to those pieces recharged.

After that, she turned on her divination-diverting ward, made a round-about trip through the city, entering and exiting carriages several times to lose any pursuers, and entered the Silk Door to change into her other body. After leaving the Silk Door, she stopped by a nice restaurant—one that had a bathroom for customer use—and re-disguised herself before leaving through the small window.

Sighing at the hassle of it all, Siobhan finally made her way to the market for the other two-thirds of her shopping spree.

This included a new internally expanded, magically lightened bag that looked different from the satchel she had been carrying around everywhere, and that had the additional feature of being able to change color from red to black. Just like her shoes—which disguised themselves by changing size—the bag could be something that would identify her when she switched bodies. No matter how expensive a good one was, she didn't want it to be another lazy mistake.

She even picked up some essential oils and fragrant extracts, prepared to make distinct scents for both of her bodies.

The last task she completed before returning to the University was to check the drop box, where she found another letter from Professor Lacer. It was quite short and simple, and only informed her that they had completed the agreed-upon preparations and requested that she make herself available for the first journal exploration session that Sunday at midnight.

Tanya had included a package of her own for Siobhan, which she waited to examine until she was back at the Silk Door. It contained two books on shamanry, obtained through the secret thaumaturge meetings that Tanya had attended on Siobhan's behalf, as well as a small box of black tar beads made from the laughing poppy—a small tribute from Tanya. To Siobhan's surprise, the latter had been obtained not from the secret thaumaturge meetings, but from Tanya's superiors among the Architects of Khronos.

Laughing poppy was not illegal, per se, but it was a restricted component that one was supposed to have a license to purchase, due to the potential for abuse.

Siobhan tucked it away in her new bag, which she stashed at the Silk Door, and then went through the whole ordeal of changing identities in reverse. Shee transferred the books into her old satchel to read during the upcoming nights.

Wednesday evening, she went through her paranoid transformation process once again. There were absolutely no signs that she was being followed or tracked, but there might not be, if her opponent was the Red Guard. This was a sensitive time, so it was better to be as safe as possible. There were things she needed to do as the Raven Queen that she didn't feel safe putting off.

First, she visited Lynwood Manor. Rather than go to the front gate, she approached from the back. At one point, she might have sneaked inside, but now that the Nightmare Pack was an ally, she thought that might be considered somewhat rude. With a mental model of the grounds' layout in her head, she sent a tendril of her shadow forward to where she knew a couple of guards would be stationed. She closed her eyes and tried to see through the light her shadow was absorbing, but managed only the vaguest impression of brightness in certain areas.

When her shadow reached the spot from her memories, she grew the end into a three-dimensional raven, which hopped around cutely.

This was immediately followed by a dog's frantic barking and a man's shout.

She froze the raven in as non-threatening a pose as possible, frowning as she tried to sense what was going on around it. '*Agh!*' she let out a mental exclamation of frustration when this continued to yield nothing useful.

Tentatively, she raised up an arrow beside the shadow raven, pointing back toward her. Then, she let the raven hop back in her direction, slow enough that the guards should have no trouble following.

The sound of the intermittently barking dog drawing closer let her know that at least *something* had noticed and was coming her way.

A couple of minutes later, the solid iron gate set into the wall in front of her opened to reveal two Nightmare Pack guards and a dog—or rather, three Nightmare Pack guards.

The dog, a medium-sized mutt whose hackles were fully raised, wore a cute yellow and black bandanna embroidered with the symbol of the Nightmare Pack, as well as a few extra badges that announced what he had been trained to do.

When Siobhan and Liza had done the blood magic rejuvenation on Anders' dog, Bear, dozens of former strays had been left behind at the Lynwood estate. Rather than dumping them back on the street, the Nightmare Pack leaders decided to keep and train them. The Pack counted several skinwalkers among their number, which made the training process much smoother. Now, at least half the enforcer teams were accompanied by a bandanna-wearing canine, many of whom were trained to track down and subdue targets.

A few of the bigger dogs could even deliver messages or supplies in small packs attached to their backs via harness.

The mutt watched the small raven dissolve back into Siobhan's shadow, then met her gaze and bristled even more, pulling back his lips to snarl at her while taking a step to interpose himself between her and his handler.

The two guards tried to bow to her, pull back the dog, and apologize all at the same time.

Siobhan waved away their words but was slightly hesitant to move past the dog when it was in such an agitated state. After a moment's consideration, she brought the free portion of her Will to bear on the creature. She impressed the certainty of her own harmlessness and friendly nature into her Will and pushed it out toward the dog.

Slowly, the dog calmed, then looked away from her gaze and wagged his tail.

She let it sniff her hand, refrained from petting it, and turned toward the mansion on the other side of the gardens.

Miles burst out of the back door before she could make it very far. He raced up and grabbed her hand, babbling about how happy he was to see her and any random tidbit about his life that popped into his mind. He dragged her to the side of the garden, where a poorly constructed tiny house had been nailed to an old tree.

Miles held his fingers up over his lips. "Shh. They might get scared if you're loud." Within the tiny house, which he had made "all by himself" with the help of some of the adult Nightmare Pack members, lived a family of sprites.

A mother sprite tended to a wriggling pile of grubs within the dimly lit interior, which was luxuriously appointed with silk scarves and cloud-cotton.

"Did you know they can sense your Will?" Siobhan whispered.

"Like you did to the dog?" Miles asked.

Siobhan blinked, surprised for a moment, but then realized that Miles must have heard it on the wind. "Well, yes."

"Can I learn to do that, too?"

"Very likely, though it will probably take a lot of practice."

"I've been doing a ton of meditations. It helps with the whispers, and when I get afraid or have the *bad* thoughts."

"That is good. The meditations should help to prepare your Will for other things, too." Siobhan remembered some of the books on mental trauma that she had skimmed through. "Do you have someone you can talk to about the *bad* thoughts?" It was always easier to give advice than to take it oneself.

Miles let out a tiny, uncomfortable grunt. "My mom, I guess."

Gera and Lynwood exited onto their back porch, and Siobhan shared a nod with them across the distance.

Miles and Siobhan stared at the sprite family for a while before making their way slowly up to the mansion, holding hands. "My birthday is soon," Miles reminded her. He looked up at her with wide, innocent eyes. "You'll come to my party, right?"

"I plan to, as long as nothing goes wrong."

"And you'll bring a gift?"

"I will."

"I know you'll come up with something amazing. Something unexpected. Something that makes people jealous." He held up a forefinger. "That last part is most important. A gift so awesome and special that other people won't be able to sleep because they can't stop thinking about how jealous they are."

Siobhan's lips quirked up. "By 'other people,' do you mean Theo?"

"Yes," Miles stated unashamedly. "But, you know, everyone else, too. Is that something you think you can handle? Something better than the book you made for him."

Siobhan rubbed one of the feathers sprouting from her hair. "This feels like a lot of pressure."

Miles patted the hand he was holding. "I believe in you," he said reassuringly.

After greeting Gera and Lynwood, Siobhan handed over the detailed sleep-proxy spell arrays that she had copied down for them. While the Lynwoods' thaumaturges were setting up and double-checking everything in preparation for Siobhan's supervision, she took a few minutes to teach Gera the esoteric humming spell.

"Thank you," Gera said, very calm and strangely loose-limbed after having practiced the spell on herself. She even smiled.

Siobhan realized that Gera must almost always be tense around her. She hadn't even known the other woman could appear so at ease.

Soon after, Siobhan supervised the first casting of the sleep-proxy spell for Millennium. Since she was not very magically powerful, and her presence as a joint-caster might make the spell more difficult to cast, she only watched from the side of the room.

Instead of ravens, which apparently everyone had felt was too sacrilegious to sacrifice, they were using a raccoon that they had prepared and boosted with the death of its brethren ahead of time. Siobhan and Liza had tested this, too, and it worked fairly well, though raccoons already slept so much of the day that they weren't quite as effective.

Still, it would be enough for Miles, since the raccoons were also less likely to die from sleeping for a few days straight. And the dreamless sleep spell would always be there as a backup, or if Miles simply preferred the comfort of sleep.

When the spell took effect and Miles started jumping about with wild, exuberant energy, Siobhan turned to Gera. "I understand that Deidre Johnson has set up an…organization, of sorts, who call themselves the Undreaming Order and have been acting in my name. I would like to see them."

Any lingering ease drained from Gera's body language. Her arms held straight to her sides, she nodded stiffly. "I will escort you, my lady."

14

UNDREAMING ORDER HEADQUARTERS

Millennium wanted to accompany them to the headquarters of the Undreaming Order—Siobhan was deeply reluctant to call it a "church"—but Gera and her brother Lynwood insisted that the boy stay home. Their refusal to involve Miles only made Siobhan more apprehensive. *'What am I about to walk into?'* She imagined a cabal of people staring out from the deep shadow of hooded cloaks, each carrying a pet raven in their arms and doing strange pseudo-rituals to give themselves imaginary powers. She rolled her shoulders to release the tension there. *'It probably won't be that bad.'*

As they walked through the dimly lit streets toward the headquarters, Lynwood tried to make awkward conversation that quickly petered out, while Gera remained almost entirely silent. Siobhan grew more tense in turn, and found herself fiddling with her mother's ring on her finger and brushing her arm against her side to feel the press of the black sapphire Conduit against her ribs. She forced herself to relax as they arrived at the building, which was a few blocks east of Lynwood Manor.

The Undreaming Order headquarters was a sturdy, two-story circular building made of white stone that was stained brown with the signs of age and neglect. The shutters in the sparse windows had all been painted black. There was no dome atop the roof, but evenly spaced ceramic tubes allowed rainwater to run off the flat surface instead.

Several enforcers and their dogs were visible along the street, some obviously on guard, but a couple seemingly just lounging around in plainclothes. Most were from the Nightmare Pack, but others she recognized from the Verdant Stag. None directly guarded the entrance.

Lynwood noticed the direction of her gaze. "About half are on the payroll. The rest...well, some volunteers have taken it upon themselves to start a protective roster. Giving a tribute of their time, as it were."

"Have you had trouble with security?"

"Some," he admitted, his amber eyes almost reflective in the light of the nearest streetlamp as he watched her warily. "Nothing that you need to be concerned about, I believe. We have handled it."

Siobhan stepped forward and opened the front door. Only darkness waited beyond. In fact, it was a little *too* dark, as if something were preventing the light of the streetlamps from passing the threshold. Siobhan wrapped her shadow around herself for comfort as she waved her hand through the doorway, feeling an almost imperceptible chill from the leather anklet that was supporting the spell.

Lynwood stared at her inky-black hand, a midnight that stood out starkly blacker than the pseudo-darkness within. "There is a second door, just a few feet in."

Siobhan stepped through the threshold. She stood in the darkness a moment, allowing her eyes to adjust, and soon made out the faintest glow of words a few feet above her head. Painted on the wall in a simple, elegant script: *Fear neither the darkness nor the unknown.*

Siobhan couldn't help the smile of surprise that spread across her face. "I like it," she announced before taking two more steps forward and opening the second door, which sat directly beneath the words.

The room beyond reminded her just a little of the University's Citadel— the main building where all of the classrooms and several labs were hosted— probably somewhat due to its shape. The walls curved around in a wide circle with doors leading to five other rooms, and the ceiling was high. At the far end, a staircase led to the second story.

Most notable, however, were the ongoing renovations.

Deidre Johnson, wearing a long black cloak with a fringe of shimmering black feathers, stood in the center of the room, supervising and directing the efforts of half a dozen workers. A large portion of one side of her head was still scarred and bare, but the hair on the other side had started to grow out again, and she wore it all styled toward her unburned side to freely expose the scars. Her back was to the front doorway, so Siobhan observed unnoticed.

One worker was scrubbing with an enchanted brush that left the stone of the walls almost sparklingly white. Another was on a ladder, stringing up decorative, full-length black curtains at intervals near the edge of the ceiling.

Siobhan squinted and reassessed. *'Not curtains, but possibly tapestries, done in silver thread on velvet?'* She made out a few familiar images—ravens, and her shadow-familiar.

"Up one inch on the left," Deidre called to the tapestry-hanger. "And make sure to pull it tight. Do you think the Raven Queen abides sloppiness?"

Where there were no tapestries, the walls sported both small recesses and directly mounted shelves, several of which displayed thematic decorations: a vase full of raven feathers; a decorative glass artifact filled with potion of moonlight sizzle that continuously circulated in a bubbling, glowing riot; a platter full of shiny, random baubles, coins, and broken jewelry; a bell jar protecting a glowing, many-petaled fungus; an empty cage made of gold fili-gree that had been torn and warped, as if something powerful had broken free from the inside.

The black-painted ceiling glittered like the night sky. It was embedded with a myriad of light crystals in the shape of varied artistic stars that sometimes grew ornate enough to look more like snowflakes, and which seemed to have been made of moonstone rather than quartz. Altogether, the large circular room was illuminated with a soft, cool ambiance, which seemed just on the edge of being swallowed by shadow.

One of the workers had a box, from which they took a heavy gold crown covered in what looked to be rubies and diamonds. They moved to put it into one of the display alcoves.

Deidre pointed and cleared her throat loudly. "What is that?"

The worker turned, and Siobhan recognized her as Martha, who worked as a caretaker for Miles. "A donation," Martha said.

Deidre frowned at the crown. "Is it real?"

"...Yes? But I think a thaumaturge made it, if that's what you mean."

"Does it do anything interesting? Any magic? Or carry some specific symbolism?"

Martha opened her mouth, then closed it again and held out the crown to Deidre helplessly.

Deidre took it, inspected it closely, and then handed it back. "Put it in my office. We'll sell it. It certainly can't go on display."

Martha accepted the crown reluctantly.

Deidre turned around and spoke loudly to the rest of the workers. "We are not interested in gold or gaudy jewels, except for the value they might provide to our flock when converted into something of real worth. Please remember, this room is meant to mimic the ideals, interests, and themes of the Raven Queen. We want luxury, beauty mixed with utility, and an aura of mystery. But definitely not gaudiness, overt opulence, or the gauche macabre. *Subtlety,*" Deidre emphasized.

Standing behind Siobhan in the doorway, Gera coughed gently.

Deidre's gaze jumped to Siobhan, then slid away twice before her eyes widened and she managed to focus past the spillover effects of the divination-diverting ward. Her loud gasp drew the attention of every other person in the room, first to her, and then to Siobhan.

After a single second of stunned silence, Deidre pressed her right hand flat against the left side of her chest and gave a slight bow. "This humble awakened welcomes you," she said, her voice suddenly rough. She swallowed. "What should I call you, guest? Lady Naught? Or perhaps you would prefer… High Priestess? Is the Raven Queen currently observing through you?"

Siobhan closed her eyes briefly. *'It's not as bad as you feared,'* she reassured herself. *'They could be doing much, much stranger things. Still, "High Priestess?" Where do they come up with this stuff?'* Internally, she sighed. *'Well, I suppose I did set this in motion, however inadvertently. Now I must take responsibility for my actions.'* She opened her eyes and allowed her shadow to stretch out beneath her as if cast by an invisible sun, its clothes and hair swaying in a nonexistent breeze. "Identity is such a malleable thing. But I am the one you call the Raven Queen. I have no need for titles. You may call me Siobhan, if you wish."

Deidre's knees half-buckled as if to throw herself to the floor, but the woman caught herself with admirable alacrity and straightened. Not all of the others had as much self-control, several kneeling or bowing deeply, and one woman even pressing her forehead to the floor. "My queen, you honor us with your presence."

"Yes."

To the side and slightly behind Siobhan, Lord Lynwood suppressed a snort, but he quickly controlled himself as Gera thrust a pitiless elbow into his side.

Siobhan ignored them. "I am here to review your activities and offer… guidance." She turned to the other workers. "And please, be at ease. My ego is not so large nor my self-confidence so low that I enjoy obsequiousness or sycophancy."

When several of the others didn't seem to take the hint, Deidre lowered her head and hissed, "Get *up!*"

"Perhaps you could show me around and explain your efforts," Siobhan said. It was not really a request.

"We'll just be going, then?" Gera asked, already taking Lynwood by the arm and stepping back.

Siobhan waved her assent, and Martha and the other workers congregated into a group that watched avidly from the far side of the room. There was enough space to provide at least the illusion of privacy.

"We've been holding meetings in here a few times a week," Deidre said, waving to the space around them. "Just a few dozen people on average, nothing big. We think we'll have enough space for a few hundred at a time, as more join."

'A few hundred? Out of Gilbratha's population, which must be a few hundred thousand, at least? That doesn't sound as bad as I was expecting. It's a good reminder that most people have the sense to avoid danger.'

Deidre brought Siobhan to the first door on the left. It opened onto a room that was shaped like a slightly curved rectangle. The space was mostly empty, except for a messy desk standing near the far wall next to several crates full of letters, packages, and random items. On the wall behind it was a chalkboard with scribbled notes to one side and a hand-drawn calendar to the other. "This is my office." There was a faint hint of fatigue in Deidre's voice just from looking at the apparently unfinished work. "With plenty of space to make it into a full administrative center, when that becomes necessary."

The next door opened onto a storage room half-filled with shelves that looked like they had come from the back of a shop somewhere. "We keep any tributes and donations that would be useful, and sell the rest. Mostly it's been stuff like food, used clothing, and old furniture. But also the decorations you saw out there, from some of your more wealthy or artistic followers. One member of the flock is amazing with the mending spell, and has been working to make sure nothing looks shoddy enough to embarrass you."

"I am not easily embarrassed," Siobhan said.

Deidre blinked at her. "But you would never give a poor gift. All of your boons are precious and rare. If *we* do so, it would make you look like you're the type to hand out cheap cast-offs. Even if people know a gift or our aid isn't directly from you, our actions will still affect your image. Even a spare pair of shoes given to a homeless man must be pristine. Don't worry, we don't throw away donations just because they're not new or pretty, nor turn anyone away because they are unwashed and ignorant. We know you can see the value hidden underneath, the worth of what a person might become. We really *try* to do our best to uphold your values."

'And what, exactly, are my values?' Siobhan thought, but did not ask aloud.

The next door, on the other side of the stairs, led to a makeshift kitchen area, with a smattering of appliances and a portable oven and cold-box that had been brought in. "One of the flock is a rather amazing cook. She comes in and makes large batches of food with whatever we have on hand, so we can have something to distribute at the meetings. You might be surprised how much of an enticement a free meal is to those who may otherwise be hesitant to visit."

This left Siobhan even more relieved. *'How many of "the flock" are really just poor people who want to scam a free meal out of Deidre and the others? The actual interest in the Undreaming Order might be significantly less than I feared.'*

The next door led to a bathroom with several cubicles. "We got hot water put in just yesterday!" Deidre announced proudly.

The final room, on the right of the entranceway, was a healer's station with only a few beds and, again, mostly empty space. "A healer gave us a few boxes of his almost expired stock," Deidre said, pointing to the supply cabinet. "Some potions don't really go bad or become dangerous once they've expired, they just lose efficacy. We'll keep those and throw out the rest. I already know we're going to have a ton of demand come winter. A lot of people would rather come to us than the Verdant Stag, since we don't require vows or repayment in coin. I think getting to choose how you repay help, and to who—to whom?" She sent a sideways glance at Siobhan, but when no help was forthcoming, added, "In any case, people find that appealing."

Siobhan frowned. "What exactly does your 'help' entail, and what of the repayment?"

Deidre turned back toward the steep spiral stairs on the far side of the bottom floor, smiling proudly at the group of workers whispering together as she and Siobhan passed. "The Undreaming Order was founded by several of us who you helped directly, my queen. We know that not even your time is given freely, except, perhaps, to the children you have taken under your wing?"

She looked to Siobhan, but when Siobhan raised one silent eyebrow, Deidre continued. "Debts must be repaid, but as you told Mrs. Dotts when you saved her from her attackers, perhaps not directly to you. To be honest, many of us might not even be able to repay you directly. What could we have that you would need? So we decided to help others as you had helped us. Of course, our powers aren't as great and our time not as valuable, but that only means we need to put in more effort."

The second floor had columns of white stone holding up the roof where there had been walls below, leaving the whole area open, except for a few free-standing curtains dividing the outer area. The floor on this level was polished marble instead of wood and held a huge Circle with the symbol of an eleven-pointed star within. Beyond the boundary of the columns, several smaller Circles ringed the room.

"The building was originally constructed by a group of wealthy time-travel enthusiasts," Deidre said with a wry twist of her lips. "They ended up massacring themselves in a magical accident about eight years ago. It was extremely gruesome, apparently, and word of the details spread quickly, along with some rumors that the place retained traces of their magic, leaving people reluctant to buy it. Which is why the Undreaming Order was able to rent it for so cheap."

This floor had no windows or shutters along the walls, only a single manhole-sized piece of crystal set into the center of the roof. The ceiling had been decorated with more light-imbued moonstones, however, which illuminated the expansive area nicely.

Deidre pointed to one of the curtained areas, and they began to walk. "We argued quite a bit about how much would be enough to pay back your benevolence for *sure*. Saving three lives? Seven? One hundred? And of course, it's not so easy to simply save the life of someone unjustly imprisoned and tortured. Those are hard to find, and we weren't sure if you would want us to try to free people from the Crowns' labor camps—"

"Definitely not," Siobhan snapped.

Deidre's scars flushed red and then white, but she nodded and continued walking. "Yes, well, we thought a much larger number of smaller rescues and help given to those in need could, well, add up, as it were." She cleared her throat before drawing back a curtain to show an area filled with simple bunk beds, all empty.

"And to those we help, all those who are not orphans, we pass along the burden. They, or their parents, must help others thrice the amount they have been helped, and so on. We can give guidance and offer opportunities for service, but the final choice of who they help and how they do so is up to them. Though we strongly suggest coming to a meeting or two so that they can get an idea of the kinds of acts you might prefer."

The second curtained area held a single cabinet that contained only three hand-made dreamcatchers. "This is where we will keep magical items that might be of some utility but aren't healing related. We have a few artifacts and potions, but they have all been assigned to one of the teams currently out on a mission of service."

Siobhan frowned. It was already after eleven, which seemed rather late to be handing out bread to the homeless or whatever it was they did.

The next area was a very sad library. In fact, it might even have been more like a sad "reading nook," as there were only two chairs and the bookcases were mostly empty.

"We are keeping both valuable and controversial texts here, as the second floor is not open to the public. So far we have some banned books on history, two magical textbooks that might be of use to someone who already had some schooling, and a few copies of the People's Voice that Lord Stag donated."

Siobhan reviewed the magical textbooks but found that both were mid-level treatises on witchcraft, with a somewhat narrow focus. Something about the bare shelves made her feel hungry and on-edge. She resisted the urge to fidget, instead checking her posture from head to toe. She lifted her chin and gestured for Deidre to continue with the tour.

The next curtained area was divided into two. On one end was a station set up with a table of locks, and then over a dozen free-standing doors and windows with their own locks. On the other end was a small obstacle course covered in bells, that Siobhan belatedly realized mimicked what one would encounter if climbing the side of a house, then walking along the rooftop, before climbing through a window and down a rappelling line.

"Lock-picking training, and then a bit of practice to help improve stealth and balance," Deidre said. "It's best to gain real skill in case you can't rely on magic. We have a few lock-picking artifacts, and some boots of silence—all assigned to the current team—but it's not really enough to ensure safety on a mission."

Siobhan stared for a long time, realizing that she had forgotten to ask a critical question. "What, exactly, is tonight's mission?"

Deidre smiled wide and proudly. "We're rescuing two children from an abusive household. We got reports from some concerned citizens. To be honest, most of the reports and requests aren't things we can help with. Many want to meet you, but we would never impose on your time with such. But even if the request is reasonable, and not just another plea to help someone find love or acquire riches, we don't have the manpower or the resources. We try to direct the sick and the starving to the Verdant Stag."

Deidre raised up a hand as if to stop Siobhan from speaking, or perhaps as if she were making some sort of pledge—fingers together, palm outward. "And, before you ask, we do make sure to do our due diligence before authorizing a mission. Children being a little too thin, well, that's not always the guardian at fault. Being shy and skittish could be a kid who's seen what happens in a dark alley at night and knows not to trust outsiders. But we take note of strange injuries, especially when they don't get any treatment. And then, what sealed it in this particular case, is that one of the flock saw the children praying in front of a little altar they put together in a hidden spot. An altar with *raven feathers.*" The reverence in her voice was obvious, and she gave Siobhan a significant, heavy look.

Siobhan pressed her fingers to her forehead to suppress her sudden vertigo. '*The Undreaming Order, acting indirectly in my name, just kidnapped a pair of children. Fuck.*' She took a deep breath, and then asked aloud, "How do you plan to deal with the repercussions?"

Deidre nodded happily, as if she had been anticipating this question. Her hand rose again, and she lifted a forefinger. "First, we'll threaten the abusive guardian into silence." Another finger rose. "Then, we'll get the children the care they need and take statements and evidence we can use if the coppers try to get involved. One of our awakened is a solicitor." A third finger. "We will care for the children until we can place them in a safe home, ideally with one of the flock."

There were so many holes and potential pitfalls in Deidre's three-step plan that Siobhan didn't even know where to start. Just as she opened her mouth to speak, the sound of the front door slamming open echoed up from below, followed by a woman's shout.

"We've got an injury! Someone fetch the healer."

Siobhan had turned, crossed the open space, and was running down the stairs before she even registered the decision to do so. Two workers had already started running to fetch a healer, and the rest stood outside the sparsely furnished healer's station. The Undreaming Order team was already within, but both Siobhan and everyone else in the room froze when she passed through the doorway.

A teenage girl that looked vaguely familiar was holding the hands of two younger children, while an old, somewhat ragged man covered in several wounds and leaning on a crutch made of sticks and rags stood at the edges of the group.

Jackal, the Nightmare Pack enforcer who had been captured while trying to protect Millennium, was currently frozen halfway onto one of the patient beds. Blood ran heavily down one arm to drip on the floor.

And finally Sharon, Oliver's cook and eminently sweet middle-aged lady, had what looked to be a battle wand in one blood-covered hand and grease-paint covering her face so that she could more easily blend into the night. She was helping Jackal onto the bed. "Ah, the Raven Queen, are you? Well met, dearie," she said, completely unperturbed by Siobhan's presence. "Would you mind healing this poor young man with some of your famous blood magic?"

15

———

BOOK OF THE RAVEN QUEEN

Siobhan
Month 8, Day 25, Wednesday 11:05 p.m.

As Siobhan stepped forward, the familiar-looking teenage girl, the two children, and the homeless man all took a simultaneous step back, almost as if the move were choreographed.

On the narrow bed, Jackal grew even paler. Someone had torn off his sleeve and used that to tie a makeshift bandage around the wound, but the fabric was completely soaked and blood was dripping from his fingertips.

"Sit up," Siobhan said.

Jackal jerked upright, even though he had to tug on Sharon's hand for support.

With one hand, Siobhan pulled out a wound cleansing potion, while the other tugged the simple knot of Jackal's bandage free. "Brace yourself."

Jackal's legs jerked involuntarily as she poured the painful liquid over a laceration so deep she would probably be able to see the humerus bone beneath if she pulled its sides apart. The bright, sharp scent mixed with the iron tang of blood.

"Slicing spell?" she asked as she retrieved a blood-clotting potion. Using both hands, she poured out the potion's grainy, slightly sticky contents and smeared them over the wound.

"Yes, my queen," Jackal forced out between clenched teeth. Sweat beaded across his pale face.

"Do not worry. This is something I can easily handle." Siobhan moved to the old and battered operating table and began to draw the spell array for her mirrored healing spell in a wax that wouldn't be easily smeared. "Bring him over here," she ordered. She placed the sopping mass of Jackal's sleeve-bandage on the table—it would do well for the Sacrifice.

Deidre and Sharon helped Jackal to move while Siobhan finished up the minimalist spell array.

She tipped a few more potions down Jackal's throat, then thrust the spelled cap of a one-liter bottle of Humphries' adapting solution into the skin above his jugular vein. Siobhan recalled her helplessness when trying to save Jameson, which seemed so long ago now. *'That is one mistake I actually did manage to learn from.'*

When Jackal's lost blood had been partially replenished, she put the free part of her Will to work knitting his flesh back together.

The workers from the central hall had sneaked in, and along with the others, had spread out a safe distance around the bed to watch in fascination.

"It's really the Raven Queen," the younger of the two children murmured, awed.

His elder sister nodded but placed her finger over her lips to signal for silence. Both children had small cloth satchels hung over their backs, which presumably held their meagre belongings.

When Siobhan finished, she examined the wound with her magnifying divination spell to make sure things were as perfect as possible. She made a few tweaks to smooth connections out where she had lacked precision or the mirroring nature of the spell had caused imperfections. People were not naturally perfectly symmetrical.

Finally, she drew back, grabbed a clipboard that was lying around, and sketched the shedding-disintegration spell on the back of it. She ran the spell over Jackal, herself, and anyone and everywhere he had left blood all the way to the front door. *'That's not enough.'* As she had experienced personally, leaving your bodily fluids lying around on the street was a very bad idea. Especially after you had committed a crime. She walked back into the understocked infirmary. "Report. What happened?"

Jackal, Sharon, and the teenage girl shared looks, each seeming to urge the others to speak. Finally, Sharon sighed and turned toward Siobhan. "We didn't have much trouble getting the children out. In through the window, a bit of chatting and silently gathering their things, and out through the window again. We left a raven feather on their sleeping mats and planned to visit their 'guardian' in the morning." Sharon glanced at the children and pressed her lips together to suppress whatever opinion wanted to slip through.

"It was on the way back that we met trouble," Jackal said.

"Two men wearing all black were trying to drag this man away against his will," the teenage girl said, pointing to the tattered vagabond.

Siobhan combed her memory for where she had met the girl before. "Ah! Betty?" She suppressed the urge to add, "the vomiter?" Betty looked much different now that she was no longer suffering from starvation and severe illness, and having recently had a bath and a haircut.

The girl's eyes widened comically.

Beside Siobhan, Deidre smiled smugly. "Truly, all that is within the grasp of shadows is known to you, my queen."

"Have we...met?" Betty asked.

Belatedly, Siobhan realized that she had no explicable reason to know either Betty or Sharon's name. "No."

"Do you know my name?" the young boy asked. "Do you know all our names?"

Siobhan wished she could smack herself in the forehead. She *should* have said that she met Betty in passing, and that the girl simply didn't remember her. It would have made more sense than knowing her name with no reasonable explanation. Perhaps it was time to put Millennium's advice into practice once more and simply push through with brazenness. "I apologize. That was rude of me. I am called Siobhan Naught, and sometimes the Raven Queen. What are your names?" she asked, blatantly ignoring the boy's question.

The other occupants of the infirmary introduced themselves with varying levels of formality.

Sharon moved to the wash basin and began to scrub away the greasepaint with soap and a washcloth. "We'd heard about the recent spate of kidnappings, and he was yelling for help, so we stopped and confronted them. They attacked. Would have hit the children if not for Jackal," Sharon added with a respectful nod. "So we fought back and managed to make ourselves enough of a nuisance that the kidnappers decided to go for easier prey, I guess."

"Thank you." The homeless man bowed deeply several times in thanks. His fingers were tight where they gripped onto his makeshift crutch, and he remained otherwise silent.

Siobhan asked for more details about the attempted kidnappers, but other than the fact that they seemed healthy, their clothes fine, and their artifacts expensive, they had no identifying features and had given away no clues. Their attempted victim had no idea why they might have targeted him, except that he was conveniently alone at the time. '*This is too worrisome to leave to chance.*'

Mentally, she designed a spell array whose output would be facing outward rather than inward, that could keep the person within the inner Circle safe and warded while destroying any pieces of them existing out in the world. All her research into sympathetic concepts, her attempts to devise a solution to the blood sample the coppers had taken, as well as her work with Professor

Lacer and her side project of warding her attic apartment, had paid dividends in knowledge. Time spent learning was never wasted, even if the knowledge wasn't immediately applicable.

This kind of spell array was distinctly different than the Circle turned inside-out that she had read about in *100 Clever Ways Thaumaturges Have Committed Suicide*. The problem was, Siobhan wasn't strong enough to make it effective over the distances necessary, and any samples behind wards would also remain safe.

"Still, it is better than nothing," she muttered to herself. After a moment of hesitation, she looked at Deidre and motioned for the woman to follow her out of the infirmary. Once they were far enough for privacy, she asked, "Does the Undreaming Order have any powerful thaumaturges?"

Deidre's forefinger rose halfway to point at Siobhan before she jerked it down again. "I am not sure if you would consider him powerful, but among our awakened, Anders is a competent thaumaturge. Several other members of the flock are also thaumaturges of varying capability. They may not be awakened yet, but we might be able to call on them if there is a need."

"Actually, just call Gera," Siobhan said. Gera was proficient with divination, if not disintegration curses, and would be strong enough for the sympathetic magic to reach quite far.

While Siobhan waited, she went up to the second story and found a free space at the edge of the room, beyond the columns. Conveniently, the previous occupants had built a simple pentagram array design into the polished marble. Using it as a guide, she drew out the spell array with a glue-based paint stick, giving an excessive amount of detail and writing a full explanation of the spell's effects around the inside of the outer Circle.

She double-checked her work for errors, then tried casting it herself while she waited for Gera to arrive. Her strength quickly hit its limits, and she was forced to drop the attempt with what was probably only a few blocks around the headquarters cleaned of any hair or skin flakes she might have shed.

Siobhan returned to the first floor to find everyone eating at a table that had been brought from the storage room in the kitchen. The children were both unnaturally thin and unnaturally cautious. They ate slowly and deliberately, watching and silently mimicking Deidre and Sharon's manners. By the time the meal was finished, Gera had arrived. Siobhan instructed the woman to go up to the second floor and cast the spell she had prepared there. "You can use the spell array I drew or, if you have someone with expertise in the area, some other version of the spell, but precautions must be taken to keep all of the Undreaming Order awakened safe from sympathetic magic."

Deidre and the others followed Gera up, leaving Siobhan alone with the children.

Siobhan deactivated her dowsing artifact and sat across the table from the two.

The boy was small enough that he had trouble seeing over the edge, while the girl watched Siobhan with weary eyes and a grim tilt to her mouth.

"Did these people ask you if you wanted to come before they brought you here?"

Both children remained silent.

Siobhan sighed and tried to soften her body language. "I want to know if you got to choose—if you wanted to leave your home—or if they brought you here against your will."

The girl's grip tightened around the handle of her water tankard. "We're not going back there. Not ever again. We're under your protection now and everyone will be too scared to hurt us. And someday, a good family that knows all about you and does what you say is going to adopt us," she said, her voice challenging but her eyes pleading.

"And I'ma eat pie on my birthday, and I won't get cold in the winter because my boots'll have stuffin' in them," the boy added.

The girl took a deep breath, as if she were about to take a frightening leap. "And we'll go to school!" Her gaze flicked to the side, and then back to Siobhan, her hand squeezed even harder around the tankard's handle.

Siobhan's chest tightened painfully, and it felt as if her heart were struggling to pump suddenly sludge-like blood through her veins. If she were to guess, that final addition was not a promise made by Sharon or the others, but the girl's sneaky way of trying to get additional concessions from the one person who she believed could make miracles come true. "If that is what you want, it will be done. But—"

Siobhan paused as the girl visibly deflated with relief, then continued. "But it may not always be easy. Your former guardian may have complaints. You will need to talk about what your life was like before you came to us."

The girl's lips turned down again.

"And it might take some time to find a family that you like enough to adopt them," Siobhan added.

The girl's grip loosened, and she shared a look with the boy. "We get to choose?" she asked.

"Both sides have to choose," Siobhan said gently. "But yes. You have to accept them. Both sides adopt the other. And if they ever were to treat you badly…"

The girl gave Siobhan a vicious little grin. "Then *you* visit in the night, right?"

Siobhan shrugged and leaned back in her chair. "Do either of you need healing?"

"We're fine, my queen," the girl said quickly.

"Did you know that I can hear the sound of a lie?" Siobhan asked languidly.

The girl gulped. "I mean…we don't have any *injuries* or noth—or anything. Just some scrapes and bruises? Nothing that hurts too bad."

"Would you be more comfortable if I healed you, or if one of the others did? Perhaps Sharon? We will need to catalogue any visible signs of violence or abuse."

"Sharon!" came the immediate response.

Siobhan tried not to let her feelings be hurt by how sure—and how relieved—the child seemed by the choice.

When the women returned from the second floor, Siobhan handed the children off to Sharon and Betty.

"Gera is still working on Jackal," Deidre said. "Thank you for creating a way for us to protect ourselves in your absence, my queen. I am ashamed to say I didn't even consider it."

Siobhan ignored the thanks, suddenly self-conscious that a real expert in divination had seen her no doubt amateurish spell creation. She waved for Deidre to convene in her office.

Now that Siobhan had seen what could come of it, the stack of correspondence in the crate beside Deidre's desk seemed eminently more ominous. '*How many of those are requests for rescue?*' Siobhan left the door open behind them so that she would be instantly alerted about any emergencies.

Siobhan hesitated. There was only one chair. "Bring another chair."

Deidre drew back her shoulders and proudly announced, "That's alright, my queen. I'll stand."

Siobhan sighed. "Bring another chair," she repeated.

When Deidre returned, hauling one of the chairs from the kitchen, she placed it in front of her desk and sat in it, leaving her own chair behind the desk for Siobhan.

"You have explained why you decided to start the Undreaming Order and much of what you do, but I have further questions. Why did you choose that name?"

Deidre blushed, but placed her hands on her knees and did not fidget as she answered. "Well, we held a vote, my queen. We awakened did. The idea came partially from what you did for Millennium, and partially from the prophetic or symbolic dreams several people have testified about and tried to interpret. But mainly, it came from Enforcer Turner's research into the concepts of lucid dreaming. Several of those who believe in your power and grace were practicing the exercises already and espousing the benefits."

Siobhan was familiar with the concept of lucid dreaming, as it was one of the techniques often recommended to manage persistent nightmares. Unfortunately, it had not helped her in the least, as what she really needed was to avoid dreaming altogether. Still, over the years she had picked up quite a lot of knowledge about it. "I remember some of those people," Siobhan said. One of the Nightmare Pack enforcers had spoken of it to her months ago. She pulled the memory up and searched it for clues. "They hope to come awake while dreaming…and pray for my guidance?"

"Well, among other things. Many consider lucid dreaming, when combined with other practices, to be the best way to get you to accept a message or request. Several people have also reported symbolic responses, such as dreaming of a raven or a shadowy form, after which they experience some corresponding positive or negative event in reality, or feel that they have been called to take some action."

That was dangerous. Not only could dreams be totally outlandish, the person interpreting them could assign almost any meaning they wished. This was part of why Siobhan found the practice of divination through symbolism and augury to be so extremely useless.

"The name 'Undreaming Order' might not exactly correspond with the desire to control one's mind even while asleep, but, well, it sounds powerful. And we did not want to draw ire by choosing a name more blatantly reminiscent of you. And…perhaps someday, those who you favor could receive boons that allow us to do what we have trained for more fully," Deidre added tentatively.

"And the 'awakened' are those with leadership positions?"

"Yes. It's somewhat presumptuous, I know."

Siobhan sighed. "The greater 'flock' that you have referred to—those among them who join without having been transferred a debt of service—what do they hope to gain from membership in the Undreaming Order?"

"Many *need* nothing in particular. But they know you do not give your aid for free. They also know that your wings often shelter the downtrodden and the helpless, and those who become your enemies or attempt to harm those under your protection receive no mercy. They hope for no particular boon, only your favor. They would shelter under your wings, and in exchange carry out your will."

Perhaps sensing Siobhan's exasperation, Deidre hurried to add, "We have not spoken on your behalf without your permission. We are ready to put orders or rewards from you into practice, if you wish. Our awakened and some members of the flock would be happy to help those under your protection or make trouble for your enemies. We could spread word of your desires and instructions to your followers, or gather a specific type of offering, whatever you want. But we have not been so presumptuous as to give commands in your name."

Seeing as people everywhere seemed to attribute actions and intent to her that she had never taken and did not endorse, Siobhan had her doubts about how well Deidre and the other "awakened" had really managed to keep their own strange opinions out of the Undreaming Order. "I would like to see the book you have been working on."

Deidre opened one of the desk drawers and carefully took out a binder. The front half was filled with pages that had been neatly printed and hole-punched, while the back half was wrinkled sheets covered in surprisingly neat and uniform cursive. The front of the binder was labeled very simply, *The Book of the Raven Queen.*

While Deidre sat watching her intently, Siobhan turned to the first page and began to read.

It was really just a collection of exaggerated tales about the Raven Queen told as first-person accounts. Sometimes, there were multiple versions of an event told from different perspectives, including the contradictions and variations that came standard with witness accounts. *'At least Deidre had the journalistic integrity to record the truth, even when it opened the book up to skepticism, rather than trying to force all the accounts to meet her narrative.'* That they were not totally fabricated did not make them any less exaggerated, however. Siobhan wondered how it was possible for people to remember something she had been involved in with technically accurate events but such wildly exaggerated details, emotional responses, and conclusions about her purpose.

Beyond that, several stories were either totally false, or were perhaps real but had nothing to do with her. She was not in control of people's dreams, coincidental miracles or misfortune, or the actions of every single individual raven in the city.

"It is a living document," Deidre explained as Siobhan got to the handwritten parts. "Meant to grow as we record and look to learn from your actions."

Siobhan took the fountain pen from Deidre's desk and marked several of the accounts. "These are either false, or someone has been impersonating me."

Deidre's eyes widened with horror. "I will remove them immediately, my queen! Should I… Do you wish any action to be taken against those who gave false reports?"

Siobhan looked down to the binder, wondering where, exactly, she would draw the line between "real" and "false" reports. For all she knew, these people actually believed what they were saying. "No," she admitted with defeat. "But do not allow people to go around believing they are true. Issue a retraction, I suppose."

The end of the binder had a list labeled: *Tenets of the Raven Queen (Extrapolated).*

Several were distinctly combative, such as the one that endorsed a commitment to revenge as a deterrent against people harming others.

Siobhan crossed out those that seemed particularly likely to lead to disaster and, after some thought, wrote a few replacement tenets in the careful, elegant script she had created for the Raven Queen. When she was finished, the simple list contained seven tenets. A couple still seemed dangerous in the right hands, with the wrong interpretation, but Siobhan still felt them to be *right*, and so did not remove them.

All thinking and feeling beings should be held to the same standards and afforded the same fundamental rights.

One's body and mind are subject to their own will alone. All beings should have the freedom to pursue their own will.

Treat others with compassion, empathy, and respect, for you never know when great power may be disguised in a humble form.

Encroaching on the rights of another opens one up to reprisal and the loss of one's own rights.

The pursuit of justice is the duty of all thinking and feeling beings, and should prevail over laws, institutions, and the authority of those with great power.

It is dangerous to meddle with things one does not understand. If one wishes to meddle, they must first understand.

Actions have complex consequences. One should strive not to cause harm through their actions, and when they inevitably fail, do their best to rectify their mistake and resolve any harm that may have been caused.

As she stared at the list, an existential dread crept up the back of Siobhan's neck like cold spider legs, accompanied by the premonition that whatever bulwark had been holding back the metaphorical tide, that threshold had now been crossed. What was to come could not be stopped. Hopefully, she would at least be able to guide it.

Siobhan looked out into the central hall, where the children had just exited the infirmary.

They were freshly bathed, and moving their limbs and pressing on certain spots with amazement. "It doesn't hurt at all!" the young boy announced, crouching down and then hopping like a frog.

Gera, Jackal, and the homeless man the Undreaming Order had rescued came down from the second floor, with Gera looking somewhat fatigued from her efforts. "It is done," she announced.

"You should do the children, too," Betty said. "Just in case."

Gera hesitated, but after watching the children for a few seconds, she nodded. "Come, then. I will show you some magic designed by the Raven Queen," she said, turning to walk back upstairs.

The little boy's pants had rips in both knees.

"Does the flock have any needs? Are you getting enough donations to help with food, clothing, a safe place to sleep, and basic healing?" Siobhan asked.

Deidre's eyes flicked toward the children passing by, and then down to her lap. She smiled to herself, then said, "Resources are always a struggle for an organization like this, my queen. People are more generous than you might expect, but many of the flock are struggling themselves. That said, we have so far been able to provide one meal a day, to mend clothing and provide footwear, and for a select few, rent a room that they can share with other members of the flock long enough to sleep. Healing… that is very expensive, my queen. Those who need it, we send to the Verdant Stag. They do not exclude those who live outside their territory from their loans."

Siobhan thought of Oliver's ideals—that everyone should be rich enough to live a satisfying life, as well as have the opportunity for an education. That given the opportunity and the right leadership, society could uplift itself. That there was no need for anyone to die from lack of coin.

She thought of the girl's request to go to school. *'What kind of skills can lift people out of hopelessness and poverty?'* she wondered. She stared at Deidre's fountain pen and then added one final tenet to the list, leaving the number at eight.

There is the potential for greatness in all thinking and feeling beings, and it is our duty to nurture that potential through caring for the innocent and helpless, offering opportunities to the hungry, and striving continuously to better ourselves.

"LET me introduce myself more formally, Deidre Johnson." She gave the "Self" part of the chant she had created, speaking clearly and slowly as she stared into the other woman's widening eyes.

"I AM a changeling like the seasons,

A daughter of shadow and light,
Of Charybdis mists and raven's flight,
And always I seek after mysteries."

SHE POINTED to the last tenet. "You, too, must continue to seek. I hope that all of the flock can learn to read, do basic math, and learn some basic meditations." The former two would set someone up for entry level schooling, or perhaps vocational training, and the latter could help to strengthen the mind against hardship and trauma. As Millennium called them, the "bad thoughts." These were basic life skills that everyone should have.

"I do not want you to force anyone who refuses, but it should be strongly encouraged. For those who can accomplish this well, there will be more to follow."

Deidre swallowed convulsively. "Even for us awakened? For me?"

"Surely, if you want it."

"*I do.*"

Siobhan chuckled. "Okay. But first, see to the flock. You might be able to source teachers from among your number, but you will likely need funds to make this possible. Here." Siobhan pulled out a Conduit from her new bag and placed it on the table. It was one of those she had taken from the Pendragon Corps, which she had put in her bag for emergencies. Having three Conduits—two of them hidden—was perhaps overkill. If the concept of "overkill" was possible when it came to something that could save one's life.

Siobhan would have kept even more, if she could think of other places to hide them. '*Perhaps at the nape of my neck, under my hair…*' she mused. She shook off the thought. Giving up one of her Conduits hurt in the part of her that was never satisfied no matter how much she had, always sure that hunger and fear and helpless desperation could return right around the corner, but she was still incredibly wealthy. She still had almost a dozen Conduits, and with the continuously rising price of celerium, even the poorest was worth more than twenty thousand gold. Siobhan could afford to put poor children through school, if not the University itself.

Deidre looked from the polished celerium to Siobhan, and then back again. Cautiously, she reached out and took the Conduit. "Your will shall be done, my queen."

16

THE DAZZLER

Month 8, Day 28, Saturday 5:30 a.m.

Saturday morning, before the sun rose, Sebastien walked out to the Flats. Professor Lacer had asked her to meet him there in class the day before, and she didn't know why. *'Best case scenario, he wants to assess my progress on the three transmutable substances he assigned. Slightly worse case scenario, he wants to test my capacity with the Henrik-Thompson—though I'm not sure why he would have us meet on the Flats for that. Worst case scenario, he's deduced something else about my connection to the Raven Queen and wants me away from any important buildings to mitigate destructive repercussions.'*

Sebastien's mind continued to spin up increasingly unlikely horrible scenarios. *'What if he wants to have a meeting with Sebastien and the Raven Queen in the same room together?'*

The way to the Flats was empty. Distant sounds from the land and sea below mixed into an almost inaudible sigh, but otherwise the night was silent and still.

Professor Lacer met her at the end of the pathway with a nod of acknowledgement, and she followed him up the pathway of white stone and across the obstacle-course-laden Flats to the northern edge of the white cliffs. The stars above reflected off the placid surface of the lake below, which continued on through the base of the white cliffs before running out into the Charybdis Gulf as well as fueling the city's canals.

Without preamble, Professor Lacer said, "It is difficult to keep a secret. Most people do not realize how difficult, and they fail to keep them so commonly that failure is almost a social expectation—what one might call 'gossip.'" His lips pursed with distaste. "But when they have an important secret, one they must ensure does not get out, many people find themselves without the tools to make that possible."

Professor Lacer didn't *seem* like he was building up to some big trap or revelation. In fact, his tone was more akin to one of his in-class lectures. Sebastien squinted. "A secrecy spell? Or a compulsion to avoid specific, related topics?"

Professor Lacer let out a huff of amusement. "That is an option, of course, and not just to bind *others* to secrecy. But not only is that magical field illegal to the masses, those kinds of spells have restrictions and downsides that I find…unpleasant. Besides, just like there is no curse without parameters that will unravel it, there is no compulsion that is infallible. I much prefer to maintain personal control of my own mind."

"Me too," Sebastien decided immediately.

"To keep a secret properly, it is best if you are the only one who knows it. As is famously said, 'Two may keep counsel, putting one away.' Or, more colloquially, 'if one of them is dead.' Unfortunately for you, at least three people know your secret." He looked at her pointedly.

Sebastien nodded slowly. *'Professor Lacer, the Raven Queen, and Damien all "know" that I might be descended from Myrddin. But really, Professor Lacer is the only one who thinks that. I really hope that is the secret he's talking about.'*

"When you have a real secret, not some little piece of gossip or an embarrassing skeleton in your cupboard, you must act as if you did not know it. Not just in action, but also in thought. It is extremely easy to slip and provide tiny clues to the truth without realizing it. When you come across information regarding your secret, you will automatically make conclusions, but you must act as if you have not. You will need to simulate a self who does not know. If the secret is entangled with many different parts of your life or affects different people in different ways, you will need to maintain the causality of two or more different realities. This…is harder than you might think, but a strong Will can help. In fact, holding contradictory information in the mind and simulating either side as truth is one of the ways the Red Guard has experimented with increasing the soundness and force of the Will."

Sebastien already practiced this in some ways. It was why she used different names for different identities, even in her own mind. But she doubted she managed to reach the level of self-hypnotization that Professor Lacer was talking about. *'It is useful advice,'* she admitted to herself, but yet, some part of her shied away from it. She tried to latch on to the discomfort and follow it deeper. *'Is that a form of lying to yourself?'* she wondered. *'No,'* she decided, '*it is a form of acting until you can outwardly embody the role. Nothing more than a mental set of clothes. Of course, wear the clothes long enough and the person might shift to fit them. And for me…how many different sets of clothes might I have to wear, around how many different people?*' Her lies, and which people knew which parts of them, or believed certain things about her, were becoming somewhat…unwieldy.

'*It's exhausting,*' she realized suddenly. '*And lonely. But the alternative is still too frightening. If I had been capable of compartmentalizing my "realities" from the very beginning, it might have changed a lot. However, it doesn't fix the risks associated with having to switch frequently between identities. This technique would work better for long-term, deep-cover Red Guard assignments.*'

Professor Lacer drew her attention back. "You must also guard against your own impulses to share more than you should. I imagine you can think of several times that you've had a personal secret and felt the strong urge to divulge that secret to someone else?"

For some reason, the first memory that sprouted to life in Sebastien's mind was a memory of looking at Ennis's back as he hurried to throw rucksacks filled with their belongings into the back of a wagon. They needed to leave before the sun rose, for both of their safety. Siobhan had stood in the road, her eyes stinging and her throat stiff. '*Father, you're hurting me,*' had sounded in her head, as clear as if she had spoken it.

But she didn't speak it. Not then, and not later, when similar things happened again and again. Occasionally, and especially as she got older, she got angry and let scathing accusations and verbal assaults meant to wound him in return spill from her tongue.

But never that small, vulnerable plea for him to see what should be so obvious. For him to *care*.

Sebastien swallowed and looked down at the heavens reflected below. Even considering that memory was a lack of proper compartmentalization, according to Professor Lacer. She was Sebastien now, and had never known an Ennis.

She had wanted to tell Damien parts of the truth several times. She had even idly considered coming clean to Professor Lacer and relying on whatever aid he could provide.

"It is a natural impulse for us to want to share with others. But consider, even when you are the one who would directly bear the consequences if your secret were known, *you* still feel the urge to tell others. Any person you share your secret with has that same inborn desire to share, and *they* will not have the same inherent motivation to remain silent. Nor can you trust that they are able to reliably model a world in which they do not know, or the consequences of sharing too freely."

Professor Lacer sighed. "Unfortunately, a lecture such as this does little to help you learn the depths and nuances of the art of secret-keeping, which is not my true expertise. And you have shown yourself to be incapable of avoiding all but reasonable danger. I can imagine several scenarios where someone who holds an unsavory interest in you might try to coerce you into truth-telling by various means. And even if not that, what of the other threats you have faced?" He clenched and released his fists. "I foresee upheaval and violence bubbling up in this city—this country—like a potion about to erupt. And I would not leave you helpless."

Professor Lacer turned to face her. "We are here so that I can give you two resources that may help you if you face danger again and cannot rely on the kindness of *random strangers* who happen to be passing by to save you," he said, his tone making it clear that he was alluding to the supposed kidnapping attempt by the Pendragon Corps.

Sebastien perked up with interest. "Resources?"

Professor Lacer gave her a wry look. "Yes, yes. Try to contain your greed. Here is the first." He reached into his breast pocket and pulled out a badly tarnished copper crown—likely a forgery of some sort, as legitimate coins were formulated to be resistant against environmental damage. "This is an artifact which you can use to signal me in an emergency. Twist it like so," he demonstrated, revealing a seam right down the middle and leaving the copper crown half tails, half heads.

He twisted it back and handed it to her. "It works on sympathetic principles, but it is strong enough to overpower the Raven Queen's boon and many other types of barriers. It has a minor enchantment so that it will be the first coin you pull out of your pocket or coin purse when you reach for it. If you activate it, I will prioritize locating and saving you. *When* should you activate it?" he asked, staring at her with narrowed eyes.

"Only in the direst of emergencies?"

"No!"

Sebastien flinched back.

He scowled at her, pressing his lips into a thin line of frustration for a moment. "You should activate it whenever you believe yourself to be in significant danger that you would have *moderate trouble* extracting yourself from on your own. This includes legal trouble, such as being arrested. It includes having been mugged and needing to walk back to the University without your shoes. It includes waking up in a strange room and not knowing where you are or how you got there! Your sense of a 'dire emergency' is so skewed that you might hesitate to contact me when facing down a dragon in single combat."

Sebastien opened her mouth to protest, but closed it again when Professor Lacer's scowl grew even more thunderous.

His tone softened. "I will not be angry if you use it and it turns out your life was not in danger. I will not be angry if you use it and you are not injured." He sighed, and even softer, added, "I will not be angry if you use it and I arrive to find you were frightened by something that has already passed and was no true threat."

Sebastien's fingers tightened tentatively around the coin. She was aware that it could be a tracking device as much as a method to call for aid. She was also aware of what it meant that Professor Lacer would allow her to inconvenience him so. A mix of warmth and wariness battled in her stomach. "Thank you," she said softly.

He cleared his throat and turned to face northward once more. "Speak no more of it. Now, for the second contingency." He held his hands in front of him, forefingers and thumbs touching in an imperfect Circle that was shaped more like a spade, with his palms angled outward. She noted a small celerium ring on this thumb instead of the much larger sphere he usually used when free-casting. He spoke softly, adding a long pause between each statement that made his words sound like poetry.

"From luminous whispers,
   Dancing stars weave dreams of light,
   And shattering radiance blooms,
   Defiant against the night."

As he spoke, tiny motes of light that looked like dust-sized fireflies converged to the center of the space between his hands. They disappeared into a tiny black dot.

When Professor Lacer had finished speaking, he paused, then thrust his palms forward. The space between his hands grew entirely black, but from the other side burst a green light so bright that even the part that refracted around the sides of his palms and through the flesh of his fingers left spots in Sebastien's eyes. She could see the path the light traveled highlighted in the particles of dust and water in the air for a long, long way.

Professor Lacer released the spell and lowered his hands. "This spell is called the dazzler. I have cast a weak and somewhat undirected example for better theatrical effect. It is not a widely known spell, though it is used by the Red Guard as well as a few members of the army's special forces. However, it is not illegal for civilians to know, as long as you can defend your use of it after the fact, and have not significantly injured innocent bystanders. Sometimes, small, flexible tricks can be surprisingly useful. This one, in particular, is special due to its…versatility."

Sebastien blinked several times to clear the lingering red blotches in her eyes.

"You can create any color of light, or even, with more advanced application, a strobe light that cycles between several colors. The green I displayed has a few advantages. If you keep the power low, that color will not do permanent harm to the human eye. So you can use it on people who you only suspect to be an enemy, or if there are allies or innocents in the direction you are beaming the light. At high power, you can and will permanently blind people who do not have access to magical healing. The green is well suited to penetrating atmospheric haze or smoke, if you need to use it to light the way in the dark or through a battlefield. However, it is highly noticeable, which can be a boon if you are hoping to use it as a signal, or a liability if you require stealth. For you, however, the green has a very compelling feature, and that is how little power it requires to seem bright."

"Green light is close to the eyes' peak sensitivity when they are adapted for the dark," Sebastien said, reciting a piece of trivia from Professor Gnorrish's class. "At night it will appear a lot brighter than a red light for the same amount of power."

"Indeed. Now, why do you think I am teaching you this esoteric spell rather than handing you a second artifact with capabilities far stronger than what you could produce on your own?"

Sebastien did not have to think long. "Because in times of dire need, you can only *really* rely on yourself."

Professor Lacer eyed her for a moment. "I would not have worded it that way, but, essentially, yes. A great many thaumaturges can only be considered such in optimal conditions. In their lab, their workshop, or with the array-drawing supplies they happen to carry with them, they are sorcerers of some capability. In an emergency, away from those resources, they act as magicians, pulling out whatever useful artifact they prepared and congratulating themselves on their foresight. But then the artifact runs out of charges, or fails to meet the specific needs of the situation—and the output cannot be modified on the fly. Or," he said more gravely, "it is taken from them by their enemy, sometimes even to be used against its owner."

"That's why it pays to be a free-caster."

"But you are not yet a free-caster, and neither of us can, nor *should* attempt to speed up that process. Esoteric spells, and to a lesser extent, gesturan spells —due to the difficulty of learning them and the time it takes to cast them—are the second-best option. This spell is something that you can cast when all else is lost, and with no external resources or components except a Conduit. At what point might this spell still fail you?"

Sebastien recalled the spell's chant and looked up at the sky. "Does it have something to do with the stars? Does this spell only work when it's dark?"

"You seldom disappoint," Professor Lacer said mildly.

The words sent a gentle rush of satisfaction through Sebastien. "I would also have trouble casting it if my fingers were cut off or my arms were badly injured. If my tongue had been cut out and I couldn't speak. If I was underwater, the water might muffle and distort the chant. Would that matter? It might not work properly if I were trapped underground without any access to the sky. Or if I had been drugged, concussed, or had Will-strain and was unable to focus." Sebastien paused, sure that she could come up with more scenarios with a little time to think, but Professor Lacer nodded.

"Being underwater makes spells that require a chant more difficult, but does not stop you from casting them if your Will is clear and forceful enough. This spell works best at night, under a clear sky where the stars can be seen. That is why I spent several hours before your arrival casting a far-reaching weather spell to ensure optimal conditions."

Sebastien stared at Professor Lacer, who didn't even seem to be bragging, and then looked up at the sky again. This time, the complete lack of clouds, the clarity of the air, and the lack of wind took on new meaning. Weather spells—effective ones—were a thing of legend. It required an immense amount of power to control the world on such a scale. "Isn't that…illegal?" Weather spells, cast poorly, could also have disastrous consequences. Only a few thaumaturges were licensed to cast them, and generally as a relief effort to stave off famine. And according to the newspapers she had been reading lately, even that was controversial.

He gave her a wry smile. "I was careful not to get caught. There were only going to be a few clouds, anyway, so the change was not too drastic."

Sebastien wondered if it would be rude to ask his thaumic capacity. 'Well, of course it's rude,' she realized. 'But he can just refuse to tell me. He's not the type to get hung up on social norms and niceties.'

She asked, but Professor Lacer raised one amused eyebrow at her and continued with his lecture instead of answering. "It can still be cast under other conditions, but you will struggle to output as strong a light compared to the amount of effort you spend gathering power. If you are sealed beneath the earth, without any external source of light, you will struggle greatly."

She narrowed her eyes. "But I might still be able to cast it? I have noticed, with enough practice and familiarity, you can bend the original rules with certain spells."

"You might," he agreed. "This is certainly one of those spells. Now, an explanation of the exact mechanisms behind how this magic works is generally reserved for a few lectures in the higher levels of my Practical Casting course, but I think we can sum it up with something you will understand." He paused, and then said, "It is the mind that sees light. The eyes are only there to send signals."

Sebastien's eyes widened slowly as the implications hit her. *'Is that transmutation, somehow directly stimulating the optic nerve? Or transmogrification, somehow utilizing the idea of light?'* "I don't understand," she announced boldly.

He chuckled. "I see that Professor Gnorrish has been training you well. I know you are familiar with one or two other esoteric spells, but this will likely be the most complicated and difficult one you have ever attempted. It is not something I would usually teach to a student, and if I did, not one below fourth term, perhaps even fifth. However, I believe you will grasp the concepts. You are skilled with light-based spells and have a rare understanding of transmogrification."

Sebastien grinned giddily and bounced on her toes a few times to bleed off some of her sudden, heady excitement.

Professor Lacer gave her a stern look. "Focus."

"I *am*."

He huffed, but his eyes held a hint of amusement. "The chant can be repeated as many times as you want to build up power, but I recommend you limit yourself to once until you are completely certain your Will can handle a second repetition, and then a third, and so forth. As you gain proficiency with the spell, you may gather more power in the space of a single chant, so gauge your level of effort carefully.

"This is partially a transmogrification-based spell. You might have wondered how I was able to create such a large amount of light while seemingly gathering so little. Part of the explanation is that the spell absorbs heat as well as light. If you are casting it without loss, it will also absorb the sound of your voice. But part of what makes it seem so bright is that it exudes not just visible light, but also the *concept* of light. *Intent* matters greatly." He paused there, as if to let some epiphany sink into her brain.

After a moment, she said, "Okay?"

"Light and the idea of light are not the same thing. Not only that, but you must lean into transmogrification to produce the effect, without any components to draw the concept from. Perhaps an example is in order." He palmed his usual Conduit and closed his other hand into a fist, palm up. "Concentrate."

As he opened his hand, a gentle, warm light shone from the area above his palm. It stayed for a moment, then began to cycle through different colors and intensities. Finally, he closed his palm again. "That was light."

He opened his palm a second time, and for a moment Sebastien thought he had cast a similar spell, though the quality of the light was somehow different. Purer, maybe. But then she glanced up and noticed him staring at her with intent, rather than down at his palm where she had expected.

And though his palm was now much lower in her field of view, the light still seemed to be shining, somehow, directly into her eyes. She frowned and looked back at it, realizing that despite the brightness, she could see his palm beneath the light. Her eyelids fluttered, and she raised a couple of fingers to her temple, rubbing gently as if the pressure would help settle her sudden sense of pseudo-vertigo.

As before, the light began to change. But the new colors weren't real colors. Or they were *more* than real colors. Sebastien scowled and bent the entirety of her Will toward discernment. In the red light, she experienced a scarlet curtain made of silk billowing past her face. The color changed, to a cold white light that had the same cold, eye-watering burn of the sun reflecting off an unbroken field of white snow. And again, conjuring a cyan ripple of coral and fish spied through crystal clear ocean water…

The colors were always associated with other imagery, so fleeting and distant that she would have never noticed, normally.

Professor Lacer closed his fist and let it drop. "That was the concept of light. You are likely to struggle with the latter. Since you are one of the few who understands how transmogrification truly works, you have a chance to succeed, with the proper application of effort and ingenuity. I will not expect you to manage a spell heavily laden with the concept of light today. If you can merely create a directed beam in the right color, I will consider it a success.

"It is best if you come up with your own imagery for the spell, but as you first learn to cast it, you will want to focus on the idea of luminous whispers, dancing stars, and dreams of light. Add to that a shattering radiance, which I have just demonstrated for you in case you have no direct experience to draw on. Take your time to consider it, and when you are ready, attempt a low-power casting. Do not worry about the color, but do keep in mind the shield of darkness behind the directed light, as well as the fact that it should go forward from where you aim and not scatter off in every direction."

Sebastien closed her eyes and pulled up memories of watching the aurora during her childhood on the Northern Islands, the dancing fire-familiar that she and her friends had watched atop a roof, and a play she had seen once that featured someone's idea of the Radiant Maiden, along with a dozen other potential memories.

When she was ready, she placed her hands in position, spoke the chant, and did her best not to get distracted by the hovering pane of half-darkness that Professor Lacer cast to cover both of their faces, just in case.

When Sebastien thrust her hands out, a bright white light flared from her palms. It was not as coherent or strong as Professor Lacer's, and she suspected that it called up none of the special memories she had used to focus it, but he did not complain, merely saying, "Try again."

An hour later, traces of light and color began to transform the horizon, as if it had slowly been absorbing the output of her repeated castings. She had tried dozens of different memories and ideas, and she was able to cast the spell in half the time it had originally taken, and at the specific frequency of green that Professor Lacer had demonstrated. It processed about half of the sound from her voice and enough heat to make her finger bones ache. But what she was most proud of was the piercing *feel* to it that spoke of cutting past defenses and burning out vulnerabilities.

She could sense it even past the darkened strip of a shield Professor Lacer had placed in front of their faces. *'Would this bypass other defenses people would normally use against light?'* she wondered. *'Or, could I learn to signal a specific person, while leaving anyone else oblivious, if the concept was clearly not meant for them? If I could get as good with this as I am with the shadow-familiar spell, perhaps I would be able to extend its possible uses to a similar degree.'*

She looked to the sun, just peeking over the edge of the planet. *'The stars are always there, even when you cannot see them. And the sun is also a star,'* she remembered.

"You are nothing if not a fast learner," Professor Lacer said. "Your concepts are still weak, but to be noticeable at all, after only an hour of practice, is…satisfactory."

Sebastien beamed with achievement. She doubted she could have cast such a spell when she had first arrived in Gilbratha just under a year ago. *'I need more practice with transmogrification. I should buy some light-based components and play with them until I get a better feel for it.'*

Professor Lacer handed her a pair of tinted gryphon-riding goggles and warned her to wear the eye protection when practicing without him, until she got better at reducing any spillover light. "If you ever need to use this spell but hope to preserve your night vision, use red light instead of green. At low enough output, a single repetition of the chant will be enough to power the light for several minutes. You will want to adjust your imagery to support that purpose," he reminded her.

Before leaving the Flats, Sebastien took advantage of the opportunity to demonstrate her progress with transmuting the items he had given her. She was able to weave the spider silk in several different patterns, and even had some immediate control over its color, though she couldn't do anything bright. She created a single strip of silk about two inches wide, depicting some stylistic herons and water lilies and using four different weaving patterns, including one that mimicked embroidery.

Professor Lacer took it, ran his thumb over the surface and examined the design in the rising light of the sun, then shoved the strip in his pocket and stared at her expectantly.

The scab-root came next. She made it as pretty as possible, resulting in a fist-sized tuber that looked more like a potato than a dirty lump with a dozen oozing wounds that had dried over. Sebastien beamed with pride. *'People probably wouldn't gag at the sight of it!'*

Professor Lacer cut through it with a slicing spell, instantly steam-cooked it, and after what she assumed to be a diagnostic divination, took a bite. He didn't even grimace, but her mouth watered in sympathetic disgust.

"I don't know any way to make them taste palatable."

"You cannot. Better to make them tasteless by cutting off the signals from your tongue to your brain. I have a spell for that, but you would probably be better off with a potion."

Finally, she transmuted a cluster of diamonds from a twig, a piece of the white cliffs, and some water from the canteen in her bag. To show off, she even transmuted a diamond the size of a grain of sand from the air.

After examining all four, Professor Lacer put the diamonds in his pocket, too. "What are these exercises useful for?"

"Survival," she replied immediately. "Even if I am dropped naked in the middle of nowhere and left for dead, as long as I have enough time to make a diamond, I will survive."

"And with what will you make that diamond?"

"Celerium is best, but if you can restrict yourself to a few thaums at a time, anything can be used as a conduit. Even a random twig." She picked one up and waved it at him. "I'd say I could channel at least twenty thaums without destroying it. My control is probably my strongest point, and I can easily restrict myself to that. The wood will start steaming and popping before it explodes, so I'd even have a warning if I were to get sloppy. Which I wouldn't."

"Good," Professor Lacer said simply. "You have met my expectations for this term. Now go off and study for the exams or something," he said, shooing her away.

Sebastien did so for a few hours, but then left the University and went through the whole hours-long process of multiple transformations. The tarnished copper crown remained in Sebastien's bag, where she had left it.

When she arrived at Liza's house as a heavily disguised Siobhan, it was already nearing noon.

The woman had been working to expand the sleep-proxy from one raven to many, which involved a large amount of math that Siobhan didn't understand. Her eyes had extra-dark bags under them, and her hair, though coiled tightly into a bun with a hairpin speared through the center, looked as if she had been spending a lot of time in an electrical storm.

"I need a research assistant for the ravens. Someone to examine, care for, and keep logs of their health so that I can estimate the efficiency of my spell designs," she said. She rubbed her temples, then looked up at Siobhan expectantly. "Someone with two hands and a working brain, that's all I need."

Siobhan hesitated. Transforming from Sebastien into Siobhan was dangerous, and she wanted to avoid doing it more frequently than necessary. But she had to be the Raven Queen to help Professor Lacer—in this body, better said "to help Thaddeus"—decrypt Myrddin's other journals.

"I can only come at certain times." She would try to find some extra time whenever she already needed to be Siobhan. It made sense to take full advantage of all the work it required to switch identities, anyway.

Liza found this barely acceptable. After helping Siobhan to re-cast her sleep-proxy spell with a fresh sleeper raven, the woman remained in a sniping, grumpy mood.

Siobhan kept her mouth tactfully shut as they left Liza's house and hailed a carriage to take them to their true destination. The shaman that Liza worked with at the Retreat at Willowdale had agreed to meet "Amelia" again and help her answer some sensitive, perhaps less-than-legal questions to do with shamanry.

He lived above a small shop that sold magical trinkets as well as spices and teas. A sign above the door mentioned making appointments with the shaman for "a reading," so presumably he had some sort of collaborative arrangement with the shop owner.

Liza nodded at an aproned man through the window, then went around to the back of the building and up the stairs there. She knocked several times, checked her pocket watch to make sure they had arrived at the right time, and then reached down to try the handle.

It opened easily. Liza's frown deepened, but she stepped through the doorway into the gloom within, and Siobhan followed.

"Renaldo?" Liza called. A kettle was sitting atop the stove but was long burned dry and the heated metal was starting to give off a strange, faint smell.

While Liza turned off the stove, Siobhan pushed aside the beaded curtain into the small living room. Her breath caught in her throat and she stiffened, arching backward as her body half tried to jump away.

The shaman was sitting in an armchair.

He was staring right at her. Or at least one of his eyes was. The other was looking off in another direction entirely. His sclera were mottled crimson, and blood and brain fluid had leaked from his nose, staining his chin and the flamboyant, bright robes beneath.

The skin of his face sagged strangely, and his mouth hung open, revealing a pale, swollen-looking tongue that seemed to want to spill out from between his lips.

Siobhan backed up as silently as she could, grabbed Liza's arm, and whispered to the other woman, "He's dead."

17

PROPERTIES OF DARK MATERIALS

Month 8, Day 28, Saturday 12:00 p.m.

Liza reached up and drew out one of her decorative hair sticks, partially loosening her mass of curls. She held it like a battle wand, her grip steady and practiced. Her left hand, bearing three chunky golden rings, came up in an outward facing fist, hinting at some kind of shield spell.

The sight jolted Siobhan into action. She drew out her own battle wand, the weight of it immediately comforting in her hand. *'Oh gods,'* Siobhan realized with a start, *'someone might have actually killed him.'* The idea made her blood run cold.

Without a word, Liza began to sweep through the house, her movements precise and controlled. Professional.

Siobhan followed behind, trying to keep her attention focused wherever Liza wasn't looking to provide a better range of cover. *'That's how the Red Guard or the military squads do it, right?'* She felt like a child mimicking what she had seen at the latest popular play. *'I'm not trained for this!'*

They moved from room to room, checking closets, under furniture, and behind curtains. *'The front door was unlocked when we arrived,'* Siobhan remembered. However, there were no obvious signs of forced entry or struggle. The house seemed undisturbed, almost eerily so, given the circumstances.

As they progressed through the bathroom and bedroom, Liza paused to examine seemingly innocuous objects like a half-empty glass on the bedside table and the positions of Renaldo's pillows.

Siobhan half-expected someone to jump out at them from every shadow. But the small apartment was empty. They made their way back to the living room where Renaldo's body lay.

Liza knelt beside him, her hair-stick wand still at the ready. She began to examine his body more closely, her expression grim and focused.

Siobhan stood back, her own wand lowered but still gripped tightly. She tried to keep from staring at Renaldo's eyes and tongue. *'Aren't we supposed to close his eyes as a sign of respect to the dead?'* she wondered.

But perhaps Liza wasn't bothered. The woman visually and then physically inspected Renaldo's neck, wrists, and ankles for any marks. Presumably, she was probing for any hidden injuries or signs of struggle. "No obvious wounds," Liza murmured. She leaned in closer, examining Renaldo's face. "No discoloration around the mouth or nose. No signs of strangulation."

"Signs of magic?" Siobhan asked softly.

Liza gave a single nod. She pointed to a polished wooden pipe that had fallen to the ground, spilling its ashy contents over the rug. "I could cast a diagnostic spell, but I'm pretty sure that's a combination of dreamwort, ghost flower—also known as elcan iris—and cat's cough."

Siobhan recognized two of the herbs Liza mentioned. Cat's cough, notorious for its addictive properties and the way it deepened one's voice with prolonged use, and elcan iris, a plant known for its bloodthirsty nature and soporific pollen. Also addictive. *'What was Renaldo doing with those?'* Aloud, she asked, "Dreamwort?"

"Dreamwort is a psychoactive," Liza added, her tone matter of fact. "Though that might not be the official name for it."

That explained why Siobhan was unfamiliar with it. She had kept far away from anything that could make her lose control of her mind, her body, and especially her dreams.

Liza leaned closer to Renaldo's face, pulling up his lip to examine his teeth. "He drank a potion, too. Recently."

Siobhan's gaze swept the room, searching for clues. As Liza moved aside, Siobhan noticed the thick lines of a Circle peeking out from beneath the intricately patterned throw rug that covered most of the floor. A spell array had been painted on the floor beneath. Siobhan moved to lift up the rug, but then noticed the small carved bear figurine that had been placed near the wall, just inside the bounds of the outer Circle and inside a much smaller component Circle.

"A magical...fetish?" she asked, pointing it out to Liza. She thought that was the right term for it, though they were rare in modern sorcery.

Along the other walls were three more components. What appeared to be a tiny bone wind chime, a finely woven cord made from human hair—'*Renaldo's own?*'—and a small bowl of what looked like dirty salt, certainly not fit for human consumption. '*Could it be dehydrated directly from the Charybdis Gulf?*'

Careful not to disturb anything, Siobhan and Liza worked together to lift the rug far enough that they could get a better look at the spell array without unduly disturbing the contents of the room.

The symbol inside was a cross—a tetragram—meant for transmogrification, focused on stability, foundation, strength, and authority.

Liza knelt to examine the array more closely. Siobhan understood the glyphs, which seemed to be about dreams, barriers, and protections, but their significance in this context eluded her. '*Is she looking for breaks in the Circle? Or some other flaw?*'

Liza stood abruptly, her eyes sweeping the room one last time. "We're leaving," she announced, her tone brooking no argument.

Siobhan blinked in surprise. She had expected more from Liza—a thorough investigation, perhaps, or some arcane ritual to uncover hidden truths. But as Siobhan stood there, staring at Renaldo's lifeless form, she found herself at a loss. The room was beginning to smell. As corpses do, this one had released its waste on death.

Without waiting for a response, Liza strode back outside.

Siobhan hurried to follow, her thoughts whirling but never quite landing on anything solid, like falling leaves caught in a twister.

Rather than return the way they had come, they walked through the back alley and exited onto the next street over. Liza had tucked most of her wand up her sleeve, but her fingers were curled around the tip.

The pair covered significant ground at a rapid clip. Though Siobhan could tell that Liza's tension remained beneath the surface, and noticed that she was searching for potential threats in dark corners and on the edges of roofs, outwardly the woman's posture had lost all hint of paranoia. Finally, after some unknown criteria had been met, Liza hailed a covered carriage.

Within the shaded interior, Siobhan hesitated, then asked the question that had been burning in her mind. "How...how did Renaldo die? What killed him?" She kept her voice low, just in case the driver might be able to overhear them past the sounds of the street and the carriage itself.

Liza's jaw clenched. "He was walking in the spirit realm," she said tersely, offering no further explanation.

Siobhan noted the worry lines etched deep around Liza's eyes and mouth. There was more to her distress than just the shaman's death. '*What will this mean for Liza? Does she know something I don't?*'

As the silence stretched on, Siobhan's mind began to wander down darker paths. '*Could the Red Guard have assassinated Renaldo?*' She had no evidence to support such a theory, but after everything she'd learned about the hidden workings of the world, she couldn't help but feel a twinge of paranoia.

She thought back to the scene they'd left behind—the spell array, the magical fetishes, the herbs. It all pointed to some kind of shamanic ritual gone wrong, but was that the whole story? Sometimes, she felt like everything she thought she'd known was only a fragile veneer over the much darker, more complex truth. And perhaps she was getting too used to her reputation and experiencing delusions of grandeur, but the timing of Renaldo's death seemed notably coincidental. Of course, she also knew that tragedy didn't have to come with any justification. That was life.

Siobhan hesitated, her hand hovering uncertainly above Liza's. Without meeting the older woman's eyes, she reached out and grasped Liza's fingers. Liza stiffened, her initial instinct to pull away evident in the tension of her muscles. But after a moment, her grip softened, and she squeezed Siobhan's hand gently.

"You're a good child," Liza murmured, her voice barely audible over the clatter of hooves.

The unexpected tenderness in Liza's tone made Siobhan's chest tighten. She swallowed hard, fighting back the sudden urge to cry. *'I'm not a child,'* she wanted to protest, but the words died on her lips.

As the carriage rattled on through the crowded streets, Siobhan felt Liza's tension gradually ebb away. The older woman took a deep breath, her shoulders relaxing slightly.

"Renaldo died of natural causes," Liza said at last, her voice low and controlled. "Will-strain, it looked like." She let out a soft, humorless chuckle. "Shamanry is dangerous, and Renaldo was always a little too *adventurous.*"

'Will-strain.' The words echoed in Siobhan's mind in a chilling tone. She didn't know why it surprised her to see the effects of magic played out once more. Really, it was much more likely than an assassination. Being a thaumaturge was like being a hunter who kept a slavering, hungry wolf at their bedside.

"There's no need for you to worry," Liza continued, her tone growing firmer. "But you shouldn't give any hint of being involved with Renaldo. That could lead to interest in you, and under any investigation, the Amelia identity will fall apart." She paused, her grip on Siobhan's hand tightening momentarily. "You should lay low for a while."

The carriage slowed, and Liza gently disentangled her hand from Siobhan's. "This is where we part ways," she said, gesturing to the door.

Siobhan alighted onto the sun-warmed pavement, the sweltering air enclosing her in an unwelcome embrace. As the carriage pulled away, she found herself rooted to the spot, a sense of weightlessness washing over her.

Siobhan shook herself from her daze. She couldn't afford to stand still, exposed and vulnerable. In the shadow of an alley with no windows, she tied up her curled hair and put on a wig. She was becoming more practiced and efficient with the elaborate disguises. As a child, she might have been excited with the thrill of secrecy. As an adult, it was an unpleasant hassle.

She set off on a meandering path through the city, her steps purposeful but unhurried. Every so often, she hailed a carriage, rode for a short distance before disembarking, and then continued on foot. The routine was familiar, almost comforting in its predictability. *'Just another day of paranoia,'* she thought wryly, grousing silently about the limitations of her transformation amulet.

'It's nice, but it would be even nicer if it had more built-in forms. Going through hours of disguising and re-disguising myself all the time is exhausting.' She sighed, imagining the convenience of being able to switch between multiple identities at will. Perhaps there would be a hint to it in one of Myrddin's journals. If so, she would definitely work on it once she had mastered the art of personal flight.

Finally satisfied that she had shaken any potential tails, Siobhan returned to her room at the Silk Door. Once there, though, she found herself unsure of what to do next. *'What's the most pressing issue?'* she asked herself, trying to impose some order on the chaos. *'Myrddin's journal. I should at least finish skimming through it before the meeting with Professor Lacer.'*

But it could still wait for a few hours, until she could move under cover of night. Or, perhaps more truthfully, until the prickling unease she had felt since discovering Renaldo's body lessened. Siobhan remained in her tiny closet room at the Silk Door, her mind split between two tasks. One part of her focused on the books Tanya had procured for her from the secret thaumaturge meetings, while the other part of her Will played increasingly difficult games of control with her shadow.

As she flipped through the pages of the first, a stray thought crossed her mind. *'If only I could split my eyes like I can my Will. I could read both books at once!'* Unfortunately, it wasn't humanly possible to unpair the eyes from one another. Not without magical modifications, at least.

The image of Renaldo's eyes, blood-burst and empty, flashed through her mind. She shuddered, immediately abandoning any desire to do such a thing to herself.

The first book, a general introduction to shamanry, tried to dispel the common assumption that shamans were only another type of diviner. The craft was far more complex, and more dangerous, than simple divination.

A shaman's true talent lay in using altered states of consciousness to interact with the spirit realm. They used various techniques to achieve these states, including meditation, various types of physical deprivation or pain, and plenty of mind-altering substances.

The book explained that shamans acted as intermediaries between the physical world and the spirit realm. They could communicate with "spirits," to seek guidance or channel their power for healing or other purposes. Siobhan found herself fascinated by the descriptions of spirit journeys, where shamans would leave their physical bodies to traverse the otherworldly landscape of the spirit realm.

One woman recounted traversing a shimmering forest where the trees whispered ancient secrets, their leaves made of starlight. Another told of soaring through endless skies filled with floating islands, each home to different spirit beings. A particularly vivid account described plunging into a bottomless ocean teeming with luminescent creatures that sang melodies of creation.

The book warned that such journeys were not without peril. Some shamans spoke of encountering malevolent entities that sought to trap or devour their essence. Others described becoming lost in labyrinths of their own fears and desires, struggling to find their way back to their physical bodies.

Shamans insisted that these were more than vivid dreams—that there was truth and knowledge to be found in the spirit realm, if one knew how to interpret it.

This sounded rather like something Ennis would say while running a scheme, and Siobhan remained deeply skeptical.

But it was a fact that spirits could temporarily possess a shaman's body in the physical world, lending their unique abilities or knowledge to the host. This possession, while potentially dangerous, allowed shamans to channel otherworldly powers for brief periods.

'*Otherworldly powers? What does that mean, exactly?*'

The book went on to give some distinctly disappointing examples: extraordinary powers of deduction, as if the shaman were merely a clever detective with a penchant for theatrics; hallucinations that miraculously led one to crucial clues in perplexing investigations; and even one spirit that allowed the shaman to "smell the truth," whatever that meant.

Siobhan scoffed, but quickly checked herself. '*There must be a reason Professor Lacer mentioned them,*' she thought. '*And probably an even more interesting reason the Red Guard restricts their practice.*' Hopefully, the latter was because of something more than just how dangerous it must be to cast magic while under the effects of a psychoactive drug. So, trying to be more open-minded, she continued.

Their magic could untangle the knots of confused or forgotten memories, coaxing clarity from the murky depths of the mind. Some, with the right training as mind-healers, could even heal mental wounds and soothe the lingering effects of trauma.

The craft, the author insisted, was "a bridge between the conscious and unconscious, the seen and unseen realms."

The spirit realm was a place of raw magical energy. It was described as a vast, ever-changing landscape filled with spirits of all kinds—from nature spirits to ancestral guides to powerful entities beyond human comprehension. Even the flora and fauna were types of spirits, and could not be relied upon to remain static. Navigating this realm was fraught with danger for the unprepared or unwary.

In the spirit realm, where the boundaries between thought and reality blurred, summoning was much more powerful. There, the summoner's Will could shape reality more directly, luring spirits with startling ease. Friendly spirits could be summoned for protection or guidance, and more powerful entities for aid in specific tasks.

Siobhan's discomfort grew as she read about induction rituals—a practice that seemed almost the inverse of summoning. Instead of calling something to the caster, induction rituals called the world to move the caster toward a goal. The magic reached into the caster's mind and the surrounding environment, nudging people and events to create "signs" that the caster could follow, and which would eventually make the long-term desired outcome more likely.

Siobhan's skin crawled. The idea of surrendering her agency, even to the ephemeral forces of her own magic, allowing it to subtly manipulate her actions and those around her, felt fundamentally wrong. This had to be at least partially transmogrification. *'How much of the common consciousness, that vast sea of shared human experience and belief, would leak into how the spell reacted?'*

She was untalented with divination. If she struggled with simple deductive spells, how could she hope to navigate the complex currents of an induction ritual? The potential for disaster seemed overwhelming.

While summoning frightened her—the idea of calling forth an entity with its own will and motives was daunting—at least she could fight against it if things went wrong. But induction... that felt like willingly stepping into quicksand—slowly sinking while unseen hands guided her descent.

Siobhan's back still prickled with unease as she reached the book's end, though the author attempted to leave off on a flowery note.

The second book's pages were worn and slightly discolored with age. Unlike the first, this one was clearly meant as a practical guide.

Unfortunately, it began with lists of omens and their potential meanings. She scoffed, remembering a study she'd recently read about the uselessness of omen interpretation. Even trained diviners barely managed to predict outcomes more accurately than untrained commoners guessing blindly.

As she skimmed through the pages, her skepticism grew. *'A black cat crossing your path means impending doom? How specific,'* she thought sarcastically. *'I'm sure that's never led to false panic.'*

Supposedly, forms within the spirit realm were more descriptive of intrinsic nature, but Siobhan felt that omens would still be entirely open to interpretation.

The book then delved into exercises for preparing to safely navigate the spirit realm. Siobhan's interest was piqued despite her skepticism. The techniques seemed sound enough. Several focused on mental discipline and visualization, such as imagining a sphere of white light surrounding oneself, or picturing complex geometric shapes rotating in three dimensions.

Others were exercises to increase awareness of one's body. These included methodically tensing and relaxing each muscle group, tracing the outline of one's body with the mind's eye, or learning to isolate and activate obscure muscles.

The book also delved into techniques for exploring and solidifying one's sense of "self" and strengthening the psyche, such as meditation on one's core beliefs and values, visualizing a mental landscape that represented different aspects of personality, and exercises to strengthen the barriers between conscious and subconscious thought.

The author's favorite method of preparation was to become lucid while dreaming, then ask some specific questions about oneself—calling on the guidance of the subconscious—and then interpret the "signs" that resulted. Some shamans used hallucinogens to do the same thing without the need to achieve lucidity in a dream. A dangerous shortcut, according to the author.

They moved on to exercises meant to help one realize when things were not as they should be—several of which Siobhan recognized as techniques for achieving lucidity in dreams, which had to be practiced while awake until they became habit. One such technique involved regularly checking the environment for inconsistencies or impossibilities, such as text that changed when looked at twice, or attempting to push one's finger through the palm of the opposite hand. None of them had ever worked for her.

And finally, methods to maintain one's mental stability and sense of self while fighting against the spirit realm's inherently corrosive effect. These ranged from simple mantras to be repeated under duress to more complex visualizations of anchors tethering one's consciousness to the physical realm. A tether made of one's own hair was one of a few components the author suggested could help in anchoring spells.

The importance of protection and grounding when working with the spirit realm could not be emphasized enough.

'It didn't save Renaldo,' Siobhan thought. '*Do these techniques actually work, or are they just fancy ways to fool yourself into believing you're protected?*'

But as she read further, a chill ran down her spine.

Accessing the spirit realm generally involved altered states of consciousness, with specific actions taken while lucid dreaming being one of the easiest entry points, if unreliable. Siobhan's hand unconsciously moved to press against her chest where her grandfather's medallion hung underneath her clothes. It was small comfort.

'What would happen if I tried to enter the spirit realm with this thing *inside me?'* The thought made her stomach churn. Will-strain was one thing, but the idea of losing control in a realm where thought could shape reality? With an Aberrant sealed inside her, waiting for any opportunity to break free? Siobhan shuddered.

As night fell, she tucked away her books, transformed back into her other body, and made her way to the attic apartment.

Once inside, she unlocked the warded chest that contained Myrddin's journal, though she left it inside the warded chest for a smidgen of extra protection. She picked up where she had left off last week, turning a small chunk of pages at a time so that she might have a better chance of skimming her way to the end before her Will gave out.

After abandoning the wing suit, Myrddin had apparently moved on to a more ambitious project. Sebastien traced a finger across the page as she took in the intricate designs for a flying balloon-carriage. The hollow metal frame resembled nothing so much as a fat shark or some kind of small whale.

Accompanying the sketches were notes on a propulsion spell that was actually quite simple, just a modified and incredibly powerful version of the gust spell.

As she delved deeper, she found a study on sky-kraken. Myrddin's notes were meticulous, detailing wing structures, hunting patterns, and defensive capabilities. At the bottom of one page, a hastily scrawled note caught her eye.

Do not attempt to create air-borne vehicles without stealth spells and heavy shielding. Artillery spells strongly recommended.

THE STUDY on sky-kraken took on new meaning, and Sebastien suppressed a snort. She was tempted to keep reading within this section, as her imagination quickly filled with other flying predators he might have encountered, or other notes he might have made about his attempt to fly the hollow whale, but she forced herself to skip farther forward.

The map that greeted her as the next pair of pages resolved looked… wrong. She peered at it for a while before finally realizing that it stretched beyond the limits of the known lands. The boundaries and topography were significantly different from what she had seen on maps while traveling with Ennis. Decent maps were expensive, though. Perhaps she had never seen a really good one.

The familiar regions were rendered with startling precision, far surpassing the crude sketches from earlier in the journal. Sebastien made a mental note to compare these maps with the most detailed ones available in the University library. She was curious to see how much had changed—or remained the same—in the thousand years since Myrddin's time.

As she turned to the next set of pages, her breath caught. It was a map again, but Myrddin had marked specific locations with X's and stars. Sebastien leaned closer, her eyes darting from mark to mark, committing each to memory. There was even one in the frozen tundra north of Silva Erde, far beyond where people had managed to explore. There were no labels, no explanations for why these spots held significance. '*What did you find in these places, Myrddin?*' she wondered, her mind spinning with possibilities.

Sebastien forced herself to turn the next set of pages before her Will grew too tired to continue. The page she turned to was titled at the top.

Attempt 21: Too chewy. Alkaline solution too strong?

BELOW WAS WRITTEN A HEAVILY annotated recipe for alkaline noodles. The whole page had been scribbled out, along with an angry note in large letters.

Wrong, all wrong!

THEN, with the turn of a page, she found herself looking down upon the final entry in Myrddin's journal. Sebastien's eyes widened as she recognized the familiar shape given form in ink lines.

'*Carnagore.*'

There weren't many details on Carnagore—presumably Myrddin had continued in one of his other journals—so Sebastien returned to the section detailing the personal flight spells.

This time, she read each page closely, making notes of what she needed to research to get closer to actually understanding. The idea of being able to fly around under her own magical power made her a little giddy. This knowledge wasn't entirely lost like some of Myrddin's other accomplishments, but it certainly wasn't the kind of thing the average thaumaturge would ever have access to. Perhaps Professor Lacer could fly at will? If so, she marveled at his restraint in acting so reserved and walking everywhere.

As the sun began to rise, Sebastien realized she had gone over the section several times and understood less than she initially thought. The complexities of the spells were far beyond her current level of comprehension. Determined to bridge the gap in her knowledge, she left and made her way to the University library.

Sebastien spent the day poring over texts on advanced aerodynamics, energy conversion principles, and the intricacies of gravity manipulation. The more she read, the more she realized how much she still had to learn. It was humbling, but also invigorating. Each new concept she grasped felt like a step closer to unlocking the secrets of flight.

With a big pile of books in her arms, she passed one group of particularly miserable-looking students. They stared at her. One of the girls hiccupped and began to cry silently.

Sebastien belatedly stamped out her huge grin and dulled the bright sparkle in her gaze. Looking away, she shuffled awkwardly back to the small table she had covered in research.

As Sunday evening approached, Sebastien reluctantly closed the books and prepared to leave. At midnight, she returned to the caves off the inner docks at the base of the white cliffs, once again as Siobhan.

Siobhan arrived at the designated cave, her footsteps echoing softly in the damp darkness but quickly fading into the distant sounds of water. The focused beam of her lensed lantern illuminated the rough-hewn walls, casting eerie shadows that seemed to dance and twist with each step. As she rounded a bend, she saw two figures waiting for her—Professor Lacer and Grandmaster Kiernan.

Both squinted, and she hurried to point the light of her lantern at the ground between them. With her other hand, she turned off her dowsing artifact. She wanted to know—to feel it—if a divination attempt was made against her.

Professor Lacer's face was an impassive mask, his eyes dark and unreadable in the dim light.

Kiernan, on the other hand, looked distinctly uncomfortable, his gaze darting between Siobhan and the professor with barely concealed anxiety.

"Miss Naught," Professor Lacer said, his voice low and controlled. "Follow me."

Without waiting for a response, he turned and began to lead the way into an upward-sloping tunnel.

Reminding herself to embody the persona of the Raven Queen in both thought and action, Siobhan fell into step behind Thaddeus, while Kiernan brought up the rear—despite the fact that she in no way trusted the man to watch her back.

After several minutes, the sound of the water faded away, leaving only their own footsteps, breath, and the rustle of their clothing, which all seemed offensively loud. Finally, they emerged into a small, circular chamber.

Thaddeus turned to face her, his expression inscrutable in the dim light of her lantern. "Miss Naught," he began, his voice low and measured, "I believe it's time we have a private discussion."

Siobhan tensed as she recognized the spark of anger in the depths of his gaze.

"Is this necessary?" Kiernan cut in, his voice adopting an overly friendly tone as he attempted to ease the mounting tension.

"Very," Thaddeus replied. He lifted a hand and cast his favorite sound-muffling spell. "Would you do the honors? It would not do to have him read our lips," he said, gesturing to her shadow.

Warily, Siobhan created a dome of darkness around the two of them, which soaked up any reflected light from her lantern.

Thaddeus's lips were pressed into a firm line of displeasure. "What are your intentions toward my apprentice?" he asked challengingly.

18

―――

THE LAND OF DREAMS

Siobhan
Month 8, Day 30, Monday 12:15 a.m.

"My intentions?" Siobhan repeated slowly, trying to buy time while she figured out how to answer Thaddeus's question. Her divination-diverting ward had not activated, meaning that he was not attempting to divine the truth. But she still preferred not to lie, if possible. He was astute, and might be able to tell even without the help of magic, but lying also wove a web that she could get tangled in someday.

Thaddeus stared at her silently, intangibly increasing the pressure to answer.

Siobhan looked to the side, refusing to be rushed. Finally, she said, "I mean Sebastien Siverling no harm. His existence is irreplaceably useful to me, and my intention is to do what it takes so that this continues to be so. If possible, I want all of Sebastien's hopes and dreams to come true."

Thaddeus scoffed. "A statement full of loopholes."

She looked back to Thaddeus and raised a challenging eyebrow.

"But I believe you mean your words, in essence," he conceded, relaxing. "I already know that he has been allowing you to access Myrddin's journals." He gave her a judgmental, unhappy look, but didn't try to forbid her from meeting Sebastien or using his identity to get past Myrddin's wards. "Are you and he...related? How is it that Sebastien came to be recognized by Myrddin's magic?"

Siobhan blinked in surprise, then suppressed a grimace. How was it that Thaddeus always managed to ask the most inconvenient questions? "Related? Well...I suppose you could say that, though the truth is far from the traditional meaning of that word. I do not know the exact mechanism for how Myrddin's journal recognizes him, or even *why*, exactly, it does so."

Thaddeus's gaze flicked away for half a second, an uncharacteristic flash of shyness twisting his features. "So you aren't...his mother? Or great, great... ancestor of some kind?"

Siobhan's eyes grew wide. *'How would that even be possible? We're the same age!'* she screamed internally. She pressed her lips together in a displeased line. "No."

"Will you tell me how you are related? And how it connects to Myrddin?"

"No," Siobhan repeated. Siobhan dropped the dome of darkness, revealing the dimly lit tunnel once more.

Following suit, Thaddeus did the same with his sound-muffling spell.

Kiernan's eyes, their corners pinched and wrinkled with agitation, darted between her and Thaddeus. He opened his mouth to question them but then closed it again. When neither of them volunteered any explanation, he grunted his displeasure to himself and rubbed his bald pate, missing the confidence and joviality he showed in front of University students. "Are we ready to continue? Myrddin's journals have been waiting to be read for over a thousand years now."

"I doubt Myrddin would mind," Siobhan said, waving for Thaddeus to take the lead once more.

Contrary to Kiernan's prior impatience and unease, the man dredged up some courage and announced, "We require a vow of secrecy, and some assurances of your good intent before we reveal the book."

This was not surprising, but they had gotten so far without bringing it up that Siobhan had hoped they would just forget. "Is my word not enough?"

Kiernan didn't back down. "No one's word would be enough with something this valuable. Not even my own."

Siobhan looked at Thaddeus. He nodded silently, and she assumed that he had already taken vows of his own. "Fine, then," she said. "Let us discuss the terms."

"In private," Kiernan rebutted, motioning upward.

They continued through the winding white cliff tunnels and occasional caves, climbing steadily upward until her legs burned despite all of the physical exercise she had been getting recently. Eventually, they reached familiar halls cut from the stone, and Kiernan opened a door to a small room, empty except for a few pieces of parchment and a complex spell array.

Kiernan handed her one of the pieces of parchment, which was already filled with the terms of the vow they hoped she would agree to.

The skin between Siobhan's eyebrows wrinkled as she read. The terms weren't as bad as they could have been. They were much more agreeable and less open to abuse than what she'd agreed to for that initial loan from the Verdant Stag, which was ironic. But with what she knew now, she still wouldn't accept some of the more blanket statements.

Approximately an hour of arguing with Kiernan followed. Despite the man's obvious discomfort with her, he didn't back down easily or let her dictate the terms with impunity.

In the end, she couldn't avoid a vow of general secrecy about what she might learn in Myrddin's journals, as well as an add-on clause that covered *conditional* pacifism while actively working on the project. Neither of them were quite happy with the final outcome, which Siobhan decided meant that it was a pretty even compromise.

As they left the small room, each with a copy of the agreement, Thaddeus raised an eyebrow at her peevish frown. "You really are bound to your word?"

Siobhan stared at him, since this had nothing to do with honesty and everything to do with magical compulsion. *'But am I really bound?'* she wondered suddenly. *'Perhaps, like the vow of secrecy I made to the Red Guard, the name I did it under could have a strong effect. Siobhan Naught might not be able to talk about what she learns from Myrddin's journals, but perhaps Sebastien Siverling can.'*

And if it were that easy, there were certainly other ways to wriggle out of vows. As evidence, the danger of making a familiar contract with an unwilling being.

Her frown eased. "I like to do what I said I would do, whether I am forcibly bound to my word or not." To herself, she added that this was only true with those she did not consider enemies. There were times when a lie was necessary. Still, she wouldn't go spreading Myrddin's secrets around like a farmer sowing wheat.

Siobhan and Kiernan followed Thaddeus to the small, warded room that held three of Myrddin's other journals.

She slowed as she was forced to push through the magical resistance around the doorway. Finally, she slipped past as if the barrier were a thick, invisible soap bubble that snapped back into place behind her.

Kiernan let out a strangled sound from behind her.

She turned, looking for whatever danger had surprised him, but found him looking back and forth between Siobhan and the threshold, his eyes wide with awe.

He pushed through the doorway himself, and as soon as Thaddeus met his gaze, pointed urgently and silently to the doorway.

"What is wrong? Has an intruder disturbed your wards?" Siobhan guessed.

Kiernan gave her a strange look that was half-scornful, half-disgruntled, and moved to examine the warding spell array around the doorway with intense scrutiny.

Thaddeus let slip a tiny smirk.

When neither of them explained what was going on, Siobhan realized that there was some other issue with the wards. She tried to see if there were any changes from the last time she had been here, as Sebastien. Even her memory wasn't perfect, especially with information she hadn't been paying attention to, and she wasn't able to tell if the wards had been tampered with or updated.

But she did remember that last time, Thaddeus had told her to "come in" just as she was about to pass the threshold. Was this one of those wards that required any strangers to be invited?

She looked at Thaddeus, but he didn't seem to be worried or suspicious. So Siobhan just cleared her throat and pretended everything was normal. *'Of course the Raven Queen can bypass wards. That fits with my persona, right?'*

Inside, the room looked exactly as Siobhan remembered from her last visit. A smaller circle of ever-burning dark red flame surrounded a white pedestal made of what she suspected to be pure salt. Atop the pedestal lay the three books, their leather covers unmarked by age or use. Siobhan kept her expression neutral, careful not to show any excessive interest in the books or admiration for the complex wards protecting them.

After a short while, Kiernan gave up on his examination.

"If you will spoof the correct identity, I will handle the rest," Siobhan said, gesturing imperiously.

Kiernan and Thaddeus each produced one half of a plate-like artifact—an exquisite creation of shimmering opal, gold, and ruby, with several small encapsulated and hidden components under opaque domes around its edges. Carefully, they notched both halves together into a single, seamless Circle, then lifted one of the books and placed it beneath.

Siobhan approached the pedestal. She felt the weight of Myrddin's legacy pressing down on her but refused to let it show. Instead, she focused on the task at hand, her mind already racing with possibilities about what knowledge these ancient tomes might contain.

Thaddeus stood on one side and Kiernan the other, both men staring at her with almost palpable eagerness.

"I am not as powerful or accomplished as Myrddin," she warned. "Accessing the contents of his journals is difficult, and can quickly push my Will to its limits. I will not be able to get through every page. I recommend we start by checking the first page of all three, to see if Myrddin left any notes. After that, I can clarify two dozen pages at most before my Will gives out, after which I will require a week or more to recover."

Professor Lacer frowned. "Will-strain?"

"Not exactly," she said, "though that could happen if I am not careful." Really, the requirement for such a long time between sessions was only meant to keep them from trapping her there for days on end when she really needed to be Sebastien.

"Do not risk damaging yourself," he warned, in a tone that reminded her of the way he spoke to her in her other body.

Siobhan smiled with delight.

"Only two dozen pages?" Kiernan complained, taking out a handkerchief and wiping some sweat off of his neck. "But each journal has a couple hundred, at least. How long will it take us to get through them, at that rate?"

"Perhaps we can spread those pages out to get a general idea of the contents covered, and then return to focus on anything that the History Department finds particularly interesting," Siobhan said, suggesting the exact same tactic she had employed on her stolen journal.

Kiernan was reluctantly appeased, and so Siobhan took a moment to center herself. Once ready, she dropped her shadow-familiar spell and bent the entirety of her Will toward entering the key to Myrddin's journal.

She slipped up halfway through and had to start over from the beginning, which only heightened the obvious tension felt by her companions. Finally, however, the glyphs stopped shifting and the contents resolved into clarity.

Kiernan couldn't restrain a reverent gasp, sidling closer until his arm pressed against Siobhan's.

She gave him a single hard look, and he retreated.

This journal did not have any special note in the beginning, as hers did. Flipping the page revealed an entire spread of gibberish equations. Siobhan stared at them impassively, unable to be impressed with what she didn't understand at all. She also didn't try too hard, as almost all of her concentration was in use simply maintaining the journal's clarity.

Kiernan squinted. "Oh, I cannot see clearly from this distance. The magic is interfering. I suppose to keep anyone from spying from afar. Can you read it, Thaddeus? Did she succeed?"

Thaddeus had stepped closer, too, looming barely an inch behind Siobhan on her left side. He was tall enough to easily read over her shoulder. "They are equations for a space-related spell," he said.

Siobhan was impressed that he was able to deduce that from the gibberish on the page, until she saw a small drawing of what looked to be a piece of paper folded in half, along with a legible note from Myrddin.

If I could just fold it and punch a hole, I could travel great distances almost instantly.

· · ·

"TELEPORTATION, IT SEEMS LIKE," she said softly.

Kiernan's eyes grew wide, and he inched slightly closer. "A working teleportation spell? How many thaums?"

Thaddeus shook his head. "It doesn't say."

"And it might not be 'working,'" Siobhan added. "This is only the one page. Myrddin could very well have abandoned development halfway through if he had too much trouble."

Kiernan looked as if he wanted to argue but restrained himself. "You would know best," he muttered.

Thaddeus moved over to the wall and opened a hidden compartment there, from which he pulled a dozen sheets of parchment. "Can you hold it?" he asked.

"Not indefinitely. But long enough for you to transcribe the page. However, it will reduce the number of pages we can access later."

Professor Lacer and Grandmaster Kiernan shared a long look. Finally, Kiernan sighed. "Skip it for now. We need to find any information on celerium. Barring that, some other immediately useful spell."

Siobhan carefully let her Will loose, and the journal slipped back into true incomprehensibility. The next journal was again missing any introductory note, and was perhaps even more unfathomable.

"I believe it has something to do with divination, based on the fact that it uses both a pentagram and a nonagon sub-array and no numerological symbol in the main array, but I've never seen anything quite like it," Thaddeus said.

The third journal started with plans for Carnagore, only slightly more advanced than what Siobhan's ended with. "I could be wrong, as Myrddin was rather flighty and liked to jump around between projects, but I believe this one is chronologically first," she said, basing that off of little more than that her journal had a prefacing note, as well as the fact that she had been able to vaguely understand several of the projects in her own entry, while the ones in these other two entries were ridiculously beyond her.

"The one with the space-bending spell," Kiernan said, casting his vote immediately. "Think how useful it could be to teleport."

"How many thaums do you imagine it takes to teleport?" Thaddeus asked conversationally.

Kiernan deflated. "We could cast it…as a group?"

"Only if you are willing to bring in the world's top experts in mathematics and natural science," Thaddeus said. "I suggest we get an overview from beginning to end, and hope that Myrddin's ideas build upon each other."

"They often do, in my experience," Siobhan offered. "I agree with Thaddeus."

And so Thaddeus carefully counted out ten pages without lifting them, then used the edge of his thumbnail to turn them all. The surface flashed with another two glyphs, but Siobhan easily matched them both with her Will, and the contents remained legible.

A half-dozen intricate diagrams spread across the pages.

Myrddin was an impressive artist, and had penned several close-up examinations and dissections of the muscular structure of a horse, and an annotation about their strength-to-weight ratio. A note rested at the bottom of the second page. As always, Siobhan mentally translated the archaic spellings and word choices into something more modern.

Next on the list: unicorn, peryton, moonspring hare, dryad, quicksilver serpent, troll, sky-kraken, dragon. Surely, that will be enough.

"Fascinating," Thaddeus said. "I imagine he hoped to combine the best properties of each into Carnagore. It would be impossible with a flesh and blood being, but with a creature made of metal…"

Obviously, Myrddin had succeeded in some capacity, as the results spoke for themselves.

The next set of pages delved into joints and tendons, interspersed with drawings of manually constructed versions, some of which were in strange shapes that Siobhan had never seen before and which would allow an unprecedented, disturbing range of motion.

After the next jump of ten pages, the focus shifted to an exploration of metal qualities. Myrddin's meticulous charts compared the tensile strength, malleability, and magical conductivity of various metals. Siobhan noticed a small doodle of a frustrated face next to a failed experiment with mithril, which was the catch-all name for an alchemically modified metal that had over a dozen different formulations depending on the time period and thaumaturge who created it. Nowadays, any respectable metal-focused alchemist used more specific names for their formulations.

This exploration soon diverged into extensive work testing various alloys, both of metals and magical components. Thaddeus raised an eyebrow at a particularly audacious combination. "He attempted to alloy a charcoal reduction of wolframite with phoenix ash? Bold."

Siobhan had no idea what that meant, so she nodded noncommittally.

Finally, they reached a section detailing Myrddin's efforts to create an alchemical metal. The pages were filled with complex alchemical formulas and ritual diagrams, all aimed at producing a "super metal" with seemingly impossible properties. Siobhan chuckled as she read Myrddin's latest note.

> Success! The metal resists heat and damage like dragon-scale, conducts magic like silver, and maintains flexibility like a yew sapling. Now, I just have to repeat this process sixty-three more times…
>
> Hmm.
>
> I realize now that I may have failed to plan ahead. I need a way to make bigger batches.

GRANDMASTER KIERNAN HAD APPARENTLY GROWN weary of squinting to try and make out the contents while remaining a safe distance from Siobhan. Instead, he had taken to pacing back and forth, casting curious, burning glances at them.

Both Thaddeus and Siobhan ignored him.

The next section was more of the same, except with detailed examinations of various animal feet, hooves, and paws.

Following this was a propulsion spell designed to improve the grip and thrust of hooves. This ingenuity had eventually led to Carnagore's speed and legendary sure-footedness.

The next pages revealed a diversion into developing a compulsion spell aimed at keeping living beings away from a particular area. Myrddin had added several layers of modification on top of the standard compulsion, implanting false memories of finding that the location did not hold what the person hoped to find, as well as triggering an adaptable hallucination that would discourage them from coming back.

Thaddeus read closely, nodding silently to himself.

"We need this," Kiernan announced immediately.

Siobhan imagined that it would be helpful to keep the Crowns from finding the Architects of Khronos. She, too, could think of more than a few personal uses for such spells, but something held her back from full enthusiasm. Was it right to manipulate someone's mind—the source of their personality—like that? It felt like true blood magic, cruel and vile in a way that much of the magic labeled as blood magic wasn't. Pretending that it didn't hurt the victim was only self-deception to avoid guilt. This was not a spell she could cast on anyone she wouldn't also attack with a hemorrhaging curse.

The next set of pages held notes on Myrddin's tests using something called "infrasound" to enhance the aversion compulsions. The notes detailed experiments with the sound frequency as well as the vibrational intensity required for humans to pick up the feeling that "something was wrong."

However, it was the next section that truly captured Siobhan's attention. Myrddin had written about the Black Wastes, noting how they, too, created a natural, deeply instinctual aversion in living beings.

The Black Wastes are troubling. Unlike other environmental taints, which I would expect to slowly improve over time, these seem to persist. I must map out their borders and come up with severity metrics that I can use to calculate whether they are changing at all.

SIOBHAN FELT a chill run down her spine, remembering the effects of the Black Wastes on the Archaeologist—once Edgar—whom she had met at the Retreat at Willowdale. That was what the Black Wastes had done to the man with the strongest mental resistance; the rest of his party were either dead or completely insane.

'*Except, perhaps, for Oliver's thief. Did she get away before they could do irreparable damage?*'

These journals had been recovered from a hermitage within the Black Wastes, which meant that at some point, Myrddin had decided to live there. '*What could have driven him to such a decision? What did he discover about the nature of that magic-warped land? And did it have anything to do with the brillig?*'

It was said that now-extinct species were the cause of the Black Wastes, but Professor Lacer also once mentioned that they were rumored to have been able to split their Wills. Like Myrddin. And like her.

She met Thaddeus's gaze and saw the knowledge of the implications in his eyes. This could be significant. Myrddin's research into the Black Wastes might hold answers to questions they hadn't even thought to ask.

Siobhan wanted to keep reading here, but Thaddeus turned to the next section. Luckily, or perhaps ominously, Myrddin was still focused on the Black Wastes. Whatever the outcome of his desire to map and measure them, his worries had not been satisfied. The left page was filled with a disturbing sketch of a twisted landscape. The right page held a single note.

Before, I would have simply done a massive divination with a heptagram, reaching out to the world itself for answers. All of the data is there, to be sure, and accessible one way or another. But now, that seems...dangerous. Some things can not only be harmful to <u>know</u>, but harmful to access. Knowledge can be poked and prodded like an open wound.

SIOBHAN HAD no idea what Myrddin might be referencing, but her own thoughts immediately jumped to the thing sealed in her mind. The thing that wanted her so badly to remember it. To *know* it. There was a reason Grandfather had made her forget.

After the next skip, Myrddin was planning an "expedition." Except the preparations did not include travel gear, arrangements to handle magical beasts, or any maps.

> I suspect that somewhere in the land of dreams exists an analogue for the Black Wastes. With the help of a friendly spirit, I may be able to find it in only a few days of exploration. I must prepare armor of magic and thought. It will surely be a dangerous trip. Still, it could be important to the Work.

THE REMAINDER of the page was covered in what looked like a coffee—or perhaps potion—spill, and Myrddin had not bothered to write over the dark stain.

Siobhan re-read Myrddin's note several times. 'The land of dreams… Is that what Myrddin called the spirit realm?' It could have been a simple, innocent turn of phrase, but something about it tickled in the back of Siobhan's mind. Unfortunately, she didn't have the spare brainpower to really dig into the thought.

Before Thaddeus could reach for the next set of pages, Siobhan turned one. She wanted to see what came of this. Who knew how long it would be until she could get answers, if they skipped past them now?

> I found it. I did not enter, because I had not prepared enough protections and I suspected my mind would be ripped apart. At this point in my life, I do not have enough sanity left to spare!

SIOBHAN WONDERED if that was supposed to be a dark joke, or if something had actually damaged Myrddin's mental health. Maybe too many expeditions into the spirit realm?

After that, the journal moved on to a recipe for spiced hot chocolate that Myrddin rated, "Delicious!"

'But where are the notes about his trip? Aren't explorers supposed to catalogue their adventures? He didn't even explain what exactly "it" was that he found!' Siobhan complained silently.

Only, in the margin at the bottom of the page, below the recipe, Myrddin had written another note in an unusually messy scrawl.

I find myself worrying about the scar that isn't healing.

SOMEHOW, she knew he wasn't talking about a physical wound.

19

A SONG OF CHAOS AND ETERNAL NIGHT

Siobhan
Month 8, Day 30, Monday 2:30 a.m.

Siobhan's left temple pulsed with the beginning of a headache. She released her Will's hold on the glyphs, allowing Myrddin's journal to revert into Delphic gibberish. She let out a soft sigh, her shoulders sagging slightly as the strain of maintaining her focus lifted. The sudden loss of meaning left her feeling oddly hollow. "I must take a break," she announced, rubbing her temples. "My Will needs time to recover."

Thaddeus nodded. "Of course. How long do you require?"

Siobhan considered for a moment. Normally, she would have cast the light-refinement spell to expedite her recovery, but as Siobhan, she shouldn't know that spell. Instead, she saw an opportunity to pursue her own interests. "Two to three hours should suffice. I would like to spend that time accessing the restricted archives, as was promised me. It would be a shame to waste this opportunity while I am here."

Kiernan's brow furrowed, his frustration evident. "But we've barely made it through one full journal," he complained, gesturing to the stack of untouched books. "Surely there must be a way to accelerate this process?"

Siobhan arched one eyebrow, a hint of challenge in her voice. "If you are dissatisfied with my pace, Grandmaster Kiernan, you are welcome to attempt splitting your Will yourself."

Kiernan's face reddened, but he remained silent.

Siobhan allowed herself a tiny, spiteful smirk.

Thaddeus ignored the byplay. "Your request is reasonable, and I have what you require." He pulled a faculty token out of his pants pocket and handed it to her. "I anticipated that you would be eager to seek after mysteries."

Her gaze rose to his, and she let out a small huff of amusement at the reference.

The token was made of surprisingly lightweight metal rather than wood or even stone, like most of the faculty tokens. It held the sky-kraken crest of the University but was much more finely detailed than her student token.

"We can return for one more session tonight before I reach my limit and need a longer break. Perhaps I can visit again in one week, assuming you will not be too busy in the aftermath of the exams and exhibitions. I hear grading homework is a grueling task."

Thaddeus and Kiernan exchanged glances, silently weighing the proposal. Finally, Thaddeus spoke. "That should be acceptable."

Kiernan deflated, running a hand over his bald head. "Very well. But we must make more progress soon. The potential knowledge contained in these journals is too valuable to dawdle."

'That potential knowledge is what keeps me so valuable.' Siobhan shifted, stretching her muscles and wriggling her toes. Her feet were beginning to ache from standing.

She and Kiernan followed Thaddeus through the winding tunnels of the white cliffs. Her steps quickened as they reached the area of warded and cryptically labeled doors that signified the restricted archives.

"The wards will recognize your new faculty token as having the same level of access as Archmage Zard," Thaddeus explained. "However, they will record a completely null entry in their records. Someone would need to purposely look for such an entry to find it, and even then, it would not reveal *who* entered." He paused, his expression growing serious. "But be warned—you must avoid being inside when Archmage Zard himself tries to enter. That might confuse the wards and give someone a clue to start investigating."

Siobhan squinted. "Am I to keep tabs on your Archmage, then?"

"Given that the man has not used the archives outside the hours of noon to five for the last thirty years, you should be safe so long as you limit yourself to nighttime visitation."

"That is acceptable."

Once again, Thaddeus led the way up through the winding tunnels of the white cliffs. As they walked, he explained that while she was free to use the library's catalogue, much of the restricted archives' content—especially the most sensitive documents—were unindexed.

"I can still make use of the catalogue. I may have other methods to find the unindexed material," she said.

Siobhan looked around as she stepped up through the metal doors that separated the restricted archives from the rest of the library. It was strange and eerie to be there in the dead of night, and as Siobhan rather than Sebastien. This body did not feel like it belonged.

Siobhan ignored the sensation and set to work, entering a catalogue request for any restricted texts with references to the Black Wastes. The artifact returned a long list, from which she selected the most promising.

"Please collect these documents for me," she said, handing a short list to both Kiernan and Thaddeus.

Thaddeus sighed, his exasperation evident as he reluctantly tucked the flimsy paper note into the pocket over his chest. He gestured for Kiernan to follow, despite the grandmaster's protests.

"This is highly irregular," Kiernan muttered, his voice tinged with unease. "We shouldn't be here at all, let alone fetching documents for... for..."

"For the Raven Queen?" Thaddeus supplied dryly. "Come now, Grandmaster. We are already neck-deep in this mess. A few more steps will not drown us."

"But we're leaving her alone! Without supervision!" Kiernan hissed, even as he walked back down the short stairwell to the lower levels.

"Oh, yes. Very serious. Especially since there is no way she could make her way around the University grounds without our supervision or consent," Thaddeus replied sarcastically. "Do you think you could stop her?"

Kiernan had no response to that.

The two men disappeared into the depths of the restricted archives, their footsteps echoing in the quiet space. As they vanished from sight, Thaddeus's low voice drifted back. "And do try not to look so terrified, Kiernan. It is unbecoming of a man in your position."

As soon as they were out of sight, Siobhan made her way to a room in which, she had noted from the catalogue, several promising titles were held. The metal identity token had no trouble getting her past the doorway. Since her new bag didn't have her favorite slate folding table, she pulled out a piece of seaweed paper and drew out a simplified, minimalist version of the keyword-searching spell that Damien had found and adapted for his newspaper research project.

Siobhan palmed a beast core, channeled through the ring on her hand, and held up the piece of paper to the often-unlabeled texts sitting on the upper left edge of a bookcase. Working quickly, she scanned that shelf, and then the next, searching for a handful of words related to the Black Wastes. The small output circle occasionally flickered as it encountered a match.

By the time Thaddeus and Kiernan returned, their arms laden with various scrolls, books, and even a couple of metal tablets, Siobhan had discovered two additional volumes that were not indexed in the catalogue, as well as the ones that had been. She had already tucked the spell array back into her bag and was sitting with the books at the room's only table.

The men placed their haul down on the table. Then, to her surprise, Thaddeus took the seat beside her and began to organize everything so it was within easy reach for both of them.

Siobhan and Thaddeus worked in silence, only speaking when they stumbled upon something noteworthy. Kiernan, yawning, pulled out a book of old poetry from the stack to occupy himself.

After a while, he perked up. "Oh, this one is my favorite. 'A Song of Chaos and Eternal Night.'"

Even Siobhan knew of that poem, having heard bits and pieces from wandering entertainers when she was young.

"It's written from the perspective of a man exiled to the Black Wastes for betraying his king," Kiernan said.

Without prompting, he began to recite the verses, his voice low and somber. The poem painted a vivid picture of the Black Wastes' horrors—a place where reality twisted and warped, where the very air seemed to corrode one's sanity. The exiled man's descent into madness was chronicled in chilling detail, each stanza simultaneously more depressing and more defiant than the last. The man never returned from his exile.

The poem ended as such:

"IN THIS REALM of twisted night,
    Where chaos reigns supreme,
    I stand, defiant in my plight,
    Against this waking dream.

THE LAND MAY SHIFT beneath my feet,
    And horrors fill the air,
    But still my mind refuses sleep,
    In depths of dark despair.

MY BATTERED MIND, though, will not break,
    Within this maelstrom of the soul,
    Through phantoms real and visions fake,
    My self-same being keeps its role.

BEYOND THIS WASTE of endless blight,

A world of order yet endures,
And though I'm lost from mortal sight,
My spirit now forever burns."

KIERNAN GAVE A SMALL, self-satisfied smile and looked to them for a reaction.

"Did the author have any personal experience with the Black Wastes?" Siobhan asked.

Kiernan blinked at her, then looked down at the pages as if they might hold the answer. "…No?"

Since the poem was useless, Siobhan returned to her reading.

Thaddeus was next to break the studious silence. "I have found some information on the brillig," he said, his tone carefully neutral as he pushed the book over to rest between them.

Siobhan eagerly leaned forward. The brillig had been so long dead—almost four thousand years—that it was difficult to find any reliable information about them.

The book, which had been written long enough after the fall of the brillig that its contents were questionable, described them as a strange-looking race, each individual unique in their appearance. Unlike the fey, who were often depicted as beautiful despite their otherworldly nature, the brillig were described as hideous and deformed. Their bodies seemed to defy natural laws, with limbs bent at impossible angles and features that shifted and changed like smoke.

Siobhan was quickly getting the feeling that the author had a bias against the brillig, as he seemed to be writing during a time of famine. He believed that if not for the Black Wastes, which were in the middle of once-fruitful land, the famine would never have happened.

With caustic derision and thinly veiled accusations, the text went on to describe the brillig's magical abilities. Each brillig was born a free-caster, but without the merit or control that would accompany such a feat among other species. They were able to perform magic without the need for a Circle or other focusing tools.

'*"Other focusing tools." What does that mean? Does he mean components, a Sacrifice, or…a Conduit? Did the brillig cast through their own flesh? And if every one of them was born a free-caster…*' She had been going to conclude that they must have been ridiculously powerful, but instead, she shuddered with the sudden realization of how horribly, *ridiculously* dangerous that would be. Could the brillig still break and become Aberrants?

Siobhan had known that they were supposedly capable of dual-casting, but the book provided more detail. It described how this ability made the brillig formidable opponents in magical combat, able to attack and defend with equal ferocity. Some accounts even claimed that the most powerful brillig could maintain dozens of spells at once, their minds compartmentalized into numerous discrete identities that contributed to their madness.

The same madness that made it necessary to eradicate them from the face of the planet.

The words sent a chill down her spine.

The book then returned to a discussion of how to mitigate the famine—through war on a neighboring country—and Siobhan set it aside.

They spent another hour skimming the texts on the table with little luck. Kiernan had set aside his book of poetry and was dozing in his chair. Together, Siobhan and Thaddeus had gone through most of the texts they had gathered, and she was beginning to despair of finding anything relevant until she grabbed an old leather case and shook out the scroll contained within. The scroll's author approached the subject of the Black Wastes with a more objective, investigative lens.

Everyone agreed that the Black Wastes were created by brillig magic—though Siobhan reminded herself that everyone agreeing did not make it true—but the exact mechanism of this feat remained a mystery. The author drew comparisons to similar, albeit temporary, effects observed when different types of magic, particularly more abstract effects, violently collided and mixed in chaotic ways.

After the attack on Knave Knoll, when she had set off her disintegration mine and accidentally exploded the rogue thaumaturge and his companions, she had witnessed something similar. The memory of the swirling fractals of unguided power, the warping of space and the screaming of the air, sent a chill down her spine. Yet, unlike the Black Wastes, those effects had been fleeting. That area of the canal had been repaired and was otherwise indistinguishable from the rest of the city.

The persistent nature of the Black Wastes was as puzzling to Siobhan as it had been to Myrddin and the author of this scroll.

The brillig's magic had somehow poisoned the land, but "poison" seemed an inadequate term for something that had endured for thousands of years. And in any case, the land was not dead. To the contrary, it was incredibly vital in its own way. It was as if they had fundamentally altered the very fabric of reality in those areas, creating a new type of land that defied the normal laws of nature.

The magic sustaining the Black Wastes would have required an immense and continuous source of power. Normal spells, even those cast by the most powerful thaumaturges, eventually ran out of energy, with the only exception being self-powering artifacts. But the Black Wastes showed no signs of weakening after millennia, and surely someone would have noticed if some kind of ultra-massive artifact was drawing power from somewhere to maintain the effects. It would be such an incredible amount of energy that she didn't see how it could have remained secret all this time.

Even if only out of greed, someone would want to fix the issue and reclaim the land.

'What if the brillig never went extinct, and they're somewhere inside, maintaining the effect?' That seemed somewhat plausible.

But a little worm of doubt continued to gnaw at the back of her mind. Where else did one see strange and impossible effects that seemed to never run out of power? Magic that had no reasonable limits?

'It's almost as if they turned the land itself into an Aberrant.'

Siobhan felt as though the world had shifted around her, leaving her just a few degrees off-center.

'No. Surely that can't be possible. At most, some powerful Aberrant is still living in the center, and the Red Guard is letting them stay because they are too powerful to deal with.'

But Siobhan remembered how often her preconceptions about magic—about society, about the world—had been shattered. Time and again, what she had believed to be common sense had turned out to be incomplete knowledge or outright lies. The more she learned about the hidden workings of the world, the more she understood how little she truly knew.

20

DOOMSDAY MACHINE

Siobhan
Month 8, Day 30, Monday 4:00 a.m.

Siobhan set aside her mind-reeling speculation about the cause of the Black Wastes and continued to read. The author of the scroll next delved into theories about why and how the Black Wastes affected the mind.

It was commonly known that the skin was a powerful and inherent barrier. That was why it was basically impossible to reach into someone's chest with magic and directly stop their heart.

The text postulated that there was a mental barrier that functioned similarly to the inherent barrier of the skin. Just as one's inherent ownership of their own body gave a powerful resistance to external magic, the scroll suggested that the inherent ownership of the mind—and the Will—protected against intangible external access.

The author believed that this mental barrier could be damaged and weakened, just as an enemy might cut and spill blood, thus opening a victim up to magical effects using that blood.

The symptoms that people showed on extended exposure to the Black Wastes would make quite a lot of sense if the nature of the land itself were infecting them. A human mind was never meant to be so malleable, so without identity.

Siobhan's thoughts jumped back to one of Thaddeus's letters, in which he had mentioned that agents of the Red Guard were attempting to create spirit world wards using mental walls and protective structures. He had thought these might allow a spirit-walking shaman to protect their mind against the erosion of the spirit realm.

'Myrddin found an analogue for the Black Wastes inside the spirit realm,' Siobhan mused. *'But how similar are they, otherwise?'* She had never experienced either, but the stories suggested they shared several characteristics.

"Have you ever walked within the spirit realm, Thaddeus?" she asked.

"Twice."

When she saw that he did not intend to explain further, she asked, "And the Black Wastes?"

He looked up from the page he had been skimming. "I have seen it from a distance, but never entered."

Siobhan nodded slowly. The first time she had met Renaldo, Liza's shaman friend, he had offered to "anchor" the Archaeologist during a visit to the Retreat at Willowdale. Siobhan did not know exactly what that meant, but it was something shamans did when walking within the spirit realm, wasn't it?

The author proposed that the mind's natural defenses were rooted in a person's sense of self, their identity, and their Will. It was this innate barrier that usually prevented external forces from directly manipulating one's thoughts or memories. Like spells that forcefully bypassed the physical barriers, there were even several known spells that bypassed the barrier of the mind. The easiest way to do so was with light, taken in through the eyes, or less easily, with sound through the ears.

The rest of the scroll was redacted.

Siobhan unrolled it to the end, finding only lines of black ink so inscrutable she couldn't even make out a depression or scratch formed by the author's pen tip against the paper.

Thaddeus glanced over. "It looks like someone along the way decided the University archives weren't secure enough for that information."

"The Red Guard?" she asked.

"Maybe."

"Is there any way to clarify what was written originally? Some sort of divination to track the way the paper's fibers were disturbed during the course of the writing?"

"Redaction spells are not so easily thwarted. There *is* no writing, any longer."

Siobhan pursed her lips with frustration. *'I suppose the Red Guard doesn't want even University faculty learning about a memory-erasing spell, or whatever the author was going to start talking about.'*

She would have liked to keep searching for more information about the Black Wastes, but her Will had recovered and the night was growing late.

Kiernan woke easily enough that she wondered if he had really been asleep, and after returning all of the texts to where they had come from, they began to make their way back down again.

Suddenly, Thaddeus halted, his eyes lighting up. "Ah, I almost forgot," he murmured, veering off into one of the side rooms.

Siobhan followed, curiosity piqued.

Thaddeus began rifling through a nearby stack of scrolls, his movements purposeful. "I want to find something for Sebastien," he explained, his voice tinged with an uncharacteristic warmth. "The boy is a genius with kinetic magic."

Siobhan had to suppress a jolt of shock and delight at such high praise from the usually stern professor, though she would never have expected a compliment for her *physical* prowess.

"Can't this wait?" Kiernan asked, dragging his hands down his face.

"It will not take long. I already know what I want, I just need to find it."

"A kinetic genius?" she asked. "Sebastien does not seem particularly athletic to me."

Thaddeus sent her an exasperated look. "I assure you, my apprentice is very talented. He gained competence with his first gesturan spell—and not a simple one—within *one week*. The amount of physical and mental precision required for such a feat, surely even you cannot scoff at."

Siobhan had thought the whole process was quite difficult. She had even wondered how someone without the ability to split their Will could ever manage to focus on everything at once. But she supposed that trying to ingrain the perfect movements, breath, and humming tone into muscle memory, while using all of one's higher-level thought processes to focus on casting the spell, might make things take longer. Apparently, much longer.

'*I'm a genius?*' She had told herself that before, of course. But mostly when she was giddy with the results of her hard work on some project, or when she was trying to reassure herself that she could handle the long and difficult path to becoming a powerful sorcerer. It wasn't as if she actually believed it. *Myrddin* was a genius.

Siobhan moved to one of the shelves and began to flip through a random book. The diagrams inside were immediately recognizable. '*This is a gesturan spell. Is this whole room gesturan spells?*'

She began to rifle through the shelves with intense excitement, only to realize that perhaps the Raven Queen shouldn't be so impressed with *anything*. She quickly tempered the outward signs of her enthusiasm.

Most everything was written in another language and beyond her comprehension. She wasn't sure how risky it might be to try to follow the diagrams without understanding the instructions. Her memory was good, but definitely not good enough to memorize multiple pages of instructions, write them out later, and get them translated.

Her eagerness was beginning to deflate when she found a small leather-bound journal that proved to be worth its weight in gold.

It was a simple primer with what might be considered the very simplest of spells, or the building blocks of more complex effects. It had a lot of pictures—and was probably meant for a child—and simple text. That text had already been translated by the original owner of the journal.

'*I can't check books out of the archives without leaving a record. Can I steal this?*' she wondered. She was hesitating over whether to consult with Thaddeus about the theft when he found whatever he was looking for.

He looked up and noticed her watching. "This sound spell should pair nicely with some light-based work I assigned recently. I am sourcing a restricted component to help him add some modifications to the latter."

"Oh?"

"The spell itself is legal. And who is to prove that any short-term memory loss was due to his harmless defensive magic?"

Siobhan blinked slowly. Suddenly, the way Professor Lacer had explained the spell to her made a lot more sense.

"Myrddin's beard," Kiernan muttered, rubbing at his eyes. "Why?"

"Sebastien...cannot modify someone's memory without this component, though? The spell itself is harmless?"

"He is a mostly normal human boy. He cannot induce memory loss without the help of components," Thaddeus said, exasperated. "Your expectations are unreasonable. Please lower your standards."

Siobhan wanted to protest that he had misunderstood her but let the matter drop.

"Oh. Did I misunderstand you? Do you think it is too reckless to give the boy such magic?"

"To the contrary," Siobhan replied, her mind whirling with the possible uses. How many times would she have been able to get out of a dangerous situation with such a spell? "It could be an invaluable tool. The more ways he has to protect himself, the better."

As Thaddeus tucked away the scroll, Siobhan made a snap decision. "I think I will do the same," she said, holding up the spell primer. "I will gift this to Sebastien, that is."

Thaddeus's eyes narrowed. "He is *my* apprentice."

Siobhan rolled her eyes in return. "I am not trying to *steal* him from you. I simply think he would find this useful, as I would have at his stage."

"Oh? Are you familiar with gesturan spellcasting yourself?" Thaddeus asked, relaxing.

"I can perform some, yes."

"How old did you say you were again?" Thaddeus asked, his tone deceptively casual.

She tilted her head to the side. "I have already answered that. I am only a couple of weeks older than the last time you asked." She stepped forward and pressed the primer into his hands with a smile. "You will have to give it to him on my behalf."

Thaddeus's gaze caught her own, and he stared down at her as if trying to read the thoughts behind her eyes. "It is only that a twenty-year-old free-caster who displays your level of power and precision, and has also mastered gesturan magic, seems…impossible."

Siobhan looked away as a wave of awkwardness washed over her. *'That is a very good point. Why didn't anyone consider this when they were coming up with the ridiculous myth of the Raven Queen?'* However, she didn't want to disabuse him of the rumors that in many ways had been protecting her, so she just hummed noncommittally.

Thaddeus's piercing gaze lingered on her, clearly noticing her evasion.

The silence stretched between them until she cleared her throat and gestured toward the doorway, where Kiernan jerked and looked away. "We have a task to complete, and I am sure Grandmaster Kiernan is waiting impatiently."

The dimly lit stone corridors seemed to stretch endlessly, the shadows cast from the overhead lights making the rough texture of the walls look like desolate mountains and valleys seen from many miles above.

Siobhan, Thaddeus, and Kiernan returned to the room containing Myrddin's journals. Despite the late hour, Siobhan found herself alert and focused, the vivifying effects of her freshly bound sleeper raven still coursing through her. As she accessed the journal once more, the glyphs yielded to her Will with surprising ease.

The next section revealed that Myrddin had moved past his interest in the Black Wastes and returned to his earlier work on aversion wards. A wry note caught Siobhan's attention:

Oops. What an embarrassing mistake!

SIOBHAN SNORTED WITH AMUSEMENT. Myrddin had apparently failed to make himself an exception to his own ward, likely resulting in being unable to return to the place he had warded, or at the very least some significant discomfort as the wards tried to influence him to leave and maybe even forget why.

As they continued, the journal shifted to space-affecting spell theory. Myrddin's meticulous notes began with standard expanded containers, a concept familiar to most thaumaturges. However, his exploration quickly progressed to more ambitious applications. Detailed diagrams illustrated the creation of expanded rooms, accompanied by complex equations that made Siobhan's head spin.

'*In this, at least, I do not have Myrddin's brilliance,*' she thought, as Thaddeus gasped at some novel approach to stabilizing and anchoring these expanded spaces. Apparently, Myrddin's method addressed several of the potential pitfalls: strange spatial anomalies, physical damage when traversing the expanded area, and the nauseating effects on the human mind as it picked up clues hinting at the true nature of any such warped zone.

The next pages delved into the compression of space for fast travel. Myrddin's excitement was palpable in his hurried scrawls and increasingly complex formulas. However, this enthusiasm was tempered by a series of cautionary notes. After that, a page was dedicated to an anti-seasickness potion.

A final note from Myrddin ended the journal.

Failure. I must declare fast travel via compressed space utterly impractical. Extensive research and investment into stabilization techniques would be necessary, as the current method induces severe nausea and bodily harm. My theory is that the living form—an intricate assembly of countless moving parts —is far too complex to maintain synchronization during these rapid spatial shifts. Even for someone as immensely wealthy and powerful as me, it is impractical.

THEY ALL KNEW which journal came next in the sequence—the one detailing Myrddin's attempts at space-folding for teleportation. However, Siobhan felt the weight of fatigue settling over her mind.

Final exams and exhibitions were set to begin in the morning, and she still needed to navigate the long process of safely leaving, transforming back into Sebastien, and returning to the University. She could already imagine the frantic energy that would permeate the campus in the early hours, as students engaged in last-minute preparations.

She would need to be back in her bed as Sebastien before then.

Kiernan's disappointment was palpable as he slumped in his chair. "Not even a hint about celerium production," he muttered, his voice tinged with frustration. "All this effort, and we're no closer to getting what we *truly* need."

Siobhan remained silent. When she had spoken with him a couple of weeks earlier, Oliver had agreed to let her examine his entry of Myrddin's journals. However, she would not be able to do so until he returned from his trip to Osham, made necessary by the strike team sent there by the Architects of Khronos.

Her gaze settled on Kiernan, studying him intently as she contemplated the internal dynamics of the Architects.

The group's recklessness troubled her. They were an association of revolutionaries, similar in some ways to the Verdant Stag, she supposed. But Oliver held all the authority within the Stags, and had a clear vision for the future and how he planned to achieve it.

She doubted the Architects were led so cleanly. Had Kiernan truly agreed to send a team to Osham, or was there a silent war being waged between influential members? The implications of such internal strife could be far-reaching and potentially dangerous.

As Siobhan's scrutiny lingered, Kiernan began to shift uneasily. He tried to meet her gaze, but his eyes kept sliding away. "Please do not misunderstand me, Queen of Ravens. I am not placing the fault at your doorstep. I was only...frustrated."

Siobhan realized she had been making the man uncomfortable, and he had thought she took offense at his complaint. She waved away his words. "It is fine."

That morning, just as the first rays of dawn began to creep over the horizon, she had become Sebastien once more and had finally succumbed to a last-minute attempt at a nap. She hoped to be as fresh as possible for the exams. Though Professor Lacer had not given her any ultimatums this term, it seemed at a minimum she should get better scores than she had on the first term's exams.

Her eyes had barely closed when a hand on her shoulder and the rattling of the ward-linked stone on her desk jolted her awake.

Damien stood over her, his face etched with worry and exhaustion.

"I need to talk to you," he whispered urgently. "Somewhere private."

Groggily, she turned off the intrusion alarm and sat up. "What is it?"

"It's my report," Damien said, his voice hoarse from lack of sleep. "On the research mission. I... I'm sure now. Well, I've been pretty sure for a while, actually. But I've just finished compiling all the data I have access to."

Sebastien realized her heart was pounding harder than it had any reason to. She threw her light blanket off and pulled on proper clothes.

Damien's eyes widened, and he spun to face away from her, then looked studiously out of the window while rubbing one of his ears awkwardly.

The usual classroom that they used for morning study group and planning sessions to overthrow certain members of the Thirteen Crowns was unavailable, having been transformed for the upcoming exhibitions. After a moment of hesitation, Sebastien led Damien to the second-floor storage room, a space that held memories of her clandestine magical practices.

It was as dusty as ever, and had actually been expanded somewhat to make room for stacked student desks and chairs cleared from other rooms in the Citadel.

As soon as they closed the door behind them, Sebastien cleared out an empty space on the floor and began setting up wards, her movements quick and practiced. Damien's evident concern prompted her to add extra layers of protection, drawing upon the knowledge she'd gained while studying how to safeguard her apartment.

Finally satisfied with their security, Sebastien turned to Damien. He reached into his bag and pulled out a thin binder, its contents a half-inch stack of high-quality paper.

Damien's hands trembled slightly as he opened the thin binder, revealing pages filled with meticulously organized data. Sebastien leaned in, her curiosity piqued by the intensity of Damien's expression.

"I've been tracking the Red Guard's magical feats." Damien stopped to cough violently, perhaps because of the dust or perhaps from neglecting his health to finish the report.

Sebastien dug into her satchel and pulled out a canteen of water for him.

When his eyes had stopped watering, Damien continued. "I've been looking for times that they perform magic similar to known Aberrant abilities. And especially anything that might resemble Newton's…effects."

Her stomach clenched. "Did you find…?" Sebastien trailed off, unable to say that horrible thought out loud. She hadn't specifically told Damien to look for Newton, but ever since she had learned what the Red Guard did with Aberrant components, the possibility that they had harvested what were essentially his remains had stayed in the back of her mind. *'Could an Aberrant feel pain if they butchered it for parts?'*

Damien shook his head. "No. I found…something else. You know I ran out of allowance already this term. So to fund further research, I had to sell some of my belongings. Titus has been too preoccupied lately to notice." A flicker of guilt crossed his face before he pressed on. "I needed access to back issues of newspapers that have gone out of business. Some of them used to provide more detailed information about rogue magic and Aberrant incidents. And then I decided to get at least one major newspaper based in the other biggest cities, too, for more comprehensive input."

He flipped through the pages in the binder, revealing complex data organized into neat graphs and tables. "To make the data-organization spells easier, I had tagged and labeled each rogue magic incident with a dozen or so pieces of relevant information. My idea was to organize and analyze the information from different angles. I could make lists ordered by location, or civilian casualty numbers, or…time."

Damien paused and swallowed, turning to another page. "This one shows the frequency of suspected Aberrant incidents over the past eighty years. That's as far back as I could go with the available newspapers."

Sebastien studied the graph, noting the gradual upward trend and occasional spikes.

Damien explained, "There's been about a thirty percent increase in Aberrant incidents since then."

"But couldn't that just be due to Gilbratha's population growth?"

Damien nodded and flashed her a small smile. "I thought of that too. So I sold my horse and bought editions of one major newspaper from Paneth and Lenore's other largest cities. The data includes all of that. The trend is the same everywhere." He flipped to another page. "And this graph adjusts for population growth. Even accounting for that, there's still a twelve percent increase over the same period."

Sebastien's mind raced, considering possible explanations, even as a sick, writhing pit began to grow in her stomach. "What about University admissions? Have they kept pace with Gilbratha's population growth?"

Damien shook his head. "That's the thing. The University has maintained a steady intake of about three thousand students per year for the last one hundred fifty years. It hasn't increased at all."

Sebastien licked her dry lips. "So, there might be more rogue thaumaturges out there with improper training, since the University isn't meeting the growing population's needs. And if other minor institutions aren't picking up the slack, the disparity between trained thaumaturges and the general population is growing wider."

Damien fumbled with the pages, his exhaustion evident in every movement. "I considered other explanations too," he said. "Maybe the data quality has changed over time, so more incidents are actually being recorded rather than passed over. Or there could be lies about the causes of rogue magic incidents, saying disasters were caused by Aberrants when they really weren't."

"Or perhaps," Sebastien mused, "as the stigma of the Blood Emperor slowly fades, people are more willing to experiment with dangerous magic."

Damien's eyes lit up with a mixture of excitement and trepidation. "Exactly! I thought of that too. But I was still worried, so I went to the University student census. I looked for all records of students leaving for 'medical reasons' or similar excuses. It wasn't easy—I had to translate the data across several different record-keeping standards."

"And what did you find?"

Damien swallowed hard and showed her yet another graph. "Over the last two hundred eighty years, the numbers are slowly but steadily rising, even adjusted for the increase in student admissions one hundred fifty years ago."

The implications hung heavy in the air between them. Sebastien's fingers tapped rapidly against the side of her leg, and she had taken out the Conduit from her pocket without realizing. Deliberately, she put it back. "It could be that the University's safety mechanisms and procedures have become less robust," she suggested. "Maybe it wasn't always normal for one in fifteen students to have a catastrophic misstep while casting magic before they reached the level of Master."

"I agree that the University is putting too much pressure on its students. There's also a chance that something about the modern teaching methods means our Wills aren't being properly trained in all facets, making them unbalanced and more likely to fail."

He paused, his gaze meeting Sebastien's with an intensity that made her breath catch. "But what if it's not any of that?" The question lingered, unanswered.

"I looked up some studies about Aberrants," he continued, turning to another section of the report. "By the time a thaumaturge graduates, one in fifteen have died, broken, or otherwise damaged their Will badly enough that they have no chance of continuing as a thaumaturge. That's about six and a half percent. Over the course of a lifetime, that rises to ten percent."

"Most of those people probably just die. What percentage are Aberrants, specifically?"

"About one percent of catastrophic failures among the student body turn into Aberrants. It's actually lucky that we haven't experienced one yet. There's an incident every year or two." He swallowed hard. "We'll see more than one before we graduate, probably."

"One percent… It seems like so few, but that's actually a huge amount. It means that from each year's new and hopeful students, eventually three will become Aberrants."

"Yes," Damien agreed, taking a deep breath. It hitched as he blew it back out again. "And that doesn't count unlicensed thaumaturges."

"How many people do those Aberrants kill, on average?" Sebastien asked, cutting to the heart of the matter.

Damien was silent for a moment, until she looked up from the report to meet his gaze. "The median Aberrant kills forty-seven people. That's a lot less for students that break at the University. There are a lot of preparations to deal with one here. Honestly, that isn't very many people, in the grand scheme of things. Most Aberrants are destroyed or removed easily, and the ones that aren't can still go inside a sundered zone. But the problem…" He shook his head, seemingly unable to continue.

"The problem is that some Aberrants turn out like Eltrocus, Metanite, or the Red Sage," Sebastien said.

"Yes," Damien whispered. "The highest death count to an Aberrant is approximately eight hundred thousand people, to Loimae, the Plague. The second-highest is three hundred twenty thousand, to the explosion when Dipsa broke. That whole city is still stuck inside a sundered zone—the largest one in the world—because it poisoned the land irrecoverably." Damien's voice grew a little stronger. "I can name at least twelve Aberrants that have killed over twenty thousand people, and there are certainly more outside of Lenore. Metanite isn't even particularly dangerous, but it's still managed to kill about two hundred people over the course of the last ninety years. I'm actually scared to speculate how many people the Red Sage might have killed indirectly. How many Aberrants are out there that the Red Guard can't stop and can't contain?"

"A thirty percent overall increase means we're thirty percent more likely to get another one like Loimae." Sebastien closed her eyes as a memory of her last glimpse of the village she grew up in flashed across the back of her eyelids. "And when that happens, it's not just the loss of life. It's the lost industry, suppressed trade, fear, and famine. The time it takes to recover, and the people who never do. The potential geniuses who die without ever contributing to society."

"And the increase in Aberrant incidents afterward."

"Because desperate people are reckless," Sebastien agreed.

Damien shook his head. "I don't think that's it. You know how our Wills grow stronger with practice? How channeling more power allows us to increase our capacity even further? That's why Archmage Zard can gain a thaum in just three hours of practice, while it takes me five."

"Yes," she said, wondering where he was going with this.

"Look at the data again." He turned the page back to the second graph, adjusted for population growth. "Look at the spikes, and then look at the trend line afterward. I don't know the cause behind all of the spikes, but some of them correspond with wars or other massive disasters, like Loimae. Every time we have a spike, the frequency of Aberrant incidents goes down again, but never back to the pre-spike baseline. And afterward, the rate of growth goes up by a few tenths of a percent. I think that the spike itself is doing something to the baseline."

Damien's hands were trembling, and though her own didn't feel much more steady, Sebastien gently drew the binder from his grasp, for some reason wary of the contents, as if they could harm her. That Aberrants might grow more likely in a similar way to her own Will's growth should have been an earth-shattering revelation, but Damien was still hesitating. There was more, something else. "Tell me," she commanded softly.

"One of these spikes"—he reached over and pointed to one about eighty years before—"corresponds with a really violent succession war in Kuth. But the thing is, University students weren't involved in that, and it otherwise only affected Gilbratha because the price of some goods rose. But the entire population of thaumaturges here had about twice as many break events as normal that year."

"No," Sebastien whispered.

The silence stretched on, as if Damien couldn't bear to contradict her.

"Did this happen again during the Haze War?" she asked.

"I can't tell for sure. We were involved in them directly, and I couldn't get good data from the East. But…students still enrolled in the University had an increased rate of break events, as did thaumaturges throughout Lenore. That's not a good data point, though, because it could have just been the stress of the War that caused a disproportionate number of breaks."

Sebastien found the spike that would have corresponded with the war. Her gaze stayed trained on the baseline afterward, which, as Damien had said, had risen more than it should have otherwise during that time period, and continued to curve upward. She realized she was breathing too hard and forced herself to slow.

"Damien, I don't know enough about math to make an educated guess, but does this seem like an exponential growth graph to you?" she asked, her voice strained and small.

Damien reached over and closed the binder. "I don't know how long we have," he said, not answering directly. "We would need an expert; I'm not skilled enough to guess at the tipping point. For any single failure of Will, there is only a tiny chance of an Aberrant being created. And for every Aberrant incident, an even smaller chance that they will be beyond the Red Guard's ability to handle. But we keep rolling the dice, Sebastien. Not only that, we keep adding more and more dice to the roll. And every time an Aberrant appears, it's another roll. Eventually, we will roll the next Cataclysm, whether it's a single Aberrant that splits the planet in two, or a thousand that exterminate us all bit by bit over the course of a hundred years."

Sebastien had considered these same fatalistic thoughts herself, though never to this degree. She had eventually determined that the only solution was to gain power. But if Damien's speculation was true, what could someone of even Myrddin's power do? What kind of future would she have in a world where magic was becoming even more dangerous?

Sebastien felt as if some part of her were detaching from her body. She noticed a faint smear of ink on Damien's jaw. A few pieces of dust floated through the air between them. Their wards muffled any noise from outside, but she could still hear faint sounds from the general hubbub of the festival-like exhibitions. Her hands were sweating. With a deep breath, she drew her focus back in. "We have to be sure. We still need more data. Are spikes in break events from somewhere across the known world really endangering every thaumaturge, regardless of involvement or proximity? Are the more powerful, uncontrollable Aberrants increasing at the same rate as the rest?"

"Do you think I'm wrong?" Damien asked.

"No," she admitted. "But I really hope you are. I hope there's something that explains all of this in any other way. If there is, we need to find that thing." Sebastien handed the binder back to Damien and pressed her fingers to her eyes until she saw stars. "Whatever the truth is, I want to believe it," she reminded herself. "No matter how horrible it is, being ignorant or refusing to believe the truth won't change reality. Only by knowing do we have any hope to change our circumstances for the better."

21

THE STARPEAK MOUNTAINS

THE THUNDEROUS POUNDING of erythrean hooves against the earth shuddered through Oliver's body as he hunched low over his beast's neck. Exhaustion etched his face, and those of his companions. Their clothes were wind-whipped and sweat-stained, and dirt had built up into lines of mud in the areas where their skin creased. The relentless pace had taken its toll, but they pressed on desperately.

Magically lightened saddles took much of the weight off the horses, allowing them to maintain their grueling pace. Extra horses were tethered behind, ready to replace any mount that faltered. Ebenezer, Oliver's new erythrean, was powerful, his eager strides eating up the road below. But he wasn't Elmira.

A pang of grief that turned to frustrated, exhausted rage shot through Oliver as he thought of Elmira. She had fallen in battle at Knave Knoll against the Architects of Khronos months ago, a senseless waste of an innocent life. For him, the loss of a friend.

Now again, the Architects were the cause of his problems.

His muscles were beyond aching and had started to scream and tremble from the constant tension of maintaining his position in the saddle. The others had taken what recovery potions they could without building up any toxicities, but the potions barely worked on Oliver.

They had been riding for almost two weeks now, trying desperately to catch up with the strike team the Architects of Kronos had sent to Osham. They had long passed the follow-up team—the people that he had first sent out before realizing the severity of the situation.

Kiernan had been away from the University when the team was authorized and sent, and Oliver had learned their purpose too late. Kiernan insisted he hadn't known about it and did not authorize it, but he wouldn't say who did, which made Oliver suspect it was someone important. It was possible that one of the Crowns had turned on their own and was colluding with the Architects, he supposed. He would dig into it when he returned.

The landscape, a mix of stony fields and scattered trees that Oliver barely registered, blurred past them. He had no energy for curiosity. The only thing that kept him going was the knowledge that they would reach the Starpeak Mountains' western pass, only a short distance from the ocean, in one more day. Already, the jagged peaks were visible, and had been for some time, though they were the foggy blue-grey that came with distance and humidity in the air.

Enforcer Huntley, observant as ever, was the first to notice something on the horizon. He called a halt, drawing Oliver out of his single-minded focus. They slowed the horses gradually, allowing time for their powerful circulatory systems to cool down somewhat. Stopping suddenly after hours of exertion at top speed could even cause cardiovascular damage.

Two massive shapes soared through the sky to the west, their wingspans dwarfing even the largest eagles.

Oliver squinted, trying to make out more details, but the fading light and haze of moisture-laden air from the ocean made it difficult to discern much beyond their general silhouettes. "Rocs," he breathed.

Enforcer Huntley dismounted and moved to stand on the side of the road. He raised a battered spyglass to his eye, adjusting the focus as he peered at the distant figures. The giant magical birds couldn't stand up to a dragon or a sky-kraken, but they were still one of the apex predators of the skies, and their wind magic meant that they could carry three times their own weight as cargo.

"I can't make out much," Huntley said. "It could be some kind of stealth spell at work, or just the damned humidity." He plucked at his shirt with distaste, fanning himself.

Oliver nodded, a knot of unease forming in his stomach, and held out a hand for the spyglass. He couldn't make out much more than Huntley.

"I don't want to jinx us, but I have a bad feeling about this," Huntley said.

"You think it's the Architect strike team?"

Huntley took the spyglass back again and fiddled with it. "It would make sense, wouldn't it? Travel stealthy on horses for most of the way so they can't be tracked, no need for any special licenses or flight records, and much less interesting and memorable to the average person who might spot them. Pick up the rocs to bypass the Starpeak Mountains entirely. No need to deal with Osham's border guard or defenses if they get enough distance and come around from the north... And it's much harder to notice and defend against a flying attack."

Oliver agreed, but he didn't say so out loud. He dismounted Ebenezer and almost collapsed.

Ebenezer laid back his ears and stared peevishly at Oliver, who ignored him, hanging onto the saddle for a bit while he shook out his legs.

Eventually, Oliver was able to hobble back and forth to loosen the muscles. "It was already tight, trying to make up for a week's head-start."

While they waited for Oliver to make a decision, Huntley gave Ebenezer a scratch on the frequently itchy spot under his mane, though Ebenezer was too exhausted to respond. One hundred twenty kilometers a day was an almost unbelievable speed. Oliver couldn't expect any more from the horses. *Or* the team.

"If they picked up rocs here, even laden with men and supplies, stopping to hunt, they could easily cover five hundred kilometers in a day," Oliver said. He took out a map, ignoring the cold rush of exhaustion that shivered down his back despite the heat, and did the math. "If so, we can't catch up to them. Not like this," he muttered. He closed his eyes and spoke louder. "Even going out of their way far enough that they can avoid sight from land and come in on the target from the other direction, they'll be there in five, maybe six more days."

"Maybe that's not them," one of the other enforcers offered with tentative optimism.

Huntley raised both eyebrows and shrugged. "Sure," he said, though his tone lacked conviction.

The weight of their situation settled over them like a heavy cloak. Oliver, at least, had some idea of what failure here could mean, and the others weren't idiots. They needed to catch the Architects before they got to Osham and stop them from ever crossing the border.

Oliver couldn't go to the Osham government himself. After his father had smuggled Oliver out of the country, the man had been disgraced. The state had charged him half the family fortune in fines and imprisoned him for six years, putting his skills as a thaumaturge to work. When he returned to freedom, his title was lowered by two ranks and much of his holdings were given to his former rivals.

Oliver had a few contacts in Osham, either leftover from his childhood or acquired more recently, but he was still technically considered a fugitive. Though little effort had been put into recovering him, if he was discovered in

Osham, some opportunistic noble might try to use his presence as leverage or turn him in to gain favor with the ruling party. He might never leave Osham again if he set foot across that border.

The team watered their horses, adding a splash of recovery-boosting potions to ease the steadfast creatures' exhaustion, and then had a quick drink from their canteens. Oliver braced himself before swinging back into the saddle.

Ebenezer let out a discontented snort, followed by an amazingly expressive whicker which meant that he expected extra treats that evening, and then some grumbling that Oliver imagined was a series of grumpy comments about how Ebenezer longed for retirement, even though he was only ten.

Oliver apologized to him, forcing himself to ignore the pained cries of his muscles as they began to ride again. He had grown soft, living in Gilbratha, and with so much luxury, for so long. "If it's not them, we have to keep going. Even if it *is* them, we need to keep going."

Ebenezer stopped grumbling and increased the pace slightly.

The Architects' plan was audacious, to put it kindly. In harsher words, it was reckless insanity. They were on their way to kidnap a group of recruits from a small military training facility near Osham's northern border.

Why? Oliver had asked himself that question many times. Kiernan either didn't know or wouldn't say. The Architects wanted a revolution, and one might think that made them and Oliver allies, but they disagreed on the *outcome* of that revolution—and perhaps the methods of execution, too.

The first motive that came to mind was ransom. Osham's government had a strict policy against negotiating with hostage-takers, a principle they adhered to with unwavering resolve. However, people might be ransomed back to their families instead, or used to blackmail powerful parents into doing the Architects some unsavory favor.

But Oliver suspected it was more than that. The Architects had proven themselves reckless, but even they must have realized that they were taking a large risk. Not only would the military facility be protected, its inhabitants ready to fight back, but Osham's response to crime—or anything they felt was a threat—was overwhelming aggression. If they failed, everyone on the strike team would die. Some of them would have their minds torn apart, and Osham would very likely decide to solve the problem of the Architects more *perma-nently*—which could blow back on the Verdant Stags.

No, risk like this required a commensurate reward. It seemed unlikely that blackmailing any one noble, no matter how powerful, would be worth it, unless they knew something he didn't. He would hesitate to take such a risk even to kidnap the premier's beloved daughter.

Even if the Architects were too short-sighted to see it, Oliver was worried about more far-reaching repercussions. If Osham thought that they'd been attacked by Lenore, when tensions were already so high due to the depleting supplies of celerium, what would they do? The state was afraid to be seen as weak. Osham's leaders blustered and used force even when a soft hand might be better. In Oliver's opinion, they did not seem to understand the consequences of creating resentment, even with the wonderful example the Blood Emperor had set.

But Oliver could think of one thing that might make this attack worth it, if the Architects had grown even more conceited and reckless. What if the recruits were Nulls?

Siobhan had told Oliver of her suspicions that one of the Architects' hired mercenaries, a rogue agent from the Red Guard, was using Aberrant parts as components, something Oliver had not even known was possible. Armed with that knowledge and Tanya Canelo's story of her near-fatal mission for the Architects, Oliver had grown suspicious that they were smuggling Aberrant parts. When he had tracked down an Aberrant-components smuggler for Siobhan, he hadn't been able to connect them directly to the Architects, but it only reinforced his suspicions.

Nulls were at a disadvantage in many ways, being entirely unable to do magic, but they had a few specific advantages. Because of the way that magic struggled to affect them, they were useful in combating Aberrants and countering magic that lacked physical components.

Unlike Lenore, which embraced magic in all its forms, Osham's deep-seated prejudice against thaumaturges—and particularly free, unleashed thaumaturges—made Nulls all the more valuable. They even bred for it, with noble lines bringing Nulls in by marriage in the hopes of producing children with the trait—children that would then serve the state and bring honor to their families.

It was why his sister had been taken. She and Oliver weren't completely oblivious to the dangers; their family had never been quite as nationalistic and fervently loyal as Osham's other leaders probably wanted. Oliver and his sister had even made a childish plan to escape and live on their own before she was drafted.

But they hadn't managed it. Four years after his last glimpse of her— looking back at him from atop the horse his family was also donating to the military, trying to smile at him bravely though her eyes glittered with unshed tears—his family had received a letter informing them of her death. Her belongings had been returned to them, but not her body. Not even ashes.

That was when his father began making plans to send Oliver away. When it was confirmed that Oliver had no chance of becoming a thaumaturge himself, his father acted. It had been twenty years since Oliver had last seen the man. He was still alive, but they didn't share correspondence very frequently, except to check on the other's wellbeing.

But even if the Osham recruits were Nulls, something still didn't add up. Didn't the Architects know about the mental conditioning programs that Osham subjected its recruits to? They were rather effective at instilling unwavering loyalty to the state. Surely, the Architects must have known that kidnapping fully indoctrinated soldiers and hoping to change their allegiance would be a long, arduous process.

But perhaps that was exactly the point, and why the strike team was moving with such urgency. Perhaps they hoped to capture recruits who hadn't yet been subjected to the full brunt of Osham's psychological manipulation. By acting now, they might hope to capture these young men and women before Osham's conditioning irrevocably shaped their minds.

The implications sent a chill down Oliver's spine. He could only think of a few things one might do with a group of Nulls.

Of course, the Architects might outfit them with artifacts and use them as a fighting force, but the problem was that most battle spells caused harm by affecting the environment. Oliver was resistant to magical effects, both good and bad, but he was just as likely to get roasted by a fireball or have his organs ruptured by a concussive blast as anyone else.

Perhaps the Architects had heard word of a specific Aberrant. If Siobhan was correct, the components from the exact right Aberrant might significantly increase the chances of a successful coup.

Or—and he wasn't sure if this was better or worse—what if the Architects hoped to *create* a specific Aberrant, kill it, and butcher it like a cow? He could understand why, with such a goal, this might seem like the perfect opportunity. Of course, it was all still speculation, but it made a little too much sense.

But perhaps a more important question was: what would Osham do in response, if they felt threatened?

The next day, Oliver and his team stopped a few kilometers from the base of the Starpeak Mountains. From afar, the mountains had been visible as a jagged wall reaching up to meet the clouds, but as they drew closer, the true scale of these geological behemoths became something they could *feel*. The mountains loomed defiant, a row of massive stone fangs that seemed to tear at the very fabric of the heavens.

The peaks, ranging from twelve to eighteen kilometers in height, vanished into the clouds far above, beyond the height where non-magical beings could survive. Even the lower troughs and valleys between the mountains, at around five kilometers high, dwarfed any other terrain Oliver had encountered. Despite their seemingly fragile appearance, with sharp, craggy edges and precarious overhangs, the Starpeak Mountains had withstood the test of time and nature's fury.

The mountain range was logistically, if not literally, impassable. During the Third Empire, several guerrilla armies had set up bases within them, and

Osham had caused more trouble for the Blood Emperor than several of the smaller countries combined.

Now, the high-altitude valleys were home to many of Osham's military bases, where they stationed both massive artillery artifacts and teams of riders flying on rocs, gryphons, perytons, and even the occasional pegasus or dragon. And yet, one might still stumble upon a small village hidden in some valley or the pseudo-peaks that lined the base of the taller mountains, populated by brave settlers who had carved out a place for themselves and learned how to survive the harsh environment.

The western pass, near the coast, offered a route through. Far to the east, the Starpeak Mountains ended abruptly near the border with Silva Erde, allowing a second path for trade. Combined with the ice oceans to the northwest and the Abyss Chasm to the north—and the magical beasts that crawled out of it—natural barriers left Osham somewhat isolated from the rest of the known lands.

The small military outpost the Architects were targeting sat close to the Abyss Chasm. The constant battles against magical beasts emerging from the chasm's profound depths provided invaluable training for Osham's soldiers, while the harvested components and beast cores from these creatures formed a significant portion of the nation's exports income.

The trade city of Malzhan guarded the mountain pass, serving as the mercantile hub through which all western trade flowed in and out of Osham. Oliver and his people split up before entering the city, leaving a couple of their number to watch the road. They did their best to discreetly gather information about any unusual activities or sightings. Hours passed as they combed through taverns, markets, and docks, seeking any whisper of the Architects' strike team.

Enforcer Huntley went to speak with the border station.

Reconvening at an inn near the city's edge, they shared their findings, or rather, the lack thereof.

"Nothing," Huntley reported snappishly, his voice filled with frustration. "No sign of any large group passing through, no unusual boat hires, not even a whiff of suspicious activity."

Another enforcer added, "I checked with the harbormaster. No unscheduled vessels have docked in the past week."

"They could have joined up with a large convoy, perhaps." Oliver said. "Anonymity in numbers."

"Or they could have smuggled themselves in as cargo."

Oliver frowned. It was more common for people to try to smuggle themselves out of Osham than in, but that might just mean the guards were laxer about searching.

"We could try to run them down—without you," Huntley said, giving

Oliver a warning stare as if he anticipated Oliver would try to throw himself into danger. "But I don't like our chances of stopping them without creating… trouble." A political incident, Huntley meant. "And if I'm honest, I think we're already too late."

"The rocs," one of the other enforcers said, eliciting weary nods all around.

Another piped up. "We could hire rocs, too. Or maybe a dragon, if there are any riders in the city."

"We're already a day behind," a woman muttered. "And what would we tell the dragon rider, exactly?"

"If our quarry has already passed the border, then it's too late to stop this quietly," Oliver said. The team exchanged uneasy glances.

After a moment of tense silence, Oliver spoke again, his voice low and determined. "We have no choice. We must inform the border officials of the impending attack."

"But sir," one of the younger enforcers interjected, "won't that compromise our alliance? The Architects are going to know who spilled."

Oliver shook his head. "Better this, than the attack succeeding and Osham blaming Lenore."

"They can use a divination relay to get the message where it needs to go quickly—quicker than a roc—and hopefully mount a response in time," he said.

With grim determination, they set about crafting a carefully worded message. Oliver ensured it contained enough information to prompt action without revealing their own involvement or the full extent of their knowledge.

Then, they spent a few hours hunting down a horn of speech owned by the local city manager, which was sympathetically connected to the border patrol's head office. No one wanted to volunteer to deliver the bad news in person, after all. That was likely to get them detained and questioned. And when the Architects caused trouble, that questioning might turn distinctly *torturous*.

As the two-way horn relay carried their warning to Osham's military command, Oliver felt a mix of relief and apprehension. They had done what they could, but it felt woefully inadequate.

Belatedly, the thought crossed his mind that the recruits might actually be better off getting kidnapped by the Architects of Khronos. But Oliver couldn't fix all the wrongs in the world. Not yet, anyway.

The border authorities' response was colored by skepticism, confusion, and aggression. The idea of a terrorist group targeting such a remote outpost seemed far-fetched to many officials.

"At least they're aware now," Huntley offered, trying to find a silver lining. "They might not believe it fully, but they'll be watching."

Oliver nodded, but the knot in his stomach only tightened. "We'll stay for a few days," he decided. "Just in case we somehow overtook the strike team without realizing it and can catch them on their way through."

Half the team brightened considerably at the promise of beds, baths, and cooked food.

But Oliver couldn't shake the feeling of impending disaster. The dread that had been building since he first learned of the Architects' plan now sat like a lead weight in his belly.

2 2

SUBSTITUTE EXHIBITIONIST

SEBASTIEN
Month 8, Day 30, Monday 7:30 a.m.

GIVING Sebastien the report on his research seemed to have released something held taut within Damien. As they and their friends gathered for breakfast, he slumped listlessly in his seat.

The food was better than normal, perhaps to encourage them to put their all into the exams. Ana pushed a plate of eggs and toast towards Damien. "You need to eat something," she said, her voice tinged with concern. "You look like you're about to fall face-first into your porridge."

"Too nervous to sleep?" Alec commiserated, his own knee bouncing rapidly beneath the table.

Damien mumbled something incoherent and halfheartedly picked up his fork.

Sebastien watched him with a growing sense of guilt. Damien's exhaustion was almost entirely due to the research project she had encouraged him to pursue, but at this rate, he was likely to perform poorly on his exams. "The quicker you eat, the quicker you can take a nap."

Damien blinked as that information burrowed past the barrier in his brain caused by sleep-deprivation and then began to shovel down the food. When the tray was empty, he pushed it aside, folded his arms on the table, and rested his head on them. Within moments, his breathing had evened out.

Sebastien unbuttoned the light summer jacket of her suit and rested it over

Damien's head to block out the light. When the others were finished, Sebastien waved them off. "You all go on ahead. I'll stay here with Damien for a bit to make sure he gets to the exam in time." They still had about forty-five minutes before the first extended test period began. Sebastien knew from experience that sometimes that could make all the difference.

The atmosphere was festive and hectic, but slightly less panicked than she remembered from the first term's exams. Even the exhibitions this term were slightly less elaborate than the first term's, except for a couple of big, planned events that were enough to draw the crowds all on their own. She assumed that, for the majority of students, it was an even-numbered term, as only those who had been held back or who had entered during the more limited Sowing Break exams were hitting milestones now.

When it was time to leave for the exam, Sebastien gently shook Damien awake. They arrived only a couple of minutes before the bell sounded, and most of the other students were already seated.

Professor Burberry was handing out sealed test papers, smiling merrily and trying to joke in an attempt to put the students at ease.

As Sebastien took her paper from the woman, Burberry leaned in close and put her hand on Sebastien's elbow to keep her from walking on. Burberry spoke in a low voice. "Mr. Siverling, I want you to know that, although we emphasize the importance of these exams, you are not in danger of failing out for the year if you put in even moderate effort."

Sebastien blinked, unsure how to respond.

Burberry continued, her voice gentle but firm. "I've had a talk with Professor Lacer about unrealistic expectations and the risks that pressuring young thaumaturges can bring. I know how hard you've been pushing yourself. Please don't hurt yourself to impress someone who's forgotten what it's like to be just starting out."

Sebastien stood there, somewhat baffled by Burberry's words, and then walked on to her seat when Burberry gave her a nod.

She guessed that somehow, word about her lack of sleep must have reached Burberry's ears. She tried to be discreet, but it was impossible to keep people from noticing when a light was glowing from her cubicle in the middle of the night. Not unless she wanted to make more elaborate renovations to the small space.

It was a stark reminder that she needed to find a more discreet way to manage her nocturnal activities. Suddenly, she realized that it had been a mistake not to sign up for any of the exhibitions. Sure, she hadn't had time to prepare anything impressive, but without an extra source of contribution points, she was unlikely to ever get out of the dormitory.

When Ana asked her what was wrong, Sebastien explained.

Ana flipped her long, honey-colored waves over one shoulder. "Is that it?

You know you can put your name down to fill in a spot if any of the other students drop out of the exhibition last-minute, right? It happens every term, for various reasons I'm sure you can imagine."

"Ah," Sebastien said. She had not known that, but it made sense. Students probably dropped out due to nerves, straining their Wills or injuring themselves during the exams, or even, occasionally, because they had died.

The Introduction to Modern Magics exam wasn't much different from the ones held in this class before. Sebastien easily poured out her knowledge into short essay questions. They had covered most of it at least briefly in class, and the rest was covered in supplemental reading, or was something they should have picked up in one of the other three mandatory core classes.

The practical portion involved casting a selection of random magic they had studied throughout the term. She moved through the tasks with practiced ease, starting with the creation of a simple, all-purpose antidote potion. She stashed the two extra vials she'd made in her satchel with a secret grin.

Next, she did a simple card-reading divination for her test proctor, being sure to sound as confident as possible. She had learned that the way they graded people on these kinds of ambivalent magic had a lot to do with their own perception.

Finally, she created a tiny vermin-repelling artifact. Despite this being the hardest of the practical tests, she doubted that just being able to detect small animals like mice and rats and then waving little clacking sticks would actually deter vermin for long. They were smarter than people gave them credit for, and hunger was a great impetus for bravery.

When she was finished, Sebastien decided to take Ana's advice and made her way through the combined crowds of students and civilians to the administration center in the library.

'*That was easy,*' Sebastien reflected. Intro to Modern Magics was supposed to be an overview of the different kinds of magic they could be learning each term, a place to consolidate and get a little extra practice or an introduction to a topic whose elective they weren't taking. For Sebastien, however, the class moved too slowly. Too much time was spent explaining things in class that they could be learning through doing some basic research on their own.

When she arrived at the administration center and announced her purpose, the faculty member at the desk lit up like a flower that had seen the sun. "Guys, it's Sebastien Siverling, and he's here to be an exhibition stand-in!"

One of the older, more portly staff members immediately pushed his way to the counter. "You won't regret this," he said, filling out Sebastien's paperwork with impressive speed.

When Sebastien explained that she was willing to fill in a spot in the exhibitions at any point that she wasn't taking an exam, with twenty minutes of forewarning, and for *any* of the classes that she was taking, the man literally grabbed her hand in both of his and bowed over it. "Thank you, Mr. Siverling."

Sebastien stood there awkwardly as they finished the paperwork and everyone beamed at her.

"We will send a runner for you if we have a spot," the man said. "Keep your student token on you."

Sebastien idled about, ate lunch, and supervised a second nap for Damien before the Natural Science exam.

Professor Gnorrish had again gone out of his way to make even his exam engaging, with interactive questions and drawings that moved across the paper in response to the students.

The most difficult and time-consuming topic of this exam was a simulated experiment. The test provided an issue and some basic information, and then asked them to go through the steps to gather data, analyze the results, and present their conclusions. The paper responded to their written answers, providing "results" based on the steps they described.

Around her, Sebastien noticed several students discreetly attempting to cast ink-erasing spells on their papers. She ducked her head and smirked at their suppressed panic. They had probably realized that they had made mistakes earlier in their experimental setup. She admonished herself to remain focused and finished in time to answer some of the extra-credit questions at the back. They wouldn't count toward her score, but were a great way to earn a few extra contribution points.

As the test period drew to a close, Professor Gnorrish stood at the front of the classroom and smiled out at all of them with pride. He cleared his throat and addressed the students, his voice carrying a hint of emotion.

"It has been my honor," he began, "to guide you all through this first year of higher learning. Natural science is not just about memorizing facts and figures, but about understanding the very fabric of our world and how magic interacts with it." He paused, his gaze sweeping across the room. "I hope that a few of you will go on to change the world with the knowledge you've gained here. Remember, true discovery comes not just from what we know, but from questioning what we don't."

Sebastien smiled back genuinely as he met her gaze.

As soon as she stepped out of the classroom, a young man lunged at her.

Sebastien jerked back, but instead of attacking, the man gestured into the distance. "Mr. Siverling?" he asked. Without waiting for an answer, he continued. "You're needed to fill in for an exhibition immediately. Please follow me!"

The runner led Sebastien to the History of Magic exhibition area. She remembered from last term that it was mostly museum-style displays of ancient relics, some reproductions of what they thought the Chalice of Plenty and the long-destroyed City of Zed looked like, and sometimes a speech or two about some historical topic.

She had nothing like that prepared.

The exhibition organizer who met her there was notably apologetic, but reminded her that she did say any of her classes, and without any extra lead time.

"It's okay," Sebastien assured them. "I just need a black curtain for a backdrop, as large as possible."

"What will you be doing?"

"An illusion play. A story about Myrddin's travels, I think."

They put up a hasty sign at the entrance and sent the poor runner to get the curtain for her while she set up a simplistic spell array on the empty, portable stage. She only used a couple of glyphs. Even outside of Professor Lacer's class, and though this was not an emergency where speed was of the essence, it was valuable to practice minimizing her reliance on a spell array.

When the curtain was set up and the organizer called the start of the exhibition, she began to absorb and bend the light within the Circle to her Will. The story she chose was one of the less well-known, about an adventure during Myrddin's travels to the East. While there, he had learned some of their magics from a local master. The scene depicted a small Eastern village nestled in misty mountains, with ornate pagodas and cherry blossom trees.

The East also had their own magical beasts, many of which were insidious and clever, and loved to slowly terrorize small communities of people. Sebastien didn't know if the story was true or whether the beasts even existed. Some of them sounded rather more like Eldritch or Nightmare-type Aberrants.

Sebastien narrated the story and did the voices herself, taking liberties with the characterization and the appearances of the monsters. She also frequently took the opportunity to interject asides about any historical truth behind the tale.

A crowd slowly grew, and she was satisfied with the couple dozen attendees gathered around by the end of her exhibition. They clapped politely—the children with extra enthusiasm—and Sebastien encouraged them to check out the other historical exhibits.

The single judge seemed to be a history enthusiast, as he took the opportunity to loudly introduce some of the other exhibits to the crowd before they could politely slip away.

The organizer bustled over to Sebastien, beaming. "Oh, that was wonderful. I wish more students would come up with ideas like that. People don't know the value of history. It's not as if it's all boring dates and lists of names. What we don't understand, we are doomed to repeat, my father always said."

They made a note on their clipboard, shared a glance over their shoulder with the judge, and then told Sebastien, "Fifty contribution points."

"Fifty?"

"Fifty."

As Sebastien walked away, she realized that the contribution points—a far larger number than her exhibition really warranted—were some kind of belated bribe for putting herself on the spot.

Tuesday started with the History of Magic exam. It retained Professor Ilma's signature requirement for deductive reasoning and a comprehensive understanding of the broader forces that shaped pivotal historical moments. Though it made for a good story, the huge movements and the shifting of power were rarely caused by a single person, good or evil.

After the main test, there was an extra credit question. "What would the world be like today if one of these significant historical figures had never existed?" It then gave a list of names to choose from.

The bell rang, cutting Sebastien off when she was only a single page of hasty scribbles into her answer. Reluctantly, she set down her fountain pen. Her fingers ached and were so stiff she had trouble relaxing them from their clawed position, as if she were still holding her pen between them.

Sebastien considered asking Professor Lacer for whatever spell he used to control his pen. She was pretty sure her mind could move faster than her fingers.

As the other students filed out of the classroom, Sebastien lingered behind. She approached Professor Ilma's desk and pulled out the borrowed books about Myrddin.

Ilma pressed them back toward Sebastien. "Keep them," the woman said with a small smile.

Sebastien blinked in astonishment, acutely aware of the books' considerable value. Especially *Enough Yarn to Last the Night: A Collection of Myths from the Life of a Man with Many Names*, which had been illustrated by hand. It wasn't just that. They were full of notes from Ilma's mentor, and surely held sentimental weight.

"Why?" Sebastien asked, unable to hide her confusion.

Ilma's eyes twinkled with an uncharacteristic warmth as she replied, "I heard about your exhibition." She gestured toward the books in Sebastien's hands. "You *read* these," she said simply, as if that single fact explained everything. Without waiting for further response, she gathered up the sealed box full of completed tests and walked out.

During the midday break between exams, Sebastien was called for another exhibition while eating lunch. The sudden summons caught her off guard, her mouth still full of food. Reluctantly, she stuffed her cheeks like a chipmunk and set her half-finished meal aside. As she hurried behind the runner, she drew several amused and curious glances from passersby.

The exhibition, she learned as they cut between cobblestone paths to get to their destination more quickly, was for Introduction to Modern Magics. However, upon arriving at the venue, Sebastien noticed on the schedule that the student whose spot she was filling was in term five, taking "Studies in Modern Magic: Elemental Influences," a more advanced specialization of the introductory course.

The organizers, seemingly unfazed by this discrepancy, began announcing her presence with great enthusiasm as soon as she arrived. *'They must have considerable faith in my ability to pull something appropriate out of my ass.'* It seemed like a risk to her, but luckily for them, she did have an idea.

Sebastien cleared a space on the white stone ground in front of the tiered rows of seating, where a sizeable audience was already beginning to gather. She measured out an area a few strides across and began scraping out a more intricate spell array than those she usually used. This was too complex to hold even half of it in her mind.

She incorporated glyphs for each of the five Elemental Planes—earth, air, fire, water, and radiance—and added drawings to represent the specific form she wanted each element to take. She had appropriate components in her satchel, many saved from various in-class practices, but she asked the organizers to get planar components for her anyway. They were expensive, and if no one stopped her, she might be able to sneak off with them afterward.

Finally, she added two central glyphs: *'lifelike-movement'* and *'detailed-molding.'* Here was one case where specificity trumped flexibility.

With the array complete and the planar components in place, Sebastien populated the circular, makeshift arena with small constructs, each made from one of the five elements. The tallest of them only reached to her knee, but she thought they were still quite fearsome looking. She didn't have the strength to make the combatants any bigger but thought it would be alright with the small size of the stands.

As the diminutive figures came to life, ready for a mock battle, the audience cheered. There were quite a few children, but several of the adults looked equally captivated.

Sebastien orchestrated the battle with careful precision. She focused on animating two elemental beings at a time, allowing them to engage in dynamic combat while the others shifted and breathed, or stalked back and forth in a loop, looking somewhat alive but not really contributing to the melee. Without dropping her shadow-familiar spell and using both halves of her Will, she didn't have the ability to do any more than that.

The audience didn't seem to mind too much, screaming and cheering as the miniature elementals clashed.

The battle progressed, each elemental showcasing its unique strengths and weaknesses. The earth golem's sturdy defense crumbled against the water sprite's eroding attacks. The air sylph danced gracefully, evading the fiery salamander's scorching strikes. But it was the Radiant angel that truly captured the crowd's love.

Wielding a child-sized spear of pure light, the glowing avatar moved with ethereal grace, smiting its opponents one by one. Finally, it stood alone, holding spear and wings high as it turned to the crowd in glory.

The audience actually shook the stands with cheers and stomping, as if they had just watched some kind of provocative blood-sport.

Sebastien looked to the judges, who seemed to be…exchanging coin under the table?

"Seventy contribution points," one stood up and yelled, which was met with resounding cheers from the audience.

Sebastien grinned, rolling her shoulders and rubbing her forehead to release some of the tension that intense concentration had caused. Again, it was more than she perhaps deserved. This had taken barely any preparation and left nothing of value behind, and yet she earned as much as she had for her Practical Casting exhibition last term.

'*More bribes for being a last-minute stand in,*' she concluded. '*But perhaps this, rather than signing up from the beginning, is the optimal strategy for earning maximum contribution points. I might do it again next term.*'

After that, the Sympathetic Science exam proceeded much as it had the previous term. Now that she understood transmogrification better, Sebastien attempted to refine her strategy slightly. She focused on discerning the connections an *average* person might make, while also seeking out more unusual associations when she could think of one that seemed particularly poetic.

She had also gotten a lot of practice with easy transmogrification tricks that term, as they ran through hundreds of examples of simple spells in Practical Casting.

As the exam concluded, Sebastien felt cautiously optimistic about her performance. She had balanced the expected responses with more creative connections. Hopefully, if she hadn't gone overboard into the realm of outlandishness, she might even impress Professor Pecanty again.

As they reconvened after the final exam of the day, Damien appeared much recovered from the previous day's exhaustion. Collectively, their group of friends decided to take the opportunity to observe some of the ongoing exhibitions rather than put any time into studying for the remaining exams.

As they wandered through the bustling grounds, eating food from stalls rather than visiting the cafeteria for dinner, Sebastien managed to maneuver them over to a Practical Casting exhibition.

An upper-term woman was presenting, and the crowd around her buzzed with excitement as she stepped onto the stage.

Without uttering a word or drawing a Circle, the woman raised her hands. A shimmering, spiral-shaped shield of wind materialized before her. As assistants launched various projectiles at her, the wind shield caught and deflected each one with graceful efficiency.

Sebastien wasn't certain if the faint glow emanating from the spell was intentional—perhaps to make it visible to the audience—or if it indicated some inefficiency in the casting. Regardless, she found herself impressed. A free-cast shield spell seemed like an eminently practical skill for any thaumaturge to develop.

Ana, standing beside Sebastien and Damien, let out a small sigh. "I'll probably never have anything like that to show for Practical Casting," she admitted.

"You can do it," Damien encouraged her.

"No, probably not. I'm barely keeping up in Professor Lacer's class, and I'm not putting in the hours to catch up to either of you. I might even end up having to re-take this term again."

Damien scrunched up his forehead. "Why are you taking the class then?"

Ana's eyes were still fixed on the woman giving the demonstration. "I'm not there because I expect to become a free-caster myself, though if I manage it eventually of course that would be a nice fringe benefit. It's where the most ambitious thaumaturges of our generation will be found. I'm hoping to network with them, to build connections for the future."

Damien looked from Ana to Sebastien, and she followed his gaze and nodded. "It's already paying off."

Sebastien grinned. "I am *the most* ambitious thaumaturge of our generation," she promised.

"Do you hope to surpass Professor Lacer some day?" Damien asked.

Sebastien shook her head, looking back to the stage, where the woman finally grew tired and dropped her shield spell. "I plan to become the most powerful sorcerer in the world."

She almost expected one of the others to laugh at her, but none of them did.

Practical Casting was Sebastien's only exam on Wednesday. The test began with a short written portion, heavily focused on glyphs. Sebastien felt confident in her knowledge in that area. However, she deliberately missed a few answers, particularly those she had learned from Myrddin's journal. She doubted even the more studious of her peers would know some of them. The decision to hold back grated at her like something was scraping against the bones of her spine, and she acknowledged that it was probably paranoia, but if anyone had a chance to deduce her secret, it was Professor Lacer.

And he was the one who had advised erasing all traces of a secret's existence. Impressing Professor Lacer with her unusual knowledge wasn't worth the risk. Besides, it wasn't as if these exam results mattered for her in the long term. She doubted she would ever have a conventional job working for someone who would care.

After the written portion, students were directed to cubicles outfitted with protective wards. Student aides bustled about, preparing to grade the practical portion, which required only a simple demonstration of a few spells from each of the nine general areas they had practiced throughout the term. They even had a bucket of components prepared for the students to work with.

Sebastien had no trouble with any of it. *'I'm learning,'* she thought with a deep satisfaction. Professor Lacer had forced them to gain a modicum of experience with a range of spells. Among many other things, this included controlling heat and its absence, creating various gems or earthen armor, and pushing an electrical current through the ground while divining for hidden metals. Over the course of the term, his students had gained a solid grasp on how to use the world around them as a source of power, as well as to create various effects.

Most of the spells weren't particularly useful outside of niche applications, but there had been so many of them, and it added up to a general level of competence and the versatility to create her own solutions to a wide range of problems.

It was a shame that so many of the spells used components, which she found generally inconvenient, but thought was probably important to discourage impatient students from trying to free-cast any of the exercises.

Still, she had several ideas for new spells to add to her spell rod, and ways to modify her existing spells for greater versatility.

After the exam, Sebastien and Damien found themselves watching a group of children who had gleefully volunteered to participate in an exhibition. A witch's elemental, resembling an enormous water blob, "ate" the kids, carrying them around in air bubbles amid shrieks of muffled laughter.

"What are we going to do about... you know?" Damien asked, his voice low and tinged with concern. "We can't be the only ones who know, right?"

Sebastien spoke vaguely, since they weren't properly safe from prying eyes or listening ears. "If it's real, then the Red Guard must know. Probably the Thirteen Crowns, too—at least the lords of each family. Surely others would have discovered it, even if by coincidence? Professors, or mind healers, or really anyone with access to the relevant data, and the right knowledge to understand what they were seeing. Except I haven't heard any rumors about it at all."

Sebastien gave Damien a small smile. "That's actually a really good sign. If this were happening, we wouldn't be the first ones to find out, and it seems like it would be very difficult to keep secret. Even if most people didn't believe it, that kind of sensationalist talk would spread quickly. As for what we do about it..."

She rubbed her tongue across the back of her teeth while she thought. "It is incredibly serious, but if you're right, it's been going on for a while now. It's not likely to reach a critical turning point overnight. We have to confirm that your hypothesis is correct before we start panicking. But if it is, I still wouldn't know what to do about it. Is *that* something that can be fixed?"

"The higher-ups might have an idea," Damien suggested. "They must have resources and contacts that you and I don't know about, right?"

Unfortunately, Sebastien was the highest-level member of their two-person organization. "Maybe," she said. "In any case, you don't need to agonize over it." She clasped his shoulder, hoping to ease some of the lingering anxiety held there. "The higher-ups are going to need more information. You just need to get the data from Harrow Hill, and they'll figure out what to do from there."

Sebastien elbowed Damien in the side gently. "Hey, hopefully, we can just leave it to the Red Guard. This is literally their job, after all." They had people like Thaddeus Lacer on their side. She couldn't think of anyone more competent.

23

DEMONSTRATIONS OF SKILL AND POWER

SEBASTIEN
Month 9, Day 1, Wednesday 2:00 p.m.

ON WEDNESDAY AFTERNOON, while she and her friends were hanging about, Sebastien was asked to fill in for a third exhibition, this time for Natural Science. She was given a few hours of advance notice, and several of her friends, intrigued, decided to follow her.

"This isn't fair," Damien complained. "Why are they scheduling exhibitions when they know the students are going to be in exams?" Sometimes, Sebastien forgot that Damien was taking the maximum seven classes each term—one more than her. He still had his Divination exam scheduled for the latter half of the day while everyone else was free.

Sebastien took advantage of the extra time to plan something different. When she arrived at the exhibition area, she made several requests to the organizers: ten pounds of cotton or any other fibrous material they could provide; a bucket each of wood, dirt, and stone; and a standing wall or chalkboard to use as a base for her spell array.

As before, they were enthusiastic about meeting her requests, and the organizer in charge of advertising started dramatically yelling stuff like, "Come one, come all, and witness a demonstration of skill and power by none other than Sebastien Siverling, the only person Grandmaster Thaddeus Lacer has ever taken as an apprentice! That's right! Sebastien Siverling, the young man that Thaddeus

Lacer chose, even when it is well known that he turned down the High Crown's own heir!" The man put a hand to the side of his mouth and leaned forward as if sharing a secret, despite the fact that he was yelling at almost the top of his lungs. "You might have read about Mr. Siverling in the newspapers."

There was a pause, and though the man's back was turned, Sebastien was still somehow sure, based on body language alone, that he had just given an exaggerated wink. "And folks, he's here today to show you the true, secret wonder of natural science. Did you think natural science was boring and useless, barely real magic? Well, think again! Prepare to be amazed!" The man continued in this vein for some time.

Sebastien had a sudden, revelatory suspicion. '*Are the organizers somehow being rewarded based on how many people their exhibitions attract? Well, hopefully they're not disappointed.*' She had something less flashy planned than an illusion play or mock elemental battle.

Once the materials arrived, Sebastien arranged the component buckets on stools of varying heights around the edges of the chalkboard spell array. By this time, a substantial audience had arrived.

When the organizers gave her the signal to begin, Sebastien smiled and turned to the crowd. "It's true that natural science is all about the magic that can be found in nature and the world around us, but it isn't just about recreating mundane phenomena. It's about understanding how and why things work the way they do. And once you understand that…it becomes much easier to bend the world to your Will in novel ways."

She turned to the chalkboard. "What you are about to see is transmutation alone. I have some basic components"—she showed off the buckets—"but with a few exceptions, I will only be using them for their *similarities* to the substances I need. It makes transmutation easier when converting dirt to different dirt, or stone into a gem. It would be equally possible for me to do all of this using only the air—it would just take a lot longer, and I doubt any of you feel like sitting around for two or three days while I work at it."

A young woman's voice from the back of the crowd yelled, "I'll sit on you for two or three days, Sebastien!"

Sebastien almost choked and was thankful for the crowd's laughter, which allowed her to gather her wits. She tried to keep her expression stoic, though whatever she had been about to say was forgotten. She cleared her throat and finished quickly. "I will not be using any duplicative transmogrification today. Observe."

With the audience's attention captured, Sebastien began to cast. She started by creating a couple of cables, which she connected to the top of the chalkboard so that she didn't have to make her creation float the whole time, in addition to everything else. From those cables, she grew a thick, circular backing of cotton fabric, dense enough that the tapestry would hang properly, rather than rippling and fluttering in the wind.

The crowd expressed their amazement with soft gasps and murmurs of appreciation, even though Sebastien felt she hadn't yet reached the truly interesting part of her demonstration.

It took her a while to grow a layer of orb-weaver silk atop the cotton base, and she worried that the audience would grow bored, but didn't notice anyone leaving.

Once the base was complete, Sebastien moved on to the art. She started with the sky. It was simple enough to transmute some of the dirt from the bucket into a light blue mineral dye. It was one of the many substances they had practiced with in Practical Casting, and while she didn't know it as well as the auxiliary exercise materials Professor Lacer had assigned her, she had no problem achieving something that was close enough. She embedded tiny particles of this dye through the silk strands, creating a gradient in the top third of the silk circle. To add depth and nuance to the color, Sebastien then discreetly applied the color-changing spell to the silken threads themselves in a slightly different shade.

Then came the ground, which took up the bottom third of the tapestry. Browns were easy, and a little boring. To remedy this, she added variety, showing the different levels of soil beneath the ground, as if the tapestry were showing a section of land that had just been sliced through and separated by an Archmage.

Green filled the middle, a base for what was to come, and then she returned to the ground and began to add texture. She molded dirt and rocks into little textured buttons of various shapes, sizes, and surface finishes, with a loop on the back for the silk to thread through, and used them to create an even more realistic illusion.

With these, she simulated the different kinds of soil beneath the earth, adding the occasional rock, hollow, flow of sand, or layer of clay. A combination of mica and mineral pigments created a subtle but obvious shimmer in places, hinting at magic.

Sebastien added a majestic tree to the tapestry, its roots spreading deep into the earth and its branches into the sky. With meticulous care, she attached slender strips of wood to the fabric, creating an illusion of depth that made the tree appear to be emerging from the tapestry itself. The audience gasped and murmured among themselves, and Sebastien looked up briefly as the organizer pushed back a few members of the crowd who had been trying to get uncomfortably close.

Next, she turned her attention to the leaves. Using a combination of transmutation and her color-changing spell, Sebastien crafted translucent, shimmering surface leaves that seemed to dance in an unseen breeze, and the shadow of depth and abundant foliage behind them. There was some applause, but she was too engrossed in creation to pay much attention to it.

Sebastien wove blades of grass into the foreground, each one a delicate, smooth line of embroidered silk. Rolling hills receded into the distance. In the sky, she placed birds in mid-flight, their wings spread wide as if caught in a moment of graceful soaring. Glittering hints of wind currents flowed through the scene, visible only as subtle refractions of light.

Velvet-soft, milky clouds drifted across the upper portion of the tapestry, their edges tinged with gold as if illuminated by a setting sun. Between the branches of the tree and beneath the earth, Sebastien added small creatures peeking out or burrowing into their homes. A fox's curious eyes gleamed from behind a root, while a family of field mice scurried along a hidden tunnel. A tiny skeleton of white stone lay in a hollow beneath the roots of the tree.

So engrossed was she in her work that Sebastien lost track of time. It wasn't until the University bell tolled the hour that she realized how long she had been working. She looked at the tapestry critically. There was more she could do, much more, but surely the audience was growing tired.

She stepped back and turned to them. "One of the first things you learn in Natural Science is that everything is connected. Our world is one big ecosystem, with life and death, what is above and what is below, all flowing from and feeding each other." She gestured to the tapestry. "This is a depiction of a simple ecosystem. Please, feel free to come up and examine it more closely once the judges have made their evaluation. Even touch it, if you like."

"*Only* after you have washed your hands!" a man in the audience cried. "And be gentle."

Sebastien eyed him curiously, but nodded. It would be a shame if her work was destroyed by carelessness.

As she stepped to the side to wait for the judges to decide if she would be awarded contribution points, the man from the audience approached.

He studied the tapestry reverently, leaning in to examine the intricate details with a monocle held to his eye. Tentatively, he brushed a finger along the tree's translucent surface leaves.

He straightened and nodded decisively to himself, reminded the rest of the crowd, "Be *careful*. It is delicate," and strode over to Sebastien.

Sebastien didn't think it was actually that delicate. Orb-weaver silk was incredibly strong, after all.

The man introduced himself and shook her hand. "Your work is extraordinary. I'd like to purchase it, if possible."

Sebastien tilted her head, surprised, then looked to the exhibition organizers.

"You can sell it as long as it remains on display for the remainder of the exhibitions."

"I'll have a glass case put up around it so that it isn't sullied," the man said, as if the deal were already done.

Sebastien hadn't even had a chance to open her mouth when Ana smoothly stepped up beside her. With a charming smile, she introduced herself to the potential buyer and began to negotiate on Sebastien's behalf. Sebastien watched, impressed with how at ease her friend seemed, as well as the ridiculous price she offered the man.

While this exchange took place, one of the judges approached Sebastien. "Impressive work," he said, nodding approvingly. "Sixty contribution points seems appropriate."

By the time Sebastien had finished slipping the paper record of her winnings into her pocket, the tapestry had been sold.

"I'll keep a thirty-two-gold sales commission, which leaves ninety for you," Ana said, writing out a cheque while they walked. She tore the cheque away and handed it to Sebastien.

Sebastien stared at the numbers. "That thing can't possibly be worth this much. I spent less than an hour on it, and the supplies probably cost less than a single gold."

Alec nodded rapidly and pointed at Sebastien. "What he said. I mean, it was *pretty*, but kind of boring, don't you think? It would have been better if he made the picture of something more interesting. Like a dragon breathing fire."

"It was wonderful," Brinn said, smiling at Sebastien reassuringly. "One of the best things I've seen all week."

Ana's honey-colored hair caught the light as she tilted her head, regarding her friends with amusement. "Oh, boys," she said, her tone both patient and slightly condescending. "You're thinking about this all wrong. This isn't just a tapestry. It's a luxury item, something unique that I've never seen before." Ana's eyes sparkled with enthusiasm as she continued. "And it's not just about the tapestry itself. It's about who made it. You're moderately famous already, and under Thaddeus Lacer's tutelage, you're likely to become even more so. He just made an investment."

"You're saying that thing could be worth even more someday?"

Ana shrugged. "Sure. But that man isn't just paying for the art. He's paying for bragging rights, for a conversation piece among other wealthy people. It will make him seem interesting, well-connected, and insightful. It's worth it."

Sebastien stroked her chin as Ana's words sank in. She found herself seriously considering asking Ana if the other young woman would like to open a tapestry shop together. The prospect of easy wealth dangling tantalizingly before her was almost too enticing to dismiss.

But then, Sebastien reminded herself of the cache of celerium hidden away, a treasure far more valuable than any tapestry she could make. And even with her reduced need for sleep, her time was still already stretched quite thin. She had no time to start up a side business.

The Defensive Magic exam on Thursday, their last of the term, was once again set up as an exhibition. This time, however, the false terrain area created from white stone had been transformed into a dense forest. Well, a *kind* of forest, if that forest was drawn by a child who made cloud-like curves for the trees and bushes instead of any actual foliage. No one would be climbing within the branches.

'*The Defense exhibitions probably take more manpower than any other exhibition type,*' Sebastien mused. In addition to what it must have taken to mold the Flats into novel terrain every term, this exam had tons of proctors watching the students through spelled silver mirrors, ensuring that as few students as possible were critically injured and making the whole thing into a huge show for the crowd, complete with betting.

This term, the contest resembled a game of capture the flag, with students divided into a dozen teams and competing against each other. Each team had a base, which had to be protected by an actively cast shield. To "win," a team needed to end the exam with two base flags—huge, red, glowing flags on poles. If they were able to protect their own flag, that would count as one.

At least half of the teams today would lose. Probably more than that, as a few outliers would likely collect more than two flags. Of course, even students from teams who had lost would still have a good chance to pass the exam based on their individual performance.

Sebastien did not have the luxury of choosing her role, unlike most of the other students.

Fekten had placed her on the shield spell. "You are to focus on protection, and nothing else. If I see any funny business from you, I'll have you disqualified faster than you can cry about unfairness and discrimination," he said.

Sebastien grimaced but didn't argue.

Fekten turned to walk away, but then paused. "Siverling, do you know the fastest way to break your Will?"

"Opposing another thaumaturge's Will," she said.

"That is correct. The shield's intermediary devices will protect you, but not completely."

It was a warning, she thought, but it almost sounded like a threat. Fekten had never quite warmed up to her again after the previous term's misunderstanding. She overheard Fekten instructing one of the test proctors to keep a close eye on her.

Despite the restrictions, Sebastien felt calm. If not for the fact that every team would probably have at least one upper-term student who was likely to take the shield-breaker role, this assignment would have been advantageous for her, and she might have selected it anyway.

The shield spell was actually a two-way device, somewhat like the Henrik-Thompson artifact. Rather than merely attacking and defending as one would in a real battle, it was all channeled through a hip-height pillar at the edge of each base. The pillar somewhat adjusted the amount of power that needed to be channeled to achieve the same effect based on the student's term, though it did not entirely even the playing field.

Sebastien thought she was quite powerful for a second-term student. In addition to that, maintaining or breaking the shield was not a matter of pure power, but a kind of mini-game in itself.

A "fire" shield was weak to a water attack, but strong against air. An earth shield was weak to air, but strong against light. Taking down the shield was as much a matter of being able to swiftly switch spells as it was of sheer capacity.

As a clear bell started the test, Sebastien grasped her Conduit in one hand with obvious, pointed motions, just so no one could mistake her for not having one. She channeled a bit of energy into the air version of the shield—the better to see approaching danger through—and settled in to wait.

Sebastien's team huddled together to strategize. Several agreed that they should send both of their upper-term students out on the attack team, which would increase their chances of capturing flags.

A young woman Sebastien didn't recognize seemed perturbed by this. "But that's a second-term student," she said, pointing at Sebastien. "Are you really going to have him manage the shield alone?"

One of the upper term students patted her reassuringly. "That's Sebastien Siverling." He turned to Sebastien. "You can handle it, right?"

Sebastien nodded easily, suppressing a yawn. She could tell that the sleeping raven bound to her was beginning to fail under the accumulated fatigue. She would need to go to Liza's and switch it out soon. "Well, probably. You should get two flags while you're out, just in case."

The upper term student smiled and pounded his fist into his open palm. "So, we'll have three flags, total. We should bring those back to base for Siverling to protect, and if there's time, we'll go out for a fourth."

A girl laughed dramatically, throwing back her head and half-covering a faux-evil laugh. "Highest scoring team! Contribution points for everyone!"

Rhett was the only other student on Sebastien's team that she recognized. He joined the attack group's ranks but didn't seem particularly pleased about the situation. She thought she heard him muttering something like, "Not even a chance to show my leadership skills."

It took a surprisingly short time for the first enemy team to arrive. A woman with a confident swagger approached, tapped her student token to the pillar, and launched her attack. Her teammates spread out, engaging Sebastien's few remaining defenders while providing cover for their shield-breaker.

Sebastien's opponent tried to take her by surprise, switching between three different attack elements within the first ten seconds. Sebastien had been a bit nervous, but at this, she calmed down. She countered each of the woman's attempts to break through with ease. Mentally, Sebastien taunted her. *'I haven't even stopped casting my shadow-familiar spell. You're just that inept.'*

The woman's initial confidence gave way to frustration and then astonishment as Sebastien had no trouble keeping up and showed no sign of fatigue.

Just as the shield-breaker had grown red-faced and seemed to be reaching the limits of her patience, a second enemy team charged out from between the white stone tree trunks, trapping the first enemy team between themselves and Sebastien's base.

The chaos of battle intensified, with ultimately harmless spells flying in all directions. The first team was wiped out, down to the last.

One of the new arrivals came to challenge the shield. The man nodded congenially at her. "All alone on shield duty, huh?"

Sebastien decided to boast, since this was only a game and didn't really matter. "I alone am enough." She almost blushed with regret, because it sounded much worse out loud. And it wasn't even true, really. If her stamina ran out, one of her teammates could step up and try to take over before the shield fell.

The man started out tentatively, testing her skill. "You're good," he complimented.

Sebastien scowled at him.

Eventually, her opponent abandoned subtlety and began hammering at Sebastien's shield with raw power.

Sweat beaded on Sebastien's forehead. She poured as much power as her Will could channel into the shield. She even dropped her shadow familiar, just to have that slight extra edge.

But it was all for naught, and the harsh reality of her relative youth—her *weakness*—could not be denied. She could not beat this man in a straight fight.

Fortunately for her team, the attack group that had gone out returned before she could fail, holding two giant flags. They fell on her attackers with berserk screams, and one boy even dropped his battle artifact and started beating a girl about the shoulders with the captured flagstaff in his hands. "For glory! For the contribution points!" he bellowed.

With both numbers and force, they managed to halve the enemy's numbers.

Sebastien's opponent let out a disgruntled "tch" and ran off with the rest of his team when they escaped. He had been seconds away from overcoming the last threads of her resistance.

Sebastien sagged with exhaustion. Her mind felt stretched thin. "Don't go out again," she told them. "I can't keep up the shield until the test ends."

Rhett managed to convince a smaller group of students to leave the flags there and try for a fourth, but the majority stayed behind to help Sebastien defend.

They ended the exam with three flags, and when all the grading was done, Sebastien's performance had earned her thirty contribution points for skill.

On Friday, with their exams completed, Sebastien and her friends found themselves free to enjoy the final day of the exhibitions like the other visitors. Thursday and Friday were geared toward showcasing the most impressive and powerful displays, many featuring students on the cusp of graduation who hoped to secure promising careers. The University, ever opportunistic, aimed to draw the largest crowds during this time, eagerly anticipating the mountains of silver and gold they would harvest from their students' efforts.

Alec's eyebrows seemed almost electrified, the bushy hairs wild with excitement as he dashed ahead of them to look at the new prizes added to the display in the Great Hall.

The grand showcase of everything available for contribution points served a dual purpose: it was both a bragging opportunity for the University to impress visitors and a tantalizing enticement for students to earn more contribution points.

Alec stood with his hands clasped together as if in prayer, drooling at an entire suit of armor imbued with the energy of the Planes of Earth and Fire, a masterpiece created by none other than Archmage Zard himself.

Sebastien could admit that the craftsmanship was intricate, and a palpable magical energy seemed to emanate from its smoldering surface. "What is Archmage Zard's specialty? Is he an artificer?"

Damien grinned. "Among other things. I think he's most famous for being an 'elementalist,'" he said, adding air quotes with his fingers.

Alec nodded. "He's done something famous with fire, earth, air, and water."

"Not Radiance?" Waverly asked.

"Not yet," Alec said. "I'm not sure what he would do with it. He likes to make stuff like this for the students, but that's mostly just a hobby. What he's really good at is affecting a huge area with gradual, powerful effects. Like smothering forest fires or diverting rivers. I heard one time he picked up a mountain and moved it. It took him three days."

"That didn't happen," Brinn said confidently. "Even Archmage Zard can't pick up a mountain. Maybe he scooped out chunks of it, piece by piece, and managed to move it that way."

"I've met him," Damien said. "He's not as interesting as Professor Lacer. He's an old man. The kind that hands out hard candies to children, even when they're already teenagers. If he were poor, he'd be the kind of man that pops out his wooden dentures to shock his grandchildren."

Ana nodded nonchalantly. "He gave me a candy one time, but the wrapper had fallen off, and it was all covered in lint from his pocket. He free-cast a spell to clean it and told me not to waste perfectly good candy."

"I've seen him around, but I've never met him," Waverly said. "He has an interest in rare magical species, I think. Sometimes he brings them home from his travels." She sighed wistfully.

Sebastien wondered if she might have encountered the renowned Archmage on the University grounds without realizing it. If he looked like any other old man, she might have simply ignored him. "Is he attending the exhibitions?"

Alec shook his head. "No, the High Crown sent him off to rescue some village that was hit by a mudslide. He's, like, building houses out of wood and digging supports and stabilizers into some mountainside."

Brinn's attention was captivated by a glass jar of what looked like herbal tea leaves. "I heard that Archmage Zard once saved an entire village from starvation in just three days."

"How?" Waverly asked, picking up a delicate crystal wand whose display very clearly said "Do Not Touch" and waving it around. "Wait, no, let me guess. He grew giant magical pumpkins?"

"Oh, me too!" Alec said. "Did he…water their fields with the blood of their enemies?"

Brinn shot him a look of disgust. "No. Shut up, you two. The village was on the coast and had been hit by a sea storm. There were rumors the storm was magically empowered by a beast of the deep, but anyway, all of their crops had failed, and they were running out of food. Archmage Zard showed up with nothing but a sack of seeds."

Brinn took the wand out of Waverly's hand and placed it gently back in its spot. "He didn't just plant a few fields. No, he created an entire agroforestry farm around the village. We're talking edible plants, bushes, and trees, all growing together in perfect harmony."

Ana interjected, "But how could he make them grow so quickly?"

Brinn grinned, clearly relishing the opportunity to explain. "That's the brilliance of it! No one knows! I have several theories. I think he might have used a combination of growth acceleration spells and some kind of sympathetic link absorbing the fruitfulness of some other region where the seeds came from. The villagers said it was like watching a hundred years pass in the blink of an eye. By the third day, they had a sustainable food source that will last for generations."

Sebastien turned her attention to the prize book and flipped through the pages of items not physically on display. Her eyes scanned the listings, searching for the section on private rooms.

She frowned. "Five hundred points for a private room?" That was beyond what she could afford. Sighing, she flipped to the next page, which detailed the four-bedroom apartments. The individual bedrooms were only about twice as big as their current cubicles, but it also offered a shared living area. The total price, while still steep, was only twice that of a single room, making each individual bedroom half as expensive.

Damien peeked around Sebastien's shoulder, growing contemplative.

Sebastien's pocket vibrated as the alarm spell she had placed on her pocket watch went off. All other thoughts fell from her head. She sucked in a breath of excitement. "It's time!" she told the others, and then hurried off, heedless of whether they were following her.

The sun had climbed high in the sky, and the most widely advertised showcase of these exhibitions was about to begin. Sebastien wouldn't miss it for anything.

After all, Thaddeus Lacer had volunteered to give an exhibition.

24

VENDETTA

Month 9, Day 3, Friday 1:40 p.m.

Sebastien and her friends arrived at their reserved seats in the temporary amphitheatre, a grand structure of white stone drawn up from the ground for the huge crowds that came to watch the Defense exhibitions. The air buzzed with excitement as spectators filed in, their chatter filling the space. Massive mirrors, sympathetically connected to those within the test area, dominated the center of the amphitheatre. For the moment, they merely reflected the eager faces of the crowd.

Alec and Rhett peppered Damien and Sebastien with questions about Professor Lacer's upcoming exhibition. "Come on, you must know something!" Alec pleaded. "He's your mentor!"

"I'm as much in the dark as you are," Sebastien admitted. Trying to be patient when everyone around her was so excited made it even harder.

Damien kept adjusting his collar and sleeve cuffs, fidgeting restlessly. "He hasn't dropped even the slightest hint. I think he enjoys the suspense."

"Maybe he's come up with something that will gain him Archmage status, and he wants to sway public opinion before going before the Council of Grandmasters," Ana said.

"What did Archmage Zard do to receive the title?" Sebastien asked. "I know you have to contribute something significant to a particular field of magic to be considered a Grandmaster, but what about after that?"

Before anyone could answer, Damien suddenly perked up. He stood, waving enthusiastically at a figure making their way through the crowd. "Titus! Over here!"

Titus Westbay, Damien's older brother, approached their group with measured steps. He wasn't wearing his uniform, which made him look younger, more like Damien. His eyes flickered briefly to Sebastien, and his expression grew somehow uncomfortable before smoothing out again, though Sebastien couldn't guess why. Maybe he still didn't trust her around Damien. Titus greeted everyone politely and acquiesced to sitting with them.

Professor Lacer walked through one of the amphitheatre's side doors, making his usual dramatic entrance with his long jacket flapping behind him. He ignored the scattered cheering that broke out and strode toward Sebastien's group. "I trust you are all prepared for an…educational experience."

Titus grinned. "Is that what they call showing off, nowadays?"

Professor Lacer sniffed condescendingly. "Perhaps not when *you* do it."

The crowd's chatter died away, replaced by a wave of silence that spread from the entrance. People began to turn, many bowing deeply as a procession made its way into the arena. A man with long, intricately braided grey hair, wearing a suit that looked like it cost an entire year of University tuition, entered. He was wearing a thirteen-pointed crown.

Sebastien's breath caught in her throat. That man was the High Crown.

A younger man walked at his side, and a retinue of Pendragon Corps guards flanked and followed behind them, their eyes sweeping for danger. The High Crown's presence seemed to electrify the air. Perhaps to the others, it was with awe, but for Sebastien, the tension was a reaction to sudden danger. "Why is he here?" she asked in a dry, brittle voice.

"Because I invited him," Professor Lacer said. He was smiling, but the expression did not reach his eyes. With a casual wave of his hand, he began to manipulate the stone of the white cliffs. A section of the amphitheatre stands —the best seats, only a little behind and to the left of Sebastien's group—rose and assumed the shape of an ostentatious throne. Then, they transformed into pure crystal, catching the light of the sun so that it almost seemed to glow. It was close enough that they would be able to hear the High Crown speak.

The High Crown smiled and nodded benevolently to Professor Lacer, and after a pause for him and the young man at his side—a whisper from Ana confirmed him to be the High Crown's heir—to wave at the crowd and accept some cheers, the older man took the throne.

Sebastien subtly shifted her position, angling herself so that she could keep them in her peripheral vision. She didn't feel comfortable turning her back on them.

On the stage, a woman with a booming voice spoke. "Welcome to the most anticipated exhibition from the University of Lenore this year! Tickets have been sold out, and you may need to squeeze in a little with your neighbors. Don't be shy, people, we're all here for the same reason. Everyone needs to be seated securely before the exhibition can begin.

"Thaddeus Lacer is the youngest Master of free-casting in a century, and also a Grandmaster of sorcery. He fought with honor and brought glory to our nation during the Haze War, and was widely recognized as a war hero after previously confidential records were released to the public. He is not only a champion duelist, but also the patent holder of several spells. This man fought and *killed a dragon!*" she roared, pointing at Professor Lacer, who was still standing beside Sebastien's group.

The crowd cheered and stomped until the stone shook.

Sebastien noted that the announcer *didn't* mention that Professor Lacer was a member of the Red Guard, even though it was widely speculated and also true. Technically, it was supposed to be a secret.

"Grandmaster Thaddeus Lacer is immensely powerful," the woman said, calming somewhat. "That is why I must sincerely caution you. Powerful magic can be uncomfortable to experience, both physically and mentally. Those who are pregnant, ill, or easily disturbed in body or mind should avoid this particular exhibition. You still have five minutes to leave for your own safety. There will be no rescue during the course of the exhibition, no chance to change your mind and leave."

Beside Sebastien, Damien shifted uncomfortably and pressed his palms flat to the legs of his pants. He noticed her attention and gave a small, awkward smile. "It's fine. It's just…a lot of these people probably don't understand what it will really be like. I hope the organizers have some way to manage anyone who panics."

As the woman returned to calling out more of Professor Lacer's various feats, Titus elbowed his younger brother teasingly. "These warnings are only making me more eager," he said, a grin spreading across his face. "I can't wait to see what you have in store for us, Thaddeus."

"My magic will tell the audience more about me than that woman ever could," Professor Lacer said with an unvarnished confidence that would have seemed like hubris on anyone else. With that, he moved to a corner of the stage and took a seat.

The announcer urged everyone to calm down and remain quiet.

People with boxes strapped to their bodies rushed through the audience, handing out handfuls of darkened glasses. Sebastien hurried to put hers on.

Professor Lacer closed his eyes, his body relaxing into a meditative pose. The crowd watched in hushed anticipation as the minutes ticked by. Whatever this spell was, it must be complex and powerful to need such concentration. Likely, he was carefully constructing the spell in his mind's eye, clarifying his intent and ensuring the forcefulness and soundness of his Will.

The tension in the amphitheatre grew palpable as Professor Lacer remained motionless. Some audience members shifted uncomfortably in their seats, while others leaned forward, their gazes fixed on the still figure of the professor.

Finally, after what seemed like an eternity, Professor Lacer's eyes snapped open. He rose to his feet with fluid grace and strode to the center of the stage. For a moment, his gaze locked with that of the High Crown.

The silence that fell over the crowd was absolute. Even the rustling of clothes and the whisper of breath seemed to have been stolen away. Sebastien's heart was pounding in childlike anticipation.

In one smooth motion, Professor Lacer raised both arms toward the sky. In his right hand, he held an enormous, bright blue beast core that seemed to pulse with barely contained power. His left hand grasped his Conduit. Both were secured to his palms by wire bindings so that he could not accidentally drop them.

An invisible pressure seemed to build against her skin. It grew steadily, pressing against her entire body until she felt as if she were being pinned to her seat by some unseen force.

The silence deepened. Even the sounds that she had not realized still filled the air dampened. The sounds of the other exhibitions, the wind, the city beneath, and even the breath in her own lungs fell away. It was a quiet so profound that she felt as if the world itself had frozen around her. It reminded her uncomfortably of the sensory deprivation spell the Pendragon Corps had put her under. If not for her ability to breathe, and blink, and her subtle grasp on her own shadow, she might have panicked.

Then, something came to fill the void that had been left behind. It was two-fold. A deep, resonant thump that she felt more in her bones than heard with her ears on one end, contrasted by a single high-pitched note, just on the edge of her hearing range. She had to concentrate to make sure she wasn't imagining it, her mind creating something to escape the discomfort. The combination of the two sounds created a disorienting effect, making her feel slightly off balance even as she sat perfectly still.

Then, almost imperceptibly at first, the world around them began to darken.

The air thickened, making it difficult to breathe, and the light continued to dim. Fighting against the ephemeral restraints, she raised her hand to shield her eyes from the sun, subtly using her shadow-familiar to shade her pupils beneath her palm. The darkened glasses would probably help, but she felt more comfortable relying on her own power when her eyesight was at stake.

The sun was being eclipsed, but not in any way Sebastien had ever seen before. Instead of the moon slowly sliding across its face from one side to the other, darkness was growing from a single point at the center of the sun's disk. The blackness spread outward like a pupil in the center of a glowing iris, consuming the sun's radiance with an eerie, unnatural progression.

Sebastien shuddered at the sudden feeling of being watched. As the darkness expanded, the pressure and sound grew more intense. The deep, resonant thump that had been vibrating through her bones increased in volume and frequency, while the high-pitched note at the edge of her hearing became more piercing. Sebastien's chest felt tight, as if an invisible hand were squeezing her lungs.

She watched in awe as the blackness finally engulfed the entire sun, plunging the amphitheatre into an otherworldly twilight. The crowd's murmurs of unease were barely audible over the oppressive soundscape of Professor Lacer's spell.

'Is he using the sunlight as an additional source of power for his spell, or does the blackness serve some other purpose?' she wondered. She had no time to ponder these questions further, as a sudden change swept through the arena.

There was a distinct 'pop,' like the sound of a soap bubble bursting but magnified a thousandfold. In its wake, a wave of energy washed over Sebastien. The fine hairs on her arms and the back of her neck stood up, as if a static charge had passed through her body. Within moments, the sensation intensified. The longer hairs on her head rose, defying gravity. Her clothes, too, started to float and billow as if she were suspended in water.

Her stomach flooded with icy cold and the muscles lining her spine twitched and fizzed with phantom impulses. She lost sensation from the mid-thigh down but had a disturbing feeling that she could not only feel the organs within her chest and abdomen, but feel the brain within her skull, quivering within its protective layer of cerebrospinal fluid.

Sebastien squeezed shut her eyes and clenched the edge of the stone seat beneath her, trying to force her racing heart and the instinctive panic that unsettled her thoughts to calm. She didn't want to miss even a second of this, no matter how her body cried out in primordial fear that something was very, very wrong.

She opened her eyes and looked at Professor Lacer, and then to the artificial eclipse above once more.

Without warning, something else washed over her. This was different, more profound. It felt as if reality itself was shifting around her. Sebastien blinked, disoriented, and found herself in an almost familiar, yet utterly alien landscape.

She was hanging in a realm of pure, intense light. The air shimmered with energy, and though she could not control her field of view—and in fact seemed to have no body at all—she could see three suns hanging in the sky, their combined brilliance nearly blinding. In the far distance stood a forest of trees whose leaves appeared to absorb light, creating dark silhouettes against the luminous backdrop.

With a jolt of realization, Sebastien understood where she was. This was the Plane of Radiance. If those trees were transported to the mundane realm, they would likely appear to be glowing, and soon after would starve to death from the lack of sufficient light. Her eyes watered slightly but didn't burn the way they would have if she were truly there. No, this was some kind of illusion.

As the strange vision of the Plane of Radiance enveloped her senses, Sebastien found that with intense focus, she could glimpse the amphitheatre around her, but her body remained frustratingly immobile. The spell's effects were overwhelming, controlling her perceptions and leaving her feeling as though she were flying through an otherworldly landscape.

Vibrant, reflective gases drifted by in mesmerizing clouds, their colors shifting and swirling in patterns that defied description. In the distance, enormous, winged creatures soared majestically. Below, lakes of quicksilver and hills of fiery diamond passed by in a continuous panorama.

Like the rest of the audience, Sebastien was initially captivated by the extraordinary spectacle. However, her attention was suddenly drawn to movement on the stage. Professor Lacer walked toward and then past her, with an uncharacteristic stiffness. Sebastien strained to follow his progress, her head barely able to shift a few centimeters against the oppressive magical pressure.

From the corner of her eye, she watched as Professor Lacer approached the High Crown's crystalline throne. The grey-haired man's body language betrayed agitation as he addressed the professor. "What is the meaning of this, Grandmaster Lacer?" he demanded, his voice tight with tension.

Professor Lacer's response was casual, almost mocking. "Leandro," he said, using the High Crown's first name with deliberate familiarity, "I invited you here because I wanted an opportunity to speak to you in a way that even your dull, arrogant mind could comprehend."

The High Crown's posture stiffened. "Is this some sort of threat, Lacer? You're overstepping your bounds."

Professor Lacer laughed, the sound devoid of humor. "A threat? Oh, Leandro. You fail to grasp the situation entirely."

"My guards will kill you if you make any move to harm me, famous hero or not."

Professor Lacer gestured broadly, encompassing the immobilized crowd and the helpless guards. "Look around you. Your protectors are useless. They have no idea you are in danger."

Sebastien realized it was true. One part of her senses was still encompassed by the Plane of Radiance, but other than her, Professor Lacer, and the

High Crown himself, no one else seemed to be aware of what was going on in the real world at all. Even the High Crown's heir, sitting on the stands to his left, was staring wide-eyed at nothing, still and oblivious.

The High Crown's voice took on a calculating edge. "I see. You're working for one of my rivals, aren't you? Name your price, Lacer. Whatever they're offering, I can double it."

"You still do not understand," Professor Lacer said, his voice dropping to a low, dangerous tone. "I do not care about these petty power struggles, your idiotic management, or your insecurity. I am not interested in your power at all." He leaned in closer, his words precise and cutting. "What upsets me, Leandro, is your utter failure to appreciate my value or my nature. You understand me so little that you actually dared to go after my apprentice."

Professor Lacer rotated the wire mesh fixtures on his hands, moving the beast core and Conduit to the backs of his hands rather than his palms. Thus free to act without dropping his spell, he reached out and grasped Leandro's face with frightening strength. The tendons in his arms stood out as he squeezed the High Crown's jaw muscles, forcing the man's mouth open.

Sebastien did her best to keep from reacting physically, watching out of the corner of her eye as she screamed internally. *'What is happening!?'*

"Let me make this perfectly clear," Professor Lacer said, his tone hard as granite and filled with loathing. "I would not have allowed such a thing even if you had fallen to your knees and groveled before me."

With a swift motion, Professor Lacer reached into his pocket, withdrawing something she couldn't quite see. With deliberate slowness, he shoved the object into the High Crown's gaping mouth.

Whatever magical pressure was keeping the audience in their seats still worked on the man, and though he twitched and strained until the tendons in his neck stood out and the blood vessels in his eyes burst from the pressure, he could not resist. He began to hyperventilate, and then to choke.

As the High Crown's face grew puce and swollen with lack of air, like a bag of blood on the verge of bursting, he suddenly swallowed in a huge, tearing gulp.

'Or,' Sebastien realized with a quivering chill, *'whatever that was just crawled down his throat.'*

Professor Lacer released the High Crown. His grip left visible marks on the man's jaw.

The High Crown gasped for air, his eyes wide with panic and confusion.

Professor Lacer's voice was eerily calm as he explained, "You have just swallowed a curse, Leandro. It is based on a magical beast from the East, the *gu*. Should you ever act against me or my apprentice again, it will activate. And when it does, hundreds of thousands of extremely poisonous bugs will be released into your body. They will breed and fight inside you, their poison artificially prolonging your life far beyond what any human body should endure. You will experience every moment as they eat each other, waging a horrible war within your body. Finally, the winning gu will grow to the size of my fist."

The High Crown's face had drained of color and was now an ashen, corpse-like grey as he stared up at Sebastien's mentor.

Professor Lacer continued. "The gu will liquify your insides and drink until your corpse shrivels, then tear its way out of your skin, ready to repeat this process from scratch." He reached into his pocket and withdrew a glowing potion. "This will heal your throat. Drink."

The High Crown shook his head frantically, his wide eyes darting around for help that wouldn't come. He opened his mouth and strained to scream, but all that came out was a tattered, hoarse rasp.

Professor Lacer forced the healing potion down his throat, too.

The other man's color improved, and now able to scream, he did so loudly, shrilly, shouting for help and spouting off codes that were meant to alert his guards to danger.

Nothing happened. No one responded.

"Feel free to seek out curse breakers," Thaddeus added, almost as an afterthought. "They will find nothing."

"I'll go to the Red Guard. They'll—"

"By all means, do so," Thaddeus interrupted, his tone growing darker once more as he smiled savagely. "They have already punished me all they are willing to, and I have done much worse than this."

He leaned in closer to the High Crown and poked him in the belly. "And remember, the gu is already within you. Do you think you have time to remove it before the curse recognizes your intentions?"

As Professor Lacer turned and walked stiffly back down to the stage, Sebastien struggled to keep her breathing even. Her forehead, palms, and back were beaded with cold sweat. When he looked at her, she was already staring blankly ahead, like the rest of the audience. It seemed dangerous to meet his gaze now, to admit that she had seen.

Perhaps he had meant her to. *But perhaps,'* she thought, *'I was partially shielded from the effects of his spell by my shadow.'* Sebastien knew that some mind-controlling effects, like light, entered through the eyes, and she had protected hers before she looked up at the sun.

The mesmerizing vision of the Plane of Radiance shifted, and Sebastien found her viewpoint descending toward a city of shining whites and rainbows below. They fell into an area on the outskirts that seemed to be a mix of temple, garden, and open-architecture palace.

Intricate spires of crystal and light reached toward the three suns, their surfaces refracting and scattering luminescence in dazzling patterns. The gardens were a riot of color, filled with plants that seemed to be made of living gemstones and metals. Instead of swaying in the wind, they pulsed in color with its movement. Reflective pools and fountains spraying mist cast prismatic rainbows across the impossibly smooth walkways.

Despite the alien beauty surrounding her, Sebastien struggled to focus on the details.

There were some gasps and sounds of awe from the audience as the vision came to rest before a humanoid—an angel. It was tall and thin, and stood next to a column holding a spear. Like the Radiant Maiden was said to, it had wings, which trailed all the way to the ground behind it but did not move in the wind as a bird's feathers might. "Go no further, strange creature," it warned, its voice carrying an undercurrent of power that tickled Sebastien's ears. "This is not a place that one can enter and exit freely."

"I am a human sorcerer from the mundane plane," Professor Lacer said, "and this form you see is merely a spell I am using to contact you."

Small sounds from the audience let Sebastien know that everyone else could hear this, at least.

"Are you one of the Radiant Maiden's host?" he asked.

The angel's demeanor shifted, becoming more guarded. "I am," it confirmed.

Professor Lacer nodded, his posture relaxed despite the gravity of the moment. "I offer to trade three lengths of enenra cloth for three of your feathers."

The angel considered the offer for a moment, its radiance pulsing subtly. "This is a fair trade," it declared. "Is that…all you have come for? You will depart afterward?"

"Immediately," Professor Lacer agreed. He drew forth some dark, tattered cloth wrapped around a board from one of his larger pockets and threw it into the sky. It disappeared into the blackness covering the sun.

The angel had the cloth in its hands, suddenly. It looked extremely out of place there, both dark and threadbare, but the angel seemed pleased with it. It plucked three of its feathers.

Sebastien looked up. Three feathers were falling from the sky. *Their* sky, in the mundane plane.

In the distance of the Plane of Radiance, an enormous form rose up with a slow flap of wings. It was a woman the size of a giant.

Her skin was a shade of brown so dark it edged on black, striking a stark contrast against her gleaming white wings—of which there were too many. Six or seven pairs, it seemed like, attached not just at the back, but at the hips and on the legs. They curved around to partially hide her form.

Her face was half covered by what might have been an elaborate headdress made of feathers, or might have been a natural growth. It drew to a point over her nose, obscuring everything above her cheeks. '*The Radiant Maiden,*'

Sebastien realized with awe. *'How many paintings of her have I seen? And not one of them does justice to her sheer presence.'*

Thaddeus bowed, and then, with a sudden rush of sensation, the vision of the Plane of Radiance dissolved.

The crowd erupted into thunderous applause, their cheers echoing off of and rumbling through the stone.

The High Crown rose abruptly from his crystalline throne, his face ashen and his movements unsteady. He stumbled down the steps, one hand pressed to his stomach as if to quell a rising nausea. He was not alone in seeming overwhelmed, and several healers began to make their way in through the side entrances. A few moved toward the High Crown, but he waved them off violently.

Damien leaned toward Sebastien, his voice low and tinged with surprise. "I suppose even someone like him can be susceptible to the effects of such intense magic."

Professor Lacer's voice rang out across the amphitheatre, drawing all eyes back to him. "What you have just witnessed is a breakthrough in planar magic," he announced, his tone carrying a hint of pride. "I have developed a new method of accessing the Elemental Planes without physically entering them. This innovation will allow for greater freedom of exploration and, potentially, open new avenues for trade with these realms."

As the High Crown neared the exit, still looking decidedly unwell, Thaddeus's gaze flickered between the retreating noble and Sebastien. His lips twitched in that subtle, familiar expression of amusement that Sebastien had come to recognize. The professor's voice cut through the murmurs of the crowd once more.

"Before we conclude, I have one more announcement that may interest you all," he declared. "In approximately one hour, right here in this arena, we will witness a duel. The High Crown's heir has challenged my apprentice to magical combat."

A collective gasp rose from the spectators, followed by excited chatter. The High Crown, who had almost reached the exit, froze. He turned slowly around. His face, already pale, seemed to lose what little color remained. "No!" he cried out, his voice a strangled refusal that teetered on the edge of a shout.

Thaddeus continued, seemingly unfazed by the monarch's outburst. "I understand the High Crown's reluctance. After all, there is an inherent imbalance in pitting someone who has achieved their Master's certificate against a second-term University student. I know the High Crown to be an honorable man who would not authorize such injustice. However, we have agreed upon a suitable handicap for Mr. Pendragon, to make things more balanced." A sly smile played at the corners of Professor Lacer's mouth. "And I believe my apprentice might just surprise us all."

The younger Pendragon looked in confusion between the High Crown and Professor Lacer, and then turned to pick Sebastien out of the crowd.

Damien turned to Sebastien. "Why didn't you say anything about this?"

Sebastien's lips felt numb. "I just found out about it," she croaked, her voice barely above a whisper.

2 5

DUELING THE HIGH CROWN'S HEIR

Sebastien felt as if the world were spinning around her. She wanted to rest her head on her knees while things settled, but instead looked desperately between Professor Lacer and the High Crown, as if one of them could free her.

The two powerful men stared unblinking at each other. Professor Lacer wore a small smile and an unusually friendly expression. The High Crown looked constipated, if anything.

Most of the stadium had fallen silent as if people were afraid to miss even the slightest detail.

'*Say no, say no, say no,*' Sebastien urged silently, trying to push a compulsion on the man with her eyes and the force of her Will alone.

Beside the man, the younger Pendragon seemed to have noticed her in the crowd. He looked to his father, and then to Sebastien. His shock turned to suspicion.

Sebastien had a very strong feeling that the young man had never requested a duel with her at all. '*What is Professor Lacer trying to do? Some display of dominance? But surely, refusing the duel isn't "acting against" either of us? Or is he trying to make Pendragon throw the duel against me?*' The latter was the only way she had any chance of winning. '*Or maybe he just hopes they'll refuse and lose face from seeming scared of the challenge?*'

When the High Crown gave Professor Lacer a single, stiff nod, his son grew incredulous. The High Crown pulled the young man away to speak with him privately, while Professor Lacer turned his attention toward Sebastien.

People broke out into cheers, clapping and stomping or hurrying to make bets with their friends. Dozens were pointing at her, as good as a spotlight being shone on a stage actor.

Sebastien's legs lifted her halfway up from her seat before her mind caught up. She opened her mouth to protest, but the words died in her throat as she caught the High Crown's venomous glare. Nothing she could say would make a difference, she realized.

Professor Lacer descended from the stage and moved to stand beside her. He placed one hand firmly on her shoulder. "You will do fine," he said, his voice cutting easily through the noise and carrying that familiar tone of absolute certainty. "After all, you have nine spell options to work with, while Frederick Pendragon only has three."

"I've never dueled before in my life!" Sebastien protested, her voice cracking slightly.

Professor Lacer paused, as if surprised, but recovered quickly. "Well, there is a first time for everything."

Sebastien stared at him, open-mouthed. She knew he had spent some time in the dueling circuit when she was a child, and of course had dominated with his characteristic overwhelming general superiority. She had read the newspaper articles about it. So, surely he had the experience to know that a second-term student who had never even competed couldn't win against a Master who had probably been dueling for fun since he was fifteen? "I'm going to embarrass us both."

"You have all the skills necessary to succeed," Professor Lacer assured her, patting her shoulder somewhat awkwardly.

Rhett pushed through the crowd that had begun to gather around them. "I can give him a crash course on the rules and strategy," he volunteered eagerly. "I know all the standard formations and techniques."

Professor Lacer nodded. "Good. Sebastien, you are to do your utmost to win, within the rules…and disregarding silly notions like 'honor.'" His tone grew graver, a subtle warning. "I believe any apprentice of mine should be able to win in a match-up like this." With that, he turned and walked away to discuss the upcoming duel with the event organizers.

"Disregarding honor? Do you think Professor Lacer is upset about Frederick Pendragon challenging you? He must be really angry about the unfairness, to say something like that," Rhett said uneasily.

Sebastien couldn't help but think that perhaps people didn't know Thaddeus Lacer quite as well as they thought they did.

What he had done was beyond reckless—it was practically suicidal. He had threatened the High Crown himself, the most politically powerful person in all of Lenore. The kind of man who could order someone's entire family line erased from existence with a single word and then forbid the newspapers from writing about it.

A stranger reached out to grab her arm, and she shifted away automatically, shaking them off.

Ana smacked that person's hand with a cane that she had acquired seemingly out of thin air. "No touching!" she growled. She took the lead, waving the cane about indiscriminately as they made their way down to the area in front of the stage.

'Professor Lacer must not be afraid of being caught or punished,' Sebastien thought. 'Likely, he's proactively prepared for the danger he just called down on his own head. Or maybe he just thinks nothing the High Crown does can harm him?' But this still felt like a massive escalation of the situation. While Lacer might be capable of defending himself against whatever retaliation came his way, she certainly wasn't.

A cold sweat broke out across her forehead as an even more disturbing thought struck her. How exactly had Professor Lacer created that gu curse? She was certain he had prepared it in advance—he'd still been actively maintaining the planar portal avatar spell during their confrontation, and he couldn't dual-cast. But the mechanics of it troubled her.

The curse needed some kind of intent-based trigger, surely? Yet the High Crown had screamed for his guards with no immediate consequences. Perhaps the curse was designed with a delay, preventing the High Crown from dying right there in the audience and implicating Professor Lacer.

But what truly unsettled her was how he had anchored it to "himself or his apprentice." True curses typically relied on binding magic rather than sympathetic connections. And her divination-diverting ward probably wouldn't even activate against it, since the curse wouldn't need to search for her to do its job.

She remembered Professor Lacer's words when he had examined Liza's ward and its properties. He had talked about a method to model his knowledge of someone and then divine for anyone who matched that hypothetical construct. It was a method of circumventing certain divination wards.

It had not worked on her, which she suspected had something to do with the fact that he didn't actually know who she was. His model was inherently incorrect.

If he did that here to anchor the curse's parameters, then "his apprentice" was very clearly a different model than "the Raven Queen." But if he had used a *piece* of her somehow, without her knowledge, she already knew that both of her bodies were equally "hers." In fact, it was almost strange how both bodies seemed to react exactly the same to sympathetic magic, even though

Sebastien's mass was higher than Siobhan's, meaning that it couldn't be a *pure* transformation.

But however it worked, if it had used a piece of her, the next time the High Crown acted against Siobhan Naught, it would either activate her divination-diverting ward or the High Crown would die a horrible, gruesome death. And seeing as Professor Lacer was fully aware of her divination-blocking "boon," the latter seemed more likely. Not only would she be suspected as the culprit, it would alert Professor Lacer to her true identity.

Sebastien could think of only one word to summarize the situation. "Fuck."

Rhett threw an arm around her shoulder. "Don't worry too much. No one expects you to *win*."

She looked at him incredulously. "Professor Lacer just said he expected me to win."

"He wasn't serious, surely?"

"He's always serious."

Rhett shifted uncomfortably, his expression worried. "What's your current thaum capacity?"

"You were there for the last test," Sebastien reminded him. "Six hundred eighteen thaums."

Rhett pinched his lips together and shook his head. "Right. Well, that's very nice and all, but Frederick Pendragon probably has three or four times that much power. Maybe more, if he's anything like you and Damien. And even with only three spell circles in his dueling ring, he can make them as large as he wants." He tugged on one of his small braids. "That must be why Professor Lacer said you don't need to be strictly honorable. You have *no chance* in a straight fight."

Damien had approached, and now elbowed Rhett in the side. "That's not true. The outcome is never determined until the end."

Rhett pinched his chin and nodded sagely. "You're right. I need to place a bet on Sebastien now. If he somehow wins, I can probably make ten-thousand-to-one profits."

Waverly sidled in between them. She adjusted her glasses and looked Sebastien up and down. "Is that true? You can win? Because I'll bet on you, too. I could use a few thousand gold that my parents don't know about."

Sebastien didn't think she could win, but she certainly had no choice but to try. "I don't have the power, but I have a few tricks up my sleeve. Professor Lacer taught me how to adjust and even completely detach the output of my spells from the physical Circle. Some of them I have enough force and clarity of Will to adjust slightly without changing anything on the spell array, if we leave the output moderately vague in the setup."

"That's huge. What spells can you cast?" Rhett asked.

"We're allowed to use components and set everything up beforehand, right?" she asked.

"Of course! You just can't free-cast or use esoteric spells, and your opponent gets one minute to examine your spell arrays before the duel starts, and vice versa," Rhett said. "You have to stay within your outer circle, and if you leave it for any reason, you lose a point. Get hit enough to cause damage by an opponent's spell, and you lose a point. Lose three points and you're out."

Sebastien nodded absently, her mind already racing through possibilities. Since this wasn't a real fight, and they would both be stuck within pre-defined areas, it opened up her options quite a lot.

She listed off her capabilities, starting with the basics she'd learned in class and moving on to some of the more creative applications she'd discovered through experimentation. With each new spell or technique she mentioned, Rhett's eyes grew wider.

"I'm still not very good with anything that requires heavy transmogrification," she admitted. "Not enough to use it in battle, anyway."

Rhett stared at her with a mixture of amazement and apprehension. "Where did you learn all this? Some of these applications... I've never even heard of using these spells this way."

"Practice," she said simply. "Lots and lots of practice. And..." She hesitated. "Sometimes desperation leads to innovation. The fact that this is a game and not a real fight to the death is the only reason some of those ideas could be viable."

"And he's Professor Lacer's apprentice," Damien added proudly. "Why do you think the man accepted Sebastien?"

Waverly rolled her eyes. "Yes, yes. So, what I'm gathering is that we should all pool our funds to bet on Sebastien."

Ana smiled. "We might make enough to fund our own pseudo-noble house. The Fourteenth Crown Family."

They were trying to put her at ease, Sebastien realized.

Waverly started to rock back and forth onto her tip-toes. "Enough for me to buy a dragon egg, do you think?"

Brinn stuck out a knuckle and rapped her on top of the head. "Waverly, you *cannot* bind a dragon familiar. Haven't you heard the many, many stories about witches who thought they could handle it?"

Waverly rubbed the top of her head and scowled at him. "But I'm better than all of them. A dragon would like me. Especially if I raised it from an egg."

"Sure, it's cute and manageable as a hatchling. Maybe it eats a few of your neighbor's pets and tries to have sex with your serving boy. But the next thing you know, it's big enough to ride, and you'll be forced into raiding Silva Erde or Kuth to pay for its upkeep and maintain your end of the contract. Or it wants its own familiar and decides it must have a sky-kraken, never mind that they eat dragons. Or…"

Sebastien tuned them out as Brinn and Waverly continued to bicker.

Damien rubbed his chin thoughtfully. "Since this isn't an official duel for rank, we should be able to provide our own components. That could be good for you, right? You can use whatever you're most comfortable with."

"Or bad," Sebastien said. "The High Crown can obtain anything money can buy."

Rhett snorted. "You're forgetting who your mentor is. Professor Lacer could probably get his hands on anything just as easily."

Ana straightened, her eyes sharp. "Components aside, your only real advantage is versatility. Nine spells versus three gives you options." She smoothed the line of her pants' seam with precise movements. "Frederick Pendragon isn't a free-caster, but he's been tutored by the best since he could walk. He's competent, and I'm sure he has some impressive tricks prepared."

"You know him?" Sebastien asked.

"I know of him. If I were in his position, I would choose three versatile spells: defense, offense, and control. He needs to make a good showing here." Ana's lips curved in a small, knowing smile. "Have you had any interaction with him before? Something that would make him challenge you to a duel?"

Sebastien shook her head.

"It's because Professor Lacer rejected him as an apprentice!" Damien exclaimed. "The High Crown must be holding a grudge."

Ana nodded slowly. "Frederick will probably treat this as a demonstration at first. He'll let you show off your repertoire, maybe even seem like he's going easy on you. Then he'll defeat you decisively." She tilted her head, considering. "If you can embarrass him early, he might drop the pretense and actually try. And if you manage to embarrass him badly enough…" Her voice lowered. "Well, people tend to make mistakes when they lose their composure."

Sebastien watched as the exhibition organizers scrambled to adjust the schedule, selling tickets on the spot and creating a betting station near the entrance. The impromptu duel had created a buzz of excitement that drew even more visitors than before. They would display it on the massive mirrors even for those who couldn't fit inside the amphitheatre itself.

On the stage, two large circles had been painted out, just touching each other. One was hers, and one was Frederick Pendragon's. Between them, a curtain had been set up to keep them from watching each other's preparation.

Rhett pulled her aside and started rushing through as much knowledge as he could pack into thirty minutes of rapid-fire lecturing.

Sebastien did her best to retain it all, despite the use of names and standard strategies that she had never heard of, while simultaneously trying to formulate a strategy that had any hope of winning.

Rhett followed her onto the stage as she began to draw out her spell arrays, continuing to spew information of questionable use.

She laid out her spell arrays with methodical precision, nine smaller Circles around the inner edge of the larger one, while still leaving her a couple of meters in the center in which to move.

Instead of a standard barrier spell, she created two more situationally useful shields: a mirror-based one that she hoped would deflect incoming attacks with minimal resistance, similar to how her divination-diverting ward worked; and a magnet-based shield that might be able to cover the places where the other failed.

Rhett hovered anxiously nearby. "This is a terrible idea," he said, gesturing at the mirror array. "Reflecting spells back is way harder than just blocking them. The backlash alone could break your Will."

"I'm not going to reflect them back," Sebastien explained. "Just…guide them away." She continued drawing her arrays: two different air-control spells —one broad and one precise—vibration control, light manipulation, stone disintegration, and stone control. That was eight, and after a moment of hesitation, she added electrical control to her ninth inner circle, just in case it would be useful to counter something Pendragon did. A lot of battle spells could be disrupted by lightning.

Her strategy relied not on casting multiple spells simultaneously, but on using most of her Will to maintain detailed control over deliberately vague spell arrays while leaving some mental power for dodging—and if Ana's advice was right, maybe taunting. Most of Sebastien's power would focus on fine-tuning the output of each spell.

This would keep Pendragon from knowing exactly what she had up her sleeve and allow her to do multiple different things with a single element from the same spell array.

The added one extra component to the broad air control spell, glad that there was no wind and hoping that Pendragon wouldn't have the time to examine it closely, or the imagination to be suspicious.

It ended up taking slightly longer than the promised hour for the duel to start, as the organizers rushed to bring properly sized dueling suits from somewhere. They were slim and stylish, made of leather and with long, flared jackets that reminded Sebastien a little of Professor Lacer's.

More importantly, they were artifacts that would offer protection, measure the impact of most spells, and monitor the body's condition to detect damage. With that, they helped the judges determine the awarding of points that might be less obvious, and also gave damage reports to the healers on standby.

Sebastien and Frederick Pendragon were ushered off to a couple of small closets cut into the side of the amphitheatre to change, and Sebastien realized an unforeseen problem. To prevent cheating, artifacts weren't allowed in the duels. And they would check.

Along with her clothes, she stripped off her warding medallion, the new sympathetically linked bracelet, the anklet she used to cast her shadow-familiar, and the harness with her black sapphire Conduit. She hesitated with Myrddin's transformation amulet. They wouldn't be able to detect it was an artifact, but she didn't want anyone to see or know about it, either.

After some hesitation, she took it off and put it in the small chest provided to keep her belongings. After physically locking it, she then used some chalk and a knotted piece of leather to cast a locking spell on it too. She paused, feeling half-naked despite the protection of the dueling suit, and then used a second spell to fuse the wooden lid of the chest to the body. *'Just in case. Without the amulet, I'll be trapped in this form.'*

Even that didn't feel like enough, and with wild scenarios of someone stealing the whole chest and running off with it, she brought it out and set it at Damien's feet in the stands. "Look after my things."

Alec leaned forward, resting his chin on his fists. "Are you afraid someone is going to steal your underwear?"

Waverly, who was sitting behind him, kicked him in the back.

Sebastien was still wearing her underwear, but... She looked up at the crowd. Maybe some of those people were the same kind who would steal her things and sit around in a circle taking turns casting divination magic on a drawing of her. Suddenly, Alec's idea didn't seem so outlandish. She looked down at Damien. "Protect my underwear," she said seriously.

Alec started giggling, and Waverly kicked him again, forcing him out of his seat and onto the floor.

Damien's mouth did a funny little wiggle, but he saluted Sebastien with equal seriousness.

Sebastien returned to the stage to do one last review of her spell arrays.

Ana approached as Sebastien finished. She gripped Sebastien's forearms tightly and tossed her hair with nonchalant confidence. "Show them what you can do."

Sebastien grinned back at her friend. "If I win, I want ten percent of whatever the group wins from betting."

The announcer's voice boomed across the arena. "And now we see a touching moment between the underdog defender and his...close friend." The suggestive tone in her voice was unmistakable.

Ana's face twisted with disgust. "Oh, please. Two ridiculously attractive people can be just friends, you know!" she called back loudly, drawing laughs from the nearby crowd.

The announcer cleared her throat awkwardly and moved on to introducing the duelists' credentials while Sebastien made her final preparations, double-checking each array for perfection.

And then the curtain came down and the timer started.

As they switched places to look at each other's spell sets, Pendragon gave her a confident smirk. Who knew what the High Crown had told him.

With dismay but no surprise, Sebastien noted the complexity and precision of her opponent's work. Unlike her, his spell arrays were full and detailed. He had done as Ana guessed. His shield array incorporated both physical and energetic protection components, with redundant fail-safes that would make it difficult to overwhelm. A force spell used sympathetic connections to mimic and amplify…physical movement? She didn't spend the rest of her limited time trying to read and parse the whole thing. His ranged attack array bristled with piercing and slicing glyphs arranged in an efficient pattern that would allow some measure of guidance, even once it had been shot.

She could tell that he knew output distancing too, though his version seemed to require guiding anchors rather than true detachment. Either that, or he was deliberately showing less capability than he possessed, hoping to catch her off guard.

When the minute ended, they returned to their own Circles and bowed to each other with formal precision. As Sebastien focused entirely on her opponent, the crowd's roar faded to a distant hum.

The instant the starting bell rang, Sebastien channeled power through her vibration array, creating a thunderous crack of sound as close to his head as she could manage. She followed it immediately with a much more subtle variation of the vibration spell, meant to disrupt the inner ear and cause vertigo. This was tricky, and she wasn't sure she was doing it right. It wasn't an application she had practiced nearly enough.

Pendragon's shield—a spherical thing that reached all the way to the ground on all sides—grew around him with impressive speed. It seemed to be made of gently glowing lines that formed hundreds of interconnected triangles. He shook his head, pressing his hands against his ears as he stumbled. Unfortunately, he regained his equilibrium quickly.

It wasn't enough for the judge to raise a flag for a point in her favor.

Sebastien's excitement at landing even a glancing blow faded as she realized the limitations of her strategy. Her sound-based attack couldn't penetrate his shield to reach his inner ear—the barrier blocked not only spells impacting against its surface, but the energy transfer she needed to supply her detached-output attack.

To bypass such protection, she would need a spell that drew power from somewhere the shield didn't reach, either physically or conceptually. The latter, at least, she had absolutely no idea how to manage.

Before she could formulate a new approach, Pendragon's shield dropped and another of his spell arrays activated with a subtle glow.

He lifted his right hand, and a giant, blue-glowing mimic of the appendage rose from the ground. The magical hand was taller than Pendragon's body.

Though several meters separated them, he smirked again and slapped in her direction.

The force-hand jumped forward and blasted through the air, coming in to swat Sebastien like she was a fly.

Sebastien squeezed her Conduit until the veins in her wrist stood out, and her mirror-shield spell blinked immediately to life. She angled it to the side to deflect the oncoming blow.

The force of his strike shattered her mirror-shield spell like glass.

Sebastien released the spell before it could harm her, but she was mentally reeling as she used her last bit of mental fortitude to throw herself bodily to the side. She landed hard and lay prone.

Displaced air brushed past her face and ruffled her hair as his attack missed by mere inches. It struck the ground on her other side with a horrible *crack*. The attack spell dissipated from its own overwhelming force, but the tremor traveled through the stone and rattled her bones and lungs.

Sebastien crawled back to her feet and met Frederick Pendragon's gaze.

He was smirking again, but none of his three spell arrays held the subtle glow of activation.

Sebastien swallowed, trying to wet her dry throat. '*If that had hit me, I wouldn't just have lost a point. I would be seriously injured.*'

26

A LESSON IN VIOLENCE

Sebastien
Month 9, Day 3, Friday 3:35 p.m.

Pendragon hadn't gained a point on Sebastien, so waiting for her to regain her footing was not a requirement of the duel itself, but arrogance. That was good. No fight was determined before the end. If he failed to take her seriously and was even a little more careless than he would normally be, that was to her advantage.

Sebastien didn't wait. She bent one part of her Will to controlling the broad air control spell's output with various on-the-fly modifications, and used the other to send several quick bursts of power through it. It was still far from free-casting, but it made her more versatile than she should have been.

Several sickle-shaped slicing spells cut from her spell array and through the air, one after the other, as fast as if she were simply snapping her fingers and creating them. Some traveled straight, but several curved around like boomerangs, targeting Pendragon from different angles and heights. They were more visible than they normally would have been, due to the tiny granules of dust and flour riding their wake.

She wasn't skilled enough to calculate the angle of travel perfectly ahead of time without actively controlling each, and so several would miss. That was fine, as they instead worked to restrict the area he could use to dodge.

Pendragon's eyes widened, and he tried to dodge anyway, but there were simply too many attacks coming at once. His triangular shield spell flashed back to life with a crystalline chime, the magical barrier forming just in time to deflect her assault.

The announcer's voice boomed through the amphitheatre as she screamed something about Sebastien's speed and control, but Sebastien tuned out the words. She couldn't afford to lose focus. She channeled power into her other air-based spell, this one meant for fine control. It was technically a modification of a spell meant for patients with lung issues, but Sebastien used it to draw extra oxygen from the air near Pendragon inward, while pushing away nitrogen. She hadn't practiced this spell long enough to be truly proficient or totally efficient with it, but she did her best to keep the spell array from glowing noticeably.

If Sebastien wanted to win, she would at least need to *try* to kill Pendragon. She remembered Ana's advice, too. She drew back her shoulders, raised one eyebrow, and called out loudly enough to be heard past the announcer and the roaring of the crowd. "I heard you were turned down by Professor Lacer as an apprentice candidate. No wonder, if you have this much trouble against a second-term student."

Pendragon stood up, still under the cover of his shield bubble, and gave her another of those irritating, condescending smiles. "You're such a child. I would be the one dishonored if I took you seriously. It would be like kicking a puppy who is biting at your shoelace."

He shook his foot in her direction and then began casting his third spell. Two seconds later, streams of golden-red light twisted up from the center of the spell array and coalesced into the slightly abstract shape of a falcon. It made a single flap in the air and then followed the violent direction of Pendragon's arm to shoot toward Sebastien like an arrow.

It was fast. Very fast. But it flew in a straight line, and Sebastien had plenty of room to dodge, although she had to make an extra duck and weave to avoid the edge of the spell's angled "wing." It shot past her, continuing on for a few meters before unraveling back into streams of light and then disappearing entirely.

Sebastien dropped her air control spell and reached for the electricity spell array. With a deep breath and a firm grip on her Conduit, she channeled as much power as she could manage into a single, concentrated spark and sent it flying outward. The electricity crackled through the air, but instead of striking Pendragon directly, it ignited the dust-filled, oxygen-rich atmosphere she had been quietly building up around him.

The resulting fireball was spectacular. Flames erupted from all sides, battering him before he even had a chance to raise his shield. The pressure wave knocked him off balance. His long hair crackled, singed half away from the heat, and his dueling suit was scorched.

The judge's flag rose, awarding Sebastien her first point.

The crowd erupted in cheers and stomping, sending a tremor through the stone amphitheatre. Sebastien didn't let the noise distract her. She immediately switched back to her fine control air spell, this time drawing in carbon dioxide and nitrogen and pushing away any remaining oxygen.

Technically, after winning a point, they were supposed to allow their opponent to recover and the judge to signal the duel's continuation. But as long as she was sneaky enough, she thought she might get away with it.

"Kicking a puppy?" she yelled. "But…Professor Lacer expects me to win." She sent back a smirk as similar to Pendragon's as she could manage. "Don't worry, it's not dishonorable to lose to someone who's simply better than you."

His expression darkened. "One point is all you'll get," he snarled, his previous pretense of casual superiority forgotten.

He activated his falcon-missile spell again. The bird of golden-red light streaked toward Sebastien, who managed to dodge again. She poured even more power into the air spell, hoping the lack of oxygen would slow his thoughts as well as his Will. She probably wouldn't be lucky enough to suffocate him into unconsciousness, but this was a form of environmental attack that could get past even his shield spell.

She caught a flash of red-gold out of the corner of her eye. Sebastien tried to throw herself out of the way, but there was no time. She dropped the air spell, and her mirror-shield spell flashed into existence in the next instant, placed perfectly between herself and the oncoming attack within a tenth of a second. It might have been the fastest she had ever cast a spell, but like before, it shattered under the impact.

Even angled to deflect rather than block, it simply couldn't withstand Pendragon's raw power. The falcon's wing caught her shoulder, shredding through her dueling jacket and tearing the skin beneath.

Sebastien gritted her teeth but couldn't hold back a scream of pain.

The judge's flag rose again, evening the score.

Blood trickled down Sebastien's side, but a quick test showed that she hadn't received enough damage to limit her mobility. There was no time to dwell on it. Her practice with light-refinement had taught her that she could push part of her Will into controlling her magic while leaving the rest to guide her body. She pushed away the burning pain and the way her arm wanted to go limp just to avoid jostling the wound. It settled unhappily in the back of her mind, no longer a distraction.

The judge gave the signal to continue.

Perhaps the suffocation plan was a little too ambitious. After all, they were in the open air, not an enclosed room. Sebastien disintegrated some of the white stone into a fine dust, instead. While dodging another strike from Pendragon's giant force-hand—which crashed into the ground where she had stood with enough strength to crack the stone—she channeled power through her broad air control spell.

The gust of wind carried the stone dust directly toward Pendragon's face. It was a basic strategy, one that any experienced duelist would know to expect. True to form, Pendragon didn't even bother raising his shield. He simply closed his eyes and turned his head slightly, letting the dust scatter harmlessly around him.

"Really?" he called out, his voice dripping with condescension. "Dust in the eyes? Is that the best Professor Lacer's precious apprentice can manage? I expected something more…impressive."

He still wasn't taking her seriously. Sebastien kept her expression neutral, refusing to let a premature smile of triumph show on her face.

She channeled power through her light manipulation array, crafting an illusion of Pendragon's own falcon spell. The false bird of golden-red light materialized above her, its wings spread wide in a perfect mimicry of his attack. But unlike Pendragon's version, which moved with devastating but predictable speed, Sebastien's illusion streaked through the air just barely slow enough that the human eye could follow.

Pendragon's eyes grew wide as the illusory falcon streaked toward him. He wasn't fast enough to throw up his shield and so stumbled backward, his arms raised in an instinctive block. When the spell hit him, it disappeared harmlessly.

He patted frantically at his chest, looking around with wide eyes. His shield still hadn't come up.

Sebastien didn't waste the opening. While Pendragon was still off balance, she poured her Will into the stone-molding spell. She stilled completely, channeling every scrap of concentration into precisely positioning the spell's output. The white stone beneath Pendragon's right boot softened and grabbed, holding just long enough to further destabilize him.

As he flailed backward, fighting to keep his footing, Sebastien returned to her broad air control spell. Three crescents of compressed air shot out in rapid succession, cutting through the space between them with lethal intent.

Pendragon's expression twisted with desperation as he realized his predicament. His shield finally came up, but her slicing spells were already past. Apparently, either the shield could only be compressed so close to his body, or he didn't have the alacrity to modify it under such pressure.

The first blade of air sliced across his chest. The second caught his shoulder, drawing a thin line of blood. The third missed as he finally managed to stumble out of the way.

The judge's flag rose again. Though she had landed two hits, the rules awarded only a single point. In truth, she felt lucky that she had managed a point at all, what with the relative weakness of the attack. Unless she had managed to hit a vital point, those cuts would have barely slowed a real enemy. But this was a duel—a game, really—and that could work to her advantage.

The announcer's voice boomed through the amphitheatre. "An absolutely brilliant strategy from young Siverling! Returning a replica of his opponent's attack was purely psychological warfare, meant to throw Pendragon off balance. And clearly, it worked spectacularly! No damage was done by the initial attack, but Pendragon was flustered and ended up losing a second point!"

Though her blood sang with the thrill of success, Sebastien forced herself to wait for the judge to deem Pendragon, and the duel, fit to continue.

Pendragon's face had turned an ugly shade of red, a mixture of embarrassment and rage twisting his features. His previous arrogance had vanished entirely, replaced by murderous intent. Like this, he looked quite a lot like his father.

Sebastien needed just one more point to win. Despite Pendragon's greater power, his Will moved like a battering ram compared to her precision and speed. If she could survive his next assault, victory was within her grasp.

Sebastien set off another barrage of air-based mini thunderclaps around Pendragon. The attacks weren't powerful enough to seriously harm him, but they were fast and numerous, designed to keep him off balance. If she was really lucky, enough damage to his eardrums might accumulate to earn her a point.

His force-hand spell glowed to life again. Instead of attempting to slap her away or squash her like a bug again, Pendragon grabbed for her. The giant blue fingers spread wide. Sebastien attempted to dodge, since defending with magic was useless anyway, but he used slower, more precise movements to pen her in.

If this continued, she would be forced out of the ring or caught and crushed until she lost another point. She leapt forward instead, launching herself in the air and attempting to use the hand as a platform to throw herself to safety.

As she was coming down on the other side, the hand reversed direction, striking her with a backhanded sweep that sent her tumbling toward the edge of the ring on the other side.

She maintained her concentration, setting off even more miniature thunderclaps around Pendragon's head. She noted in a small corner of her mind that several of the faculty standing on the side for emergencies had tensed, their hands moving toward their Conduits.

Unfortunately, Pendragon maintained his composure despite the assault.

Sebastien cast her reflective shield spell between herself and the edge of the ring. The shimmering barrier materialized between her and the ground, but Pendragon's force-hand crashed down after her. She found herself caught between the two magical constructs. Her ribs creaked as the air was knocked from her lungs, and her shield shattered like weak glass.

She smashed into the stone and rolled immediately to avoid being crushed by the magical hand. Whether from the impact of the blow or crossing the boundary, she lost another point.

She climbed slowly to her feet, trying to ignore the screaming hindbrain panic that she couldn't get her lungs to accept air. Her gaze met Professor Lacer's; her mentor was standing off to the side, ready to intercede in the case of a real emergency. His expression was stoic and unreadable.

As breath returned to Sebastien's lungs, she moved back into the ring and nodded to the judge. She drew on her electrical spell array, watching as Pendragon's falcon missile coalesced and streaked toward her, its golden-red light casting strange shadows.

Sebastien dodged again to make sure it wouldn't clip her from its initial strike, but her real defense was a small arc of electricity that cracked out and through the oncoming attack, searing her eyes with its light.

The electricity wasn't as potent as she'd hoped, but it disrupted the falcon's form. The construct's wings flickered and wavered as the energy interfered with its structure. Sebastien resumed her barrage of thunderclaps against Pendragon while keeping her eyes fixed on the faltering missile. The falcon construct went only a few more meters before unraveling, dissolving into streamers of light that faded away.

Sebastien remained tense, watching for another surprise attack or some indication that the spell had only pretended to fail, but Pendragon was already activating his shield array once more, the familiar triangular lines of the barrier beginning to form around him.

At first, Sebastien thought her constant barrage had gotten to him.

His composure cracked once more as he sent her a very unbenevolent glare of pure rage. But then, he gripped both hands in a white-knuckled grasp around his Conduit, and the triangle-shaped lines making up his shield flexed and warped for a moment, like a soap bubble about to burst. That was the only warning she got.

The shield exploded outward toward her in a wave of crystalline force. The triangular patterns stretched and distorted as they expanded, creating a translucent wall of magical pressure that threatened to push her straight out of the ring. The raw power behind it made her teeth ache, and she slid back.

But Sebastien leaned into it and hunkered down, one knee pressing into the white stone beneath her. She channeled power through her mirror-shield spell, angling the edge like a wedge to slice through his expanding shield. The pressure parted around her in a small area, just enough to keep her from being thrown backward. Her boots scraped against the ground as the force continued to push her, but she didn't shift more than a few inches.

As the ongoing wave of his shield's explosive power began to taper off, she pulled on the only spell she hadn't yet used—the magnet-based shield. This would be the most difficult spell application yet. Remaining in her half-kneeling position, she turned all of her Will toward acting faster than Pendragon could respond.

The magnetic shield had been meant to help draw physical attacks off course, and probably had several other potential applications based on natural science, but she didn't have a strong enough grasp on the concept to do much beyond the obvious. Still, augmented by a powerful component, it might be enough.

She would have liked to target Pendragon specifically—perhaps his clothes—but didn't have the time to figure that out, if it would even work without a sample of what she wanted to attract. Instead, she directed an attracting force toward his general direction with all the power she could muster. She didn't distance the output, as the difficulty might decrease the force she could apply.

Although it failed to send him flying through the air, it was enough to pull him off balance. As he struggled to catch himself, one flailing arm crossed the plane that separated their sides of the dueling area. She grabbed the limb and yanked him across into her Circle.

Then, just to make *sure* she would get the point, she punched him in the face.

Pendragon reeled back, his eyes wide and round. His hands lifted to cup his face protectively but drew away bloody. His expression twisted with shock at first, and then outrage as his gaze snapped to her.

A stunned silence fell over the amphitheatre as the judge raised his flag one final time. "The winner is Sebastien Siverling!" the announcer's voice boomed, breaking the tension.

Sebastien kept her eyes locked on Pendragon, muscles tensed for any potential retaliation.

His face went pale before flushing crimson from his collarbones to the tips of his ears. His fists clenched at his sides as his gaze darted between the crowd and his father, who was standing at the base of the stands rather than sitting on the crystalline throne.

The High Crown's limbs were rigid, and though he wasn't scowling, his lips were set with disgust, and the look in his eyes was dark.

With mechanical stiffness, Frederick Pendragon executed a formal bow to Sebastien, then to the judge, before striding off the stage, his back ramrod straight.

Sebastien returned the formal gestures, though her movements were somewhat hampered by her injuries. When she straightened, she caught Professor Lacer's eye. He gave her a single, subtle nod.

Before she could think to do anything else, her friends descended upon her in a jubilant swarm.

There was a lot of jumping and screaming until they belatedly realized that she was still injured. Alec tried to kneel so that he could give her a piggy-back ride over to the healer. While she was busy arguing, the healer managed to pry her friends away, scolding them harshly for obstructing his ability to do his duties.

He brought her over to the side of the amphitheatre to be examined, after which she was treated on the spot with a few spells and potions, including an expensive Radiant healing salve that knitted the flesh of her shoulder back together with barely any scarring.

"Magic is amazing," Sebastien said with a chuckle, rolling her shoulder and noting only a faint ache left behind. "I love it."

While the others were waiting, they had gone to collect their winnings. Waverly handed Sebastien a few dozen gold with a regretful expression. "The odds against you weren't nearly as bad as we expected. I definitely can't buy a dragon. Maybe a pixie, but I don't really fancy a life of collecting all their dust and dander."

'So people actually believed I might be able to win? Professor Lacer's reputation must carry more weight than I realized,' Sebastien thought.

She opened the wooden chest, changed back into her regular clothes, and re-cast her shadow-familiar spell with profound relief. All of her hidden accessories remained untouched. The familiar weight of them against her skin provided an unexpected measure of comfort.

Sebastien decided to leave quickly to avoid any further dramatic events, but Professor Lacer intercepted her. He gave her perfunctory congratulations on her win, passed on a slip for a hundred contribution points from the judge, and then hesitated with uncharacteristic awkwardness.

"I should have brought this up earlier, but the days slipped away. I wish to discuss your living arrangements for Harvest Break. I am able to assign you accommodation in one of the premium dormitories that will be vacant, if you feel uncomfortable returning to Dryden Manor."

Sebastien blinked.

"And if you need me to, I can *handle* any issues with Lord Dryden personally," he said, a hint of malice sneaking into his tone.

Sebastien's eyes narrowed with sudden suspicion. "Have you been talking to Titus Westbay?"

"He made me aware of the possible issue. I understand that you would likely also be welcome at Westbay Manor, but I thought you might prefer your privacy."

Sebastien gave an angry huff and ran a hand through her hair. "Titus Westbay is an incorrigible gossip and a rumor-monger. You should take anything he says with a grain of salt. And thank you for the offer, but I'm staying in my own apartment over the break," she stated firmly.

She braced for Professor Lacer to pry or argue, but he shifted topics smoothly. "Here." He reached into a pocket and pulled out two leather-bound notebooks. "These are manuals on gesturan spellcasting. Study them over the break, along with the dazzler. When you think you're ready, contact me to schedule a time to practice some of its more advanced applications."

Before they could discuss details, her friends swept her away, insisting on a celebratory dinner. As they led her off to the edge of the white cliffs and they stood in line for the transport tubes, she glanced back at the University grounds, which were still teeming with students and visitors.

It seemed like a lifetime since she had come to Gilbratha, but it still felt surreal to realize that her first year at the University was over.

27

ROUND TABLE

Gera
Month 9, Day 4, Saturday 8:00 a.m.

Gera's constantly running divination took in the others sitting at the round table they had set up in the center of the Undreaming Order's second floor. Deidre, Anders with his dog lying by the foot of his chair, Jackal, Martha, Sharon, Enforcer Turner, the artificer Liza, and Healer Nidson were all in attendance.

Most, like Gera, were particularly dedicated members of the Undreaming Order, though the latter two were only adjacently involved in their efforts and had been called to this meeting for their outside perspectives and their particular areas of expertise. Gera could not see them, but she could sense each contour and movement of their bodies, along with everything else in a moderate radius around her.

She cleared her throat, pressing her fingers gently against the newspaper lying on the table in front of her. "We are here today to discuss what I believe might be the latest move by the Raven Queen. Sebastien Siverling dueled and defeated Frederick Pendragon, heir to the High Crown, yesterday afternoon."

Several of those around the table nodded, but Liza narrowed her eyes. "Let's get this over quickly, shall we? I have places to be."

Nidson yawned and pinched the bridge of his nose. The man had been up late working on a particularly tricky injury to one of the flock—a woman who had been half flayed by her husband. Nidson was not a true member of the

Undreaming Order, but he was happy to work for gold when they encountered an injury that their simple stock of potions and bandages couldn't heal. Deidre especially appreciated that he tended to undercut his prices whenever he felt moved by the more pitiful patients, but the man obviously had little time for rest. "Pardon me, but I fail to see how the latest gossip is relevant? Do you believe the Raven Queen somehow sabotaged the match?" he asked.

"Those who do not follow news of the Raven Queen closely might not be aware," Gera said, "but she places special importance on Sebastien Siverling. We…" She shared a look with Deidre. "Well, we do not know why. However, she has bestowed upon him a boon of anti-divination, and she admitted before the Red Guard that they have some sort of special connection."

Liza looked down and raised her fingertips to her mouth, but it didn't completely cover the secret, amused twitching of her lips.

Gera didn't need to be a prognos to know the other woman thought she knew something the rest of them didn't. She turned her head so that it seemed she was staring pointedly.

Liza looked up and noticed. She calmed her expression quickly. "Yes, I do think I heard somewhere that they have a special connection. But I don't have any extra details. I wasn't even aware of the duel. What happened to make a meeting like this necessary?"

Deidre eagerly volunteered to read the story in the newspaper. The account was somewhat less sensationalized than usual, considering the people involved and the power they wielded. Neither the High Crown nor Frederick Pendragon had been available for comment, but the Ambassador to the Public had been quoted. "A friendly duel between two young men is meant to be a learning experience, and young Lord Pendragon was very gracious in allowing a serious handicap and holding back so that Mr. Siverling could display all of his skills, despite his relatively much weaker power."

"I was there," Martha, Millennium's personal caretaker, said. "The fight was quite exciting, but I didn't even know the half of what Mr. Siverling was actually doing until I saw an analysis of it in the paper. A lot of it was invisible."

Young Enforcer Turner grinned giddily and clenched a victorious fist. "And he punched Pendragon in the face! That was the absolute best part of the whole thing."

Sharon, their cook, grinned as if she had won the match herself. "Young Sebastien is such a hard worker, he deserved to win. I swear, I've never met a sweeter young man, and he never lets his unfortunate circumstances hold him back."

Anders reached into his satchel, pulled out a bowl and a canteen, and set some water on the floor for his dog. "It's relevant because of the fact that Frederick Pendragon was completely outclassed in skill levels, if not power, and by the end of the day, the whole city will be gossiping about it, if they aren't already. Am I right?"

"Yes," Gera said.

"Politics is warfare by other means," he said sagely. "Undermining the High Crown's authority by throwing their competence into doubt and delegitimizing the worthiness of his heir."

"It fits her methodology," Deidre agreed. "She loves to make her enemies look foolish."

Sharon pursed her lips with mild disapproval, but said nothing. She seemed much more interested in caring for and feeding the needy, and opposing the kidnapping and torture of children, than reveling in the Raven Queen's more vicious exploits.

"I do have a few contacts within Pendragon Palace, and some skill in divination," Gera said. "There is no evidence that Frederick Pendragon challenged Sebastien Siverling to a duel at any point before their meeting at the exhibitions. I believe it is highly likely that Thaddeus Lacer acted on behalf of the Raven Queen to challenge Pendragon."

Martha leaned forward. "I saw Siverling's face when the duel was announced. He seemed totally shocked. Do you think...he didn't know about it ahead of time?"

"The Raven Queen must have been very confident in his skills," Enforcer Turner said. "As expected from someone she found worthy enough to bestow a boon on. I wish I could fight like that."

Sharon's lips pursed even tighter, as if she were sucking on a lemon. She obviously did not approve of Sebastien's involvement in that fiasco, and would not be convinced that the Raven Queen's boon was a pure positive. She seemed to feel that the boon painted a target on Siverling's back, and even if it was intended to protect him, it could put him at risk from the Raven Queen's enemies.

"Why the High Crown accepted the duel, I do not know," Gera said.

"Perhaps he thought there was little danger of losing," Anders offered. "That would be the obvious reaction. In truth, Siverling does seem to have gotten quite lucky. He took advantage of being underestimated. But that doesn't matter, since all that most people will really consider is the headline. Sebastien Siverling bested Frederick Pendragon in a duel."

"And punched him in the face," Enforcer Turner repeated, grinning. "Just from hearing that, I feel he's fifteen percent more likable. We could definitely be friends."

Jackal had taken out a tiny dagger from somewhere and was giving himself a manicure with its razor-sharp edge. "So, what is her plan with all this? To be honest, after what happened, I expected something more...dramatic."

"It's only step one of her plan!" Deidre said, glaring at him. "Well, probably."

Gera pressed out her palms, motioning for them to be calm. "The Raven Queen has put herself in opposition to the established powers from the time she came to Gilbratha. Several months ago, she sent a letter to the High Crown requesting a meeting to discuss peace, and he turned her down and promised to apprehend her. That part was in the papers. After what happened later, I doubt there is any chance for him to escape unscathed. So, I wonder, was it a sense of fairness that led her to make that overture, or was it a trap, leading him to make himself more firmly her enemy so that she could feel justified in taking him out? Or maybe she was just taunting him. After all, if she really wanted to meet, there's no chance his security could stop her. However, I agree. After what he did, the man is lucky to still be alive."

Anders shuddered and reached down to pet Bear's head for comfort.

Deidre absently rubbed her burn-scarred ear. "I think we might be able to guess at some of her plans by examining the things she's stated publicly. The letter to the Edictum Council, for one. At first, I thought it was just a poetic promise of retribution, but...doesn't it sound kind of like a prophecy?"

Liza scoffed. "Please don't tell me you believe in prophecy."

Sharon rolled her eyes at Liza, then stared back defiantly as the taller, darker woman glared at her.

Deidre ran a hand through her hair and pulled it to the side, brazenly showing off the burn scars covering the other side of her scalp. "Even if you don't want to call it a prophecy, do you think it is wise to discount a possible *warning* by the Raven Queen? I'm not saying she can see into the future, but I would be entirely unsurprised if she has ways of knowing things the rest of us don't. I have been compiling and rereading the Book of the Raven Queen, and as I begin to under-stand her better...I've become increasingly troubled by the contents of her letter."

Deidre reached into the satchel at her side and pulled out the binder with the latest version of her work. "Listen.

"ON A COLD WIND BLEW STRIFE.
   The thief of fire,
   Will be a light in the darkness,
   A candle against the night,
   And will laugh as she feasts.

SAVE YOUR TEARS FOR YESTERDAY.
   As you dream of cracked roads,

And tend your garden of sticks.
For madness makes no plans,
And there is but one cure for the living.

A SCREAM into the void echoes.
Black eyes see nothing,
But a fortune of dust,
Empty bellies and sharp teeth,
And payment in bone."

ENFORCER TURNER SHUDDERED. "Okay, you've convinced me. Creepy. But what does it mean?"

"She is the thief of fire," Healer Nidson said. "I think it's an allusion to one of the old myths, where humans stole knowledge of fire from the Titans. And the fire would be—"

"The book the University brought back from their expedition," Sharon interrupted.

Healer Nidson nodded at her. "Yes, ma'am. Knowledge, essentially."

"So she will be a light in the darkness, a candle against the night?" Martha asked. "What is the night?"

Anders rubbed the stubble forming on his chin. "If we continue with the theme, then the night would be ignorance, right? But I feel like the second verse is a lot more interesting. Cracked roads and a garden of sticks seems like a prediction that everything that her enemies have built, both industry and personal wealth, will be destroyed."

"What about, 'Save your tears for yesterday?'" Martha asked.

Enforcer Turner shrugged. "Because once it happens, it's already too late to cry about it."

Sharon leaned over to read from the binder in front of Deidre. "'Madness makes no plans?' Is she calling herself mad?"

"That's not about her," Deidre said confidently. "She's a chess-mistress with plans within plans. Every domino she knocks over hits two or three different objectives at once."

Martha hesitated. "Perhaps she is mocking her enemies for being 'mad' and not properly preparing for what's to come? Reacting improperly to the danger she represents?"

"Or to an external threat," Anders said, his mouth growing grim. "'But one cure for the living...' I can't think of anything other than 'death' that would complete that riddle. If we assume that she's talking about something that will be severe enough that people will either wish or *need* to die to escape it... A Blight-type? A Nightmare-type? Or an illness curse?"

Healer Nidson's gaze sharpened. "Biological warfare?"

Sharon pressed her lips together and shook her head. "It could simply mean that things will be so hopeless that people will wish to die to escape. 'A scream into the void echoes.' That obviously hints that there will be no salvation, no one who can help. And the black eyes, are those hers?"

Enforcer Turner nodded sharply. "Definitely. You remember what she said when we were escaping from the Pendragon Corps, right, Anders?"

"Yes. She said a few lines from the letter, but clarified. 'Your screams will echo into the void,' and, 'my eyes see nothing but a fortune of dust.' She screamed it in her eldritch-horror voice, the one that echoed and warbled." Anders reached for Bear's head again and took a calming breath as the dog pressed itself against his chair, the creature's sheer weight causing it to scrape a few centimeters across the floor. "I couldn't forget it even if I wanted to."

Jackal, Turner, and Deidre echoed his shudder.

Jackal shared an uneasy look with the others. "Okay, I admit, this is starting to seem quite unsettling. I feel like maybe we should have put more importance on this from the beginning. Because the last verse is predicting poverty, famine, and violence. I mean, hopefully it's...exaggerated?"

Deidre snorted. "If anything, the Raven Queen is prone to *understating* things. She prefers to impress people with actions, not words. If she feels the need to exaggerate, then the reality would probably be cataclysmic."

Gera's back prickled with a sudden wave of cold at the other woman's choice of words. "Let us turn our attention back to the beginning. After reading the whole thing, that part seems to take on new meaning. Would she say that if she were going to be the one to bring about this ruin? Why would she need to be a light in the darkness or a candle against the night if she were in control of what's coming?"

"She's—" Deidre's voice broke, and she cleared her throat before continuing. "The Raven Queen is not all-powerful. But if she considers herself merely a candle compared to a world of night, then things must be very, very bad."

Sharon tapped the binder. "You have the tenets she handed to the Undreaming Order, right? I respected her quite a bit more when I heard them. I don't believe that young woman—or incredibly ancient sorceress, whatever you want to call her—would willingly place innocents at risk. It's why I'm willing to be a part of her organization. But if we consider that the letter was only meant as a threat to her enemies, then the first verse doesn't make sense."

Healer Nidson tapped his fingers rhythmically against the tabletop. "So we must conclude that it was meant as a more general warning."

Martha looked to Gera. "Millennium has had some unpleasant episodes recently. Do you think…he might be hearing hints of what's to come?"

Gera grimaced. "I hope not. If he is, then it means things are not far off. But if it is as serious as we suspect, and something the wind could bring rumors of, I imagine his reaction to the whispers would be much worse." She was again grateful that her son no longer dreamed, and only rarely needed to sleep, even if it did mean that he got up to a huge amount of mischief while most of the household was at rest.

"We should begin to stockpile food," Sharon said firmly.

"Do you think she's already doing that?" Turner asked. "She said she would 'laugh as she feasts.'"

"She's a powerful thaumaturge. She'll never go hungry. But do you think she can feed the entire city?" Sharon asked. "I think that's a little too unreasonable."

The young man shrugged. "Why not? She just needs to go out and kill a whale or a kraken once every few weeks. I work so hard on her behalf, I don't believe she would let me starve."

Deidre slammed her hand onto the table and pointed an accusing finger at Turner. "You have a fundamental misunderstanding of the situation and your position!" she declared. "True, the Raven Queen protects her own. But do you think she'll accept people into her flock who refuse to prepare or better themselves, who just want to do barely enough and then shelter under her wings and suck off her tit? She has standards!"

Bear let out a deep, rumbling growl, staring over the edge of the table at Turner, who shrank back, chastened.

Anders patted the side of Bear's neck. "If we had no idea, that would be one thing. But she's warned the entire city so blatantly already. Being completely unprepared for disaster would be due only to willful ignorance at this point. Especially after she literally handed us the resources to prepare."

"The celerium," Deidre agreed. "It was much more than was needed to hire a few extra teachers to come give lessons to the flock."

"What kind of medical supplies will we end up needing? Can we speak to her? I need details to properly stock the infirmary," Nidson said.

Liza cleared her throat. "How, exactly, do you all believe that the Raven Queen knows these things? Are you sure her predictions are accurate?"

A moment of silence followed. Finally, Deidre spoke up. "I'm not sure about her exact capabilities, but she told me directly that she was a seeker of mysteries, and that she wanted the flock to be, too. It seems reasonable that she has some methods to learn things the rest of us can't."

"What about Lord Stag?" Anders asked. "They've collaborated in the past. Is he doing anything in particular? Something we could emulate?"

Gera frowned. After hesitating for a moment, she said, "I sense that man has his own agenda. He collaborates with the Raven Queen, true, but he is not her follower. Still, he *has* been preparing local food production facilities. Not nearly enough to make a difference in a famine, however. But it's undeniable that several powerful factions, including the Thirteen Crowns, have been stockpiling celerium and powerful components. People are still disappearing off the street, and an unusual number of long-distance caravans and fleets of ships have been going missing. The army is recruiting. Prices for food, basic potions, and clothing are rising, and with the ice storms in the northern islands and the drought in Kuth..."

Liza nodded slowly. "That's all true. But if she wanted you to do something about it, why hasn't she given you more detail or specific instruction?"

Gera could write to the Raven Queen in the linked journal the woman had given her and schedule a meeting. "We should ask her for clarification," she agreed.

"Wait," Deidre said. "She *did* already give instructions. I just, well, I took them at face value."

Jackal scowled at her. "What *exactly* did she say?"

Deidre swallowed and looked at the ceiling as she tried to remember. "She wanted us to continue our current efforts, obviously. Feeding, clothing, and healing the flock. But in addition to that, she said that she wanted us to seek after mysteries, like her. And, um, specifically, she wanted every single member to learn to read, do basic math, and learn some basic meditations."

"Meditations?" Turner asked.

"They can help to settle the mind, but most use them as a way to stabilize and prepare the Will," Gera said. "She prescribed some mental exercises for my son, but he mostly keeps up with them in preparation to—" She stopped, her blind eye widening. "In preparation to learn magic. She told him she would teach him some magic one day."

Enforcer Turner leaned forward so hard and fast he almost fell from his chair. "Wait, are you serious?"

Deidre's eyes had gone wide, and she was staring into the mid-distance as if watching the descent of the Radiant Maiden into their midst. "She said that, for any who complete those lessons, there would be more to come. Is that what she meant?" Her voice went high and squeaky with feverish intensity. "Do you think that's what she meant!?"

Liza raised her eyebrows. "Several of you are already thaumaturges. Would you need to complete the meditations, as well? Setting aside the illegality of teaching magic to others without, at minimum, a Master's certification, how would she afford to outfit every single member of the Undreaming Order with basic components and a Conduit? And beyond that, it takes a very long time to become a competent sorcerer. If the majority of the flock were to be of any use, she would need to wait years."

Deidre laughed somewhat maniacally. "She can just hand out celerium worth thirty thousand gold without twitching an eyebrow. I don't think we need to worry about her resources." She turned a feverishly intense gaze on Gera. "What are these meditation exercises, exactly? I need a list. We should buy reference books. Or maybe some meditation tutors. Monks are good at that, right? We need to hire some monks, real ones, like from the Isles of Coldpine."

"I don't think they're the kind of monks you need, unless you plan to sprint bare-chested into battle," Anders muttered, but Deidre wasn't listening.

Liza's lips twitched again. The woman crossed her arms and leaned back in her chair. "It's not common knowledge, but I have heard some rumors from those with special channels that what the Raven Queen stole was a method to create celerium. But are you sure that's what she's planning? Could she have had some other reason for her instructions?"

"The lucid dreaming," Enforcer Turner piped up immediately, only slightly less excited than Deidre. "The exercises to prepare for that can be a little like meditation." Of them all, the young man was perhaps the most enthusiastic about the practice, though Gera had heard several of the other members of the flock complain that it was just an excuse for him to take a midday nap.

Deidre flipped frantically through her binder. "Gera, you heard her sing that song to the Red Guard, right?"

"Yes," Gera said. The atmosphere among the others was getting to her, and her fingers twitched and trembled. She clasped her hands together in her lap. "She sang it in the eldritch-horror voice, as you called it. But like a lullaby."

Deidre found the page where she had recorded her interview with Gera and recited the song quickly.

"HUSH NOW, child, do not weep.
    Close your eyes and sink to sleep.
    In slumber's realm, you may roam,
    But heed me, child, stay close to home.

FOR SHOULD you wander far and wide,
    Your soul may find a place to hide.
    In the realm of dreams, beware,
    Dark creatures roam with wicked stare.

FOR IF YOU stray too far, too deep,

In the land where nightmares sleep,
Your soul may wander, lost and torn,
And those you've left behind, forlorn.

SECRETS IN THE DARKNESS KEEP,
For with the dawn, all shadows flee.
Sleep now, child, do not fear.
Morning comes soon, bright and clear."

SPOKEN THIS WAY, it was much less disturbing than the original rendition.

Anders and Jackal shared a knowing look. "It's obviously a warning," Anders said.

Jackal pointed his small dagger at the other man. "Yes. A threat to them about the kind of power she controls. I mean, we already know that dreams—and nightmares—are part of her domain. If she were going to teach me any magic related to that song, I would definitely want to stabilize my Will as much as possible." He turned to Deidre. "There has got to be information about the best ways to grow the other facets of the Will besides capacity, right? I agree, we need that."

"I can source some mind-healing potions and supplies if you allocate me some of that thirty thousand gold budget," Nidson said. "But I would like to return our attention to the coming danger. Is it possible that the Undreaming Order is meant to be a stabilizing influence during the coming disaster? It would be a good reason for her to go to all the trouble to create an altruistic organization. After all, this doesn't serve her personally in any way."

"We exist to keep more people alive?" Sharon murmured, staring at the table.

Anders pressed a fist to his mouth, absentmindedly petting Bear as the dog whined and placed its drooling head in his lap. "It would have been a good reason to reach out to the Verdant Stags, too, since they'll surely serve a similar purpose." There was a moment of silence as the weight of this possibility settled over all of them.

"We won't let her down," Deidre declared solemnly, meeting each of their gazes individually.

Jackal slipped and winced as he cut the side of his finger with the tiny dagger. "Should we try to help with the High Crown, too?"

"But she never asked you to prepare for any of this," Liza said.

Deidre rolled her eyes. "Do we need the Raven Queen to explicitly say to prepare when she's already warned of the coming danger? We'd be stupid not to listen to her. And otherwise, she's literally *told us* what to do already. If she really needed our help with the High Crown, she would have said something. And in exchange, she would have given us something big. It's probably less hassle for her to just handle it herself. What can we do that she can't?"

Enforcer Turner pinched his chin thoughtfully. "But that doesn't mean we can't still build up small amounts of favor by assisting, just like we do when helping people in her name, right?"

"But we don't know her plan," Martha said. "If we start trying to embarrass and undermine the High Crown, is there any danger in doing it…too well?"

Surprisingly, Sharon was the one to let out a dark chuckle. "How could a little embarrassment ever make up for his crimes? I don't have any special capabilities, but if you need my limited skills for that, I would be *delighted* to assist."

"I don't see the harm in it," Deidre agreed. "But the focus of our efforts and resources should be on carrying out her actual orders as well as possible. This is going to be a huge undertaking, if we do it right. We might need to buy up some of the surrounding buildings. I'll start working on a plan. We need to expand and improve our efficiency, and figure out how to manage a much larger flock without letting people slip through the cracks. Maybe some kind of reward or recognition program meant to increase our members' sense of loyalty and belonging. I don't want to tell everyone that the Raven Queen plans to teach them magic. We want people who are here for the right reasons, not a sense of greed."

"Maybe a ranking or badge system for various contributions and achievements?" Sharon offered. "We can all collaborate on the plan. I'm going to need a bigger kitchen, and some helpers. And…we should keep an eye on Sebastien. He's a wonderful, sweet young man, and I worry he might run into danger, caught up between these powerful forces."

$$2\ 8$$

THE RIVER OF OBLIVION

AFTER THEIR END-OF-TERM CELEBRATORY DINNER—WHERE Rhett boasted loudly and incorrigibly that it was all his teaching that led to Sebastien's win—Sebastien herded and packed her drunk companions into carriages headed for their respective homes, then took a couple of hours to safely switch to her other body. As Siobhan, she returned to the University in the dead of night.

She stopped at the base of the cliffs and tested to see if the fake version of Archmage Zard's token would work to activate the transport tubes. It did, which meant that she could enter and exit the grounds without implicating her Sebastien identity. To be safe, she had left her student token and the sympathetic emergency tracker Professor Lacer had given her behind.

However, rather than taking the transport tubes, Siobhan moved into the open base of the cliffs where the water from the northern lake flowed through, past the small docks there, and into the white cliff. She found the meeting spot from the last time she was here, when Thaddeus had led her and Grandmaster Kiernan up through the stone tunnels and caves to the small room where they kept Myrddin's journals.

With a bit of concentration, she was able to remember the path that Thaddeus had led them on. *'This is safer than leaving a record of my passing, and leaves me much less likely to be caught in some theoretical ambush.'* Even though the long climb made her legs burn, it was nothing compared to some of the things Professor Fekten put them through.

When she finally reached the restricted archives underneath the library building, she stopped to breathe in the smell. Like the wind before a storm, the air felt charged with the promise of knowledge and power that lay within the iron-doored rooms. And it was all just waiting for her to absorb it. This made Siobhan a bit giddy, and since she was alone with no one to judge her for childishness, she grinned to herself and skipped up to the main floor of the library.

She used one of the indexing artifacts to search for restricted books on several different topics. Some might not be indexed, but she had found that they were often shelved by category. Once she found a room with a heavy concentration of texts about shamanry, for instance, she could go there and do a keyword search along all the shelves to find extra relevant material.

After compiling enough texts that she would have trouble reading them over the next week or two, she sat down eagerly at one of the small tables in an out-of-the-way room in the restricted archives. Before she left, she would mis-shelve the texts she still wanted to read so that they would be waiting and ready for her return.

Her first area of study was break events. She hoped to find some special, restricted information about what caused them, but found nothing new. Disappointingly, much of it was even the same tired propaganda about immoral magic corrupting the Will, which she was ninety percent sure was bunk. What few new ideas were posited had little to no basis in factual research. Most were based largely on singular anecdotes that weren't even provided by the person who experienced the break event—for obvious reasons. Siobhan skimmed increasingly quickly and managed to get through her entire stack of books and scrolls on that topic without finding anything useful.

Despite the lack of new information about the causes of break events, she did find several descriptions of unusual or particularly dangerous Aberrants, a few of which were notable.

One particularly interesting Aberrant had caused chaos in a small town near the border of Silva Erde. According to the scroll, this creature could implant false memories into anyone who met its gaze. The victims would suddenly "remember" years of friendship or romance with the Aberrant, complete with detailed shared histories and emotional connections. The Red Guard had only managed to identify the threat because the false memories contradicted each other: one victim remembered the Aberrant as their childhood sweetheart; another was unwaveringly confident it was their long-lost sibling who had been studying abroad for the past decade; and a third knew the Aberrant as their mother, despite having a living mother already. Each was convinced of their version of events, unwilling to believe the others, and even the man whose memories contradicted *themselves* could not distinguish which was real.

When it was killed, they still mourned, as even knowing that they had been deceived did not erase the memories and the emotion that came with them. The man who had remembered it as his mother was forced to leave active duty and see a mind-healer for several years to try to heal the damage his dissonant memories had done to his psyche.

Siobhan wasn't sure that she would have been able to make such a difficult decision. Damien was probably the closest person to her at this point, and, perhaps, one of the only people in the world who was her friend without any benefit to himself. She'd never had siblings, but maybe this was a little like what having a brother was like. *'If I found out he was an Aberrant all along, would I be able to kill him?'*

A small journal that ended halfway through, leaving mostly blank pages behind, described an Aberrant whose power manifested through lies. It had a huge, toothy mouth, and would seal that mouth against the ear of its victim and whisper some falsehood to them. The lies would burrow into the victim's ear canal and take form by consuming brain matter, eventually eating their way out through the opposite ear. These "larvae of falsehood" would then grow into monstrous forms that reflected the nature of the original lie, bringing destruction wherever they went.

Siobhan shuddered and scratched at her own ears, which suddenly felt quite strange. She was sure it was a psychological reaction, but not so sure that she didn't stop and take a moment to cast the airway-clearing spell on the sides of her head. All it retrieved was a bit of earwax, which Siobhan saved in a small, empty jar with some distaste. Earwax was a spell component. *'Even if it is gross, better to use my own than someone else's.'* She eyed the jar. *'Probably.'*

The third case that caught her attention detailed an Aberrant that created doorways to what seemed to be an alternate, empty version of their world. Those who stepped through would find themselves completely alone except for an overwhelming sensation of being watched and pursued. Though no other beings were ever seen in this parallel world, victims reported an intense, primal urge to run. When "caught" by whatever unseen force stalked them, they would simply drop dead without apparent cause. If their bodies weren't retrieved within an hour, the corpse would vanish. If left unguarded, the doorway itself would disappear and reappear in a new location. In this case, none of those who went through a previous iteration of the doorway would be found, alive or otherwise, when the new doorway opened.

The Red Guard tried to burn the doorway down but discovered that only caused it to change location. Eventually, they "solved" the problem by cutting the entire doorway out of the building it appeared in, complete with some of the wall and ceiling, and carting it away. Presumably, they would set a guard on it to keep it from moving forever more.

Siobhan closed this last book with a shudder. Her hands trembled slightly as she reached for the canteen of water at her side, which was faintly stale. The silence felt oppressive, the shadows in the corners more menacing than before.

She tried to imagine what it would be like to face such horrors again and again. The Red Guard walked into situations where a single misstep, a moment's hesitation, or even just meeting the wrong creature's eyes could lead to fates worse than death. Even if their bodies survived, their minds could be forever warped. It took a certain kind of courage to sign up for a job like that.

The light-refinement spell *might* help against some of the more straightforward effects, like the larva of falsehood or the implanted memories. But what about others? Some, she would be completely helpless against.

'I wonder if this is why the Red Guard places certain restrictions against shamans working in the spirit realm.' Aberrants created from break events involving the spirit realm would be horrifically dangerous and difficult to deal with. Even just imagining the possibilities set her ill at ease.

Siobhan's fingers ghosted over the delicate skin of her temple. Somewhere in there was something malignant, not so different from the monsters she had been reading about. If she was to burn it out, she needed answers, and she had several ideas for where to begin her research.

One of her first thoughts had been to learn more about binding magic and curses, since it was likely that some of those principles had been used to seal the thing in her mind. After all, Grandfather *probably* hadn't engraved a spell array for a containing artifact on her skull.

But after thinking about it some more, she was skeptical that avenue would yield results unless she just happened to get lucky. True curses all had a particular way to break their effect, but similar to understanding how an Aberrant might be countered, it was important to understand the original magic that had created them.

Without knowing exactly how the Aberrant had been sealed away in the first place, trying to undo or modify that binding would be more likely to break something important than to succeed. In a mathematical analogy, if you wanted to cancel out a number, you needed to add it to the exact negative that would leave the equation at zero.

She wasn't desperate enough to risk destroying her own mind just to get rid of the creature imprisoned within it. If things got to that point, she would be better off just turning herself in to the Red Guard.

Siobhan's second stack of texts focused on magical seals, as that was her next idea for a solution. She pulled the first tome toward her, its leather binding cracked and worn with age. The musty smell of old paper filled her nostrils, and she sneezed as she opened it, revealing densely packed text and diagrams.

As she read through the semi-impenetrable material, searching more for a general understanding of the concepts than a deep grasp on the specifics, her initial excitement faded.

Some people considered certain wards a type of seal, as technically, anything that kept something contained inside was a seal. But most of the ones she found had nothing to do with the mind and were meant to keep livestock or prisoners in.

There were extensive details about the mathematical principles behind containing physical—and magical—matter, complete with case studies of failures and the catastrophic consequences that followed. One particularly graphic example described what happened when someone attempted to seal a herd of magical deer without properly accounting for their ability to phase through solid matter. The resulting explosion of desperate animals trying to escape had destroyed half a village.

Only two texts even approached anything close to what she needed. The first described an attempt to create a room of absolute stillness by sealing away all energy. The researchers had tried to create a barrier that would contain heat, sound, and even magical energy itself. They had failed, but the theory behind their attempt was interesting, as was their theory of "absolute zero."

The second potentially useful text detailed the sealing of a wraith-like Aberrant in a tower. However, the method relied on gathering shed particulate matter from the creature to attune the wards specifically to it. Siobhan couldn't exactly gather pieces of whatever was sealed in her mind without defeating the purpose of the seal entirely.

She closed the last book with a sigh, rubbing her tired eyes and contemplating her notes. While the research hadn't provided an immediate solution, she reminded herself that the entity in her mind had been sealed away for eight years already. It was unrealistic to expect answers after a single night.

'*Knowledge is never a waste*,' she reminded herself. Even Professor Lacer had mentioned that if one learned enough in several different fields, they would realize that at its base, the theory was all connected.

Siobhan moved on to investigating artificial intelligence and consciousness transfer. She found several restricted texts on the topic. Golems were an example of this, though often extremely simple or clumsy due to the complexity required to encode lifelike functions. It was impressive to have one that could not just carry your belongings, but also sweep your floor without destroying your furniture.

One particularly enlightening tome spoke of magical consciousness transfer—blood magic of the less harmless variety.

The book explained that moving minds between vessels was purely in the realm of transmogrification, as transmutation required a deeper understanding of consciousness than humanity possessed. There had been quite a few experiments during the Blood Empire. The process always resulted in some loss of fidelity, like trying to pour soup through an increasingly fine sieve. The more complex the original consciousness, the more was lost or twisted in transference, and the greater the risk of complete mental dissolution. Often, the existential torture of the technique drove the transferred mind to insanity.

The author described it as trying to force one's entire foot into a hollow cube, pressing and bending and twisting until the flesh fit. Even if the cube technically had the volume to accommodate the foot, it was not designed to do so.

The author made the obvious connection to Carnagore, Myrddin's infamous metal beast. Because of the creature's complex functions that seemed to make autonomous, complex decisions, it had been rumored to be a magically transformed living horse, or at least to house a horse's consciousness. Of course, other parts of Carnagore's myth refuted this idea, such as turning into a statue at the top of a mountain.

Another chapter discussed binding spirits into physical vessels, which was how shamans allowed contracted spirits to temporarily inhabit their bodies, sharing power and knowledge. Theoretically, spirits might also be bound into other physical forms besides the shaman themselves, if one knew how to prepare a vessel and give the spirit some method of anchoring and empowering itself.

'Shamanry again. I really think the answer might lie somewhere in this craft.' She didn't remember her grandfather doing much that she could classify as shamanry, but he had been quite old and accomplished, and she had been learning magic for only a short while when he died.

She looked at the pile of unread books and scrolls on the table. Fewer were related to the craft than she would have hoped. If she didn't find the answer within these, she might be reduced to physically searching through every room for texts containing relevant keywords.

She pushed aside the other texts to create a smaller pile focused on shamanry, but froze as a scroll inside of an ornate case caught her attention with its first few paragraphs.

'This…is about the guiding light ritual? The one I used to create a personal symbol!?' She bounced in her seat, holding back a cackle of excitement. All the other texts were forgotten as she began to read.

The scroll was old, its paper yellowed and cracking at the edges, but the text within was clear, if semi-archaic in wording and spelling.

The scroll contained three additional functions that could be added to the symbol's utility, each requiring short rituals. The first modification would allow her to sense through the symbol, though the scroll warned it could be somewhat disorienting. The second allowed her to receive a simple "ping" of awareness—like a gentle tap on the shoulder of her consciousness—when someone with the symbol wanted her attention.

But it was the third function that made her breath catch. The scroll detailed a method of sending dream messages to another person who possessed a copy of her symbol. The recipient would need to complete their own ritual and keep the symbol close to their head while sleeping, but it would allow direct mental communication, albeit only through dreams.

The technical explanation fascinated her. Normal mental barriers made direct mind-to-mind communication nearly impossible, but dreams provided a natural lowering of those defenses, and a conduit of sorts for channeling them.

The final third of the scroll's length contained exercises that would help the thaumaturge send actually *coherent* messages. Several techniques were similar to those used by shamans to safely interact with or traverse the spirit realm, apparently. There was a reason that in some ancient cultures that realm had been called the river of oblivion. Even without facing any particular dangers—of which there were a myriad—existence there wore away at the mind and the Will.

'This is probably why the scroll was included in my search results for shamanic practices,' she thought. *'I am very lucky tonight.'*

She read through the scroll again, doing her best to commit the entire thing to memory. An alarm spell she had placed on her pocket watch alerted her that sunrise was coming soon. Siobhan had to leave, and though she would have loved nothing more than to continue her research, it had been a long week, and she was growing weary.

'It's a good chance to visit Liza. I need the sleep-proxy spell refreshed, anyway.' She changed her disguise—though not her body—before leaving, so that she could travel unnoticed. When a wave of dizziness hit her on her way back down through the tunnels, she realized how long it had been since dinner. After leaving, she stopped at a restaurant and ploughed through almost an entire table of dishes by herself.

With her stomach literally bulging, she arrived at Liza's apartment. However, no one answered the door, even after she annoyed the metal lion knocker into trying to bite her.

Frustrated but resigned, she transformed back into Sebastien, traveled a strange route to avoid any tail, and returned to her own attic apartment. She took a short nap and then checked the linked journals that she had given to Liza and Gera.

Within Liza's, she found two messages waiting. One notified Sebastien that Liza had to leave because she'd gotten a lead on a replacement shaman, and specified a very early time that Siobhan needed to arrive by if she wanted Liza's help to renew the sleep-proxy spell.

The second message was longer, and was partially faded, as if perhaps it had been transcribed from Liza's original notes by some sort of image-copying spell. This one contained calculations for converting the sleep-proxy spell into an all-day ritual that could be performed by someone with a much lower capacity than Liza's. Below that was a hastily scribbled message.

I may be gone for several weeks. Based on what I've seen of your Will, you should be able to handle this. Please don't cause any huge disasters while I'm gone.

P.S. Here is the password for my house. Say it to Mr. Lion. Also, water my plants and take care of the animals.

THE PASSWORD WAS a strange series of letters and numbers that ended with the phrase, "I'm an arrogant young prat who keeps too many secrets from the amazing, beautiful, and talented Liza, but at least I can be trusted to look after her house. I won't snoop in her things or burn the place down."

Sebastien snorted with amusement, but after reading through the details of the extended sleep-proxy ritual, let out a few choice curse words.

If she tried to avoid sleeping for much longer, her raven would die, and if that happened, it was possible that she would pass out from the sudden fatigue.

The extended ritual would require significant magical stamina—more than the average thaumaturge of her power could safely sustain. There was a limit to human concentration, after all. The only consolation was that she could break up some of the sections and rest in between. Still, attempting such complex magic in her current state would be foolish. Ideally, she would drop the linking spell and sleep for a while—real sleep—before casting a replacement.

29

———

A SEXY STATUE

SEBASTIEN
Month 9, Day 5, Sunday 10:00 a.m.

SEBASTIEN WASTED no time sitting down to review the modifications Liza had made to the sleep-proxy spell. She closed her eyes and ran through the whole solo casting process in her head to make sure she had a firm grasp on it. Visualization wasn't as useful as actual practice, but it was a good secondary method when one needed to minimize the chances of screwing up.

Then, she heaved a deep sigh, let out a few childish whimpers of unwillingness, and went through the whole rigamarole to return to her other form with the lowest possible chance of being caught or tracked. Again. By the time she finished, she'd resorted to fidgeting with her shadow under the cover of her clothes just to stave off the frustration at all the wasted time and effort. '*If there is any actual magic that would allow me to shape-shift or otherwise avoid the Red Guard's attention, I need to find it, because this is getting older than Myrddin.*'

Liza's lion door knocker was very suspicious and angry looking, but after she gave the password, it begrudgingly let her in.

Liza's plants were already watered and her animals fed, so Siobhan went down to the warded cells that used to be an apartment below. Much of the sleep-proxy spell was already set up, but she made several adjustments to the spell arrays per Liza's instructions.

When she had checked thrice to ensure an absence of silly mistakes, Siobhan cast her dreamless sleep spell on a cot in one of the other cells at the maximum power she could bring to bear. Then, she set an alarm spell on her pocket watch that should wake her in four hours, hopefully before the dreamless sleep magic ran empty.

The last few times she had slept, it had been Liza who cast the spell for her in between refreshing the sleep-proxy spell. The older woman had never commented on the need, but the strength of her Will had reassured Siobhan. No dreams had wormed their way past its protection.

Now she was apprehensive. She hauled the cot close to the sleeping raven before releasing it from the binding magic, just in case. It was unlikely, but she didn't want to leave any chance that she might collapse on the floor, completely unprotected.

The raven didn't wake up right away; it would need some time to recover from the stress on both its mind and body.

Siobhan lay down immediately, closing her eyes as the world seemed to roll around her with sudden, dizzying fatigue. For a few seconds, she worried that her anxiety might keep her from sleeping, and then all conscious thought faded into oblivion.

Some time later, Siobhan realized she was dreaming. Her heart jumped and adrenaline ran through her body strong enough that she *almost* woke herself, sensations from the real world poking through. But, as she realized her dream wasn't frightening and held no hint of the thing sealed in her mind, her fatigue managed to pull her back under the surface.

She was flying over Gilbratha, exulting in the air, the sun, and most of all, the freedom. The joyful emotion came from somewhere in the back of her mind, but was somehow distant, more like a memory of emotion than something she was actively experiencing.

Siobhan instinctively realized that she was a passenger in this experience, lacking not only the ability to control this body, but also the desire to do so.

The bird—because this body was a bird—flew lower. It swooped down in a daring, skilled maneuver to snatch a cookie out of a young girl's hand.

The child screamed and began to cry, and the bird gave a raucous, cawing laugh as it flapped away, gaining height again.

It landed on a rooftop to eat the cookie, delighting in the taste. If it were a human, it would have been making lewd sounds as its eyes rolled back in its head with pleasure. It was sad when the cookie was gone, even though the treat had stuffed its belly. From the roof, the bird watched the passersby down below, taking particular note of any that wore black feathers. They, Siobhan knew somehow, would be more likely to feed it or trade their shiny trinkets in exchange for a few coos.

Siobhan woke to her pocket watch's alarm but was slow leaving behind her drowsiness. She put her feet on the cool floor and stared down at her toes, worrying about the dream. Nothing should have slipped past her dreamless sleep spell.

She looked at the sleeper raven, which had begun to stir. It was experimentally stretching its wings and hopping about the healing enclosure. *'Did I just experience the raven's dream?'* she wondered. *'Was that some kind of magical backlash stemming from the inherent inequality in the binding magic between us?'*

She didn't know enough to be sure, but reassured herself with the knowledge that none of Liza's much-enhanced ravens could have escaped, and no matter how disturbing the unexpected experience had been, Siobhan was not harmed by it.

Siobhan chugged some water, jumped around, stretched until she was entirely awake, and then spent the next eleven hours casting with minimal breaks between steps.

It was an entirely different level of effort than keeping her shadow-familiar going all day, but she thought the practice with that might have helped, along with the hundreds of hours of light-refinement that might have incrementally strengthened her Will.

When the final step was completed and the fresh raven bound to her, Siobhan collapsed to her knees. She took half an hour to simply rest, letting her mind and body relax as the magic rejuvenated her in an entirely different way.

She would have tried for some light-refinement, but the sun had long set. She was to meet with Thaddeus and Kiernan again that night, but not for a couple of hours yet.

In the meantime, she had an easy ritual to do to expand the utility of her guiding light symbol. It was a moonless night, which was perfect for the additional ritual that would allow her to receive a "ping" from someone on the other end of a symbol. It was honestly extremely easy, only needed to be completed once, and just used an alternate version of the standard chant's final verse. She did so on one of Liza's tiny balconies, then rushed off toward the University, making sure to leave her student token as well as the emergency artifact Thaddeus had given her behind.

The men again met her at the base of the white cliffs, and they walked in relative silence. Kiernan was antsy, often rubbing at his short white beard and sighing. When they neared the level of the hidden journal room, he abruptly asked her, "How likely do you think it is that we'll find an answer to the celerium problem within these three books?"

"I truly do not know," Siobhan said. If she had to guess, it was probably the fourth journal that was closest chronologically to the one Oliver had stolen, and the most likely to hold the answers the Architects of Khronos and the Thirteen Crowns both so desperately wanted.

Kiernan turned to Thaddeus. "And how likely do you think it is that the Crowns' expedition actually turns up a fresh deposit?"

"It does not seem too implausible, though I would need to know more about their exploration plan to make an educated guess. I would be more concerned about their ability to maintain a hold on any new deposits they find, so far from our base of power."

Siobhan raised her eyebrows. "An expedition to find celerium?"

"I am surprised you did not already know of it," Thaddeus said.

"They are sending one to the north, through Ironpine Forest and maybe even beyond, and one to explore the ocean," Kiernan said. "I'm not sure how feasible the latter really is, because their surveying spells will need to reach vast distances through water, and even if they do find something, how are they going to set up the infrastructure to mine it past all the magical beasts?"

Siobhan hesitated to reveal her lack of knowledge, but her curiosity won out. "Surveying spells? I find myself ignorant of the methods your people use to search for celerium."

Thaddeus's voice took on a tone that reminded her of the classroom. "I assume you are hinting at the fact that celerium can only be used to scry for other celerium mined from the same deposit?"

Siobhan nodded as if she had, in fact, known that. This was probably another bit of "common knowledge" that she had somehow never picked up during her rather non-standard education.

"The surveying spells look for telltale hints at the presence of celerium and search for more natural signs of its presence, rather than scrying for celerium directly. History has shown there to be about a one in three chance to find a second or even third source of celerium nearby the initial deposit. If we were to find celerium in the ocean, I imagine we would quickly look to deepen our relationship with the Plane of Water and call on its denizens for aid."

Kiernan was squinting at her. "Do you know another way to search for celerium?"

"No. I have never had the need to do so."

Kiernan snorted uncharitably and muttered something unintelligible under his breath.

Siobhan ignored him. "I imagine your new spell to make planar exploration and communication so much easier would become quite valuable then, Thaddeus."

"Oh, you know, just doing my part," he said as he opened the door to the small, warded room. He didn't even smirk, which Siobhan thought must have taken exceptional self-control.

She managed to get into the third journal—the second of the three the University held—on the first try tonight, and as before, they eagerly read Myrddin's words.

He started up where he had left off in the previous journal, with space-magic theory. Except now, he was considering trying to punch a hole through folded space to travel instantly. As they jumped forward a few pages, Myrddin worked on creating a small space almost entirely separated from the rest of reality, warded to the gills against both mundane and super-esoteric threats.

Thaddeus seemed very impressed, reading over things several times and muttering to himself.

Siobhan, by contrast, found it slightly boring. Sure, it was insight into incredible magic as well as the mind of the world's greatest thaumaturge. But she couldn't understand a smidge of the actual theory, and only knew generally what was going on due to a few pictures and passages where Myrddin talked to himself in plain-speak, such as one particular note:

> I can test it with a pebble. Inside the separated space, even if things go wrong, the failure shouldn't cause catastrophic spillover damage.

"HE SHOULD USE a grape instead of a pebble," Siobhan muttered. "Grapes are much more similar to the human body. And I hope he has a plan to completely excise that pocket space from the rest of reality in case things go wrong."

Thaddeus looked at her, then back to the page. "Do you understand this?"

Siobhan would have liked to brag, but she feared that one of them might ask her to explain things if she lied. "Only a little." She paused, then added, "Not very much," just to make doubly sure that they didn't misunderstand.

But when they turned to the next section and found that Myrddin had decided to stop with the attempt to develop true teleportation magic entirely, fearing that he might "destroy the world," Thaddeus gauged her reaction carefully. "What do you think about that?"

"Myrddin was not a complete idiot," she said, nodding appreciatively. "He seems like the kind of person who actually tried to learn from his mistakes. I admire that. It is harder than it seems." She knew from experience how easy it was to fall back into the same bad patterns. She pointed to a spot further down the page, where Myrddin had said:

> I cannot truly be sure of the outcome or the viability of my void bubble in controlling any backlash. Instant travel is not important enough to risk the lives of everyone in existence, as well as any hope for their future. Also, I live here, and I like my planet un-crumbled.

. . .

"I ALSO LIKE MY PLANET UN-CRUMBLED," she joked. Neither Thaddeus nor Kiernan seemed to find it amusing.

Following his experimentation into teleportation, Myrddin developed a soft cookie recipe with some kind of chewy, melty candy mixed in. Only after having satisfied this sudden and inexplicably intense craving—after spending six weeks traveling to find the perfect ingredients and going through twenty-three batches of test cookies—did Myrddin return to his more magical experiments.

He was back to Carnagore again. This time, he was starting to put together all the research and theory from before and creating the horse's body. Every single piece was some kind of super, magically conductive material, often created by Myrddin's own hand via alchemy or other rituals.

Over the next few dozen pages, this work continued. Several times, Myrddin made mistakes or had insights that required him to redo things or adjust his plans. When he finally completed the body, dozens more pages were spent on cascading spell arrays—which would be made entirely out of celerium. These would control Carnagore's movements and add a few magical effects, like a propulsion spell on the hooves, a few moments of lightness and gravity-like force propulsion to allow Carnagore to do a single huge leap or pour on extreme speed if required.

He created the spell arrays separately, on a kind of three-dimensional invisible wire-frame. Finally, he meshed the spell arrays and the body together and added a beast core to the power center.

Siobhan was becoming quite excited. *'Will I get to ride my very own Carnagore someday?'* Sure, even with the instructions, actually creating the artifact would be a huge feat of thaumaturgy—maybe even enough to qualify someone for Grandmaster—and that wasn't even considering the cost. It still sounded strangely appealing, in the way something like riding a dragon never had. A dragon could betray you, or die, or just be generally a jerk. Carnagore was an artifact.

'I will name mine something different, though. Something less edgy.'

The next set of pages was filled with Myrddin's disappointment, and Siobhan's in turn. The Carnagore prototype was nothing like the stories, and obviously nothing like Myrddin's vision. It jerked when it moved, looked somehow strange and uncanny when it walked, was too stupid to path-correct and avoid damaging its surroundings, and a dozen other failures that Myrddin noted along with anecdotes of its embarrassing mishaps.

After that, Myrddin created a monitoring spell that would help him come up with better math for how quadrupeds moved. He just needed to place down the monitoring artifacts and leave them for a few months.

The next section was filled with several notes from Myrddin, as his thoughts seemed to keep interrupting whatever else he tried to work on.

I do not understand why people insist on blaming me for their cattle acting strangely. When I went to get milk this morning, the farmer of course did not dare say anything to my face, but I cast a spell and overheard him and his neighbors gossiping about how I insisted on casting "strange magic" on their cattle. I swear, one of them even insinuated that I had a "perverse interest" in their goats!

My interest in their goats is solely based on the way that cute, small one named Caramel dances along the top of the fence like some kind of cat! It is impressively nimble, and I believe any normal, totally non-depraved person would think so.

HE HAD DRAWN a picture of an adolescent goat hopping along a stick-woven fence. This was followed not long after by another note.

I had nothing to do with the cattle supposedly acting strangely. If you find your cow watching you through your bedroom window at night, perhaps the dumb thing was attracted by your snoring, Bernard! It certainly isn't "scheming against you," and if it is, I didn't have anything to do with it! If I wanted to harm you, I would simply vaporize your body and make everyone forget you ever existed.

AND FINALLY:

The Widow Gray asked me to make her cow produce mead instead of milk today, and no matter how I tried to explain that such a thing would require much more complex work than a simple chant and wave of my hand—and that the cow most likely would not survive the extensive physical changes—she was unconvinced. Ever since I did that water-into-wine trick down at the tavern a few years ago, people have been strangely fixated on this idea. She believed I simply was not properly incentivized to do the work for her, so she took out her wooden teeth and offered me—

HE HAD CROSSED the rest of that paragraph out.

> Well, in any case, I made her an artifact that will speed up the fermentation process of whatever source beverage she puts into the jar. I have a suspicion she will add milk. If she comes to me complaining that it is creating yogurt and not mead, I think I will scream.

AND THEN, he got back to Carnagore's movement spell arrays, even adding a control array to let him give simple directions with his voice as well as the standard methods by which most horses were trained. His reaction was less than enthused.

> The metal beast looks natural, but not quite graceful. There is more to be done. Still, it is a beautiful, enormous metal horse that can jump over a house (must add better cushioning spells on the back) and I look quite dashing riding it about.
>
> I should know by now that the common man will be impressed with any old thing, but that birdbrain Tarquin said that my creation was impractical, stomps around like a hippopotamus, and is obviously some kind of compensatory measure for the "size of my wand." As if the metal beast were no better than some blasting trinket!

THERE WAS MORE, but again, it was angrily crossed out.

"He had not yet named it Carnagore," Siobhan noted. Thaddeus grunted his agreement.

Myrddin's next project was to transmute a body of flesh from scratch—apparently something he had learned how to do years ago and practiced every few years. Unfortunately, he didn't get into the details of how he achieved it.

> I am still a genius and a better sculptor than any god, but it is not going to work for my purposes. So many things are missing. Also, I realize now my lack of foresight. What am I going to do with this body? I cannot simply dump it, lest someone find it and inevitably accuse me of murder or dark rituals to some eldritch entity. Vaporizing it seems such a waste, after all that work, and it feels quite strange to bury it, as if it were once human.
>
> I suppose I shall just transmute it into dirt.
>
> Or maybe...a sexy marble statue?

. . .

THIS WAS FOLLOWED by a sketch of an alluringly posed naked man that looked...suspiciously like Sebastien, except with black hair and a little more meat on his bones.

Siobhan's heart jumped, and she forcibly caught her breath in her throat. She stared at the likeness, her mind completely blank of any way to explain it or play it off.

She felt Thaddeus shift beside her and slowly turned her head to meet his gaze.

"Does that look like Sebastien to you?" he asked.

30

SPITE

SIOBHAN
Month 9, Day 6, Monday 3:00 a.m.

SIOBHAN LOOKED BACK to the tasteful nude of her other form drawn in Myrddin's journal. "It does look a little like him," she admitted, trying to keep her voice from cracking with nerves. She must have succeeded, because Thaddeus flicked a glance to Grandmaster Kiernan and then helped her turn to the next section of pages.

The older man had stationed himself on the other side of Thaddeus despite the distance making it difficult to see past the incoherency defenses on Myrddin's journal. He was too uncomfortable to stand next to Siobhan, so he was constantly squinting and rubbing at his temples as he tried to see what the two of them could.

Siobhan concentrated on the two new glyphs that flashed up, which succeeded in both keeping the contents coherent and partially distracting her from the issue. Surely, Thaddeus had more to say about the uncanny resemblance to Sebastien, but perhaps he did not want to discuss it in front of Kiernan.

Myrddin had left behind whatever the purpose of his last project was, and was now attempting to cultivate a pepper with "perfect hotness and sweetness." That would have been reasonable, except that he wanted versions that additionally had flavors of cumin, paprika, lemon, and garlic. An all-in-one spice. By this point, Siobhan shouldn't have been surprised that he seemed to manage it. He modified the seeds with magic, then sped up their growth immensely through several rounds of testing and tweaking.

"Surprisingly efficient," Thaddeus said, pointing out some notes about the overall energy requirements for a round of peppers from seed to harvest.

Siobhan tried to note the details, since this was the kind of thing that Oliver's warehouse farms might benefit from, but most of the work had been done on previous pages, and what was left was still beyond the limit that her meagre leftover mental capacity could parse.

Myrddin was more self-satisfied by this achievement than most of the ones that had come before, calling himself an "unparalleled genius and a master chef" and lamenting only that the new pepper varieties had sterile seeds.

Jumping another ten pages ahead found Myrddin again considering the human body. In archaic wording and strange spelling that Siobhan automatically translated into modern vernacular in her head, he had written:

The perfect body would be able to be controlled effortlessly and instinctively while remaining hyper-receptive to magic. Obviously, current humans are a failure of design in the latter aspect. Perhaps it is ironic that I say so. After all, the wonder and complexity that is life is beyond me. I do not even know where to start figuring out how the human brain works.

THERE WERE some calculations where Siobhan didn't even understand all the mathematical symbols, and then he continued:

It seems like the human brain should not, in fact, work. It is so tiny, to store so much, and the electrical impulses aren't even really that fast. Is it possible there's something we've all been missing? Crazy theory, but perhaps memories are not, in fact, stored in the brain, only accessed and retrieved by it. Of course, that brings into question the topic of the soul, which is even more mystical and unfathomable.

I am not known to be humble, but I do not understand how thought or personality works well enough to even consider trying to replicate it through transmutation. It is a feat I would be more likely to approach through transmogrification, but...

Perhaps there is another avenue to achieve my purpose.

Siobhan's eyes were glued to the words as her heart leapt in her chest. She didn't know what exactly Myrddin was trying to do or for what purpose, but there was a chance—a small one—that his research here could provide insight into her own problem. Unfortunately, they jumped forward again.

There was no writing on this set of pages. Instead, the book displayed a moving painting of a meadow in springtime. Siobhan would have called it a painting, but it was not like any she had seen before. The faintest of brush-strokes and the fact that it was set into a pair of spread pages were the only clues to what it was.

Beside her, Thaddeus wavered in shock. The flowers of the painting swayed gently in the wind. Bugs crawled through the dirt and bees alit on petals. Birds occasionally swooped through the air. The *light* was impossibly accurate, shadows and reflections and subtle counter-reflections beyond what a human could create. Even a master illusionist would have struggled.

Siobhan could smell the flowers.

Thaddeus reached toward the page, and she shot out a hand to catch his. "Do not touch it." The painting was so lifelike that it brought to mind the idea of stepping through a doorway to another world. "You might be trapped within."

Thaddeus drew back his hand, and she released his fingers. "Thank you," he said. "Is it a trap, then?"

"I do not know what it is. I only have an instinct of eldritch danger."

Thaddeus stared at the painting for a while longer before turning to the final page of the journal.

Here, Myrddin had written another note:

What is the Will? Oh, yes, I have heard many explanations since I came here, each more vague and platitudinous than the last. It is the manifestation of our thought-weight, the proof of the soul, and the tool with which we bend reality like a pewter spoon.

But <u>what is it?</u> How does it work?

Everything has an explanation, but the Will, perhaps even more than the magic that can be accomplished with it, seems to subvert the rules of physics and reality as I know them. Obviously, this means that I understand neither the rules of physics nor reality.

If I can find the answer, it may solve several of my other problems and be a huge step toward completing The Work.

AFTER THAT, he had made a long list of experiments to try. Some she could understand, or at least parse together from their individual words, but others were seemingly gibberish. Quantum superposition? What did that even mean? Had Myrddin made those words up?

He had drawn a star next to one of the ideas, which was just, "Try portable spirit-realm viewing spell."

Why was it special? Did he think that idea was particularly likely to bear fruit? As far as she had seen, there had been no such thing written in the journals so far. Either they had missed it somewhere in the pages they had skipped, or Myrddin hadn't written it down.

Thaddeus sighed as he closed the book. "One more to go."

Kiernan eyed the shifting cover wistfully. "A shame that we have only three of the five. What wonders could have been contained in the pages of the other two?" He looked to Siobhan pointedly, half-suspicious, half-jealous.

Siobhan ignored his passive-aggressive comment. "Perhaps we should stop here for the night." She could have kept going for a while longer, but not through an entire extra book, and pushing too hard might be detrimental to the fresh sleeper raven bound to her. She had done her best, but she was no Liza.

After they made plans for the next review session, Siobhan still had several burning questions for Thaddeus, but before she could ask to speak with him in private, he motioned upward and said, "I have recently acquired a lovely spiced wine, as well as some pine-nut infused coffee. Would you care to partake?"

Kiernan looked between the two of them, but when no additional invitation for him was forthcoming, he put on a grandfatherly smile and ushered them toward the door. "Yes, yes, you young people get along amongst yourselves. I'm afraid these old bones must retire for the night. Or morning, as it may be. Don't get into any trouble now, you hear me?"

Thaddeus, confident and seemingly unconcerned that either of them might be seen, led Siobhan up and across the University grounds to his cabin, where he made her a cup of coffee, shuddering in distaste as she diluted it with cream until it matched the color of her skin. Finally, he sat across from her with a steaming mug of spiced wine. "The drawing," he said without preamble.

Siobhan nodded. There was only one way she could play this, really. "It was not detailed enough to certainly be a replica of Sebastien, but it is too strange to be coincidence. I will be clear, I do not know why that drawing resembles him so. Do you have any theories?"

Thaddeus tapped his forefinger against his mug. "I have some thoughts," he corrected. "We already knew that Sebastien was special, in being able to pass the identity lock on Myrddin's journals. Since he is very obviously not

Myrddin himself, that ability leads one to certain avenues of explanation. However, by all accounts, he looks nothing like Myrddin. Tell me, Siobhan. Do you know anything about Sebastien's origins? Anything about his parents?"

Siobhan knew that no divination was being cast on her, but she was uncertain about her ability to get away with a lie, even so. Still, she would try. "I understand that he was orphaned young, then raised by a thaumaturge for a time. I do not believe he could tell you of his parents if he wanted to, or that anyone would be able to track them down. I am aware of the coincidence of his last name, but in my opinion, the idea that he is descended distantly from some pre-Third Empire royalty is complete bunk."

Thaddeus nodded easily. "To be sure. However, I wonder if perhaps Sebastien's appearance and skill are not mere coincidence." He shifted uncomfortably, staring into the dark liquid in his hands. He lifted his gaze to hers, wearing an expression that she couldn't read. "There have been programs to create…certain kinds of special children, not limited to nor ended with the fall of the Blood Empire."

"You think Sebastien is one of those? An…engineered child?"

"I am not jumping to such conclusions. However, I will note that there were no records of any statues in Myrddin's hermitage. If Sebastien were a descendant of Myrddin, which I previously considered a plausible theory, the bloodline would be incredibly diluted. It would be a very strange coincidence if he looked anything like such a distant ancestor. Additionally, I have to wonder, who was that body modeled after? Who was the *flesh* modeled after?"

Siobhan stared at him wordlessly.

"Again, I am only throwing out thoughts. I do not know enough to make conclusions, and I have no way to find that information, either. However, if my thoughts are in any way connected to reality… It is a horrible thing, to grow a child for the sole purpose of their utility."

"I agree."

Thaddeus sighed and took a deep gulp of his wine. "Let us speak of other things."

Perfect. Siobhan leaned back on the couch. "I do have something I wish to discuss. Something delicate. Do not be alarmed."

Thaddeus raised his eyebrows. "Saying, 'Do not be alarmed,' has never actually worked. If anything, after hearing that, I am more alarmed."

Siobhan gave him a small smile. "I want to know about what you did to the High Crown."

Thaddeus stilled. "You…know about that? How?"

"I watched. Before you ask, I will not tell you how."

He smirked. "You are a shapeshifter. You were in the crowd, disguised as a commoner."

She didn't reply, and his smile widened. "Or you can spy through your ravens?"

Siobhan took a polite sip of her coffee.

"You spied on the High Crown's nightmares. Tell me, has he taken any action to try to uncover the solution to my curse?"

She blinked at him guilelessly.

He chuckled. "Alright. Well, are you hoping to blackmail me with knowledge of my crimes?" He didn't seem particularly worried about that possibility.

"Of course not," she admitted. "I just want the details. Why did you do it and how does it work?"

"I did it for the reasons I stated. Leandro Pendragon feels free to act as he likes because he does not understand that the position of the High Crown does not confer absolute power, no matter what the laws say."

"Magic is a strength above all other forms of power," Siobhan agreed. "How does the curse work? Not the effects—I heard your description of those —but the trigger and the binding."

"Well, obviously the activation was delayed. It would not have done if the High Crown were to defy me out of stupidity and meet a gruesome death right there among the crowd. I may have somewhat exaggerated my immunity to retribution." He shrugged. "However, the risks were worth it."

"How sensitive is the trigger? Does it work on his intent, or your judgement?"

"Intent and severity of the offense. A few threats will do nothing. It will be triggered by bodily harm, imprisonment, attempts at assassination, that kind of thing."

"So if he were to accidentally harm Sebastien, he will be safe?" If that were the case, then there was a good chance that harming the Raven Queen wouldn't count, since it would be unintentional harm to Sebastien. It wasn't enough to reassure her, however.

Thaddeus narrowed his eyes. "Do you think he will attempt to 'accidentally' harm us? I am not sure he is clever enough to think of it, let alone pull it off."

"I do not know him well enough to say, though I judge him to be spiteful to the point of foolishness. Of the binding method... I assume you took into account the boon I gave to Sebastien? If there is any sympathetic magic involved in the triggering—"

Thaddeus waved a hand at her. "Not to worry, the curse is nothing so rudimentary. It works on my conception of Sebastien as well as the High Crown's —so that he cannot use some sort of geas to change his understanding of his enemies' identities. 'By accident,' as you said. In exchange for power, and to make other methods of breaking the binding more difficult, the curse will break on its own in three years and three days. By then, I hope to make Sebastien strong enough to protect himself somewhat."

Siobhan hummed ambiguously. "And the duel, then? It seems it would only raise the High Crown's ire and make an enemy of his heir."

Thaddeus was silent for a moment, though his lips twitched a few times as if he wanted to say something but was holding himself back. "So you do understand consequences?" Before she could respond, he continued. "I called the duel for multiple purposes. It was a handy way to suppress the High Crown and immediately set the man's response precedent. If I could start him out submitting to the curse and refusing to dare to trigger it, he would be more likely to continue on that path. After all, to do otherwise would be to admit he was wrong. Secondly, I called for the duel out of spite." Cooly, he took a sip of wine. "I think you can understand that motivation."

Siobhan felt strangely insulted, but couldn't think of a rebuttal in time.

"Thirdly, the duel was a convenient way to give Sebastien experience combatting someone more powerful in a safe environment, but where the stakes still *felt* very real."

Siobhan tilted her head to the side. "You thought Sebastien needed... combat experience?"

"Fekten's class is useful, but far from enough. Sebastien is too talented and has too easily surpassed his peers. I will add that the duel worked. I saw Sebastien take a large step closer to free-casting with my own eyes. Despite the simplistic spell arrays, he showed significant improvement in his control over his spells' output, and extensive clever modifications. Apparently, he only needed the proper incentive."

Siobhan stared down at her lap. What Thaddeus had actually seen was her using one part of her Will to shore up the other, splitting the workload, so to speak. A trick shortcut to success, just as her tether method for spell distancing had not been true detachment. But of course she couldn't say so.

Thaddeus had done a lot for her, in both of her forms. And he was incredibly powerful. But he also took drastic action like this without warning, which made him somewhat dangerously unreliable. No matter how powerful he was, he was not omniscient or all-powerful, and could not reliably protect those who were allied with but much weaker than him. Maybe his threat to the High Crown would keep her safer, but the possibility wasn't guaranteed enough that she felt comfortable with the accompanying risk.

And something about the look in his eyes when he spoke of spite... It was a little unsettling.

She set her empty coffee mug down and stood. "Will you walk me to the lifts?"

Thaddeus seemed somewhat reluctant but didn't argue. Once they were outside again, he said, "I gave the gesturan reference books to Sebastien."

"Oh? Perhaps you can explain why Sebastien has no idea that I was the source of one of them? You took credit for my find."

Thaddeus cleared his throat. "So you heard that, too? Obviously, it was too public a venue for me to mention your name, and I did not want to put off his education for something so trivial."

Siobhan huffed, but gave Thaddeus a small smile so that he would know she was not really angry. "Well, just as long as you do not mind me taking credit for your work at some point."

Thaddeus's steps slowed for a moment. "That is…acceptable, I suppose." When he got to the lifts, he activated one on her behalf, then stood at the top for a while, watching her descend.

Siobhan returned to Liza's before dawn, since she didn't want to compromise her attic apartment with her presence in this form, and it was too much of a hassle to go through the long process of multiple disguises to become Sebastien again.

Over the next few days, she spent the daylight hours working on light-refinement and practicing gesturan magic from the two texts Professor Lacer had given her. Her night hours were spent mostly in the restricted archives. They contained less on shamanry than she had expected from what was most likely the largest library in the country, but she had found a few interesting tidbits.

The best was something from a mostly redacted book—a condition that made her more interested in the pieces of information that were left behind, because surely the rest of it must have been especially useful. Apparently, it was possible to get hints about how a spell worked by examining the magic from the spirit realm, where there would be a "conceptual echo" of it.

'This was probably what Myrddin meant by a spirit-realm viewing spell,' she realized, her heart jumping with excitement. 'And maybe it worked, because he ended up making the transformation amulet and a much better version of Carnagore.'

It might, just possibly, be a safe way to examine the thing trapped inside her mind, or the magic of the seal itself, without contacting the Aberrant again or allowing it any sort of freedom. 'Finding a way to do that should be my number one priority,' she thought.

During the few night hours she was not squirreled up in the restricted archives, she had completed the other two short add-on rituals for the guiding light symbol. She had been lucky to get the correct kind of night weather for the other two sub-rituals in such a short period of time, but other than sensing through the symbol, she needed help to ensure she had completed her part correctly.

Really, the whole process had been easier than she would have expected for such a useful piece of magic. With the expanded utility functions, it was basically an alternative emergency communication system.

'Why is the ritual not more well-known? The limitation here is really the number of shapes that can be easily made into a personal symbol. To implement it on a large scale, nations would need to put in place some kind of mathematical method to create symbols that are just distinct enough from each other not to cause problems with the magic, but which could have thousands or even millions of subtle permutations. Though…who knows if those kinds of symbols would actually "take" with this kind of spell, being by necessity disconnected from the conceptual identities of the people who would be using them.'

Then, Siobhan realized that she was a bit of a hypocrite, and not for the first time. A spell like this could be a rather large tactical advantage, and despite often lamenting the secrecy so ingrained into thaumaturge society, she had no plans to share the guiding light ritual with the masses, either. Maybe someday. When she was much, much stronger, she would be able to share some of the less sensitive magic she had learned.

On Wednesday evening, she left Liza's house, avoided the door knocker's petulant attempt to bite her, and headed out for the Undreaming Order. Surely, someone there would be willing to help her test her new magic.

3 1

DREAM MESSAGES

SIOBHAN—DISGUISED as yet another alternate version of her female form —took a rather nice carriage from Liza's to the Undreaming Order headquarters. It cost a couple of extra silvers, but she was tired of walking back and forth across what felt like the entire city over and over. She was, technically, rich now, and could afford to pamper her weary feet. Even if the idea of paying for unnecessary things like suspension spells and a nice padded seat still made her cringe.

The carriage offered all the local newspapers, except for The People's Voice, which she wasn't sure really counted. Several of the headlines were talking about a recent attack on Osham. Siobhan chose one and began to skim through it, wondering if it had anything to do with the Architects. The details of the actual attack were vague, and the article mostly focused on how Osham was demanding "restitution." Their demands, she noted, were excessive and ridiculous.

She hadn't finished reading the article by the time the carriage arrived at her destination, but she could guess how the High Crown would respond. He would be outraged and double down with bluster and the metaphorical great fist of his power. Siobhan snorted with distaste and hopped out.

The area in front of the building had been spruced up with some repair and cleaning spells, and even the street looked strangely new. People were apparently repaying their debts in whatever way they could. Again, guards were stationed nearby, but instead of the stoic reserve that she would have expected, they smiled and greeted the people who passed, often by name. One eyed her, and she smiled back, hoping she seemed harmless. She looked nothing like herself, once again, but that didn't mean they wouldn't guess at her identity anyway.

Siobhan stepped through the artificial darkness of the entryway and into the large, circular room beyond.

Over a hundred people were seated at rickety old school desks within, though the room could have fit twice that number. A platform had been raised to hold a man and a large chalkboard, and the lights had been turned up bright enough so that people could see without squinting. The Undreaming Order was holding a math lesson.

The kitchen was busy, no doubt preparing the meal that had lured these people here for basic education. Siobhan moved around the outer wall of the room, feeling odd as she she watched children and adults alike take notes. *'This is happening because of me. I am indirectly providing a basic education to a hundred people.'* It was surreal. Suddenly, she felt that she might understand why Oliver so enjoyed philanthropy. It was a kind of power that felt different from mastering magic. It wasn't as heady an achievement, but she felt a deep, warm satisfaction.

Several people were in line for the healer's room, and another station was set up for people registering their good deeds. She eavesdropped for a while, hiding a chuckle as a woman proudly reported her efforts to feed the local ravens and had her contribution duly noted by the scribe on duty.

Siobhan slipped past to the administrative office, which was filled with several desks now, as well as shelves along the wall to hold records and supplies.

Deidre was there, going through some sort of ledger. She looked up when Siobhan sat in the seat before her, scowling at the younger woman. It took two seconds for her to recognize Siobhan, and to her credit, she reacted rather subtly. Her eyes widened, her throat convulsed with a hard swallow, and her body stiffened. Then, she said, "Welcome." Her eyes darted to either side, unsure, as she looked at the other administrative workers. She looked back to Siobhan and mouthed, "Secret?"

Siobhan shrugged, nodded, and pointed at the ceiling. There was no use making a scene by announcing herself as the Raven Queen.

Deidre stood. "Let me show you the way, Miss."

A few others glanced toward them, but everyone else was too busy to pay Deidre and Siobhan much attention.

The second floor was much less busy, though a few of those who called themselves the awakened were there, reading, practicing stealth or lock-picking, or meditating. Here, the two of them received a lot more scrutiny. "Who is she?" one of the awakened asked Deidre.

Deidre hesitated.

"I am Siobhan Naught." She moved her shadow as if an invisible light were orbiting her. "But please, carry on as you were. You know I do not stand on ceremony."

The others did not, in fact, carry on as they were, electing to stare instead. Thankfully, no one kneeled or bowed.

Deidre took Siobhan to a new addition at one end of the room, where some of the dividing curtains had been replaced by copper walls and a door. Deidre knocked on the wall as they entered, producing a dull tone. "Lead-centered for the protection, copper plated for magical conductivity. It's supposed to be for the eventuality that one of our awakened gets in trouble with the law and needs a safe place to stay while we handle the situation. I am not sure if the privacy measures meet your requirements, but this is the best I can offer." There were two bunk beds within, as well as a shelf with some non-perishable foods and bottles of water.

It was more than Siobhan had expected, and though she hadn't considered what she was about to share particularly sensitive, she decided that the protections were, in fact, welcome. She sat on one of the lower beds and motioned for Deidre to do the same. "I have been working on some magic that requires a collaborator. This person does not need to be very magically power-ful, but they would need to trust me to perform potentially invasive mental magic on them. It should be harmless, but as I have not tested it yet, I cannot absolutely guarantee—"

Deidre shot to her feet. "I'll do it. I'll do it!" She tapped both of her feet on the ground rapidly, running in place like she was trying to ascend an invisible stairwell with the world's tiniest steps, then threw her arms up in victory. "I *knew* it!" she squealed. Then, she seemed to realize that she was still in the room with Siobhan and sobered, sitting back down and placing her hands primly on her knees. She cleared her throat. "I would be happy to assist you, my queen. I have little experience with spellcasting, but I have no qualms about blood magic or whatever experiments you want to do. I have been prac-ticing basic meditations to stabilize my Will, and have managed to success-fully cast the most rudimentary of spells. My capacity is still meagre, but I can assure you, you will find no one with more dedication than me."

Siobhan was reminded of a cat that had slipped and fallen from a fence, but afterwards sat down and licked itself as if nothing had ever happened. If Deidre was going to pretend her outburst hadn't happened, Siobhan would play along. She pulled one of her thirteen-pointed star light coasters out of her bag and handed it to Deidre. She had left the invisible mark of her personal sigil on it, along with a few others. Unfortunately, she had discovered that despite the ease of creating the sigils, she could not do so endlessly, as whatever space in the back of her mind held awareness of them separate from her other mental processes was limited. *'Perhaps it will grow with time. For the moment, I will have to choose who gets one wisely.'*

"That is just a coaster with a light crystal, but I have embedded it with magic that will allow communication. I can find the coaster at all times, past any of the usual wards or intervening materials." She gestured around the small room. "Walls like these would not impede me. If you carry it with you, I will be able to find you. I can sense through it, seeing and hearing whatever is near." In fact, it was easier than trying to sense through her shadow, though more than a bit disorienting, and sounds were muffled and somewhat indistinct.

"If you complete one ritual, you may draw my attention with it," Siobhan continued. "If you complete a second, and keep it under your pillow while you sleep, I should be able to send you a dream. To be more specific, I will be able to send you a short message through a dream. If it works, it will be coherent enough that you can remember the message when you wake."

Deidre did not seem to find this at all alarming, nor did she question why Siobhan needed any special preparation to do this, despite controlling people's dreams supposedly already being one of her abilities. The other woman could barely hold back her excitement as she absorbed the instructions for both rituals with unblinking, ravenous zeal. "If only I had understood your plans better, I would have started practicing meditation and basic spells weeks ago! Will I be too weak, do you think?"

"You only need a handful of thaums. Twenty or less, I would estimate." They went up to the roof for the first ritual, which required only some basic supplies and Siobhan's sigil. The flock was halfway through setting up a series of garden beds protected by small glass houses. Deidre beamed at Siobhan's nod of approval.

Deidre needed to be in sight of the night sky, so there was no good way to keep her activities undeniably private. Under the unblinking eyes of the stars, she went through a process similar to what Siobhan had done to create the sigil in the first place.

Siobhan almost thought she could feel the tug on that particular tether in her mind as Deidre repeated the chant that would, if effective, allow her to draw Siobhan's attention when needed. It used a portion of Siobhan's personal chant, slightly modified.

"I, Deidre Johnson, call out.

    I call to she who is a changeling like the seasons.

    The daughter of shadow and light.

Of Charybdis mists and raven's flight.
She who seeks always after mysteries.
I, Deidre Johnson, call out.
By my Will, I beseech your regard."

WHEN IT WAS FINISHED, Deidre went back inside, into the small metal bunk room, and spoke the chant once more. One of the ephemeral tethers in the back of Siobhan's mind flared with light that reminded her somehow of a bright, clear bell's tone. It was very faint, likely because Deidre was so weak, but there was nothing in the part of her mind where the tether to the sigils existed to distract her, so even the faintest change could draw her attention. Siobhan closed her eyes and followed that tether to the source.

Deidre was kneeling on the floor with the light coaster pressed between two praying hands. "Can you hear me, my queen?" she added hesitantly.

The knowledge from the sigil came as if Siobhan had knowledge of the area in a bubble around it, rather than seeing through a window or an eyeball. She could see Deidre and her surroundings, but also knew everything that was in the woman's pockets, and the fact that she had a mole on her back. The latter two were both somewhat indistinct, as apparently the lack of direct light did have some effect on her perception. Siobhan had no way to reply, so she made her way back down from the roof. She opened the door, closed it behind her, and tried to hold back the giddiness of her own smile. She had a reputation to maintain, after all. No matter how accidentally she had gained it. "I could indeed hear you."

Luckily, Deidre was just as excited as she was, and was definitely too busy holding back a happy dance to notice Siobhan's expression.

Siobhan explained the second ritual, which needed to be completed on a cloudy night when no celestial lights could be seen. "I know of no way to retract the permission you will be giving afterward, though I suppose if the sigil—the coaster—is far enough away from your head while you sleep, it would serve the same purpose."

Deidre wrote it all down, memorized it, and then burned the instructions to ash. "I will complete it as soon as possible. Several times, perhaps, to ensure it works properly and there are no surprise gaps in the clouds while I am casting. And I will take a sleeping potion afterward. I am not sure I will be able to sleep, otherwise. That will not affect the spell, will it?"

Siobhan didn't know, but finding out would be useful, so she approved it.

When Siobhan was ready to leave, Deidre stopped her. "Could you perhaps give us more details about the coming disaster?"

Siobhan wondered what she was talking about. "The disaster?"

"The one that will cause widespread death, destruction, and famine," she said, though it sounded somewhat like a question.

"Do you mean…the celerium running out? There are at least half a dozen others, but that is the big one, I think." It was true that if the magical element of industry became a bottleneck, everything else could begin to fail, too. Hopefully, it would not come to that. Even if the journal Oliver held contained no hint of a solution, they would have years yet to start preparing for critical depletion. Surely, even if everyone had to walk around with huge orbs of thaumaturge-created gemstones to cast, life would find a way to continue on. There would just be some upheaval during the transition. Maybe the Crowns' expedition would even find a new source before then.

"Ah." Deidre blinked at her, wide-eyed. "But you have a method to create celerium. Is that true?"

"I am impressed with your information network," Siobhan said. Most still didn't know what had actually been in Myrddin's stolen journal. It wasn't, technically, the truth, but she didn't think it wise to explain the whole situation with the two stolen journals to Deidre.

With a blush, Deidre said, "Well, I don't know that it's so impressive. Just some basic deduction and a few rumors." However, the confirmation had relaxed her quite a bit. "Then…is there anything particular we should prepare?"

Deidre's caution pleased Siobhan. As she had learned personally and repeatedly, one could never be too prepared for disaster. "A little of everything, I suppose. The kinds of things you might want to buy at the last minute, and that everyone else would be trying to buy, too. The kinds of things you cannot make locally. If you do not have it on hand by the time you need it, it is already too late."

Deidre nodded like this was something profound.

"I do not wish to cause a premature panic. Do not mention this to those who do not need to know, but feel free to consult with the other awakened that you trust. Also, do not bother trying to buy up celerium."

"Of course not," Deidre agreed, rubbing her palms together with a faraway look. "Though if it is not too bold to say it, my queen, many would find a gift of celerium an irresistible lure to the cause, or a handsome reward."

Siobhan almost choked on her own saliva. "Hmm." Internally, she screamed. *'Is Deidre really hinting that she wants some more celerium? Does she think I can just hand it out like rock candy?'* She calmed somewhat, and realized, *'Maybe she just needs something with a better capacity for her own growth as a thaumaturge.'* Siobhan knew well how frustrating of a bottleneck that could be. After a long moment of hesitation, and the reminder that she might one day be able to turn beast cores into replacements, she pulled out the extra Conduit that she had taken to keeping in a secret pocket inside her bag. "Here. You may sell this and use it to buy several lesser Conduits, celerium or otherwise. Use one for yourself and keep the rest for those who need them."

Owning a Conduit was the difference between practicing magics passed down by one's family or being able to get a job as an Apprentice—or not. Or, for someone like Deidre, who couldn't afford a formal education, it could be the difference between being able to use her skills to survive or not. And it wasn't as if Siobhan was doing anything with her hoarded celerium in the meantime, anyway.

Deidre took it with thanks and a bow, but none of the extreme gratitude that such a generous gift really deserved.

'Don't be childish,' Siobhan reminded herself. *'You're coming to enjoy the feeling of superiority a bit too much.'*

Before she left, Siobhan gave Anders, Jackal, and Sharon a coaster with her sigil on it, keeping one for herself. She explained that if they should find anyone with those same coasters, they should provide aid if those people were in need—without giving away any secrets.

Over the next few days, she continued her research in shamanry and practiced the exercises that would stabilize her Will for sending dream messages. Some of the exercises were stranger than others. A few, she had learned when trying to find a way to deal with the nightmares, and others were new.

Periodically, she would stop and recall exactly what she had been doing for the last twenty minutes, from the first moment to the last. This was considered one of the harder exercises, but Siobhan had never found memory tricks difficult. As a side benefit, it helped to better connect the things she was learning to other knowledge, so they were recalled more readily outside of intensive searching. To add on to that, she would analyze the logic of what she was experiencing and how she had gotten where she was. To make this exercise harder, she could try to remember everything in reverse order, from the last moment to the first.

There were prospective memory exercises that required her to remember to perform an action when a trigger was met. For instance, Siobhan set a trigger so that when she saw a woman in a red dress, Siobhan would tap her right thigh three times. When she heard a rooster's crow, she would murmur to herself, "The rooster crows, but is it dawn?" and other things of that ilk.

There were other, more physical exercises, too, like examining the structure of her hands in detail, or doing particular movements that used a range of specific muscles.

Some of the exercises involved recalling your dreams. Those, she ignored.

She got a chance to try out the magic only a few days later. It required nothing but her Will, a bit of power, and the smoke from a stick of specially formulated incense.

Since the spell did not work on sympathetic principles, she didn't bother to leave the massive stone barrier of the restricted archives. She ran through the exercises to stabilize her mind against turbulence and decoherence first, and then reached through the tether leading to Deidre. Her message was fairly short, but complex enough to test how well the person on the other end could receive information and retain it.

Prepare three dog biscuits, one silver coin, and a jar of honey. Feed the dog biscuits to Bear with regards from me. Place the silver coin on the roof. Use the jar of honey to create some stick-candy and distribute it to the young members of the flock. If you received this message, relay my instructions in full.

Wake up!

She tried to imbue the last order with urgency and an imagined sense of adrenaline to ensure that if Deidre had taken any sleeping potion, she would be able to overcome its soporific effects.

Then Siobhan returned to her studies. Fifteen minutes later, she felt the ping from Deidre's copy of her sigil and reached out to sense through it. Siobhan grinned as Deidre repeated her own words back to her, word for word.

'One more drop of true power, acquired.'

3 2

CONCEPTUAL BEINGS

SIOBHAN
    Month 9, Day 11, Saturday 1:00 a.m.

SIOBHAN WAS SYSTEMATICALLY WORKING her way through all the texts she could find that dealt with shamanry. She still felt that the practice was unpleasantly wishy-washy and poorly documented by its practitioners, but she was nevertheless becoming something of a theoretical expert in the craft. As she finished one book, she picked up the next in her quickly dwindling list, *Spirit Guides and Familiar Bonds: Divergent Practices in Traditional Magic.*

The author posited that, while shamanry was often considered a sub-craft of divination, in many ways, it was actually a type of witchcraft. Witches set out an enticement-laced summoning Circle and negotiated a contract with their prospective familiar, who they could then use to channel their magic. Technically, if Empress Regal had been a magical beast instead of a normal raven, Siobhan could have used the raven-summoning spell as the first step toward entering into a contract with her.

Witches had the advantage of easy casting of spells that fit within their familiar's range of abilities, decreased chance of Will-strain, and an up-front advantage in power over modern sorcerers. Sometimes, depending on the power of the familiar, that advantage might last for decades. They had the disadvantages of reduced versatility, the fact that a familiar could die, and having to fulfill the terms of whatever contract they had bound themselves to. Developing a familiar's power required work and dedication, just like developing one's own power with sorcery. While one could technically have more than one familiar—if the contracts allowed—doing so by necessity meant that progress for each would slow further.

The author argued that shamans could do similarly, either for service within the spirit realm or outside of it. Due to the transitory nature of the spirit realm, these contracts were almost always short term rather than for life. Within the spirit realm, the contract was a standard enough process, though summoning a spirit had a few quirks that were different from summoning a magical beast in the real world, seeing as they had no identifiable, concrete species.

Outside of the spirit realm, however, spirits required a body to reside in as part of the terms of the contract, without which they had no way to interact with the mortal world. Most often, shamans allowed the spirit to temporarily reside in their own bodies.

Hypothetically, if one could create the right body and a strong enough anchor, the spirit could be hosted in a different form. However, in practice, this was impossible for any larger and more complex spirit. No one had figured out how to make a permanent anchor, or, more importantly, a body that could properly house a spirit. It faced similar problems to any other method to encapsulate a mind within a body different from its own.

The book delved into theories about how to create a good anchor and the least-horrible body depending on the spirit's characteristics. It did not theorize about ways to overcome the current limitations on either. Anchors were all distinctly temporary, and bodies meant only for the simplest of spirits. Done incorrectly or with too small a capacity, trying to stuff a spirit inside a body would both damage the spirit and result in poor integration.

Siobhan found the sections detailing how to actually bind a spirit much more fascinating. Beings in the spirit realm could coalesce from spirit matter easily, almost by random coincidence, but they might disperse just as easily unless they had either the luck or power to stabilize their existences. Part of the reason they agreed to contracts with shamans was the stability it created for them by the very nature of the binding.

Spirits had no name—and should not be given one. '*What happens if you do?*' Siobhan wondered. The book didn't say. Without any horrifying cautionary tales, she had a hard time taking warnings of danger seriously.

Instead, spirits should be described. If she knew a specific one she was looking for, she might summon them using words like, "The friendly spirit who knows the shaman Siobhan Naught, who loves flowers and knows the color ultraviolet, who has walked with Siobhan Naught through the Valley of End and has been contracted to aid her."

But the author brought up something critical. "How do you bind a conceptual being, who has no body and is made of thought-stuff, to their word?"

Spirits were unlikely to lie, and many believed doing so was somehow dangerous for them. This made it even harder for them to break contracts than for beings from the mortal world or the Elemental Planes. Nevertheless, they were happy to mislead and misdirect, and they *could* lie. There were several records of them doing so if they found the benefits great enough.

In the real world, the spell array worked the binding magic. In the spirit world, glyphs were less conceptual and more real. Though Siobhan did not fully understand what this meant, apparently spells would take physical form and needed to be molded and set, like clay. The author suggested the form of a collar and leash, which made Siobhan's insides squirm with discomfort.

Intent was even more important than normal in the weaving of a spell. Even if both sides agreed to the same terms, each might have a different personal interpretation of those terms. In that case, the one who was stronger would take precedence, their Will guiding the contract's actual effects. To ensure agreement in intent, the forming of contracts was often accompanied by moralistic storytelling and common fairy tales, where each side explained to each other their interpretation of the story as it pertained to their contract.

Siobhan grew increasingly convinced that this might be how Myrddin created Carnagore. *'If you could create a body that could react to Will, wouldn't that be the perfect solution to house a being with no real-world physical form?'* Siobhan thought as she finished the book. *'Then, you would just need to solve the body causing insanity to the transferred consciousness.'*

Obviously, none of the methods the rest of the world knew about were good enough. But maybe Myrddin had come up with something new.

Siobhan sat for a while, staring into the shadows between shelves and in the corners of the room. Even she became weary of studying for hour after hour, especially when she wasn't sure how much of what she was learning was actually helping her.

With a sigh, she roused herself and began to look for the next hidden text that held relevant keywords about divination and shamanry. What she really wanted was some insight into Myrddin's spirit realm viewing spell—which she hoped might allow her to examine magic through it without needing to enter it—but she had been trying to find information about it for the last few days without much luck. She was holding out hope that the instructions would be somewhere within one of Myrddin's journals, but knew she couldn't depend on that.

After a few more scrolls and some actual clay tablets, she began to consider calling it a night before the frustration built beyond her limits. She flipped rapidly through a pamphlet that turned out to be a treatise on the immorality of shamanism, which appeared to be written by a particularly syco-phantic student as part of a failed Master certification attempt. Siobhan snorted and tossed it aside, wondering if it had, perhaps, been placed in the restricted section by mistake.

"And that, I think, is enough," she told herself, beginning to organize the materials still in front of her.

A tiny, leather-bound book caught her eye. It had the wraparound tie common to journals, and was hidden inside a fake larger book that had some of its interior cut out to act as a secret compartment.

Siobhan hesitated before taking out the journal. *'Curses. I'd better check for curses. If the person who handles the shelving in here didn't know about the hidden book, it might not be safe.'* There were several restricted rooms that required higher clearance than the rest, which she had not attempted to enter, even as desperate as she was for answers. Thaddeus had warned her about the curses and traps that a certain kind of thaumaturge liked to build into their grimoires.

The secrecy of hiding a book within another book seemed overkill, especially since someone could have just blacked out the parts they didn't want seen even by people with access, like she had found with several of the more promising texts.

She ran through the limited number of curse and trap detection spells she knew, which were mostly child's play, then cobbled together her own spell that gave her a bit of trouble in the casting since it was so new. None of them found anything concerning.

Siobhan considered going off to research more danger detection spells, but couldn't hold back her curiosity.

The small, leather-bound book unwrapped to reveal handwritten research logs. It would have reminded her of Myrddin's own journals, except that she could understand everything they had written, including the calculations and spell arrays. These, thankfully, were complete and coherent, from beginning to end.

The author, unnamed, had been working with a team to develop a spell, which, based on its casting method and effects, they had dubbed—somewhat ominously—the "crown of madness." And it was what she had been looking for.

Well, not exactly. It was not Myrddin's spirit realm viewing spell, but it did approximate it, for a different purpose. This spell was created not to examine the echo-manifestation of magics cast in the real world, but to explore the spirit realm and communicate clearly with spirits.

"Clarity of intent is all-important," the author said. "The more powerful the spirit, the more harmful it is for them to lie, true. However, the more powerful spirits often have the most to gain from the downfall of a mortal walking their realm. They are more likely to be able to utilize and repurpose the mortal's inherent stability. Additionally, spirits know well their reputation for truthfulness, and they occasionally leverage it when they think the risk is worth it."

This spell allowed one direct insight into the often-incomprehensible spirit realm, as well as both the intent and nature of its denizens. Unfortunately, the very purpose of the spell came with inherent downsides. When casting it, spirit realm insights didn't need to be interpreted—they were unavoidable, and understanding was gained directly from exposure.

The journal's author noted in a shaky hand how the spell had already caused thirteen career-ending incidents for either the thaumaturges casting it or those who were in the spell's area of effect. Two of those had been break events resulting in Aberrants.

"It must be the inherent instability of casting a spell that affects your own mind," Siobhan read. "It degrades your concentration, which is a death sentence for a thaumaturge. One of the Aberrants opens up doors to...other places. Some of them are horrifically dangerous, just because of the way they spill over into *here*. But one of those doors leads to a place where the magic is more advanced than any I've seen before, and has spread throughout society all the way to the poorest of the poor. That world seems to have other doors to elsewhere, though they call them rifts, and harvest some kind of energy from the existence of the rifts, which can be used to empower people or directly charge their artifacts. It seems like some new form of magic."

Siobhan stared at the words, trying to imagine such a place. Would sorcery even work there? And had this new world been created by the Aberrant, or was it already out there, just...existing? Was there any way to tell? Siobhan preferred the idea of the latter. If Aberrants had the ability to create entirely new worlds with new types of magic, that level of power was terrifying. *'What if it wasn't a new world at all, but an illusion? What if, after you walk through and the door closes, there's nothing on the other side but annihilation?'*

After that, there were several almost reverent write-ups about the worlds behind the Aberrant's doorways, but the journal ended before its pages were filled.

On the last page, the author's handwriting grew worse. More hurried. "I fear the Red Guard is coming for us. I cannot speak for the others, but I will not wait here to receive them. They will slaughter all of us for the affront of keeping an Aberrant alive and secret from them, if not for the original research itself. I am going through the door to the world of rifts, wondrous artifacts, and buildings of glass that reach toward the clouds."

Siobhan's fingers were trembling. She closed the journal and then opened it again to the first page and read through the whole thing once more, tying strings of connection to all the relevant information to ensure she would be able to recall it with fidelity. Then she wrapped the leather cover and cord back around, put it back into the larger book, and slipped it onto the shelf she had taken it from.

'*This spell is dangerous. As they said, a spell that directly affects your ability to apply your Will couldn't be safe. It was a failed design from the start. For most humans. But I... I can split my Will. One part could concentrate on holding the spell while I stabilized my control with the other. Kind of like I did when dueling with Pendragon. If it worked like that, it might make the spell safe enough for me to cast. And I have light-refinement to make me harder to damage and heal up the effects of exposure to the spirit realm afterward.*'

Siobhan rubbed her chapped lips together, trying to ground herself with the physical discomfort of the scratchy feeling. "Don't go crazy, now," she whispered to herself. "Pride will be your downfall." It was unrealistic to think that she was really any better than the thirteen thaumaturges who had failed to safely cast or endure this spell before. People who thought like that ended up dead.

This was recklessness, with no defense. "And I am not yet that desperate," she confirmed aloud.

HARROW HILL ARCHIVES

Damien
Month 9, Day 11, Saturday 11:00 a.m.

Damien left Harrow Hill's old archive room, leaving behind the two administrative interns that he'd commandeered for the organization and cataloguing project. They were still knee deep in dusty old records, slowly working through their respective boxes. The three of them had made great progress since the term ended, but Damien couldn't feel happy about it.

He walked past a room whose walls were covered in information about the Raven Queen and cabinets filled with files of civilian reports, professional profiles and projections, and engagement strategies to keep any team that might meet her alive and uncursed. There was only one man in the room, reading through the stacks of reports about potential Raven Queen sightings with lifeless eyes.

In Damien's opinion, they didn't *really* hope to catch her anymore. Not after she had thwarted all of their plans so repeatedly and thoroughly. Not after the Red Guard had met with and refused to deal with her, despite the High Crown's rage. Of course, the coppers couldn't actively give up, but it was telling that none of the engagement strategies had them trying to incapacitate her. Any who met her were supposed to politely ask for her to turn herself in and defend themselves if necessary, but otherwise avoid angering her.

The coppers had plenty of other problems to deal with, anyway. The next room was devoted to the team trying to figure out what was happening to the dozens of poor and homeless people that were disappearing. Considering that it was unlikely anyone knew about or reported the disappearance of the average homeless person in the Mires, the number of missing was likely much higher than that.

Damien smiled and exchanged some pleasantries with one of the frustrated coppers working within. He wasn't technically authorized to know anything about ongoing cases, but his Family connections meant none of them tried too hard to keep confidentiality. Many assumed that he would work at Harrow Hill after he attained his Mastery and graduated. "No breaks in the case?" he asked.

The man squeezed his pen, rubbing his thumb over its grip as if he wanted to grind it away. "Plenty of leads, but all of them somehow come to a dead end. The only thing I'm sure of is that someone powerful, and probably wealthy, is behind it. If not for the fact that the Titans-damned Undreaming Order keeps rescuing these people, I would say the Raven Queen was behind it."

Damien would have been more interested in the mystery, but there was enough evidence to be sure that the disappearances weren't caused by an Aberrant. He made some commiserating noises.

"Tell your brother I need more men, or at least a stipend, to post rewards for civilian information."

"I'll tell him, but you know how it is," Damien said.

"Goddamn penny-pinching Pendragons," the man growled under his breath, his grip growing tight enough that Damien thought the pen might actually break. "Does the High Crown think punishing us with empty pockets will increase our performance?"

It was dangerous to complain like that aloud, especially with the High Crown so recently sensitive to discontent. One never knew the hidden allegiances of those who might be listening in, even if they were your coworkers. Damien made a noncommittal grunt and continued on.

When he got to Titus's office, he stopped outside, adjusting his clothes and smoothing his hair. It was unfair how Titus's hair always managed to look so perfect, without any of the stiffness or sheen that would have indicated a hair wax. Damien made a mental reminder, for what was probably not the first time, to look for spells that could style and set his hair. It was hard to remember things like that when his mind and efforts were devoted to so much more important problems. Maybe one day, he would go bald from the stress.

Damien shuddered at the nightmarish thought as his scalp tingled in distress.

Upon knocking and opening the door, Damien found his brother reading the latest edition of *The People's Voice*, the simple publication run by the Verdant Stags, and which always featured opinion interviews with civilians.

This issue was about the Verdant Stags' latest expansion of their territory, which would only see more of their newspaper spreading everywhere.

As Damien entered and closed the door behind himself, Titus set down the paper. "The Ambassador to the Public has been urging me to shut down the Verdant Stags' press. Unfortunately, due to the way the law is written—since the Verdant Stags are not selling the newspapers but giving them away as free literature to people who buy other items from their owned or affiliated businesses—we have no actual recourse to shut down the press or charge anyone with a crime. Not unless they slip into the dangerous zone of suggesting insurrection or otherwise encouraging criminal action."

"Have you found any of that?"

"Not directly, but we've noted a few issues in the last few months that skirt the line. They're growing bolder."

"But they have solicitors who will argue they've done no such thing," Damien guessed. In the couple of weeks that he had been working at Harrow Hill, he'd already gotten an idea of how the Verdant Stags were run.

"One already came to visit us. He insists that truthfully publishing quotations from citizens who might be angry or reckless is not encouraging criminal acts. And then he pointed out that clause at the back of every single issue that *directly and specifically* states that the writers of *The People's Voice* encourage no reckless or criminal action, and merely hope to inform the people of events and the general sentiment toward those events, without adjusting the narrative for personal gain."

That seemed like petty quibbling to Damien. "But the Verdant Stags choose what events to report on, as well as what quotes to publish. Surely that argument won't stand?"

"Of course, not against the interests of the Thirteen Crowns. But it makes things difficult when every person we arrest will have a solicitor holding on to them, kicking and screaming through as hasslesome a legal process as they can manage. And some of the judges..." Titus shook his head. "We need a change in the law if they want results."

Some of the judges would rule in the criminals' favor, either because they had been bribed, threatened, or simply believed in the cause of the Verdant Stag. Damien didn't agree with that stance, but he could, increasingly, understand it. The Verdant Stags were undeniably a boon to those in their territory, and the people loved them. Who could blame them? They provided many of the services that the Crowns were supposed to, and more beyond that, without imposing nearly as much tax on the general citizenship.

One of Titus's teams had recently met a team of Stags while out on patrol. Some civilians had used the green emergency flags to call in a squad of enforcers to handle some emergency. When the coppers had tried to arrest the gangsters, they had been beaten half to death. Not by the Stags, but by the civilian bystanders, who took offense to the idea that the Stags might be kept from responding to the emergency.

The thought of it filled Damien with weary frustration, and he knew Titus was no different, though his brother's frustration was tinged with anger. Damien wished he couldn't understand the civilians, but some sickened part of him whispered that maybe they were right. He had probably been reading too many decommissioned and pseudo-seditious newspapers.

"The Verdant Stag is tricky," Damien said, swallowing the rest of his doubts back down into that pit in the bottom of his stomach that was getting more and more full.

"This new organization run by the Raven Queen might be even worse."

"The Undreaming Order?"

"Them," Titus agreed. "They're certainly growing even faster than the Verdant Stags." He stood and moved to his office's window, looking out over the grounds contained by a tall stone wall. "On the surface, they're solely a charitable organization. But they worship the Raven Queen, and that should tell you all you need to know about them." Titus turned to Damien. "They're *dangerous*. What have you heard about them, Damien?"

He replied quickly and easily. "They're going around doing charity work on a mass scale and preaching about some tenets of the Raven Queen. It's actually a fairly ingenious...business model? Not exactly the right term for it, but you know what I mean. Everyone they help must pay on to others three times the help that they themselves received, all in the name of the Raven Queen."

Titus nodded. "However, it's only the Raven Queen's reputation that manages to keep things in order. They're all working on an honor system, more or less."

Damien shrugged. "I'm not sure a little loss here and there actually matters. With the exponential growth of the model, even if some people don't pay it forward, on a large scale it will be hardly noticeable. And a few visits by the Raven Queen to any notable offenders will probably be more than enough to keep the majority in line."

"Well, what the public might not know is that the Undreaming Order is suspected in *several* crimes. Kidnapping, assault, arson, bribery, blackmail, and the list goes on."

"But you haven't arrested them," Damien said, moving to stand at the other side of the window. "Which must mean that you don't have any concrete evidence. Or you're afraid of angering the Raven Queen?" At the idea of her descending to break her followers out of jail, he shuddered. If the Pendragon Corps couldn't stop her, how were the coppers supposed to?

Titus tapped a forefinger on the window glass, his eyes trailing a raven flying over the wall. "Both, I suppose," he admitted with a sigh. "But we cannot worry too much about the latter when we also don't have the former."

"What is all the charity for?" Damien wondered. "I mean, is she just trying to change public perception of her? Is it a front for something more nefarious? Or, like *The People's Voice* suggests, does she actually care about helping people who *deserve* help?"

Titus opened his mouth, his lips twisting as if to scoff, but he fell silent for a long moment. "I don't know," he admitted. "But it worries me. This city is full of cracks, Damien. I don't know if you can sense them, but they're just getting deeper. This is yet one more fault line. One good quake will rip the whole thing apart."

Damien suppressed a shiver at the helpless foreboding in Titus's voice. "Surely there must be something we can do to keep it together. That's why the coppers exist, isn't it?" Damien knew it sounded naive. He knew that, in practice, it didn't always work that way, but surely, when it counted most, honor should come first?

Titus leaned against the window's edge and stuck one hand in his pocket, idly jingling the coins within. "The overarching problem is that the coppers don't have enough funding. We're expected to maintain patrols we don't actually have the manpower for, in addition to investigating crimes both big and small, in a population that is growing increasingly hostile to us. I want to put my people through continuing education to increase their skill sets and ability to resolve conflicts with something other than violence and hardline authority. I want to hire people who can only be enticed by more than the paycheck we offer. Those who value justice. Those who cannot be bribed. I want to implement better reporting and emergency response systems throughout the *entire* city."

Titus sighed and pulled out a copper crown from his pocket. It was tarnished and sat dully between his forefinger and thumb. "That's what I want. What I get is funding on a level that means I can barely afford to keep the shifts fully staffed. When I complain, I am told that I spend too much on pensions for our retired or injured comrades. I refuse to cut the pensions, Damien, I *refuse*."

He squeezed the copper crown in his fist. "Pensions are the kind of support beam that, if removed, send the entire structure tumbling down. My men need to be able to rely on having a future when they get old, or if something goes wrong."

"You could... The Family could afford to donate," Damien suggested hesitantly.

Titus scoffed. "That is a slippery slope, and there is a good reason no Westbay has been foolish or desperate enough to do that since Lenore was first established. Father would disown me if I tried. Plus, if the High Crown felt that the coppers were becoming a privately funded army..."

"It might make him nervous. But if they're not funding us, where is the gold going? It's not as if tax revenue has fallen, right? Does the High Crown really not understand that we need more funding?"

Titus's eyes grew dark, like rain clouds creeping in over a grey autumn sky. "They're making a mistake. But even Father won't listen."

"Have they given up on retrieving whatever the Raven Queen stole, then? Something of Myrddin's isn't valuable enough to justify funding its retrieval?"

"Something of Myrddin's? How did you know? Is that just common knowledge now, rumors spreading throughout the city?"

"I just made an educated guess," Damien said, "Ana's the one who collects all the gossip, not me, but I wouldn't be surprised if the information has leaked by now." What he didn't say was that his guess was informed largely by Sebastien's intense interest in Myrddin. His friend had been studying the man with the same intensity he reserved for an interesting new spell, and would actually look up from whatever he was doing if he heard someone talking about Myrddin in passing. Once Damien had the idea, it seemed to fit so perfectly, and this confirmed it.

"If you can't catch her," Damien said, "maybe you should set up a meeting. She has shown she'll meet with people, like the Gervins, for instance. In fact, don't you have her ring?" At Titus's sharp look, he rubbed the back of his head. "I heard that somewhere." In reality, Damien had seen the ring in the Gervins' safe when he and Sebastien…"explored" it.

Titus sighed. "She might be willing to meet, if we could somehow ensure she trusted us not to betray her, but that ring was a fake. We discovered that after we arrested Malcolm Gervin and confiscated the contents of his safe."

"*Fake?*" Damien was more discomfited by this surprise than he would have expected, though he wasn't sure why. "What happened? Did someone switch it out?"

"The way I see it, there are three possibilities," Titus said, holding up three fingers. "One, the Raven Queen took the original herself, though I'm not sure why she would leave a fake in its place. Maybe some cruel joke." His forefinger dropped. "Two, the Gervins never had the real thing in the first place. Ennis Naught gave them a fake, which, given the man's history, wouldn't be so surprising. But in that case, she probably didn't know about it, seeing as she broke into Harrow Hill with a raven's body just to ask him about it." His second finger fell. "Three, the ring was real, or original, however you want to say it, but it was never a proper Conduit from the beginning. In that case, she would have cared about it for the sentimental value. Or maybe she didn't know it wasn't celerium, either. I don't know which is more likely. But we can't exactly call for a meeting and then give her a silver band and some broken quartz shards, can we?"

"What do you plan to do, then?"

"I would, in fact, very much like to meet with her, if only to talk. But I cannot imagine a scenario in which the High Crown agrees to anything of the sort. No, he would order us to lie to her and then try to arrest or kill her when she showed up."

"And you would fail," Damien said succinctly.

Titus groaned, twisting and stamping his foot dramatically, like a toddler on the verge of a tantrum. "Agh, even my little brother holds so little faith in our capabilities!" He straightened and sobered. "Well, that is, in fact, the most likely outcome."

Damien patted his shoulder. "Cheer up. Your faithless little brother has ordered a delivery of roasted kebabs."

"Street food?" Titus asked, his lips staying straight though his eyes lit up. "You know street food isn't assured to be hygienic," he complained, but he was already moving to clear space on his desk, motions fast enough to bely his excitement. "Did you get honey drizzled squid, or just more of that disgusting eel you like?"

"Squid. But...I can't stay to eat with you. I'm meeting Sebastien and Ana for lunch."

Titus looked up from his desk, his hands falling along with his expression. "You're abandoning me?"

Damien grinned. "Allow me to repeat, I am your *faithless* little brother."

"How is Sebastien? I haven't seen him since that whole fracas with Frederick Pendragon."

"Oh, good, good," Damien said, inching toward the door. "Just doing genius things, as usual."

"And Ana? I heard she's been busy with the business recently."

"You know Ana, she'll rip apart a business opportunity with her bare teeth and then smile like a demure, pretty lady." With that, Damien ran off before Titus could invite himself along to lunch.

3 4

BENEATH WALLS OF STONE

Damien picked up a paper from a scruffy-looking boy hawking at the corner, but refused the follow up attempt to sell him "high quality" foreign cigars. Damien didn't consider himself an athlete or a prospective professional duelist, but he still didn't fancy having his lung capacity reduced or having to take a lung-clearing potion to strip away tar buildup.

He frowned at the headline as he flagged a carriage. Osham's premier was insisting that Lenore pay restitution for that attack last week. And, of course, he wanted that done in the form of celerium and rare components.

Damien wondered how the Thirteen Crowns would respond. No one wanted to make an enemy of Osham, but at the same time, conceding to their demands would not only be admitting that they were behind the attack, but also showing that they could be threatened into concessions. Only a weak nation would actually pay them. The High Crown would either refuse outright or find some other, indirect way to appease Osham's premier.

If Damien were the High Crown, he would try some kind of joint project to strengthen ties between their two nations, or an exchange program or something. But Damien was not the High Crown, nor even the leader of his Family, which meant there was little use worrying about it.

There was construction work near the restaurant where he was meeting

Sebastien and Ana, causing a traffic jam. Damien hopped out of the carriage to walk the rest of the way, leaving the newspaper behind. The sidewalk was packed with other pedestrians, the flow of people moving slower than Damien would have preferred.

In front of him, two women were walking with their heads tilted close together. The taller one said, "He came by the house again. I saw him through the window this morning, before I turned on the lamp. He was standing out on the street just...watching."

The shorter one hooked her friend's arm and pulled her closer. "That's not okay."

"I know—"

"No, *listen* to me. That's not okay. You told him you weren't interested, and now he's stalking you!" Their conversation grew louder as they seemed to forget they were out in public.

"Stalking? I'm not sure I'd say he's *stalking* me."

"What about when he showed up at your work with flowers and told everyone there that he was taking you out, even though you already said no?"

"Well—"

The short one kept talking, as if already anticipating her friend's response. "What if he was doing this to *me*? Would you agree that he was stalking me, if I were the one telling this story? Would you be worried about me, knowing what you know about him? Think about it."

There were a long few seconds of silence, and then the tall one said, "Okay, he's stalking me. And I would be worried for you. But what do we do about it?"

Damien wondered if he should say something. His first instinct was to tell her to go to the coppers. Except, unless the man had been violent toward the tall girl before, there wasn't much the law allowed the coppers to do. At best, they could visit him and give him a warning, hoping that he would be scared into rethinking his actions.

The short woman spoke as if to answer Damien's thoughts. "His uncle is the owner of that construction company that just got a contract with the Moncrieffe Family. I'm not sure we can rely on the coppers to take your side."

Damien ground his teeth together.

"And those bruises on my arm have already faded, so there's no proof of anything, really," the tall one said, nodding morosely as she absently rubbed her shoulder.

Damien brightened. A prognos could observe her testimony as well as the man's and judge who was lying, which would serve as good evidence toward violence. It wasn't their usual job to work on domestic disputes and other "small" crime, but Damien suddenly realized that it *should* be. He opened his mouth, but then closed it again, suddenly awkward.

Before he could come up with a way to insert himself into the conversation, a slender girl, probably younger than Waverly, sidled up to them. She slipped a small, folded pamphlet, no bigger than a palm, into both women's hands. "I overheard what you were saying," she said in a low voice. "If you want someone to actually listen to your problem and take action to fix things, come to the Undreaming Order."

"I've heard of you guys," the shorter woman said with obvious suspicion.

"Then you know we keep our promises," the girl responded confidently. She had a certain way about her—a conviction—that even Damien found compelling. He couldn't help but believe her. Or at least believe that she believed. "All you have to do is learn a little about the Raven Queen and submit a request for help."

"But you want payment, don't you?" the shorter one snapped back.

"Of course we do," the girl said. "Just like the coppers or the gangs want payment for their help. The difference with us is, you get to decide how you pay your debt, and to whom. You even get to decide when to pay it. Though if you leave it unpaid, there is always a chance the Raven Queen will call it due."

"Then it isn't exactly our choice, is it?"

The girl shrugged. "That's part of the deal. She's never called a debt from the flock due yet. If you want to be sure you can avoid that, pay forward the help you receive immediately. We have a ton of different recommended ways to volunteer if you have no coin. Nothing is free, but the Raven Queen only takes what you can afford to give. They helped me, and they can help you, too. The protection of the Raven Queen's wings stretches as far as the darkness does."

Damien was so engrossed in their conversation that he almost tripped over the curb as they moved from crossing the street back to the sidewalk.

The tall one asked hesitantly, "What exactly can you do to help me, and what would I have to do in return?"

"We have several options of varying severity that we can use in a situation like yours, depending on the specifics. I think the most effective and efficient is a curse that will compel him to stay away from you. It's not that hard to pay back. A few weeks of working in the kitchen or helping our cobbler make shoes during your spare time every day, that kind of thing. If you have a chance to save someone and you take it, that will repay a good chunk of your debt, too. You have to learn the Raven Queen's tenets, but you don't have to join the Order unless you want to."

"...Why are you doing this? All of you, I mean."

The girl grinned, her eyes sparkling with pride and satisfaction. "If you learn the Raven Queen's tenets, you'll understand a little bit. If you learn— really learn—about who the Raven Queen is, you'll understand even more.

I've paid back my original debt several times over now. I continue creating good in her name so that I might gain her favor."

The three young women veered off in a different direction than Damien was going. He considered following after them, but when someone jostled him in the shoulder and cursed him for blocking the middle of the sidewalk, he instead continued on toward the restaurant. The conversation kept playing over in his head, especially the last bit. But when he found Sebastien sitting at a table on the balcony while a waitress tried to flirt with him, Damien's thoughts returned to the reason for their meeting.

Or rather, the reason they had agreed to meet earlier than they told Ana— so that they could discuss sensitive topics.

Damien walked inside and told the host he was meeting a friend. "The reservation should be under Westbay, and I saw my friend up on the balcony." He made to walk past, but the host nearly jumped at him in excitement.

"You're Damien Westbay!?" the man asked, his voice tight with excitement.

"I am," Damien said calmly, but inside he felt a little pleased with the treatment. That he, a younger son of the Second Crown Family, was known by name was a little flattering. Hopefully the man wouldn't get too familiar, though. Sometimes it got awkward to be stared at and gossiped about.

"Yes, you're Sebastien Siverling's friend!" the man exclaimed. "Do you think a few of us could get Sebastien's autograph? I know he doesn't like to be crowded. He's so down-to-earth," the man gushed. "Maybe we could give you a notebook or something and you could get the autographs on our behalf?"

Damien scowled. "Sebastien doesn't give out autographs," he stated succinctly, moving around the other man. He made his way up to the balcony and sat down with a huff.

Sebastien acknowledged him with a glance and then returned to watching people in the street below. He seemed aloof and a little tired. The waitress was nowhere to be seen. Likely, Sebastien had sent her away.

Damien observed the languid confidence in Sebastien's body, the deep-seated self-assurance in his eyes, and knew that things like this would happen again. Damien would be recognized as "Sebastien Siverling's best friend." Damien ran his finger around the rim of his water glass, wondering how he felt about that. It was…fine, as long as they both did things that mattered. As long as Sebastien didn't completely outclass him and leave him behind.

But Damien wasn't as talented as Sebastien. He worked hard, but already Sebastien's skill was outpacing his own. In twenty years, Damien would be a fantastic thaumaturge. Sebastien would be…something more. There was a reason Thaddeus Lacer had taken Sebastien as an apprentice but refused Damien. Refused him even after he completed extra exercises and worked harder than anyone else in the class besides Sebastien himself.

But Sebastien couldn't do everything, no matter how ambitious he was. There simply wasn't enough time in the day, or in a single life, no matter how far magic stretched things. If Damien could specialize correctly, he could shore up Sebastien's weak points and remain indispensable.

Damien activated the privacy wards engraved into the circular table. "We've indexed about thirty percent of the archives," Damien said. "There's a lot of missing information when you get near Lenore's founding, but we've been taking three boxes from each decade, rather than trying to do things from beginning to end. I wanted to get answers quicker."

The full force of Sebastien's attention fell to Damien, and with it, just the faintest sense of ephemeral pressure, recognized somewhere in the back of Damien's mind.

"We still have a lot of work to do, and I suppose what the data is showing could reverse once we process the rest, but so far…" Damien cleared his throat. "Already, the trend is clear. Both overall break events and Aberrant incidents are increasing faster than the population of both the general populace and thaumaturges. I…don't anticipate any dramatic reversals in the data. In fact, if things reversed at this point, I would be more suspicious that someone had begun tampering with the reports."

Sebastien stared at Damien for a few moments, then slowly sat fully upright and squared his shoulders, his chin lifted perfectly as if to balance a tome atop his head. This was the way that Sebastien armed himself for battle, Damien had noticed. "I understand. Thank you, Damien."

Damien tried to mimic Sebastien's posture, suppressing the urge to bounce his knees up and down or take nervous sips of his water. "There's something else. As far as I can tell, Aberrants aren't increasing uniformly across all levels of strength. They are disproportionately weighted toward the weaker end. Which makes sense, in a way, because obviously people are more likely to break when they're young and inexperienced. But I…" He looked away and swallowed down the lump in his throat. "I wonder if it's deliberate, somehow. I know that sounds crazy, but—" His voice broke, and he had to close his eyes for a moment.

"Because if you knew break events were increasing, and you couldn't stop it, maybe you would try to ensure the Aberrants created were as weak as possible," Sebastien said in a low, horribly calm voice. "And it would be a good reason for the University to push its students so hard. For those who will break, let them break early. But just because it has a certain internal logical consistency doesn't make it true."

He leaned forward and tapped the table to bring Damien's attention back to his face. "It could just be that practice and experience strengthen the Will in ways that make a break event less likely, just as would be the case in all other dangerous endeavors that require high levels of skill."

Damien nodded gratefully, some of the sick tension leaking from his body. "I guess all of this has made me overly paranoid."

Sebastien smiled without humor. "Maybe. Unfortunately, I've found that no matter how hard I try, I'm never quite paranoid enough."

"Well, if they aren't influencing society so that weak thaumaturges are more likely to break, do you have any idea of what they *are* doing? Because I've thought about it a lot, and I don't believe that you and I are the only ones who know about this. It's just an amazingly well-kept secret."

Sebastien pursed his lips and looked into the distance again. "I've been thinking about that, too. I understand that they wouldn't want to panic the public. It's not as if any one group, even the Red Guard, could simply stop anyone new from becoming a thaumaturge, even if they wanted to. People would simply do it in secret and with poorer training, or, more likely, the Red Guard would find themselves no longer welcome in most countries. The only thing to do, really, would be to discover why it's happening and then try to combat it at the source. Perhaps they are doing so already. Though…with knowledge of the crisis being so restricted, it means that many of the brightest minds who might put their efforts toward finding a solution are instead working on other problems. That is inefficient. I wonder if revealing the truth and allowing the panic would be more efficient, on balance."

Damien struggled to imagine all of the repercussions of such an announce-ment and after a moment shook his head to draw his thoughts back from the chaos. "Is this enough for you to make another report to the higher-ups?"

"Yes."

"Do you think they'll give us any follow up missions, or will this go to someone more…well, qualified?"

Sebastien's expression pinched, as if the implied label of "unqualified" pained him. "I'm not sure, but it's hard to imagine what two second-term University students could really do from here."

"And surely, this is enough to take me from a provisional member to a full member, right?"

Sebastien hesitated before nodding. "I think so. But things might not be quite like you expect."

Before he could say more, Ana stepped out onto the balcony, shielding her face from the sudden brightness. She was early. "I can't believe you both arrived before me," she said, smiling. But Damien knew her well enough to see the spark of knowledge hidden in her eyes. She may not have known what they were discussing, but she knew that they had met early on purpose, and the privacy wards were obvious. It was difficult to keep secrets from her.

Sebastien pulled out a small box from his jacket pocket and handed it to her. "Surprise," he said, completely deadpan.

Ana blinked down at the box, truly surprised. "What is this?"

"Something for Nat. Well, for you and Nat to share."

"It's not her birthday."

Sebastien nodded. "She wrote me a letter complaining about how she doesn't have an interesting older brother to bring along and show off on outings with her friends."

Ana closed her eyes and pressed her fingers to her forehead.

"I cannot attend her friend's party this weekend, so I got her this as an apology. It's just a few fancy pastries from the Glasshopper."

Ana smiled lopsidedly, then groaned and shook her head, and then smiled again as she slipped the box into her bag. "I will give it to her, and she can share them at the party with those she likes best while bragging that they are a gift from Sebastien Siverling, most recently in the papers for trouncing Frederick Pendragon in a duel. It will give her a nice share of social clout, and I am sure she will feel great satisfaction in refusing to share with Cecilia Cyr." She sat down and gracefully lifted two fingers to grab the attention of a waiter. "But Sebastien, please do not feel obligated to indulge her so. If you give her an inch, she will take a mile, and the next thing you know, she'll be your Apprentice and setting fire to the Charybdis Gulf."

Sebastien's eyes had just begun to crinkle with a laugh when the sirens started.

Ana froze, white-faced.

Damien, for some reason, was looking outward, as if he might see what had happened. That didn't make sense. He would have felt it before he saw it, probably, but he hadn't sensed a break event.

After a short pause, Sebastien turned and grabbed Ana by the forearm. "Get up. We need to move before the panic starts. Get to a shelter."

Damien had sensed the backwash from a break event before, more than once. He was a much stronger thaumaturge now than he had been then, which should have increased his "sensory range." Either the person who had broken was very weak, or ground zero was quite far away. But Sebastien was still correct. Distance did not immediately equal safety, and a weak thaumaturge could still produce a deadly Aberrant. Already, people in the restaurant and the street below were beginning to call out, "Aberrant!"

Down on the street, Ana looked around frantically for one of the signs that should point the way to the nearest shelter, but Sebastien had no time for that. "Follow me. I know the way."

"What, did you memorize a map of the city?" Ana asked jokingly, as they jogged along behind Sebastien.

"Yes," Sebastien said, his head swiveling back and forth as he observed and processed everything he was seeing, leading them with surprising skill through the crowd and past potential obstacles. He hesitated at one corner for a moment, and then turned north, despite the fact that Damien was pretty sure there was a shelter to the south only a kilometer or two away.

Damien didn't say anything, because Sebastien probably knew that, too.

They got to the shelter within twenty minutes, filing in through the outer doors, then the second set, and then the final inner set of lead and iron. A couple of the light crystals embedded into the huge, arched ceiling were empty of charge, and a few others were flickering, a sure sign of shoddy work by the artificer that created them. Damien scowled. It created a depressing, eerie effect that only exacerbated the tension of all those huddling within.

Ana was staring at the latest page in her pink notebook, waiting sense-lessly for words to appear. They wouldn't, not so far beneath the barrier of metal and stone.

There was a strange pulse, and Damien could have sworn his flesh rippled like water for a moment. Apparently, he wasn't the only one, as screams erupted all around him. The light crystals took that perfect moment to cut out all at once.

Sebastien grabbed Damien's arm and pulled him back against one of the support columns, and a moment later, a sphere of bright light bloomed above their heads, revealing Ana's terrified face on Sebastien's other side. He was casting from the thirteen-pointed star light coaster, though he kept its distinguishing face tucked to his palm. He'd slipped his other hand into his satchel, and Damien saw the dull glint of a battle wand's base gripped between his fingers.

It took almost fifteen seconds for the backup lights to come on.

By that time, many people had already succumbed to panic, rushing toward the doors, trampling on others, and screaming with the kind of terror that was infectious.

"My skin is maggots!" one man nearby shrieked. "I'm being eaten alive by worms!"

It took the coppers stationed within fifteen minutes to suppress the panic. They did so with silencing and stunning spells, and a good few bruises and broken bones when the magic ran out. "It's all in your head!" their squad leader called out. "No Aberrant magic can reach through these walls and wards. The most they can do is make you *think* they have. The Red Guard personally warded this shelter with the most powerful magic known to man. We are safe so long as we don't panic and start tearing each other apart."

Sebastien had let his light spell go by then, and the three of them huddled close, refusing water as the coppers began to pass it out.

"Nightmare-type?" Damien asked, whispering so low under his breath that no one could hear it more than a couple of feet away within the echoing cavern.

"Probably," Ana agreed.

"It's not true, what the copper said," Sebastien whispered back. "The Red Guard can't ward against everything, every potential effect an Aberrant might have. That's literally impossible. We don't even understand how Aberrants themselves work, let alone half the magic they propagate."

"They do the next best thing and cast stabilizing magic," Damien said. "They ward against what they can and cast opposing magic to try and catch the rest. It works pretty well. *Very* well, usually. Their spells to resist change are probably the best in the world."

Sebastien's eyes narrowed at that, and his lips pressed together as if he were holding back words as his eyes scanned the ceiling. After a moment, he asked, "Why didn't we feel the break event?"

Damien explained his thoughts from earlier, but hesitated before adding new ideas. "Or, a roaming Aberrant could have approached the city. Sometimes everyone misses them until it's too late, if some stupid sorcerer breaks doing experiments out in his cottage in the middle of nowhere."

"Or we did feel the break event, but we forgot it. If it's a Nightmare-type," Ana contributed, her voice low and her eyes dull.

They fell into silence for a long while then, outwardly if not within their own heads. Perhaps an hour had passed when a girl came to crouch beside them.

"You!" Damien said. It was that same girl from earlier, who had been inviting the young women to get her cult to perform a curse for them. "You're with the Undreaming Order."

The girl blinked, then smiled at him, though her eyes kept being drawn back to Sebastien. "I am. I'm here to offer you the services of a mind healer. We just purchased his services. He can help calm you if you need it, right now, or deal with any long-term effects of the mental strain. We're set up over there," she said, turning and pointing. "We also have an Apprentice healer who's gotten permission from the coppers to cast, considering the circumstances. She can fix cuts, bad bruises, and broken bones as long as the break is clean."

"Thank you," Sebastien said, "but we're fine."

The girl nodded but hesitated before moving on. "Do you...remember me?"

Damien looked between the two of them. "You know her?"

"I do," Sebastien said.

The girl smiled brightly, even more so than when she spoke about the Raven Queen. "He saved my life," she told Damien.

"Wait, what?"

"It was nothing," Sebastien muttered.

"Why don't I know about this?" Damien asked.

"Because he didn't do it for praise," the girl said, full of conviction. With one last smile and nod at Sebastien, she left.

Damien turned on his friend. "What happened?"

Sebastien groaned and leaned his head back to thunk against the support column. "Why don't you ask Titus? He's the one who actually saved her life, technically. He paid the healer's bill."

"*What?*" Damien asked, even more shocked and outraged. "When did you go around saving people's lives with Titus?"

"He wanted to keep it a secret from you," Sebastien said, unrepentant.

Damien tried to pester Sebastien into telling the story, but his friend refused, and eventually Ana snapped at him to shut up. A few hours into their stay, she dozed off, using Sebastien's satchel as a pillow. Damien took the opportunity to talk to Sebastien again. "Why did you take us to this shelter, instead of the one to the south?"

Sebastien looked at him in silence for a moment, and then said, "There are parts of the map of the city that are a little blurry in my mind. I think they're —at least some of them—Red Guard bases. This one was a lot closer to one of those blurry spots, and potentially the protection of their agents. So, I led us here. Just in case."

Damien opened and closed his mouth again, then finally said, "You memorized the entire city. Yes, totally normal." His eye twitched. "So normal, in fact, that the parts you *can't* remember are suspicious. And based on that suspicion, you deduced the location of secret Red Guard bases." He let out a choppy, semi-hysterical laugh. "Why hasn't anyone else ever thought to do that?"

Ana shifted and smacked Damien, mumbling sleepily for him to be quiet.

Damien held his knees to his chest and rocked back and forth. "I'm the normal one," he muttered to himself.

Sebastien patted him on the back. "Do you want an anti-anxiety potion?"

Reluctantly, Damien acquiesced. Of course Sebastien was a genius. Damien already knew that. It just didn't seem fair that he could be so good at magic *and* everything else. Damien consoled himself with the fact that he still had better hand-eye coordination, footwork, and more luxurious hair.

The Aberrant was eventually handled, and they were let out of the shelter that evening, about an hour before sunset.

Ana rushed off immediately toward home and her sister. The Lilies had several shelters, and the Crown Family homes often had personal shelters of their own, so Damien was sure Nat would be fine.

As Sebastien and he walked through the grumpy, dispersing crowd, Sebastien stopped for a second. "I have a contact who might be able to get us some answers about all this," he said.

Damien knew immediately that he was talking about the Aberrant problem.

"I will go to them and try to get some information that will guide our next steps. Something actionable I can pass on to the higher-ups," Sebastien added after a short pause.

Damien wondered if his "contact" was Professor Lacer. But if that were the case, Sebastien would have probably just said so, right?

3 5

A SHROUD OF LACE

Siobhan
   Month 9, Day 12, Sunday 1:00 a.m.

Siobhan stopped on the wide street in front of the canal entrance through the northern white cliffs and looked around for anyone out late enough to notice her.

Pain prickled up through Siobhan's shoulders, into her neck and the base of her skull. With a wince, she rolled her neck and rubbed at her muscles, trying to relieve some of the tightness. Her eyes were dry and faintly gritty, but neither blinking nor yawning soothed them. It had been a week already since she refreshed her sleep-proxy spell, and the fact that the fatigue was slipping through so clearly showed Siobhan just how far she still needed to go to catch up to Liza's skill. '*All the stress today was as bad as casting for a few hours straight. And it wasted my time and kept me from* actually *casting the sleep-proxy.*'

She resolved to do so in the morning, after she got back to Liza's and had a chance to take a nap. '*Next time, I need to refresh the spell earlier, before it gets so strained that I need to rest first.*'

Only half of her tension was because of the Aberrant incident. Which was absurd, really, considering that an Aberrant incident should arguably be one of the worst things someone could experience on any particular day. But Siobhan kept thinking of the things she hadn't been able to say to Damien.

The Red Guard might be working in secret to understand and fix the underlying problem causing the increasing number of break events. But she couldn't forget that they *used* Aberrants as components.

It was one of the things—perhaps the biggest thing—that made them so ridiculously powerful.

And yes, it made sense that they needed special tools to deal with such anomalous, dangerous enemies. But if they could reduce break events, maybe they could stop them entirely. And if they did so, what would happen to all of the power they wielded?

She also remembered that they restricted research into certain applications of shamanry. What if that wasn't because the craft was so horrifically dangerous and likely to create the kind of Aberrants that even the Red Guard would struggle to neutralize? What if it was because certain aspects of shamanry touched on this colossal secret?

Siobhan reminded herself that they took vows. She didn't know the details, but presumably those vows would prevent them from working for their own self-interest, even if mortal nature would have encouraged it. They existed to protect the world from the things that might destroy it. She crossed the street, went over the bridge at the base of the cliffs, and then passed under the towering white stone. When she got to the place where they had convened before, only Kiernan was there.

He had been pacing back and forth and jumped when he noticed her, then nodded formally and put his hands in his pockets. After a second of silence, he pulled his hands out of his pockets and instead crossed his arms.

Siobhan eyed him curiously, but when she determined he had no intention of speaking, she turned to press her back against the wall and closed her eyes. After a few minutes of waiting for Thaddeus, her scattered and anxious thoughts grew too uncomfortable to remain cooped up with, and she turned her attention to her shadow instead. First, she practiced sensing through it, which had grown much easier than when she first attempted it.

She made it harder by sending it back the way she had come, and then around a few corners, over the bridge, and into an alley on the other side of the street to explore. In the past, she wouldn't have been able to do this. Originally, she couldn't send the spell around blind corners or beyond the range of her vision. She wasn't sure why it was easier now. *'It could be that I've memorized so many of the details of the city that my grasp on its location remains firm. But it's probably the fact that if I can see with my shadow where it goes, I do not need to see with my eyes to direct it.'*

She fell into fantasizing about how useful such a capability could be and ended up cackling a bit to herself. Abruptly, she remembered that she was not alone and opened her eyes.

Kiernan was staring at her. His eyes slowly trailed down to her feet as her shadow returned to pool around her. "Is…something wrong?"

"No, I was just scouting a bit."

Kiernan nodded, and then kept nodding for a bit too long, still staring at her shadow. "Yes, yes. Well…it's just a bit *unusual* to watch." He hesitated, then added, "Is it true that you can travel through it?"

Siobhan tilted her head to the side. She could cover an area with it and then walk through the darkness to appear elsewhere, but she was mostly sure that was not what he meant. "Not in the way you think," she said. There was no point in making herself seem less impressive or powerful, not when the Raven Queen's reputation had become such an asset for her. '*Sometimes fate works in ludicrous ways,*' she mused.

Next, she brought up a delicate filament of her shadow to hang in front of her and began to weave it into a lace-like pattern, growing ever-outward from the center like the facets of a snowflake. She added more filaments, working faster and faster until she had filled the air in front of her from ceiling to ground with a beautiful shroud. Once, such fine control would have been difficult, but now controlling her shadow was almost as easy as thinking, and the only difficulty was keeping the design firm in her mind. Honestly, at this point, she was unsure how to continue improving the shadow-familiar. '*Maybe I can try to absorb other types of energy beyond light and heat. It's not a built-in function of the spell, but neither was sensing through it.*'

Kiernan had retreated further into the tunnels and was pacing again. The sound of his footsteps scraping the white stone and his absentminded sighs were irritating her.

Siobhan halted her lacework and spun toward the old man. "Why are you so agitated?" she snapped.

Kiernan stopped. At first, his gaze avoided hers, but he steeled himself to look directly at her. "I am merely concerned about the late arrival of our third colleague."

Siobhan's eyes narrowed. "Truly?"

Kiernan swallowed heavily. "Yes?" When she continued to stare at him silently for an uncomfortably long moment, he grew more and more tense until seeming to pop like a balloon. "I am under a lot of pressure recently." Siobhan only had to remain silent for a few more seconds for him to elaborate. "Desperate times make for strange bedfellows."

Siobhan wasn't sure who he was alluding to. '*Me?*' she wondered. But that seemed unlikely. Someone new. Someone from one of the Thirteen Crown Families, perhaps? Based on the goals of the Architects of Khronos, she could see why Kiernan would be conflicted about allying with someone from the group that they wanted to overthrow.

However, if that was the case, it wasn't good for her. The animosity between two of the strongest factions in Gilbratha was part of what had created a safe pocket for her to exist within. Each side felt an incentive to keep the other from gaining control of her—and her knowledge. If they allied, she could be put into a situation with no safe exits. "If you take a viper to bed, do not be surprised if you wake up to a bite," she warned. "That is the viper's nature."

Kiernan's face crumpled into an exasperated frown. "I know that. But I am not in a position to unilaterally make decisions." He glanced back at the lace shroud, grimaced, and said, "I believe Professor Lacer may not make it tonight. I will take my leave rather than continue to wait. Until we meet again." He bowed, then edged past her, scurrying around the construction of darkness and out toward the street where the transport tubes waited.

Siobhan considered, but decided to keep waiting. She pretended to grab the shadow lace with her hand, forcing it to drape like actual fabric, which she threw around her shoulders like a cloak. Then, she sent an undefined blob of it to the mouth of the cave system so that she could monitor the street. While keeping this stable in the back of her mind, she bent the other part of her Will to practicing small gesturan spells.

Doing all of this at once was quite a stretch for her. Even with the ability to split her Will, each part only had so much available concentration. She couldn't keep track of any details while sensing through her shadow so lack-adaisically, but she would at least know if anyone walked by.

The primer she had found, and which Thaddeus had then gifted to her, contained the most basic of exercises. Gesturan magic was heavily based on the elements, and so there were three exercises for all five. The movement to create a ball of water was different than a ball of fire—which made a lot of sense when she thought about it in terms of natural science. She was about halfway through the primer, and could gather all five base elements and shape them into a ball. She could then sling that ball around her body before shooting it off with a thrust of her hand for all of the elements except Radiance and Fire, neither of which would naturally cohere and then stay together when launched as easily as Water, Earth, or even Air.

Based on the drawings, the final set of exercises dealt with forming the element into a disc and then exploding it outward, but she hadn't gotten to that yet. Perhaps after a couple more weeks of practice.

Even these, the most basic of exercises, took a long time to cast and a precision that the average person apparently found difficult. That was inconvenient in a way, but they didn't require any components, not even chalk or a place to draw a Circle. *'I wonder if learning different crafts like this helps me get closer to free-casting. After all, I am training myself not to fall into any particular ruts in my casting process.'* Modern sorcery, esoteric spells, alchemy, and gesturan spells all had their own process to access the fabric of magic and call forth a response.

As for the spell Professor Lacer had gotten her personally, she had yet to make much progress on it. It allowed one to create sounds, with great variety and control. Hypothetically, she could create the sound of an instrument, or an explosion to knock out someone's eardrums, or even mimic her own voice. So far, she could barely create some hair-raising, eerie, off-tune screeching sounds.

Her greatest feat was a simple tapping that reminded her of a pebble falling onto stone, which was a big improvement over a haunted violin's wail of sorrow and hatred.

Movement on the street caught the attention of the part of her Will that was idly watching, and she dropped her attempt to turn her pebble sound into a more hollow drumming. A few people had passed so far, but this time, it was finally the one she wanted.

Siobhan stepped out of the shadows of the cave and raised a hand.

He tensed and spun to face her between one step and the next, his Conduit in his hand.

Siobhan let out a small snort. That was Thaddeus Lacer's version of tripping or jumping in surprise.

He looked around, then made his way toward her, by the water's edge. "I was busy with our response to today's Aberrant. I assumed neither of you would wait for me."

"Kiernan has left already. I waited because I wanted to talk to you about something different," Siobhan said. For some reason, her heart began to race at the words, like it was a prelude to confessing some terrible secret.

3 6

VIOLATION

Siobhan
Month 9, Day 12, Sunday 3:00 a.m.

For some reason, Siobhan couldn't force her mouth to form the words of the question she really wanted to ask. Instead, she said, "Thaddeus, you are a *special* agent, correct? I am unsure of the exact nature of and responsibilities carried by that title within the Red Guard. Why were you involved with this Aberrant incident? You are not on an emergency response team; you have a position at the University. Was there some special reason for you to be involved today?"

Thaddeus raised an eyebrow. "You do not already know the Red Guard's structure and policies?"

Siobhan let out an unladylike snort. "There is more that I do not know than which I do."

He paused, as if surprised, but then nodded sagely. "A sentiment only grasped by those who know enough to realize the scope of things. Still, I am curious. Did the Red Guard not exist when Myrddin was alive?"

Siobhan peered into the darkness of the tunnel ahead, which seemed particularly eerie beyond the radius of Thaddeus's floating sphere of light. "No? They were established around eight hundred years before the current era, significantly after the time that people speculate Myrddin died, correct?" She frowned, wondering why he would ask such a strange question. She turned to him. "Unless you know something I do not?"

"No. As I said, I was merely curious."

She narrowed her eyes. "Was that some kind of…test? Even if the timeline worked and I could have gotten some clues about the Red Guard from Myrddin's writings, consider how much would have changed between the Red Guard of then and today. I could be sure of nothing, let alone the specific role of a special agent."

Thaddeus nodded easily, though something about the way his mouth twitched told her he was holding in a thought, or perhaps a private joke. He sighed. "The point of the Red Guard was that they would not change. Faithful to the mission first, and above all. But, of course, an unchanging order… That goal was always impossible."

He sucked in a deep breath and rolled his shoulders as if to relieve some tension. "To answer your question, I usually get called in to assist if the Aberrant is particularly strange and understanding its anomalous effect is difficult. It is not my job, true, but I am knowledgeable enough to make an initial assessment and recommend the best follow-up procedure."

Siobhan wondered what, exactly, said follow-up procedures might be. How much of it dealt with ensuring the safety of the world, and how much with managing the processing of Aberrant components? Perhaps, to the Red Guard, those were the same thing.

"I am also sent out sometimes if a team needs a great deal of extra power applied in specific ways. And sometimes, I participate on a voluntary basis, out of personal interest."

"You have given me three reasons. Which was the cause for your involvement this time?" Siobhan asked, avoiding a damp spot on the floor.

"You should know I cannot give confidential information," Thaddeus said, but she knew him well enough to detect amusement in his voice. Thaddeus had a wry, subtle sense of humor that she suspected most people were completely oblivious to. He was surprisingly ironic and sarcastic.

"You cannot, or you do not wish to?" Siobhan asked mildly, with pure curiosity.

He let out a huff. "This Aberrant required my presence for none of the above reasons. Or, perhaps, the last one. I do find the situation quite interesting, though I might not have gotten involved of my own volition."

Curiosity flared up in Siobhan like a grass fire—sudden but soon futile as it realized there was nothing else to consume. She wouldn't ask for the details. Sebastien might have been able to, but the Raven Queen couldn't.

Looking at the ground, Thaddeus's lips lifted in a tiny, pleased smile, but he didn't volunteer anything further.

Siobhan edged slightly closer to the question she wanted to ask. "How many Aberrant incidents have there been in the last twelve months? In Gilbratha specifically," she added.

"I am aware of four."

"Oh." That was one more than Siobhan had been aware of. *'Were there no alarms for the fourth?'* she wondered. Aloud, she asked, "Is that usual?"

"Four is perhaps a little fewer than average. Especially considering that two were very low-powered, from thaumaturges with Wills yet to reach even the Apprentice standard. But Aberrant generation rates are certainly not consistent. An area can go for quite a while without one and then suddenly get bombarded. It happens frequently enough that it has become a bit of a superstition among the Red Guard." He turned to her and added, "There is even a theory that the stress of experiencing another's break event makes one more likely to break themselves."

Siobhan's insides twisted a little. "Is that a true theory? One backed by reasonable evidence?"

Thaddeus gave a small, sideways-tilted nod that might have, in someone else, expressed uncertainty. But Siobhan could see the spark of mischief was still in his eyes and knew otherwise. It was true.

"How long does the increased risk last? Forever? Or is it like Will-strain, and subsides with time?"

"That is difficult to test *properly*," he said. "It is unethical, you see." The spark of mischief grew stronger. "I believe the increased risk is temporary, but I could be wrong. One can only look at the data over time to see the correlation."

This was all the encouragement Siobhan needed to ask the question she had wanted to all along. She spoke before she could second-guess herself. "Are the overall incidents of severe Will-strain and Aberrant formation increasing?" Her heart thumped in her chest, sending blood rushing through her ears, and she stealthily blew out a deep breath to compose herself.

Thaddeus stopped walking, which did not help to calm her.

He pushed his lower jaw forward and back several times, then flexed his hands. Staring at the floor, he asked, "Why would you ask that?" in a deceptively mild tone.

Siobhan swallowed. She had never seen him so discomfited, and this kind of reaction seemed abnormal. He had some idea of the answer, obviously, or the question wouldn't have affected him so. "I have reason to believe it," she said softly, relieved that her voice didn't crack.

Thaddeus was silent for a bit, though the flexing of his hands and jaw had stopped. He started walking again and reached into one of his jacket's inner pockets. "Were there fewer Aberrants during Myrddin's time?" His tone was conversational again, but this did nothing to alleviate Siobhan's tension.

Would he skirt around actually answering her question until the end? Would he take her to the Red Guard and have her ask her question again, but to someone like Captain Aisling? Or would he lie? Because at this point, if he told her there was nothing to worry about, she would not believe him.

His jacket gave a small tearing sound, like he had fumbled a button or tie and instead impatiently managed to rip a seam. "Did it seem as if losing control badly enough for Will-strain or a break event was more difficult or less likely in those days?" he asked, walking ahead of her into the dark.

"Again, I do not know," she said, following him. '*Why do people seem to keep assuming that I know things about Myrddin's time beyond what I could learn from one of his journals? Aside from the one I own, Thaddeus has read along beside me the whole time, and yet he still keeps asking these insinuating questions.*'

Thaddeus paused as they came to an intersection and waved for her to take the lead.

"It does seem likely, based on the trends that I have seen," she admitted. "But the frequency could be on some kind of wave cycle, rising and falling again, rather than an ongoing increase." It was the first time she'd had the idea, and the possibility comforted her. She hoped he would say that was how it worked. Or at the very least, that there was some way to stop the rising tide.

The light orb Thaddeus had been casting winked out.

Siobhan began to turn, feeling uneasy, but before she could face him, a sudden spike of outright terror slammed into her. Blood and flames flashed behind her eyes. The image was accompanied by a skittering and scrabbling just behind her right ear, but somehow also *in her brain*. She sucked in a breath so hard and sharp she choked on it and jerked away into the wall, still trying to turn and look back to face the skittering thing.

But instead, she saw Thaddeus. He was barely illuminated by the faint glow of a spell coalescing a few inches from the end of his fist, which was outstretched toward her. In it, he gripped a bracelet of strange, thick glass beads, while the other hand held his Conduit.

There was just enough time for his eyes to widen before the spell hit her.

Instead of slamming into her dead center, as it might have if she hadn't flinched away, the magic caught her right arm and a bit of her side. The glow flared slightly as something rope-like grasped around her arms and tried to constrict her torso. But the magic was more than that.

Spreading from the point of impact, her body went painlessly limp, as if the flesh were asleep. It reminded her of the few times she had gotten stuck at the boundary between waking and sleeping, and no matter how she tried, the commands from her mind were ignored by her slumbering flesh. It had been terrifying then, and it was terrifying now, as she fell into the rough stone wall and began to slide down.

She struggled against the feeling, using her left leg, which was farthest from the impact and least affected, to try to shove herself away from Thaddeus. Instead, she stumbled from the combined resistance of the ephemeral bonds and her body's sudden lack of balance. The dead flesh felt heavier than it should have been.

A flash of helpless fatigue reached her mind, but it was not strong enough to bring her down. With an effort of pure Will, she grasped enough control to turn and try to shamble away.

Before she could take a second step, Thaddeus tackled her.

She crumpled like a soggy noodle, and his weight crushed most of the air out of her. Her attempts to struggle were about as effective as a bug under a boot, and only half as coordinated. "Why?" she choked out.

Thaddeus's breath hit her left ear as he responded, and the rumble of his strained voice passed through his chest and into her back, where they were pressed together. "I do not want to kill you. If you do not know, if you *cannot* know, then I will have no obligation to do so. Luckily for the both of us, I am good at memetic spells. Hold still, do not fight, and it will be over quickly."

If she'd had breath to do so, Siobhan might have laughed at the insulting absurdity of that statement.

The paralysis spell fell away, the rope-like bindings dissipating, though the sleep-dead effects lingered. Perhaps Thaddeus thought she would listen to him and comply. Perhaps he thought she had no chance of escape, even if she struggled. Or perhaps he simply had no choice, as he could not cast his memetic attack against her while also maintaining the paralysis.

Siobhan bucked and twisted, and though she did not throw him off, she managed to turn around to face him. She smashed her palm up toward his face, though she could barely make out his features. She had heard that you could kill someone by shoving their nose bridge back up into their skull.

She didn't want to kill Thaddeus, either, but when a much weaker prey animal fought against a predator, they had no chance of survival if they weren't prepared to fight to the death.

Her hand slipped off and away, but his grunt and the warm, metallic splatter of blood that dropped onto her chest and neck told her that she'd at least hurt him.

Her hands scrabbled wildly for his left arm, grasping it and following it down to the fist at the end. She grabbed the strange bracelet and tore at it like a rabid dog, even reaching up to bite at it when it refused to break and scatter apart in her hands. She had a guess as to what it was—rare components, encapsulated inside reinforced glass beads, for the spells that even Thaddeus Lacer could not cast entirely without support. If she could get it away from him, she might have a chance.

Thaddeus cursed and punched her in the side of the head with the hand gripping his Conduit.

Stars burst across her vision but entirely failed to light up the darkness. Her ear rang, and she whimpered involuntarily.

"Just stop!" Thaddeus bit out. "I won't kill you." He cast something, and the stone softened under her like a thick pudding, some of it reaching up as if to bind and entomb her.

In desperation, she pulled on her shadow, which had almost no definition against the surrounding darkness, lifting the entirety of it up to hover beside them, attached only by a thin string. She made it as cold as her Will could achieve, as cold as the dark side of the moon, as cold as the disappointment of Thaddeus's betrayal.

Then she formed it into a spike and slammed it into Thaddeus's left ear, as if driving a nail into his brain.

He jerked away as if he had been physically struck.

His knees lost the security of their hold around her hips, and she bucked to throw him off. She scrambled out of the hole in the stone her body had sunk into and scrabbled away, at first on her hands and knees, but quickly back to her feet. The adrenaline coursing through her made her light and strong, helping to shake off the lingering sleep from her limbs. She threw herself forward, knees high and steps landing on the ball of her foot, for maximum speed.

She drew her shadow around her like a cloak, profoundly grateful for this spell that had been with her so long—almost since the beginning. Thaddeus's reaction to her shadow's attack had probably just been an automatic, instinctive reflex to jerk away from the invasion of his ear, but that was enough. It was the chance she had needed. It would have to be enough.

Thaddeus muttered a low, angry curse, and then went silent.

Siobhan let her shadow's trailing end billow out to fill the entire hallway behind her as she fled into the darkness of unknown tunnels as if her life depended on it. Hopefully, it would blind Thaddeus as he tried to follow.

3 7

——— ———

A DESPERATE ESCAPE

Siobhan

Month 9, Day 12, Sunday 3:15 a.m.

'*THE QUESTION I asked is not allowed,*' Siobhan thought as she raced into the darkness. She fumbled the light coaster out and used it to shine the way, confident that Thaddeus couldn't see it through the shadow-familiar billowing out to fill the space left behind. '*The Red Guard has decided that those who know must die.*' She would leave trying to figure out *why*, exactly, for a less critical moment. Thaddeus's decision to try to make her forget was…understandable. Better than immediately trying to murder her, she supposed.

Except that, for her, she might legitimately prefer to die rather than have her mind tampered with once more. It would be a violation of her very being, and she couldn't allow it. No matter what, even if she had to become the kind of wild animal that gnawed its own leg off to escape a trap.

Siobhan couldn't tell if Thaddeus was following her—her own wild breath and the echo of her footsteps were too loud. But if he was, he would catch up quickly. His stride was longer than hers, and this body simply couldn't handle the same physical exertion as her other. Still, he would be blinded, and even the bravest man would fear running blindly into the darkness.

As she ran, she reached into her bag and retrieved two potions by feel and memory alone. First, a fleetfoot potion. She felt the wind rush through her muscles and lighten her body as if she was filled with smoke rather than flesh.

Second, quintessence of quicksilver. She'd gotten a tiny little vial of it in the Night Market. Not to play around with—especially not after her experience with the beamshell tincture—but for a situation where she needed what was essentially a short-term performance enhancer to save her life.

She let the metallic powder fall onto her tongue, where it seemed to coalesce into a thick liquid and easily rolled to the back of her mouth. She choked down the surprisingly disgusting concoction. Many products of alchemy were unappealing, but her body instinctually rejected this one. She had no comparisons by which to describe the taste and smell, except that it was the complete antithesis of food, and the droplets had such strong surface tension that they refused to break apart on her tongue. If not for her self-control, she would have gagged it out.

But she immediately understood why people became addicted to it. It seemed to slow time while also doubling her brainpower. Even tiny details became noticeable, and her memories bobbed so close to the surface that she might have been able to relive them at will. She had known that memories were connected, and often used mnemonic techniques based on this to help her memorize new information. But now, just the taste of the air on her tongue called up a dozen different connected memories, both mundane and significant, and each she effortlessly scoured for something useful to her current situation.

'*My mind can hold all the thoughts.* All of them.' Of course, she immediately realized this was unfounded, semi-maniacal hubris, but the rush was undeniable.

She realized her panic was making her inefficient, so she adjusted her posture for maximum speed with minimum effort and forced her breaths to come in through her nose and out through her mouth in a rhythm that matched her footsteps, like Fekten had taught.

When she came to an intersection, she sent a part of her shadow, formed to look generally like her but as cold as could be, running in the opposite direction. She sent the greater mass of her shadow to follow it, too. If he was sensitive to the false clues, he might be fooled. Such a ruse was unlikely to be effective, but it might increase her chances of escape by a single percent or so.

She slowed for a moment, holding her breath just long enough to listen. She was able to note faint sounds of movement that, without the aid of the quicksilver, were so faint that they might normally have gone unobserved.

Thaddeus was up and moving, but he was far behind.

Siobhan continued forward, this time at a slower pace that would make less noise and leave her the energy to react to any surprises with full force. Her shadow-clone was getting very far from her down the tunnel in the other direction now, so she stopped and made it pretend to hide.

She had a very serious problem to deal with now. She didn't know the way out. She hadn't memorized the entire network of caves, tunnels, and hallways cut through the white cliffs.

She stopped again to listen at another intersection, this one split between a more natural, rough-looking pathway and a man-made hallway. She even licked a finger and held it up to feel for wind and sniffed the air in the hope that the quintessence of quicksilver would bridge the gap in her knowledge and help her come up with a deduction.

After two seconds of contemplation, she chose the more natural terrain, both because it was sloped downward—and thus hopefully toward an exit— and because it would be harder to navigate without sight.

The part of her shadow "hiding" several hundred meters in the other direction absorbed a sudden flash of light, though Siobhan herself couldn't see it past the shadow plugging the tunnel behind her.

She moved slowly in her physical body, trying to sense through the distant shadow. *'Was he fooled?'* But the flash of light had disappeared as quickly as it came, and she didn't sense any indication of his presence. Perhaps he had already realized the ruse and turned around. Or perhaps the light had been some kind of scouting spell, sent in advance. She couldn't assume she had even the slightest idea of the extent of his capabilities.

The rough tunnel led down to an even rougher cave that, under the faint illumination of a bottle of moonlight sizzle kept mostly concealed inside her hand, looked remarkably like the inside of a shark's mouth. Hundreds of huge jagged teeth were formed of stone, all of it somehow both slippery with damp but also rough enough to scrape off skin. Moss-like growths of some magical species absorbed heat and let off an extremely faint glow, but left the air so cold her breath was visible.

On the far side, there seemed to be a low tunnel, through which she could hear the echoes of a drip. With all the dripping going on in the cave, she would never have been assured of finding something on the other side without the quintessence of quicksilver, but it made parsing all the information and making these kinds of deductions unnaturally easy.

She had made it most of the way to the small tunnel when another spike of fear rose up from nowhere, giving her the unmistakable impression that she was being chased and the monster was right behind her. As though a dream was peeking into reality, she had a flashing, waking nightmare that she was sneaking a look through the peephole of a doorway, only to see an eye pressed to the other side, watching her back.

Siobhan flinched and fell to the ground behind some stalagmites only a second before a powerful wave of divination rolled over her. She pressed herself to the rough stone, taking what minor protection the jagged shield provided, and crawled forward into the small tunnel. The scent of mineral-laden water and the half-musty, half-vegetative smell of algae and other small organisms that could survive the dark filled her nose and mouth with their nuance.

She scraped her hands and knees and tore her dress as she crawled. If she had been wearing her new, fancy battle dress, that wouldn't have happened. *'Hells, if only I had outright bought all of that warded jewelry from Liza, too. I could have just gone around all the time looking like I was prepared for a meeting with the High Crown. Always, always, it seems I regret my own complacency. If I get out of this alive, I must beat it into my thick head that there is no such thing as being over-prepared or overly paranoid.'*

The farther she got into the tunnel, the more the stone pressing all around her provided protection from Thaddeus's magic. Unfortunately, it was meagre protection in the face of the crushing pressure of his attempt to find her.

Thaddeus was too strong, had too clear an idea of where she might be, and was confident enough to pit his strength against that of the Raven Queen. If not for the weight of stone between them, the claws of his magic would have sunk in and rent apart her fragile, slippery shell. Every moment, the invasive sensation grew stronger.

Siobhan came out of the tunnel on the other side and lurched to her feet, but the terrain here was almost impassable, and she was once again reduced to climbing over obstacles. She had to put the light-coaster crystal side down in her mouth and clench it between her teeth because she needed both of her hands just to move. She skidded down the side of a crevasse and then lifted her body up the other side, flailing to raise one leg over the edge as she cursed her weak woman's arms. Without the ability to move fast, to put dozens or hundreds of meters more matter between them, she had only minutes left. Possibly seconds.

With a brain running on quicksilver, that was quite a long time.

There was no guarantee any amount of intervening material or distance would save her. A person of Thaddeus Lacer's power might be able to pierce through the white cliffs entirely, even if he were standing atop them and she tunneled all the way to the base.

The loss of blood to the disks in her back was growing as she Sacrificed it for power, which was very unfortunate at a time when she needed to be at her best physically. Her mind scrabbled uselessly for options as she felt the divination continue to scan for her like a million spotlights sweeping back and forth, every moment growing in intensity and number until it felt like they would sear right through her.

It might have been hopeless, but that imagery gave her an idea. This divination spell might be invisible, but that didn't mean it wasn't transmitting energy. She might not be able to see it, but whatever tendrils, waves, or rays it used, they carried magic in them—a source of power that allowed them to recognize and return the information they had gleaned to their caster. In that way, they weren't so different from sound or light waves.

What was sound, if not a kind of vibration, a form of heat? She could Sacrifice that for power. And as for light, she already had plenty of practice doing so. How different could energy that she could not see and did not understand the form of be?

Liza's artifact, so greedily drinking the blood that passed under the surface of the skin in her back, was able to "shunt aside, reflect, capture, discourage, and devour any non-mundane possibility of information leaking to magical observation." That was what Liza had said. But it was relatively weak, and her Will too feeble to bolster it the way she needed.

Still, if she could handle the divination rays, it could handle keeping the fact that she'd done so a secret. It could disguise the empty spot in the world that she created.

So Siobhan bent her Will, and her shadow, to devouring the unseen. *'Don't focus on the fact that you don't actually understand what a divination wave is,'* she told herself. She stopped moving and held her hands cupped together in front of her mouth, as if casting the shadow-familiar for the first time. *'Focus on the idea of an invisible spotlight, devoured by your shadow just like all that is visible. Your shadow is an empty space, devoid of heat and life, devoid of communication, devoid of thought and the concept of information itself.'* She wasn't sure how well this attempt to add a bit of extra transmogrification flavor to the shadow-familiar would work, but without true understanding, she needed whatever glue she could find to hold the magical effect together. *'Devour, and arise.'*

Her shadow obeyed.

The pressure eased. The disks in her back warmed and began to draw less of her blood, and the part of her Will assigned to empowering the divination-diverting ward was suddenly applying far more force than necessary.

Siobhan spat out the light coaster and pressed her hands to her mouth to muffle a deep-throated laugh. Had the answer been this easy, this simple, all along?

'Well, perhaps not.' Siobhan lowered her hands, put the light coaster back in her mouth, and continued to scramble across the cave room. She hadn't had the skills to do something like this from the start, and even if she had understood the concepts involved, her control over the shadow-familiar spell might not have been strong enough. She could do quite a lot with it now that hadn't been within its original parameters.

'I'm a genius!' she concluded, mentally patting herself on the back.

After a while, Thaddeus seemed to give up on finding her, and she made her way to the far side of the gnarled, twisted cave area. She squeezed through a fissure that led into a hallway and began to search for a way out again. She had been walking for a few minutes, and the fleetfoot potion had worn off, when another feeling of warning bloomed in her mind, seemingly from nowhere.

This one was less directed than the previous two, and though she spun around looking for danger, she saw nothing. She had barely turned to start running again, one hand in her pack to retrieve another fleetfoot potion, when the magic hit.

A ripple went through the stone like a wave on the edge of a pond, and as it passed, the stone melted. As if springing a trap, tendrils of liquid stone exploded upward and wrapped around her. She tried to rip through them, but every step, every movement, set off more.

The wave continued on, leaving the stone as hard as if nothing had happened, except for the new, melted appearance of the walls and the bindings reaching up from the floor to Siobhan's hips.

She reached for the spell rod nestled in the dip of her spine and pulled it out. Her fingers felt for the engraved symbol indicating the stone-disintegration spell. She twisted that segment, causing the circular spell array painted on orb-weaver silk and framed in metal to spring outward. Pulling from the beast core nestled against her skin beside the black sapphire Conduit, Siobhan had turned the stone around her ankles to rough sand and almost freed herself when the wave of liquid stone returned from where it had come.

This time, the remaining tendrils squeezed down hard enough around her legs to bruise the flesh, and as if they were somehow sentient and had "found" her physically and thus had no need for a divination, her ward broke in the same moment that it attempted to activate. She had no chance to resist.

Dread covered her in a cold sweat, and she redoubled her efforts to disintegrate the stone, adding panicked yanks of her legs to the effort to escape. It only took her fifteen seconds to get free, but every second her sense of foreboding grew stronger. Half of it was her own natural response, and the other half was another of those strange daydream-sensation warnings. It was telling her that she had put her hand in the cookie jar without realizing that in the doorway behind her, the monster who owned those cookies loomed.

She had freed herself and taken two steps when Thaddeus burst out of the side of the hallway a few meters in front of her. The stone closed up behind him, leaving no sign of his passage. He skidded to a stop and took several deep, gasping breaths. He opened his hand and let the shards of a depleted beast core fall to the ground, where they clinked and scattered.

'Did he just cast some sort of stone-traversal spell and sprint toward me in a straight line, diving right through everything in between?' She had heard that skolex worms —giant, predatory, sand-worms—did something similar to ease their movement through the ground, deep in the Tataroc Desert.

The unnatural foreboding dropped away, replaced by a real and present dread that needed no augmentation and was all her own. Her skin prickled and the air felt thicker with every breath as he glared at her, already gaining control of his breath.

"I found you," he said.

Siobhan gritted her teeth as helpless frustration burned the back of her throat. *'What am I supposed to do against Thaddeus Lacer!? This is just unfair.'*

38

ICARUS BURNING

Siobhan
    Month 9, Day 12, Sunday 3:25 a.m.

Siobhan turned to run, and Thaddeus sprinted after her. As she had guessed before, he was quicker. His legs were longer, and each step propelled him forward with more strength. She managed to get the second fleetfoot potion up to her lips and drink it without choking, but that only let her slightly exceed his speed.

"Titans damn you, Siobhan," he cursed in a low voice between gasps for air.

For a moment, she considered switching into her other body. It might fare somewhat better against Thaddeus. But even now, she hoped to preserve that identity's safety. There was still a chance she would get to use it again. If she could break away from his line of sight a second time, she might be able to switch and then pretend that she was somehow, actually, Sebastien. Who was in the tunnels either for a legitimate reason or via some nefarious magic of the Raven Queen's. And the Raven Queen herself, nowhere to be found. '*We seem to have switched places!*' she imagined saying.

Siobhan shook her head. How likely was a ruse like that to actually work? At the very least, it would make Sebastien more suspicious. At worst, Thaddeus would dig deeper and realize the great deception she had been pulling off —that Siobhan and Sebastien were like a change of clothes, each housing the same being.

Beyond that, she would need to find a place to wash up, switch outfits, and possibly deal with any new injuries that came from physically ripping through her clothes, all of which were currently sized for a significantly smaller body. Even if she wanted to, there was no *time*.

Thaddeus ignored the veil of shadow trailing behind her, simply pouring so much light into the darkness that she couldn't absorb it all.

Despite skidding around corners and fleeing with a reckless abandon that eventually led to her coming into another cave—this one a dead end—she didn't manage to lose him.

Siobhan stumbled to a stop, her legs trembling, her teeth clenched around the light coaster. She let it fall into her hand to better gasp for air. Darkness encroached on the edges of her vision as she swung the light coaster around, trying to find a way out. She almost missed it at first—a hole toward the back of the cave, near the ceiling. Luckily, there were minimal barriers between it and her across the floor, but she would have to climb the wall to reach it. Everywhere her light had passed, hairy moss on the cave walls and floor seemed to have captured some of the light, glowing gently.

However, it was too late. Thaddeus had caught up.

Siobhan tucked her spell rod back into the holster sewn into the inner back of her dress along the curve of her spine. With her hand free, she drew out her battle wand from the holster on her thigh. She fired without checking the spell currently selected. A trio of slicing spells shot out, one at the center and two curving in through either side. This wand was filled with some of the most powerful battle spells legally available, enough so that she had winced when buying it, due to her history of somehow losing every single battle wand she got her grubby mitts on.

Without even a blink or a twitch, Thaddeus threw up an instant, effortless shield that blocked all three slicing spells. His nose had stopped bleeding, but there was obvious bruising beneath his eyes already, and some crusted blood around his nostrils and in his mustache. "I apologize for underestimating you," he drawled. He was breathing hard, but clearly less winded than her. His stamina was better than hers, too. "A sleep-based spell, on a master of shadow and nightmare? I should have known not to attack you within your own domain of expertise."

Siobhan ignored him, switching to a concussive blast spell and throwing a couple of those as she backpedaled to put more distance between them. She put the light coaster back between her teeth, illuminating the upper half of her face from below while a thin strip of shadow over her eyes kept her from blinding herself. With her now-free hand, she scooped up a rock.

Thaddeus's shield absorbed the first spell, and with timing that must have been born from long experience and exquisite reflexes, he dropped the shield spell, lifted the hand with the beaded bracelet once more, and cast a roiling, purple-tinged spell, then brought the shield spell up again just in time to catch the second concussive blast.

Thaddeus's purple counterattack spell was so efficient that it barely glowed, but Siobhan's eyes were still well enough adjusted to the dark that she could clearly make out its writhing edges in the split second that it shot toward her.

Her warding medallion screamed with sudden cold, and the combination of fleetfoot potion and the much longer-lasting quintessence of quicksilver allowed her to take a single, small step to the side.

She cringed from the combination of freeze-burn on the delicate skin of her chest and the instinctive fear of that hungry magic, lifting her arms to brace around her head. The attacking magic slid off and to the side, and a piece of her warding medallion broke. She could tell because of the sudden pause in its sinking temperature, and the way the purple spell seemed to stutter as the force driving it away gave out.

"So, that was your free-cast deflecting spell?" Thaddeus asked. "I am pleased to see it in person. Very smooth," he praised.

Siobhan had almost forgotten about the warding medallion—a reminder that the quintessence of quicksilver only gave the *illusion* of omniscience. '*Why didn't it activate against Thaddeus's attack before?*' It was a rhetorical question, though. Even Grandfather couldn't have anticipated literally every spell that someone might cast against her with nefarious intent, nor created wards detailed enough to nullify them all. And even if he might have noted a spell to force sleep paralysis, the warding medallion hadn't been finished when she took it.

It was telling, though, that Thaddeus didn't imagine that her own defense could have been based on an artifact. Just because none were visible and her clothing was obviously too poor of a quality to carry any powerful magic didn't explain it. He had a blind spot toward her, an expectation that she was *competent*. She wasn't sure how she might use that misconception against him.

Siobhan darkened the thin strip of her shadow to protect her eyes from flash blindness as she switched the spell on the battle wand again, and then again half a second later. This time she shot out a huge ball of fire packing a massive blast in its center, followed by a flare of lightning that shot right through its center. The fireball disguised the lightning, which in turn destabilized the fireball, exploding it slightly early and continuing on to strike at Thaddeus while he was hopefully off guard from the explosion.

Finally, she hurled the jagged rock she had picked up earlier with so much force she almost cracked a tooth against the coaster. It never even hit Thaddeus's shield, slamming instead against a secondary shield that sprang up a few inches in front of the first.

Siobhan's thoughts stuttered in confusion, but she had no time to wonder.

The shield blinked back out of existence, as if it had never been there. *'Of course he would have a basic automatic defensive artifact, you idiot!'* she scolded herself.

With her free hand, she reached into her satchel, hooked a vial of acid and a vial of liquid fire between her fingers, and then hurled them both at Thaddeus with enough force to break the delicate glass.

Without waiting to see the result, she switched the wand's current spell again, and this time sent out a barrage of stunning spells, hoping that, at the very least, some of the soporific powder contained in the spell would get past Thaddeus's shield.

The fact that he wore no obvious or excessive jewelry that could store spell charges was a mark of confidence more than modesty. He could cast anything he needed, and would be able to access the Red Guard's supplies during the rare occasion that he went up against something truly dangerous. But a basic defensive artifact against things like thrown stones would catch the sort of random, mundane attacks from commoners that might take him by surprise, or that someone like her might try to slip past a more arcane-focused defense. However, if she cracked a vial of acid or liquid fire over it, it might allow the liquid through while stopping the shards of glass.

In truth, she didn't have much hope. While a single shield that defended against *everything* was almost impossible to make, most of her offensive options were rather mundane and relatively low-powered. They weren't meant to deal with a Grandmaster who could probably have been certified as an Archmage if not for politics.

When the crackling, red light of the stunning spells faded, she saw that the stone was scorched and cracked around Thaddeus, liquid fire smoldered at his feet, and dust filled the air. But the man was still standing, completely unharmed. Rather than the shield she had been expecting, he had created armor for himself. It reminded her of a dark, smoky chitin, except that it glittered scintillatingly. Smooth lines covered his entire body in articulated segments, which came to blade-like edges at his shoulder and knees.

Thaddeus swiped a hand over his face, and the plate there grew transparent so that she could see his expression in the eerie green glow of the moss that had been enlivened by her light show and the flames on the ground. He raised one eyebrow. "Are you underestimating me?"

Siobhan bit back a scoffing laugh of despair. A physical suit of armor rather than an actively cast shield would mean that he could take blows that he would normally have had to stop attacking to deal with. Whatever substance he had made it from, whatever clever internal structure it used, his armor could deal with fire, force, lightning, acid, and seemingly protected against particulate substances and poison, too. To add insult to this, he had gone so far as to add artistic flourishes to make himself seem more menacing. *'Is he holding back?'* A small part of her sparked with twisted, bitter hope. *'Trying to give me a chance to escape, maybe? Or maybe he just wants a good challenge.'* Whatever the case, she would take any advantage she could get. "Please let me go," she asked, imbuing her voice with as much sincerity as possible. "I won't ever tell anyone what I discovered. I can swear a vow to it, if you want. Does the Red Guard really care about this so much? What does it harm if I know the truth? We're already allies, Thaddeus, *please.*"

Begging was revolting, and for a moment she thought she might actually gag, but her pride was worth little against stakes like these. Even if she knew the begging wouldn't save her, as it never had. She would take any chance she could grasp, no matter how slim.

Thaddeus's eyebrows scrunched together in an expression of pain. "I wish it were that easy. Unfortunately, I do not make the rules, and I cannot stop what has been set in motion. But I promise you again, when I defeat you, I will not kill you. If you give up fighting, it will be gentle, and as painless as I can make it." He pointed one armor-covered index finger at her and another spell shot forward. This one *screamed*, like invisible lightning, and seemed to crack through the world in much the same way. Unlike lightning, it was slow enough that she had time to backpedal and dodge to the side, but it seemed to be drawn to her with some sort of homing function.

As it approached, the medallion began to draw in heat again, and Siobhan gritted her teeth against the cold burn. She wished there were some way to feed the artifact heat like she could feed blood and power to her divination-diverting ward, but unless she wanted to take it out and risk it being forcibly removed from her possession, there was no safe way to do so. Burning herself with fire was as dangerous as with cold. The crackling attack slid around her invisible, slippery ward and tried to come in from the side, so that the deflection had to keep turning to match it.

A scream of pain slipped past her clenched teeth as the warding medallion literally froze the skin and cloth in a small area around itself. She scrambled to put physical distance between herself and Thaddeus's spell, just to buy a few microseconds of reprieve.

Thaddeus frowned as he followed the magic's path with his gaze, a hint of strain in the fine wrinkles at the corners of his eyes.

'He's directing it.' Siobhan reached into her satchel and drew out a philtre of shadow-perception.

She took a sip, then dashed it on the ground between them as she backpedaled from the inexorable, screaming spell. Clouds of darkness exploded outward but did nothing to obscure her perception. If anything, the temporary ability to parse all the information her senses were giving her might give her an extra edge. She tucked the light coaster away in a pocket.

Unfortunately, the lack of sight did not seem to hamper Thaddeus nearly enough, or perhaps the homing function was built into the spell, after all.

In desperation, Siobhan brought her shadow up and sank it into the crackling, screaming battle spell like an enveloping maw, with the intent to rip from it whatever power drove it. She was not able to absorb the spell itself, but the barrier of her shadow did seem to work to cut off whatever was connecting it to Thaddeus.

As with divination, an actively cast spell like this required a source of power, even if she couldn't see its path or trace its flow.

Thaddeus gasped and stumbled, wide-eyed.

Without him, it expended itself on ripping apart the clouds of magical darkness within a few seconds, while Siobhan took the time to slip away unseen. Not toward the hole at the back of the room that seemed to lead to a tunnel just big enough to crawl through. Thaddeus was too clever not to have noticed it already. Instead, she moved toward the side of the room, where she had seen an outcropping of stone a few meters above head height, just wide enough to lie on and be partially hidden. While she moved, she took more potions from her bag and downed them, one after the other. Bark-skin, to add some protection to her flesh. Feather-fall, to ease the climb. A draught of shadowed concealment, chugged to the last drop. An aptly named sticky-fingers salve, good for just thirty seconds. The last had two common uses: pickpocketing, and burglary. It allowed her to grip the cave wall well enough that, with the feather fall, she could climb up the side like a lizard.

Her mentor righted himself, the fist holding his Conduit pressed to his chest and his face twisted with shock and suspicion as he looked around blindly for her. "What was that? How did you do that?" The words were gritted out between clenched teeth, his voice tight.

Siobhan remained silent as she settled onto the ledge, pressing herself fully into the hard stone. She pulled the spell rod out again and lined up a few battle potions by her stomach with careful, precise movements, fighting the desperate urge to pant for air.

Thaddeus cast a gust spell so powerful that it picked up the shards of the philtre of shadow-perception and the remnants of unexpanded liquid still pouring from it and buffeted it all toward the back of the room. The clouds of darkness escaped through the tunnel near the ceiling, confirming for Siobhan's benefit that it was, in fact, traversable, though it would be an uncomfortably tight fit even for this body.

Siobhan's ears popped at the sudden change in air pressure, and even though she was on the edge of the spell's effects, she pressed her no-longer-sticky fingers to the ground and closed her eyes at the sudden fear she, too, would be blown away. The feather-fall potion's magic faded even as the gust spell died down.

All of the potions seethed in Siobhan's stomach, urging her once again to vomit, and a hot wash of horror chilled her skin. If Thaddeus had hit her directly with even such a basic spell, she probably would have been blown across the room and bashed against the wall. Bark-skin wasn't enough to protect against such a blow. Her warding medallion might not be, either.

As the wind died down, Thaddeus looked around the cave that had been flash-cleaned with narrowed eyes. He brought up his light orb again, doing a full, careful spin, and then dropped the light to send out a wave of divination that she very carefully ate with her shadow as it washed over her. It went on for a while, long enough that her quicksilver thoughts had time to spin.

'What horrible wrong turn did I make that put me here, at this moment, in this situation?' Her memories flowed like liquid, and she concluded that this was inevitable since she had first gone to visit Thaddeus in his cottage. She had become too comfortable with him, felt a little too safe. She knew the kinds of things the Red Guard did to protect their secrets, and yet she'd somehow failed to internalize that Thaddeus, too, was an agent. Siobhan squeezed her eyes tight in regret and shame at her own stupidity. Even if she'd decided to ask him for the truth, she could have done so in a safer manner. The same way she had gone to treat with the other Red Guard agents.

'Do I have any options right now if he doesn't just give up and walk away? If he finds me?' She had over twenty minor spells in her spell rod, and she could detach their output to fight with them while simultaneously continuing to hide her physical location. But she couldn't see even those that were meant for battle instead of just general utility—a drilling spell, for instance—doing much harm to Thaddeus. Would an unlocking spell make his armor fall apart? She doubted it. Even if she could come up with something that could get past his armor, he could cast a shield even faster than she could attack. She had more battle potions with various effects, but none of them seemed likely to be effective.

She had left the emergency copper coin with the tracking spell in it behind, but even if she'd had it, she doubted Sebastien's safety would come before the compulsion of Thaddeus's vows.

'Ah! I should have reminded him that the Red Guard gave me the authority to do restricted research!' Except...he had been there for that agreement, which had been pretty specifically about shamanry. He knew about her expanded leeway, and it wasn't enough to stop him from being compelled to kill her. She believed, at least, that if that knowledge would have loosened his vows, he would have drawn upon it already. He didn't want to kill her. Just scrub her brain with a metaphorical scouring potion.

If only she had that promised rare component that would help her modify the dazzler, she could possibly just erase the last twenty minutes from Thaddeus's mind and fix this whole thing. The idea filled her with vindictive satisfaction, but she quickly brought herself back to reality.

The gesturan spells she knew were far from developed enough to be useful. Sitting around casting for several minutes just to launch a fist-sized clod of dirt or ball of water was a terrible idea. At Siobhan's current level, that kind of magic was only good for surviving the type of emergency that didn't require any fighting.

Her only advantage over Thaddeus was that he could only do one thing at a time. He could switch between spells slightly faster than her, but that didn't make up for his limitation. If she added on the possibility of attacking with an artifact, potion, or even a physical blow of some sort, she had a chance to hit him—but she had nothing that could get past the armor.

She briefly considered trying to carve out a piece of the ceiling and drop it on him while he was distracted.

Her disadvantage was that if he found her, a single spell from him could end things.

Thaddeus drew in a long-suffering breath through his nose, then winced and lifted a hand as if to touch it, though he stopped himself halfway.

Another flash of warning rose up from the back of her mind. She didn't need to interpret the memories to know that Thaddeus didn't really think she had escaped and was going to cast some kind of revealing spell. Based on his prior success, it was likely he would try something that she had no defense against.

All she could do was misdirect and deceive, and so she needed to do that better than she ever had before.

Before Thaddeus could finish preparing his powerful spell, she dropped a thread of shadow down the side of the wall in front of her, ran it over to a spot a few feet behind Thaddeus, and lifted it into an imitation of herself. She made the false fabric of its skirt and the tips of its hair cold enough to waft fog, and despite his armor, Thaddeus noticed almost immediately.

He whipped around to face her shadow, and Siobhan took advantage of his movement to snap open one of the segments of her spell rod without being heard. The illusion spell drawn on it was vague, so that she could use it for quite a lot with the right application of Will.

The problem with illusions was that they had no shadow. They were all light, and even the more complex ones that could block out the sight of whatever came from behind them looked unnatural, visibly ephemeral and a little too glowy. She had practiced adding shadow to her illusions when she made Theo's birthday present, the illustrated book telling of his adventures with Empress Regal. Since then, she hadn't gotten nearly enough practice with illusions to be comfortable enacting her current plan. But she had been practicing magic all the time, including the incredible detail that any truly lifelike illusion required.

And so, now, she brought all of her concentration to bear and added a second, detached-output spell where the face of her shadow form hung in the air. From within the lightless dark, her face appeared, as if rising to the surface of a sheet of water. Its eyes were closed. Every lash was drawn in shadow and light, her skin scattered with pores and faint texture, and the sweat beaded on her upper lip and around the edges of her hairline reflected light from the moss and still-burning liquid flames.

Siobhan watched intently, wishing she had the eyes of an eagle so that she could see her work in more detail. Her quickened thoughts ceased to feel like enough, and the rest of the world fell away as every part of her mind and Will poured into creating something even realer than reality.

Her illusory form's hair and clothing remained a midnight void, as if only the face were peeking out from an elaborate costume, which wafted with fog and fluttered in an illusory wind. She knew her own face better than most, perhaps, due to being able to take it on and off and having spent so much time disguising it to look like other versions of itself. She poured in everything she knew about it, even the scent, the way breath felt flowing through her nostrils, and the exact way the world faded from sight every time she blinked. These were not visual, and shouldn't have mattered for a simple illusion, but they were *real*, and she had learned that such things mattered when practicing magic.

Thaddeus's eyes were wide, and rather than attack, he took a single step back.

'This is where reputation comes in handy. If it were Sebastien doing this, Thaddeus would look for more reasonable explanations instead of wondering what strange magic I've cast.'

Thaddeus regained his composure quickly and cast a probing attack.

Siobhan's illusion twirled out of the way with unnatural, fey-like speed, then immediately fell still again. Looking up through its lashes in a way that was more menacing than flirtatious, it gave him a slow, mocking smile.

Behind Thaddeus on the other side, Siobhan sent down another few dozen threads of shadow. These, she formed into ravens, and sent them flying through the air in a complex pattern. Of course, they made no sound, but Thaddeus somehow noticed and half-turned his head to see them out of the corner of his eye.

While turning, he stepped carefully to the side and backed up so that he could see both Siobhan's illusory form and the whirling mass of ravens at once.

She let a few, frost trailing from the longest and sharpest edges of their wing feathers, swoop in a little closer to Thaddeus as if threatening him.

It was a true testament to his wariness that he didn't immediately attack, instead saving his magic for defense.

After a moment, when the tension was reaching its peak, she sent her illusion "running" back to the entrance of the cave, while the ravens coalesced into an almost indistinguishable mass and flew through the tunnel on the other side.

Thaddeus looked from one to the other and then let out a deep sigh. He lowered his head and reached up as if to pinch the bridge of his nose but ended up knocking his hand into his armor's face plate. After a few seconds, he turned and walked after her illusory copy.

Still lying up on the ledge within the cave, Siobhan remained still and silent, wrapped in a thin shell of her shadow just in case she needed to immediately devour an attempt to scry her. Minutes passed, and she continued to send her shadow outward in either direction, using what she could sense through it to direct it. If the stone turned to liquid again, she would stay perfectly still and hope that it didn't react to her.

Enough time passed that the potions she had taken, except for the quintessence of quicksilver, began to wear off. The sweat cooled on her skin, and her shadow stretched far enough that she had to stop and let it return to her body.

'*Am I safe?*' she wondered. Some part of her wanted to keep hiding here, but another part of her considered that Thaddeus might retrace his steps if he couldn't find her.

Siobhan sat up, and her instincts screamed a warning like a half-remembered daydream, as a small sound against the stone behind her warned her to turn her head.

Thaddeus stood over her, taking up the small remaining space on the ledge, and she had no idea if he'd been there all along, invisible and silent, or if he had stepped out of the stone wall at that very moment.

Surely, if it were the former, she would have noticed his presence? He was breathing hard, and a sheen of sweat coated his temples and the sides of his nose. With the quintessence of quicksilver, even the tiniest hints could be analyzed and reveal relevant information. The hair on her arms would have shifted, or a waft of his scent would have slipped through.

He had left his armor behind somewhere. Perhaps it conflicted with the spell that allowed him to travel through stone. So, as he crouched down over her, she could hear his low murmur clearly.

"You are very clever, and very skilled. But I know your love for tricks, Siobhan. If the test is set by you, given two answers to choose from, the third will always be correct."

3 9

DELAYING TACTICS

Thaddeus jogged in the general direction that Siobhan had flitted, his mind replaying the strangely stunning sight of her almost completely swallowed in darkness. Whatever magic she had worked made her inhumanly fast, and though he could cast several spells to increase his speed in various ways, she vanished so quickly that he could not be sure which turn she had taken at the next intersection.

To be truthful, he was not entirely certain that he should be following her, and not the dense cloud of ravens she had sent streaming into the small hole at the other side of the cavern. Were they a decoy, or the preparation for some nasty surprise? Siobhan always seemed to think three or four moves ahead, and though Thaddeus prided himself on his intelligence and deductive reasoning, he did not know enough about the range of her capabilities.

His left ear tickled, and he flinched, slamming his fingers against it in an instinctive attempt to shelter it from attack. However, he felt no pain or sense of invasion, and when he drew his fingers away, they were wet with a smear of dark, thick blood.

With a grimace, Thaddeus cast a spell to cleanse himself from head to toe. His small wound from her attack earlier was already healed, but a phantom ache remained.

Siobhan had not even managed to destroy his eardrum with her icepick to the side of the head, but the attack had been effective, nevertheless. Extreme vertigo was a particularly useful attack against rival thaumaturges, because it was difficult to control the Will past the disorientation.

He had been, embarrassingly, taken off guard. She had not even had a Conduit in her hand, and he had not noted the ring that she must have used to cast, despite being the one to give it to her. It was so small, compared to his own Conduit, and compared to the kind of capacity she had displayed. That amount of celerium was only useful for a low-level Master…and, admittedly, emergencies. Out of all people, Thaddeus, who perhaps knew more about her than anyone else in the city, should not have underestimated her like that.

She had run, and Thaddeus had managed to cast a healing spell on himself after a bit of fumbling around.

She had continued to use that Conduit throughout the entirety of their fight, controlling it through the back of her finger despite the increased difficulty. Did she not have any better options, or did she simply prefer to keep her hands free for more mundane attacks?

Fighting her had been nothing like he had expected.

Thaddeus had listened to the reports and even watched the memories of people who had gone up against her, but he had expected that when faced with someone of his power, she would fight more—well, more like him.

Instead, she had made strange, unconventional choices that left him off-balance and confused.

He suspected she had been utilizing her ability to dual-cast more than was obvious, though at least one of her spells always seemed to be something weak and simple, again using that spell rod that Sebastien had developed. He had long since deduced that dual-casting came with more limitations than she advertised. If she were able to simultaneously free-cast two powerful spells, he might have lost their contest.

Or, perhaps she simply knew that her own strength was less than his and judged that the only way to win was through the advantage of versatility that her abilities granted.

What was the point of the battle potions? And the rock? Surely she did not think they would work against him. Was it some sort of test to gauge exactly how his shield worked, to set him up for a later surprise?

More likely, she had been trying to buy time for some reason, keeping him busy without hurting him.

Thaddeus rolled his shoulders against the unpleasant, prickling tension the thought brought. If not for the armor, he might have rubbed at his face. It was true, they had been fighting, nominally, but nothing she had done would be lethal against someone like him. Instead of trying to kill him, or even simply incapacitate him when he was temporarily off-kilter from the spike of bitter cold to his eardrum, she had simply run away.

And then, when it seemed she could not stop him without hurting him, she had pleaded with him. He had never even considered such a possibility. Siobhan Naught, the Raven Queen, was not the type to beg. Against an enemy, no matter how much stronger than her they might be, she would go down fighting like a dragon until the last spark of light left her eyes.

Did she not consider Thaddeus an enemy, even now?

If not for his vows… Thaddeus squeezed down on his Conduit so hard that he feared something might break. The laughably, tragically ironic part of it all was that he did not even know why they required this.

He could guess, of course, and he had.

The tragic truth was that the Red Guard was failing, on multiple fronts, and most of those who might have been able to do something about it were either too blind or too prideful to admit it. They sanctioned and punished him, but really, they feared that he might succeed where they could not.

He had considered and discarded the idea before, but perhaps Siobhan would be the type of person to appreciate his research. She likely even had deep knowledge and insights into areas that he had not yet had the time or inclination to explore.

For instance, the way she had severed a spell from his control. If he had been a lesser thaumaturge, slower to reel in his Will, she might have forced an accident. Severing magic that worked on other magic was a rare skill to start with. He had never met anyone who could sever the Will of a caster from a *detached* spell.

At any other time, in any other situation, Thaddeus would have spent some time theorizing about this ability and attempting to develop his own severing spell to achieve this. As evidenced, it would be useful against other extremely high-level thaumaturges. Instead, he stopped for a moment, taking deep breaths in through his nose and out through his mouth, and cast a gentle spell to speed his recovery. He had been trying to distract himself, to chase her ineffectively for a moment, but the vow would not allow him to continue when he could do better.

He tried a few divination spells, just in case, but of course, found nothing. He thought back to his tests on Sebastien's bestowed version of this ability. If it was the same kind of magic, only weaker, that suggested that its one great weakness was that it could be overwhelmed by sheer application of power.

Thaddeus considered attempting to pit his strength directly against Siobhan's, despite the disadvantage that the stone and distance between them would put him at. She was powerful, but he had no reason to believe she was noticeably more powerful than him. Before he could attempt it, he froze with a sudden realization. "She has been tricking me," he said aloud.

He turned around, but rather than take the same route back through the winding halls, he cast his earth-tunneling spell to sprint back in a straight line. His armor melted around him and the pieces clattered to the floor behind him, but it was only a minor loss, as he could reform it with a few seconds of effort and a beast core, of which he still had several remaining. He moved quickly, pausing several times to breathe and recover when he exited into hallways or small caves. If he ran out of breath while halfway through the stone, it would be quite a hassle to drop the earth-tunneling spell without harming himself and transmute stone into air while entombed. The return cost him another beast core, and he was glad to be so well prepared.

Thaddeus aimed to arrive at the side of the cavern on a small ledge he vaguely remembered, which should allow him to overlook the room, while potentially avoiding triggering any alarms or other forms of observation. His aim was accurate, but the ledge was occupied.

He almost tripped over Siobhan's prone form and managed to school his expression of surprise only a fraction of a second before she turned and met his gaze. He did not want to show weakness or admit that she had outmaneuvered him mentally. He had thought he might find some clues, or even, potentially, her having fortified the cavern or taken the time to set up some spell too powerful to free-cast. But there was no sign of that. Why was she still here?

4 0

———

THE DARK DESCENT

Siobhan raised her right hand with the palm outward as shadow coated the appendage like a liquid. While Thaddeus's attention was drawn to this seeming attack, her other hand reached into her boot and pulled out the thin knife sheathed inside. In one smooth motion, she drew it and stabbed at the side of his knee.

His automatic shield spell popped out again, stopping her thrust as if the knife in her hand were the wrong side of a powerful magnet.

Basic shield spells like this did have a weakness, though, or they would be popping up all the time at dinner or at the barber's. Their parameters reacted to speed and force, not the mere proximity of anything categorized as a blade.

Siobhan understood her failure in a moment faster than a blink and reacted. Before he could respond to her attack, she snapped out her free hand, grasped his ankle, and yanked it toward her with a full body heave.

He lost his balance and began to fall. His lower back would have hit the rough stone at the edge of the short ledge, and his upper body would have swung over the side.

He, of course, cast some kind of spell to catch himself halfway, but she was already trying again with the knife, this time bringing it in with what she felt was excruciating slowness.

Despite her analysis of the shield artifact's likely weaknesses, it again stopped her from stabbing him, but she got much closer.

Instead of drawing away for a third attempt, she kept pressing, using both arms and the weight of her body. Her knife inched closer as one second passed, and then two, and Thaddeus began to right himself.

A vibration spell cast on the blade would likely do the trick, as a lot of physical wards were weak against extremely rapid pounding or drilling. She could do that, but even though her spell rod was right next to her, she couldn't spare the time or both of her hands to open the right array.

In desperation, she threw up her shadow between them, surrounding Thaddeus's head and trying to suck all of the heat from it. Freezing the inside of his nostrils and the film of liquid over his eyes might be possible, if she focused hard enough, and might buy her a smidgen more time.

He blew through her shadow with some kind of Radiant beam that seared through the protection over her eyes and *burnt* at her shadow as if it was mere fog.

In desperation, she continued to attack with most of her shadow, while a small bit of it coated her hands and the knife blade. *'Pierce! Pierce!'* she screamed in her mind, pouring desperate intent into the magic. If she could stop Thaddeus's earlier spell as she had, was it so different to create a single point where the shield spell's power failed?

But it was different, enough that even as she sank to within millimeters of Thaddeus's flesh, she could not get through. Her shadow was so depleted, and it *hurt*, and she drew it back from attacking Thaddeus to instead protect her own flesh.

Then the thing in the back of her mind surged, flooding her with a desperate hunger for *power* that was at once deeply familiar and entirely alien. She remembered sensations she was sure she had never felt, and the edge of an eldritch understanding brushed her mind. True void contained an emptiness that could never be filled, a cold that could never be warmed, and a hunger that would cry out forever, for at the end of time, there was *nothing*. And a shadow had no meaning if there was no light.

The shadow devoured, and the knife sank into the flesh of Thaddeus's knee.

Siobhan and Thaddeus let out almost identical, wrenching gasps, though for different reasons.

She firmed her grip and threw her body to the side, forcing the slim strip of metal to move through his joint.

The flesh made a wet ripping sound, and the cartilage, or perhaps the tendons, snapped and cracked like a roasted chicken leg being torn from the rest of the meat. A burning hot spray of blood followed her hand, coating her fist as she yanked it back.

Thaddeus's gaze stayed locked on hers as he drew in a choked gasp. The leg buckled under him.

Siobhan grabbed the spell rod, then shoved herself up and over the rocky edge of the ledge. She fell awkwardly, scattering a few of the battle potions she'd had waiting, and landed with jarring force on her left leg. Holding her breath until she was out of the radius of their effects, she limped away. As the pain lessened, her speed increased, until she was once again sprinting through the winding, hive-like tunnels cut through the white cliffs.

She pushed herself to the edge of her capabilities, but she couldn't deny the despair coursing through her. She had thrown everything she had at Thaddeus. What more was she supposed to do?

But she didn't fall down and give up or just resign herself to failure. If Siobhan were the type to simply accept reality when everything seemed hopeless, she would never have made it this far.

Siobhan took her third fleetfoot potion of the night, ignoring the nausea that followed. She slowed slightly so that she could breathe well enough to chant, pulled her shadow in around her body, and began to cast a second spell.

Thaddeus healed himself and caught up with her in less than a minute. This time, instead of running after her, he flew. It *looked* a lot like lounging on an invisible chair, but in effect, it was flying. He grabbed her by her hair and yanked hard enough that her neck wrenched and her feet flew out from under her.

But she had been watching behind herself with her shadow and was prepared for his arrival. As she fell backward and he flew onward, several strands of her long black hair between his fingers, she released the spell she had been building up. The dazzler flashed out like a spear of light and took Thaddeus in the face.

The black star sapphire Conduit pressed into her side shattered with enough force to send several shards ripping into her skin.

In shock, scrambling to release all of the magic under her Will's grasp before the much-decreased capacity of the largest shard still under her command gave out, Siobhan couldn't react to anything else.

She hit the ground. Her breath exploded out. A shock of pain and lightning seared from her back into her extremities as the spell rod tried to forcibly take the place of her spine. Her head smacked down a split second later, and she saw stars, but didn't pass out.

Her open mouth gasped helplessly for air, but she managed to roll over with clumsy, almost drunken motions. With the help of the wall, she climbed to her feet.

Thaddeus was reeling much as she had been, his invisible chariot spell dropped and his hands grasping at his face, which was bleeding again.

However fast he was with a shield spell, he hadn't been able to move faster than the light—especially since the dazzler's tell-tale gathering process had been hidden under her shadow, leaving him no warning. By its nature, by the time you perceived it, it had already hit you. Failing to re-create his earlier armor had been a mistake, though even it might not have saved him. Light was difficult to defend against, especially when it carried a few transmogrification concepts suited to travel and piercing.

Siobhan thanked whatever gods might be for non-forced errors in her enemies. Then she braced herself, kicked him in the side of the head while he was down, and stumbled on.

Fireflies danced across her sight. If not for the wall to orient her, she would have fallen at least twice before her diaphragm opened up enough for her to suck in a shallow sip of life-giving air. She stumbled on faster and had the presence of mind to pull an expensive healing potion from her bag. She took a moderate mouthful, re-corked the vial, and put the rest away as cleansing light swept through her body, fixing a half-dozen moderate and again as many minor wounds.

Then she ran again. She was too tired to sprint at full speed, and when she heard Thaddeus get up and start chasing after her once more, the sharp rapping sound of each step indicating that he'd re-created his armor, she almost cried. Belatedly, she realized that she should have kicked him harder. She should have smashed his face in until he passed out. Some part of her still didn't want to kill him, apparently. Siobhan cursed that peabrained, self-sacrificing, moronic part of her.

She flipped the ring on her middle finger—her mother's ring—around and made a fist to ensure she wouldn't lose contact. The stone was set deep enough that it could touch the back of her finger most of the time, but adjustments of her finger positioning or grip could create a small gap between herself and the celerium, causing a catastrophic failure. She cast the shadow-familiar spell again.

As soon as she spoke the last words of the chant, those foreign daydream-thoughts screamed out from the back of her mind, vivid and urgent. Two children wearing crimson cloaks fled from a bestial wolf through an ominous forest, hand in hand. One pushed the other into a small den dug out at the base of a tree and turned to face the wolf, alone.

'*Oh, gods,*' Siobhan thought.

The daydream tried to persuade her again. The child facing down the wolf pulled back its hood to reveal glowing yellow eyes and a pointed maw full of fangs. It gave a rattling, growling screech of threat toward the wolf, which hesitated.

'*This is a bad idea,*' she recognized. '*But it won't break my Will. And aside from that, I feel like things literally cannot get any worse for me at this moment. Even if that thing were to side with Thaddeus and turn on me, he would likely still be distracted fighting it, which could give me a chance to escape. If it tries to run and start hurting people, that gives me an opportunity, too. Surely, dealing with me cannot be more important than dealing with an Aberrant. Best-case scenario, it does what it promises and then runs out of energy and goes back inside, just like last time.'*

She tried to come up with a better option, but Thaddeus had begun to cast another spell already.

Siobhan detached her shadow.

For a single second, nothing happened, and she simply ran on without it.

Then the dissonance hit, flipping the world upside down and inside out. But she was prepared, and the sensory confusion didn't hit her as hard as last time. She stumbled a bit, but didn't fall.

As if her left-behind shadow were a hole in the ground and the thing in her head was crawling out of it, a black hand reached up and grasped the stone. An arm followed, and then an entire body. A copy of Siobhan stood up between Thaddeus and Siobhan herself. It opened its eyes, and the glowing-amber circles of its irises reflected off Thaddeus's dark armor.

It lunged at him with inhuman speed. One hand formed into a claw that sank through the clear face panel of his armor, going for the eyes with single-minded intensity.

Blood and a thick clear fluid splattered on the inside of his faceplate as he flinched back with a curse. But his response was immediate and devastating. Light erupted from the hand holding his component bracelet in a blazing wave.

Siobhan felt a phantom pain, like she was standing too close to a roaring bonfire, as the Radiance tore through her shadow once again.

The being wearing her shadow screamed, too high-pitched to seem remotely human, on the edge of breaking glass. But she sensed it absorbing some of the light—not as much as she could have channeled herself, but enough to matter. Undeterred by the damage, as soon as the spell dropped, it tried to leap on Thaddeus. Not as a human might have done, but like some sort of shadow-kraken or octopus. It wrapped itself around his torso and head, sank through the faceplate again, and tried to crawl into his orifices.

Thaddeus, of course, responded with even more light, bursting outward directly from his skin like the surface of the sun. He followed that up with some kind of ripping attack that somehow affected the shadow despite its selective ephemerality.

Siobhan did her best to put the input from her shadow into the back of her mind as they battled, but she couldn't help flinching each time Thaddeus let loose some new spell. Eventually, after a short time that somehow felt like an eternity of battle and running, her shadow became too damaged. *'What happens if it "dies?" What happens to me if my shadow gets completely ripped apart, and dissipates or something?'* She didn't want to risk releasing the spell, because rather than bringing her shadow back, it might just sever the connection between her and it, giving complete control to the thing currently wearing it.

Apparently, the thing felt the same sense of insecurity, because it rushed back toward her in a blur, too fast for her senses to track. But it didn't reattach to her this time. Standing slightly hunched but somehow still taller than her, it looked back the way it had come. "There is no hope in a fight against that man," it said to her in its strange, muffled voice. Its words held the ring of truth, echoed by the frustrated despair she felt from it.

Siobhan slowed at an intersection, now hopelessly lost. She turned toward the left, but it pinched at her sleeve and pointed to the right. She hesitated, muttered a curse, and turned to the right instead. By this point, it was obvious that the thing had some additional sense for magic that she did not, and unless this was all a very elaborate ruse, it sincerely didn't want her captured by the Red Guard and was willing to collaborate to keep her free.

"I offer another way to escape, one that the enemy cannot track nor follow," it said.

Siobhan glared at it, panting heavily as she willed her legs to keep moving, step after step. Her mouth was so dry.

"I can create a door," it said, a spike of hunger hidden underneath a bed of truthfulness.

Siobhan scoffed. "No."

"Why!?" it cried.

"At least Thaddeus doesn't want to kill me, though that might change if he realizes what you really are. Surely, he's taken vows to destroy Aberrants, too. Or at least capture them." she added with a cruel smile.

The thing's frustration and fear grew to a fever pitch, and the shadow rippled as it looked over its shoulder once more. "You will be as bad off as I, if we cannot escape," it promised.

"But I will be *worse* off if I take your poisoned deal."

It gritted its teeth and wriggled strangely, as if its limbs had fallen asleep, or as if it was trying to stomp about and throw a tantrum but had forgotten what that looked like. "Fine. I vow that I shall not harm you this night, on my magic. I vow that I shall not harm you this night, on my memories and dreams. I vow that I shall not harm you this night, on my future. I have thrice vowed your safety, human. Until the sun rises, you are safe with me."

Thaddeus slammed past her divination-diverting ward easily.

Siobhan shuddered from the sense of being watched, pinned like a butterfly for observation. Without her shadow, she could not stop him.

The divination fell away, but she was not relieved, because she knew something else would be coming next.

Another pulse of magic flashed out, this time seeming to turn the very air into syrup. It was as if the effects of gravity and energy were reduced.

Siobhan had heard people describe dreams where they tried to run but bounced instead, their bodies too light and weak to affect the world even enough to flee. Siobhan leaned forward until her fingers touched the wall and the ground and tried to use them to pull herself forward faster. *'Swimming isn't the answer. Would a directed gravity spell propel me?'* she wondered, already reaching for the spell rod. It was a little banged up, but after a few smacks, the spell array she wanted sprang open.

A directed gravity spell did indeed work, but she knew that, inevitably, Thaddeus would be faster. While he was casting this, he couldn't move directly through the stone or fly, but there was no way he would have cast something that disadvantaged them equally.

Even her lungs found it difficult to process the air like this, and her weariness reached a crescendo.

A rippling, gurgling sound approached, echoing strangely, but definitely growing closer.

Siobhan let out a low sob of exhaustion.

The creature wearing her shadow stepped in front of her, unaffected by Thaddeus's spell. "Choose now. There is no time." Its form lost coherence for a moment, and then became a hooded, flapping cloak of darkness that held no head, and no body. When she looked closer, it seemed more like a cloak-shaped window to…*elsewhere.*

It was very dark beyond, but she could make out the light of distant fires. *'What magic is this?'* she wondered.

But the rippling sound was upon her now, and when she turned to look behind her, there was Thaddeus, his eyes healed and the inside of his faceplate clean of gore. His arms were outstretched and hands pressed together to carve the way as his jacket, worn on top of his armor, flapped about like some sort of tail fin and propelled him powerfully forward. It should have looked ridiculous. Instead, it was terrifying.

The air regained its viscosity, and as she tumbled to the ground, Thaddeus's Will tightened, preparing something devastating and final. She didn't need a daydream flash to tell her so.

She met his gaze through his faceplate. He was serious now, and she could sense his determination to break her like a constrictor snake broke the bones of its prey. He had lost all patience with their game of cat and mouse.

Siobhan threw herself backward through the cloak, and when she had passed, it collapsed to nothing behind her.

41

THE WOMB AND THE GRAVE

Month 9, Day 12, Sunday 3:50 a.m.

On the other side of the strange cloak-window to elsewhere, Siobhan climbed to her feet. Everything was deeply, existentially wrong, and she had opened her mouth to scream in pain and fear when the thing at her side reached out and took her hand.

And suddenly, she wasn't so sure what had been wrong. Somewhat embarrassed, she closed her open mouth and turned her mind to observation.

Here, the thing was no longer mimicking her, or even wearing her shadow.

Siobhan looked down quickly, relieved to find that her body cast its own shadow once more. With an effort of Will that felt...*strange*, but not as if something were opposing her, she managed to make it wriggle a little. Assured that it was solely under her control, she looked back up.

The thing was seemingly flesh and blood, and truly androgynous. Though some features reminded her of her own face in the mirror, some were totally different—and yet still strangely familiar.

Siobhan did her best not to make any mental connections to certain memories.

It had quicksilver sclera surrounding its golden irises, which, as always, seemed to be lit from within. Its skin was threaded with glowing red veins, as if lava ran under the surface rather than blood. It loomed hungrily over her, staring intently, but as she grew apprehensive, it bared its teeth in frustration and turned to lead the way.

When she didn't immediately follow, it tugged impatiently on her hand.

She considered breaking this physical connection between them, but remembered the feeling of wrongness when she had first fallen into wherever this was, and a sense of foreboding stopped her. Instead, she adjusted her grip so that she could hold on to it in return, no matter how loathsome this mimicry of intimacy was. The solidity of another hand in her own was like a candle against the dark, a small piece of comfort that made no sense based on how she felt about the creature leading her.

The creature's clothes were not quite real, ever-shifting. As Siobhan looked closer, she saw that the fluttering layers and folds kept giving glimpses to else-where, but the shape of it somehow created an optical illusion of disconnected limbs, tortured bodies, and doorways.

Siobhan tore her eyes away. *'Better not to focus on that. There's definitely some mind-affecting magic involved.'* "Where are we?" she asked, looking around. They were walking through a starless night, on a path made of huge paving stones and bordered on either side by smooth boulders the size of a person.

"We are outside reality, in a place that is somewhat stable and realer than some, that still bears the marks of a path I left."

Siobhan did not understand. *'Am I…inside the seal that Grandfather made?'* she wondered. But that didn't seem right. She looked around and realized that the giant stones bordering the path were actually carved. They were walking by the feet of giant, humanoid statues. And the flames she had seen earlier were high above, held in equally giant lanterns. The statues' faces were hundreds of meters away, too far to see in the darkness.

As she kept looking, she realized that the flames had a form. She squinted, and they seemed to grow brighter, or perhaps her eyes were simply adjusting to the lack of light. The edges and color gradients of the flames grew more distinct, and suddenly, it was clear that the flames were each a body. People-shaped. And they had been all along!

The flame people seemed to notice her attention and began to bang on the edges of the lanterns they were trapped within, calling soundlessly down at her. As she and the thing walked on, hand in hand, the flame people grew desperate.

Siobhan caught the faint whooshing and crackle of flames, but almost as if they were molded to be more than meaningless background noise. *'Is that words? Are they speaking?'* She couldn't understand it.

The thing yanked her hand roughly, forcing her attention back to it.

She suddenly realized that she could see so much better than when she first entered, though it was still just as dark, and her eyes should have already been well adjusted. However, she could tell now that the huge paving stones beneath their feet were edged with blood rather than mortar. And as she and the thing walked along them, the edges sank.

The thing yanked her hand again, even harder, and squeezed with pent-up anger until Siobhan's fingers creaked.

She tried to pull away, but there was no give to its grip.

It turned to her with a snarling mouth suddenly filled with sharp teeth. "Cease, you stupid mortal. Do you have no sense of danger?" It turned back, and they walked in silence for a few moments before it huffed and turned to look at her again, overflowing with bottled frustration. "Some part of me believes that *withholding information* is a kind of harm, apparently." It shuddered, but in a way that no mortal being could. Its body fractured into shards and mist for a fraction of a second, so quick her eyes almost missed it, and then pulled together looking slightly different. Still androgynous, still a little like her, but everything was just faintly *off* in a way that she struggled to understand, as the new appearance seemed to overwrite the other in her memories.

"This place eats your thoughts and creates corpses from your memories," it said. "Its land is shifting like the sea, and all who walk through its borders and breathe its air will be made more like it. Fight to remember yourself, lest you lose yourself."

Siobhan belatedly understood. "This is the spirit realm?"

It didn't answer.

She was fascinated despite the danger but did not indulge her curiosity by further paying attention to her surroundings, though it went against her nature to hold back so. Biting her lip for the small spike of pain that would help clear her mind, Siobhan recalled the shamanry exercises she had learned before. Reluctantly, she dropped the shadow-familiar spell so that she would have more mental space to work with. It didn't seem to have any effect on her, nor on the being. '*Will it be free, now?*' Judging from its lack of reaction, it hadn't even noticed.

Siobhan counted her fingers, wiggled her toes in her shoes, and mentally repeated her name, her current situation, and her purpose. She recalled the shape of her face and the taste of her favorite foods. She clenched her muscles, one by one, and focused on the feel of her clothes across her skin. With two pieces to her Will, it was actually easier to keep some part of herself focused on self-stabilization than it might have been. When one would get distracted, the other would draw it back in.

For someone with so much experience remaining utterly focused while casting spells, the shamanry exercises should have been easy. To the contrary, it was like even existing in this world put her in a half dream-like state. She was a doll made of old, fraying yarn, and the very air was filled with hooks that pulled free strands of her being as it passed.

The thing tugged her hand again, walking faster with legs that seemed longer than hers, even though they were the same height. She could feel its anger and deep resentment. "Hurry. I do not have the power to remain for long, and without me, you will die." It sneered at her, leaking disgust mixed with an undefined longing. "Your physical body was never meant to exist here."

"Why are you helping?" she asked.

It didn't answer, but she could feel a faint fluctuation in its emotions.

Siobhan went back to putting her full attention toward the self-stabilizing exercises for a moment, and then asked, "Do you think he might have found you while he was wiping my memories? Is that why you're helping?"

It prickled with a feeling that she decided was best described as revulsion or aversion, an emotional feeling akin to the goosebumps she had experienced one day when she came upon a dog eating the entrails of another dog.

"Are you afraid of what might happen to you if my mind were damaged, or I died?"

It turned to snarl at her in a way that reminded her of the daydream-promise it had sent her earlier—a vulnerable, small thing making itself appear more threatening than it felt. And oh, it hated her so for asking.

That was alright. She hated it, too. Siobhan wondered about the way it had fractured earlier. In a place like this, the appearance it showed might be more connected to its true identity than anything else she had seen. She considered asking its name, but she didn't want to risk that. Instead, she asked, "Have you been absorbing power from my shadow this whole time? I had wondered where the extra might be going, but I just considered it part of the entropic mystery. All magic loses some of the energy in translation from source to effect, and no one knows where it might be going..." She nodded to herself, concluding that the answer was, "Yes," even though the thing remained silent.

There was a certain irony in the fact that she had been drip-feeding the creature even as she kept control of her shadow all the time for the feeling of safety it gave her.

"How did you know that Thaddeus was about to attack me? Can you sense magic?" She already knew that it couldn't actually tell what she was thinking or know everything that she experienced.

"Can you shut up?" it asked.

"Well, I'm saving your life—maybe life isn't the right word. Your continued existence—by letting you escape with me, so I think the least you could do is show a little gratitude by answering my questions," she snapped back with a fake smile.

Its outrage welled up so strong and fast that it couldn't keep it all inside. "Saving *my* life? *Letting* me escape with you!?"

Before it could continue its rant, she interjected. "So how did you know?"

"You've been feeding me all that power, so I had enough to spare to take a peek through the cracks, you horrible, self-centered *bitch*. What do you think I am? Do you have any idea of the *power* I could wield, if not for being trapped in the seal?" It turned to grin at her, giving a pointed look to their clasped hands and then at its own feet. "Well, mostly sealed," it amended. "This place speaks plenty about the mortal plane, for those that have eyes to see."

Siobhan suddenly noticed that the creature didn't have a shadow of its own. In a place like this, was that a hint at its nature? It was not a complete being. Could it even survive without her, or someone, to host it?

Siobhan felt her attention start to slip and focused on stabilizing herself for a while again before she felt safe to talk. "So…you can sense magic?"

"I can see everything, even the wretched desires at the bottom of your black, putrid heart."

That was a lie. It could sense magic, via the spirit world, through the cracks in the seal Grandfather had made. It was a very useful ability, to know what was coming even before the magic was fully cast. Even one second's lead could give her a huge advantage against an enemy. It might even work as a minor divinatory ability, what with the magical components, artifacts, and concoctions people like her often carried around.

She frowned suddenly, looking around again. They had been traveling along the paving stone path between giant statues for a long while now. At least she thought it had been a long while. Trying to pull on the memories to check felt…dangerous. "Does distance here correspond to distance and location in the real world? Because if you plan to dump me out of this place at the height of the white cliffs, a thousand meters walk away from where we entered, I warn you that you'd better do it after the sun rises. You promised me thrice to do no harm."

"Haven't you heard any of the stories? Neither time nor space are absolute. But I can control the narrative. Close your eyes."

Very reluctantly, she did so. Ironically, it made it somewhat easier to keep some part of herself focused on remembering who she was.

The thing tugged on her arm, jerking her sharply to the left, and they walked into what she was very sure had been a statue before. They met no resistance. She felt a sort of tension release in it, even as its weariness grew, and opened her eyes.

They were in a wasteland city that somehow reminded her of the fake, miniature city the faculty had built for the first term's Defense exam. This city, however, was wrong in subtle ways, like some intelligent being had built it while blind, having only ever heard stories about humans and their cities, but never seen civilization themselves. There were no doors anywhere. How were people supposed to enter the buildings?

Also, the windows looked a little like eyes. Not in their shape. Just...in their presence, the mood they gave off.

And the thing was fracturing again. This time, it took a little longer for its form to settle back together, some of the seams taking a while to heal. Its face had grown paler and gained the subtle greenish tint of illness and fatigue.

The wind blew through the city. They were very high, evidenced by a certain thin quality of the air that she recognized instinctually.

The creature studiously did not look at the windows that looked increasingly like eyes, and told her to close her own once more.

They turned another corner, and Siobhan felt the change in the creature that indicated it had done something again. "Go through," it said, tugging her forward impatiently.

Siobhan opened her eyes. There was a doorway in front of them, though the creature was holding its edge with a white-knuckled grip and straining tendons that made it seem as if it had just ripped open the wall and was holding the doorway's existence in place by force.

The doorway's edges looked a little like a cloak, and there was sky beyond it.

This sprouted a visceral horror in Siobhan, and not because she thought that the creature was about to push her into a very long fall to her death. In fact, she could not remember why she was so horrified, and there was some comfort in that.

"Go, before you are trapped and we die," it told her, some honesty leaking through as it grew desperately tired and began to fracture once more.

Siobhan stepped through.

The thing held her hand until the last moment.

As she passed the threshold, gravity spun on its axis, and suddenly she was stepping *upward*. Reeling with sudden vertigo, Siobhan fell to the ground. The immediate absence of unreality hit her body and mind like an illness hex. She heaved up the remnants of potion liquid as her body shivered with waves of alternating hot and cold and her skin screamed at the sensation of air and clothing and ground as if it had been scraped raw.

The spirit realm had been affecting her more than she realized. Siobhan hugged herself, and after the overwhelming sensations faded a bit, checked her extremities. She was alright, but suddenly sure that she had begun to lose the length of her hair, the tips of her fingers, and the proper, complex movement of a human's foot. If she had stayed much longer, there might have been permanent effects. Her *thoughts* were tender. No one she had ever heard of had walked through the spirit realm in their physical body—she hadn't even known it was possible—so she wasn't sure if the self-stabilizing exercises had been working as intended, if she just wasn't skilled enough with them, or if this was simply a measure of how dangerous the spirit realm really was.

Siobhan took a deep, shuddering breath and looked around. She was atop the white cliffs, at the edge. It was still closer to Thaddeus than she would have liked. And unfortunately, the being sealed in her mind hadn't seen fit to leave her somewhere convenient. She was at the northern edge of the cliffs, near the Flats, and looking out over the view of the farmland, roads, and lakes to the north of Gilbratha. Why hadn't it taken her somewhere farther? And how much time had passed?

She wondered where the creature was. Had it gone from the spirit realm back into the seal in her mind? Was it just loose, now, waiting to ambush any shamans whose spectral bodies got too close? She felt for the space in the back of her mind where it lived, like tonguing the empty gum where a tooth had once been. The seal was still there, she thought. And the creature had felt no overwhelming triumph when they entered the spirit realm. If that had been its key to freedom, she probably would have sensed it.

Just as she began to consider the best way to get as far away as possible, as quickly as possible, a wave of divination came up through the ground and broke her divination-diverting ward. Thaddeus was becoming wise to her tricks, it seemed, and realized that she needed at least a little time to react. With the lingering rawness from time spent in the spirit realm, there was also an increased sensitivity, and she thought she felt the moment when the divination found what it was looking for—her neck and chest.

Or rather, Thaddeus's own blood, spilled at the beginning of their fight and now long dried. He'd pulled out some of her hair, too, but if he hadn't held on to it, then getting clean might buy her some time to gain distance and better wards.

She was walking quickly along the side of the cliffs and preparing to cast the shedding disintegration spell when something latched on to her. She tripped, caught herself, and turned to see nothing…except, belatedly, a finger-width sized hole in the cliff's stone a few feet behind her.

She screamed as a horrible pulling and tearing sensation tried to rip her toward the tiny hole.

Half a second later, Thaddeus was there, floating two feet off the ground. Behind him, the hole in the stone had become a man-sized tunnel stretching diagonally down into the darkness until she could not see the end. An instant later, he released whatever space-warping spell he had cast, and the tunnel collapsed back down to the diameter of a finger.

Siobhan turned and leapt off the side of the cliff.

PERFIDIOUS

Thaddeus
   Month 9, Day 12, Sunday 4:00 a.m.

THADDEUS PANICKED when Siobhan seemingly threw herself to her death, just for a moment. Despite knowing that she was a powerful thaumaturge, some instincts were hard to break.

Soon after she began to fall, she had taken out that strange pseudo-tome that Sebastien developed and sprouted ephemeral wings of condensed air. They were cast weakly but were enough to slow her.

Just as she had begun to show a hint of gliding rather than merely falling, Thaddeus reached out and again cast the spell to create a line between them, as he had done only seconds before to pull himself up through the stone. Thaddeus braced himself for the discomfort, set himself as the anchor, and yanked her toward him. With the help of the spell, both distance and the intervening matter were shunted aside, replaced with a small pocket of space sourced from one of the beads on his component bracelet. The space could not touch the rest of the world, and the rest of the world could not touch it, not even with gravity or friction. Only magic could pass through, which made it somewhat ineffective as even a short-term shield.

Her natural magical resistance was not enough to stop him, and without inertia to slow or endanger her, she arrived within grasping distance in a quarter of a second.

The effort of the spell drained Thaddeus's second-to-last beast core.

Though he was almost exhausted from the series of powerful spells he had been casting for the last fifteen minutes since she disappeared, first to find her again, and then to catch her, he quickly followed up with a paralysis spell. He was sure to cast one that had nothing to do with sleep, shadows, or anything else that might be within her area of expertise.

She crumpled to the ground, her eyes glaring up at him like two black coals even as her face went slack.

Thaddeus followed the paralysis with several different incapacitating spells, put her directly into a coma while bypassing sleep entirely, and then tied a complex wire frame around her hands and each of her fingers so that they could not move or curve into a Circle.

Then, Thaddeus took a few minutes to rest, simply closing his eyes and breathing as he knelt beside her. It was a beautiful, cool night, and the air was crisp with the promise of autumn. Thaddeus could not appreciate it.

It had been a while since he pushed himself to the edge of his capacity like this, not just in power, but in complexity. He spent a lot of time practicing to grow his Will, of course, but his stamina was most efficient at about seventy percent of his maximum performance. Anything over that, and he burnt out quickly.

Against most enemies, he still would have come out on top, but she had almost escaped. If he had been just a few seconds slower, or if she had jumped and flown off a little sooner, he might not have managed to catch her due to sheer fatigue. Or, he would have run out of beast cores, which would have handicapped his ability to power his spells.

He opened his eyes, checked his work, and pulled the strange expanding spell array device and her Conduit ring from her hands. Her fingers were so slender, and her hand was so much smaller than his. Somehow, lying still like this, her entire being seemed smaller than he remembered.

Thaddeus looked for a beast core, but either she had dropped it somewhere over the edge of the cliff, or she had been pulling from some other source of power. Thaddeus briefly contemplated this implausibility before setting it aside. Beast cores were valued for a reason, but there were always other potential sources of power, if one had the Will to utilize them. Using the material of the cliff, he molded a sarcophagus of stone around her. If she were to wake somehow, which would normally have been out of the question—but with her, still seemed a distinct possibility—he was not entirely sure if his efforts would hold her.

He then cast half a dozen divination spells on her just to ensure she showed no signs of suddenly springing to wakefulness. Moderately reassured, he cast a cleaning spell on her body to get rid of the traces of both their blood. Very carefully, he followed this up with a mild healing spell, just in case she had gotten more injured than he realized during their battle.

She had again passed up the opportunity to try to kill him. She wouldn't have succeeded, of course, but she hadn't even tried when he seemed at his most vulnerable.

He could not be sure if she had still been pulling her punches at the end. Some of the abilities she had displayed were nothing less than Grandmaster-level. That knife should not have been able to pierce his defenses. And after that, the spell he had cast to hold the blade in place within his knee had been ignored entirely, as if he were pouring energy into a bucket with no bottom.

He could not help but think of Myrddin's famed void shield, though he reminded himself that the mechanism between the two feats could be entirely different.

He recalled the cloak-shaped gateway into darkness and amended his earlier estimation of her power. Perhaps she had even reached Archmage-level.

That contrasted against the low-powered dazzler, which seemed a strange coincidence. Had she been mocking him with the choice? The spell could have been learned on her own, true, but he also considered the possibility that she had been watching when he taught Sebastien, or perhaps picked it up from the young man later. Had it been some kind of message? Its secret purpose was to erase memories, after all...

If so, he could not parse the hidden meaning, but it left him feeling vaguely uneasy. He had not seen Sebastien for a while—longer than Thaddeus had expected Sebastien would be able to stay away, even with the gesturan primer and sound spell to occupy him. What had Siobhan been doing with the young man during that time?

With a deeply weary sigh, Thaddeus picked up her understated purse, cast a levitation spell on Siobhan's sarcophagus-entombed body, and began to walk toward his cottage while she floated beside him. He strongly suspected that the cloak-shaped gateway had been a function of her shadow spell, though he remained unclear on the details. She had been swallowed up by it and disap-peared from the world entirely, not a trace of her or the spell itself remaining. It did not seem to be a planar portal—how would she have contained the spillover energy while free-casting? It also was not a fabled teleportation tech-nique—she had been gone for some time, he believed, and then been caught again shortly after returning.

If he had to guess, she was either traveling as a shadow, or perhaps somehow through the spirit realm, though he was not sure how that would be possible with a physical body. Could she have dispersed and remade her flesh? Somehow shielded it? Thaddeus shook his head and forced himself to stop speculating. He had too little information about that spell. There might be some other option he failed to even consider.

He sighed and looked wistfully at her face, the only part of her left free from the stone. He wished he could ask her about these things, but after he was done, she would not remember, and he would not be able to explain how he knew.

One of the most common mistakes that even intelligent people made was the inability to change their minds when presented with new evidence. Thaddeus had previously stated quite firmly that it was foolish to believe she might be a witch, and the shadow-creature a powerful demon familiar. He had believed her when she claimed to be a sorcerer.

But he noted that all the most powerful abilities she displayed tonight had been related to the shadow, even from the beginning.

That was further evidence that he had missed something important. How was she able to cast a Grandmaster or Archmage-level spell with that Conduit? Did she have another, hidden somewhere? Surely even she would not have cast through her own body.

The shadow had been the spell she used to sever one of his attack spells from his control. It had also seemed to *become* her, for a moment, a fey, entrancing being of half-flesh, half-shadow, though he now suspected that had been some kind of illusion.

Later, though, it had managed to injure him with a very physical attack, before attempting to worm its way inside him. Intimately aware of the effects this had had on Mr. Jorgensen, the *former* Pendragon Corps member, Thaddeus had responded with alarmed fury. He believed he had managed to harm the... shadow-familiar. For that was what she called it.

Thaddeus let out a low chuckle. Siobhan had a reputation for truthfulness. Obviously, she had outwardly trivialized the utility and danger of that spell to the point of outright lying. He distinctly remembered her calling it "harmless." But at the same time...could she have been offering the plain truth to their faces?

Because if she were a witch as well as a sorcerer, it would explain a lot about her strangely lopsided abilities. But how could she have possibly contracted something so powerful? Had Raaz Kalvidasan known how to create a hereditary binding? There was a reason no sane person contracted a familiar magnitudes more powerful than themselves.

Or perhaps she was not a witch, but something new? Something that would explain two Wills within a single body, and all the clues about her that didn't fit together. Something that would explain why, when things got truly serious, the shadow so often took Siobhan's own form? What if the Raven Queen had always been a shadow?

"Stop speculating," Thaddeus reminded himself. Sometimes, it was hard not to let his thoughts run away with themselves, even though he knew that people, including himself, were prone to filling in missing information in ways that supported their conclusions, rather than the truth. It was only that so little about Siobhan Naught made sense, he could not help but try and fit the pieces together and fill in the blanks. "The simplest explanation is almost always correct. I am confused, and I do not understand. The only thing I can truly anticipate from my past experiences is being surprised," he reminded himself, a small chastisement for his wild, fantastical theories.

Thaddeus opened the door to his cottage and guided her carefully over the threshold. He had no way to learn the truth. Obviously, nothing she said could be trusted. He wondered if she had lied to him at other times, about other things, too.

It was still possible that her abilities seemed so lopsided because of heavy specialization and a lack of well-rounded education. Or that she knew she had less readily available power sources than Thaddeus, and was saving it all for her final escape attempt.

He settled her with a gentle thud on his living room floor, then pushed the furniture toward the walls to clear space. He disintegrated the stone around her and sent it out of the cottage, then stared down at her peaceful, barely breathing form. His lips moved against his will, as if to say something to her insensate form, but no sound escaped.

Apologies were useless, and he would not insult her with them, even if she would never know. He had gotten himself into this situation when he got involved with the Red Guard. Despite all his painstaking work to loosen the shackles of his vows, this particular issue was not an area where he had succeeded yet, and thus he had little choice.

Thaddeus was a slave. The thought sent a white-hot bolt of rage through his brain, and he had to take a moment to breathe with his eyes closed before he could continue. He repeated his earlier divinations to ensure she was not somehow near to waking, then retreated to the side room for several restricted components and a potion that would keep her in a coma for the next few hours.

As he began to prepare the spell array, he considered stripping and searching her, as was standard safety protocol with prisoners. The vow did not force him to do so. He decided against it. She was incapacitated, and the idea of her lying there naked felt somehow distasteful, like plucking the feathers from a beautiful bird. Some part of her dignity would be lost. What he was doing was already bad enough.

Mind-altering spells were some of the most difficult magic Thaddeus knew. Before casting, he took a moment to set aside the small part of him that was still violently, wrathfully fighting back against the compulsion of his vow. There was no room for internal conflict. For what came next, his performance needed to be perfect.

Thaddeus tore a hole in the barrier of her mind as if he were slicing open the belly of a rabbit to expose the organs. Then he reached in and grasped for the conversation that had started this, the question that should never have been asked. It was a struggle to connect his own memory of that moment to Siobhan's, as her mind writhed and fought against him like a panicked, rabid animal fighting against the snare. But once he had the thread of the memory, he could follow it to all the pieces that connected to it.

This spell did not allow him to see what those memories were, only that they lit up when the memory of her question was stimulated. Truly accessing another person's memories, by necessity, required one to experience them. Connecting two minds like that was dangerous for both parties, and in his current state of relative fatigue, especially so. He did not *have* to, and so he did not.

Thaddeus found it helpful when casting this spell to visualize thoughts as a web, though such a simplistic representation was by nature incorrect. Memory connected to memory, but also to personality, and to the Will. It was impossible to excise the Will from a living being, and he did not want to purge any part of her identity.

Therefore, he was very careful as he pulled on the memories, stripping them from their fellows, all the way back to the source. Several times, he was forced to pause for fear of damaging her, as her mind, still strangely agile, began to tear itself apart in her desperation to resist him.

Her struggles were exceptionally powerful, and several times, he almost thought they would cause him to lose control of the spell. If given enough time, she might have even overcome the potion he fed her earlier, well before her system had physically processed it.

Despite the trouble she caused him, Thaddeus admired her tenacity. This was the kind of mind that created an unparalleled Will.

Nevertheless, by working and resting bit by bit, like reeling in and giving line to a fish until it exhausted itself, Thaddeus prevailed. He loosed his grip on the spell and looked up toward the ceiling, still kneeling beside her insensate body. Sweat dripped from his face and soaked his clothes, despite the weak temperature-controlling spells embedded in his jacket.

He knew that it was likely a certain kind of person would eventually come to ask the same questions again, but he refused to go so far as to try to strip the curiosity out of her. If events one day replayed themselves, hopefully by then he would be able to make his own choices.

He stood up, drank, and ate—and took a peek in her purse while he recuperated. There were a few standard supplies, but he suspected there was more he could not access. If he wanted to spend the time, he could break into it, but it would make keeping Siobhan from becoming suspicious more difficult. With a sigh, he returned to cast a second spell, this one to twist her thoughts and hide the fact that he had removed memories.

This spell was similar to the first, but dealt with creating connections and healing rather than carving away slices and slivers. He wove her mind and memories together around the hole he had created. Each thought that might otherwise have led to the realization that something was wrong, he bent around the edge of the hole and connected to another mundane thought.

The process was complex, and he was forced to adjust his weaving several times as certain thoughts and memories refused to bind properly to each other.

Even now, Siobhan fought him, though more feebly now that she had forgotten what was happening, who was doing this to her, and why. Her thought web was peculiar—less fluid than most, yet with more connections than normal. Perhaps it would lead to a strange form of creativity based on widespread experience rather than the more typical intuition. It certainly made reconstruction difficult.

But Thaddeus was persistent and meticulous. When he was done, the hole, empty of gleaming strands of memory, was left only with the faint ghostly shimmer and shadow of the underlying parts he could not remove. Otherwise, it was clean work. The wound was patched and would heal fully with time.

Finally, Thaddeus cast a spell to create new memories. Many among the Red Guard found this the most difficult, and it was because no two minds were alike. People were prone to noticing when a thought did not sound like their own or when memories felt alien. However, Thaddeus had a way to get around that.

Using one's own mind against them required fourth order connections and a delicate touch, but given the slightest suggestion and a few nudges, people were incredibly good at filling in the gaps. He believed it was a design flaw in the brain.

This meant he could not definitively and precisely control what she filled in the gap in her memory with, only push her in the right direction and provide key points for her to latch on to. But whatever she created, it would feel natural to her.

When it was done, he gave her a healing potion, carried her back down to the base of the white cliffs, and laid her gently on the ground. He put her ring back on her finger and her Conduit in her pocket, then fixed the damage that her clothing and other belongings, including her strange spell stick, had sustained. He cast a spell to detangle her hair.

He hesitated for a long while. Procrastinating, really. Finally, he walked over the bridge to the place where she surprised him earlier that night. From there, he free-cast a spell to wake her.

She gasped like a corpse risen from the dead, mouth gaping open, chest arched up as her fingers scrabbled at the fabric over her breasts as if to peel everything back until she could tear at her own heart.

Thaddeus sprinted to her side and free-cast a general-purpose healing spell on her, one that would forcefully calm her body's signs of panic. He knelt on one knee and caught her confused, fearful gaze. "I deeply apologize, Siobhan." His voice cracked, and he paused to swallow. "I attacked on instinct when you surprised me." He ran a hand roughly over his face and said truthfully, "This has been an incredibly trying day, and I am on edge. But that is no excuse."

He remembered belatedly that he should have questioned her about the source of her knowledge, and barely held back an expression of triumph at his successful evasion of the Red Guard's geas. He had managed not to think about it for long enough, and it was *too late now*. And this was one more small sliver chipped away from the walls of his prison. He had time, and he had the Will. One day, he would be free entirely.

Siobhan looked wildly around with wide eyes, settling slowly as she seemed to piece together what had happened. She nodded, and in a hoarse voice, said, "I bear at least half the blame. I cannot believe I thought giving a bit of a scare to Thaddeus Lacer was a good idea. Though whatever you cast, I am surprised you managed to take me down before I could react." She gave a tight smile and sat up. "This is a bit embarrassing."

Thaddeus gave her a small, joking smile and helped haul her to her feet. "I promise not to tell anyone."

43

———————

BIFURCATION

Siobhan
  Month 9, Day 12, Sunday 7:00 a.m.

Siobhan woke to a mind—a self—tearing itself in two.

Most of her remembered coming to wait for Thaddeus, hoping to discuss the situation with the emergency shelters that had become obvious to her the day before, and then ending up waiting a very long time indeed. But a piece of her Will, more separate from the rest than any part of her had ever been, remembered differently.

This other version of events was dream-like and incoherent, and it *hurt* in a way the less horrifying version of events didn't. That made her believe it might be real. The feel of the shards of her shattered black sapphire Conduit digging into her side under her clothes made her sure. She tried to remember what had happened in that other version, but her knees gave out under her as a terrible spike of pain seemed to lance through the spot between her eyebrows. It was as if someone had hammered a construction nail right through her skull in a single blow.

'*Just like I did to Thaddeus's ear, maybe,*' she thought semi-coherently as he grabbed her around the waist and supported the weight of her body.

He was shaking her, saying her name in a tone full of worry, but her eyes couldn't even focus on his face. It felt like something critical within her had frayed and was coming apart at the seams, like her heart would rip and claw its way out of her chest. She had never realized how deeply horrifying it would be to have lost her grip on reality. Because that was what it was. She did not know what was real. *She* didn't feel real.

Although her Will could split into two threads, it could not work against itself. It was the same reason she hadn't been able to scry herself while simultaneously empowering her divination-diverting ward.

To stop this terrible wrongness, she pressed the part that knew something horrible into a ball, all facing inward, tiny and quiet, and shoved it to the back of her mind. The pain and confusion eased immediately, but did not disappear.

"I deeply apologize, Siobhan." Thaddeus's voice cracked. "I attacked on instinct when you surprised me." He rubbed his face wearily. "This has been an incredibly trying day, and I am on edge. But that is no excuse."

Siobhan looked around desperately, though she didn't know what she was looking for. Something to explain what had happened, maybe. Some hint that the world wasn't real, perhaps.

But her survival instincts had been honed for so long that they were ingrained in her. *'When weak, show strength,'* she heard in an echo of Grandfather's voice. She nodded, and in a hoarse voice, said, "I bear at least half the blame. I cannot believe I thought giving a bit of a scare to Thaddeus Lacer was a good idea. Though whatever you cast, I am surprised you managed to take me down before I could react." She gave a tight smile and sat up. "This is a bit embarrassing."

She braced herself, and, with Thaddeus's help, managed to stand upright, one hand to her temple.

"I promise not to tell anyone," he said, though his smile seemed mocking.

Siobhan almost punched him in the face, but managed to hold back, since there was a reasonable chance that such impulsiveness would get her killed.

"Are you alright?" Thaddeus asked.

"I am fine, thank you. I suppose I am lucky that you did not cast something more lethal," she said, trying for a smile as the other part of her quaked in fear of this man who was acting so concerned for her. She pressed it down further.

"I was busy with our response to today's Aberrant. I assumed neither of you would wait for me," Thaddeus said.

Siobhan blinked. Surely, this had happened already? After a moment, she said, "Kiernan has left already. I waited because I wanted to talk to you about something different." For some reason, her heart began to race at the words.

'This is a test,' she realized. *'If I think of it like that, everything makes sense. And if that's true, then I am in terrible danger.'* Perversely, that knowledge calmed her. She pushed back her shoulder, lifted her chin, and smiled coolly despite the spike of phantom pain that was now stabbing through her left eye. She waved

toward the street. "Walk with me?" She wanted desperately to avoid going into the tunnels.

Thaddeus nodded easily, clasping his hands behind his back like a scholar.

Instead of trying to come up with a lie, Siobhan called upon her false memories, even though a large part of her instinctively wanted to ignore them. What if Thaddeus knew what had been planted and wanted to ensure it had taken root properly?

A distant bell tolled the hour, and the sun would soon begin to rise, though its face would be obscured by the towering white cliffs surrounding the city for another hour or two. "I cannot believe I was practicing in a fugue that whole time. It is no wonder that my head is throbbing now," she said, watching him carefully with her peripheral vision.

Thaddeus frowned slightly. "A hazard of the occupation. A strong Will requires great focus, which sometimes has downsides. Sebastien often forgets to eat, and when I was young, I at times became so engrossed in study or some small project that I would put off going to sleep for an hour, and then suddenly find it was dawn."

Siobhan couldn't play along with this casual conversation. She had to move things along and end them quickly. "I wanted to speak to you about the emergency shelters."

"What about them?"

"Obviously, there are too few to house Gilbratha's growing population. I think the Red Guard must be concerned, but who will build more? Is that the responsibility of the Thirteen Crowns?"

Thaddeus showed no outward signs of relief that the topic was only indirectly related to Aberrants, this time. "The Red Guard is aware of this issue, but funding for these projects is supposed to come from the rulers of whatever area the emergency fortifications are built in. In this case, yes, the Thirteen Crowns. The High Crown has been dragging his feet, either because he does not want to pay, or because he still hopes to leverage new shelters against the Red Guard politically, in exchange for favors and concessions. Do not worry. We might not technically have any authority to force action, but in practice, few manage to hold out against pressure from the Red Guard for long. Three new shelters should go into production by this time next year, with the capacity to hold fifty thousand each."

That would be enough to keep up with Gilbratha's growth for a while, Siobhan guessed. "And at least two of them will be built in the Mires?" she asked, arching one eyebrow.

Thaddeus chuckled. "That, I cannot say. But if my input is allowed, I will press for that. Are you satisfied?"

"I am never satisfied, but I suppose that will have to do."

"Let us discuss our joint project, then. Soon, it will be time to start transcribing. I wonder… Perhaps some of the information should be left out of that transcription. More dangerous applications of magic that you would not trust just anyone with, for instance." He gave her a subtle, sidelong look.

Siobhan blinked. Thaddeus was suggesting that they collaborate to hide some of the contents of Myrddin's journals. Or rather, to keep that information exclusive to themselves—and the Red Guard. Obviously, giving such powerful information to people who had treated her as an enemy, and who would still want to control her in the future, was suboptimal. With the way the books worked—obscuring view from those who weren't right next to her while she held the Will-based key in mind—it might be possible. "You did not take any vows that would interfere with that?" she asked.

It was a small test of her own, but again, Thaddeus didn't outwardly react. He shook his head. "The wording was much too loose to bind me to anything, and they did not even think to do an intent-aligning ritual before the binding magic."

Siobhan smirked. "Intent-aligning rituals? Such things are considered blood magic, are they not? At least, when not performed by a member of the Thirteen Crowns."

Thaddeus shot her a look but didn't respond.

"I agree to your proposal," she said, even though the thought of being trapped in a small room with Thaddeus made her fingers clench. It was what she would have done if things were normal. A hopeless, sardonic thought bloomed from the part of her mind that was hiding and trying not to be noticed. *'I might not see the time where I have to follow through on that promise.'*

The city had woken up around them, and when Thaddeus yawned, Siobhan bought him a black coffee from a cafe just opening up for the morning, then left while he was staring absent-mindedly into its steaming darkness. She looked over her shoulder with a smile.

He was watching her leave over the rim of the cheap cup. He smiled back, as if nothing were wrong.

Siobhan didn't get far—barely out of his sight—before she stumbled with dizziness. She reached up to touch wetness on her upper lip and pulled away fingers smeared with blood. The edges of her vision were beginning to spark and waver. *'Will-strain.'* She pressed her lips together, but a muffled sob burst out anyway, splattering more blood from her nose. *'It's getting worse, and I don't know what to do.'*

She moved into a narrow alley, out of sight of the morning commuters. Obviously, she needed to resolve the dissonance, but even if she wanted to simply accept the modifications—the heinous violation of her being—she didn't know how to stop knowing the truth. The other part of her could not let it go, could not un-know it. "Is this it, then? All I have done, to end like this?" she whispered, tasting iron and salt.

"No," she whispered, and then again, louder, "No."

She took less than a minute to plan out her next actions, even though such hasty consideration was sure to miss something. She had maybe two hours left before the quintessence of quicksilver wore off, and who knew what would happen then? Could she survive the crash in this state? Her mind had an expiration date, and every second spent like this brought it closer. When she knew what to do, she took the main part of her Will, the part that had been mutilated, and rolled it into an inward-facing ball, too, so that less of it could interact with the other.

It was only a visualization method, but it helped somewhat.

Thinking as little as possible, and contemplating the last several hours not at all, she walked like a puppeteered corpse through the streets, moving to complete the simple steps of the plan she had set for herself. She would prepare a few potions to help her recover and force her to sleep, and would get out of the city while she healed. Both to be as far away from danger as possible, and also because, in the case of a break event, she hoped to put as few innocents in danger as possible.

Siobhan mentally pulled the parts of her Will apart from each other. They didn't want to go. Some kind of magnetism seemed to keep them together, but every bit of distance she managed seemed to ease the severity of the still-accruing damage, so she kept pulling. It also gave her something to focus on other than her mismatched memories.

The world changed.

Siobhan jerked in surprise, looking around with confusion and sudden fear. It was as if she had blinked and time moved forward without her. The light, the noise, even her body was different. She looked at her hands—pale, thin-fingered, and larger than the hands of the body she had just been wearing. She was in a different part of the city, and not anywhere she had originally planned to go.

Sebastien—yes, Sebastien, she confirmed—had a sudden moment of panic that Thaddeus had found her again and this time did a better job. Her breath rasped in and out roughly but couldn't keep up with the rapid beating of her heart. Absently, she wiped away more blood from her nose. When someone walking through the crowd suddenly appeared right in front of her, she realized that she was missing some vision in her right eye, a blank area that was not dark but simply empty, as if her brain no longer recognized it.

"Sebastien!" a familiar voice called.

It took her a moment to realize, and then another moment to find the source.

Damien, Ana, and Nat were standing on the sidewalk across the street from her, staring at Sebastien as traffic passed between them.

After a moment to think, she recognized her location, a street a kilometer or so north of Waterside Market. *'Why am I here?'* she wondered. She had planned to move south after getting what she needed. *'Was I heading back toward the University for some reason?'* There were faint stirrings of memory, but as she tried to dig into them, someone bumped into her shoulder, and she fell.

"Sebastien!" Damien cried out. He rushed across the street and helped her back to her feet.

"I have Will-strain," she said in a low, hoarse voice. "It's getting worse, and I need to get out of the city. I'm worried…" She swallowed, noting absently how dry her mouth and throat were. "I'm worried about a break event."

Damien sucked in a sharp breath, and his grip on her arm grew almost painful for a moment.

'Wait, is it possible for my Will to break when I'm not even actively casting anything?' It was a sign of how muddled she was that she hadn't realized this earlier. "Maybe not a break event," she reassured Damien. *'But that probably doesn't preclude the chance of death by massive brain hemorrhage.'* She was already seeing strange movement and hints of silhouettes that didn't exist out of her peripheral vision and in the blank part of her right eye's visual field.

"Carriage, I need a carriage here!" Damien screamed, waving his arm toward the street.

One stopped, but the driver eyed Sebastien uncomfortably.

"Is that Will-strain?" someone in the crowd asked.

Someone else said, "I heard when a thaumaturge is about to break, they bleed out of all their orifices. Look at him, he can't even keep his eyes straight in his head."

Soon after, there was a noticeable bubble of cleared space around Sebastien and Damien, and the carriage moved on.

Ana elbowed her way through the crowd, dragging Nat by the hand behind her.

"I need a carriage here!" Damien screamed again, even more frantically. "Fifty gold for the first one that stops!"

Sebastien swayed, and the ground rose up to meet her.

With a grunt of effort, Damien dragged her upright again, and suddenly there was a carriage stopped in front of them.

An older woman with round cheeks and sharp eyebrows threw open the door. "Sebastien Siverling?" she asked, looking him up and down. "Get in, get in!"

4 4

———

THE KEY TO AN UNKNOWN LOCK

Damien
Month 9, Day 12, Sunday 9:00 a.m.

Damien worked with Ana to shove Sebastien's somewhat larger frame into the stranger's carriage, and all three of them climbed in after him. "It is Will-strain," he admitted, his heart aching with every too-fast, panicked beat. "But you're not in danger unless Sebastien tries to cast something."

"'M not that stupid," Sebastien slurred.

"We need a mind healer, then?" the middle-aged woman asked. At Damien's nod, she screamed, "To Order Headquarters!" to the driver. "Post-haste, as if the denizens of all the greater hells were at your heel!"

The carriage jerked forward, and from above came the driver's frantic ringing of a bell as he in turn yelled, "Make way, make way!" to the rest of the street.

Sebastien flinched from the noise, leaning away from the woman and into Damien's side.

Ana was busy checking Sebastien's eyes and trying to get him to do simple response tests to judge the severity of the Will-strain, but he wasn't being cooperative.

Nat, by contrast, was sitting totally still and silent, her hands fisted together around her dress at the knees, and her face pale.

Damien was the only one who seemed to notice the destination their supposed benefactor had given the driver. "Undreaming Order Headquarters?" he asked, trying not to let his sudden dismay and suspicion show.

"We can help," the woman said. "And there is a mind-healer already visiting today."

"You're one of them?" Ana asked, narrowing her eyes.

"I serve the Raven Queen," the woman agreed. "But there is no reason to be alarmed. I wish you no harm, and the other awakened will be eager to help. This is what is best for young Mr. Siverling. I assure you, there is nowhere you can take him where he will be as well cared for and protected."

Damien shifted uncomfortably, feeling at his coin purse, which certainly did not have the fifty gold he had promised within. "Could I write you a cheque? Who do I make it out to?" He realized that he didn't have any cheques on him, either. "Or you could send an invoice to Westbay Manor…"

"Oh, it's fine," she said, waving her hand dismissively.

Damien clenched and unclenched his jaw before forcing himself to speak. "No, it's not fine. I don't want Sebastien or any of us racking up a debt with the Raven Queen."

The woman shook her head. "You misunderstand. The payment for helping this young man has already been made. It is actually I who is lucky to have been passing by at the perfect moment." She pursed her lips thoughtfully. "Or perhaps it was not luck, but fate."

Ana leaned forward and clasped Sebastien's hands, which were smeared with streaks of dried blood, between her own. "What happened?" she asked. "Were you trying to cast a new spell, or…?"

Sebastien tried to speak but started coughing violently instead.

Damien fumbled in Sebastien's satchel for the canteen of water he knew the other young man kept and then helped Sebastien to drink a few sips.

"I was attacked," Sebastien mumbled, his eyes seemingly unable to focus. One was particularly bloodshot, perhaps because Sebastien kept rubbing it roughly. "A spell to wipe my memory and then to keep me from finding out that it was done." He blinked several times and tried to sit up but was obviously too dizzy to manage. "Wait. That's a secret. I shouldn't have told you." He looked at Nat. "Don't say anything, okay?" he asked earnestly. "I don't want you to get hurt."

Her chin trembling, Nat nodded gravely. "Are you…going to be okay?"

Sebastien lost focus on her and began mumbling something about how he had half-forgotten, half-remembered, and it was tearing his mind apart. "I—I have to stop thinking. I'm going away before it gets worse."

"Wait!" Ana leaned forward until she almost fell off the bench seat. "Who did this to you?"

Sebastien chuckled but didn't answer.

It was still late summer, but Damien had gone cold, the hair along his arms rising with goosebumps. He knew of one other instance of something like this. Newton's family. And he knew who had been behind that.

The middle-aged woman pulled a potion out of her purse. "Would a deathly sleep potion help? It causes a coma for a few hours at safe doses."

Sebastien's eyebrows rose. "It might help. A coma is beyond dreams, right?"

The woman leaned over and groped Sebastien's arms and chest, looked him up and down, then muttered a few calculations to herself and poured out three drops from her bottle like an absolute expert, as if she dosed people with the deathly sleep potion regularly. "That should last for ninety minutes."

Sebastien slumped to unconsciousness almost as fast as the drops hit his tongue, without even a hint of wariness against this strange woman.

Nat's face crumpled as Sebastien's expression went slack, and she forcibly held back a sob so strong it wracked through her body.

Ana seemed to find the woman's actions dubious, too. "Who are you?" she asked bluntly.

The woman was entirely undaunted. "Everyone calls me Mrs. Dotts. You may, as well. You're Mr. Siverling's friends, then? If I had to guess, Anastasia Gervin and Damien Westbay."

"You know us?" Nat asked.

"Oh, I've read about Sebastien Siverling and his friends in the papers, dear. This must be your older sister."

Nat nodded. "And Sebastien and I are friends, too. It's just that the papers haven't written about me."

"Oh, really?"

"Of course! We watch street shows together, and we've even gone out to breakfast, just the two of us. Sebastien said his favorite foods are all the things with butter, salt, and sugar."

Mrs. Dotts lifted a hand to her mouth and laughed like someone in a play. "Ho, ho, ho! It seems Mr. Siverling and I share the same taste in food!"

The young girl and middle-aged woman kept up this pointless chatter until the racing carriage finally arrived, and then Mrs. Dotts took charge and started snapping orders and throwing hand-signs like some kind of spy. "I've got Sebastien Siverling in critical condition after being attacked by a botched memetic spell. We need maximum secrecy, as the attacker may still be after him. Second floor only, bring him around from the side door. Call the mind healer up right now. Siverling is currently under the effects of the deathly sleep potion, which will wear off in slightly over an hour."

To Damien's surprise, the Undreaming Order people took only a moment to respond, and some even moved in formation like some kind of trained copper squad. Those in charge seemed to be wearing dark clothing, and though it wasn't a uniform, all had some kind of rank or achievement pins displayed on their left breast, some more than others.

As several of them were rushing Sebastien off on a stretcher, the same teenage girl they had met during the most recent Aberrant incident rushed out to meet them. "Oh, gods! It's Sebastien!" she wailed dramatically.

Damien almost tripped.

She looked around frantically. "We have to save him!"

Nat let out a single sob before managing to get her breathing back under control. She glared silently at the older girl.

"That's what we're about," Mrs. Dotts snapped back. "Stay quiet and out of the way if you want to help."

Damien flinched as a woman with horrible burn scars covering half her head threw open the side door, her other hand wrapped tightly around the wrist of a scholarly looking man. "Up to the second floor!" she urged. "We'll get him in the warded box."

For a moment upon reaching the top of the stairs, Damien thought he saw a familiar thirteen-pointed star in the marble floor. But no, the huge design might have been meant for casting some enormous spell, but it had only eleven rays.

When they finally got settled inside a strange metal box-like room sitting inside near the wall, the burned woman thrust the mind healer at Sebastien.

Contrary to Damien's expectation, the man waved his hands around anxiously. "This is…beyond my expertise. I work with *children* who have experienced trauma. I'm not some battlefield healer who deals with blood magic mental effects! You need—you need an expert."

"Who?" the burned woman demanded.

"Um, well, probably Tricia Adway, but she's employed by the Retreat at Willowdale right now. I don't know if she does emergency care. If not her, then—"

The burned woman turned to the teenage girl and snapped, "Go, Betty!"

Betty sprinted off like a long-legged racehorse.

The burned woman turned to Mrs. Dotts. "Get this healer's address and go to her home as well. We must cover all bases to ensure maximum speed of retrieval." She turned back to the healer. "The deathly sleep potion may wear off before someone competent arrives. Is it safe for us to dose him again?"

"W-well, I wouldn't. Maybe a mind-stabilizing potion? If you have the funds to afford one, I would recommend it."

"Gold is not an issue," Damien said.

Ana nodded, tapping one foot impatiently. "As long as it's *definitely* safe for someone in his condition?"

"I think Titus took one when I was little," Damien said. "I only remember Father was livid, but Titus got better quickly."

The healer nodded rapidly. "It shouldn't have any negative side-effects. It does slow down the thoughts, but it also creates a protective jelly that fills the mind and makes it less likely for wounds to accrue or bleed out. That's a metaphor, of course—I learned about it in school. It's like how poor commoners will wear a cast over a broken bone if they cannot afford quicker healing." He shifted uncomfortably. "To be clear, the potion is not meant to be used for brain injuries."

The man was at least competent enough that, after accidentally bringing up the possibility, he knew how to cast a divination spell to check for said injuries. He was stymied by Sebastien's boon for a moment, but with some whispered threats from the burned woman, Deidre, the bewildered man managed to overcome, and eventually announced the mind-stabilizing potion safe.

Another few people set out for all the best apothecaries in the city to try to buy one of these rare potions, and Damien only then realized the remaining Undreaming Order members were watching Sebastien like googly-eyed fish.

Deidre questioned Damien and the Gervin sisters about Sebastien's situation, then went to a small but beautiful altar area set against the outside room's wall. She kneeled and said a prayer to the Raven Queen, but this prayer seemed to segue into making a...report? Then, she sat on the edge of one of the nearby empty bunk beds, took a swallow of potion, and told one of the others to wake her in twenty minutes if she did not arise on her own.

"What's going on?" Nat asked.

Deidre smoothed out her clothes and arranged her hair neatly, almost proudly making sure that her scars were fully revealed. "I have just sent a prayer directly to the Raven Queen. The ability to do so is a great privilege for me alone among her awakened followers. I will now sleep and wait for a revelation. Do not worry, young miss. Everything is going to be okay. Why don't you go play with the other children down below?"

Nat shook her head and stepped back toward Sebastien, as if she were afraid someone would forcefully drag her away. Her lashes were wet with tears that had slipped past her control, but her expression was firm and determined. "I will stay."

Ana, who had been wiping the traces of blood away from Sebastien's face and hands, scowled through the metal room's open door at Deidre. "Are you really just going to go to sleep right now?" she scoffed.

"Sleep connects me with the Raven Queen, a being who is more powerful than either of us will ever be, and whom I serve," Deidre bit back. "The kind of being who could solve all of this with a single spell and a bit of blood sacrifice if she deigns to."

Ana's mouth fell open. "Blood sacrifice!?"

Deidre rolled her eyes. "She would use a goat, or something, and then we could all eat it for dinner. Or maybe thirteen young men all around Mr. Siverling's age would come down with a sudden case of amnesia."

"It's illegal," Ana muttered, not bothering to disguise her look of distaste. "I don't care if we get to eat the goat afterward if I have to spend a month in Harrow Hill for it."

Privately, Damien thought that both he and Ana would probably Sacrifice quite a lot of goats if it would help Sebastien. Ana just didn't like Deidre, for some reason.

Deidre ignored her and laid back with her hands resting together over her chest.

Unfortunately, after twenty painful minutes of waiting around, it seemed that the Raven Queen did not respond. When Deidre woke, she suppressed a troubled expression. "This matter is up to us."

Damien cursed the Raven Queen in his mind, uncaring about the rumors that said she could hear when her name was called. Despite his earlier reluctance to be involved with her or the Undreaming Order, he realized now that he would very much appreciate the assistance of someone so powerful in the mental arts. Surely, as a Westbay, he could offer her something worth her time without being forced to owe her a favor?

The mind-stabilizing potion arrived before the actually competent mind healer. When Sebastien woke, he groaned and whimpered and didn't seem to see Damien standing on the right side of his bed until Sebastien turned his head far enough to see him with the left eye. He reached up to rub at that eye again, and Damien grasped his hand and pressed it back down.

A drop of water fell on Sebastien's arm, and Damien only then realized that he was crying. With shaking hands, he brought the potion to Sebastien's mouth.

Sebastien resisted, turning his head away.

"Trust me. This will help," Damien said.

Sebastien let slip a few helpless, frustrated tears of his own, but he swallowed the potion down to the last drop. This seemed to ease his pain somewhat, and while they waited, Damien explained the situation, though he wasn't sure how much Sebastien understood.

When Healer Adway, an older woman with long, steel grey hair and midnight-dark skin finally arrived a couple of hours later, she had Sebastien's situation diagnosed within fifteen minutes. Damien didn't like the way her eyes widened at first, nor the way her lips thinned afterward. But she didn't waffle about and wring her hands.

It took her another hour to set up an incredibly complex spell array, which Damien watched carefully, wishing he could help. "He has already started fixing the damage. Honestly, it's astounding, and if I hadn't seen it myself, I would have thought it impossible," she said. "However, without help, there is no way he will make it before the Will-strain kills him. He already has some moderate swelling of the brain. I will stabilize the situation and aid his efforts."

"He's going to live?" Nat asked, speaking for the first time in several hours.

"He and I will fight for his life together," the healer said.

This was not a "Yes," and Damien knew that everyone in the room understood that.

Healer Adway spent several hours that day casting until she reached exhaustion. Her wrinkles seemed deeper and her eyes more sunken as she reported with evident embarrassment that, though he seemed to be asleep, Sebastien was still working to heal himself, fighting for his life. "I would force him to stop, but I'm not sure the strain of pushing himself so hard is any worse than the damage caused by the attack. Either way, we will run out of time soon. I will rest for a while and then return to supporting his efforts."

Nat did end up going down to the first floor when it got dark, but instead of playing with the other children, she pestered the awakened for information about how the Undreaming Order worked, asking surprisingly insightful questions for a child her age. They were trying to set up for a night service, and she was so underfoot that the workers set her to doing basic paperwork in Deidre's office. Anything to keep her busy. In part, it was a kindness, meant to keep her mind off of the interminable wait.

When it grew late, Damien went down and found her and Deidre working side by side with almost identical postures. The sound of fountain pens scribbling on paper filled the room.

Nat frowned over a ledger. "We need better preservation on the potatoes. We lost three whole bags this week to spoilage."

Deidre responded without looking up. "Put in a work order to the thaumaturges with a qualified preservation or cleansing spell."

Nat stuck out her tongue as she stamped the paper she had just finished. "How much credit for that?"

Damien interrupted. "It's time to go home, Nat."

She scowled at him, looking quite like her older sister Ana at that moment. "Are *you* going home?"

Damien didn't bother to answer.

Ana strode past him and moved to stand over Deidre's other shoulder.

Deidre slammed the ledger she was working on shut, stood up, and the two women had a short staring contest. Then Deidre smirked, raked her hair to the side with her fingers, and leaned a little closer to Ana. "It's time to go home, kid."

Nat pouted and stood to leave, but Damien felt that maybe the words had been meant for Ana, who whirled around and stalked right back out again, a faint blush of suppressed anger staining her cheeks.

In the morning, Sebastien was still meditating and working to piece his mind back together. The mind-healer uncomfortably explained that Sebastien should be sleeping at times, too, but that he wouldn't stop even when she warned him to rest. She couldn't keep up. "I would force a potion down his throat to knock him unconscious, except he does seem somehow able to manage this insane level of effort. He's getting better. I just worry that when he finally cannot continue anymore, there won't be a second chance."

"If anyone can handle it, it's Sebastien," Damien said. He believed it, despite the curdled mass of anxiety lodged in his chest. "If you're worried, give him more of the mind-stabilizing potion."

The old woman hesitated. "It's two thousand gold per vial. I cannot purchase it on credit."

"I'll write a cheque for it right now," Ana called, coming up from the stairwell on the other side of the room. She walked over to them, wrote the cheque on the spot, and handed it to one of the Undreaming Order's awakened. Then she nodded to the healer, grabbed Damien by the arm, and pulled him away.

When they had reached relative solitude on the other side of the room, she spoke. "Do you have any ideas about who did this to Sebastien? I haven't been able to sleep, and I've been thinking about it all night. He was attacked with blood magic bad enough that it could have killed him. And whoever did it is likely still out there. They're powerful enough and have the right connections to know those spells, but they're too shit a thaumaturge to cast them right. Still, I'm sure they desperately want to avoid being caught. I think we should bring in a prognos to investigate. Can you report this to the coppers and get your brother to assign a task force to the case?"

Damien hesitated, remembering Sebastien's warning not to say anything about what he had told them, and his own speculation about the source of the attack. He looked over his shoulder at his seemingly sleeping friend.

One of the Undreaming Order people was setting up an artifact to blow cool air on Sebastien. They all seemed to be putting in an unreasonable amount of effort into caring for Sebastien, but Damien wasn't sure why. Based on Mrs. Dotts' words, it couldn't be because they thought Sebastien would be a valuable debtor. Damien remembered that the Raven Queen had saved Sebastien the last time he was attacked. Why couldn't she have saved him this time, too?

Damien shook away the petulant thought, absently rubbed at a wrinkle on the side of his pants, and admitted, "It might not be safe to call in the coppers."

Ana squinted at him but nodded slowly. "I see. It's true they're not blood magic experts. The Red Guard, then? Do you think they would look into this as a favor to Professor Lacer, maybe?"

Damien closed his eyes. "Not them, either."

He opened his eyes again to find Ana staring at him as if she could peer into his soul if she tried hard enough. "Do you know who did this, Damien?"

"I don't!" he denied quickly. Surely, hopefully, please-let-it-not-be the Red Guard. It could have been some rogue thaumaturge living in the seedy underbelly of the city who wanted to erase a witness to some terrible crime. That was the kind of thing Sebastien seemed likely to get caught up in. Or...maybe the Pendragon Corps? Frederick Pendragon and the High Crown both had a reason to bear a grudge, after all. The only other option Damien could think of was someone within their own, unnamed order of the thirteen-pointed star, no matter how unlikely it seemed. Damien didn't really know anything about the other members, except that Sebastien trusted them, and that Oliver Dryden had failed to be accepted.

From Ana's expression, Damien wasn't sure that she entirely believed his denial, but she navigated conversations like a duelist navigated footwork, and changed the topic. "What could Sebastien have had in his head that someone was willing to carve out with magic?"

Their research project on Aberrants, of course. This popped into his mind like the obvious answer, but Damien tried to think of other alternatives. Sebastien had met the Raven Queen several times. Maybe it had something to do with her. However, Damien was sure she wasn't the perpetrator. Even if she were to do something like this, she wouldn't botch it. Either she would have murdered Sebastien and made a huge spectacle of his corpse, or the memories would have been erased from both Sebastien's and Damien's heads, and no one, including them, would have ever realized it.

"I won't force you to tell me," Ana said. "I don't know what idiotic schemes you boys have been getting yourselves into, but I *do* need you to tell me if I need to intervene. Should I station guards outside this building, or beside Sebastien's sickbed?" Her eyes brightened. "Or...hire some mercenaries? The kind that create permanent solutions and 'remove' problems?" She made quotes in the air with her fingers and wiggled her eyebrows meaningfully, but there was no hint of teasing in her eager expression.

Damien cleared his throat. "I don't know who we would have murdered, so maybe...not that."

"It's not murder, Damien. It's *removing problems*. One of those is a crime. The other has plausible deniability."

Damien closed his eyes again and rubbed at the bridge of his nose. He was too tired for this.

"Even if you don't like my suggestions, I think we need to make sure that someone is with Sebastien at all times. Just in case."

Damien agreed.

When Sebastien developed a high fever that couldn't be mitigated by the standard potions and salves, he helped apply cloths dipped in ice water to Sebastien's head to make sure his brain remained cool.

Sebastien still refused to actually sleep, though most of the time he was unresponsive enough to seem unconscious.

Over the next three days, the Undreaming Order headquarters saw a surprising amount of people come and go. Deidre gave a couple of sermons that Damien couldn't help but overhear while sitting next to Sebastien's bedside. Damien didn't really understand the appeal of such a dangerous, vengeful, anarchist like the Raven Queen as a leader. Nevertheless, many of the people below seemed to prefer it over a leader characterized by their kindness and honor. This was indicated by the stomping, laughing, and cheering at each mention of the Raven Queen's various punishments and acts of revenge.

Nat came back every day to check on Sebastien and do paperwork.

Ana was there for a short inspection a couple of times a day, and with each visit, looked increasingly irritable and vengeful.

Perhaps the strangest part was that everyone in the Undreaming Order was a little too friendly to Damien. They happily sat with him next to Sebastien's bedside whenever the exhausted mind-healer was forced to rest. They eagerly listened to stories of Damien and Sebastien's various escapades. Everyone seemed to love hearing about incidents when Sebastien was rude to people without realizing, and there was uproarious laughter as Damien explained that Sebastien had an arch-nemesis that he didn't even know existed because he was so oblivious to people he found boring.

Damien was worried at first that they might try to proselytize or brainwash him, but they were surprisingly subtle. And he couldn't deny the fact that they were doing good. The amount of people they were feeding, healing, and clothing was one thing. But the schooling... Somehow, that hit Damien the hardest.

It was strange to realize that all these people following the Raven Queen were actually, truthfully, doing a lot of good. It wasn't just something to read about in *The People's Voice*. It was really happening. Of course, they were all strangely vengeful, and at least all the "awakened" were *definitely* criminals, but they truly believed they were the good guys.

Maybe because of that, it was difficult to see them differently.

On the evening of the third day since Sebastien was cursed, Ana came by to check on him, sneer at Deidre, and drop off an artifact shaped like an innocent bunny keychain. It was packed with rending spells, which would literally rip someone limb from limb and spill their entrails over the ground. Which was very illegal.

Damien took it gingerly. "It has a safety switch, right?"

Ana smiled innocently and didn't answer the question. "It's for Sebastien, but you should keep hold of it until he wakes. Again…just in case." The smile dropped from her face. "We have to protect Sebastien, Damien. He's smart, but sometimes I think he's *too* smart. It makes him think he can handle everything on his own, even when he really, *really* can't."

Damien slipped the bunny keychain into his pocket. "Just in case," he agreed.

45

EUNOIA

Sebastien
Month 9, Day 12, Sunday

THE PROCESS of sewing her mind back together was painful, precarious, and exhausting. Once Sebastien had started, the smooth edges of the memetic wound in her mind were left frayed. They would further unravel and cause more damage if not tended to immediately, so she couldn't stop. She wasn't sure how long it took.

The other half of her Will had retained a ghostly version of her original memories, but they were damaged and confused. She couldn't simply use them to replace what Thaddeus had built. But she also found strange, echo-like, almost imperceptible remnants of the original memories hiding on what was somehow a lower level than the false ones. She latched on to those echoes, reinforced them with the part of her Will that mostly remembered, and tore apart the pieces of memory usurping their place. In this way, she built herself back together from the roots up. The real memories fit with the echoes in a way that the false ones didn't, though she imagined if she had let the false ones sit there long enough, perhaps the echoes would have changed to match them.

As necessary as this work was, her body seemed to find it unnatural—or perhaps it simply couldn't stand the pain. When the sleeper raven bound to Sebastien died, she almost went with it.

She broke into a high fever, which was more frustrating than anything, as it slowed and muddled her thoughts and made the whole process at least three times more difficult. She recognized the distinct smell and taste of fever-reducers, but whatever their magic was targeting, her fever came from a different source and was unaffected.

Without the other potion they kept feeding her that seemed to fill her mind with a thick, cushioning syrup, her mistakes might have ended her. That potion made the work harder, too, but it also gave her leeway. When she lost her grip, it slowed the destructive, whip-like lashing of the threads. When she made a mistake, it partially isolated the wound and dampened the metaphorical bleeding.

At times, the mind-healer supported her work, easing the pain and doing some kind of magic to hold things in place for her so that she could work more efficiently. But the woman, glimpsed only in fractured moments when Sebastien managed to open her eyes, was only able to cast this wondrous magic for six to ten hours every day, spread out over several shorter sessions.

Sebastien would have failed—not for lack of desire, or lack of Will, but for the sheer scope of the insurmountable wound—if not for a monumental revelation.

While one half of her Will tried to hold in place the countless threads of the tapestry that created Siobhan Naught and Sebastien Siverling, and the other re-wove the picture that should have been, there was yet room for thought. More than there should have been. And when she grasped at this extra space, she found *herself* again.

Her Will, without very much scope or power, but undeniable. A third facet of herself. Another split. When this had happened, she wasn't sure. It didn't give her any extra power to work with, as no matter how many parts her Will could split into, she was still limited to less than a thousand thaums. But she didn't need power. She needed finesse.

And this was, in effect, a third pair of hands with which to weave.

And so she lived.

When she finished, she fell into a deep sleep. And for the first time since she was a small child, when she dreamed, those dreams were mundane. She had trained herself to realize their approach so that she could wake on command, but she almost didn't recognize what was happening, because they weren't nightmares. Nor were they memories. And nowhere was the touch of the thing sealed in her mind. It wasn't until the fever ran its course that the hints of nightmare began to creep back in. When they did, she was too weak to fight against them, but she did not meet the creature with the glowing amber eyes. It was mostly incomprehensible: eggs cracking to reveal yolks of crimson blood, twisted brimstone limbs, and a doorway leading to a hungry sky.

She slept until the wounds in her mind began to heal. Unfortunately, her head was still throbbing when she jerked to wakefulness, and she felt somehow both ravenous and nauseated at the same time. She croaked for water, and Natalia hurried to help her sit up and drink.

Nat looked tired and her eyes were a little bloodshot, but she smiled widely at Sebastien and immediately launched into an update on everything that had happened while she had been unaware. She acted as if Sebastien had simply been on a trip or taking an extended nap, rather than fighting for her life. "And this," she said, holding up a key ring from which a rabbit-shaped bauble hung. "It's super cute, but actually it's loaded with seven super-powerful rending spells, guaranteed to overpower the inherent barrier of the skin as long as you can open up a cut. It works by creating several closely scattered areas of extreme, localized gravity." She leaned forward to whisper. "Ana bought it at the Night Market. You just grab it and punch the ears into whoever you want to kill," Nat said, demonstrating with a shadow-punch into the air.

Sebastien belatedly wondered if she was still dreaming. But no, this was reality.

"I'm sure you know that's illegal, but since whoever attacked you is a criminal, too, I think it's fine. Just don't get caught," Nat said seriously, placing the key ring on the small table beside Sebastien's narrow bed. "Ana couldn't get a license for it, even with some bribes."

Somehow, Sebastien found this bizarre interaction comforting. Nat was a lot like her older sister. Sebastien found spending time with them comfortable because they somehow always knew what to say. Or, perhaps, what *not* to say. Tears, frantic questions, and admonitions to be safe would have just made Sebastien feel worse right now.

"I'll go get Deidre, Damien, and the others," Nat said. "They'll all be ecstatic that you're awake. Damien stayed awake for almost three days until someone cast a sleep jinx on him, and now he's been asleep so long that me and some of the others started betting if he would wet the bed. I bought you some cream-filled pastries that are *super delicious*, but we have to ask the healer before you can eat them." Nat patted Sebastien's arm sympathetically, then turned to leave.

"Wait." When Nat paused, Sebastien adjusted her pillow to better support her back and said, "Bring a strong thaumaturge, too. I probably won't be able to stay awake for very long, and I need a spell cast before I go back to sleep."

The person they ended up getting to perform Sebastien's signature dreamless sleep spell had a few thousand thaums under their belt, and though no one said anything, all the Undreaming Order members gave each other significant looks as Sebastien explained the magic.

Nat brought up the cream-filled pastries, and Sebastien almost cried while eating them, a sure sign that her Will-strain was quite severe. Nat puffed out her chest like a prideful rooster and promised sincerely to handle all of Sebastien's dessert intake until she was better.

Damien gave his own significant looks to Sebastien, no doubt wanting to know what had happened, but had enough sense to keep silent when surrounded by outsiders. He didn't manage to hold back his own tears completely, but at least he turned his back when they fell, so she didn't have to watch and feel even worse about it.

She considered trying to make a joke to lighten the mood, but humor had never been her strong suit. It wasn't even as if she could assure him there was no need to worry. She was pretty sure that she had almost died. Without all the time spent casting the light-refinement spell and the third fracture in her Will, she probably would have.

Sebastien ate and drank under the eager urging and too-friendly gazes of the Undreaming Order's awakened, took a few potions to ease the pain and speed her recovery, and when she was alone, took some time to examine herself.

Her side, where the black sapphire Conduit had shattered, bore the faint lines of several jagged scars, but pressing on the skin caused no pain, assuring her that no pieces of the gem lingered inside.

She found them in her satchel, along with the clothes she had been wearing, her hidden holster, and her mother's ring. The memories were less clear than usual, but she remembered finding a place to change and clean up, then going to her attic apartment to take her most important and valuable belongings. She had changed her plans and decided to leave via one of the white cliffs' northern tunnels so that she could send a high-cost, discreet runner to Damien on the way, warning him as soon as possible. She hadn't gotten that far. *'I was running on the third Will, then,'* she realized. *'But it was too weak to stay coherent?'* Normally, Sebastien would have been insatiably curious about this phenomenon, but at the moment she could only muster the energy for things that would keep her alive.

Checking her satchel, she found everything where she had put it. The warding medallion and transformation amulet were both still around her neck. *'Thank you, Grandfather. You saved my life once again,'* she thought, rubbing the golden, engraved surface of the medallion. She stared at the place where one of the surface glyphs had completely melted. With a pang in her chest, she tucked the medallion away again. *'Thank you,'* she repeated.

The knife in her boot was clean, as if Thaddeus's blood had never touched it, and a quick test with the dowsing artifact proved that her divination-diverting ward was still working just fine.

She stared blankly at the wall of the metal room for a few moments, wondering if there was anything she was missing. She smacked her lips together, grimaced, then rubbed some tooth-cleaning paste in her mouth and went back to sleep for a few hours—this time without dreams.

When the nightmares began to slip through again, she awoke and felt for the vague edges of the seal, a black, blank space in the very, very back of her consciousness, a place she might never go if she didn't have a reason to look. She wasn't sure what she was trying to find, exactly, only that she was worried. *'Are the dreams getting stronger, or am I just weak?'* She'd had trouble waking herself, almost as if the creature feeding her nightmares had wrapped its tendrils around her to hold her under the surface.

She opened her eyes to find Damien sitting beside her, squinting down at a horribly mutilated attempt at knitting, or perhaps crochet. Sebastien had never been able to tell the difference. They were alone.

"You have to destroy all of the research," she said.

Damien jerked, and she realized he'd been on the verge of falling asleep.

She repeated herself. "No one can ever know what you found," she told him, trying to drill the importance of this into him with the strength of her gaze alone. "*No one.* If you trust and care for that person, doubly so."

He let out a low breath, just on the edge of a whistle, and set down his mangled yarn. "I was afraid that might be the case. It's such a waste."

"Our lives are more important."

Damien nodded. "I'll handle it, don't worry." He hesitated. "Who did this to you?"

Sebastien couldn't tell him the truth. The knowledge might endanger him. She was so tired and weak. A strange urge to laugh filled her chest, almost overwhelming, but instead, tears burned and bubbled up from the back of her eye sockets. "I'm sorry," she whispered. "I can't protect you from what I got you into. I can't even protect myself." When she closed her eyes, the tears slipped down her temples into her greasy, matted hair.

"Are you in danger right now?" Damien asked. "Is someone going to be looking for you, to hurt you?"

"No. At least as long as no one realizes what I know. What *we* know."

Damien pressed his lips together grimly. "We are going to have to swear quite a lot of the Undreaming Order members to secrecy. And…actually, it's possible that news of your injury will have already gotten out. Is that a problem?"

"It would be better if that didn't happen." It might make Thaddeus suspicious.

"Umm…don't worry. I'll talk to Ana about it, and we'll handle it. You don't need to worry, just rest."

Strangely, Sebastien did feel somewhat reassured when she thought that Ana might handle it. She had seen the way Ana "handled" things at the University—that is, the few details of her machinations that Ana was blatant enough to explain to Sebastien directly. Keeping secrets and spreading false rumors was well within the other woman's capabilities.

"Tell Deidre, too. She'll help, I think."

Damien returned with Deidre shortly after. The woman shut the metal door behind them. "Your friend told me a little about the situation. Do not worry, Mr. Siverling. Secrecy is the nature of those who strive to follow in the Raven Queen's shadow. We have not been spreading news of your situation or even your presence, and we will cooperate with whatever story you wish to tell. However, I do have a question." She leaned closer and whispered, "Do you have any idea why the Raven Queen isn't responding? Was she involved in whatever…*incident* brought you here?"

Damien's eyebrows rose.

'*Seriously? Weren't you literally* just *bragging about being able to keep a secret, Deidre?*' Sebastien lamented silently. Aloud, she tried to keep her expression normal. "I have no idea. She didn't do this to me, if that's what you're wondering. Is there some kind of emergency you need her help with?"

Deidre stared at him. "Well, I thought she might heal you."

Sebastien blinked slowly at her. "Why?"

Deidre shifted awkwardly, looking between Damien and Sebastien. "Well, just…on a whim. She likes children."

Sebastien gave a tired sigh and closed her eyes. "I haven't been a child for a long time. And I need another dreamless sleep spell."

The next time she woke, it was to Ana, who had moved the cold-air blowing artifact too close to Sebastien's head, chilling her ears.

Ana left it there, sat down primly, and crossed her legs. "What have you gotten yourself involved in, Sebastien?" she asked matter-of-factly.

Sebastien sucked in a few deep breaths to try to clear the fog from her brain, then sat up and drank from the glass of water on the bedside table.

Perhaps Ana sensed that Sebastien was stalling for time to think of a good lie, so the other woman spoke before she could. "You and Damien are involved in some kind of secret project. Something that both of you feel is more important than school, despite *your* obsession with being the best. Something that involves sneaking out in the middle of the night and a serious amount of danger. Something that maybe involves gold, because I've noticed the way you no longer flinch when you need to pay a handful of silver for some food. I am very upset."

Sebastien rubbed the crusted sleep from the corners of her eyes.

Ana took a deep breath. "Yes, I'm furious about you stupid boys putting yourselves in danger, getting into situations that you obviously can't handle— don't argue, the fact that you're here, right now, *like this*, is evidence that you really *can't* handle it."

Sebastien met Ana's blue-eyed, surprisingly chilling glare, then looked down at the thin sheet covering her legs like a chastened child.

Ana took a deep breath. "But what I'm most upset about is that you didn't invite me. I kept waiting for one of you to mention something, but you never did." She smacked a hand to her chest, her pitch rising with anger. "I pulled you two into my scheme to take down my uncles, but when you were the ones to get into something, you didn't even *tell* me about it, let alone bring me onto the team!"

Sebastien opened her mouth, then closed it again. "Sorry?"

Ana glared at her. "Not good enough."

"What we're doing, it's not whatever you think. It doesn't…pay. It's more like…homework projects for charity work? *Not* like the Undreaming Order's charity work," she hurried to clarify.

Ana rolled her eyes. "Your little secret involves the gaining of other types of power, right? Power that just happens to not be wealth."

Sebastien couldn't deny it, though she wasn't sure that was exactly true in Damien's case.

Ana nodded, as if Sebastien's silence was answer enough. "Of course, *you* wouldn't be interested in anything that didn't involve gaining power. Well, I'm interested in other types of power, too, you dim-wit," she snarled. "Even if it's just *connections* with important people, some of whom happen to be my friends." That last part was said in a smaller, more vulnerable tone.

Sebastien wasn't sure if that was deliberate—a calculated manipulation. Nothing about Ana gave away a lie. Sebastien cupped her face in her palms, then tried to run her fingers through some of the tangles in her hair. '*Do I have to run a fake organization for a second person now?*' Even the thought of it was exhausting.

"I know it's not safe. I don't care," Ana said, as if anticipating Sebastien's next argument. "If you thought it wasn't worth it, you wouldn't be doing it."

"I have special circumstances," Sebastien muttered. Ana opened her mouth to argue, but Sebastien held up a hand to cut her off. "Can we please talk about this when I'm feeling better? I just…can't right now. I can't."

All the fight went out of Ana. She scooted her chair closer, leaned forward, and hugged Sebastien. "Okay," she said softly.

"Thank you," Sebastien whispered.

Ana just patted her back silently, then went to call the thaumaturge to re-cast Sebastien's dreamless sleep spell, and after eating and drinking some more, Sebastien lay back down. As she was drifting off, she thought she heard Oliver's voice, but by the time she woke again, there was no sign of him.

4 6

———

A PIG TEAMMATE

Oliver
   Month 9, Day 17, Friday 6:00 p.m.

OLIVER SLOWED Ebenezer to a walk as he approached Gilbratha's north-western entrance tunnel. The line was long, and as the tunnel itself was fairly narrow, moving slowly. But it was still easier than trying to take a horse—even an erythrean—through the northern lake access, which required getting onto and off of a barge. His eyes kept being drawn up to the white cliffs, like most of the people entering the city. When one had been living in Gilbratha for a while, it was possible to forget how imposing the surrounding stone wall was. Many cities were built with walls, some even quite large and reinforced against magical beast attacks. But none compared to Gilbratha's towering, white stone circle, wide enough to build atop and tall enough to be seen from over a day of travel away.

Ebenezer let out a tired whicker, and Oliver gave a commiserating hum of agreement. "Finally back," he murmured. The late afternoon sun warmed his back uncomfortably, and he scratched at his neck, which had gotten sunburned a couple of times during their journey to the Starpeak Mountains and back.

"I've been dreaming about my bed," one of his enforcers said. "So soft, so comfortable, so clean." Two members of the group had enough elementary magical knowledge to set up wards against vermin, and one man knew a basic cleansing spell that had made him extremely popular, but it wasn't the same as a soaking in a hot bath with high-end soap and some softening salts.

Oliver patted Ebenezer's neck. "Soon, you'll be back at the manor. Fresh hay, sweet oats, and the biggest carrot the servants can find."

Ebenezer pawed at the ground and snorted impatiently at the people in line ahead of them. He craned his neck to either side, then tried to sidle around, obviously intent on cutting past everyone in front of them and going straight to the entrance.

"Behave," Oliver said.

Ebenezer laid his ears flat and bared his teeth. After a moment of hesitation, he flicked his tail at the left side saddlebag and tried to walk forward once more.

"I'm not going to bribe the gate guard just to save you half an hour," Oliver said.

Ebenezer twisted his head to the side and gave Oliver a one-eyed glare.

"Two carrots," Oliver bargained.

Ebenezer walked forward once more.

"Three. That's my final offer."

Ebenezer snorted, then reluctantly moved back to their spot in line. He waited three seconds, then looked back and gave a triumphant whinny, obviously showing off to the other horses.

Oliver rolled his eyes in exasperation and thought longingly of the tub in his home. Luxuries were easy to become accustomed to and hard to give up. He had grown soft.

Alas, a quick wash in one of the rooms at the Verdant Stag would have to do for the moment, because the disaster he had gone on this trip to avert had not, in fact, been averted. He and the team had stayed in Malzhan for two days, and though they had been questioned twice by local authorities, nothing seemed to have come of it. And, of course, Osham wasn't giving out any details about what had happened. Deciding that he had done all he could and hoping to avoid any complications, Oliver had decided to leave, and they had returned at a quick but more sustainable speed than the rush that had taken them to the Starpeak Mountains.

But a couple of days ago, he had picked up a newspaper and seen Osham's premier decrying the unannounced attack and kidnapping and demanding ruinous levels of restitution from Lenore.

Apparently, quite a few of those kidnapped young men and women had been from influential families in Osham, though many were technically from branch lines or conceived by concubines. This was further evidence toward Oliver's theory about what could make them act so recklessly. Breeding a Null was a sign of status in Osham, after all. The Architects must have been desperate to be willing to take such risks. Oliver wondered again what they hoped to do with those young men and women and cursed the fact that he had not infiltrated his supposed allies' ranks well enough to have learned about their plan ahead of time.

Despite Oliver's attempts to inform Osham of the truth, according to the papers, they were blaming Lenore as a whole and not the Architects specifically. He wasn't sure if that was a tactic to give Osham the upper hand when asking for restitution, though it seemed that if they had really wanted their children back, they would have been more interested in the truth. Either that, or they knew something he didn't. Oliver had been musing on this for a long time now, his mood growing ever darker.

"You can all go home. Rest for three days, and then come to the Verdant Stag for assignments," Oliver told them.

They let out weak cheers, except for Huntley, who seemed even more shifty than normal, watching the pedestrians as if he expected one to lunge at Oliver with a hidden knife at any moment.

Oliver and his companion began riding toward the Verdant Stag, moving slowly through the late afternoon traffic. He had considered calling upon his various contacts and plants to report on the situation within the city—and the Architects—over the next couple of days. To remain inconspicuous, such things couldn't be too blatant, after all. He also should probably make a visit to the city's best information broker. But he was fed up. Those things could come later.

Instead, he would go straight to the source. He gave the orders as soon as he arrived at the Verdant Stag and then went to take a bath and have a nap.

The Stags' preparations were fairly simple, and late that night, when most of the city was asleep, a team of enforcers broke into Grandmaster Kiernan's home and kidnapped the man. Luckily, he was not a free-casting battle sorcerer, and had been completely unprepared for organized and well-funded violence. Oliver had been preparing for something like this for a long time, after all.

Some part of Oliver had wanted to go with the team, but hands-on work like that was what subordinates were for. And he had to deal with the paperwork that had accumulated while he was gone. So much paperwork.

But less than two hours after they had departed, the team returned. An enforcer knocked on Oliver's office door and informed him that Kiernan was ready for him.

Oliver tidied his appearance and put on his mask before going down. Kiernan knew his face already, but this wasn't about keeping secrets. It was about intimidation. The smooth, featureless surface and the artificial darkness filling the eye holes were rather unsettling. Of course, it didn't hold a candle to the Raven Queen's repertoire of intimidation tactics, but that was fine, since Oliver was trying to build a reputation as a generally benevolent leader who was only occasionally ruthless and bloodthirsty.

There had always been a hidden room attached to the wine cellar beneath the Verdant Stag. But after the fighting and destruction that had led to so much renovation, Katerin had suggested they take advantage of the situation to expand their underground holdings. Now, the footprint beneath the ground was larger than the building above. For now, all the wards were holding strong, and the damp hadn't seeped in, though Oliver found the low ceilings oppressive. There was something about knowing you were deep beneath the surface that created a feeling of pressure.

When he arrived, he found Enforcer Huntley standing outside, leaning against the wall. The man pushed himself upright and entered the small square room ahead of Oliver, then moved to lounge against the far wall, placing himself so that he could see both Kiernan and Oliver at the same time. The man may have seemed at ease, but Oliver knew from experience that he was ready to move at any time, despite how unlikely it was that Oliver would be in danger here.

The room was completely bare except for Kiernan, who was tied up in a chair in the exact center with a bag over his head. A light crystal affixed to the ceiling shone down on him like a spotlight, and it was slightly blue-purple, without any of the comforting feel of light taken from the sun. Kiernan had been stripped, searched, and was now wearing a simple vest that came down to his knees, without even laces or a button that could be used to make a Circle. He had no Conduit, no artifacts—even his teeth had been examined— and his limbs and hands were tied so that he could not gesture or cast something esoteric.

"Who's there?" Kiernan demanded. "How dare you attack a University professor in his home! This is illegal! Arrestees must be made aware of their accused crime." He fell silent for a moment, then changed tactics. "Do you know who I am? Is this a kidnapping? Are you looking for ransom, maybe? I assure you, there are those who will pay handsomely." When no response came, he rocked violently in his chair, which was too heavy to tip over.

Oliver ignored him, letting him ferment blindly for a while longer. According to his files on the man, Kiernan was known to be a free-caster. But there was a huge chasm of skill between technically being a free-caster and being Thaddeus Lacer. Kiernan had been known to cast a small cloud that, after about fifteen minutes of accumulation, could rain out a few dozen drops, as well as a spell that created the ringing tone of a bell—used to call waiters and servants to attention. Even if Oliver were worried that the man might have some other tricks up his non-existent sleeve, Kiernan wouldn't be able to try them without a Conduit unless he was willing to sign his own death warrant by break event. Few who had ever come face to face with an Aberrant were that bold.

Finally, when Kiernan had gone still and silent, panting heavily within the cloth hood, Oliver stepped forward and ripped it from his head.

Kiernan jerked back in surprise. His eyes squinted against the light from above, but his eyebrows rose. "You!" he said with both outrage and shock.

"Me," Oliver agreed.

"Are you insane? Don't you know my position within the Architects—" Kiernan cut off as Oliver shoved the bag against his mouth. Perhaps fearing that he would be gagged, the man clamped his jaw shut viciously.

"Let me help you with some basic deductive reasoning, Grandmaster," Oliver said kindly. "Obviously, I know exactly who you are. All of the threats you want to use about how you're powerful and connected... I know those things, too. And yet, I dared to do this. So what kind of situation do you think you are in right now?"

Kiernan was not a complete idiot, and as the blood drained from his face, so, too, did most of his bravado. Still, he lifted his chin defiantly. "Is this really necessary? We are allies. Why have you brought me here?"

Oliver stared at him silently, letting his expressionless, ever-staring mask convey everything Kiernan needed to know.

The man swallowed. "Are you turning on the Architects of Khronos? You think to betray us?" he managed with some composure.

"Have you ever heard of this saying, Grandmaster? I heard it during my years of traveling, and it always stuck with me. 'We fear not Titan-like opponents, but pig teammates?' How is it possible for me to carefreely maintain our previous arrangement when my supposed allies are doing the equivalent of stealing a dragon's egg and bringing it back to our shared house? Should I just be implicated along with you when the dragon comes calling?" He let out a single, short bark of a laugh. "Hah! What if you start trying to make an omelette, also without my knowledge?"

Oliver leaned forward and crouched in front of Kiernan, speaking in a soft voice directly into his face. "Do you understand the implications of what you've done? Kidnapping a group of Nulls?"

Kiernan was neither surprised, nor did he refute the accusation, which confirmed Oliver's suspicions.

Oliver stood straight and took a couple of steps backward till he stood on the edge of light and dark. "Do you think Osham is the type to just let this go? And what about the Thirteen Crowns? The Red Guard? There are only so many things that Nulls would be useful for, especially that would require so many of them."

Kiernan looked down and to the side. He shook his head silently, though the hunching of his shoulders and the pained expression on his face exposed his great antipathy toward what Oliver was saying. He seemed more despairing and embittered than defiant.

"Where are they, and what are you doing with them?" Oliver asked.

Kiernan spoke in a dull, toneless voice. "They're in a safe place where they can't cause trouble for us."

"Is that really the answer you want to give me? Because…" Oliver tilted his head to the side a little too far for comfort. "With this kind of pig teammate, it seems wiser to slaughter it first, so that maybe it can act as appeasement when the dragon comes looking. I will not allow the Verdant Stags to be implicated because of what you've done."

Kiernan pressed his lips together and closed his eyes. His face was pale when he met Oliver's gaze again. "You'll cut ties with us, despite our cooperation being so profitable? What other buyer will you find for such a quantity of illegal materials? And you forget how much we know about you, Oliver Dryden. I'm sure the High Crown would be amenable to a little anonymous tip, especially if it led to him getting a public win over a source of discord."

Oliver remained still and silent for a handful of breaths. Then he reached up and took off his mask. He smiled in the way that he usually avoided—too gleeful, too honest, too disturbing.

Kiernan's face went slack as any blood that had remained drained away.

"Simply cutting ties? That's so mundane and harmless," Oliver said. "You know that's not what I meant. As for the materials, I'm sure I can find a use for them all on my own. And as for my name…" He stepped forward, fully into the light, until he could loom directly over Kiernan, so close their knees almost touched. "You're mistaken if you think I'll cling to it. If I cannot be Oliver Dryden, I will still be Lord Stag. I never intended to get out of this unscathed."

Kiernan's eyes shook.

Oliver turned to leave.

"Archmage Zard is one of us!" Kiernan burst out. His voice broke from the force, and he started coughing violently.

Oliver turned back around. Archmage Zard? That was…bad news. And they had kept it well hidden. He must not normally be involved in much of their operations. Or, perhaps the Architects were more internally fractured than Oliver had known, working in distinct cells to increase security.

When Kiernan spoke again, his voice was slightly rough. "Archmage Zard was the one who insisted on pulling off that operation. He's been growing impatient for years now. I never—I never wanted that. We're supposed to have a council of worthy leaders, but he's an Archmage. It turns out, he can actually just do whatever he wants without majority approval, especially if he leads the attack himself. How were we supposed to stop him? And I—I understand why you're angry! I do! But you can't do this. Zard won't stand for it. He'll eliminate you and all your people and tell the High Crown he was doing him a favor. The only thing you can do is put a smile on your face and pretend this never happened. I won't tell anyone. I'll even swear a vow, if I must."

With someone like Zard, who was apparently drunk on some cocktail of greed and narcissism, acting freely and recklessly, there was little chance that Oliver would be able to influence the Architects onto a more acceptable path. Even if some of them wanted to, what Kiernan had said was true. How could they stop him?

That was fine. Oliver had already reached his limit with them. This had never been a permanent arrangement. To end things now was sooner than he would have liked, but they were forcing his hand. He turned to leave once more.

"Wait. Wait! You have to let me go," Kiernan said incredulously. "Zard will be suspicious. You can't just leave me here."

Oliver reached the doorway and looked over his shoulder as Huntley moved to follow him out. "You aren't leaving, Grandmaster Kiernan."

Kiernan was silent for two seconds and then began to scream, heaving violently against his bonds as he realized he was well and truly wrecked.

Huntley closed and locked the heavy door behind them, and Kiernan's screams cut out abruptly and entirely. "Interrogation?" he asked simply.

Oliver nodded. The coppers might not have succeeded in getting anything useful out of Kiernan and his comrades when they questioned them, but the coppers were working under certain restrictions that Oliver wasn't.

As he turned toward the stairs that would lead them back up into the Verdant Stag, Oliver mused on his next steps. Time was running out, so he would need to accelerate his preparation and expansion. He had to be ready when the right moment to act decisively came. And if there was any meat to be gotten off of the metaphorical corpse of the Architects of Khronos, he would need to ensure the Verdant Stags got a few bites.

47

SUDDEN SHOWERS

THE NEXT DAY, Sebastien left the Order's headquarters. Damien and Deidre had argued with increasing passion about who she should stay with until she put her foot down and picked Damien. In part, this was just to keep him from becoming even more suspicious of their strange behavior and deducing a possible connection between Sebastien and the Order. She had no reasonable excuse to want to stay with these people, and she was still far from ready to be on her own.

The first day at Damien's was entirely uneventful in a way that left Sebastien feeling strange, but on the second day, Titus came home for dinner. He stared at Sebastien a little too long, then looked at Damien. "I didn't know we had company."

Damien nodded with forced obliviousness. "I invited Sebastien to stay with us for a few days. He's set up in the green guest room."

"Hmm." Titus spent a lot of his time at dinner asking probing questions about and directly to Sebastien. Things like, "So how did you do on your end of term exams?" and, "What kind of job are you hoping to get after graduation?" Damien let her answer a few, but then started monopolizing the conversation with such rambling monologues about himself that he couldn't even eat properly.

After dinner, Titus called Sebastien into the drawing room and spent a long time very determinedly beating her at the dueling board and other games.

The next day, he came home with a letter from Professor Lacer. "He was alarmed that you were not at your stated residence, and might have gone looking for you, had I not informed him that you were here with Damien and entirely safe." He yanked at his tie, loosening its grip around his neck. "Please. You are both adults now. Do not make people treat you like children by being so inconsiderate."

Sebastien hoped it was not obvious that all the blood had left her face in a single rush. Somehow, when she spoke, her voice did not crack. "My apologies. I will write him a letter in return. It had not occurred to me that he might be concerned about my whereabouts."

Titus didn't seem to notice anything, though Damien stared at her a moment too long.

Still, they were both quickly distracted by dinner, and then games. Titus's dominance recurred, aided by Sebastien's distraction, until Damien got fed up. He enlisted the help of several of the servants, and they all teamed up to crush Titus in a variety of games—even those that didn't inherently involve team-work—until he pleaded mercy.

Damien cast her dreamless sleep spell for her, but he was not as skilled nor as powerful as her, and the nightmares continued to command undue strength. Several times, they snuck up on her so subtly that she almost didn't realize she was dreaming, and they fought to keep her under the surface when she tried to wake. Sebastien was still recovering, and in no shape to do anything about it. Not that she knew *what* to do about it. She did have one idea how to find out, but the crown of madness, which should allow her insight into whatever magic had been worked on her via its traces in the spirit realm, was dangerous.

Sebastien spent four days at Westbay Manor, and though she cast no magic during that time, she did probe through her own mind, checking on the healing process and exploring recent changes. *'What does it mean that there are now three pieces to my Will? What even is the Will, that it can split like that? Has my brain expanded, or is it just running, in effect, three times as hard as an average person's when I have all three pieces of my Will active at once? Why don't I get any stupider when I'm focused on two different things at once? And...how was the third Will born?'* She recalled her memories from the period she had blacked out. It was almost like a new, infant version of her had been birthed, and took some time to find its feet. Now, it felt indistinguishable from the other two facets.

She had missed the Saturday-night-Sunday-morning meeting with Thaddeus and Kiernan. She had no good solutions for how to handle that whole situation, so she set it aside for the future. Perhaps she would really just leave Gilbratha this time. But something small and weak inside held her back from committing to that decision. In a small attempt to mitigate potential repercussions, she left a letter for Thaddeus in the dead drop box she had set up before, apologizing for her absence and explaining that she had Will-strain and was recuperating. This was in addition to the lighthearted note she sent him in her normal handwriting, as Sebastien.

Thankfully, he was not so worried that he came to visit. She didn't know that she could have withstood that.

There had been no scrying or other attempts at sympathetic magic. Either Thaddeus hadn't kept any strands of her hair, he was not trying to find or harm her, or he had simply judged sympathetic magic to be infeasible. She had gone to a lot of effort to convince the University and the Thirteen Crowns of that. Thaddeus knew that he could overpower her automatic defenses, but he had no way to guess at her distance or her wards, and if the memory modifications had worked as intended, he would have no good excuse to be scrying for her.

Damien assured her that all the traces of their research project had been destroyed, loathe as he was to do so, and that Ana had helped spread some rumors about Sebastien that had nothing to do with having her brains scooped out like someone digging into the center of a watermelon with a spoon.

Apparently, it was best for the rumors to be both faintly outrageous as well as contradictory. So, some people might hear that Sebastien was spending time at Pendragon Palace, where the High Crown was considering him as a replacement heir in lieu of the failure, Frederick. Others might hear that he had been seen leaving on a ship whose captain had once been arrested for piracy, before he bribed his way to freedom. And yet others would hear about a trio of young men who were disguising themselves as Sebastien Siverling to run various cons on people just wealthy enough to be worth it but not so rich as to be dangerous.

When she could cast the light-refinement spell, she did so. It was a strain to both her body and mind, but a pleasant one, and left her feeling as refreshed as she was shaky and exhausted. It also helped with the sudden flashbacks—memories of being overpowered in the dark confines of the white cliff tunnels—and the prickly feeling of being hunted even when she knew she was as safe as it was possible to be.

Which was not *perfectly* safe, and perhaps that was really the problem.

At first, Damien argued hotly that she was being reckless to start casting so early, but she knew her own mind. It was only a little bruised, a little sore. Perhaps it should have taken longer to heal. Perhaps having three sides to her Will made her heal three times as quickly? Eventually, she had to just ignore Damien and prove that she could handle it. If anything, she felt a little stronger than she had been before this whole fiasco.

Damien settled down after the first fifteen minutes, watching the whole thing with fascination. However, when Sebastien offered him the light-refinement instruction manual, he immediately gave up with the somewhat petulant declaration that he would continue to focus on modern sorcery. "I can't do everything. I have to focus if I'm going to be good enough."

Sebastien understood the desire for excellence, even if she did not want to limit her interests to achieve it. So, even though it was a little disappointing, she didn't offer him the gesturan primer, either.

She spent a lot of her time on a balcony near the Charybdis Gulf, looking out over the water and the city beyond. The weather was changing rapidly, and with that came several sudden showers. At times, she could watch the rain pour down in blinding sheets over one part of the city while the sun still shone brightly in others.

As she sat and watched one such shower crawl over the city at a rate only slightly faster than the average pedestrian could run, an unbidden flashback to the moment Thaddeus had caught her took over her mind for half a second.

Sebastien gasped, leaning forward and hugging herself to ward off a sudden chill. She had been powerless. Everything she could bring to bear, and more that she shouldn't have, had been useless against him. *'I'm still so weak.'*

She remembered the look in his eyes as he had crushed her beneath his Will. She remembered the desperate, intangible battle for her mind. She remembered being flayed of her protections and unraveled from her core.

And then she remembered his smile afterward. How he had said, "I promise not to tell anyone," as if they shared a secret joke.

She understood that he'd had no choice. He could have killed her and he hadn't, and though he also hadn't planned it this way, she was here, still sane, still *herself*. This was one of the best possible outcomes for her misplaced trust.

But some part of her still couldn't help but hate him.

She hunched forward further and hugged herself tighter, letting out a low, stifled moan. With the noise came the tears she had been trying to hold back. Her body convulsed, almost breathless, and she opened her mouth in a soundless scream.

She had trusted him.

Sebastien cried for long minutes with only the occasional audible sob slipping out, and then, quite suddenly, she became too exhausted to continue. She lay sprawled over the chair just breathing for a bit, then forced herself upright and cleaned away the evidence of her breakdown.

By the time Damien joined her half an hour later, the rain had reached Westbay Manor and she was wrapped in a thin blanket, scribbling in her grimoire.

'What if he betrays me, too?' The thought came without warning. She took the

steaming mug of hot chocolate Damien offered her and turned her gaze back out over the gulf. *'Don't be silly,'* she told herself. *'In this case, I am the one betraying him.'* She stifled an ironic laugh. *'I guess I absorbed more from Ennis than I thought.'*

On the evening of the fifth day, she left for Liza's, again despite Damien's protests. She wanted to re-cast the sleep proxy spell. It might take her more than a single day to get through all the steps, with her Will still slightly tender, but she *longed* for the freedom and safety of eschewing sleep once more.

True storm clouds, more ominous than the sudden showers and cheerful drizzles they had been getting all week, had rolled in since that afternoon, and as the wind picked up, the rain came with it. Instead of trying to cast a shield barrier, Sebastien stopped by the front of an enterprising shop and bought an umbrella for the usurious price of five silvers. It was a good umbrella, high-quality, bright red, and wide enough to block out the rain driving in from a slight angle.

She traveled most of the way as Sebastien, slipping into and out of carriages and a couple of different pubs. Normally, she wouldn't have gone to Liza's in her male form, but with the woman being gone anyway, and the fact that Thaddeus must have reported what happened to the Red Guard, she was wary about using her original body. What if they wanted to do some kind of follow-up to ensure the memory modifications had worked? What if they decided her continued existence wasn't an acceptable risk, no matter how Thaddeus had tried to mitigate the situation? She disguised herself, of course, wearing a black-haired wig and darkening her eyebrows and eyelashes to match with a color-changing spell. A little highlighter to soften the angles of her nose and round her cheeks, and she was unlikely to be recognized.

When she got closer to Liza's, she drew her cloak's hood farther down her face and popped up the collar of her jacket underneath. If someone were watching Liza's house, hopefully she would remain entirely nondescript, except for her height.

She planned to stop and watch for any signs of a lookout before entering, but as soon as Liza's apartment block came into view, Sebastien saw that the light was on inside.

Liza was home.

She suppressed a groan, hesitated for a while, and then turned to walk off in a different direction than she had come. She would change into Siobhan close by, hurry to Liza's, and then change back again as soon as she was finished.

She changed the color of her umbrella first, giving it a midnight-blue hue, then changed into her battle dress. She remembered how she had wished she were wearing it the last time she was in this body. *'This might actually be advan-*

tageous,' she realized. '*I can buy a few thousand gold of warded artifacts from Liza while I'm there. Everything she rented me last time, and more.*'

With excitement quickening her movements, she changed forms and began to make her way back. While she walked, she allowed herself an extended daydream about a life where she made and sold beautiful, treated-silk umbrellas for a living. Each one would be a unique work of art, and she wouldn't take commissions. Ana would handle sales and marketing, of course. Their worries would be mundane and small; the worst they would have to deal with was thieves and jealous rivals.

Siobhan got lost enough in this daydream, distanced from the world beyond the edge of her umbrella, that she almost didn't notice when things started to go strange around her. Silhouettes with no faces watched from the windows, and the street was already empty of other pedestrians.

Siobhan's heart sank all the way down to the bottom of her shoes and then ripped free of her body entirely. '*The Red Guard. It's their shitty, "destined to meet under the rain," spell again. If I had stayed Sebastien, would they have caught me? Whatever they're doing, there's no sympathetic magic involved, which means it might have more to do with the* idea *of me than my actual self. And their idea of me is the Raven Queen.*' Despite that shaky inference, the only comfort she could find in this moment was that if they *had* found her as Sebastien, they might have grown suspicious about what that meant.

But then, that comfort was ripped away by another thought. '*What if they watched me transform?*'

48

RED GUARD PRESSURE

SIOBHAN
Month 9, Day 20, Monday 10:40 p.m.

'*Is that even Liza with the light on in her apartment, or was it one of them, waiting for me?*' Siobhan wondered. She closed her eyes and listened to the crashing noise of the rain for a moment. It was exhausting to be so wary all the time, and there were so many dangers to juggle. Too many. '*If I make it past tonight, something has to change. I cannot go on like this.*'

Siobhan didn't run. She had tried that last time and knew it wouldn't work. She kept walking until she found a nice, well-lit street corner, and then she waited.

It didn't take long. Three people stepped through the surrounding rain barrier and into the light: Captain Aisling, the androgynous agent that had fought with her the last time they trapped her with this spell, and an old, hunch-backed man with a cane. Thaddeus was not there. He could have been watching along with whoever was casting the spell, or even casting it himself, but the stupid lizard part of her brain that couldn't make calculations like that still found his absence immensely relieving.

Siobhan lifted her jaw, raising the umbrella higher so that she could glare out from under its rim. "Why the ambush? Special Agent Thaddeus Lacer was to be our intermediary. Is it betrayal, then?"

Captain Aisling shook his head and waved a hand in denial. "No, definitely not betrayal!" he assured her.

She was tentatively relieved that he made no mention of nor gave any signs that they had known she was Sebastien only half an hour before. Surely, the fact that she had been disguising herself as Thaddeus Lacer's apprentice would have been noteworthy enough to comment on, even if they hadn't immediately jumped to the conclusion that they were the same person.

Captain Aisling stepped to the side to make way for the old man to pass, a hint of wariness slipping through his disciplined, placid expression.

As the old man stepped closer, Siobhan saw that one of his eyes was an artifact, slightly larger than the other and bulging out of the socket. One of his hands was made of intricately carved wood covered with crystalline glyphs so tiny they looked like little sparkles rather than symbols. They were high-end prostheses, which gave new meaning to the hunched curve of his back and his limp. When Siobhan was younger and more immature, she might have found the evidence of so much flesh replaced by artifice off-putting, but now it only spoke to her of a man who had experienced hardship and found his own way to overcome it.

He looked her up and down, once with his eye of flesh, and then several times with the eye of metal and glass. "There is no convenient, immediate way to get a message to you through Agent Lacer, and I simply couldn't wait to meet you. Writing letters and waiting for a response as if you were halfway across the world is criminally inefficient." He had a faint accent that she couldn't place.

Captain Aisling gave a single nod. "We hope you will forgive the intrusion, Queen of Ravens. We just want to have a friendly discussion. Analyst Hite is a researcher with a particular interest in the project you have been tasked with." Hite was pronounced "Hee-tay," and she tentatively placed him as being from the East.

"Well met," Siobhan said, nodding to the old man. Something about the way Captain Aisling's manner was so perfectly neutral and unoffensive put her on edge.

Hite took another step closer to her, peering even closer still, as if he could see inside her. And maybe, with his artifact eye, he could. "I've heard you have the ability to cast two spells at the same time. The reports say you call it 'splitting your Will.' How does it work? Are there two people in there? Did the two halves of your brain develop separately? Have you always been able to do this, or did the ability develop at some point?" With every question, his words came faster, and he inched a little closer, until she could smell him.

He didn't stink, but the skin of Siobhan's back still prickled with unease and a sense of danger. Hite's eyes, both of them, held a look that creeped her out in a way that had nothing to do with his physical form.

She tried to keep that from her expression and tone as she replied. "I do not know how this ability came about. I at first believed it to be a natural skill that I merely developed with a bit of effort, as you might learn to raise both of your eyebrows separately. It *feels* natural, still."

She couldn't remember if she had ever split her Will before Grandfather died. It was unlikely. She'd just been a fledgling thaumaturge at that point, and after all the horror stories Grandfather had told her about magic gone wrong, she'd had at least a moderately developed sense of self-preservation. Had Grandfather or her mother ever cast multiple spells at once? She was pretty sure the first time she had done it knowingly was when she had needed to block a scrying attempt from Eagle Tower while simultaneously casting the reverse-scrying spell she'd come up with to find her blood.

Hite pursed his thin lips into a pout. "Really? But all of the subjects that attempted it died."

Aisling winced and weakly muttered something about "criminals."

"You have been tasked to help us find actionable information on the ways that a consciousness may be encapsulated, stored, and transferred properly, without causing unfeasible degradation. Possibly the secret of Carnagore, possibly the secret of yourself." Hite lightly reached forward and touched her arm. "What have you learned?"

"Please do not touch me. I treasure my personal space," Siobhan said.

Something soured in Hite, but Captain Aisling immediately apologized. The other agent, whose name Siobhan still didn't know, shuffled uncomfortably, glancing at Siobhan's shadow.

Siobhan wished she still had her black sapphire Conduit. Being ready to cast at any moment without *seeming* ready was a great advantage. "The Carnagore we are learning about in Myrddin's journals right now is a wondrous artifact, but nothing more. It is not the answer you are looking for. That may yet change, however. We are still going through the journals. I am also not the answer you are looking for," she added, hoping it sounded believable.

"You still have nothing new? It has been a month since we assigned you this task!"

'*Has it only been that long?*' she wondered. '*It feels like half a year, or more.*'

Hite turned to Captain Aisling. "Why are you letting her run around so ineffectually? If we just brought her in for study, I could peel open her head for something actually new and interesting."

The muscles along Siobhan's spine tightened with a sudden, cool dread.

"We have an agreement," Aisling said, his hands still carefully loose and unthreatening at his sides. "And no reason to bring in people for study who remain cooperative."

"Is she actually being cooperative?" Hite argued.

The unnamed agent's eyes kept flicking from Siobhan's shadow to Hite and back again. They were both afraid of the old man. And if *they* were, then Siobhan should be absolutely terrified.

"I am making progress," she offered, taking a cue from Aisling and keeping all signs of threat from her tone and body language. "Though I am not certain whether it will lead to an answer."

Hite jumped on the offering like a starved lizard snapping up prey. "Oh, wonderful! Tell me, does it have anything to do with creating an artificial brain using a crystalline matrix? I've long thought the answer could lie there, but there are so many roadblocks and unexpected difficulties." He didn't wait for her response at all, waving one arm about as he continued excitedly. "I think the crystalline matrix may still require partitioning, but how to do so? And do you think it's better to create a duplicate in the target body, or try to transfer the original consciousness? There has been some argument, seeing as the first option could be considered a form of death, and many people feel uncomfortable. You know, that whole idea that the copy of them is no longer *them* once it diverges for even a second. It seems like an issue that might create problems with proper assimilation and settling..." He continued on like that for a while longer, growing increasingly incomprehensible, and then stopped abruptly, looking expectantly at Siobhan.

"I *do* think the answer could involve solving those problems," she lied. She had no idea what he was talking about. "However, I suspect the process has met a failure point from the very beginning, and the answer lies in a more... undefined craft, like shamanry. Transmutation and transmogrification should support and build from each other in a more *integrated* way." She very much doubted that she would come to the answer through natural science faster than the Red Guard could do so. If she found a solution, it would be through the privilege of access to better resources, along with taking full advantage of shortcuts and approximations—such as transmogrification.

Unfortunately, Hite's expression twisted further. "Are you trying to put me off with empty assurances? Have you discovered nothing, or is it that you wish to keep your knowledge to yourself? Perhaps you *should* come to one of the research centers. They have better resources there. We could have one of the other subjects pray to you, if that is necessary for the shadow to possess them. If there are secrets left inside you, I will be sure to extract them." He stepped closer and patted her arm again. "Don't worry, I won't let you die. You are too valuable for that, if you are what we suspect."

Captain Aisling stepped forward, one hand going to the wand on his belt, though he did not draw it. "*Analyst* Hite, allow me to remind you that I am the ranking officer in charge of this region, as well as this case. I have authority here, including making decisions about allied assets."

Hite continued staring up at Siobhan for a moment, then spun to face

Aisling. "I will remind you in turn that you may have authority, but I have higher clearance. The directors are interested in my research." He turned back to Siobhan and eyed her speculatively.

The unnamed agent had put a hand on their battle wand, too, and was starting to breathe noticeably faster, their gaze continually flicking to Siobhan's shadow.

'He's considering trying to capture me right now,' Siobhan realized. *'Are the others going to fight him, or help him?'* She remembered what Thaddeus had said to the High Crown about the Red Guard not being willing to punish him further, even for placing a curse on this nation's most powerful ruler.

Maybe Hite really could get away with it. If she were captured successfully, there would be no downside for them. And after all, Hite had not directly bound himself to the oath she and Aisling agreed to. He might not technically have the authority to go against it, but the only thing stopping him was bureaucracy—questions of hierarchy, authority, and punishment.

'What do I do? The dazzler is probably my best option for an effective surprise attack —if their standard equipment wards aren't set to handle it—but I'm not good enough to do it without the chant and a good bit of lead-up time. If I were carrying Thaddeus's tracking device, I might even be desperate enough to try to signal him right now.' She wished she had another disintegration mine, though if she had, she probably would have used it against Thaddeus in the tunnels.

The androgynous agent was looking at Siobhan's eyes, now, and shook their head subtly.

'A signal not to attack?'

They cleared their throat, and though their voice quavered slightly, they spoke clearly. "The Raven Queen has always dealt in good faith. This project is the kind of problem that cannot be solved in a day, or even a month. Sometimes it is more efficient to collaborate than to use force, especially when *novel* ideas are required."

Hite stiffened, straightening slightly.

"Perhaps an outside perspective is what we really need, since obviously this problem has stumped our own researchers until now."

As Hite slowly turned around, Captain Aisling moved to stand in front of the other agent like a human shield. "Agent Holland may speak roughly, but it is true that when new research avenues are available, they should be taken advantage of. All that we have to lose is a little time."

Hite was silent for a long time, but eventually snorted and swung back around to Siobhan on one leg in a move that no human knee could have allowed. "How long could you possibly need?"

"Another year for preliminary leads, perhaps," she suggested, somehow knowing that this reasonable request was useless.

"You have three months to prove your worth as an independent researcher," he snapped back. "I will not allow the Red Guard to waste such a potential resource." He turned to look over his shoulder at Aisling. "*Time* is precious, too."

49

———————

NO WAY OUT

Siobhan
Month 9, Day 20, Monday 11:00 p.m.

After Analyst Hite let her go and the rain stopped, Siobhan did not go back to Liza's. Instead, she turned around and headed for one of the few dozen places across the city that she knew was safe to stop and change forms in.

She mulled over her latest problem along the way, too overwhelmed to be truly panicked. There was only so much stress that a human body could take before it became numb. She had three months to prove herself useful. It was possible she might have a good clue about encapsulating and transferring consciousnesses for Hite by that point, but would that really satisfy him?

Siobhan didn't believe Hite was going to take "No" for an answer, even from Captain Aisling. She also didn't think she had the leverage to have Hite removed by one of these "directors." Especially since the old man technically hadn't done anything egregious yet. In fact, bringing herself to their attention might make things even worse. There was no guarantee any of them would be as reasonable as Aisling.

'*Could I assassinate Hite?*' she wondered longingly. She was willing, but it seemed unlikely, and even if she succeeded, she might get caught.

She blew out a long, slow breath. Since the chances of being able to avoid capture if the Red Guard became determined to find her were so minuscule, she needed to finalize her preparations to run. To disappear forever. Something in her chest squeezed painfully, as if she really might just disappear, without the support and structure of the life she had built here. She would be entirely alone.

She shook her head. *'Don't be ridiculous. I would figure it out. I always have before. I have the gold, and I have some of the steps in place already. Identity papers, and such. I still need to create more robust escape routes, prepare living arrangements, and see about alternative learning opportunities.'* The next time she got caught in an emergency situation, she needed a real way out.

She remembered the way the creature in her mind allowed her to escape through the spirit realm, but cut off that dangerous line of thought before it could get too far.

'Thank goodness I refused to take vows that would allow the Red Guard to restrict my freedom. That was worth it.' She still didn't actually want to leave. So, in the time she had, she would do what she could.

She got to a small inn, where she stripped off the clothes she had been wearing. Her first instinct was to burn them. Yes, this seemed paranoid, but Hite had touched them. Who knew what he could have left behind?

However, this battle dress had cost her so much gold, and only been possible for her to purchase because of her connection through Liza. So instead, she cast the shedding-disintegration spell with a broader focus, destroying not only her own, but all biological remnants. Then she cast a scouring spell. Still feeling uneasy, she filled the room's empty wash basin with water, then added a cleansing potion. Finally, she used a heating spell to boil the water for a few minutes.

When she was done, she removed the water from the fabric with another handy spell and packed the battle dress away. Luckily, she had a spare shirt and pair of pants, and a light cloak to cover it all. Long gone were the days when she had to steal clothes from homeless people.

She considered becoming Sebastien again, but felt that between the potential danger of being followed as Siobhan and someone from the Red Guard learning her other identity, being tracked was the lesser evil. It would be a neat trick if they had terrified her just to secretly watch how she responded. Ennis had told her that breaking in and trashing a place, then hiding and watching how the owner responded was a great way to find the location of hidden safes. Then, if one acted quickly enough, they could raid the contents before security measures were increased. Or, go back to the scene of the crime impersonating a ward expert and just steal the safe outright.

She could afford to have Siobhan Naught's identity associated with Oliver Dryden, no matter how undesirable that would be. She could not afford to give up her other name, her last and strongest line of defense.

In fact, Hite was not Siobhan's most urgent problem. She needed to deal with the seal in her mind, which might be cracking further. However, even the thought of going back to the restricted archives to search for more information on shamanry made her heart race. Thaddeus might find her there. The thought of being alone with him made her want to flee.

Siobhan stepped back into the street, looked both ways, and headed toward Dryden Manor. *'I should see if I can figure out how urgently I need to come up with a solution to the sealed creature. And maybe some clues about how to actually do that. Whatever I learn will inform my next steps.'*

When she arrived at Dryden Manor, she climbed up the side of the building and tapped politely on the window of Oliver's still-lit office. Just in case, it was better to not seem so familiar that she could nonchalantly walk in the front door.

He jumped so hard he almost fell out of his desk chair. When he turned to see her face in the window, his body relaxed, falling out of the automatic fighting stance he had adopted. He rubbed his eyes, his head bowed like some kind of exasperated nanny, before letting her in.

Oliver was tanned and had grown a short beard in the time since she last saw him. Unlike Thaddeus's, it was neat, trimmed, and didn't look as if it was desperately trying to escape from his face. He looked her up and down quickly, but upon seeing that she had no wounds, his expression fell flat. "The window, Siobhan, really? Are you, perhaps, getting a little too caught up in your own mystique?" he asked, closing and locking it before drawing the curtains.

She rubbed her forehead tiredly. "Who knows? I'm not sure of anything anymore."

Oliver stared at her for a moment, his eyes narrowed, and then moved to one of the bookcases near the door. He moved a set of books, reached into the empty space left behind, and turned a dial set into the wall. "Did something happen?"

Siobhan shivered as some indefinable part of her sensed the activation of powerful wards. He must have had them added recently. She took a place on one of his upholstered settees before the fire, as the earlier rain had left her slightly damp and chilled. "A lot has happened," she admitted.

Oliver puttered about for a moment, bringing back two glasses of alcohol and a dish of candied nuts. He sat beside her. "I heard about some of it. I'm glad to see you recovered. I came to visit twice, but you were sleeping both times, and your young friend Damien did his best to hurry my exit, just short of resorting to force. What happened?"

Siobhan took the nuts, at first just intending to stall for time to think while she ate, but immediately realizing that she was famished. She shoved an entire handful into her mouth, heedless of basic manners.

Oliver nudged the second glass of alcohol closer.

She hesitated, but then took a small sip of the honey-colored liquid. It was disgusting, of course, but though swallowing it made her shudder, its warmth was welcome. "I'll start from the beginning. I made a deal with the Red Guard after you left, mostly as planned." She tried to be succinct, but somehow ended up speaking for a long while.

When she skipped past Damien's fatal discovery and Thaddeus's attack with a few vague, non-incriminating sentences, Oliver reached out and touched her forearm. "Stop." He hesitated, searching her eyes. "Whatever put you into the care of the Undreaming Order almost killed you. I'm sure it was…traumatic, but you know you can tell me anything, right? I was incredibly worried."

She pressed her lips together.

Oliver's eyes wavered with some emotion she couldn't decipher. "Is it too hard to talk about?" he asked gently.

She ran her tongue over the inside of her teeth for a moment, then leaned closer to his ear and spoke in her softest voice. "It's just dangerous for you to know. It might even be dangerous to say out loud."

"We're under the cover of some very strong wards."

She shook her head silently.

They shared a long, meaningful stare as Oliver seemed to put something together in his mind. He let out a low breath. "Okay. But if that's the case, then you're not safe, either. Is there anything that I can do to help?"

Siobhan smiled bitterly. "Not with that. There's something else." She explained her recent encounter with the Red Guard, and more specifically, Agent Hite.

When she was done, Oliver rolled his glass back and forth between his palms, staring into the swirling liquid and ice. "This is a problem," he agreed. "As much as I would like to, I cannot guarantee that the Verdant Stag can protect you from the Red Guard. We simply do not have either the power or the capability."

Siobhan waved a dismissive hand. "That isn't why I came to you. I need your help with something else."

"Getting out of Gilbratha?" he guessed.

"I won't leave just yet, but yes. I have a few identity papers. I need to make sure they have some assets in their name and backgrounds that could get me access to schooling." She rummaged within her bag and pulled out a small stack of the navy-colored booklets.

"How did you get these? I didn't…"

Siobhan raised an eyebrow. "I have other contacts besides you, Oliver."

He flushed slightly. "Right."

"That's not all." Siobhan hesitated as her instincts toward secrecy warred with her need for help. Was there anyone else she could go to about the thing in her head? Everyone involved with the Undreaming Order thought she was powerful and in control—it was part of their reason for whatever loyalty they held. She didn't know how they might respond if disillusioned.

Oliver had betrayed her once already, but he had never acted maliciously toward her, and he still considered himself her ally even though he knew a large part of the danger that trailed behind her like a fancy gown's decorative train. She might have trusted Liza, but she still remembered Oliver's warning about the woman before Siobhan had first met her. Liza had a code of honor, but Siobhan could not buy her *loyalty*, and she wasn't sure where the woman's personal limits lay, nor even how she really felt about Siobhan. Would an Aberrant be a step too far? Thaddeus Lacer would have been capable of handling the situation, but she could no longer trust him. Damien and Ana… might have stood by her. Damien, at least. But they would both be rather useless against this kind of predicament. She could afford to hire a stranger, but just like Thaddeus, she couldn't trust one.

All in all, Oliver was her best choice. She couldn't handle this alone.

"You're usually so bold. Seeing you hesitate like this is making me wary," Oliver said with a half-joking smile.

Siobhan closed her eyes, took a deep breath, and then speared him with her gaze. "Oliver, I am choosing to trust you with a dangerous secret. The second-most dangerous one I know. If you betray me, you had better make sure to murder me too, else I will come for you and kill you if it's the last thing I do."

The smile fell from Oliver's face. He remained silent for a long while, his gaze assessing her in return. "This dangerous thing, it's worse than potentially being kidnapped by the Red Guard or being hunted for high treason by the Thirteen Crowns?" When she didn't respond, Oliver set his glass on the table between them and leaned forward. "But you need help, and you have no other options," he stated. He looked into the fire for a moment, then turned back to her. "Okay then. Tell me."

Siobhan still hesitated.

"I am sure that I could use a favor from the Raven Queen soon, too," he said.

Though she knew it shouldn't have, this eased her discomfort. "Something specific?"

"A spot of trouble has arisen with the Architects, but I'll tell you about that once we have some time. There's nothing to be done about it right this moment, and I don't believe it's any immediate threat to you, otherwise. Don't worry, I won't pressure you into doing anything you find objectionable," he added, offering a very small, self-conscious smile.

Siobhan was curious and alarmed, but she felt like if she added even one more tiny stressor to the seething mass stretching her thin, she might burst. *'Later. I'll deal with that later.'* At first in a halting voice, and then with more confidence, she explained the situation with the thing in her head from beginning to end.

It was the first time she had ever told anyone, and as the truth spilled into the world, it left her feeling free, but also untethered and out of control, like a hot air balloon loosed to the mercy of the wind.

Oliver remained calm throughout, though little twitches of his fingers and flutters of his lashes gave away his internal distress.

"I want to try looking at myself in the mirror while casting the crown of madness. Since it gives insight into the spirit realm, I think I might be able to see some hints about the seal, but I'm worried about safety. It certainly isn't safe for others, and it isn't as if I know anyone else with a split Will who could test it for me—even if I was inclined to put someone at risk for my own benefit. Who knows what else the creature can do? Who knows how safe viewing it through the spirit world might be?" Siobhan concluded. "I need backup."

"Well...you came to the right person." He grinned. "As a Null, I might not be able to help you cast any powerful spells, but I do have a good chance at helping, and it should be safer for me to watch over your experiments than anyone else. Who knew my condition would come in handy some day?"

Siobhan's mouth fell open. "You're...you're not a Null."

Oliver's grin fell away, replaced by what looked like genuine confusion, which morphed into suppressed amusement. He pressed his fingertips to his lips and cocked his head to the side. "I'm rather sure I am? I think I would know."

"What!? But—but you have all those books about magical theory!" she exclaimed, waving to the bookcases lining the surrounding walls. "And you have so many stories about foreign magic, a-and... *You* were the one who taught *me* how divination difficulty scales with distance!" she blurted, pointing at him accusingly.

Oliver nodded slowly. "Yes, well, I may not be able to cast magic, but I can still learn about it. It is important to understand how the world works if you hope to change it. And you'll recall, if you think closely, that none of the stories of my travels entail *me* casting magic. As for being able to teach you some basic calculations, I wanted to be a diviner before I was confirmed to be a Null. I thought maybe I could find out what happened to my sister. But I assure you, Siobhan, I have never cast even the tiniest spell during my thirty-three years on this planet, and not for lack of trying."

Siobhan fell silent, one hand pressed to her mouth. '*How did I not realize this? It's true, I've never seen or heard him talk about casting magic. I just assumed, someone so educated, intelligent, and ambitious...*' She let her hand fall limply into her lap.

'*Ah. I see. I am a bigot. I associate all of those traits with magic, and so him being a Null was inconceivable to me.*' A blazing blush seared her forehead down to her neck. She leaned forward in as much of a bow as she could perform while sitting. "I'm very sorry for my assumptions."

Oliver laughed, leaned over the table between them, and nudged her up by her shoulders. "It's not going to be a big deal, is it?"

"It won't," she promised, trying to get her embarrassment under control.

"Okay. Well then, let us plan," he said, rubbing his hands together like an eager storybook villain.

50

A CROWN OF MADNESS

Siobhan
Month 9, Day 23, Thursday 3:00 p.m.

It took a couple days of preparation before Siobhan felt safe enough to attempt the crown of madness. Most of that time was spent waiting for Oliver's contacts to give them some portable and very specific wards based on some of the more unusual containment spells she had read about in the restricted archives. Siobhan wasn't good enough with artificery or warding to even fully understand them, let alone create the wards herself.

She had gone to Liza's place again the next day after her encounter with the Red Guard, only to find the woman no longer there. Liza had instead left a blisteringly angry letter about Siobhan's neglect of her plants and animals, which might have died if not for much of their care being automated via various artifacts. When the letter got to the dead raven beginning to rot in its cage, Liza's tone had softened somewhat, allowing worry to peek through her rage.

But even if she was worried, it hadn't been enough for her to stay and look for Siobhan. Liza was gone again, and who knew when she would be back?

Siobhan had deflated. She had hoped for Liza to help with the wards, but they ended up working with what they had. A small part of her wondered if maybe the Red Guard had gotten to her, but if that were the case, she probably wouldn't have left the letter. And whatever Liza was doing, there were few people as generally competent as her. If anyone could protect themselves, it was Liza.

While Siobhan and Oliver waited on the wards, she re-cast the sleep proxy spell, played around with the utility of splitting her Will into three pieces, and practiced light-refinement to speed her healing and give her mind extra stability for what was to come. She hoped it would be enough. *'It's just a viewing spell,'* she reassured herself. *'Everything I know says it shouldn't let the thing out of the seal. And beyond that, the creature shouldn't have much power left, since I haven't cast the shadow-familiar or swallowed any beast cores since the fight with Thaddeus.'* In fact, she felt strange without the shadow-familiar spell, as if it had become a sort of security blanket.

They set everything up at Liza's, since the woman wasn't there to object and her house was already configured and warded for magical experiments. It was probably one of the safest places in the entire city. When they were finally ready, Siobhan cast the light-refinement spell once more, cleansing and energizing her mind before moving down to the lower cells with Oliver.

If anything went wrong, he could trigger a series of increasingly obscure and powerful wards to keep her—and anything else with her—contained. He also had an entire collection of potions on hand to heal her, stabilize her mind, purge foreign influence, and a dozen other things. Some of them had been almost impossible to get and were only available because of Oliver's connections to the Night Market and a wide selection of smuggled goods.

Surely there was more that they could have done, but with the requirement of secrecy, their options were limited.

She shared a glance with him. They both nodded silently, and she stepped into the prepared cell. Her hand was clammy around her Conduit, which she held as much for comfort as utility.

She wore only a thin cotton night-dress, appropriate for sleep. All her other artifacts and sources of magical interference, including the transformation amulet and warding medallion, waited outside the cell. She did not want any insights to be contaminated.

One part of her Will would block out all external distractions and focus only on casting the spell. Another would notice and interact with the spirit realm and allow itself to be distracted and enlightened. The third would watch and wait to be needed. All would experience the effects, technically, but only one would pay attention to them. She hoped this would allow her to avoid the pitfall that previous casters had fallen into.

Rather than an extensive spell array, casting the crown of madness required a simple artifact, some of the caster's blood, and a ritual.

The artifact was a crystal singing bowl with a basic spell array engraved into the bottom, which would activate as the bowl was being played. Rather than discrete charges, there was a total amount of power that could be used up, and it would drain progressively faster the longer any particular casting session went on.

The bowl was a pale cream and mostly smooth, except for a razor-sharp edge cut into one side, just below the rim. Siobhan held it in front of her in her left hand, her Conduit in her right, and dragged her right thumb across the sharp edge. The wound began to drip blood immediately. She dabbed her thumb onto both temples, then the space between her eyebrows. This "crown" of blood was probably what the spell was named after.

Then she brought her thumb down to the rim of the singing bowl and began to drag it across the rim in a slow circle.

The crystal began to sing at once, creating a ringing sound similar to what one could create with a damp finger on the rim of a wine glass. Except the sound Siobhan was creating here was much deeper, too profound and resonant to reasonably come from such a small bowl.

The hair across her body rose as an ephemeral chill rolled across her. The sound grew heavier and more complex, as if matched by a host of invisible counterparts. The ringing tones dug into her bones and pulled at her mind, and the blood from her thumb dripped slowly down the inside of the small bowl and pooled in the center.

The blood would act as an attractor for spirits, who craved such material for its power, but that was not her purpose today. She whispered the chant, since she would actually rather *not* be heard by whatever might be listening, at least this first time.

"CRYSTAL SINGS TO pierce the veil,
    Blood burns bright to mark the way.

BY BLOOD and song I seek the path,
    Through veils of flesh and bone and breath,
    Below the world of mortal things,
    Where truth eternal softly sings.

I AM the blood that feeds the deep,
    I am the song that breaks the sleep.
    Grant me sight beyond the seeing,
    Grant me truth beyond mere being.

SONG TO BRIDGE the space between,

Blood to bind what lies unseen."

WHOEVER HAD CREATED this spell had been a bit of a poet. Chants almost never actually *needed* to rhyme, though many people found those that did more appealing, or more impressive. What did she know? Perhaps the denizens of the spirit realm appreciated it, too.

However, the results of the chant were immediate and obvious, if somewhat hard to define. The world was tinged with an eerie tint, and she felt as if she were being watched. She had an impression of surreality, or perhaps unreality, as if all the world was a shallow, shoddy dollhouse and perhaps she was merely a doll, too, who existed for the amusement of a much greater, outside force.

'The spirit realm isn't here. It isn't affecting the world, only my perceptions,' she reminded herself. As she continued to ring the bowl, she noticed that the lines of the room she was in were all wrong and the angles had gone skewed in a way that would make it very difficult to hold up the roof. She blinked at it in confusion.

Siobhan swayed a bit until the third part of her Will gave the one observing the spell's effects a nudging reminder that she probably didn't want to fall over. She sat down. The stone was strangely soft and warm beneath her, like shaved skin from a frankly enormous giant's inner thigh. She stared at it in wonder, too. Was each bump and divot in the stone one of the giant's pores? The hair on her arms shifted, and she was suddenly quite suspicious that an invisible entity had just brushed across her, though, admittedly, it had felt like a slight breeze.

The third part of her Will found this fascinating, too, but forced itself to remain undistracted, and reminded the part actively casting this spell of that. Her prior experience with the spirit realm, though limited, helped somewhat. When she felt stable, she stood up again.

Siobhan had set up a big, gilded-edge oval mirror to observe herself while she cast the spell, and now she turned to it. She saw herself, at first, looking a bit strange and dramatic, but not in any particularly insightful way. With a step closer, and then closer again, she was able to peer into one of her eyes. She looked into the dark pools until she seemed to fall through the hole. The darkness extended for a long time, with galaxies of breathtaking colors and sparks of memory flashing by in fascinating attempts to distract her, but she kept her focus on her mission.

Eventually, she saw a cube in the darkness of her eye. It was stone, and just about the size of a jail cell. There were no windows and no doors, and it looked as if it would last a millennium…or, no, as if it had already weathered a millennium. It was cracked in places, and a crimson fungus grew out from the inside, slowly widening the gaps like weeds growing up through cobblestone.

A thin strand trailed outward from the stone box to her, though she could not see where it connected. There came a repetitive tapping from the inside that reminded her of a bird's beak on stone.

Light from the corner of her eye caught her attention, and Siobhan looked away from the mirror to her shadow. Its eyes were glowing out at her again, though it still stretched in the opposite direction of the light and lay flat on the floor, just like a non-magical shadow should.

Siobhan blinked, and for a fraction of a second, she saw something else in place of the shadow. She blinked again to repeat it. A skeleton wearing tattered shroud-cloth lay there, so long dead and removed from the *before* that who it once was would never be recovered.

Siobhan smiled at it, even though she had hoped it wouldn't appear. She was not afraid, though perhaps she should have been. "Will it be another request to remember you, then?"

It remained silent, but she could feel its surprise, its wonder, and its wariness.

She wondered if the spell would give her insight into the truth, beyond just her natural sense of the creature's emotions. "What would happen if I do remember you?" she asked.

It spoke in an even softer, stranger voice than normal. "I will fashion your dreams into a pickaxe to break out of this place with, and your memory into a guideline to lead me to freedom."

Siobhan tilted her head to the side, breathing deeply of the smell of old resin mixed with the salty scent of sea aster, and below it all, brimstone. "And once free?"

The glowing eyes curved as if smiling. "I will build a place for myself."

Siobhan swayed slightly as the world rose and fell like an ocean wave. The ringing of the bowl felt as if it might shake her soul loose from her body. "What does that even mean?"

A faint sense of hunger and spite flowed from the shadow up through her feet. "I will eat your soul and wear your body like a fine garment."

Siobhan chuckled and blinked heavily, then shook her head. She knew she was reacting abnormally. There was fear in her, and anger too, but it was all an undercurrent, with a cocoon of gauze filtering and muffling her responses. *'I feel like I'm dreaming,'* she realized. *'And that could be dangerous.'*

Above it all, as always, there was her intrinsic desire to *know*, and with the knowing, to grasp control. Aloud, she said, "But, see, if you wanted me to let you out, why would you tell me that? Now I'm even more inclined to kill you."

She hesitated as a strange feeling filtered up through the shadow connected to her feet. "Ah, but that's what you want, too."

A flash of fear came, then something confused, and then a boiling, tar-like rage that coated everything.

The scent of cloves and copper burned her nostrils, and the air dug into her ears and tickled the fine hairs inside. She did not flinch away.

It didn't know what it wanted. It was just desperate to escape in any way possible. To cover the fear, it snarled and snapped, a response that was familiar to her. "I *want* to trap you in here with me until you go insane and break us both free. Or you could just open the veil." Its form shifted for a moment, the shadow deepening to become a doorway. Instead of the place from before, the dark hall filled with statues of giants, it was a brightly lit scene. A dirt road led up to a country home, rough-built but large enough for a family, with a small tower at the back.

Siobhan almost choked, and a rush of fear and longing pushed aside some of the soft film protecting her from the spirit realm. She preferred it that way and, with an effort of Will, did not let herself be drawn back under. "I will never go back there."

It chuckled. "You made a mistake, Siobhan. To be sure, this spell gives me no way out, and I cannot harm you, but you seem to have forgotten that I, too, can peek into the spirit realm and read the signs your kind leaves in your wake. This spell forces *understanding*."

With a sudden rush of foreboding, Siobhan grasped what the thing meant, but it was too late. For a moment, she wondered at her mistake, but realized quickly that it had always been coming to this. Since that night when Grandfather died, some version of this moment had always been inevitable. Siobhan kept her eyes open and her Will primed for battle.

The world rippled like an oil painting melting in a fire, or a whirlpool sucking her down into the depths. All she could see was the creature's glowing-amber eyes, looming close.

It whispered to her, "Seven steps back in time...lies the source of all your nightmares. Walk with me."

Siobhan fell into an ocean of memories. They poured over her, and she drowned.

THE STORY CONTINUES in *A Practical Guide to Sorcery Book VI: A Builder of Dreams.*

Preorder it now: https://geni.us/BODEBWide

IF YOU WOULD LIKE access to:

- The chance to read the latest pre-release chapters of the upcoming book as I finish them
- Illustrated excerpts from Siobhan's grimoire and portraits of the characters
- Exclusive short stories/bonus chapters/deleted scenes not available elsewhere
- Over 105 hours of audiobook content, including all exclusive bonus content in audio
- And other story-related goodies and opportunities…

Consider supporting me on Patreon:
https://www.patreon.com/AzaleaEllis

GLOSSARY OF MAGICAL TERMS

Aberrant

Thaumaturges who have lost control of the magic they channel, but instead of dying, have been changed. They are usually much more magically powerful than they were in life, and almost always have physical mutations. Some Aberrants merely mutate into a dangerous beast-like being, rabid for death and destruction. Some mutate into grotesque or phantasmagorical forms, and have esoteric magical effects. Some mutations remain minor, while the mind and powers are twisted insidiously.

Uniformly, an Aberrant is no longer human, having lost their previous thoughts and desires. Almost all Aberrants are malicious, even those with seemingly benign effects. It is believed one is more likely to break and become an Aberrant with a corrupted Will from casting immoral magics.

Abyss Chasm

A deep fissure stretching across northern Osham, from which magical beasts crawl out in large numbers.

Adder stone

A stone with a hole worn through the middle by natural means, it is said that adder stones impart clarity of mind and vision, and one can look through the hole to reveal illusions. Useful on their own, or as a component in spells.

Adhel juice

Mixed with honey, it creates a strong sticky substance. It can be cleared through applying oil.

Adze

A magical insectoid creature most prevalent in the few areas of the Tataroc Desert with year-round water—and static communities—the adze is a nocturnal bloodsucker. Upon its hatching, the first person with an eligible disease that the adze drinks from will be cured, as the adze absorbs it, but after that all other victims will instead be infected by its bite. Each time a disease is absorbed, it is added to the adze's collection and passed on along with the others. This can lead quickly to the annihilation of entire communities, making the adze one of the most feared magical beasts. Anyone who hatches one is to be put to death, along with all those who knew and did not stop them.

Alchemy

A ritual form of spellcasting that uses organic and inorganic components to create magical concoctions. The most common method of performing alchemy is through the use of a cauldron to create potions, philtres, draughts, and tinctures. It is the least expensive way to save a particular magic for instant use at a later time, but not the most efficient way. As with all ritual spells, the magic woven into alchemical concoctions is semi-permanent.

All-purpose antidote potion

A mild antidote to common poisons and venoms, the all-purpose antidote is best used on mild irritants, or to buy time for a more thorough solution to serious toxins. It can be used in lieu of a sobering potion to diminish the effects of alcohol.

Animation spell

Animation spells give temporary and false life to an inanimate object, such as in the case of the Glasshopper's eponymous confections.

Anti-anxiety Potion

Also known as a calming potion, this is a weaker and less addictive version of the elixir of peace. The University infirmary keeps a large amount on hand for students struggling with stress.

Anti-coughing philtre

Suppresses the urge to cough. As coughing is often useful to clear liquid from the lungs, this philtre is used when there are extenuating circumstances, like broken ribs, that may cause more damage.

Arcanum
A magical institution, teaching "secrets" of magic and the arcane.

Artificery
A craft of magic that embeds a pre-cast spell in an object for later release, or enchantment—changing the object's state. Battle wands, light crystals, and self-cleaning chamber pots are examples of artifacts. Enchantments and Wards are a sub-set of Artificery.

Auger
A drilling artifact created in Osham. Though meant for mining and construction, it can also be utilized to brute-force wardbreak.

Autography spell
This spell, frequently used in divination, allows the user to free write without conscious thought.

Avery Park
An area of greenery around southwest Gilbratha.

Avis Siverling
A court sorcerer who served the Krell line and married a daughter of King Krell.

Ball of light spell
Causes a spherical section of the air to glow with the illusion of a ball of light. Brightness, color, size, and location can be controlled.

Banshee
A humanoid magical creature that is dangerous to humans, and attacks with their voice through incapacitating screams and songs with a soporific effect.

Banshee's Breath
A battle philtre that creates a swirling storm that shrieks like the deadly wail of the banshees it was named for. While not deadly, the philtre may cause hearing loss and destruction within its area of effect.

Bark skin potion
Grows a protective layer of bark over the skin of the drinker, while still allowing them most of their range of motion. While not as strong as plate mail armor, it is much lighter, and more effective than chainmail against atmospheric attacks. When damaged, chunks of bark will fall off, which can be useful against spreading attacks like rotting curses or acid.

Battle wand
A wand-shaped artifact charged with offensive spells. For law enforcement, this is most commonly a stunning spell.

BCE
Before the Current Era.

Beacon spell
An esoteric spell that creates an invisible and untraceable tracking mark.

Beamshell tincture
A highly addictive magical potion that infuses the user with energy, often used to treat narcolepsy or insomnia. Beamshell creates an energy debt, and addicts frequently push through it until they collapse, starved and dehydrated. It's even riskier for thaumaturges, with high chances of Will-strain.

Beast core
Beast cores, which resemble raw gems, are harvested from dead magical beasts, and can be used to power spells in place of other sources of energy. They come in many different colors, though the color itself is not as important as the brightness and clarity, with brighter and clearer cores being easier to draw energy from.

Beast cores contain a total energy value of thousands of thaums, up to millions of thaums, and are generally rated either by their total energy value, or their per-second capacity if they were drained completely over the course of an hour.

When drained, beast cores will shatter and crumble, and cannot be recharged. Due to this, they are a rather expensive source of power, and are most commonly used for emergencies, for high-power spells that make it inconvenient to use lesser sources of power, or by those who have the coin to spend in exchange for convenience.

Beast cores become exponentially more expensive as their quality increases, similar to celerium.

Beast king

A figure shrouded in mystery and fear, the beast king is sleeping in Silva Erde, deep below the ground. While details about him are vague, diviners consistently find that if he wakes from his long sleep, calamity will follow.

Berserker potion

Temporarily increases a soldier's performance at the cost of some serious side effects, including addiction.

Bewitchment hex

Draws the attention and interest of the victim.

Bini frog

A magical amphibian often found in northern peat bogs, when under duress or unable to find others of their species, the Bini frog will change sexes, allowing themselves to lay eggs as a female and then fertilize them as a male. Notably, their male form has corrosive skin, a defensive which may have led to an initial imbalance of sexes and required this adaptation.

Black star sapphire

A gem that can be used (as can many gems) as a Conduit. It is not as robust as celerium. As components, star sapphires can be used in space-bending spells, and it is said that a black star sapphire was used in a spell to travel within and through shadows faster than any mortal could otherwise move.

Blight-type Aberrant

These Aberrants spread their anomalous effect, physically or otherwise, expanding their area of influence. If allowed to get out of control, they can cause true devastation. The first priority for this type of Aberrant is containment.

Blood clotting potion

Poured on a wound, clots blood and can stop excessive blood loss. It can allow someone to wait till medical attention arrives when otherwise they might bleed out. Not typically considered a battle potion, because it does not have offensive effects.

Blood Emperor

The Blood Emperor was the leader of the Third Empire, also known as the Blood Empire. His invading forces, from an unknown land beyond the northern ice oceans, conquered the continent about three hundred years ago. His empire was eventually overthrown, but his policies shaped much of modern society even after the Third Empire's downfall. However, atrocities committed in the name of learning and power caused a severe backlash against all forms of blood magic and its practitioners.

Blood print vow

A spell that binds two or more parties to an agreement spoken while casting, bound by a thumbprint of blood. If at least one of the vowers cannot cast magic, a third party binder must be present to do so.

Blood-regeneration potion

Boosts blood regeneration, but takes time and places strain on the body.

Bogles

Known for disguising themselves as scarecrows or other inanimate objects when spotted, bogles may cause mischief to human homes and settlements, but rarely serious harm.

Brillig

A powerful race with strong affinity to magic, now extinct, or close to it. It is said that they created the Black Wastes.

Caidan's Theorem

If distance is measured in meters, a divination spell with the base cost B will require B x distance/100 $\wedge$ (B/100) thaums to cast.

Calming spell

Forces calm and docility on the target.

Carnagore

Myrddin's most famous self-charging artifact, a horse made of white metal, who he rode into battle. The name Carnagore has roots in the words "hooves of dawn."

Cat's cough

An herb. Commonly smoked, it is addictive and gives a raspy, deep voice over time.

Cataclysm

An apocalyptic event that destroyed civilization over ten thousand years ago, and which is still shrouded in mystery.

Chameleon spell

Allows a non-living object to partially blend in with its surroundings.

Charybdis Gulf

The sea inlet that bisects the main area of Gilbratha from the Lilies—the rich area where many of the nobles and socialites live—to the east. The Charybdis Gulf is dangerous, containing magical water beasts that will drown a swimmer and even capsize small fishing boats, yet despite this remains a large source of income and food, especially for the poorer citizens.

Cinder Stag

A powerful Aberrant that is contained within a sundered zone, the Cinder Stag still manages to affect the world outside the sundered zone with karmic flames of retribution that can follow a chain of cause-and-effect back to its source.

Circle

Facilitates the three main elements of magic. It places a physical boundary around a spherical domain controlled by the thaumaturge, signifying that the things within are theirs to trade away and change as they wish.

Cockatrice

Two-legged dragon-like creature with a rooster's head. (And more or less the shape of a chicken.) Weasels are their natural enemy. Can be the familiar of a witch.

Cold box artifact

Sometimes referred to as an ice box, this is an artifact which keeps the contents placed within it chilled or frozen by siphoning out their heat.

Compass divination spell

Uses two halves of a spelled, linked bone disk as a sympathetic beacon and a stick with one burnt end. Using one half of the bone, the burnt end of the stick will point toward the other half, like a compass.

Comprehensive Compendium of Components

A restricted book that contains its namesake, including components that are illegal and unethical.

Concussion-modified fireball spell

Adds a force effect to the fireball spell, similar to an explosion.

Concussive blast spell

Shoots ball of force which expands and weakens with distance, but can cause severe damage to a human (particularly their internal organs) or even break through walls at close range. It is often visible as a waver or fogginess in the air, but much less conspicuous than a fireball or stunning spell.

Conduit

Channels the thaumaturgic energy being converted as a spell is cast. For most sorcerers, this is a celerium crystal, which is resistant to the destructive effects of channeling magic. Witches may use their familiars as Conduits, and those sorcerers who cannot afford celerium may use lesser gems, such as diamonds or sapphires.

Contact stunning spell

Set into a ring artifact, releases the spell on firm, sudden contact, like a punch.

Continue-motion spell

A complex, finicky spell that allows the caster to demonstrate an action as one of the inputs of the spell. The spell will continue this action, *exactly*, for as long as it is empowered. It is good for things like stirring a pot continuously, spinning thread, or weaving cloth, which require relatively simple, repetitive movements.

Coppers

Law enforcement, named for the copper nails in the soles of their boots, the distinctive sound of which announces their approach wherever they go.

Craft

Specific path of magic: Sorcerer, Artificer, Witch, Magician, Shaman, Animist, Gestura, etc.

Deafening hex

Causes deafness, usually temporary, though some variations will persist for a period of time after the caster stops focusing on the hex. Some variations can be used to some effect against a banshee in place of a vibration-canceler.

Devil

They possess living beings.

Dingleberry bushes

Dingleberry bushes are named for their small, hard brown fruits that smell like feces and rot even before they fall to the ground.

Dipsa

An Aberrant that wiped out an entire city and poisoned the land such that a sundered zone was required to contain the effects. It holds the record for the second-highest death count.

Disintegration mine

A magical land mine developed in the Haze War.

Dissolving tincture

A concentrated alchemical concoction that will dissolve other substances it comes into contact with, the dissolving tincture has many variants that can be adapted to the type of material the alchemist wishes to dissolve. Similar to a strong acid, but more versatile.

Distagram

A long-distance messaging artifact recently created by a University graduate that operates by using different frequency bands.

Diviner's sight

Special magical sight of the divination realm, which reveals that which might not be seen with the normal eye. It is a catch-all term that includes any ocular enhancements, such as the ability to see in the dark.

Doorjamb alarm ward

A small ward spell, carved into the underside of a door, will alert the caster when the door is opened.

Dorienne invisibility spell

A spell that uses the self-camouflaging dorienne fish to create true invisibility through which light can pass. The dorienne fish itself sees through its skin and adjusts its pigment on one side of its body to what it sees on the other to appear invisible.

Dowsing artifact

An artifact composed of two glass and copper spheres which use divination to try to locate an object or element. Siobhan uses her dowsing artifact to activate her anti-divination wards and move about the city unnoticed.

Dragon scales

A magical component sourced from the notoriously contrary, spiteful, and difficult creatures.

Drake

A miniature dragon creature, the size of a house cat. Not as intelligent or powerful. Can be the familiar of a witch.

Draught of borrowed gills

This concoction allows someone to breath underwater by dropping a small, living fish into a mucousy concoction and then gulping the whole thing down whole. The fish is kept alive within a bubble of potion within the stomach for a few minutes, during which time the fish's ability to filter oxygen from water is transferred to the drinker's lungs.

When the fish dies and the draught's effect wears off, the drinker must expel the water from their lungs quickly to avoid drowning. Often, use of this potion in dirty water can lead to complications and long-term side effects, so it should not be used recreationally.

Dream-walking

Often practiced by shamans, it is a form of divination that sends their consciousness into the dream of another, most often for exploration or healing purposes.

Dreamless sleep spell

Keeps one from dreaming, using crystal and eagle feathers as components, and cast on the pillow Siobhan uses, or anywhere under her head. Uses alcohol and herb tincture as the Circle, which evaporates quickly and isn't uncomfortable to sleep on.

Dryad

A creature of living wood, shaped like a humanoid woman. They come in different sub-species of trees, and can be very small when young. Sometimes they disguise themselves as trees before the unwary or unobservant, and short bursts of activity are often followed by long periods of "sleep."

Dueling board

A game where the pieces shoot fake spells at each other and dodge attacks under the control of the players.

Dysentery sustaining potion

Diluted in large amounts of water, will keep a patient with diarrhea or dysentery hydrated with a small amount of calories and the immediately necessary electrolytes and minerals, and slightly slows the rate of expulsion, allowing absorption.

Earth disintegration and stone creation spell

One of Professor Lacer's practice exercises. Dirt or stone can be turned to sand and back again to stone using either transmutation, which creates the effect through natural processes, or through duplicative transmogrification, which copies the properties of existing material.

Earth-aspected weta

Magical beast with a very tough hide.

Elcan irises

A deadly, flesh-eating plant with purple-streaked flowers whose long, tapered petals open and turn to follow prey as it passes, releasing sweet-smelling pollen into the air. They lure their prey with their beauty and the soporific properties of their pollen.

Eldritch-type Aberrant

A rare and highly dangerous aberrant whose anomalous effects are based on abstract concepts.

Elemental Planes

The five known Elemental Planes are accessible through planar portal spells from the mundane plane, where humans and other mundane races live. Each Elemental Plane corresponds to an element: Radiance, Fire, Air, Water, and Earth. Creatures, plants, and even the water and soil from the Elemental Planes will be imbued with the energy of their plane, and are powerful spell-casting components. Each Elemental Plane has sapient creatures, some of which are humanoid and can even cross breed with humans.

Elementals

Beings from the Elemental Planes. On the mundane plane (Earth), they are most often encountered as the familiars of witches, who use them as a Conduit to channel magic. When sapient and humanoid, they have specific labels.

Radiance—Angels

Fire—Demons

Air—Sylphides

Water—Undine

Earth—Erdgeist

Elixir of euphoria

An alchemical concoction which, in low doses, combats depression, but is more often sold recreationally for the eponymous euphoria. Highly addictive.

Elixir of peace

Imparts a sense of well-being, and can be used in small doses to combat depression and anxiety, or for its recreational effects in larger doses. It is used in war to give soldiers who are dying some peace in their last moments.

Eltrocus

A powerful Aberrant that the Red Guard is unable to fully neutralize.

Enenra

Magical beasts native to the East, enenra are creatures that seem to be made from smoke and tattered cloth, said to be born from bonfires and visible only to those of pure heart and mind.

Energy-reflecting spell

A general-purpose ward. A more expensive and inefficient defense than setting wards against more specific spells or incidents.

Enkennad's draught of shadowed concealment

A powerful potion that allows the user to disappear from view, blending subtly with the shadows.

Erlkings

Their name coming from the words "alder king" the erlkings are a magical creature found in woodland areas, sometimes conflated with the fey by the ignorant. They are known to secrete poisonous substances from their hands, the most potent of which allows them to kill with a simple touch, and to enjoy chasing children and lost travelers who have intruded on their domain.

Erythrean horse

Horse with partial magical lineage. They are extremely expensive, but don't look much different from a normal horse.

Etherwood leaves

A luxury leaf for smoking. They are dark blue. The smoke is smooth and calming, great for blowing smoke rings, but nonaddictive.

Ever-inking pen artifact

Comes as a set with an inkwell. Spelled to automatically refill the ink cartridge of the pen with ink from the inkwell whenever not in use. More expensive ones refill based on the rate of expenditure, and some very expensive ones maintain a folded space within the pen's ink cartridge, so the user never needs worry about their inkwell running dry.

Fabric cutting spell

This spell creates a short-range slicing blade of air that extends outward in an arc, the shape of which can be controlled to some degree by the caster's Will. Unlike many similar spells, it doesn't require the target to be within the Circle, as it uses compressed air as the cutting edge. At longer distances the cutting edge, visible as a faintly glowing shimmer in the air, degrades severely.

With practice and enough power, it can be used to overcome the inherent magical barrier that living creatures possess, and injure a human or animal.

Fever reducing potion/balm

Cools the head, with some cooling to the body as well, along with pain relief. Encourages comfort, allows sleep, and should be given in conjunction with a sustaining draught.

Fey

A powerful race with strong affinity to magic, now close to extinction. They were supposedly so agile they could dance between raindrops without ever being hit.

Fey flowers

A fluorescent flower prized as a component for its rarity and power.

Fiend-type Aberrant

These Aberrants have monstrous physical mutations and use physical attacks. Any magical effects are touch-based. These are the most common type of Aberrant, and generally the weakest.

Finger bone divination

Human finger bones can be used in (illegal) divination, after being processed and etched with symbols and glyphs. The diviner will shake them while casting the divination, throw them, and then read the spell's output in the way they have fallen, with certain glyphs in certain positions or crossing others. Depending on the amount of bones and what output options have been etched into them, this type of divination can have nuance and impart a greater amount of information than similar methods like dice-throwing or card reading.

Fireball spell

Shoots a ball of fire at about 12 meters per second.

Fleetfoot potion

Fractionally increases movement speed, but not reaction speed.

Flesh-fusing potion

A more powerful version of the skin-knitting salve, this potion is meant to seal larger wounds, ideally after the use of the blood-clotting potion.

Flicker-feather bird

Small birds that blink in and out of visibility with every flap of their wings.

Forest of Nod

The mythical forest that is said to be the center of the world, if it ever existed, the Forest of Nod's location has been lost to time. Some suggest that it still exists, beyond the known lands civilization was able to reclaim after the Cataclysm, and some insist that it is, in fact, one of any number of forests that now go by a different name.

Fortner's

A high class, bespoke clothing shop.

Free-casting

Casting magic at will, without the stabilizing external Word of a physical spell array, a ritual, or special movements. The Word, and sometimes the Circle as well, is instead held solely in the mind. This feat is extremely difficult, and only a few are proficient in it.

Garden of wonders

An element of a children's tale, which the University Menagerie seems to exemplify.

Gasping-tentacles spell

A spell which creates temporary tentacles growing from a solid, nonliving surface. Used to bind or obstruct movement from a distance, and often employed as a nonlethal method of detainment. Gone wrong, can strangle a victim to death.

Gestura

A sect of thaumaturges who practice a different type of craft, controlling the elements through sympathetic connections to their body movements. They are slowly dying out due to the difficulty in learning the craft and its lack of versatility.

Glow slime

A phosphorescent magical slime that slowly releases the light it absorbs during the daytime or from decaying plants with an eerie glow through the night.

Glow spell

Perhaps the most rudimentary light output spell possible, can cause an object to let off a diffuse glow.

Gold duplication spell

A duplicative transmogrification spell that copies a source of matter. As with most attempts to create matter through magic, only the most skilled thaumaturges can create a truly perfect copy that will have the same magical properties as the original, and thus duplicated gold or other substances are often worth less than the authentic originals.

Golden apple

Fruit from a magical tree that closely resembles a gold-skinned apple, and are said to improve organ function and thus increase a person's lifespan.

Gregorian snail

Magical animal. Mucus can be used as a thickening agent in most salves and lotions, especially those meant for the face.

Gremian

A small, humanoid stick creature that desperately wishes to fly once again, and goes so far as to nest in the trees and crack eggs on their bark-like skin to feel closer to birds. They are an excellent familiar for a beginner witch to practice a binding contract with.

Group proprioception potion

It allows everyone who drank from the same batch instinctively know where the others were for a short period of time. Its main component is a magical sea lichen that connects and disconnects any singular part of itself at will, still somehow communicating with the greater whole to capture prey and then confine it until it starved to death.

Grubb's barrier spell

A weak barrier spell that only protects against physical projectiles, with a minimum requirement of under 200 thaums to cast.

Gryphon

Creature with the head and wings of an eagle, with the body, legs, and tail of a lion. Can be domesticated and flown.

Guld fish

Minnow-sized fish that glint as if they are made of precious metals polished to a high sheen.

Gust spell

Creates a simple gust of wind, with the size and speed depending on the size of the Circle and the amount of power fed to it.

Hag

A magical humanoid. They have a natural predilection to the dark, and good night vision. They have some facility with hexagon/hexagram spells, dealing with balance. Hags who integrate with society may sell good luck talismans (or cursed objects.)

Hangover-relief draught

Taken in doses of a liter or more, this draught rehydrates, replenishes electrolytes, and mitigates the pain of a hangover. The University infirmary stocks many doses.

Harrow Hill Penitentiary

Gilbratha's jail, a stout stone building in the shape of a cross, within a circular wall that encloses the grounds.

Headache-relieving salve

Minty. An alchemical concoction that relieves headache pain and helps to rejuvenate the senses.

Healing potion

Generalized healing potions, of which there are many different variations of different strengths and capabilities, are an extremely effective method to preserve an injured or ill patient's life. They can be used for most types of wounds or illnesses, and are both convenient and practical. However, due to the price of components—many of which are from the Plane of Light—and the abundance of magical energy packed into these potions, they are expensive.

Hellfire

Is sometimes bright neon green.

Hemorrhaging curse

This curse causes the target's blood vessels to rupture and encourages excessive, forceful blood loss. It can sometimes be recognized by the shape of its glowing force as it travels.

Henrik-Thompson

A measure of scale for maximum Will capacity. It is measured by a crystal ball in an array that filters incoming energy and outputs a portion of it as light through the glowing crystal. It's the most widely-used metric, likely due to the fact that Will-capacity is the easiest to test, and often shows correlation to the overall caliber of a thaumaturge's Will. The brighter the light, the more power (thaums) is being channeled per second.

Homunculus

Very small people, who outwardly seem indistinguishable from humans, but are argued to be a different species due to their facility with certain magics.

Human fingernails

A component in some spells, human fingernails are illegal due to the restrictions against blood magic.

Humphries' adapting solution

An alchemical concoction that can be spelled directly into the veins to take the place of blood in a blood-loss emergency. Expensive, and the shelf-life isn't super long, so it may not always be on hand. Can also be used to keep creatures from the Plane of Water alive on the mundane plane, which was its original purpose.

Hydra

Multi-headed snake. The number of heads ranges from two to nine, with more heads generally indicating a more powerful, intelligent creature, as information processing and bodily processes are divided among the heads based on their individual priorities and specialties.

Ice lion

A predatory, large, shaggy cat that lives near the northern ice oceans.

Ignore pain spell

Muffles pain slightly, allows mind to detach from the focus pain draws, effects wear off quickly once spell is released, but it can allow someone to prepare to heal themselves. Recommended strongly against using this to do things like set bones or put sockets back into place, in case the sudden shock of pain causes the caster to lose control of the spell. Muffles pain by about 15%, so of moderate usefulness. May be good for exercise pain. Esoteric magic.

Impotence curse

A curse that removes the victim's ability to successfully complete intercourse, either through removing their libido, or suppressing their physical ability to copulate.

Improved hearing spell

An esoteric spell that uses hands cupped behind the ears to gather and direct amplified sound, and thus improve selective hearing.

Information collating spell

A spell used to search through, organize, and classify information in a wide range of documents.

Injury-protection ward

Makes physical damage less likely over a set diameter. Very expensive, but nebulous and thus not very powerful. Still can make a difference, either over time, or in dangerous circumstances.

Jentil

Giants, who are known for building megalithic monuments.

Kaiseki Ryori

A decadent, luxurious, high class dining establishment specializing in Eastern cuisine. They have many private rooms and are owned by the Nightmare Pack.

King Krell

The ruler of Lenore before the Blood Emperor, who had a daughter who married the court sorcerer, Avis Siverling.

Kitsune

A sometimes fox, sometimes woman. In human form, the kitsune will still have her tails, more depending on how old and powerful she is, up to nine. They often use their tails to cover their bodies, wrapping around it in place of clothing, and are considered seductively attractive, though they do not appear often in Siobhan's part of the world.

Knave Knoll

A jail that temporarily housed the Morrow prisoners for the Verdant Stags and fell in the attack orchestrated by the Architects of Khronos.

Kreidae spider

A magical creature known for stealth and ambushes. Its silk is highly coveted for its transparency and use in camouflage or invisibility cloaks.

Kuth

A small country to the east of the Tataroc Desert and south of Silva Erde.

Kuthian frog

Has sedative saliva, which is dried, powdered, and used as a component in stunning spells. Upon release from the spell, the treated saliva quickly degrades and becomes inert.

Landrum's nourishing draught

As with many spells, there are multiple variations of the nourishing draught.

Should be diluted in large amounts of water, which will thicken with the concoction. It contains vitamins, minerals, and electrolytes, as well as some complex sugars/starches. When given frequently, will keep the patient hydrated and with the resources their body needs to continue fighting. The nourishing draught should be created over low heat, to avoid killing the vitamins. Sometimes, it is then dehydrated for long-term storage.

Some versions also induce repeated swallowing, for patients who are insensate and cannot wake to drink. For those with extended nausea, some versions can also help them keep something down, though not stop diarrhea.

Laughing poppy

A component in a sedative potion which is known to cause allergic reactions, preferred for its ability to tranquilize without causing depression.

Light crystal

A non-celerium crystal made into an artifact spelled to release light on command. The rich use them in place of candles or lamps, as they are much brighter and require less maintenance. But, though they also last longer than a candle or lamp, they are expensive enough that the common person cannot afford to buy one, even if it would save them money in the long run.

Light Sacrifice

Light can be used as a source of magical power just like heat, matter, and kinetic force. Converting light within an area to magical power will create an area of darkness, as the light is absorbed before it can pass through or be reflected.

Light-show spell

Cast on an object, this spell creates many pulsing lights of different colors, and is meant to draw the eye and be visually enchanting. Good for traveling performers, distracting wildlife, or to cast on the harlequin above a baby's crib

Limb-regrowing potion

A newer, specialized type of regeneration potion that uses lizard components, such as that of the axolotl, to regrow missing limbs.

Lineage test spell

A divination spell that uses a piece of the target to confirm the existence of other members of their bloodline over several weeks. It is known to give unreliable results, and does not by itself allow one to track down the supposed offspring.

Lino-Wharton messenger spell

A power spell with several pre-requisites. It binds a raven to a controller, allowing the controller to speak through the raven at a distance to transmit messages, or to complete simple tasks.

Liquid fire potion

When exposed to air, this potion catches fire.

Liquid stone potion

Expands like an aerosol foam and hardens quickly upon contact with air. Can be used as a barrier or a splint for broken bones, among other things. Not permeable to air, or malleable once hardened, so it can suffocate if it lands on the face. Liquid stone's expansion is purposefully inhibited when in contact with living flesh so that those who carry it do not accidentally entomb themselves if a vial breaks accidentally.

It is softer than normal stone, similar with a similar durability as sandstone.

Loimae, the Plague

An Aberrant with the highest recorded death count, at approximately eight hundred thousand people.

Loomis anti-awareness field

A spell, in artifact form on Siobhan's heirloom Conduit ring, that dissuades people from noticing or remembering a small object.

Lore-master

A scholar who focuses on the stories of old, on the little-known or forgotten facets of magic and the creatures who use it.

Lotus flowers/bulbs

These flowers grow in the mud. Each night, they return to the mud, and then miraculously re-bloom in the morning. In transmogrification, they signify rebirth, self-regeneration, cleansing, and enlightenment.

Lugubrious

A powerful Aberrant.

Lung-sealing philtre

When breathed in, this philtre creates a sealed bubble inside the lung, which can apply internal pressure to a puncture wound and keep someone from drowning in their own blood.

Lycanthrope

A type of skin-walker, lycanthropes take on and off the skin of a wolf, transforming into the animal at will. Divested of their wolf skins, they lose the ability to transform. A Lycanthrope's animal skin can be used to give a thaumaturge a lesser version of the animal-transformation skill practiced by the skinwalkers themselves, or as a component in taming and binding spells.

Magician

A person who uses magical artifacts rather than cast spells themselves. Often derided as scammers, charlatans, and unworthy by "true" thaumaturges. An artificer who uses their own artifacts is not considered a magician.

Malediction

A curse spoken with a wronged person's dying breath brings long-term misfortune to the cursed party. These are considered baseless superstitions by most.

Mandrake root

A root plant whose tuber takes the shape of a humanoid being, and which can incapacitate and even kill with their cry if pulled from the muffling earth. They grow more expensive with age, and can be difficult to keep alive. They enjoy being sung to, and may die if not given enough personal attention even if conditions are otherwise optimal. The mandrake root's similarities to the human form make it valuable for spells that would otherwise need a human, such as simulacrum or surrogate spells, and they are most well known for their ability to receive, as a surrogate, a curse transferred from a human victim. They are also used in hallucinogenic spells and concoctions.

Map-based location divining spell

A divination spell that guides a drop of spelled mercury over a place-anchored map to find a location based on a sympathetic connection.

Memory spiders

A magical spider whose web, consumed whole without missing a single strand of silk, is said to be able to bring forth lost memories.

Mending spell

Repairs mundane objects, but requires all the pieces as well as components that would otherwise be required to mend the objects by hand. The mending spell is able to achieve somewhat finer control and dexterity than one might with their hands and fingers.

Mermaid

Mermaids are magical cephalopods. They lure prey by sticking tentacles above water and making them look like a human woman, who asks for help. When the victim gets too close, the "mermaid" suddenly comes apart into a mass of tentacles that grab them and drag them into the water to be eaten.

Metanite

A powerful Aberrant that the Red Guard has been unable to destroy or contain. It is a void-black form, which destroys everything it touches, but moves very slowly. The Red Guard uses space magic to adjust its path and evacuation to keep people safe from it.

Mimeo-motion spell

A more complex version of the continue-motion spell, the mimeo-motion spell allows duplication of the copied motion in multiple places. It is used most commonly for mass-producing books.

Mind-muddling jinx

Causes the victim trouble reading, comprehending, and focusing. As with all harmful spells classified as jinxes, it is not permanent, and cast lightly, the victim may not realize they have been affected.

Mirrored healing spell/Flesh-mirroring spell

Using blood of the injured person as a Sacrifice, this spell can mold flesh and bone to match the mirrored side of the body, and thus heal injuries without the need for rare and expensive components.

Uses glyphs "blood," "mirror," and then the physical part in need of mirrored healing, like "tooth." One large Circle around the whole area, and then two inner Circles, meeting in the middle, one which has the good side and one the injured side. Uses a pentagram inside a pentagon, for the combination of transmutation and transmogrification this spell requires. Relies more on the Will and Sacrifice than the clarity or complexity of the written Word. Requires a detailed, focused image of what the caster wants to happen. Using the wounded person's own blood is especially efficient.

Mnemonic-link tracking spell

Creates a sympathetic link between an object and the target, but depends on the caster's extreme familiarity with the target, and best augmented by an item that has a direct connection to the target.

Moon-orb weaver

A spider prized for its shocking strength, beauty, and efficiency in channeling magic.

Moonbeams & fairy wings

Moonbeams and fairy wings, harvested (from the Menagerie) at night, have mind-altering (recreational drug) effects.

Moondew drosera

This carnivorous magical plant is bioluminescent, and preys primarily on insects and other small creatures. It resembles a succulent during the day, and at night, its spines drip with glowing mucous that lures creatures into its sticky grasp.

Moonseeds

Commonly used in their dried form, similar to pepper, moonseeds are berries from a twining vine. The moonseed vine is nocturnal, growing off-white berries that resemble the pitted moon once dehydrated.

Myrddin

An extraordinarily powerful sorcerer who lived over a thousand years before. He has many incredible feats to his name, some based in reality and others in fiction, and has become enough of a household name that he's occasionally used in curses, E.G. "Myrddin's crusty black butthole."

Mystic-type Aberrant

A long-range subset of Blight and Nightmare-type. These Aberrants effect people at range, often with methods that are difficult to trace.

Nightmare-type Aberrant

This type of Aberrant is the most difficult to deal with, as they use stealth, memetic control, or subversion.

Okora's instant cottage

A spell that raises material from the ground to create a small cottage in the shape of a small model cottage used as a component. Size is dependent on power input and spell array parameters. It is easiest to cast with loose material that can be compacted together, such as snow or mud.

Orbs and Amulets

The Conduit shop at the north end of Waterside market

Osham

A neighboring country to Lenore, known for its innovations in machinery and artifacts.

Osher tree

Young sapling that can uproot itself and move short distances. Sometimes confused for a dryad, but an osher has no humanoid form and is not considered to be intelligent.

Output detachment

The practice of generating spell output outside of the bounds of the circle and an important step on the way to free-casting.

Paired movement ward

When the ring holding a banner to the base of the spell is ripped away, the sympathetically linked counterpart held elsewhere also detaches. Spell must be cast ahead of time, with both halves of the pair together.

Paneth

A bustling city and popular tourist destination just to the north of Gilbratha.

Paper bird spell

Used to send letters or messages. The paper birds are spelled to take flight and deliver themselves to set destination or recipients. Unsuitable to fly in heavy winds or rain. They are created from special ingredients that make Siobhan feel they are not as practical as she suspected.

The special paper used to make them requires flicker-feathers from the sparrow-like bird of the same name, which the University cultivates in the Menagerie.

Password puzzle artifact

In the Night Market, inside a component shop, a stone puzzle disk that must be solved with magic to make the center rise up, allowing access to the warehouse in back and the half-troll, Harvester.

Pendragon corps

The High Crown's personal guards and military force, kitted in the most expensive protection and battle spells that money can buy. Fighting against them is considered treasonous.

Pendragon Palace

The home of the High Crown, the head of the Thirteen Crown Families and leader of the country of Lenore. It is built atop the white cliffs, to the northeast of Gilbratha.

Perimeter alarm ward

Alerts the caster within when a perimeter has been breached.

Philtre of darkness

After brewing, when this concoction is suddenly exposed to air (e.g. when the bottle is smashed) the roiling liquid within bursts into clouds of magical darkness, which not even powerful night-vision can penetrate.

Phoenix ashes

An incredibly rare spell component, the ashes of a phoenix that has reached the end of one of its many life cycles are used to incubate the phoenix's egg as it rebirths itself. They are used in powerful healing and fire spells, and even supposed spells that can affect one's destiny. Most famously, they were said to have been used by Myrddin to resurrect his recently-deceased lover. They sell for about a hundred gold crowns per gram, and are highly illegal, as phoenixes are on the verge of extinction due to overhunting.

Piercing spell

A shaped spell that, unlike the area-effect concussive blast spell, is focused on penetrative power, and can gouge out a few inches of stone in a narrow diameter.

Pixie

Humanoid creatures with very delicate, multi-petaled flesh wings that constantly regenerate, dropping dandruff and little peels of dry skin. This "pixie dust" is an expensive magical component, and many humans keep them to harvest it. They are intelligent and mischievous, even sometimes malicious, prone to irritation and insults.

Planar divination-diverting ward

Protects against divination. The recipient will feel pressure under any type of divination/scrying attempt, and can add their Will to the artifact's inherent shielding capabilities to divert stronger and more determined attempts. The ward does not directly oppose a scrying spell, but turns aside, deflects, and hides instead, using its connection to the five Elemental Planes. The effects may also spill into the physical world, making it harder for people to notice and focus on the user.

When actively diverting, the embedded disks may be painful as they consume the user's blood for power.

Planar portal

A portal to one of the other Planes.

Plane of Darkness

The undiscovered sixth Elemental Plane, the Plane of Darkness, is a hypothetical plane that has long been hypothesized to balance the Plane of Radiance, creating an Elemental hexagram. However, despite innumerable attempts to access the plane, it remains entirely theoretical.

Plane of Radiance

One of the five known Elemental Planes, the Plane of Radiance hosts the element of Light in its many forms *and connotations*. Creatures and plants of the radiant element are very valuable spell components, and the most powerful, sentient Elementals from the Plane of Radiance are often called angels. The Plane of Radiance has sympathetic connections to the ideas of light, cleanliness, knowledge, strict justice, and healing. Excessive exposure has been known to cause toxicity.

Planes-damned

A curse word, referring to the Elemental Planes.

Portable office

A wooden block that unfolds into a chair and desk made out of hundreds of smaller segments, created by Liza. She sells them for ninety gold.

Portable shield artifact

A small golden sphere with legs that blooms with a semi-opaque shielding spell that isolates the person nearest to it.

Potion of feather-fall

It uses a (preferably white) feather as a main component, and seems to reduce the effects of gravity on the imbiber, allowing them to jump from a high place without injury.

Potion of moonlight sizzle

A potion that lets off a soft blue, bright glow that mimics the light of a full moon from its sizzling bubbles when the bottle is shaken. It's powerful enough to illuminate a small room on its own, and when sold at a reasonable price, much more affordable than light crystals or candles.

Potion of night vision

Allows one to see more clearly in the dark, in monochrome.

Prognos

Skilled in divination, have a single large eye in the middle of their head. It's said the best prognos diviners can see into the past to discover the identity of a criminal, but that's a myth. They are simply perceptive. They mature slowly and have longer lives than most humans.

Purple lobster

A luxury food.

Puzzle band rings

A wedding ring, historically used to keep women from cheating on their husbands, with the thought that they would be unable take the ring off for their infidelities and then fit the ring back together in time to keep their misdeeds secret.

Quintessence of quicksilver

The powder of a potion boiled down into a solid and then crushed. It temporarily frenzies the mind, making you smarter and granting a liquid creativity. Gives the illusion of power and lowers inhibitions. The effects of a single dose last about six hours on those who haven't built up a tolerance, and the come-down crash lasts a day or two. Long-term users lose their ability to focus and display various memory problems, becoming dependent on quintessence of quicksilver to function normally.

Radiant explosive

An intensely powerful, burning and cleansing explosive using properties from the Elemental Plane of Radiance.

Radiant Maiden

The progenitor of the Order of the Radiant Maiden. She is a powerful Elemental from the Plane of Radiance. These humanoid, often-winged beings have been referred to as angels.

Raven summoning spell

A spell originally designed to summon the Raven Queen, which, instead appears to be a mild area-effect compulsion that summons nearby corvids.

Red Sage

A powerful Aberrant that is contained within a sundered zone, but still manages to meet people. It has three eyes, each of which are said to see the future. All prophecies that it gives come true, but it seems that the Red Sage can either choose who it meets through a sort of subtle summoning (and thus control the prophecies it gives) or it chooses what to prophecy—it can be bribed to give a better fortune. However, in coming true *all* prophecies cause great suffering and destruction, if not to the recipient, then to the people and world around the recipient. Two of its prophecies—and eyes—are in constant use, and ensure its continued existence and ability to affect the world. The Red Guard facilitates the prophecies from its third eye coming true to try and mitigate the damage, and attempts to control who can meet the Red Sage.

Refinement of the Nine Heavens
Originally mistranslated as "Nine Light Filters," this esoteric spell was developed by the gestura to absorb sunlight and to heal and repair the body and mind. It also claims to speed up the caster's recovery time, improve mental strength, and reduce the need for sleep and the chances of experiencing Will-strain.

Regeneration-boosting potion
This potion boosts the body's natural immune response, lending some of its power to boost the healing effect and taking the rest from the stored energy and nutrients of the injured person's body. It will struggle to fix anything larger than a small dagger wound, a bone fracture, or a hand-size burn. It takes time to work and is uncomfortable, and cannot be used in quick succession, but is much cheaper than a real healing potion.

Retreat at Willowdale
The Retreat is a long-term treatment center where people with magical damage can be housed safely or, ideally, rehabilitated and healed.

Revealing spell
Uncovers non-physical illusions and can see through non-magical darkness. Usually cast via a wand, issued to some coppers. A revealing spell shoots vibrational and magic waves, which penetrate and bounce back to the wand.

Reverse-scrying spell
A divination spell with the base of a map-based sympathetic divination, but which targets instead the other sympathetic end of the connection which is being used to scry. Used to find the finder, historically most often in warfare.

Revivifying potion
Boosts organ function and energy levels. Can be used for many different illnesses, but is expensive due to its high magical load.

Roc
An avian magical beast with a similar head shape to its smaller mundane counterpart, the ossifrage, adult rocs can achieve a wingspan of 140-180 feet. Their powerful wind magic allows them to fly at great heigh for long distances, even while carrying cargo. They often use wind magic to pummel and blow their prey to death.

Rune-inscribed basin
A basin for far-viewing, a type of divination that uses water to see distant places, generally from the point of view of another surface of water. The basin can be used to contact other powerful diviners if they cast at the same time, with the same intent. Far-viewing in this manner does not transmit sound.

Sacrifice
What you give up for the effect of a spell. It can be an object, like a blob of mud used to create a brick, or energy, like the heat from a flame. Components can have either a natural or a sympathetic link to the effects of the spell.

Scab-root
A twisted, gnarled root adorned with pustules that looks remarkably like an infected scab. It is a slow-growing, endangered plant from the southwestern region of the known lands, and contains nearly every possibly nutrient a human needs to survive. Its taste is as appetizing as its appearance suggests.

Scourge-type Aberrant

The most common classification of Aberrant, Scourge-types have a short to mid-range effect whose anomalous effect is clear, allowing quantification and elimination or containment.

Selby-Forman binding

A variation on conjuration/elemental binding used in the Second Empire.

Self-charging artifacts

Artifacts that contain the parameters to not only cast a spell, but to gather and transform the energy for that spell as part of their activation and release process. Creating a self-powered, or self-charging, artifact is a Grandmaster-level feat said to be pioneered by Myrddin, who supposedly came up with several methods, some of which have now been lost.

Self-powered artifacts cannot cast truly endless spells, as eventually the spell array breaks down—and more quickly with heavy use, but they are still widely coveted.

Self-cleaning chamber pot artifact

Cleans and dries the nether regions, then processes the waste, removing the liquid from fecal matter and dehydrating urine into a thick paste, which it stores in a sealed container for later removal. An auxiliary spell keeps the smell from filtering out away from the chamber pot.

Sempervivum apricus

A low-growing succulent plant from the Plane of Radiance. Its juicy leaves grow in complex rosettes, glimmering with tiny motes of light that travel beneath the semi-transparent skin along with the water and nutrients. It is technically a "low-light" plant in the Plane of Radiance, and thus is able to survive on the mundane plane in areas with bright sunlight and long days, or with the help of artificial sunlight sources. They propagate by sending out root offshoots that grow into new baby plants.

Sensory deprivation spell

A spell array developed by the Pendragon Corps to keep enemy spies from killing themselves upon capture. It separates the mind from the body and traps the victim in a black, empty void.

Shade (dust)

Shades are predatory creatures that take humanoid forms and live in barren, arid areas such as deserts, where they will prey on the sleeping or stalk the lost traveler until they collapse from exhaustion. They are made of a fine powder which can be gathered and used as an expensive magical component.

Shadow-familiar

An esoteric ritual spell that gives the user control of their own shadow, allowing it to move, stretch, and take unnatural shapes. Powered by electromagnetic radiation. "Life's breath, shadow mine. In darkness we were born. In darkness do we feast. Devour, and arise."

Shaman

A thaumaturge who specializes in contacting the spirit realm for the purpose of divination, including dream walking, as well as certain types of mental healing and wards. They often use mind-altering or hallucinogenic substances to facilitate contact, and can sign contracts with spirit realm beings, much like a witch with a familiar. Though the practice is dangerous dangerous, shamans may send their consciousness into the spirit realm for exploration.

Certain paths of magical research within this field are heavily discouraged by the Red Guard.

Shaman-king Deon

He ruled in Qusnia, a country that exited to the southeast of current Lenore in the distant past

Shipp evidence box

Metal cube meant to put evidence in stasis. Has a transparent setting to allow examination of the contents within.

Silk Door

An upscale brothel known for its cleanliness and discretion, and frequently used by Siobhan under the assumed name of Silvia Nakai to conceal her whereabouts.

Silva Erde

A neighboring country that Lenore frequently trades with, known for its celerium mines. The Beast King is rumored to be buried deep beneath its forests.

Silver-billed woodpecker
A magical creature that can never develop its magic correctly if it's helped out of its shell.

Simple locking spell
Learned from one of the warding books Katerin bought Siobhan, this spell locks a container that can be opened and closed, without need of a key or even a physical locking apparatus. Does not stop one from breaking in physically or magically, but will require some extra effort.

Simple unlocking spell
Used to bypass either mundane locks, or negate the simple locking spell. Cannot unlock a locking spell cast with greater power.

Sinus-clearing spell
A variation on the water falling spell, used to draw off liquid and thus clear the airways. Esoteric magic taught to Siobhan by a hedge-witch.

Siren
Sometimes confused for mermaids, sirens are not in fact associated with aquatic animals, but with avians. Sirens have brightly colored feathers that sprout from the scalp and sides of their face where ears and hair would be on a human. They are best known for their mesmerizing voices, which are said to cause sailors to steer their ships into submerged rocks or even directly into cliff-sides in an attempt to get closer to the enchanting sound of the siren song.
Largely carnivorous, sirens are intelligent beings and those who are willing to integrate into human society are rare and coveted for their abilities.

Skin-knitting salve
An alchemical concoction that mends small cuts over the course of about an hour. It can heal a deep scratch, cut, or a second-degree burn, but not a serious wound, and most (less expensive) versions will leave minor scarring.

Skinjacker
A creature used in cautionary tales to children, which can take over a person's form and replace them.

Skolex worm
Magical worm-like beasts that can grow hundreds of meters long, the skolex has no eyes, and hunts through vibration alone. When devouring its prey, the skolex's mouthparts one up in four directions simultaneously, revealing multiple inward-facing rows of serrated and hooked teeth which ring the entire mouth opening. The teeth are coveted for their piercing ability and how difficult wounds formed with them are to heal.

Sleep-proxy spell
Using the principles of binding magic, one can allow a magically boosted creature to sleep in the place of another being.

Slingshot spell
Created by Siobhan based on a Practical Casting exercise, it uses the glyphs "line," "movement," and "circle" to send a projectile revolving around a central axis. When it is released, the projectile shoots out, similar to a stone out of a shepherd's slingshot.

Smoke cloud philtre
A battle philtre that creates a sudden and thick smoke cloud when released from its container. Considered a battle potion.

Sobering potion
This potion speeds up the process of filtering alcohol from the body, but can cause an overwhelming need to urinate and, if overused, lead to dehydration.

Sound muffling spell
Creates a bubble of stilled air that suppressed the ability of vibrations to travel through it, and thus muffles sound.

Space-bending spells
This type of magic can bend, and even fold space. They are extremely difficult and expensive. If a smaller area is filled with more space than it could normally hold, that space must come from somewhere, which will in turn be smaller than it normally is. There are usually visually-disorienting signs of the spell when you try to gain perspective or mentally measure the space.

Spark-shooting wand

Artifacts charged with firework-like sparks of light. Can start a fire, with the right tinder, be used as a distraction, a signal, or a threat, though the spark-shooting spell is a non-combat spell.

Speer's philtre of stench

A powerful, physically painful stench that causes tears, mucus buildup, and vomiting, like a combination of a stink bomb and pepper spray. Used as crowd control to non-lethally incapacitate a large number of people. It has magical as well as physical properties.

Spell rod

A cylindrical baton containing segments that expand into spell Circle frames. It is based based loosely on the portable war Circles used by the army, and looks like the escrima of the East.

Spirit

Ephemeral, small and often harmless beings, it is argued whether spirits are technically "alive" or merely accumulations of a concentrated type of magical energy over time, or perhaps imprinted residue from once-living beings. They may be summoned and contracted, but often have little ability to exert influence on the mundane world. Shamans often communicate with spirits to gain information through their particular brand of divination.

Spirit-trapping spell

Useful for trapping spirits for communication or contracting. There are many variations on this type of Circle.

Sprites

Tiny, insect-winged humanoids. They have some measure of intelligence, but are not considered sapient "people," rather more akin to interesting bugs.

Star-maple wood

A wood with properties from the Plane of Radiance, it can be used in regenerative and healing spells, as well as other spells using the Radiant attribute, or for its beauty. As it can be molded into an accessory while still living, it is rather valuable. As an accessory, sometimes is used to enhance beauty through improving health.

Starpeak Mountains

An unnaturally tall mountain range that separates Osham and Lenore, with only two passable routes on either side.

Stunning spell

Red projectile spell. When high-powered, can leave scorch marks and a little steam or smoke at the point of impact. Uses a combination of low-current electricity and sedative material (the powdered saliva from a Kuthlan frog), contained within a field of force, to incapacitate the target.

Summoning ritual

Summoning is said to slightly skew fate to cause a being that meets your requirements to come into contact with you. It has inconsistent results, and clarity of wording and intention is very important. One can summon spirits, animals, or even another person who has the capability to help you with a certain problem. Once summoned, you may come into contact with a being that meets your requirements as if through coincidence after some time has passed, or more directly and immediately. Some question the efficacy, hypothesizing that the vagueness of most types of summoning rituals leads to false interpretations of fulfillment.

Sundered zone

The strongest barrier spell known to man. From the outside, it looks like a perfect white dome, with all light reflected. They are used to quarantine Aberrants that cannot be killed. The sundered zones cannot be exited by the thing they were created to contain or anything tainted by them, but can technically be entered by sapient creatures who are able to give their informed consent.

Sylphide

Powerful, humanoid elementals from the Plane of Air, given to song, laughter, and knowledge carried on the wind.

Tataroc Desert

Known for its dryness, a line of standing stones through this desert signifies Lenore's border to the east.

The Bitter Phoenix

A tavern with a private back area where people partake of the illegal quintessence of quicksilver, and a powerful diviner will sell you information or make connections for the right price.

The Black Wastes

An area where dangerous magic has infected the land itself. The environment shifts rapidly, with deadly and mutated land, flora, fauna. Time spent in the Black Wastes causes paranoia, hallucinations, and makes it difficult to find your way. They have an analogue in the spirit realm.

The Charmed Highlands

An area where celerium is mined.

The citadel

The main University building, where the classes are held, and which also contains the supervised casting rooms. It looks like a coliseum made of white stone, with shimmering spelled windows and tall columns. It is huge and towering, and laid out in rings, like a cross-cut of a tree stump.

The Dawn Troupe

A powerful Aberrant which is not contained within a sundered zone. It manifests as a group of wealthy, attractive horse-riders with weapons and musical instruments. This Aberrant appreciates intelligence and talent, and will give boons to those who meet it and impress it. The Dawn Troupe can be bargained with, and never breaks its promises. The Red Guard has agreed not to attempt to contain it, and as long as it receives a certain amount of people interacting with it—usually to attempt to gain one of its boons—it does not leave a certain area to go on a hunt. The Red Guard allows people to know about the boons so they will risk their lives to try for one.

The Elementary

A shop in the Night Market which secretly sells, in the back room, items from the Elemental Planes. Their supplier, Harvester, is a half-troll.

The Gervin Family

The Fourth Crown Family. They control much of the textile industry, as well as the high-end fashion industry.

The Mires

Gilbratha's slums, which get worse further toward the south of the city. The Mires are named for the sticky, stinking waste that lines the streets and wafts from the canals. They spread beyond the bounds of the white cliffs, which have been sunk, broken, or taken apart for use as building materials on that side of the city.

The Nightmare Pack

A gang consisting mostly of non-humans, which holds territory that houses a large percentage of non-humans. They are led by Lord Lynwood, a lycanthrope, and his adopted prognos sister, Gera.

The Red Guard

A special, semi-autonomous branch of law enforcement which handles rogue magic beyond the abilities of the normal coppers. Their operations are confidential.

The Surior Mountains

An area where celerium is mined.

The Thaumaturgic University of Lenore

The most prominent and prestigious arcanum in the country, and the only one that can give a Mastery certification. It is matched in status only by Pendragon Palace, and looks down upon the city from atop the northern side of the white cliffs. Its grounds are extensive, and its structures include areas dug into the white cliffs themselves.

Every year, thousands of students, both new to magic and who have come from other arcanums to achieve their Mastery certification, take the entrance exam.

The Westbay Family

The Second Crown Family. They control the Gilbrathan coppers, and often have influence in the army as high-ranking commanders.

Timed alarm spell

Cast on a time-keeper such as a pocket watch, goes off at a set time to alert anyone nearby to the conditions of the spell being reached.

Titan

A gargantuan, powerful, humanoid being prevalent in the early days of recorded human history, who survived the Cataclysm. A Titan might simply walk by and decide to crush half a human city like a child kicking an anthill. They had enormous appetites and were entirely omnivorous, in the true meaning of the word. Extremely magically powerful. Now extinct.

Tome

A large, expensive book created with high-quality material meant for channeling magic. It has very thick pages, with a spell array drawn on each page. This allows the holder to carry portable spell arrays, open to any particular page, and cast the spell as quickly as they can place any necessary components and/or Sacrifices. Each tome usually carries between 12-20 spell pages.

Turtle creation spell

Uses a turtle egg and duplicative transmogrification to create an anatomically-correct, edible, dead turtle.

Under-bed dust bunnies

A magical creature that is spontaneously generated from the fluffy dust under a bed in a magical environment. Supposedly.

Unicorn/Pegasus

A magical, horse-like beast with a valuable horn on its head. The pegasus is the progressed form of a unicorn, the wings growing after an intense accumulation of magic.

Unnamed subtle curses

Uses sea spray gathered on a moonless night. "I swam through an ocean of uncertainty."

Utility wand

A wand artifact with multi-purpose spells meant to be widely useful for a variety of emergency situations, not simply battle.

Vampire

Sentient, magical, humanoid beings, who often prey on humans for their blood. They often have blood-red hair, pale skin, and a mouth full of canine teeth. They are weak to things from the Plane of Radiance, and a common weapon against them is water imbued with energy from the Plane of Radiance. They have a natural predilection to the dark, and good night vision.

Vibrational self-calming spell

Esoteric, rather than using a written spell array, it uses the hands over the chest to form the Circle, and the vibration of the voice as a sympathetic component for forcibly calming the body. The longer you draw out the hum, the further it "stretches" your body into a calm state. Repeat ad nauseam.

Wakefulness brew

A pseudo-alchemical concoction, but more commonly classified as "kitchen magic," this spell marginally boosts the rejuvenating effects of caffeinated beverages. Better quality base materials take the wakefulness magic more smoothly, just as in standard alchemy.

Ward against untruth

The strongest legal wards against lies create a moderate vague compulsion, and are thus utterly useless against a strong thaumaturge who can imbue their lies with their Will. Illegal wards create stronger compulsions, but are considered blood magic as they take away the free will of a human.

Wardbreaker

A specialist in diverting, subverting, and breaking wards.

Waterside Market

A sprawling market within Gilbratha proper that has a lot of shops in the streets around. People of all ages and races can be seen, as well as thaumaturges who practice many different crafts, a testament to Gilbratha's diversity. Sells everything from food to magical animals. There are stalls as well as shops, with stalls being cheaper, but shops having a better selection.

Whiskerton's whiskey of well-being

An expensive magical whiskey guaranteed to impart an additional sense of warmth and wellbeing by the shot, in addition to the standard effects of liquor.

White cliffs

Gilbratha is built within a gargantuan circle of white stone cliffs that have been drawn up from the ground in what is undoubtedly a legendary feat of magic. These cliffs are intact to the north, but have sunk, crumbled, and been demolished for other purposes toward the poorer south.

The Thaumaturgic University of Lenore as well as many Crown Family houses have been built into and atop the cliffs, and nearer the bottom are many buildings placed on the staggered plateaus. Tubes run down from the University to transport people and goods, powered by magic.

Will

The Will makes magic possible. The stronger a thaumaturge's Will, the more power they can channel, the less defined the Word needs to be, and the less power will be lost in conversion from input to effect. There are different facets to a strong Will.

Will-strain

Caused by over-exertion when casting magic. It starts with headaches, dizziness, and inability to concentrate. With more moderate strain, judgment is impaired. Sometimes thaumaturges display difficulty modulating emotions, with rapid swings from one to the other. Then hallucinations, with the more severe ones resulting in paranoia and even accidental harm to oneself or others. Beyond this, Will-strain damage is irreversible, and results in complete insanity and at times, the loss of higher brain functions. In extreme circumstances, loss of control while casting will lead directly to a "break" and the creation of an Aberrant.

Wit-sharpening potion

While it doesn't actually increase intelligence, it will temporarily make the drinker more aware and improve performance in situations that require multitasking. In too high a dose, it can cause overstimulation through increased sensory input. It is somewhat addictive.

Witch

A thaumaturge who uses a summoned contracted creature, often from one of the Elemental Planes, to cast spells, rather than using an inanimate Conduit like sorcerer.

Word

The Word guides the transformation of energy or matter, steering the effects of a spell. It can be any type of instruction, though with sorcery it is most often written into the Circle as an array of glyphs and numerically-significant symbols. These are often supplemented with speech or written instructions, especially for complex effects.

Wortcunning

Magical herbalism, the study of plants and herbs, specifically for their healing and magical properties.

Wound cleansing potion

There are many different versions of this potion, and they come in different strengths and act in different ways. Uniformly, however, they work to clear the wound of dirt and debris, as well as kill any infectious agents such as viruses or bacteria. Formerly, this was understood to be overwhelming the "bad humors," and so, wound-cleansing potions often have strong scents due to components like distilled alcohol and herbal oil extracts.

Yak urine

Used to help dyes stay color-fast.

ALSO BY AZALEA ELLIS

Did you know I have my own little online shop? You can support me directly and get my latest book **earlier than it releases anywhere else**, along with special Inner Circle and full-series discounts.

You can also get extra story content that's not available on retailers, like bonus chapters and novelettes. My books are available in ebook, paperback, and audiobook format.

To buy from me directly go to: books.azaleaellis.com

Seeds of Chaos Series (Complete)

Book I: Gods of Blood and Bone

Book II: Gods of Rust and Ruin

Book III: Gods of Myth and Midnight

Book IV: Gods of Smoke and Stars—A Seeds of Chaos Adventure

Book V: Gods of Ash and Amber

A Practical Guide to Sorcery Series

Book I: A Conjuring of Ravens

Book II: A Binding of Blood

Book III: A Sacrifice of Light

Book IV: A Foreboding of Woe

Book V: A Cauldron of Bitterness

Book VI: A Builder of Dreams

A Practical Guide to Sorcery Additional Stories (Available Exclusively from Azalea

Book 2.1: Codename: Moonsable (Short Story)

Book 3.1: Good Advice (Bonus Chapter)

Book 3.2: Preventative Measures (Bonus Chapter)

Book 3.3: The Honeymoon Suite (Novelette)

Book 4.1: Harry Harold Had no Hands (Rhyme)

Book 4.2: Immovable Objects (Bonus Chapter)

Book 4.3: Recruitment Drive (Deleted Blooper Scene)

The Catastrophe Collector: A Practical Guide to Sorcery Spinoff Series

Book I: Larva

Book II: Bloom

More books may have been published since you purchased this copy. Find a complete list on AzaleaEllis.com

Here's a Quick Link to All my Books

www.azaleaellis.com/the-books/

ABOUT THE AUTHOR

I'm the type of person that often has a wacky, shocking, or silly–but totally *true*–story to tell about my life.

(Like the time my brother and I were chased through a secluded strip of woods in the middle of the city, for over a mile, by a naked man with an erection.)

(Or the time a trucker threw an open bottle of pee out his passenger side window without looking right as I was walking by. You can guess what I got splashed with.)

I've got an active imagination that tends toward the outrageous and the macabre, which led to me being voted "most likely to borrow someone else's car to transport a dead body."

I write books about things that interest and excite me. I'm always in the middle of teaching myself something new, and if I'm not overwhelmingly busy I tend to get antsy. I believe that the impossible is only so if we believe it to be so. Therefore, nothing is impossible.

If you'd like to get updates from me, both about my books and about what I'm up to from time to time, the newsletter is the place to be, as I tend to be very scarce on other social media.

https://www.azaleaellis.com/newsletter

For more information:
www.azaleaellis.com
author@azaleaellis.com